"A YOUNG GIRL WAS DANCING."

Book II., Chap. III.

NOTRE-DAME

OR

THE BELLRINGER OF PARIS

BY

VICTOR HUGO

WITH ILLUSTRATIONS

GEORGE ROUTLEDGE & SONS

LONDON: BROADWAY, LUDGATE HILL

NEW YORK: 9 LAFAYETTE PLACE

AUTHOR'S PREFACE.

SOME years ago, while visiting the Cathedral of Notre-Dame, or, to speak more properly, exploring every corner of it, the author of this book discovered, in a dark corner in one of the towers, this word, in Greek capital letters, engraven upon the wall—

'ANA'ΓKH.

These characters, black with age and deeply cut into the stone, with certain peculiarities of form and posture belonging to the Gothic calligraphy, as if to declare that they had been traced there by some hand of the middle ages—and, above all, the dismal and fatal meaning they conveyed—struck the author forcibly.

He asked himself, he strove to imagine, what suffering spirit it might be, who had determined not to quit this life without stamping this memento of crime or misfortune on the walls of the old cathedral.

Since then the wall has been washed over, or scraped—I remember not which—and the inscription has disappeared. For thus it is that the wonderful churches of the middle ages have been dealt with for two hundred years past. Mutilation attacks them in every direction, from within as well as from without, the priest smears them over—the architect scrapes them—then come the people and demolish them.

Thus, excepting only the frail memory here preserved of it by the author of this book, nothing now remains of the mysterious word engraven in the gloomy tower of Notre-Dame—nothing of the unknown destiny which it so mournfully recorded. The man who wrote that word upon the wall, passed away several centuries ago from among men—the word, in its turn, has passed away from the walls of the church—the church itself will soon, perhaps, pass away from the face of the earth.

It is upon the text of that word that this book has been written.

CONTENTS.

BOOK I.

BOOK II.

BOOK III.

BOOK IV.

BOOK V.

BOOK VI.

BOOK VII.

BOOK VIII.

BOOK IX.

BOOK X.

NOTRE-DAME.

BOOK I.

CHAPTER I.

THE GREAT HALL.

EXACTLY three hundred and forty-eight years, six months and nineteen days have passed away since the Parisians were awakened by the noise of all the bells within the triple walls of the city, the university, and the town, ringing a full peal. Yet the 6th of January, 1482, was not a day of which history has preserved any record. There was nothing remarkable in the event which thus put in agitation so early in the morning the bells and the good people of Paris. It was neither an assault of Picards or of Burgundians; nor a shrine carried in procession; nor a revolt of scholars in the *vigne de Laas*, nor an entry of their most dread lord the king; nor a grand hanging up of thieves, male and female, at the Justice de Paris. Neither was it the sudden arrival, so frequent in the fifteenth century, of some ambassador and his train, all covered with lace and plumes. Scarcely two days had elapsed since the last cavalcade of this sort, that of the Flemish envoys commissioned to conclude the marriage treaty between the Dauphin and Margaret of Flanders, had made its entry into Paris, to the great annoyance of Monsieur le Cardinal de Bourbon, who, to please the king, had been obliged to give a gracious reception to that rude train of Flemish burgomasters, and entertain them at his Hôtel de Bourbon, with one of the rude dramatic exhibitions of the time, while a beating rain drenched the magnificent tapestry at his door.

But on the 6th of January, that which set in motion the whole *populaire* of Paris, as old Jean de Troyes phrases it, was the double holiday, united since time immemorial, of the *jour des rois*, or festival of the kings, and the *fête des fous*, or festival of fools.

On that day, then, the last of the Christmas holidays, in 1482, a bonfire was to be made in the Place de Grève, a maypole planted at the Chapelle de Braque, and a mystery performed at the Palais de Justice. Proclamation to that effect had been made the day before, by sound of trumpet, at the crossings of the streets, by the provost's men, dressed in fine hacqueton, or sleeveless frocks, of violet colored camlet, with large white crosses on the breast.

The crowd of people accordingly took their way in the morning from all quarters of the town, leaving their houses and shops shut up, toward one of the three places appointed. Each one had made his choice, for the bonfire, the maypole, or the mystery. It must be said, however, to the praise of the ancient good sense of the Parisian cockneys, that the greater part of the multitude directed their steps toward the bonfire, which was perfectly seasonable, or toward the mystery, which was to be performed in the Grande Salle, or great hall of the Palais de Justice, well roofed and windowed; judiciously leaving the poor ill-dressed maypole to shiver all alone, under a January sky, in the cemetery of the Chapelle de Braque.

The people flocked chiefly into the approaches of the Palais de Justice, because it was known that the Flemish ambassadors who had arrived the day but one before, intended to be present at the performance of the mystery and the election of the Fools' Pope, which was likewise to take place in the Grande Salle.

It was no easy matter, on the day with which our narrative opens, for a person to make his way into that great hall, although it was then reputed to be the largest single apartment in the world—whence its popular designation as La Grande Salle, the great hall *par excellence*. It is true that Sauval had not yet measured the great hall of the castle of Montargis. The open space in front of the Palais, thronged with people, presented to the gazers from the windows the appearance of a sea, into which five or six streets, like the mouths of so many rivers, were every moment discharging fresh floods of human heads. The waves of this multitude, incessantly swelling, broke against the angles of the houses, which projected here and there like so many promontories, into the irregularly-shaped basin of the Place. In the center of the high Gothic front of the Palais, the great steps, incessantly ascended and descended by a double stream, which, after being broken by the intermediate *perron* or staircase leading from the basement story, spread in broad waves over its two lateral declivities—the great steps, we say, poured their stream incessantly into the Place, like a cascade into a lake. The shouts, the peals of laughter, the clattering of those thousands of feet, made all together a great noise and clamor. From time to time this noise and clamor were redoubled ; the stream which carried all the multitude toward the steps of entrance was checked, disturbed, and thrown into an eddy. This was occasioned by the thrust of some archer, or the horse of some one of the provost's sergeants, prancing about to restore order, which admirable expedient the *prevôté* has handed down to the *connétablie*, the *connétablie* to the *maréchaussée*, and the *maréchaussée* to our gendarmerie of Paris.

At the doors, at the casements and small round attic windows, and on the roofs, swarmed thousands of goodly bourgeois faces, looking calmly and soberly at the Palais or at the crowd, and exhibiting a most perfect satisfaction ; for many of the good people of Paris are quite content with the spectacle of the spectators— nay, even a wall behind which something is going on is to them an object of no small interest.

If it could be given to us to mingle, in imagination, among those Parisians of the fifteenth century, and to enter along with them, all thrust about, squeezed, and elbowed by the crowd, into that immense hall of the Palais, which was found so small on the 6th of January, 1482, the spectacle would have both interest and attraction for us, for we should find around us the most striking kind of novelty, that of great antiquity brought suddenly before the eye.

With the reader's permission we will endeavor to retrace, in idea, the impression which he would have received in crossing with us the threshold of that great hall, amidst that motley throng in surcoat, hacqueton, and cotte-hardie.

And first of all our ears are filled with the buzzing of the multitude, and our eyes dazzled by the objects around us. Over our head is a double vault of Gothic groining, lined with carved wainscoting, painted azure, and sprinkled with golden fleurs-de-lis. Under our feet, a pavement of black and white marble in alternate squares. A few paces from us, an enormous pillar— then another—then another, making, in all, seven pillars in the length of the hall, supporting, in a central line, the internal extremities of the double vaulting. Around the four first pillars are little shops or stalls, all glittering with glass and trinkets; and around the three last are oaken benches, worn and polished by the breeches of the pleaders and the gowns of the procureurs. Around the hall, along the lofty walls, between the doors, between the windows, between the pillars, we behold the interminable range of the statues of all the Frech kings, from Pharamond downward; the *rois fainéans*, or do-nothing kings, with their eyes upon the ground and their arms hanging down; the valiant and battling kings, with their faces and hands boldly lifted up to heaven. Then, in the long pointed windows, glows painted glass of a thousand colors; at the large entrances of the hall are rich doors finely carved; and the whole—vaults, pillars, walls, cornices, and door-cases, wainscoting, doors, and statues—are splendidly illuminated from top to bottom with blue and gold, which, already a little tarnished at the period to which we have carried ourselves back, had almost entirely disappeared under dust and cobwebs in the year of grace 1549, in which the early Parisian antiquary, Du Breuil, still admired it by tradition.

Let the reader now imagine that immense oblong hall, made visible by the wan light of a January day, and entered by a motley and noisy crowd, pouring along by the walls and circling round the pillars; and he will at once have a general idea of the scene, of which we will endeavor to point out more precisely the curious particulars.

It is certain that if Ravaillac had not assassinated Henry IV., there would have been no documents relative to the trial of Ravaillac deposited in the registry of the Palais de Justice, no accomplices interested in causing the disappearance of the said documents, and therefore no incendiaries obliged, for want of any better expedient, to burn the registry for the sake of burning the documents, and to burn the Palais de Justice for the sake of burning the registry—in short, no fire of 1618. The whole Palais would have been still standing, with its old Grande Salle; we might have said to the reader: "You have only to go to Paris and see it;" and so neither we should have been under the necessity of writing, nor he of reading, any description of it whatever. All which proves this very novel truth—that great events have incalculable consequences.

It is indeed very possible that Ravaillac's accomplices had nothing at all to do with the fire of 1618. We have two other very plausible explanations of it. The first is, the great fiery star, a foot broad and half a yard high, which, as every Parisian knows, fell from the sky right upon the Palais, on the 7th of March, just after midnight.

The other is, this noble quatrain of the old humorist Theophile:

> "Certes, ce fut un triste jeu
> Quand à Paris dame Justice,
> Pour avoir mange trop d'epice,
> Se mit tout le palais en feu."*

---

* This stanza is unfortunately not translatable. The sense depends on a play of words, the word epice signifying "spice" and also fees.—TRANS.

Whatever may be thought of this triple explanation, political, physical, and poetical, of the conflagration of the Palais de Justice in 1618; the fact of which unfortunately there is no doubt, is the conflagration itself. Owing to that catastrophe, and above all to the divers successive restorations which have made away with what it had spared, there now remains very little of that original residence of the kings of France, of that palace the elder sister of the Louvre, and so ancient even in the time of Philippe-le-Bel, that it was then sought to discover the traces of the magnificent buildings erected there by King Robert, and described by Helgaldus. Nearly all has disappeared. What has become of the chancery chamber? What of the garden in which St. Louis administered justice, " clad in a cotte of camlet, a surcoat of tiretaine without sleeves, and over it a mantle of black sendal, lying upon carpets with Joinville ? " Where is the chamber of the Emperor Sigismund?—that of Charles IV.?—that of Jean-sans-Terre? Where is the staircase from which Charles VI. promulgated his edict of pardon?—the flag-stone on which Marcel, in the presence of the Dauphin, murdered Robert de Clermont and the Marshal de Champagne?—the wicket at which the bulls of the anti-pope Benedict were torn, and through which the bearers of them set out on their return coped and mitred in derision, and thus making the *amende honorable* through all Paris?—and the great hall itself, with its gildings, its azure, its pointed arches, its pillars, its immense vaults all variegated with carving? —and the gilded chamber?—and the stone lion which knelt at its door, with his head bowed down and his tail between his legs, like the lions of Solomon's throne, in the posture of humiliation appropriate to Strength in the presence of Justice?—and the rich doors?—and the beautiful stained glass ?—and the carved iron-work, the perfection of which discouraged Biscornette?—and the delicate cabinet-work of Du Hancey? " What has time, what has man done with all those wonders?" asks our author. " What has been given us in exchange for all this, for all that Gaulish history, for all that Gothic art?

In art we have the heavy, lowering arches of M. de Brosse, the awkward architect of the Portail Saint-Gervais; and as for history, we have the gabbling reminiscences of the great pillar, still resounding with the prattle of the Patrus. Here is not much to boast of. Let us go back to the real Grand Salle of the real old Palais."

The two extremities of that vast parallelogram were occupied, the one by the famous marble table of a single piece, so long, so broad, and so thick that, say the old court-rolls in a style which might have given an appetite to Rabelais' Gargantua, " never was there such a slice of marble seen in the world,"—the other by the chapel in which the reigning king, Louis XI., had caused his own figure to be sculptured kneeling before the Virgin, and into which he had conveyed, regardless that he was leaving two niches empty in the file of the royal statues, those of Charlemagne and St. Louis, two saints whom, as kings of France, he supposed to be very influential in heaven. This chapel, which was still quite new, having scarcely been built six years, was all in that charming taste of delicate architecture, miraculous sculpture, and bold and exquisite carving, which characterizes the close of the Gothic era, and which we find perpetuated through the first half of the sixteenth century in the fantastic fairy-work of the period of the revival. The little pierced *rosace* or rose-shaped window above the entrance of the chapel was, in particular, a masterpiece of grace and lightness ; it had almost the airiness of lace. In the middle of the hall, opposite to the great door, an *estrade* or short projecting gallery, covered with gold brocade, fixed against the wall, and a private entrance to which has been contrived by means of a funnel window of the gilded chamber, had been erected for the Flemish envoys and the other personages invited to the performance of the mystery.

It was upon the marble table that, according to custom, this exhibition was to take place. It had been prepared for that purpose early in the morning ; and the rich slab of marble, scrawled all over by the heels of the lawyers' clerks, supported a high wooden frame-work, the upper surface of which, visible from every part of the hall, was to form the stage, while its interior, hidden by drapery, was to serve the actors as a dressing-room. A ladder, placed, with great simplicity, outside, established a communication between the stage and the dressing-room, serving alike for entrance and for exit. No character ever so unexpected, no turn of events, no stroke of stage effect, but had to ascend this ladder. Innocent and venerable infancy of the art and of machinery!

Four sergeants of the bailiff of the Palais, the appointed guardians of all the popular pleasures, whether on holidays or on execution days, stood on duty at the four corners of the marble table.

The piece was not to commence until the twelfth stroke of noon from the great clock of the Palais. This was undoubtedly thought very late for a theatrical performance; but it had been necessary to consult the convenience of the ambassadors.

Now all this multitude had been waiting since the early morning. A good many of these worthy people, in the greatness of their curiosity, had stood shivering since daybreak before the great steps of the Palais; some even affirmed that they had lain all night against the great door, to be sure of getting in first. The crowd was growing denser every moment; and, like a body of water overflowing its borders, began to ascend the walls, to squeeze round the pillars, to inundate the architraves, the cornices, the window-cases, every architectural or scriptural projection. The general impatience and uncomfortableness, the freedom allowed by a licentious holiday, the quarrels incessantly produced by the pressure of some sharp elbow or iron heel, and the wearisomeness of long expectation, infused, long before the hour at which the ambassadors were to arrive, a tone of sourness and bitterness into the clamors of this shut-up, squeezed, trodden, and stifled multitude. Nothing was heard but complaints and imprecations against the Flemings—the *prevôt des marchands*—the Cardinal de Bourbon—the bailiff of the Palais—the Lady Marguerite d'Autriche—the sergeants of the wand—the cold—the heat—the bad weather—the Bishop of Paris—the fools' pope—the pillars—the statues—a door shut here—a window open there—all to the great amusement of the tribes of scholars from the University, and of lackeys from all quarters, scattered among the crowd, who mingled up with this mass of dissatisfaction all their mischievous tricks and jests, thus goading, as it were, the general ill-humor.

Amongst others, there was a group of these merry devils, who, after bursting out the glass of a window, had boldly seated themselves upon the entablature, and from thence cast their looks and their railleries by turns within and without the hall, upon the internal and the external crowd. By their mimic gestures, their peals of laughter, and the jocoseness with which they exchanged calls with their comrades the whole length of the hall, it was evident enough that those young clerks did not share the weariness and exhaustion of the rest of the assemblage, and that they very well knew how, for their own particular enjoyment, to extract from what was already under their eyes an entertainment which enabled them to wait patiently for the other.

"Upon my soul, it's you, Joannes Frollo de Molendino," shouted one of them to a little light-complexioned fellow, with a pretty, roguish face, clinging to the foliage of one of the capitals; "rightly are you called John of the Mill, for your arms and legs look very much like the sails. How long have you been here?"

"By the devil's mercy," answered Jehan Frollo, commonly called *Du Moulin*, or of the Mill, "above four hours; and I'm in good hopes that they'll be deducted from my time in purgatory. I heard the King of Sicily's eight chanters strike up the first verse of the high mass of seven hours, in the Sainte Chapelle."

"Fine chanters, truly," returned the other, "with voices still sharper than the points of their caps. Before founding a mass in honor of St. John, it would have been as well if the king had inquired whether St. John be fond of hearing Latin droned out with a Provençal accent."

"It was all for the sake of employing those cursed chanters of the King of Sicily that he did it," screamed an old woman in the crowd beneath the window. "What think you of a thousand livres parisis for a mass, and charged, too, upon the farm of the salt-water fish of the fish-market of Paris!"

"Peace, old woman!" replied a portly personage, who was stopping his nose at the side of the fish-seller; "it was quite necessary to found a mass. Would you have had the king fall sick again?"

"Bravely spoken, Sir Gilles *Lecornu*, master furrier to the king's wardrobe!" cried the little scholar clinging to the capital.

A burst of laughter from the whole tribe of the scholars greeted the unlucky name of the poor furrier to the king's wardrobe.

"Lecornu! Gilles Lecornu!" said some.

"*Cornutus et hirsutus*," answered another.

"Oh, to be sure," continued the little imp at the top of the pillar; "what have they to laugh at? Is not worthy Gilles Lecornu brother to Maître Jehan Lecornu, provost of the king's household, son of Maître Mahiet Lecornu, first porter of the Bois de Vincennes—all citizens of Paris—all married, from father to son?"

This grave appeal redoubled their gayety. The fat furrier, without answering a word, strove to escape the looks fixed upon him from all sides; but he exerted himself in vain, for all his efforts served only to wedge more solidly between the shoulders of his neighbors his great apoplectic face, purple with anger and vexation.

One of these neighbors, however, fat, short, and reverend-looking, like himself, at length raised his voice on his behalf.

"Abominable!" he exclaimed, "that scholars should talk thus to a townsman. In my time they would have been first beaten with a fagot and then burned with it."

At this the whole tribe burst out afresh.

"Hollo! who sings that stave? who's that ill-boding screech-owl?"

"Oh! I see who it is," said one; "it's Maître Andry Musnier."

"Because he's one of the four sworn booksellers to the University," said the other.

"All goes by fours in that shop," cried a third; "there are four nations, the four faculties, the four attorneys, and the four booksellers."

"Well, then," resumed Jehan Frollo, "we must play four hundred devils with them all."

"Musnier, we'll burn thy books."

"Musnier, we'll beat thy lackey."

"Musnier, we'll kiss thy wife——."

"The good fat Mademoiselle Oudarde——"

"Who's as fresh and buxom as if she were a widow."

"The devil take you!" muttered Maître Andry Musnier.

"Maître Andry," said Jehan, still hanging by the capital, "hold your tongue, or I'll drop upon your head."

Maître Andry looked up, seemed to calculate for a moment the height of the pillar and the weight of the young rogue, multiplied in his mind that height by the square of the velocity, and was silent.

Jehan, being thus master of the field, continued triumphantly—

"Yes, I would do it, though I am brother to an archdeacon."

"Fine fellows, in truth, are our gentlemen of the University, not even to have taken care that our privileges were respected on a day like this: for here are a maypole and a bonfire in the Town; a mystery, a fools' pope, and Flemish ambassadors, in the City; and in the University, nothing at all!"

"And yet the Place Maubert is large enough," observed one of the young clerks posted in the recess of the window.

"Down with the rector, the electors, and the attorneys!" cried Joannes.

"We must make a bonfire to-night in the Champ-Gaillard," continued the other, "with Maître Andry's books."

"And the desks of the scribes," said his neighbor.

"And the wands of the beadles."

"And the spitting-boxes of the deans."

"And the buffets of the attorneys."

"And the tubs of the electors."

"And the rector's stools."

"Down, then," said little Jehan, winding up the stave, "down with Maître Andry, the beadles, and the scribes —the theologians, the physicians, and the decretists— the attorneys, the electors, and the rector!"

"Ah! then the world is at end," muttered Maître Andry, stopping his ears.

"Apropos! the rector himself! here he comes through the Place!" cried one of those in the window-case.

They all now strove to turn themselves toward the Place.

"Is it really our venerable rector, Maître Thibaut?" asked Jehan Frollo du Moulin, who, as he was clinging to one of the internal pillars, could not see what was passing outside.

"Yes, yes," answered all the rest, "it is he—he himself—Maître Thibaut, the rector."

It was, in fact, the rector and all the dignitaries going in procession to meet the ambassadors, and crossing at that moment the Place of the Palais. The scholars, all crowded together at the window, greeted them as they passed by with sarcasms and ironical plaudits. The rector, marching at the head of his band, received the first broadside, and it was a rough one.

"Good-day, monsieur le recteur! Hollo! good-day to you!"

"How has the old gambler contrived to be here? has he really quitted his dice?"

"How he goes trotting along on his mule—its ears are not so long as his."

"Hollo! good-day to you, monsieur le recteur Thibaut! *Tybalde aleator!*—Ah! you old noodle! you old gamester!"

"God preserve you! did you often throw twelve last night?"

"Oh! what a scarecrow countenance; all blue and battered through his love of dice and gaming."

"Where are you going to now, Thibaut, *Tybalde aa dacos*—turning your back on the University and trotting toward the town?"

"No doubt he's going to seek a lodging in the Rue Thibautodé," cried Jehan du Moulin.

The whole gang repeated the pun with a voice of thunder and a furious clapping of hands.

"You are going to seek lodgings in the Rue Thibautodé, aren't you, monsieur le recteur, the devil's own gamester?"

Then came the turn of the other dignitaries.

"Down with the beadles! down with the mace-bearers!"

"Tell me, Robin Poussepain, who's that man there?"

"It's Gilbert de Suilly, *Gilbertus de Soliaco*, chancellor of the college of Autun."

"Here, take my shoe—you're better placed than I am—throw it in his face."

"*Saturnalitias, mittimus ecce nuces.*"

"Down with the six theologians with their white surplices!"

"Are those the theologians? I thought they were the six white geese that Ste. Geneviève gave to the Town for the fief of Roogny."

"Down with the physicians!"

"Down with the disputations, cardinal, and quadlibetary!"

"Here goes my cap at yon chancellor of Saint Geneviève—I owe him a grudge."

"True—and he gave my place in the nation of Normandy to little Ascanio Falzaspada, belonging to the province of Bourges, because he's an Italian."

"It's an injustice!" exclaimed all the scholars.

"Ho, there! Maître Joachim de Ladehors! Ho! Louis Dalmille! Ho! Lambert Hoctement!"

"The devil smother the attorney of the nation of Germany!"

"And the chaplains of the Sainte Chapelle, with their gray amices, *cum tunicis grisis?*"

"*Seu de pellibus grisis fourratis.*"

"Hollo! the masters of arts! All the fine black copes; all the fine red copes!"

"That makes the rector a fine tail!"

"It might be a doge of Venice going to marry the sea."

"Now, again, Jehan! the canons of St. Geneviève!"

"The devil take all the canons together!"

"Abbé Claude Choart! Doctor Claude Choart, are you seeking Marie-la-Giffarde?"

"She's in the Rue de Glatigny."

"She's making the bed for the king of the ribalds."

"She's paying her four deniers, *quatuor denarios.*"

"*Aut unum bombum.*"

"Would you have her pay you in the nose?"

"Comrades, there goes Maître Simon Sanguin, elector of Picardy, with his wife mounted behind him."

"*Post equitem sedet atra cura.*"

"Courage, Maître Simon!"

"Good-day to you, monsieur l'électeur."

"Good-night, madame l'électrice."

"Now, aren't they happy, to be seeing all that?" said Joannes de Molendino, with a sigh, from his perch on the capital.

Meanwhile the sworn bookseller to the University, Maître Andry Musnier, whispered in the ear of the king's furrier, Maître Gilles Lecornu:

"I tell you, monsieur, the world's at an end.   ever were there seen such breakings-out of the   nolars! It's the accursed inventions of the age that   e ruining everything—the artillery—the serpentine –the bombards—and, above all, the printing-press that German pest! No more manuscripts—no more books! Printing puts an end to bookselling—the   nd of the world is coming!"

"I see it is, by velvet's coming s much into fashion," sighed the furrier.

At that moment it struck twelve.

"Ha!" exclaimed the whole crowd, with one voice of satisfaction.

The scholars held their peace.

Then there was a great shuffling about, a great movement of feet and heads, a general detonation of coughing and blowing of noses, each one striving to place
himself to the best advantage for the spectacle. Then
there was a deep silence, every neck remaining outstretched, every mouth open, every eye turned toward
the marble table—but nothing appeared. The bailiff's
four sergeants still kept their posts, as stiff and motionless as if they had been four painted statues. All eyes
then turned toward the gallery reserved for the Flemish
envoys. The door remained shut, and the gallery
empty. The multitude had been waiting since the
early morning for three things, that is to say, for the
hour of noon, for the French embassy, and for the mystery; but only the first of the three had kept its time.

This was rather too bad.

They waited one—two—three—five minutes—a quarter of an hour—but nothing came. The estrade remained solitary; the stage, mute. Meanwhile impatience was succeeded by displeasure. Angry words
circulated about, though as yet only in whispers. "The
mystery! the mystery!" was uttered in an undertone.
The heads of the multitude began to ferment. A storm,
which as yet only growled, was agitating the surface of
that human sea. It was our friend Jehan du Moulin
that elicited the first explosion.

"The mystery! and the devil take the Flemings!"
cried he, with the whole force of his lungs, twisting
himself, like a serpent, about his pillar.

The multitude clapped their hands. "The mystery!"
they all shouted, "and let Flanders go to all the devils!"

"We must have the mystery!" immediately resumed
the scholar; "else, for my part, I would have us hang
up the bailiff of the Palais by way of play and morality."

"Well said!" exclaimed the people, "and let us begin
the hanging with his sergeants?"

A great acclamation followed. The four poor devils
of sergeants began to turn pale and look anxiously at
each other. The multitude pressed toward them, and
they already saw the slight wooden balustrade which

separated them from the crowd bending inwards under the pressure.

The moment was critical.

"Bag them! bag them!" was shouted from all sides.

At that instant the hangings of the dressing-room which we have described above were lifted up to make way for the advance of a personage, the first sight of whom sufficed to stop the eager multitude, and changed their anger into curiosity as if by enchantment.

"Silence! silence!" was now the cry.

This personage, but little reassured, and trembling in every limb, came forward to the edge of the marble table, making a profusion of bows, which, the nearer he approached, approximated more and more to genuflexions.

Tranquillity, however, was almost restored. Only that slight murmur was heard which is always exhaled from the silence of a great crowd.

"Messieurs les bourgeois," said he, "and mesdemoiselles les bourgeoises; we shall have the honor of declaiming and performing before his eminence monsieur le cardinal, a very fine morality, entitled The Good Award of our Lady the Virgin Mary. I play Jupiter. His eminence is at this moment accompanying the most honorable embassy from monsieur the Duke of Austria, which is just now detained by hearing the harangue of monsieur the rector of the University, at the Baudets gate. As soon as the most eminent cardinal is arrived, we shall begin."

It is certain that nothing less than the intervention of Jupiter was necessary to save the four unhappy sergeants of the bailiff of the Palais. If we had had the happiness of inventing this very true and veritable history, and had consequently been responsible for it before Our Lady of Criticism, it is not in this place, at all events, that we should have incurred any citation against us of the classical precept, *nec Deus intersit*, etc. Besides, the costume of Seigneur Jupiter was a very fine one, and had contributed not a little to calm the irritated assemblage by attracting all their attention. Jupiter was clad in a brigandine covered with black velvet and gilt nails; his head-dress was a bicoquet decorated with silver-gilt buttons; and but for the rouge and the great beard which covered each one-half of his face— but for the scroll of gilt pasteboard strewed with passe-quilles and stuck all over with shreds of tinsel, which he carried in his hand, and in which experienced eyes easily recognized his thunderbolts—and but for his flesh-colored feet, sandal-bound with ribbons *à la Grecque*— he might have borne a comparison, for the severity of his aspect, with a Breton archer of that day, of Monsieur de Berry's corps.

CHAPTER II.

PIERRE GRINGOIRE.

HOWEVER, while Jupiter was delivering his speech, the satisfaction, the admiration unanimously excited by his costume, were dissipated by his words; and when he arrived at that unlucky conclusion, "as soon as the most eminent cardinal is arrived, we shall begin," his voice was lost in a thunder of hooting.

"Begin directly! The mystery! the mystery directly!" cried the people. And above all the other voices was heard that of Joannes de Molendino piercing through the general uproar, like the sound the fife in a charivari at Nimes. Begin directly!" squeaked the scholar.

"Down with Jupiter and the Cardinal de Bourbon!" vociferated Robin Poussepain and the other young clerks nestling in the window.

"The morality directly!" repeated the crowd immediately; "begin! begin! The sack and the rope for the players and the cardinal!"

Poor Jupiter, all haggard, aghast, pale under his rouge, let fall his thunderbolts, took his bicoquet in his hand; then, bowing and trembling, he stammered out:

" His eminence . . . . the ambassadors . . . . the Lady Margaret of Flanders . . . ."—he knew not what to say. But the fact was, he was afraid he should be hanged—hanged by the populace for waiting, or hanged by the cardinal for not having waited—on either hand he beheld an abyss.

Happily, some one came forward to extricate him and take the responsibility on himself.

An individual who stood within the balustrade, in the space which it left clear around the marble table, and whom no one had yet perceived, so completely was his long and slender person sheltered from every visual ray by the diameter of the pillar against which he had set his back—this individual, we say, tall, thin, pale, light complexioned—still young, though wrinkles were already visible in his forehead and his cheeks—with sparkling eyes and a smiling mouth—clad in a garment of black serge, threadbare with age—approached the marble table, and made a sign to the poor sufferer; but the other, in his perturbation, did not observe it.

The new-comer advanced another step forward.

" Jupiter," said he, " my dear Jupiter ! "

The other did not hear him.

At last the tall, fair man, losing all patience, shouted in his ear, " Michel Giborne ! "

" Who calls me ? " said Jupiter, as if starting from a trance.

" I do," answered the other personage.

" Ah ! " exclaimed Jupiter.

" Begin directly," returned the other, " satisfy the people, and I take upon myself to appease monsieur the bailiff, who will appease monsieur the cardinal."

Jupiter now took breath. " Messeigneurs les bourgeois," cried he, at the utmost stretch of his lungs, to the multitude who continued to hoot him, " we are going to begin directly."

" *Evoe ! Jupiter ! plaudite, cives !* " cried the scholars.

" Noël ! Noël ! " cried the people ; that cry being the burden of a canticle sung in the churches at Christmas, in honor of the Nativity, whence, apparently, it was adopted by the populace as a general mark of approbation and jubilation as long as the season lasted.

Then followed a deafening clapping of hands, and the hall still shook with acclamations when Jupiter had withdrawn behind his tapestry.

Meanwhile, the unknown, who had so magically changed the tempest into a calm, had modestly retired under the penumbra of his pillar, and would no doubt have remained there, invisible, and motionless, and mute as before, if he had not been drawn from it by two young women, who, being in the first line of the spectators, had remarked his colloquy with Michel Giborne Jupiter.

" Maître," said one of them, beckoning to him to approach.

" Hush! my dear Liénarde," said her fair neighbor, pretty, blooming, and quite courageous by virtue of her holiday attire—" it is not a clerk, it is a layman. You should not say *Maître*, but *Messire*."

" Messire!" then said Liénarde.

The unknown approached the balustrade.

" What is your pleasure with me, mesdemoiselles?" asked he, with an air of complaisance.

" Oh, nothing," said Liénarde, all confused. " It's my neighbor here, Gisquette-la-Gencienne, that wants to speak to you."

" No, no," rejoined Gisquette, blushing; " it was Liénarde that said '*Maître*' to you—I only taught her that she ought to say, *Messire*."

The two girls cast down their eyes. The gentleman, who felt quite disposed to enter into conversation with them, looked at them, smiling: " You have nothing to say to me, then, mesdemoiselles?"

" Oh, no, nothing at all," answered Gisquette.

" No, nothing," said Liénarde.

The tall, fair young man now made a step to retire; but the two curious damsels were not inclined to let him go so soon.

" Messire," said Gisquette, with the impetuosity of water escaping through a sluice, or a woman taking a resolution, "then you're acquainted with that soldier that's going to play Our Lady the Virgin in the mystery?"

"You mean the part of Jupiter," returned the unknown.

"Oh, dear, yes," said Liénarde; "is she stupid? You're acquainted with Jupiter, then?"

"With Michel Giborne," answered the unknown, "yes, madam."

"He has a fierce-looking beard," answered Liénarde.

"Will it be very fine, what they are all going to say?" asked Gisquette, timidly.

"Very fine, indeed, mademoiselle," answered the informant without the least hesitation.

"What will it be?" said Liénarde.

"The Good Award of Our Lady the Virgin—a morality, if it please you, mademoiselle."

"Ah! that's different," returned Liénarde.

A short silence followed, which was broken by the stranger. "It is a morality entirely new," said he, "which has never yet been played."

"Then it's not the same," said Gisquette, "as what was played two years ago on the day of the entry of monsieur the legate, and in which three beautiful girls performed——"

"As sirens," interrupted Liénarde.

"And quite naked," added the young man.

Liénarde modestly cast down her eyes. Gisquette looked at her, and did likewise. The other continued, smiling, "It was a very pretty thing to see. But to-day it is a morality made on purpose for the Lady of Flanders."

"Will they sing bergerettes?" asked Gisquette.

"Oh, fie!" said the unknown. "What! in a morality! We must not confound one kind of pieces with another. In a *sottie*, indeed, it would be quite right."

"That's a pity," rejoined Gisquette. "That day there were, at the fountain du Ponceau, savage men and women fighting, and making different motions, singing little motets and bergerettes all the while."

" That which is suitable for a legate,' said the stranger, very dryly, " is not suitable for a princess."

" And near them," continued Liénarde, " was playing a number of bass instruments, that gave out wonderful melodies."

" And to refresh the passengers," resumed Gisquette, " the fountain threw out, by three mouths, wine, milk, and hyppocrass, and everybody drank that liked."

" And a little below the Ponceau fountain, continued Liénarde, " at the Trinity fountain, there was a Passion performed without any speaking."

" Oh, yes, don't I remember it ! " exclaimed Gisquette : " God on the cross, and the two thieves on each side of Him ! "

Here the young gossips, getting warm in the recollection of the legate's entry, began to talk both at once.

" And further on, at the Porte-aux-Peintres, there were other characters very richly dressed "—

" And do you remember, at St. Innocent's fountain, that huntsman following a hind, with a great noise of dogs and hunting-trumpets ? "—

" And then at the Bouchere de Paris, those scaffolds that presented the Bastile of Dieppe "—

" And when the legate was going by, you know, Gisquette, they gave the assault, and the English all had their throats cut "—

" And what fine characters there were against the Châtelet gate ! "

" And on the Pont-au-Change, which was all covered over with carpeting from one end to the other."

" And when the legate went over it, they let fly from the bridge above two hundred dozen of all kinds of birds. Wasn't that a fine sight, Liénarde ? "

" There will be a finer to-day," at length interrupted their interlocutor, who seemed to listen to them with impatience.

" You promise us that this mystery shall be a fine one," said Gisquette.

" Assuredly," returned he. And then he added, with

peculiar emphasis, "Mesdemoiselles, 'tis *I* who am the author of it."

"Really!" said the young women, all amazed.

"Yes, really," answered the poet, bridling up a little —"that is to say, there are two of us—Jehan March-and, who has sawn the planks and put together the woodwork of the theatre; and myself, who have written the piece. My name is *Pierre Gringoire.*"

The author of the Cid himself could not have said with a loftier air, "My name is Pierre Corneille."

Our readers may have observed that some time must already have elapsed since the moment at which Jupiter retired behind the drapery, and that at which the author of the new morality revealed himself thus abruptly to the simple admiration of Gisquette and Liénarde. It is worthy of remark that all that multitude, who a few minutes before had been so tumultuous, now waited quietly on the faith of the player's promise—an evidence of this everlasting truth, still daily experienced in our theatres—that the best means of making the audience wait patiently is, to assure them that the performance will commence immediately.

However, the scholar Joannes was not asleep. "Hollo!" shouted he suddenly, amidst the peaceful expectation which had succeeded the disturbance. "Jupiter! madame the Virgin! you rowers of the devil's boat! are you joking to one another? The piece! the piece! Begin! or we'll begin again!"

This was enough. A music of high and low-keyed instruments now struck up in the apartment underneath the stage; and the hangings were lifted up; and four characters in motley attire, with painted faces, came out, clambered up the steep ladder already mentioned, arrived safe upon the upper platform, and drew up in line before the audience, whom they saluted with a profound obeisance, whereupon the symphony was silent, for the mystery was now really commencing.

The four characters, after receiving abundant payment for their obeisances in the plaudits of the multitude, commenced, amidst a profound silence, the de-

livery of a prologue, which we willingly spare the
reader. However, as still happens in our own time, the
audience paid more attention to the dresses they wore
than to the parts they were enacting—and in truth they
did right. They were all four dressed in gowns half
yellow and half white, differing from each other only in
the nature of the material; the first being of gold and
silver brocade, the second of silk, and the third of wool,
and the fourth of linen. The first character carried in
the right hand a sword; the second, two golden keys;
the third, a pair of scales; and the fourth, a spade: and
in order to assist such indolent understandings as might
not have seen clearly through the transparency of these
attributes, there might be read in large black letters worked at the bottom of the brocade dress, JE M'APPELLE NO-
BLESSE (my name is Nobility); at the bottom of the silk
dress, JE M'APPELLE CLERGÉ (my name is Clergy); at the
bottom of the woolen dress, JE M'APPELLE MARCHAN-
DISE (my name is Trade); and at the bottom of the linen
garment, JE M'APPELLE LABOR (my name is Tillage).
The sex of the two male characters, Clergé and Labor,
was clearly indicated to every judicious spectator by
the comparative shortness of their garments and the
cramignole which they wore upon their heads; while
the two female ones, besides that their robes were of
ampler length, were distinguishable by their hoods.

It would also have argued great perverseness, not to
have discovered through the poetic drapery of the prologue, that Labor was married to Marchandise, and
Clergé to Noblesse, and that these two happy couples
possessed in common a magnificent golden dolphin
which they intended to adjudge only to the most beautiful damsel. Accordingly, they were going all over
the world in search of this beauty; and after successively rejecting the Queen of Golconda, the Princess of
Trebizond, the daughter of the Cham of Tartary, etc.,
etc.; Labor and Clergé, Noblesse and Marchandise,
were come to rest themselves upon the marble table of
the Palais de Justice, and deliver at the same time to
the worthy auditory as many moral sentences and

maxims as might in that day be expended upon the members of the faculty of arts, at the examinations, sophisms, determinances, figures, and acts, at which the masters took their degrees.

All this was in truth very fine.

Meanwhile, in all that assemblage upon which the four allegorical personages seemed to be striving which could pour out the most copious floods of metaphor, no ear was so attentive, no heart so palpitating, no eye so eager, no neck so outstretched, as were the eye, ear, neck, and heart of the author, the poet, the brave Pierre Gringoire, who a moment before had been unable to forego the satisfaction of telling his name to two pretty girls.

He had returned to the distance of a few paces from them, behind his pillar; and there it was that he listened, looked, and enjoyed. The benevolent plaudits which had greeted the opening of his prologue, were still resounding in his breast; and he was completely absorbed in that species of ecstatic contemplation with which a dramatic author marks his ideas dropping one by one from the lips of the actor, amid the silence of a crowded auditory. Happy Pierre Gringoire!

It pains us to relate it—but this first ecstasy was very soon disturbed. Scarcely had the lips of Gringoire approached this intoxicating cup of joy and triumph, before a drop of bitterness was cruelly mingled in it.

A tattered mendicant who, lost as he was among the crowd, could receive no contributions, and who, we may suppose, had not found sufficient indemnity in the pockets of his neighbors, had bethought himself of finding some conspicuous perch from which to attract the attention and the alms of the good people. Accordingly, while the first lines of the prologue were delivering, he had hoisted himself up by means of the pillars that supported the reserve estrade, to the cornice which ran along the bottom of its balustrade; and there he had seated himself, soliciting the attention and the pity of the multitude by the display of his rags, and of a hideous sore that covered his right arm. However, he did not utter a word.

The silence which he kept allowed the prologue to proceed without any distraction ; and no sensible disorder would have occurred but that, as ill luck would have it, the scholar Joannes espied, from his own perch upon one of the great pillars, the beggar and his grimaces. The young wag was seized with an immoderate fit of laughter ; and, regardless of the interruption to the performance, and the disturbance to the general attention, he cried out in a tone of gayety, " Look at that sham leper there asking alms ! "

Any one that has ever thrown a stone into a pond full of frogs, or fired a gun among a flock of birds, may form an idea of the effect produced by these unseasonable words dropped in the midst of the universal attention fixed upon the heroes of the mystery. Gringoire started as if he had felt an electric shock. The prologue was cut short ; and all heads were turned tumultuously toward the mendicant ; who, far from being disconcerted, found in this incident a good opportunity of making a harvest, and began to cry out with a doleful look, half shutting his eyes, " Charity ! if you please."

" Why, on my soul," cried Joannes, " it's Clopin Troillefou. Hollo ! friend---so thy sore wasn't comfortable on thy leg, that thou'st put it on thy arm."

So saying he threw, with the dexterity of a monkey, a small white coin into the old greasy hat which the beggar held out with his diseased limb. The beggar received without flinching both the alms and the sarcasm, and continued in a piteous tone, " Charity ! if you please."

This episode had considerably distracted the auditory ; and a good many of the spectators, with Robin Poussepain and all the clerks at their head, merrily applauded this whimsical duet which had been struck up thus unexpectedly in the middle of the prologue, between the scholar with his shrill clamorous voice, and the beggar with his imperturbable drone.

Gringoire was grievously dissatisfied. Having recovered from his first stupefaction, he was tearing his lungs with crying out to the four characters on the

3

stage, "Go on!—what the devil!—go on;" without even deigning to cast a look of disdain upon the two interrupters.

At that moment he felt some one pulling at the skirt of his coat; he turned round, not without some little ill-humor, and had much ado to smile. Nevertheless he found it necessary to do so, for it was the pretty arm of Gisquette-la-Gencienne, which, extended through the balustrade, thus solicited his attention.

"Monsieur," said the girl, "will they go on?"

"To be sure," answered Gringoire, much shocked at the question.

"Oh, then, messire," she resumed, "would you just have the courtesy to explain to me——"

"What they are going to say?" interrupted Gringoire. "Well—listen."

"No," said Gisquette, "but what they have said already."

Gringoire started as if touched to the quick. "A plague on the little stupid witless wench!" muttered he, and from that moment Gisquette was utterly ruined in his estimation.

Meanwhile the actors had obeyed his injunction; and the , observing that they were once more trying to make themselves heard, had again set themselves to listen—not, however, without the loss of many a poetic beauty, in the sort of soldering that had been made of the two parts of the piece which had been so abruptly cut short. Gringoire whispered to himself this bitter reflection. However, tranquillity had been gradually restored; the scholar held his tongue, the beggar was counting some coin in his hat, and the piece had resumed its ascendency.

It was really a very fine composition, and we really think it might be turned to some account, even now, by means of a few modifications. The exposition, rather long indeed, and rather dry, was simple; and Gringoire, in the candid sanctuary of his own judgment, admired its clearness. As may well be supposed, the four allegorical personages were a little fatigued with traveling

over the three known quarters of the world without finding an opportunity of suitably disposing of their golden
dolphin. Hence a long eulogy upon the marvelous fish,
with numberless delicate allusions to the young prince
betrothed to Margaret of Flanders—which young prince
was at that time in very dismal seclusion at Amboise,
without the slightest suspicion that Labor and Clergé,
Noblesse and Marchandise, had just been making the
tour of the world on his account. The dolphin afore-
said, then, was young, was handsome, was vigorous, and
above all (magnificent origin of all the royal virtues!)
was son of the lion of France. "Now, I declare," says
our author, "that this bold metaphor is admirable, and
that dramatic natural history, on a day of allegory and
of a royal epithalamium, finds nothing at all shocking
in a dolphin the son of a lion. On the contrary, it is
precisely those rare and pindaric mixtures that prove
the poet's enthusiasm. However, to have disarmed
criticism altogether, the poet might have developed this
fine idea in less than two hundred lines. It is true that
the mystery was to last, according to the order of monsieur the provost, from noon till four o'clock, and that
it was necessary to say something. Besides, it was very
patiently listened to.

All at once, just in the middle of a fine quarrel between Mademoiselle Marchandise and Madame Noblesse, at the moment when Maître Labor was pronouncing this wondrous line,

Beast more triumphant ne'er in woods I've seen,

the door of the reserved gallery, which had until then
been so unseasonably shut, opened more unseasonably
still, and the stentorian voice of the *huissier*, doorkeeper or usher, abruptly announced, "Son Eminence
Monseigneur le Cardinal de Bourbon!"

CHAPTER III.

THE CARDINAL.

POOR Gringoire! The noise of all the great double petards let off on St. John's day—the discharge of a score of cracking arquebusses—the report of that famous serpentine of the Tour de Billy, which, at the time of the siege of Paris, on Sunday, the 29th of September, 1465, killed seven Burgundians at a shot—the explosion of all the gunpowder stored up at the Temple gate— would have split his ears less violently at that solemn and dramatic moment, than those few words from the lips of an usher, " His Eminence Monseigneur le Car dinal de Bourbon."

Not that Pierre Gringoire either feared the cardinal or despised him; he was neither weak enough to do the one, nor self-sufficient enough to do the other. A true eclectic, as he would nowadays be called, Gringoire was one of those firm and elevated spirits, calm and temper- ate, who can preserve their composure under all circum- stances—*stare in dimidio rerum*—and who are full of reason and of a liberal philosophy even while making some account of cardinals. Invaluable and uninter- rupted line of philosophers—to whom wisdom, like an- other Ariana, seems to have given a clew, which they have gone on unwinding from the beginning of the world through the labyrinth of human affairs. They are to be found in all times, and ever the same—that is to say, ever conforming themselves to the time. And not to mention our Pierre Gringoire, who would be their rep- resentative of the fifteenth century if we could succeed in obtaining for him the distinction which he deserves, it was certainly their spirit which animated Father du Breul in the sixteenth, when writing these words of sub- lime simplicity, worthy of any age: " I am a Parisian by my birth-place, and a *parrhisian* by my speech; for *parrhisia* in Greek signifies liberty of speech, which liberty I have used even to messeigneurs the cardinals, uncle and brother to monseigneur the Prince of Conti. albeit with respect for their greatness, and without offending any one of their train, and that is a great deal to say."

So there was neither hatred for the cardinal, nor contempt of his presence, in the disagreeable impression which it made upon Pierre Gringoire. On the contrary, our poet had too much good sense and too threadbare a frock not to attach a particular value to the circumstance, that many an allusion in his prologue, and in particular the glorification of the dolphin, son of the lion of France, would fall upon the ear of an *éminentissime*. But interest is not the ruling motive in the noble nature of poets. Supposing the entity of a poet to be represented by the number ten, it is certain that a chemist, on analyzing and pharmacopœizing it, as Rabelais says, would find it to be composed of one part of self-interest with nine parts of self-esteem. Now, at the moment that the door opened for the entrance of his eminence, Gringoire's nine parts of self-esteem, inflated and expanded by the breath of popular admiration, were in a state of prodigious enlargement, quite overwhelming and smothering that imperceptible particle of self-interest which we just now discriminated in the constitution of poets—an invaluable ingredient, by-the-way, a ballast of reality and humanity, without which they would never touch the earth. It was enjoyment for Gringoire to see and feel that an entire assemblage (of poor creatures, it is true, but what then?) were stupefied, petrified, and asphyxiated by the immeasurable tirades which burst from every part of his epithalamium. We affirm that he himself shared the general beatitude; and that, quite the reverse of La Fontaine, who, at the performance of his play of "The Florentine," asked, "What poor wretch has written that rhapsody?" Gringoire would willingly have asked the person nearest to him, "Whose masterpiece is this?" Hence it may be supposed what sort of effect was produced upon him by the sudden and untimely arrival of the cardinal.

All his fears were but too fully realized. His eminence's entrance threw the whole auditory into motion. All eyes were turned toward the estrade, and there was a general buzz: "The cardinal! the cardinal!" repeated every tongue. The unfortunate prologue was cut short a second time.

The cardinal stopped a moment upon the threshold of the gallery; and while casting his eyes with great indifference over the assemblage, the tumult redoubled. Everybody wanted to obtain a better view of him, each one stretching his neck over his neighbor's shoulder.

He was in truth an exalted personage, the sight of whom was worth almost any other spectacle. Charles, Cardinal de Bourbon, Archbishop and Count of Lyons, and Primate of Gaul, was allied both to Louis XI., through his brother Pierre, Seigneur of Beaujeu, who had espoused the king's eldest daughter, and at the same time to the Burgundian duke, Charles-le-Téméraire, through his mother, Agnes of Burgundy. Now, the ruling, the characteristic, the distinctive feature in the character of the Primate of Gaul, was his courtier-like spirit and his devotedness to power. Hence, it may well be supposed in what numberless perplexities this double relationship had involved him, and among how many temporal shoals his spiritual bark must have tacked about, to have escaped foundering either upon Louis or upon Charles, the Charybdis and the Scylla which had swallowed up the Duke of Nemours and the Constable of Saint-Pol. However, Heaven be praised! he had got happily through his voyage, and had reached Rome without any cross accident. But although he was now in port—and indeed, precisely because he was in port—he never recollected, without a feeling of uneasiness, the various chances of his political life, which had so long been perilous and laborious. So, also, he used to say, that the year 1476 had been to him both a black and white year; meaning thereby that he had lost in that one year his mother, the Duchess of Bourbonnais, and his cousin, the Duke of Burgundy, and that one mourning had consoled him for the other.

However, he was a very worthy man ; he led a joyous cardinal's life ; was wont to make merry with wine of the royal vintage of Challuau ; had no dislike to Richarde-la-Gamoise and Thomasse-la-Saillarde ; gave alms to pretty girls in preference to old women ; and for all these reasons was in great favor with the good people of Paris. He always went surrounded by a little court of bishops and abbots of high lineage, gallant, jovial, and fond of good eating ; and more than once had the good devotees of Saint Germain d'Auxerre, in passing at night under the windows of the Hôtel de Bourbon, all blazing with light, been scandalized by hearing the same voices which had been singing vespers to them in the daytime, striking up, to the sound of glasses, the bacchanalian sentiment of Benedict XII., the pope who had added a third crown to the tiara— *Bisbamus papaliter.*

No doubt it was this popularity, so justly acquired, which preserved him at his entrance from anything like ill reception on the part of the crowd, who a few moments before had been so dissatisfied, and so little disposed to pay respect to a cardinal, even on the day when they were going to elect a pope. But the Parisians bear little malice ; and besides, by making the performance begin of their own authority, the good citizens had had the better of the cardinal, and this triumph satisfied them. Moreover, Monsieur le Cardinal de Bourbon was a handsome man—he had on a very handsome scarlet gown, which he wore in excellent style—which is as much as to say, that he had in his favor all the women, and, consequently, the better part of the audience. Certainly it would be both injustice and bad taste, to hoot a cardinal for being too late at the play, when he is a handsome man, and wears handsomely his scarlet robe.

He entered, then ; saluted the company with that hereditary smile which the great have always in readiness for the people ; and stepped slowly towards the *fauteuil* or state chair of scarlet velvet placed for his reception ; looking as if some other matter occupied his mind. His train—what a Frenchman might now call his staff—of bishops and abbots, issued after him upon the estrade, not without exciting redoubled tumult and curiosity among the spectators below. All were busied in pointing them out, or in telling their names, each one striving to show that he knew at least some one of them; some pointing to the Bishop of Marseilles (Alaudet, if we remember right); some to the *Primicier* or Dean of St. Denis; others to Robert de Lespinasse, Abbot of the great neighboring monastery of Saint-Germain-des-Près, the libertine brother of a mistress of Louis XI.—all their names being repeated with a thousand mistakes and mispronunciations. As for the scholars, they swore. It was their own day— their feast of fools—their saturnalia—the annual orgies of the *basoche* and the *école*. No turpitude but was a matter of right, to be held sacred that day. And then there were mad gossips among the crowd—Simone Quatre-livres, Agnès-la-Gadine, Robine Pièdebou. Was it not the least that could be expected, that they should swear at their ease, and profane God's name a little, on such a day as that, in such good company with churchmen and courtezans? And accordingly, they made no mincing of the matter; but amidst the uproarious applause a frightful din of blasphemies and enormities proceeded from all those tongues let loose, those tongues of clerks and scholars, tied up all the rest of the year by the fear of St. Louis's branding-iron. Poor St. Louis! how did they banter him in his own Palais de Justice! Each one of them had singled out among the newly-arrived company some one of the cassocks, black, gray, white, or violet. As for Joannes Frollo de Molendino, and his being brother to an archdeacon, it was the red robe that he audaciously assailed, singing out as loud as he could bawl, and fixing his shameless eyes upon the cardinal, "*Cappa repleta mero !*"

All these particulars, which are thus clearly detailed for the reader's edification, were so completely drowned in the general hum of the multitude, that they were lost before they could reach the reserved gallery; though, indeed, the cardinal would have been little moved by them; so intimately did the license of the day belong to the manners of the age. He had something else to think of, which pre-occupation appeared in his countenance—another cause of solicitude, which followed closely behind him, and made its appearance in the gallery almost at the same time as himself. This was the Flemish embassy.

Not that he was a profound politician, or concerned himself about the possible consequences of the marriage of madame, his cousin, Margaret of Burgundy, with monsieur, his cousin, Charles, Dauphin of Vienne—nor how long the patched-up reconciliation between the Duke of Austria and the French king might endure—nor how the King of England would receive this slight toward his daughter. All that gave him little anxiety; and he did honor every night to the wine of the royal vineyard of Chaillot without ever suspecting that a few flasks of that same wine, revised and corrected a little by the physician Coictier, and cordially presented to Edward IV. by Louis XI., might possibly, some fine morning, rid Louis XI. of Edward IV. *La moult honorée ambassade de Monsieur le Duc d'Autriche* brought none of these cares to the cardinal's mind, but annoyed him in another respect. It was, in truth, rather too bad, and we have already said a word or two about it in the first pages of this volume, that he should be obliged to give good reception and entertainment— he, Charles de Bourbon—to obscure burghers; he, a cardinal, to a pack of scurvy échevins—he, a Frenchman and a connoisseur in good living, to Flemish beer-drinkers—and in public too! Certes, it was one of the most irksome parts he had ever gone through for the *bon plaisir* of the king.

However, he had so perfectly studied it, that he turned toward the door with the best grace in the world, when the usher announced in a sonorous voice, " Messieurs the Envoys of the Duke of Austria!" It is needless to say that the whole hall did likewise.

Then appeared, two by two, with a gravity which strongly contrasted with the flippant air of the cardinal's ecclesiastical train, the forty-eight ambassadors from Maximilian of Austria, having at their head the reverend father in God, Jehan, Abbot of Saint-Bertin, chancellor of the Golden Fleece, and Jacques de Goy, Sieur Dauby, high bailiff of Ghent. A deep silence now took place in the assemblage, a general titter being suppressed, in order to listen to all the uncouth names and mercantile additions which each one of these personages transmitted with imperturbable gravity to the usher, who then gave out their names and callings, pell-mell and with all sorts of mutilations, to the crowd below. There were Maitre Loys Roelof, échevin of the town of Louvain; Messire Clays d'Etuelde, échevin of Brussels; Messire Paul de Baeust, sieur of Voirmizelle, president of Flanders; Maitre Jehan Coleghens, burgomaster of the city of Antwerp; Maitre George de la Moere, principal échevin of the *kuere* of the city of Ghent; Maitre Gheldolf vander Hage, principal échevin of the *parchons* of the said city; and the Sieur de Bierbecque, and Jehan Pinnock, and Jehan Dimaerzelle, etc., etc., etc., bailiffs, échevins, and burgomasters—burgomasters, échevins, and bailiffs—all stiff, sturdy, drawn-up figures, dressed out in velvet and damask, and hooded with black velvet *cramignoles* decorated with great tufts of gold thread of Cyprus—good Flemish heads after all, with severe and respectable countenances, akin to those which Rembrandt has made stand out with such force and gravity from the dark background of his picture of "Going the rounds at night"—personages on every one of whose foreheads it was written, that Maximilian of Austria had done right in "confiding to the full," as his manifesto expressed it, "in their sense, valor, experience, loyalty, and good endowments."

There was one exception, however, to this description; it was a subtle, intelligent, crafty-looking face—a sort of mixture of the monkey and the diplomatist—to whom the cardinal made three steps in advance and a low bow, but who, nevertheless, was called simply Guillaume or William Rym, counselor and pensionary of the town of Ghent.

Few persons at that time knew anything about Guillaume Rym—a rare genius, who, in a time of revolution, would have appeared with *éclat* on the surface of events; but who, in the fifteenth century, was confined to the practice of covert intrigue and to "live in the mines," as the Duke de Saint-Simon expresses it. However, he was appreciated by the first "miner" in Europe—he was familiarly associated in the secret operations of Louis XI.—all which was perfectly unknown to this multitude, who were amazed at the cardinal's politeness to that sorry-looking Flemish bailiff.

CHAPTER IV.

MASTER JACQUES COPPENOLE.

WHILE the pensionary of Ghent and his eminence were exchanging a very low bow, and a few words in a tone still lower, a man of lofty stature, large-featured, and broad-shouldered, presented himself to enter abreast with Guillaume Rym, looking something like a mastiff dog by the side of a fox. His bicoquet of felt and his leathern jerkin were oddly conspicuous amidst the velvet and silk that surrounded him. Presuming it to be some groom who knew not whither he was going, the usher stopped him with "Hold, friend! you can't pass here."

The man of the leathern jerkin shouldered him aside. "What would this fellow with me?" said he, in a thundering voice, which drew the attention of the whole hall to this strange colloquy. "Seest thou not I'm one of them?"

"Your name?" demanded the usher.

" Jacques Coppenole."

"Your description?"

"A hosier, at the sign of the Three Chains at Ghent.'

The usher shrank back. To announce échevins and burgomasters might indeed be endured—but a hosier! —it was rather too bad. The cardinal was upon thorns. All the people were looking and listening. For two days his eminence had been doing his utmost to lick these Flemish bears into rather more presentable shape, and this freak was too much for him. Meanwhile Guillaume Rym, with his cunning smile, went up to the usher: "Announce Maître Jacques Coppenole, clerk to the échevins of the city of Ghent," said he to the officer in a very low whisper.

" Usher," then said the cardinal aloud, " Announce Maître Jacques Coppenole, clerk to the échevins of the illustrious city of Ghent."

This was an error. Guillaume Rym, by himself, would have snatched the difficulty out of the way; but Coppenole had heard the cardinal's direction. " No! *Croix-Dieu!*" he cried, with his voice of thunder: " Jacques Coppenole, hosier. Dost thou hear, usher? Neither more nor less. Croix-Dieu! a hosier—that's fine enough. Monsieur the archduke has more than once looked for his *gant* in my hose."

This play upon the word *gant*, a glove, pronounced exactly alike *Gand* or *Ghent*, the great manufacturing town in Flanders, occasioned a burst of laughter and applause from the people below.

We must add that Coppenole was one of the people, and that the auditory around him were of the people also ; so that the communication between them and him had been quick, electric, and, as it were, on equal footing. This lofty air which the Flemish hosier gave himself, by humbling the courtiers, had stirred in the plebeian breasts a certain latent feeling of dignity, which, in the fifteenth century, was as yet vague and undefined. They beheld one of their equals in this hosier, who had just borne himself so sturdily before the cardinal—a welcome reflection to poor devils accustomed to pay respect and obedience to the servants of the sergeants of the bailiff of the Abbot of Sainte-Geneviève, the cardinal's train-bearer.

Coppenole made a stiff bow to his eminence, who returned the salute of the all-powerful burgher, formidable to Louis XI. Then, while Guillaume Rym, *sage homme et malicieux*, as Philippe de Comines expresses it, followed them both with a smile of raillery and superiority, they moved each to his place—the cardinal thoughtful and out of countenance—Coppenole quite at his ease, thinking, no doubt, that, after all, his title of hosier was as good as any other, and that Mary of Burgundy, mother of that Margaret for whose marriage he was now treating, would have feared him less as a cardinal than as a hosier ; for no cardinal would have stirred up the people of Ghent against the favorites of the daughter of Charles the Rash ; nor could any cardinal, by a single word, have fortified the multitude against her tears and prayers, when the Lady of Flanders came and supplicated her people on their behalf, even to the foot of their scaffold, while the hosier had only had to raise his leathern elbow to cause both your heads to be struck off, most illustrious seigneurs, Guy d'Hymbercourt and Chancellor Guillaume Hugonet.

Yet the poor cardinal had not gone through all his penance ; he was doomed to drain the cup of being in such bad company, even to the dregs.

The reader has doubtless not forgotten the audacious mendicant, who at the time of the commencement of the prologue, had climbed up to the fringes of the gallery reserved for the cardinal. The arrival of the illustrious guests had not in the least disturbed him ; and while the prelates and the ambassadors were barreling themselves up like real Flemish herrings within the narrow compass of the gallery, he had put himself quite at his ease, with his legs bravely crossed upon the architrave. This piece of insolence was extraordinary ; yet nobody had remarked it at the first moment, every one's attention being fixed elsewhere. He, for his part, took notice of nothing in the hall ; he was moving his head

backward and forward with the unconcern of a Nea-
politan, repeating, from time to time, amidst the general
hum, and as if by a mechanical habit, " Charity, if you
please!" and indeed, among all present, he was probably the only one who would not have deigned to turn
his head on hearing the altercation between Coppenole
and the usher. Now it so chanced that his hosiership
of Ghent, with whom the people already so warmly
sympathized, and upon whom all eyes were fixed, went
and seated himself in the front line of the gallery, just
over the place where the beggar was sitting ; and it excited no small astonishment to see the Flemish ambassador, after scrutinizing the fellow beneath him, give
him a friendly slap upon his ragged shoulder. The
beggar turned round. Surprise, mutual recognition,
and kindly gratulation, were visible in both faces ; then,
without giving themselves the slightest concern about
the spectators, the hosier and the leper fell into conversation in a low voice, holding each other by the hand;
while the tattered arm of Clopin Trouillefou, displayed
at length upon the cloth of gold that decorated the
gallery, had somewhat the appearance of a caterpillar
upon an orange.

The novelty of this singular scene excited such noisy
mirth among the crowd, that the cardinal quickly remarked it : he leaned gently aside ; and as, from the
point where he was situated, he caught only an imperfect glimpse of Trouillefou's ignominious garment, he
exclaimed, " Monsieur the bailiff of the Palace, throw
me that fellow into the river."

" Croix-Dieu ! monseigneur le cardinal," said Coppenole, without leaving hold of Clopin's hand, " this is
one of my friends."

" Noël ! Noël !" cried the mob. And from that moment Maitre Coppenole was at Paris, as at Ghent, " in
great favor with the people ; for men of great stature
are so," says Philippe de Comines, " when they are thus
disorderly."

The cardinal bit his lip. He leaned toward the Abbot of Sainte Geneviève, who sat next him, and said in a

half-whisper: " Pretty ambassadors, truly, monsieur the archduke sends us to announce the Lady Margaret."

"Your eminence's politeness," returned the abbot, "is thrown away upon these Flemish grunters—*Margaritas ante porcus.*"

"Say rather," rejoined the cardinal, smiling, "*porcus ante Margaritam.*"

The whole of the little court of churchmen were in ecstasy at this *jeu de mot.* The cardinal felt a little relieved. He was now even with Coppenole, for he too had had his pun applauded.

And now, such of our readers as have the power of generalizing an image or an idea, as we say nowadays, will permit us to ask them whether they figure to themselves quite clearly the spectacle presented, at the moment at which we give this pause to their attention, by the vast parallelogram of the great hall of the Palais.

In the middle of the western side is a spacious and magnificent gallery, with drapery of gold brocade, which is entered, in procession, through a small Gothic doorway, by a series of grave-looking personages, announced successively by the clamorous voice of the usher; while on the first benches are already seated a number of reverend figures wrapped in velvet, ermine, and scarlet cloth. Below and all about this gallery, which remains still and stately—below, in front, and around, are a great multitude and a great hum of voices. A thousand looks are cast from the crowd upon every face in the gallery—a thousand muttered repetitions are made of every name. The spectacle is indeed curious and well worthy the attention of the spectators. But, at the same time, what is that down there, quite at the extremity of the hall—that sort of mountebank stage, with four puppets in motley upon it, and four others below? And at one side of the stage, who is that white-faced man in a long black coat? Alas! dear reader, it is Pierre Gringoire with his prologue.

We had all utterly forgotten him; and that is just what he had apprehended.

From the moment at which the cardinal entered,

Gringoire had been incessantly exerting himself for the salvation of his prologue. He had first of all enjoined the actors to proceed, and elevate their voices; then, finding that no one listened, he had stopped them; and for nearly a quarter of an hour during which the interruption had continued, he had been constantly beating with his foot and gesticulating, calling upon Gisquette and Liénarde, and urging those near him to have the prologue proceeded with—but all in vain. No one could be turned aside from the cardinal, the embassy, and the gallery—the sole center of that vast circle of visual rays. It is also credible, we regret to say it, that the prologue was beginning to be a little tiresome to the auditory at the moment that his eminence's arrival had made so terrible a distraction. And after all, in the gallery itself, as on the marble table, it was still in fact the same spectacle—the conflict of Labor with Clergé, of Noblesse with Marchandise; and many people liked better to see them in downright reality, living, breathing, acting, elbowing one another in plain flesh and blood, in that Flemish embassy, in that episcopal court, under the cardinal's robe, under Coppenole's jerkin, than tricked out, painted, talking in verse, and packed up, as it were, in straw, under the yellow and white gowns in which Gringoire had muffled them.

Nevertheless, when our poet saw tranquillity a little restored, he bethought himself of a stratagem which might have saved the performance.

"Monsieur," said he, turning to one of the persons nearest him, of fair round figure, with a patient-looking countenance, "suppose they were to begin again?"

"Begin what?" said the man.

"Why, the mystery," said Gringoire.

"Just as you please," returned the other.

This demi-approbation was enough for Gringoire, and taking the affair into his own hands, he began to call out, confounding himself at the same time as much as possible with the multitude. "Begin the mystery again!—begin again!"

"The devil!" said Joannes de Molendino; "What

is it they're singing out at yon end?" for Gringoire made as much noise as four people. "Tell me, comrades, isn't the mystery finished? They want to begin it again; that's not fair."

"No! no!" cried all the scholars together, "down with the mystery!—down with it!"

But Gringoire only multiplied himself the more, and cried out the louder—"Begin again!—begin again!"

These clamors attracted the attention of the cardinal. "Monsieur the bailiff of the Palais," said he to a tall, dark man standing a few paces from him, "what possesses those fellows that they make that infernal noise?"

The bailiff of the Palais was a kind of amphibious magistrate, a sort of bat of the judicial order, a sort of compound of the rat and the bird, of the judge and the soldier. He approached his eminence, and with no small apprehension of his displeasure, he stammered out to him an explanation of the people's refractoriness—that noon had arrived before his eminence, and that the players had been forced to begin without waiting for his eminence.

The cardinal laughed aloud. "I'faith," said he, "monsieur the rector of the University should e'en have done likewise. What say you, Maître Guillaume Rym?"

"Monseigneur," answered Rym, "let us be satisfied with having escaped one half of the play. 'Tis so much gained, at any rate."

"May those rogues go on with their farce?" asked the bailiff.

"Go on—go on," said the cardinal, "'tis all the same to me; I will be reading my breviary the while."

The bailiff advanced to the edge of the gallery, and called out, after procuring silence by a motion of his hand—"Townsmen! householders! and inhabitants!— to satisfy those who desire the play to begin again, and those who desire it to finish, his eminence orders that it shall go on."

Thus both parties were obliged to yield, although both the author and the auditors long bore a grudge

4

on this score against the cardinal. The characters on
the stage accordingly took up their text where they
had laid it down; and Gringoire hoped that at least the
remainder of his composition would be listened to.
This hope, however, was soon dispelled, like the rest of
his illusions. Silence had indeed been somehow or
other restored in the auditory; but Gringoire had not
observed that, at the moment when the cardinal had
given his order for the continuance of the play, the
gallery was far from being full, and that subsequently
to the arrival of the Flemish envoys, there were come
other persons forming part of the cardinal's train, whose
names and descriptions, thrown out in the midst of his
dialogue by the intermitted bawling of the usher, made
considerable ravage in it. Only imagine, indeed, in the
midst of a dramatic piece, the yelp of a doorkeeper,
throwing in, between the two lines of a couplet, and
often between the first half of a line and the last, such
parentheses as these:

"Maître Jacques Charmolue, king's attorney in the
ecclesiastical court!"

"Jehan de Harlay, esquire, keeper of the office of
horseman of the night-watch of the town of Paris!"

"Messire Galiot de Genoilhac, knight, seigneur of
Brussac, master of the king's artillery!"

"Maître Dreux-Raguier, commissioner of our lord
the king's waters and forests in the domains of France,
Champagne, and Brie!"

"Messire Louis de Graville, knight, councillor, and
chamberlain to the king, admiral of France, keeper of
the Bois de Vincennes!"

"Maître Denis le Mercier, keeper of the house of the
blind at Paris!" etc., etc., etc.

This became insupportable. All this strange accompaniment, which made it difficult to follow the tenor of
the piece, was the more provoking to Gringoire, as he
could not disguise from himself that the interest was
going on increasing, and that nothing was wanting to
his composition but to be listened to. It was, indeed,
difficult to imagine a plot more ingeniously or dramatic-

ally woven. While the four personages of the prologue
were bewailing their hopeless perplexity, Venus in person—*vera incessu patuit dea*—had presented herself before them, clad in a fine cotte-hardie, having blazoned
fair upon its front the ship displayed on the old city
escutcheon of Paris. She was come to claim for herself the dolphin promised to the most beautiful. She
was supported by Jupiter, whose thunder was heard to
rumble in the dressing-room ; and the goddess was about
to bear away the prize—that is, in plain terms, to
espouse monsieur the dauphin—when a little girl dressed in white damask, and carrying a marguerite or daisy
in her hand, a lucid personification of the Lady of
Flanders, had come to contend with Venus. Here
were at once *coup-de-théâtre* and preparation for the catastrophe. After a proper dispute, Venus, Margaret,
and those behind the scenes, had agreed to refer the
matter to the award of the holy Virgin. There was
another fine part, that of Don Pedro, King of Mesopotamia ; but amid so many interruptions it was difficult
to discover what was his share of the action. All these
personages climbed up the ladder to the stage.

But it was all over with the play ; not one of these
beauties was felt or understood. It seemed as if, at the
cardinal's entrance, some invisible and magical thread
had suddenly drawn away every look from the marble
table to the gallery, from the southern extremity of the
hall to its western side. Nothing could disenchant the
auditory ; all eyes remained fixed in that direction ;
and the persons who successively arrived on that side,
with their cursed names, and their faces, and their
dresses, made a continual diversion. The case was desperate. Except Gisquette and Liénarde, who turned
aside from time to time when Gringoire pulled them
by the sleeve—except the lusty patient man that stood
near him—no one listened to, no one looked at, the
poor abandoned morality. Gringoire could see in the
faces of the auditory nothing but profiles.

With what bitterness did he see all his fabric of
poetry and of glory thus falling to pieces ! Only to

think that this multitude had been on the pc nt of re-
belling against monsieur the bailiff through their impatience to hear his composition : and now that they had
it, they cared nothing about it—that same performance
which had begun amid such unanimous acclamation!
Everlasting ebb and flow of the popular favor! Only
to think, that they had been near hanging the bailiff's
sergeants !—what would he not have given to have recalled that blissful moment! However, the usher's
brutal monologue ceased at length ; everybody had arrived : so that Gringoire took breath ; and the actors
were going on bravely, when all at once Maître Coppenole, the hosier, got upon his legs, and Gringoire
heard him deliver, in the midst of the universal attention to his piece, this abominable harangue :

"Messieurs the bourgeois and hobereaux of Paris—
Croix-Dieu! I know not what we're doing here. I do
indeed see, down in that corner, upon that stage, some
people who look as if they wanted to fight. I know
not whether that be what you call a mystery; but I do
know it's not amusing. They belabor one another with
their tongues, but that's all. For this quarter of an
hour I've been waiting to see the first blow—but nothing comes—they're cowards, and maul one another only
with foul words. You should have had boxers from
London or Rotterdam; and then indeed we should
have had hard knocks, which you might have heard the
length of this hall—but those creatures there are quite
pitiful. They should at least give us a morris-dance or
some other piece of mummery. This is not what I
was told it was to be—I'd been promised a feast of
fools with an election of a pope. We at Ghent, too,
have our fools' pope ; and in that, Croix-Dieu! we're
behind nobody. But we do thus :—a mob gets together, as here for instance ; then each in his turn goes and
puts his head through a hole and makes faces at the
others; he that makes the ugliest face according to
general acclamation, is chosen pope. That's our way,
and it's very diverting. Shall we make your pope after
the fashion of my country? At any rate it will not be

so tiresome as listening to those babblers. If they've a mind to come and try their hands at face-making, they shall have their turn. What say you, my masters? Here's a droll sample enough of both sexes to give us a right hearty Flemish laugh, and we can show ugly phizzes enow to give us hopes of a fine grinning-match."

Gringoire would fain have replied, but amazement, resentment, and indignation deprived him of utterance. Besides, the motion made by the popular hosier was received with such enthusiasm by those townsfolk flattered at being called hobereaux (a term in that day somewhat approaching to gentleman as now used in England in addressing a mixed multitude, though in this day it is no longer used complimentarily), that all resistance would have been unavailing. All that could now be done was to go with the stream. Gringoire hid his face with both his hands, not being so fortunate as to possess a mantle wherewith to veil his countenance like the Agamemnon of Timanthes.

CHAPTER V.

QUASIMODO, THE HUNCHBACK.

IN the twinkling of an eye, everything was ready for putting Coppenole's idea into execution. Townspeople, scholars, and basochians had all set themselves to work. The small chapel, situated opposite to the marble table, was fixed upon to be the scene of the grinning match. The glass being broken out of one of the divisions of the pretty rose-shaped window over the door-way, left open a circle of stone through which it was agreed that the candidates should pass their heads. To get up to it they had only to climb upon two casks which had been laid hold of somewhere or other, and set one upon another just as it happened It was settled that each candidate, whether man or woman (for they might make a she-pope), in order to leave fresh and entire the impression of their grin, should cover their face and keep themselves unseen in the chapel until the moment of making their appearance at the hole. In a moment the chapel was filled with competitors, and the door was closed upon them.

Coppenole, from his place in the gallery, ordered everything, directed everything, arranged everything. During the noisy applause that followed his proposal, the cardinal, no less out of countenance than Gringoire himself, had, on pretext of business, and of the hour of vespers, retired with all his suite; while the crowd, among whom his arrival had caused so strong a sensation, seemed not to be in the slightest degree interested by his departure. Guillaume Rym was the only one who remarked the discomfiture of his eminence. The popular attention, like the sun, pursued its revolution; after setting out at one end of the hall, it had stayed for awhile at the middle of it, and was now at the other end. The marble table, the brocaded gallery, had each had its season of interest; and it was now the turn of Louis XI.'s chapel. The field was henceforward clear for every sort of extravagance; the Flemings and the mob had it all to themselves.

The grinning commenced. The first face that appeared at the hole, with eyelids turned up with red, a mouth gaping like the swallow of an ox, and a forehead wrinkled in large folds like our hussar boots in the time of the Empire, excited such an inextinguishable burst of laughter, that Homer would have taken all those boors for gods. Nevertheless the Grand Salle was anything but an Olympus, as no one could better testify than Gringoire's own poor Jupiter. A second face, and a third, succeeded—then another—then another—the spectators each time laughing and stamping with their feet with redoubled violence. There was in this spectacle a certain peculiar whirling of the brain—a certain power of intoxication and fascination—of which it is difficult to give an idea to the reader of the present day, and the frequenter of our modern drawing-rooms. Imagine a series of visages, presenting in succession every geometrical figure, from the triangle to the trapezium, from the cone to the polyhedron—every human expression, from that of anger to that of lust—every age, from the wrinkles of the new-born infant to those of extreme old age—every religious phantasm, from Faunus to Beelzebub—every animal profile, from the jowl to the beak, from the snout to the muzzle. Figure to yourself all the grotesque heads carved on the Pont-Neuf, those nightmares petrified under the hand of Germain Pilon, taking life and breath, and coming one after another to look you in the face with flaming eyes—all the masks of a Venetian carnival passing successively before your eye-glass—in short, a sort of human kaleidoscope.

The orgie became more and more Flemish. Teniers himself would have given but a very imperfect idea of it. Imagine, if you can, the "battle" of Salvator Rosa bacchanalized. There was no longer any distinction of scholars, ambassadors, townspeople, men, or women. There was now neither Clopin Trouillefou, nor Giles Lecornu, nor Marie Quatre-Livres, nor Robin Poussepain. All was confounded in the common license. The Grande Salle had become, as it were, one vast furnace of audacity and joviality, in which every mouth was a shout, every eye a flash, every face a grin, every figure a gesticulation—all was bellowing and roaring. The strange visages that came one after another to grind their teeth at the broken window, were like so many fresh brands cast upon the fire; and from all that effervescent multitude there escaped, as the exhalation of the furnace, a humming noise, like the buzzing of the wings of ten thousand gnats.

"Curse me," cries one, "if ever I saw anything like that."

"Only look at that phiz," cries another.

"It's good for nothing."

"Let's have another."

"Guillemette Maugerepuis, just look at that pretty

bull's head—it wants nothing but horns. It can't be thy husband."

"Here comes another."

"Bless the pope! what sort of a grin's that?"

"Hollo! that's not fair. You must show nothing but your face."

"That devil, Perette Calebotte! That must be one of her tricks."

"Noël! noël!"

"Oh! I'm smothered!"

"There's one that can't get his ears through"—etc. etc.

We must, however, do justice to our friend Jehan. In the midst of this infernal revel, he was still to be seen at the top of his pillar like a ship-boy on a top-sail. He was exerting himself with incredible fury. His mouth was wide open, and there issued from it a cry which, however, was not audible—not that it was drowned by the general clamor, all intense as that was—but because, no doubt, it attained the utmost limit of perceptible sharp sounds, of the twelve thousand vibrations of Sauveur, or the eight thousand of Biot.

As for Gringoire—as soon as the first moment of depression was over, he had resumed his self-possession. He had hardened himself against adversity. "Go on," he had said for the third time to his players—"go on, you talking machines," then pacing with great strides before the marble table, he felt some temptation to go and take his turn at the hole in the chapel-window, if only to have the pleasure of making faces at the ungrateful people. "But no—that would be unworthy of us—no revenge—let us struggle to the last," muttered he to himself—"the power of poetry over the people is great—I will bring them back. We will see which of the two shall prevail—grinning, or the belles-lettres."

Alas! he was left the sole spectator of his piece.

This was worse than before; for instead of profiles, he now saw nothing but backs.

We mistake. The big, patient man whom he had already consulted at one critical moment, had remained

with his face toward the stage; as for Gisquette and
Liénarde, they had deserted long ago.

Gringoire was touched to the soul by the fidelity of
his only remaining spectator; he went up to and accosted him, giving him at the same time a slight shake
of the arm, for the good man had leaned himself against
the balustrade, and was taking a gentle nap.

"Monsieur," said Gringoire, "I thank you."

"Monsieur," answered the big man with a yawn,
"what for?"

"I see what annoys you," returned the poet; "all
that noise prevents you from hearing as you could wish;
but make yourself easy—your name shall go down to
posterity. Will you please to favor me with your
name?"

"Renauld Château, seal-keeper of the Châtelet of
Paris, at your service."

"Monsieur," said Gringoire, "you are here the sole
representative of the Muses."

"You are too polite, monsieur," answered the seal-
keeper of the Châtelet.

"You are the only one," continued Gringoire, "who
has given suitable attention to the piece. What do you
think of it?"

"Why—why," returned the portly magistrate, but
half awake—"it's very diverting indeed."

Gringoire was obliged to content himself with this
eulogy; for a thunder of applause, mingled with a prodigious exclamation, cut short their conversation. The
fool's pope was at last elected.

"Noël! noël! noël!" cried the people from all sides.

It was indeed a miraculous grin that now beamed
through the circular aperture. After all the figures,
pentagonal, hexagonal, and heteroclite, which had succeeded each other at the round hole, without realizing
that idea of the grotesque which had formed itself in
the imagination of the people excited by the orgie, it
required nothing less to gain their suffrages than the
sublime grin which had just dazzled the assemblage.
Maître Coppenole himself applauded; and Clopin

Trouillefou, who had been a candidate (and God knows his visage could attain an intensity of ugliness) acknowledged himself to be outdone. We shall do likewise. We shall not attempt to give the reader an idea of that tetrahedron nose—that horse-shoe mouth—that small left eye overshadowed by a red bushy brow, while the right eye disappeared entirely under an enormous wart—of those straggling teeth with breaches here and there like the battlements of a fortress—of that horny lip, over which one of those teeth projected like the tusk of an elephant—of that forked chin—and, above all, of the expression diffused over the whole—that mixture of malice, astonishment, and melancholy. Let the reader, if he can, figure to himself this combination.

The acclamation was unanimous; the crowd rushed toward the chapel, and the blessed pope of the fools was led out in triumph. And now the surprise and admiration of the people rose still higher, for they found the wondrous grin to be nothing but his ordinary face.

Or rather, his whole person was a grimace. His large head, all bristling with red hair—between his shoulders an enormous hump, to which he had a corresponding projection in front—a framework of thighs and legs, so strangely gone astray that they could touch one another only at the knees, and when viewed in front, looked like two pairs of sickles brought together at the handles—sprawling feet—monstrous hands—and yet, with all that deformity, a certain gait denoting formidable vigor, agility and courage—a strange exception to the everlasting rule which prescribes that strength, like beauty, shall result from harmony. Such was the pope whom the fools had just chosen. He looked like a giant that had been broken and awkwardly mended.

When this sort of cyclop appeared on the threshold of the chapel, motionless, squat, and almost as broad as he was high—squared by the base, as a great man has expressed it—the populace, by his coat half red and half violet, figured over with little silver bells, and still more by the perfection of his ugliness—the populace recognized him at once, and exclaimed with one voice: "It's

Quasimodo the ringer! It's Quasimodo the hunchback of Notre-Dame! Quasimodo the one-eyed! Quasimodo the bandy-legged! Noël! noël!" The poor devil, it seems, had a choice of surnames.

" All ye pregnant women get out of the way!" cried the scholars.

" And all that want to be so," added Joannes.

The women, in fact, hid their faces.

" Oh, the horrid baboon!" said one.

" As mischievous as he's ugly," added another.

" It's the devil!" cried a third.

" I've the misfortune to live near Notre-Dame; and at night I hear him scrambling in the gutter."

" With the cats."

" He's constantly upon our roofs."

" He's cast spells at us down the chimneys."

" The other night he came and grinned at me through my attic window. I thought it was a man. I was in such a fright!"

" I'm sure he goes to meet the witches—he once left a broomstick on my leads."

" Oh, the shocking face of the hunchback!"

" Oh, the horrid creature!"

The men, on the contrary, were delighted, and made great applause.

Quasimodo, the object of the tumult, kept standing in the doorway of the chapel, gloomy and grave, letting himself be admired.

One of the scholars (Robin Poussepain, we believe) came and laughed in his face, rather too near him. Quasimodo quietly took him by the waist and threw him half-a-score yards off among the crowd, without uttering a word.

Maître Coppenole, wondering, now went up to him. " Croix-Dieu! Holy Father! why, thou hast the prettiest ugliness I ever saw in my life! Thou wouldst deserve to be pope at Rome as well as at Paris."

So saying, he clapped his hand merrily upon the other's shoulder. Quasimodo stirred not an inch. Coppenole continued: " Thou art a fellow whom I long to feast with, though it should cost me a new douʒain of twelve livres tournois. What say'st thou to it?"

Quasimodo made no answer.

"Croix-Dieu!" cried the hosier, "art thou deaf?"

He was indeed deaf.

However, he began to be impatient at Coppenole's motions, and he all at once turned toward him with so formidable a grinding of his teeth, that the Flemish giant recoiled like a bull-dog before a cat.

A circle of terror and respect was then made round the strange personage, the radius of which was at least fifteen geometrical paces. And an old woman explained to Maître Coppenole that Quasimodo was deaf.

"Deaf?" cried the hosier, with his boisterous Flemish laugh. "Croix-Dieu! then he's a pope complete!"

"Ha! I know him," cried Jehan, who was at last come down from his capital to have a nearer look at the new pope: "it's my brother the archdeacon's ringer. Good-day to you, Quasimodo."

"What a devil of a man," said Robin Poussepain, who was all bruised with his fall. "He shows himself —and you see he's a hunchback. He walks—and you see he's bow-legged. He looks at you—and you see he's short of an eye. You talk to him—and you find he's deaf. Why, what does the Polyphemus do with his tongue?"

"He talks when he likes," said the old woman. "He's lost his hearing with ringing the bells. He's not dumb."

"No—he's that perfection short," observed Jehan.

"And he's an eye too many," added Robin Poussepain.

"No, no," said Jehan, judiciously; "a one-eyed man is much more incomplete than a blind man, for he knows what it is that's wanting."

Meanwhile, all the beggars, all the lackeys, all the cutpurses, together with the scholars, had gone in procession to fetch from the wardrobe of the basoche, the pasteboard tiara and the mock robe appropriated to the Fools' Pope. Quasimodo allowed himself to be arrayed

in them without a frown, and with a sort of proud do-
cility. They then seated him upon a parti-colored
chair. Twelve officers of the brotherhood of Fools,
laying hold of the poles that were attached to it, hoisted
him upon their shoulders; and a sort of bitter and disdainful joy seemed to spread itself over the sullen face
of the cyclops when he beheld under his deformed feet
all those heads of good-looking and well-shaped men.
Then the whole bawling and tattered procession set out
to make, according to custom, the internal circuit of the
galleries of the Palais, before parading through the
streets.

CHAPTER VI.

ESMERALDA.

WE are delighted to have to inform our readers that
during all this scene Gringoire and his piece had held
out. His actors, goaded on by himself, had not discon-
tinued the enacting of his play, nor had he ceased to
listen to it; he had taken his part in the uproar, and
was determined to go to the end, not despairing of a
return of public attention. This gleam of hope revived
when he saw Quasimodo, Coppenole, and the deafening
train of the Fools' Pope march with great clamor out
of the hall, while the rest of the crowd rushed eagerly
after them. "Good!" said he to himself—"there go
all the disturbers at last!" But, unfortunately, all the
disturbers made the whole assemblage; and in a twinkling the great hall was empty.

It is true there still remained a few spectators, some
scattered about, and others grouped around the pillars
—women, old men, and children—weary and exhausted
with the squeezing and the clamor. A few of the scholars, too, still remained, mounted on the entablature of
the windows, and looking out into the Place.

"Well," thought Gringoire, "here are still enow of them to hear the end of my mystery. They are few, but they are a chosen, a lettered audience."

But a moment afterward, a symphony which was to have had the greatest effect at the arrival of the Holy Virgin, was missing. Gringoire discovered that his music had been carried off by the procession of the Fools' Pope. "Pass it over," said he stoically.

He approached a group of townspeople who seemed to him to be talking about his piece, and caught the following fragment of their conversation:

"Maître Cheneteau, you know the Hôtel de Navarre, which belonged to Monsieur de Nemours."

"Oh, yes—opposite to the Chapelle de Braque."

"Well—the Government have just let it to Guillaume Alixandre, heraldry-painter, for six livres eight sols parisis a year."

"How rents are rising!"

"So!" said Gringoire, with a sigh—"but the others are listening."

"Comrades!" suddenly cried one of the young fellows at the windows, "La Esmeralda! La Esmeralda in the Place!"

This word produced a magical effect. All who remained in the hall rushed toward the windows, climbing up the walls to see, and repeating, "La Esmeralda! la Esmeralda!" At the same time was heard a great noise of applauses outside.

"What is the meaning of La Esmeralda?" said Gringoire, clasping his hands in despair. "Ah, my God! it seems to be the turn of the windows now!"

He returned toward the marble table, and saw that the performance was interrupted. It was precisely the moment at which Jupiter was to enter with his thunder. But Jupiter remained motionless at the foot of the stage.

"Michel Giborne!" cried the irritated poet, "what are you doing there? is that your part?—go up, I say."

"Alas!" exclaimed Jupiter, "one of the scholars has just taken away the ladder."

Gringoire looked. It was but too true. All communication between his plot and his catastrophe was cut off. "The fellow!" muttered he; "and why did he take that ladder?"

"To go and see La Esmeralda," cried Jupiter in a piteous tone. "He came and said, 'Here's a ladder that nobody's using;' and away he went with it."

This was the finishing blow. Gringoire received it with resignation. "The devil take you all!" said he to the players; "and if they pay me, I'll pay you."

Then he made his retreat, hanging his head indeed, but still the last in the field, like a general who has fought well. And as he descended the winding stairs of the Palais, "What a fine drove of asses and dolts are these Parisians!" grumbled he. "They come to hear a mystery, and pay no attention to it. They've attended to everybody else—to Clopin Trouillefou—to the cardinal—to Coppenole—to Quasimodo—to the devil!—but to our Lady, the Virgin, not at all. If I'd known it, I'd have given you Virgin Mary, I dare say, you wretched cockneys! And then, for me to come here to see faces, and see nothing but backs!—to be a poet, and have the success of an apothecary! True it is that Homerus begged his bread through the villages of Greece, and that Naso died in exile among the Muscovites. But the devil flay me if I understand what they mean with their Esmeralda. Of what language can that word be?—it must be Egyptian!"

BOOK II.

CHAPTER I.

FROM CHARYBDIS INTO SCYLLA.

THE night comes on early in January. The streets were already growing dark when Gringoire quitted the Palais. This nightfall pleased him; he longed to reach some obscure and solitary alley, that he might there meditate at his ease, and that the philosopher might lay the first unction to the wound of the poet. Besides, philosophy was now his only refuge; for he knew not where to find a lodging for the night. After the signal miscarriage of his first dramatic attempt, he dared not return to that which he occupied in the Rue Grenier-sur-l'Eau, opposite to the Port-au-Foin; having relied upon what the provost was to give him for his epithalamium to enable him to pay to Maître Guillaume Doulx-Sire, farmer of the duty upon cloven-footed beasts brought into Paris, the six months' rent which he owed him, that is to say, twelve sols parisis, twelve times the value of all he possessed in the world, including his breeches, his shirt, and his bicoquet hat. After considering, then, for a moment, provisionally sheltered under the wicket-gate of the prison belonging to the treasurer of the Sainte-Chapelle, as to what place of lodging he should select for the night, all the pavements of Paris being at his service, he recollected having espied, the week before, in the Rue de la Savaterie, at the door of a counselor to the parliament, a footstone for mounting on mule-back, and having said to himself that this stone might serve upon occasion as an excellent pillow for a beggar or a poet. He thanked Providence for having sent him this happy idea; but as he was preparing to cross the Place du Palais in order to reach the tortuous labyrinth of the City, formed by the windings of all those sister streets, the Rue de la Barillerie, Rue de la Vieille-Draperie, Rue de la Savaterie, Rue de la Juiverie, etc., which are yet standing, with their houses of nine stories, he saw the procession of the Fools' Pope, which was also issuing from the Palais, and rushing across the Place with loud cries, with great glare of torches, and with Gringoire's own band of music. This sight revived his anguish, and he fled away from it. In the bitterness of his dramatic misadventure, everything which recalled to his mind the festival of the day irritated his wound, and made it bleed afresh.

He turned to cross the Pont Saint-Michel, but found boys running up and down it with squibs and crackers.

"A plague on the fireworks!" said Gringoire; and he turned back upon the Pont-au-Change. There were attached to the front of the houses at the entrance of the bridge, three drapels or pieces of painted cloth, representing the king, the dauphin, and Margaret of Flanders · and six smaller pieces or drapelets, on which were portrayed the Duke of Austria, and the Cardinal de Bourbon, and Monsieur de Beaujeu, and Madame Jeanne of France, and Monsieur the bastard of Bourbon, and we know not who besides, all lighted by torches—and a crowd stood admiring them.

"Happy painter, Jeanne Fourbault!" said Gringoire with a heavy sigh; and he turned his back upon the drapels and drapelets. A street lay before him; and it seemed so dark and forsaken, that he hoped there to forget all his mental sufferings by escaping every ray of the illuminations, and he plunged down it accordingly. He had not gone far before he struck his foot against some obstacle; he stumbled and fell. It was the bundle of may which the clerks of the basoche had placed in the morning at the door of a president of the parliament in honor of the day. Gringoire bore this new accident heroically; he arose, and reached the water-side. After leaving behind him the Tournelle Civile and the Tour Criminelle, and passing along by the great wall of the king's gardens, on that unpaved strand in which he sank to the ankles in mud, he arrived at the western point of the City, and gazed for some time upon the small island of the Passeur-aux-Vaches, or ferryman of the cows, which has since disappeared under the brazen horse and the esplanade of the Pont-Neuf. The islet appeared to his eyes in the darkness as a black mass beyond the narrow stream of whitish water which separated him from it. He could discern upon it, by the rays of a small glimmering light, a sort of hut in the form of a beehive, in which the ferryman sheltered himself during the night.

" Happy ferryman! " thought Gringoire, " thou dream-est not of glory! thou writest not epithalamiums!— what are royal marriages, of Duchesses of Burgundy, to thee! Thou knowest no Marguerites but the daisies which thy April greensward gives thy cows to crop!— while I, a poet, am hooted—and shiver—and owe twelve sous—and my shoe-sole is so transparent that thou mightest use it to glaze thy lantern! I thank thee, ferryman! thy cabin gives rest to my eyes, and makes me forget Paris! "

He was awakened from his almost lyric ecstasy by a great double St. John's rocket (so called from the cus-tom of discharging it on St. John's day) which suddenly issued from the blessed cabin. It was the ferryman himself, taking his share in the festivities of the day, and letting off his firework.

This rocket made Gringoire's hair stand on end.

" Oh, cursed holiday! " cried he, " wilt thou follow me everywhere—oh, my God! even to the ferryman's hut ? "

Then he looked upon the Seine at his feet, and felt a horrible temptation.

" Oh! " said he, " how gladly would I drown myself— if the water were not so cold! "

Then he took a desperate resolution. It was—since

he found that he could not escape the fools' pope, Jehan Fourbault's paintings, the bundles of may, the squibs and the rockets—to plunge boldly into the very heart of the illumination, and go to the Place de Grève.

"At least," thought he, "I shall perhaps get a brand there to warm my fingers; and I shall manage to sup on some morsel from the three great chests of sugar plums that will have been set out there on the public side-board of the town."

CHAPTER II.

THE PLACE DE GRÈVE.

THERE now remains but a very small and scarcely perceptible vestige of the Place de Grève, such as it existed formerly; and that is, the charming turret which occupies the northern angle of the Place, and which, already buried under the ignoble washing which encrusts the delicate lines of its carving, will soon, perhaps have totally disappeared, under that increase of new houses which is so rapidly consuming all the old fronts in Paris.

Those who, like ourselves, never pass over the Place de Grève without casting a look of pity and sympathy on this poor turret, squeezed between two paltry houses of the time of Louis XV., can easily reconstruct in their mind's eye the assemblage of edifices to which it belonged, and thus imagine themselves in the old Gothic Place of the fifteenth century.

It was then, as now, an irregular square, bounded on one side by the quay, and on the three others by a series of lofty houses, narrow and gloomy. In the daytime you might admire the variety of these buildings, all carved in stone or in wood, and already presenting complete specimens of the various kinds of domestic architecture of the Middle Ages, going back from the fifteenth to the eleventh century—from the perpendicular window which was beginning to supersede the Gothic, to the circular arch which the Gothic had supplanted, and which still occupied underneath it the first story of that ancient house of the Tour-Rolland or Roland's Tower, at the angle of the Place adjoining to the Seine, on the side of the Rue de la Tannerie. By night, nothing was distinguishable of that mass of buldings but the black indentation of their line of gables, extending its range of acute angles round three sides of the Place. For it is one of the essential differences between the towns of that day and those of the present, that now it is the fronts of the houses that look to the squares and streets, but then it was the backs. For two centuries past they have been turned fairly around.

In the center of the eastern side of the Place rose a heavy and heterogeneous pile formed by three masses of buildings in juxtaposition. The whole was called by three several names, expressing its history, its purpose, and its architecture ; it was called the Maison-au-Dauphin, or Dauphin's House, because Charles V., when dauphin, had lived in it—the Marchandise, because it was used as the Hôtel-de-Ville, or Town House—and the Maison-aux-Piliers (*domus ad piloria*) or Pillared House, on account of a series of large pillars which supported its three stories. The Town had there all that a good town like Paris wants; a chapel to pray in ; a plaidoyer, or court-room, for holding magisterial sittings, and, on occasion, reprimanding the king's officers ; and, at the top of all, a magazine stored with artillery and ammunition. For the good people of Paris, well knowing that it was not sufficient, in every emergency, to plead and to pray for the franchises of their city, had always in reserve, in the garrets of the Hôtel-de-Ville, some few good rustý arquebusses or other.

La Grève (as this ancient square was familiarly and elliptically called) had then that sinister aspect which it still derives from the execrable ideas which it awakens, and from the gloomy-looking Hôtel-de-Ville, of Dominique Bocador's erection, which has taken the place of the Maison-aux-Piliers. It must be observed that a permanent gibbet and pillory, a justice and an échelle, as they were then called, erected side by side in the middle of the square, contributed not a little to make the passenger avert his eyes from this fatal spot, where so many beings in full life and health had suffered their last agony ; and which was to give birth, fifty years later, to that St. Vallier's fever, as it was called, that terror of the scaffold, the most monstrous of all maladies, because it is inflicted not by the hand of God, but by that of man.

"It is consolatory," here observes our author, "to reflect that the punishment of death, which, three centuries back, still encumbered with its iron wheels, with its stone gibbets, with all its apparatus for execution permanently fixed in the ground, the Grève, the Halles, the Place Dauphine, the Croix du Trahoir, the Marché aux Pourceaux, or Hog Market, the hideous Montfauçon, the Barrière des Sergens, the Place aux Chats, the Porte Saint-Denis, Champeaux, the Porte Baudets, the Porte Saint-Jacques,—not to mention the innumerable échelles of the provosts, of the bishop, of the chapters, of the abbots, of the priors having justice—not to mention the judicial drownings in the River Seine—it is consolatory to reflect that now, after losing, one after another, every piece of her panoply—her profusion of executions—her refined and fanciful torments—her torture, for applying which she made afresh every five years a bed of leather in the Grand-Châtelet,—this old queen of feudal society, nearly thrust out of our laws and of our towns, tracked from code to code, driven from place to place, now possesses, in our vast metropolis of Paris, but one dishonored corner of the Grève— but one miserable guillotine—stealthy—anxious— ashamed—which seems always afraid of being taken in the fact, so quickly does it disappear after giving its blow."

CHAPTER III.

BESOS PARA GOLPES.

WHEN Pierre Gringoire arrived at the Place de Grève, he was in a shiver. He had gone over the Pont-aux-Meuniers, or Miller's Bridge, to avoid the crowd on the Pont-au-Change and Jehan Fourbault's drapelets; but the wheels of all the bishop's mills had splashed him as he went by, so that his coat was wet through; and he thought that the fate of his piece had rendered him yet more chilly. Accordingly, he hastened toward the bonfire which was burning magnificently in the middle of the Place, but a considerable crowd encircled it.

"You damned Parisians!" said he to himself (for Gringoire, like a true dramatic poet, was subject to monologues), "so, now you keep me from the fire! And yet I've some occasion for a chimney-corner. My shoes let in wet—and then, all those cursed mills have been raining upon me. The devil take the Bishop of Paris with his mills! I wonder what a bishop can do with a mill! Does he expect, from being a bishop, to turn miller? If he only wants my malediction to do so, I heartily give it him, and his cathedral, and his mills! Let us see, now, if any of those cockneys will stand aside. What are they doing there all this while? Warming themselves—a fine pleasure, truly! Looking at a hundred logs burning—a fine sight, to be sure!"

On looking nearer, however, he perceived that the circle was much wider than was requisite to warm themselves comfortably at the bonfire, and that this concourse of spectators were not attracted solely by the beauty of a hundred blazing logs.

In a wide space left clear between the fire and the crowd, a young girl was dancing. Whether she was a human being, a fairy, or an angel, was what Gringoire, skeptical philosopher and ironical poet as he was, could not at the first moment decide, so much was he fascinated by this dazzling vision.

She was not tall, but the elasticity of her slender shape made her appear so. She was brown; but it was evident that, in the daylight, her complexion would have that golden glow seen upon the women of Andalusia and of the Roman States. Her small foot, too, was Andalusian; for it was at once tight and easy in its light and graceful shoe. She was dancing, turning, whirling upon an old Persian carpet spread negligently under her feet; and each time that, in turning round, her radiant countenance passed before you, her large black eyes seemed to flash upon you.

Around, every look was fixed upon her, every mouth was open; and, indeed, while she was dancing thus, to the sound of the tambourine which her two round and delicate arms lifted aloft above her head—slender, fragile, brisk, as a wasp in the sunshine—with her golden corset without a plait—her parti-colored skirt swelling out below her slender waist—her bare shoulders—her fine-formed legs, of which her dress gave momentary glimpses—her black hair and her sparkling eyes—she looked like something more than human.

"Truly," thought Gringoire, "'tis a salamander—a nymph—a goddess—a bacchante of Mount Mænalus!"

At that moment one of the braids of the salamander's hair came undone, and a small piece of brass that had been attached to it rolled upon the ground.

"Ah! no," said he, it's a gypsy." All the illusion had disappeared.

She resumed her dance. She took up from the ground two swords, the points of which she supported upon her forehead, making them turn in one direction while she turned in the other. It was indeed no other than a gypsy. Yet, disenchanted as Gringoire found himself, the scene, taken altogether, was not without its charm, not without its magic. The bonfire cast upon her a red flaring light, which flickered brightly upon the circle of faces of the crowd and the brown forehead of the girl, and, at the extremities of the Place threw a pale reflection, mingled with the wavering of their shadows—on one side, upon the old dark wrinkled front of the Maison-aux-Piliers—on the other, upon the stone arms of the gibbet.

Among the thousand visages which this light tinged with scarlet, there was one which seemed to be more than all the rest absorbed in the contemplation of the dancer. It was the face of a man, austere, calm, and sombre. This man, whose dress was hidden by the crowd that surrounded him, seemed to be not more than thirty-five years of age; yet he was bald, having only a few thin tufts of hair about his temples, which were already gray; his broad and high forehead was beginning to be furrowed with wrinkles; but in his deep-sunken eyes there shone an extraordinary youth, an ardent animation, a depth of passion. He kept them constantly fixed upon the gypsy; and while the sportive girl of sixteen was dancing and bounding to the delight of all, his reverie seemed to grow more and more gloomy. From time to time a smile and a sigh encountered each other on his lips, but the smile was yet more dismal than the sigh.

The girl, having at length danced herself quite out of breath, stopped, and the people applauded with fondness.

"Djali!" cried the gypsy.

Gringoire then saw come up to her a little white she-goat, lively, brisk, and glossy, with gilt horns, gilt feet, and a gilt collar, which he had not before observed; as, until that moment it had been lying squat upon one corner of the carpet, looking at his mistress dance.

"Djali," said the dancer, "it's your turn now;" and sitting down, she gracefully held out her tambourine to the goat. "Djali," she continued, "what month of the year is this?"

The animal lifted its fore foot and struck one stroke upon the tambourine. It was, in fact, the first month of the year. The crowd applauded.

"Djali!" resumed the girl, turning her tambourine another way, "what day of the month is it?"

Djali lifted her little golden foot, and struck six times upon the tambourine.

"Djali!" said the gypsy, each time altering the position of the tambourine, "what hour of the day is it?"

Djali struck seven strokes, and at that very moment the clock of the Maison-aux-Piliers struck seven. The people were wonderstruck.

"There is witchcraft in all that," said a sinister voice in the crowd. It was that of the bald man who had his eyes constantly upon the gypsy.

She shuddered and turned away. But the plaudits burst forth and smothered the sullen exclamation. Indeed, they so completely effaced it from her mind, that she continued to interrogate her goat.

"Djali!" said she, "how does Maître Guichard Grand-Remy, captain of the town pistoliers, go in the procession at Candlemas?"

Djali reared up on her hind legs and began to bleat, marching at the same time with so seemly a gravity, that the whole circle of spectators burst into a laugh at this mimicry of the self-interested devotion of the captain of pistoliers.

"Djali!" resumed the girl, emboldened by this increased success, "how does Maître Jacques Charmolue, the king's attorney in the ecclesiastical court—how does he preach?"

The goat sat down upon his posteriors and began to bleat, shaking its fore-paws after so strange a fashion, that, with the exception of the bad French and worse Latin of the preacher, it was Jacques Charmolue to the life, gesture, accent, and attitude; and the crowd applauded with all their might.

"Sacrilege! profanation!" cried the voice of the bald-headed man.

The gypsy turned away once more. "Ah!" said she, "it's that odious man!" Then putting out her lower lip beyond her upper, she made a little pouting grimace which seemed familiar to her, turned upon her heel, and began to collect in her tambourine the contributions of the multitude.

All sorts of small coins, grands blancs, petits blancs, targes, liards à l'aigle, were now showered upon her. Ir taking her round, she all at once came before Gringoire; and as he, in perfect absence of mind, put his hand into his pocket, she stopped, expecting something. "Diable!" exclaimed the poet, finding at the bottom of his pocket the reality, that is to say, nothing at all; the pretty girl standing before him all the while, looking at him with her large eyes, holding out her tambourine, and waiting. Gringoire perspired profusely. Had all Peru been in his pocket, he would assuredly have given it to the dancer; but Gringoire had not Peru in his pocket—nor, indeed, was America yet discovered.

Fortunately an unexpected incident came to his relief. "Wilt thou be gone, thou Egyptian locust?" cried a harsh voice from the darkest corner of the Place. The girl turned away affrighted. This was not the voice of the bald-headed man; it was the voice of a woman—it was one, too, of devotion and of malice.

However, this cry, which frightened the gypsy, highly delighted a troop of children that were rambling about there. "It's the recluse of the Tour-Rolland," cried they with inordinate bursts of laughter—"it's the sachette that's scolding. Hasn't she had her supper? Let's carry her something from the town side-board." And they all ran toward the Maison-aux-Piliers.

Meanwhile, Gringoire availed himself of this disturbance of the dancer to disappear among the crowd. The shouts of the children reminded him that he too had not supped. He therefore hastened to the public buffet or sideboard. But the little rogues had better legs than he, and when he arrived they had cleared the table. They had not even left one wretched camichon at five sous the pound. There was nothing now against the wall, but the light fleurs-de-lys intermingled with rose-trees painted there in 1434 by Mathieu Biterne; and they offered but a meager supper.

'Tis an unpleasant thing, after going without one's dinner, to go to bed supperless. 'Tis less gratifying still, to go without one's supper, and not know where

to go to bed. Yet so it was with Gringoire. Without
food, without lodging, he found himself pressed by
Necessity on every side, and he thought Necessity
very ungracious. He had long discovered this truth—
that Jupiter created man in a fit of misanthropy, and
that throughout the life of the wisest man his destiny
keeps his philosophy in a state of siege. For his own
part, he had never found the blockade so complete.
He heard his stomach sound a parley, and he thought
it very ill ordained, that his evil destiny should reduce
his philosophy by simple starvation. He was sinking
more and more deeply into this melancholy revery,
when he was suddenly startled from it by the sound of
a fantastically warbling voice. It was the young gypsy
singing.

Her voice had the same character as her dance and
as her beauty. It had an undefinable charm—something clear, sonorous, aërial—winged, as it were. There
was a continued succession of swells, of melodies, of
unexpected falls—then simple strains, interspersed with
sharp and whistling notes—then a running over the
gamut that would have bewildered a nightingale, yet
ever harmonious—then soft octave undulations, which
rose and fell like the bosom of the youthful songstress.
The expression of her fine countenance followed with
singular flexibility every capricious variation of her
song, from the wildest inspiration to the most chastened
dignity. She seemed now all frolic, and now all majesty.

The words that she sang were in Spanish, a language
unintelligible to Gringoire, and which seemed to be unknown to herself, so little did the expression which she
gave in singing correspond with the sense of the words.
For instance, she gave these four lines, from an old
ballad of the time of the Moors, with the most sportive
gayety:

> Un cofre de gran riqueza
> Hallaron dentro un pilar;
> Dentro del, nuevas banderas
> Con figuras de espantar.

And then, a moment after, at the tone which she gave
to this stanza—

> Alarabes de cavallo
> Sin poderse menear,
> Con espadas, y a los cuellos
> Ballestas de buen echar.

Gringoire felt the tears come to his eyes. Yet joyful-
ness predominated in her tones, and she seemed to
warble, like a bird, from pure lightness of heart.

The gypsy's song had disturbed Gringoire's revery,
but it was as the swan disturbs the water. He listened
to it with a sort of ravishment and forgetfulness of
everything else. It was the first moment, for several
hours, in which he felt no suffering.

The moment was a short one, the same female voice
which had interrupted the gypsy's dance, now interrupted her song. "Wilt thou be silent, thou hell
cricket?" it cried, still from the same dark corner of
the Place.

The poor cricket stopped short, and Gringoire stopped
his ears. "Oh!" he cried, "thou cursed, broken-
toothed saw, that comest to break the lyre!"

The rest of the bystanders murmured like himself.
"The devil take the sachette!" cried some of them.
And the old invisible disturber might have found cause
to repent of her attacks upon the gypsy, had not their
attention been diverted at that moment by the procession of the Fools' Pope, which, after traversing many a
street, was now debouching upon the Place de Grève,
with all its torches and all its clamor.

The procession, which our readers have seen take its
departure from the Palais, had organized itself on the
way, and been recruited with all the ragamuffins, the un-
employed thieves, and disposable vagabonds in Paris, so
that when it reached the Grève it presented a most
respectable aspect.

First of all marched the tribes of Egypt. The Duke
of Egypt was at their head, with his counts on foot,
holding his bridle and stirrup; behind them came the

Egyptians, men and women, pell-mell, with their little children squalling upon their shoulders; all of them, duke, counts, and people, covered with rags and tinsel. Then followed the kingdom of Argot, that is, all the rest of the vagabond community, arranged in bands according to the order of their dignities, the moines or monks walking first. Thus marched on, four abreast, with the different insignia of their degrees in that strange faculty, most of them crippled in some way or other—some limping, some with only one hand—the courtaux de boutanche, the coquillarts, the hubins, the sabouleux, the calots, the francmitoux, the polissons, the piètres, the capons, the malingreux, the rifodés, the marcandiers, the narquois, the orphelins, the archisup pôts, the cagoux — denominations enough to have wearied Homer himself to enumerate, and some explanation of which will occur as we proceed. It was with some difficulty that you could discern, in the center of the band of cagoux and archisuppôts, the King of Argot himself, the grand-coësre, as he was called, sitting squat in a little wagon drawn by two large dogs. After the nation of the Argotiers came the empire of Galilee. Guillaume Rousseau, Emperor of the empire of Galilee, walked majestically in his robe of purple stained with wine, preceded by mummers dancing warlike dances, and surrounded by his mace-bearers, his suppôts, and the clerks of the chambre des comptes. Lastly came the members of the basoche, with their garlanded maypoles, their black gowns, their music, worthy of a witches' meeting, and their great candles of yellow wax. In the center of this latter crowd, the great officers of the brotherhood of Fools bore upon their shoulders a brancard, or chair carried upon poles, more loaded with wax-tapers than was the shrine of Ste. Geneviève in time of pestilence; and upon this chair shone, crosiered, and mitred, the new Fools' Pope, the ringer of Notre-Dame, Quasimodo the hunchback.

Each division of this grotesque procession had its particular music. The Egyptians sounded their balafos and their African 'ambourines. The Argotiers, a very unmusical race, had advanced no further than the viol the bugle-horn, and the Gothic rubebbe of the twefth century. The empire of Galilee had not made much greater progress. You could but just distinguish in its music some wretched rebeck of the infancy of the art still confined to the re, la, mi. But it was around the Fools' Pope that were displayed, in magnificent discordance, all the musical riches of the age; there were rebeck trebles, rebeck tenors, and rebeck counter-tenors; not to mention the flutes and the cuivres. Alas! our readers will recollect that it was poor Gringoire's orchestra.

It is not easy to give an idea of the expression of proud and beatific satisfaction, to which the melancholy and hideous visage of Quasimodo had attained in the journey from the Palais to the Grève. It was the first feeling of self-love that he had ever enjoyed. He had hitherto experienced nothing but humiliation, disdain for his condition, disgust for his person. So that, deaf as he was, he nevertheless relished, like a true pope, the acclamations of that crowd whom he hated because he felt himself hated by them. What though his people were a people of fools, an assemblage of cripples, thieves, and beggars—still they were a people, and he was a sovereign. And he took in earnest all the ironical applause and mock reverence which they gave him; with which, at the same time, we must not forget to observe that there was mingled, in the minds of the crowd, a degree of fear perfectly real; for the hunchback was strong; though bow-legged, he was active; though deaf, he was malicious—three qualities which have the effect of moderating ridicule.

However, that the new Pope of the Fools analyzed the feelings which he experienced, and those which he inspired, we by no means imagine. The spirit that was lodged in that misshapen body, was necessarily itself incomplete and dull of hearing; so that what it felt at that moment was to itself absolutely vague, indistinct, and confused. Only, joy beamed through, and pride predominated. Around that dismal and unhappy countenance there was a perfect radiance.

It was, therefore, not without surprise and dread that all at once, at the moment when Quasimodo, in that state of demi-intoxication, was passing triumphantly before the Maison-aux-Piliers, a man was seen to issue from the crowd, and, with an angry gesture, snatch from his hands his crosier of gilt wood, the ensign of his mock papacy.

The person who had this temerity was the man with the bald forehead, who, the moment before, standing in the crowd that encircled the gypsy, had chilled the poor girl's blood with his words of menace and hatred. He was in an ecclesiastical dress. The moment he stood forth from the crowd, he was recognized by Gringoire, who had not before observed him. " What!" said he, with a cry of astonishment. " Why, 'tis my master in Hermes, Dom Claude Frollo, the archdeacon! What the devil can he want with that one-eyed brute? He's going to get himself devoured!"

Indeed, a cry of terror proceeded from the multitude. The formidable Quasimodo had leaped down from his chair ; and the women turned away their eyes, that they might not see him tear the archdeacon to pieces.

He made one bound up to the priest, looked in his face, and then fell upon his knees, before him. The priest snatched his tiara from his head, broke his crosier, and rent his tinsel cope. Quasimodo remained upon his knees, bowed down his head, and clasped his hands. They then entered into a strange dialogue of signs and gestures, for neither of them uttered a word ; the priest erect, angry, threatening, imperious ; Quasimodo prostrate, humble, suppliant. And yet it is certain that Quasimodo could have crushed the priest with a single gripe. At last the priest, roughly shaking Quasimodo's powerful shoulder, made him a sign to rise and follow him, and Quasimodo rose accordingly.

Then the brotherhood of Fools, their first amazement being over, offered to defend their pope, thus abruptly dethroned. The Egyptians, the Argotiers, and all the Basoche, came yelping round the priest. But Quasimodo, placing himself before the priest, put the muscles of his athletic fists in play, and faced the assailants, gnashing his teeth like an enraged tiger. The priest resumed his sombre gravity, made a sign to Quasimodo and withdrew in silence. Quasimodo walked before him, scattering the crowd as he passed along.

When they had made their way through the populace and across the Place, the mob of the curious and the idle offered to follow them. Quasimodo then placed himself in the rear, and followed the archdeacon backwards, looking squat, snarling, monstrous, shaggy, gathering up his limbs, licking his tusks, growling like a wild beast, and impressing immense vibrations on the crowd by a mere look or gesture.

At length they both plunged down a dark narrow street, into which no one ventured after them; so effectually was its entrance barred by the mere image of Quasimodo gnashing his teeth.

"All this is wonderful enough," said Gringoire to himself, "but where the devil shall I find a supper?"

CHAPTER IV.

THE DANGER OF FOLLOWING A PRETTY WOMAN IN THE STREETS BY NIGHT.

GRINGOIRE, at a venture, had set himself to follow the gypsy girl. He had seen her, with her goat, turn down the Rue de la Contellerie; and, accordingly, he turned into the Rue de la Contellerie likewise—"Why not?" said he to himself.

As a practical philosopher of the streets of Paris, Gringoire had remarked that nothing is more favorable to a state of revery than to follow a pretty woman without knowing whither she is going. In this voluntary abdication of one's free-will—in this fancy subjecting itself to the fancy of another, while that other is totally unconscious of it—there is a mixture of fantas-

tic independence with blind obedience, a something intermediate between slavery and freedom, which was
pleasing to the mind of Gringoire, a mind essentially
mixed, undecided, and complex—holding the medium
between all extremes—in constant suspense amongst
all human propensities, and neutralizing one of them by
another. He likened himself with satisfaction to the
tomb of Mahomet, attracted by the two lodestones in
opposite directions, and hesitating eternally between
the top and the bottom, between the roof and the pavement, between fall and ascension, between the zenith
and the nadir.

Had Gringoire been living in our time, what a fine
medium, what a *juste milieu*, he would have kept between the classic and the romantic! But he was not
primitive enough to live three hundred years; and 'tis
really a pity. His absence leaves a void which, in these
days of ours, is but too sensibly felt.

However, for thus following the passengers through
the streets, especially the female ones, which Gringoire
readily did, there is nothing that better disposes a man
than not to know where to go to bed.

He walked along, therefore, all pensive, behind the
young girl, who quickened her step, making her pretty
little four-footed companion trot beside her, as she saw
the townspeople reaching home, and the taverns shutting up, the only shops that had been opened that day.
" After all," he half thought to himself, " she must have
a lodging somewhere—the gypsy women have good
hearts — who knows?"—And there were some points
of suspension about which he went on weaving this
web in his mind—certain very flattering ideas, or shadows of ideas.

Meanwhile, at intervals, as he passed by the last
groups of bourgeois closing their doors, he caught
some fragment of their conversation which snapped the
thread of his pleasing hypotheses.

Now, it was two old men accosting each other.

"Maître Thibaut Fernicle, do you know, it's very
cold?"

6

(Gringoire had known it ever since the winter had set in.)

"Yes, indeed, Maître Boniface Disome. Are we going to have such a winter as we had three years ago, in the year '80, when wood rose to eight sols a load, think you?"

"Bah! it's nothing at all, Maître Thibaut, to the winter of 1407, when it froze from Martinmas to Candlemas—and so sharp that the ink in the pen in the parliament's registrar's hands froze, in the Grande Chambre, at every three words—which interrupted the registering of the judgments!"

Then farther on, there were two good female neighbors, talking to each other through their windows with candles in their hands that glimmered through the fog.

"Has your husband told you of the mishap, Mademoiselle la Boudraque?"

"No, Mademoiselle Turquant, what is it?"

"The horse of Monsieur Giles Godin, notary at the Châtelet, took fright at the Flemings and their procession, and ran over Maître Philipot Avrillot, lay-brother of the Celestines."

"Did it indeed?"

"Yes, indeed."

"A paltry hack-horse, too! That was rather too bad —had it been a cavalry horse, now, it would not have been so much amiss."

And the windows were shut again. But Gringoire had completely lost the thread of his ideas.

Luckily, he soon found it again, and easily pieced it together, at the sight of the gypsy girl and of Djali, who were still trotting on before him, two slender, delicate, and charming creatures, whose small feet, pretty figures, and graceful motions he gazed at with admiration, almost confounding them together in his contemplation; their common intelligence and mutual affection seeming those of two young girls; while for their light, quick, graceful step, they might have been both young hinds.

Meanwhile, the streets were every moment becoming

darker and more solitary. The curfew had long ceased
to ring, and now it was only at long intervals that a
person passed you on the pavement, or a light was to
be seen at a window. Gringoire, in following the gypsy,
had involved himself in that inextricable labyrinth of
alleys, courts, and crossings which surrounds the ancient sepulchre of the Holy Innocents, and may be
compared to a skein of thread raveled by the playing
of a kitten. "Very illogical streets, in truth!" muttered Gringoire, quite lost in the thousand windings
which seemed to be everlastingly turning back upon
themselves, but through which the girl followed a track
that seemed to be well known to her, and with a pace
of increasing rapidity. For his own part, he would
have been perfectly ignorant as to his "whereabout,"
had he not observed, at the bend of a street, the octagonal mass of the pillory of the Halles, the perforated
top of which traced its dark outline upon a solitary
patch of light yet visible in a window of the Rue Ver-
delet.

A few minutes before, his step had attracted the
girl's attention: she had several times turned her head
towards him, as if with uneasiness: once, too, she had
stopped short; had availed herself of a ray of light that
escaped from a half-open bakehouse, to survey him
steadily from head to foot; then, when she had taken
that glance, Gringoire had observed her make that little
mow which he had already remarked, and she had gone
on without more ado.

This same little mow furnished Gringoire with a subject of reflection. There certainly was disdain and
mockery in that pretty little grimace. So that he was
beginning to hang down his head, to count the paving-
stones, and to follow the girl at a rather greater distance; when, just after she had made a turn into a
street which took her for a moment out of his sight, he
heard her utter a piercing shriek.

He quickened his pace. The street was quite dark.
However, a twist of tow steeped in oil, which was burning in a sort of iron cage, at the foot of a statue of the

Virgin at the corner of the street, enabled Gringoire to discern the gypsy struggling in the arms of two men, who were endeavoring to stifle her cries, while the poor little goat, all wild with affright, hung down its head, bleating.

"Hither! hither! gentlemen of the watch!" cried Gringoire; and he advanced bravely. One of the men who had laid hold of the girl, turned toward him. It was the formidable visage of Quasimodo. Gringoire did not fly—but he did not advance another step.

Quasimodo came up to him, threw him four paces off upon the pavement with a backstroke of his hand, and plunged rapidly into the darkness, bearing off the girl, her figure drooping over his arm almost as flexibly as a silken scarf. His companion followed him, and the poor goat ran behind with its plaintive bleat.

"Murder! murder!" cried the unfortunate gypsy.

"Stand, there! you scoundrels! and let that wench go!" was all at once heard in a voice of thunder, from a horseman, who suddenly made his appearance from the neighboring crossway.

It was a captain of that description of household troops which were still called archers (from the cross-bows which they carried before the invention of fire-arms), armed cap-à-pie, with his espadon, or great two-edged sword in his hand. He snatched the gypsy from the grasp of the amazed Quasimodo; laid her across his saddle; and, at the moment when the redoubtable hunchback, having recovered from his surprise, was rushing upon him to seize his prey a second time, fifteen or sixteen archers, who followed close upon their captain, made their appearance, each brandishing his broadsword. They were a detachment going the counter-watch, by order of Messire Robert d'Estouteville, keeper of the provostry of Paris.

Quasimodo was surrounded, seized, and bound. He roared, he foamed, he bit; and had it been daylight, no doubt his visage alone, rendered yet more hideous by rage, would have put the whole detachment to flight. But, being in the dark, he was disarmed of his most formidable weapon, his ugliness. His companion had disappeared during the struggle.

The gypsy girl gracefully gained her seat upon the officer's saddle; leaned both her hands upon the young man's shoulders, and looked fixedly at him for a few seconds, as if delighted with his fine countenance and the effectual succor he had rendered her. Then speaking first, and making her sweet voice still sweeter, she said to him, " Monsieur le gendarme, what is your name?"

" Captain Phœbus de Chateaupers, at your service, my fair one," said the officer, drawing himself up.

" Thank you," said she.

And while Captain Phœbus was curling his moustache *à la Bourguignonne*, she glided down from the horse like an arrow falling to the ground, and fled with the speed of lightning.

" *Nombril du Pape !* " exclaimed the captain, while he made them tighten the bands upon the limbs of Quasimodo, " I'd rather have kept the wench."

" Why, captain," said one of the gendarmes, " what would you have? The linnet is flown—we've made sure of the bat."

CHAPTER V.

SEQUEL OF THE DANGERS.

GRINGOIRE, quite stunned with his fall, had remained stretched upon the pavement before the good Virgin of the corner of the street. By degrees, however, he recovered his senses. At first, he was for some minutes in a sort of half-somnolent revery, which was not altogether disagreeable, and in which the airy figures of the gypsy and the goat were confounded in his imagination with the weight of Quasimodo's fist. This state of his feelings, however, was of short duration. A very lively impression of cold upon that part of his body which was in contact with the ground, suddenly awoke him, and brought back his mind to the surface. " Whence is this coolness that I feel? " said he hastily to himself. He then perceived that he lay somewhere about the middle of the gutter.

" The devil take the humpbacked Cyclop! " grumbled he, and he strove to get up. But he was too much stunned, and too much bruised; so that he was forced to remain where he was. Having, however, the free use of his hand, he stopped his nose, and resigned himself to his situation.

" The mud of Paris," thought he (for he now believed it to be decided that the kennel was to be his lodging:

Et que faire en un gite à moins que l'on ne songe?)

"the mud of Paris is particularly offensive. It must contain a large proportion of volatile and nitrous salts. Such too is the opinion of Maître Nicholas Flamel and the hermetics."

This word hermetics reminded him of the Archdeacon Claude Frollo. He reflected on the scene of violence of which he had just before had a glimpse; that he had seen the gypsy struggling between two men; that Quasimodo had a companion with him; and the sullen and haughty countenance of the archdeacon floated confusedly in his recollection. " That would be strange," thought he; and then, with this datum and upon this basis, he began to rear the fantastic framework of hypothesis, that house of cards of the philosophers; then suddenly returning once more to reality, " Oh, I freeze! " he cried.

The position was in fact becoming less and less tenable. Each particle of water in the channel carried off a particle of caloric from the loins of Gringoire; and an equality of temperature between his body and the fluid that ran under it was beginning to establish itself without mercy.

All at once he was assailed by an annoyance of quite

a different nature. A troop of children, of those little barefooted savages that have in all times run about the streets of Paris, with the everlasting name of gamins, "and who," says our author, "when we were children also, used to throw stones at us all as we were leaving school in the evening, because our trowsers were not torn,"—a swarm of these young rogues ran to the crossway where Gringoire was lying, laughing and shouting in a manner that showed very little concern about the sleep of the neighbors. They were dragging after them some sort of a shapeless pack; and the noise of their wooden shoes alone was enough to waken the dead. Gringoire, who was not quite dead yet, half raised himself up.

"Hollo! Hennequin Dandèche! Hollo! Jehan Pincebourde!" cried they as loud as they could bawl; "old Eustache Moubon, the old ironseller at the corner is just dead. We've got his straw mattress, and we're going to make a bonfire with it. This is the Flamings' day!"

And so saying, they threw down the mattress precisely upon Gringoire, whom they had come up to without perceiving him. At the same time one of them took a handful of straw, and went to light it at the Blessed Virgin's torch.

"*Mort-Christ!*" muttered Gringoire, "am I now going to be too hot?"

The moment was critical. He was about to be fixed between fire and water. He made a supernatural effort, such as a coiner might have made in trying to escape when they were going to boil him to death. He rose up, threw back the mattress upon the gamins, and took to his heels.

"Holy Virgin!" cried the boys, "it's the old ironseller's ghost!" And they too ran away.

The mattress remained master of the field. Those judicious historians, Belleforêt, Father Le Juge, and Corrozet, assure us that the next morning it was taken up with great solemnity by the clergy of that part of the town, and carried in great pomp to the treasury of Sainte-Opportune's church; where until the year 1789, the sacristan drew a very handsome income from the great miracle worked by the statue of the Virgin at the corner of the Rue Mauconseil, which, by its presence alone, in the memorable night between the 6th and the 7th of January, 1482, had exorcised the deceased Jehan Moubon, who, to cheat the devil, had, when dying, slyly hidden his soul within his mattress.

CHAPTER VI.

THE BROKEN LEG.

AFTER running for some time as fast as his legs would carry him, without knowing whither, whisking round many a corner, striding over many a gutter, traversing many a court and alley, seeking flight and passage through all the meanders of the old pavement of the Halles, exploring what are called in the elegant Latin of the charters *tota via, cheminum, et viaria*, our poet all at once made a halt, first because he was out of breath, and then because a dilemma had suddenly arisen in his mind. " It seems to me, Maître Pierre Gringoire," said he to himself, applying his finger to his forehead, " that you are running all this while like a brainless fellow that you are. The little rogues were no less afraid of you than you were of them—it seems to me, I say, that you heard the clatter of their wooden shoes running away southward while you were running away northward. Now, one of two things must have taken place ; either they have run away, and then the mattress which they must have forgotten in their fright is precisely that hospitable couch after which you have been hunting ever since the morning, and which the Lady Virgin miraculously sends you to reward you for having composed, in honor of her, a morality, accompanied with triumphs and mummeries—or the boys have not run away, and in that case they will have set a light to the mattress, and that will be exactly the excellent fire that you're in want of, to comfort, warm, and dry you. In either case—good bed or good fire—the mattress is a present from heaven. The ever-blessed Virgin Mary that stands at the corner of the Rue Mauconseil, perhaps caused Jehan Moubon to die for the very purpose; and 'tis folly in you to scamper away at such a rate, like a Picard running from a Frenchman, leaving behind you what you are running forward to seek—blockhead that you are!"

Then he began to retrace his steps, and ferreting about to discover where he was—snuffing the wind, and laying down his ears—he strove to find his way back to the blessed mattress—but in vain. All was intersections of houses, courts, and clustering streets, amongst which he incessantly doubted and hesitated, more entangled in that strange network of dark alleys than he would have been in the labyrinth of the Hôtel des Tournelles itself. At length he lost patience, and vehemently exclaimed, "A curse upon the crossings! the devil himself has made them after the image of his pitchfork!"

This exclamation relieved him a little; and a sort of reddish reflection, which he at that moment discovered at the end of a long and very narrow street, completed the restoration of his courage. "God be praised," said he, "there it is! There is my blazing mattress!" And, likening himself to the pilot foundering in the night-time, "*Salve*," added he, piously, "*salve, maris stella!*"

Did he address this fragment of a litany to the Holy Virgin, or to the straw mattress? We really can not say.

He had no sooner advanced a few paces down the long street or lane, which was on a declivity, unpaved, descending quicker and becoming more miry the farther he proceeded, than he observed something very singular. The street was not quite solitary; for here and there were to be seen crawling in it, certain vague, shapeless masses, all moving toward the light which was flickering at the end of the street; like those heavy insects which drag themselves along at night, from one blade of grass to another, toward a shepherd's fire.

Nothing makes a man so adventurous as an empty stomach. Gringoire went forward, and soon came up with that one of the larvæ which seemed to be dragging itself along most indolently after the others. On approaching it, he found that it was nothing other than a miserable stump of a man, without legs or thighs, jumping along upon his two hands, like a mutilated father-long-legs with only two of its feet remaining. The moment he came up to this sort of spider with a human face, it lifted up to him a lamentable voice: "*La buona mancia, signor! la buona mancia!*"

"The devil take thee!" said Gringoire, "and me along with thee, if I know what you mean." And he passed on.

He came up to another of these ambulatory masses, and examined it. It was a cripple, both legless and armless, after such a manner that the complicated machinery of crutches and wooden legs that supported him made him look for all the world like a mason's scaffolding walking along. Gringoire, being fond of noble and classical similes, compared him, in his mind, to the living tripod of Vulcan.

This living tripod saluted him as he went by; but staying his hat just at the height of Gringoire's chin, after the manner of a shaving dish, and shouting in his ears, "*Senor Cabarellero, para comprar un pedaso de pan!*"

"It appears," said Gringoire, "that this one talks too; but it's a barbarous language, and he's more lucky than I am if he understands it." Then striking his forehead through a sudden transition of idea: "Apropos! what the devil did they mean this morning with their Esmeralda?"

He resolved to double his pace; but for the third time something blocked up the way. This something, or rather this somebody, was a blind man, a little man, with a bearded Jewish face, who, rowing in the space about him with a great stick, and towed along by a great dog, snuffled out to him with a Hungarian accent, "*Facitote caritatem!*"

"Oh, come!" said Pierre Gringoire, "here is one at last that talks a Christian language. Truly, I must have a most almsgiving mien, that they should just ask charity of me in the present extenuated state of my purse. My friend," said he, turning to the blind man, "last week I sold my last shirt; that is to say, as you understand no language but that of Cicero, *Vendidi hebdomade nuper transitâ meam ultimam chemisam.*"

Then, turning his back upon the blind man, he went forward on his way. But the blind man quickened his pace at the same time; and now, also, the cripple and the stump came up in great haste, with great clatter of the platter that carried one of them, and the crutches that carried the other. Then all three, shoving one another aside at the heels of poor Gringoire, began to sing him their several staves:

"*Caritatem!*" sang the blind man.

"*La buona mancia!*" sang the stump.

And the man of the wooden legs took up the stave with, "*Un pedaso de pan!*"

Gringoire stopped his ears. "Oh, tower of Babel!" he cried.

He began to run. The blind man ran. The wooden legs ran. The stump ran.

And then, as he advanced still farther down the street, stump men, wooden-legged men, and blind men came swarming around him—and one-handed men, and one-eyed men, and lepers with their sores—some coming out of the houses, some from the little adjacent streets, some from the cellar-holes—howling, bellowing, yelping—all hobbling along, making their way toward the light, and wallowing in the mire like so many slugs after the rain.

Gringoire, still followed by his three persecutors, and not well knowing what was to come of all this, walked on affrighted among the others, turning aside the limpers, striding over the stumpies, his feet entangled in that ant-hill of cripples, like the English captain who found himself beset by a legion of crabs.

The idea just occurred to him of trying to retrace his

steps. But it was too late; all this army had closed upon his rear, and his three beggars were still upon him. He went on, therefore, urged forward at once by that irresistible flood, by fear, and by a dizziness which made it all seem to him like a sort of horrible dream.

At last he reached the extremity of the street. It opened into an extensive place, in which a thousand scattered lights were wavering in the thick gloom of the night. Gringoire threw himself into it, hoping to escape by the speed of his legs from the three deformed spectres that had fixed themselves upon him.

"*Onde vas, hombre?*" cried the wooden legs, throwing aside his scaffolding, and running after him with as good a pair of legs as ever measured a geometrical pace upon the pavement of Paris. Meanwhile the stump-man, erect upon his feet, clapped his heavy iron-sheathed platter upon his head, while the blind man stared him in the face with great flaming eyes.

"Where am I?" said the terrified poet.

"In the Court of Miracles," answered a fourth specter who had accosted them.

"On my soul," returned Gringoire, "I do indeed find here that the blind see and the lame walk—but where is the Saviour?"

They answered him with a burst of laughter of a sinister kind.

The poor poet cast his eyes around him. He was in fact in that same terrible Cour des Miracles, or Court of Miracles, into which no honest man had ever penetrated at such an hour—a magic circle, in which the officers of the Châtelet and the sergeants of the provostry, when they ventured thither, disappeared in morsels—the city of the thieves—a hideous wen on the face of Paris—a sink from whence escaped every morning, and to which returned to stagnate every night, that stream of vice, mendicity and vagrancy which ever flows through the streets of a capital—a monstrous hive, into which all the petty hornets of society returned each evening with their booty—a lying hospital, in which the gypsy, the unfrocked monk, the abandoned scholar—the worthless of every nation, Spaniards, Italians, Germans—of every religion, Jews, Christians, Mahometans, idolaters—covered with simulated sores, beggars in the daytime, transformed themselves at night into robbers—an immense dressing-room, in short, in which dressed and undressed at that period all the actors in that everlasting drama which robbery, prostitution, and murder enacted upon the pavements of Paris.

It was a large open space, irregular and ill-paved, as was at that time every place in Paris. Fires, around which strange groups were gathered, were gleaming here and there. All was motion and clamor. There were shrieks of laughter, squalling of children, and screaming of women. The arms and heads of this crowd cast a thousand fantastic gestures in dark outline upon the luminous background. Now and then, upon the ground, over which the light of the fires was wavering, intermingled with great undefined shadows, was seen to pass a dog resembling a man, or a man resembling a dog. The limits of the different races and species seemed to be effaced in this commonwealth as in a pandemonium. Men, women, beasts; age, sex; health, sickness; all seemed to be in common among this people; all went together mingled, confounded, placed one upon another, each one participating in all.

The weak and wavering rays that streamed from the fires enabled Gringoire, amid his perturbation, to distinguish, all round the extensive enclosure, a hideous range of old houses, the decayed, shriveled, and stooping fronts of which, each perforated by one or two circular attic windows with lights behind them, seemed to him, in the dark, like enormous old women's heads, ranged in a circle, looking monstrous and crabbed, and winking upon the diabolical rebel.

It was like a new world, unknown, unheard-of, deformed, creeping, swarming, fantastic.

Gringoire, growing wilder and wilder with affright, held by the three mendicants as by three pairs of pincers, and deafened by a crowd of other vagrants that

flocked barking round him—the unlucky Gringoire
strove to muster presence of mind enough to recollect
whether he was really at a witches' sabbath or not ; but
his efforts were vain ; the thread of his memory and his
thoughts was broken ; and, doubting of everything—
floating between what he saw and what he felt—he put
the insoluble question to himself—"Am I really in
being? do I really exist?"

At that moment a distinct shout was raised from the
buzzing crowd that surrounded him, of " Let's take him
to the king! let's take him to the king!"

"Holy Virgin!" muttered Gringoire, "the king of
this place must surely be a he-goat!"

"To the king! to the king!" repeated every voice.

They dragged him along, each striving to fix his
talons upon him. But the three beggars kept their
hold, and tore him away from the others, vociferating,
" He is ours!"

The poet's poor doublet, already in piteous plight,
gave up the ghost in this struggle.

In crossing the horrible place his dizziness left him.
After proceeding a few paces the feeling of reality had
returned to him. His apprehension began to adapt
itself to the atmosphere of the place. At the first moment, from his poet's head, or perhaps, indeed, quite
simply and prosaically, from his empty stomach, there
had risen a fume, a vapor, as it were, which, spreading
itself between him and the surrounding objects, had
allowed him to survey them only in the incoherent
mist of a nightmare in that dark shrouding of our
dreams, which distorts every outline, and clusters the
objects together in disproportioned groups, dilating
things into chimeras, and human figures into phantoms.
By degrees this hallucination gave way to a less bewildered and less magnifying state of vision. The real
made its way to his organs—struck upon his eyes—
struck against his feet—and demolished, piece by piece,
all the frightful poetry with which he had at first
thought himself surrounded. He could not but perceive at last that he was walking, not in the Styx, but

in the mud ; that he was elbowed, not by demons, but by thieves ; that not his soul, but, in simple sooth, his life was in danger—seeing that he was unaccompanied by that invaluable conciliator who places himself so effectually between the robber and the honest man—the purse. In short, on examining the orgie more closely and more coolly, he found that he descended from the witches' revel to the pot-house.

The Court of Miracles was, in truth, no other than one great public-house—but it was a public-house, a cabaret, of brigands, in which blood flowed almost as frequently as wine.

The spectacle which presented itself to him when his tattered escort at length deposited him at the term of its march, was little adapted to bring back his mind to poetry, though it were the poetry of hell. It was more than ever the prosaic and brutal reality of the tavern. Were we not writing of the fifteenth century, we should say that Gringoire had descended from Michael Angelo to Callot.

Round a great fire which was burning upon a large round flagstone, and the blaze of which had heated red-hot the legs of an iron trivet which was empty for the moment, some worm-eaten tables were set out here and there, as if by chance, without the smallest geometrician of a waiter having condescended to adjust their parallelism, or mind that, at least, they should not meet at too unaccustomed angles. Upon these tables shone some pots flowing with wine and beer, around which were grouped a number of bacchanalian visages, reddened by the fire and the wine. There was one man with a fair round belly and a jovial face, noisily throwing his arms round a girl of the town, thick-set and brawny. Then there was a sort of false soldier, a *narquois*, as he was called in the Argotian tongue, who whistled away while he was undoing the bandages of his false wound, and unstiffening his sound and vigorous knee, which had been bound up since the morning in a thousand ligatures. On the other hand there was a malingreux preparing, with celandine and ox-blood, his

jambe de Dieu, or sore leg, for the morrow. Two tables
higher up, a coquillart, with his complete pilgrim's habit
(from the coquilles or shells of which this denomination
arose) was conning a spiritual song, the complaint of
Sainte-Reine, the psalmody and the nasal drone included. In another place a young hubin was taking a
lesson in epilepsy from an old sabouleux, or hustler,
who was teaching him the art of foaming at the mouth
by chewing a piece of soap; while four or five women
thieves, just by them, were contending, at the same
table, for the possession of a child stolen in the course
of the evening. All which circumstances, two centuries
later, "seemed so laughable at court," says Sauval,
"that they furnished pastime to the king, and an opening to the royal ballet entitled 'Night,' which was divided into four parts, and danced upon the stage of
the Petit Bourbon." And "never," adds an eye-witness,
in the year 1653, "were sudden metamorphoses of the
Court of Miracles more happily represented. Benserade
prepared us for them by some very pleasant verses."

The loud laugh everywhere burst forth, and the ob-
scene song. Each one let off his own exclamation,
passing his remark, and swearing, without attending to
his neighbor. The pots rattled, and quarrels were
struck out of their collision, the smashing of pots thus
leading to the tearing of rags.

A large dog, sitting on his tail, was looking into the
fire. There were some children mingled in this orgie.
The stolen child was crying. Another, a bouncing boy
of four years old, was seated with his legs dangling upon a bench which was too high for him, with his chin
just above the table, said not a word. A third was
gravely spreading over the table with his finger the
melted tallow running from a candle. And a fourth, a
very little one, squatting in the mud, was almost lost in
a great iron pot which he was scraping with a tile, drawing from it a sound, enough certainly to have agonized
the most obdurate nerves.

There was a barrel near the fire, and upon the barrel
was seated one of the beggars. This was the king upon
his throne.

ιhe three who had possession of Gringoire brought
him before this cask, and the whole bacchanalia were
silent for a moment, excepting the caldron tenanted by
the child.

Gringoire was afraid to breathe or to lift up his eyes.
"*Hombre, quita tu sombrero!*" said one of the three
fellows who had hold of him; and before he could understand what that meant, another of them had taken
off his hat—a wretched covering, it is true, but still of
use on a day of sunshine or a day of rain. Gringoire
heaved a sigh.

Meanwhile the king, from the top of his barrel, put
the interrogatory, "What is this rascal?"

Gringoire started. This voice, though speaking in a
tone of menace, reminded him of another voice which
that very morning had struck the first blow at his mystery, by droning out in the midst of the audience,
"Charity, if you please!" He raised his eyes—it was
indeed Clopin Trouillefou.

Clopin Trouillefou, arrayed in his regal ensigns, had
not one rag more or less upon him. His sore on the
arm had indeed disappeared. He held in his hand one
of those whips with lashes of whitleather, which were,
at that time, used by the sergeants of the wand to drive
back the crowd, and were called boullayes. He had
upon his head a sort of coiffure formed into a circle and
closed at the top; but it was difficult to distinguish
whether it was a child's cushion or a king's crown, the
two things are so much alike.

However, Gringoire, without knowing why, had felt
some revival of hope on recognizing in the king of the
Court of Miracles his cursed beggar of the Grand Salle.
"Maître," stammered he, "—— Monseigneur —— Sire
——How must I call you?" said he at last, having
mounted to his utmost stretch of ascent, and neither
knowing how to mount higher nor how to come down
again.

"Monseigneur—Your Majesty—or Comrade—call me
what you like, only despatch. What hast thou to say
in thy defense?"

7

"In my defense!" thought Gringoire; "I don't like that." He replied, hesitating, "I am he—he who this morning——"

"By the devil's claws!" interrupted Clopin, "thy name, rascal! and nothing more. Hark ye—thou art before three mighty sovereigns: me, Clopin Trouillefou, King of Tunis, successor to the Grand Coësre, supreme sovereign of the kingdom of Argot; Mathais Hungadi Spicali, Duke of Egypt and Bohemia, that yellow old fellow that thou seest there with a clout round his head; and Guillaume Rousseau, Emperor of Galilee, that fat fellow, that's not attending to us, but to that wench. We are thy judges. Thou hast entered into the kingdom of Argot without being an Argotier—thou hast violated the privileges of our city. Thou must be punished, unless thou art either capon, a franc-mitou, or a rifodé, that is to say, in the Argot of the honest men, either a thief, a beggar, or a vagrant. Art thou anything of that sort? Justify thyself—tell over thy qualifications."

"Alas!" said Gringoire, "I have not that honor. I am the author—"

"That's enough," interrupted Trouillefou; "thou shalt be hanged. It's a matter of course, messieurs the honest townsfolk. Just as you treat our people amongst you, so we treat yours amongst us. Such law as you give to the Truands, the Truands give to you. If it's a bad law, it's your own fault. It's quite necessary that an honest man or two should now and then grin through the hempen collar—that makes the thing honorable. Come, my friend, merrily share thy tatters among these young ladies. I'll have thee hanged for the amusement of the Truands, and thou shalt give them thy purse to drink thy health. If thou hast any mumming to do first, there is down there, in that mortar, a very good stone God the Father that we stole from Saint-Pierre-aux-Bœufs. Thou hast four minutes' time to throw thy soul at his head."

This was a formidable harangue.

"Well said! upon my soul. Clopin Trouillefou

preaches like a holy father the Pope!" cried the Emperor of Galilee, breaking his pot at the same time to prop his table-leg.

"Messeigneurs the emperors and kings!" said Gringoire coolly, for his resolution had somehow or other returned to him, and he spoke quite firmly, "you do not consider. My name is Pierre Gringoire—I am the poet whose morality was performed this morning in the Grande Salle of the Palais."

"Ah! it's you, master, is it? I was there, *par la tête Dieu!* Well, comrade, is it any reason, because thou tiredst us to death this morning, that thou shouldst not be hanged to-night?"

"I shall not so easily get off," thought Gringoire. However, he made another effort.

"I don't very well see," said he, "why the poets are not classed among the Truands. A vagrant, forsooth—why, Æsopus was a vagrant. A beggar—well, Homerus was a beggar. A thief—was not Mercurius a thief?"

Clopin interrupted him. "Methinks," said he, "thou'st a mind to matagrabolize us with thy gibberish. *Pardieu!* Be hanged quietly, man; and don't make so much ado about nothing."

"Pardon me, monseigneur the king of Tunis," replied Gringoire, disputing the ground inch by inch; "it's really worth your while—Only one moment—Hear me—You'll not condemn me without hearing me?——"

His unfortunate voice was in fact drowned by the uproar that was made around him; the little boy was scraping his kettle with more alacrity than ever; and, as the climax, an old woman had just come and set upon the red-hot trivet a frying-pan full of fat, which yelped over the fire with a noise like the shouts of a flock of children running after a mask in carnival time.

Meanwhile, Clopin Trouillefou seemed to confer a moment with the duke of Egypt, and with the emperor of Galilee, who was completely drunk. Then he called out sharply, "Silence!" and as the pot and the frying-pan paid no attention to him, but continued their duet, he jumped down from his barrel, gave the caldron a kick which rolled it and the child half a score yards off; gave the frying-pan another, which upset all the fat into the fire; and then gravely reascended his throne, regardless of the smothered cries of the child, and of the grunting of the old woman, whose supper was evaporating in a beautiful white flame.

Trouillefou made a sign; whereupon the duke, and the emperor, and the archisuppôts, and the cagoux, came and ranged themselves about him in the form of a horse-shoe, of which Gringoire, upon whom they still kept rough hands, occupied the center. It was a semicircle of rags, tatters, and tinsel—of pitchforks and hatchets—of reeling legs and great naked arms—of sordid, dull, and sottish faces. In the midst of this Round Table of beggarhood, Clopin Trouillefou, as the doge of this senate, the king of this peerage, the pope of this conclave, predominated—in the first place, by the whole height of his cask—and then, by a certain lofty, fierce, and formidable air, which made his eyeballs flash, and corrected in his savage profile the bestial type of the Truand race. He might be compared to a wild boar among swine.

"Hark ye," said he to Gringoire, at the same time shaking his shapeless chin with his horny hand, "I don't see why thou shouldst not be hanged. To be sure, thou dost not seem to like it, and that's but natural—you bourgeois aren't used to it. You think it very shocking. After all, we don't wish thee any harm. There's one way of getting off for the moment. Wilt thou be one of us?"

It may be supposed what an effect this proposal produced upon Gringoire, who saw life just about to escape him, and felt his grasp of it beginning to fail. He caught at it energetically. "That I will—certainly, assuredly," said he.

"You consent," said Clopin, "to enlist yourself among the men of the petite flambe?"

"Of the petite flambe—exactly so," responded Gringoire.

"You acknowledge yourself a member of the franche-bourgeoisie?" added the king of Tunis.

"Of the franche-bourgeoisie."

"A subject of the kingdom of Argot?"

"Of the kingdom of Argot."

"A Truand?"

"A Truand."

"In your soul?"

"In my soul."

"I will just observe to thee," resumed the king, 'that thou wilt be none the less hanged for all that."

"The devil!" exclaimed the poet.

"Only," continued Clopin, quite imperturbably, "thou wilt be hanged later, with more ceremony, at the expense of the good town of Paris, upon a good stone gibbet, and by honest men. That's some consolation."

"Just so," answered Gringoire.

"There are other advantages. As being a franc-bourgeois, a free burgess, thou wilt have to pay neither toward the pavements, the lamps, nor the poor; to which the burgesses of Paris are subject."

"Be it so," said the poet; "I consent. I am a Truand, an Argotier, a franc-bourgeois, a petite-flambe, whatever you please—and indeed I was all that beforehand, monsieur the king of Tunis; for I am a philosopher; and, as you know, *Omnia in philosophiâ, omnes in philosopho continentur*——"

The king of Tunis knit his brows. "What dost thou take me for, friend? What Jew of Hungary's cant art thou singing us now? I don't understand Hebrew. Because a man's a robber, he's not obliged to be a Jew. Nay, I don't even rob now—I'm above all that—a cut-throat, if you like, but no cut-purse."

Gringoire strove to slip in some sort of an excuse between these brief ejaculations, of which each succeeding one came bouncing out with increased momentum. "I ask your pardon, monseigneur—it's not Hebrew, it's Latin."

"I tell thee," rejoined Clopin, in a rage, "that I'm no Jew, and that I'll have thee hanged, *ventre de syna-*

gogue ! as well as that little marcandier of Judea that
stands by thee, and whom I hope to see, one of these
days, nailed to a counter like a piece of bad coin as he
is !"

So saying, he pointed with his finger to the little
bearded Hungarian Jew, who had accosted Gringoire
with his *Facitote caritatem !* and who, understanding no
other language, was surprised to see the ill-humor of the
king of Tunis vent itself upon him.

At length, Monseigneur Clopin's passion subsided.
" Rascal," said he to our poet, "then thou'rt willing to
be a Truand ?"

" Undoubtedly," answered the poet.

" Willing isn't all," said Clopin, surlily.   " Good-will
doesn't put one onion more into the soup, and's of no
use at all but for going to heaven—and there's a difference between heaven and Argot.   To be received in
Argot thou must prove that thou art good for something ; and to do that, thou must feel the mannequin."

" I'll feel anything you like," said Gringoire.

Clopin made a sign ; whereupon some Argotiers detached themselves from the circle, and returned in a
minute.   They brought two posts, terminated at the
lower extremity by two broad feet, which made them
stand firm on the ground.   To the upper extremities
of these two posts they applied a cross-beam ; and the
whole formed a very pretty portable gallows, which
Gringoire had the satisfaction of seeing erected before
him in the twinkling of an eye.   Everything was there,
including the rope, which gracefully depended from the
transverse beam.

" What can be their meaning ?" thought Gringoire to
himself, with some uneasiness.   But a noise of little
bells which he heard at that moment put an end to his
anxiety, for it proceeded from a stuffed figure of a man
which the Truands were suspending by the neck to the
rope, a sort of scarecrow, clothed in red, and so completely covered with little bells, and hollow jingling
brasses, that there were enough to have harnessed thirty
Castilian mules.   These thousand miniature bells jin-

gled for a time under the vibrations of the rope; their sound dying away gradually into a profound silence, which resulted from the state of perfect rest into which the body of the mannequin was speedily brought by that law of the pendulum which has superseded the use of the hour-glass.

Then Clopin, pointing to an old tottering joint-stool, placed underneath the mannequin, said to Gringoire, "Get upon that."

"*Mort-diable!*" objected Gringoire, "I shall break my neck. Your stool halts like one of Martial's distichs—it has one hexameter leg and one pentameter."

"Get up," repeated Clopin.

Gringoire mounted upon the stool, and succeeded, not without some oscillations of his head and his arms, in recovering his center of gravity.

"Now," proceeded the king of Tunis, "turn thy right foot round thy left leg, and spring up on the toe of thy left foot."

"Monseigneur," said Gringoire, "you are then absolutely determined that I shall break some of my limbs!"

Clopin shook his head. "Hark ye, friend," said he, "you talk too much. It all amounts to this: you're to spring up on your toe—you'll then just be able to reach up to the mannequin's pocket—you'll put your hand into it—pull out a purse that's in it—and if you do all that without jingling one of the bells, well and good— thou shalt be a Truand. We shall then have nothing more to do but belabor thee soundly for a week."

"*Ventre-Dieu!* I shall not care to do it," said Gringoire. "And suppose I make the bells jingle?"

"Then thou shalt be hanged. Dost thou understand?"

"No, I don't understand it at all," answered Gringoire.

"Hark ye once more. You're to put your hand in the mannequin's pocket and take out his purse. If one single bell stirs while you're doing it, you shall be hanged. Now do you understand?"

"Well," said Gringoire, "I understand that. What next?"

" If you manage to draw out the purse without making any jingle at all, you're a Truand, and will be soundly belabored for eight days together. You understand now, I dare say."

" No, monseigneur, I don't understand this time. Where is my advantage? To be hanged in one case, or beaten in the other!"

" And to be a Truand into the bargain," rejoined Clopin—" to be a Truand! Is that nothing? It's for thy own advantage we shall beat thee, to harden thee against stripes."

" I am greatly obliged to you," answered the poet.

" Come, quick!" said the king, striking his barrel with his foot, and making it ring. " Pick the mannequin's pocket, and let's have done with it. I tell thee, once for all, that if I hear the smallest tinkle, thou shalt take the mannequin's place."

The whole company of Argotiers applauded the words of Clopin, and ranged themselves in a circle round the gallows with so pitiless a laugh that Gringoire saw plainly enough that he gave them too much amusement not to have everything to fear from them. He had, therefore, no hope left but in the faint chance of succeeding in the terrible operation which was imposed upon him. He resolved to risk it : but he first addressed a fervent prayer to the man of straw from whose person he was going to do his best to steal, and whose heart was even more likely to be softened than those of the Truands. That myriad of bells, with their little brazen tongues, looked like so many asps with their mouths open, ready to hiss and to sting.

" Oh!" said he, in a low voice, " and can it be that my life depends upon the smallest vibration of the smallest of those bits of metal? Oh!" he added, clasping his hands, " ye bells, tinkle not—ye balls, jingle not!"

He made one more effort with Trouillefou. " And if there come a breath of wind," said he.

" Thou shalt be hanged," replied the other, without hesitation.

Finding that there was no respite, delay, or subterfuge whatsoever, he bravely set about the feat. He turned his right foot about his left leg, sprang up on the toe of his left foot, and stretched out his arm: but the moment that he touched the mannequin, his body, which was now supported only by one foot, tottered upon the stool, which had only three, he mechanically caught at the mannequin, lost his balance, and fell heavily to the ground, quite deafened by the violent vibration of the scarecrow's thousand bells; while the figure, yielding to the impulse which his hand had given it, first revolved on his own axis, and then swung majestically backwards and forwards between the two posts.

" *Malédiction !* " he exclaimed as he fell; and he lay with his face to the ground as if he were dead.

However, he heard the awful chime above him, and the diabolical laughter of the Truands, and the voice of Trouillefou, saying, " Lift the fellow up, and hang him in a trice."

He rose of himself. They had already unhooked the mannequin to make room for him. The Argotiers made him get upon the stool again. Clopin came up to him, passed the rope round his neck, and, slapping him on the shoulder, " Good-bye, friend," said he ; " thou'lt not get away now, though thou shouldst be as clever as the pope himself."

The word " Mercy ! " expired on Gringoire's lips—he cast his eyes round, but saw no gleam of hope—all were laughing.

" Bellevigne de l'Etoile," said the king of Tunis to an enormous Truand, who stepped out of the ranks, " do you get upon the cross-beam."

Bellevigne de l'Etoile climbed nimbly up to the transverse bar ; and an instant after, Gringoire, looking up, saw him with terror squatted just above his head.

" Now," continued Clopin Trouillefou, " as soon as I clap my hands do you, Andry-le-Rouge, push down the stool with your knee; you, François Chante-Prune, hang at the rascal's feet ; and you, Bellevigne, drop upon his shoulders ; and all three at the same time—do you hear? '

Gringoire shuddered.

"Are you ready?" said Clopin Trouillefou to the three Argotiers, about to throw themselves upon the poet. The poor sufferer had a moment of horrible expectation, while Clopin was quietly pushing into the fire with the point of his shoe some twigs which the flame had not reached. "Are you ready?" he repeated, and he held his hand ready to give the signal. A second more, and all would have been over.

But he stopped as if something suddenly occurred to him. "Wait a moment," said he ; "I'd forgotten. It's customary for us not to hang a man without first asking if there be a woman that'll have anything to say to him. Comrade, it's thy last chance ! thou must marry either a she-truand or the halter."

Gringoire took breath. This was the second time he had come to life again within half an hour ; so that he could not venture to rely very much upon it.

"Hollo !" shouted Clopin, who had reascended his cask: "hollo, there ! women ! females ! is there among you all, from the witch to her cat, ever a jade that'll have anything to say to this rogue? Hollo ! Collette la Charonne ! Elizabeth Trouvain ! Simone Jodouyne ! Marie Piédebou ! Thonne-la-Longue ! Bérarde Fanouel ! Michelle Genaille ! Claude Rouge-orielle ! Mathurine Girorou !—Hollo? Isabeau-la-Thierrye ! Come and see ! A man for nothing ! Who'll have him?"

Gringoire, in this miserable plight, was, it may be supposed, not over inviting. The Truandesses displayed no great enthusiasm at the proposal. The unhappy fellow heard them answer : "No, no—hang him ! it'll please us all !"

Three of them, however, stepped out of the crowd, and came to reconnoitre him. The first was a large, square-faced young woman. She carefully examined the philosopher's deplorable doublet. The coat was threadbare, and had more holes in it than a chestnut-roaster. The woman made a wry face at it. "An old rag!" muttered she; and then, addressing Gringoire, "Let's see thy cope."

"I've lost it," said Gringoire.

"Thy hat?"

"They've taken it from me."

"Thy shoes?"

"They've hardly a bit of sole left."

"Thy purse?"

"Alas!" stammered Gringoire, "I've not a single denier parisis."

"Let them hang thee—and be thankful," replied the Truandess, turning her back upon him.

The second woman, old, dark, wrinkled, of an ugliness conspicuous even in the Court of Miracles, now made the circuit of Gringoire. He almost trembled lest she should want to have him. But she only muttered, "He's too lean," and went her way.

The third that came was a young girl, fresh-complexioned, and not very ill-looking. "Save me!" whispered the poor devil. She looked at him for a moment with an air of pity, then cast down her eyes, made a plait in her skirt, and remained undecided. He watched her every motion—it was his last gleam of hope. "No," said the girl at last; "no—Guillaume Longue-joue would beat me." And she returned into the crowd.

"Comrade," said Clopin, "thou'rt unlucky." Then, standing up on his barrel, "So nobody bids?" cried he, mimicking the tone of an auctioneer, to the great diversion of them all—"so nobody bids? Going—going—going—" then turning toward the gallows with a motion of his head, "gone."

Bellevigne de l'Etoile, Andry-le-Rouge, and François Chante-Prune again approached Gringoire. At that moment a cry was raised among the Argotiers, of "La Esmeralda! la Esmeralda!"

Gringoire started, and turned toward the side from which the shout proceeded. The crowd opened, and made way for a clear and dazzling countenance. It was that of the gypsy girl.

"La Esmeralda!" said Gringoire, amazed, in the

midst of his emotions, by the instantaneousness with which that magic word linked together all his recollections of that day.

This fascinating creature seemed to exercise, even over the Court of Miracles, her sway of grace and beauty. Argotiers, male and female, drew up gently to let her pass by; and their brutal countenances grew kindly at her look.

She approached the sufferer with her elastic step, her pretty Djali following her. Gringoire was more dead than alive. She gazed at him for a moment in silence.

"So you're going to hang that man," said she gravely to Clopin.

"Yes, sister," answered the king of Tunis, "unless thou wilt take him for thy husband."

She made her pretty little grimace with her under lip. "I take him," she said.

And now Gringoire was firmly persuaded that he must have been in a dream ever since the morning, and that this was but a continuation of it. In fact, the turn of events, though gratifying, was a violent one. They undid the noose, and let the poet descend from the stool. The violence of his emotion obliged him to sit down.

The duke of Egypt, without uttering a word, brought forth a clay pitcher. The gypsy girl presented it to Gringoire. "Throw it on the ground," said she. The pitcher broke in four pieces. "Brother," then said the duke of Egypt, laying his hands upon their foreheads, "she is thy wife—sister, he is thy husband—for four years. Go your way."

CHAPTER VII.

A WEDDING NIGHT.

In a few minnutes, our poet found himself in a little chamber with a Gothic-vaulted ceiling, the windows and doors well closed, and comfortably warm, seated before a table which seemed quite ready to borrow a few articles from a sort of small pantry or safe suspended just by; having a good bed in prospect, and tête-à-tête with a pretty girl. The adventure had something of enchantment. He began seriously to take himself to be a personage of the fairy tales; and now and then he cast his eyes around him, as if to see whether the fiery chariot drawn by two hippogriffs, which alone could have conveyed him so rapidly from Tartarus to Paradise, were still there. At intervals, too, he fixed his eyes steadfastly upon the holes in his coat, by way of clinging to reality, so as not to let the earth altogether slip from under him. His reason, tossed to and fro in imaginative space, had only that thread left to hold by.

The girl seemed to pay no attention to him. She was going backwards and forwards, shifting first one article and then another, talking to her goat, making her little mow here and there. At length she came and sat down near the table, and Gringoire could contemplate her at leisure.

"You have been a boy, reader," our authority here exclaims, "and perhaps you have the happiness to be so still. It is quite certain, then, that you have more than once (and for my own part, I can say that I have passed whole days in that manner, the best spent days of my life), that you have followed from brier to brier, or the brink of a rivulet, on a sunshiny day, some pretty demoiselle fly, green or blue, checking its flight at acute angles, and kissing the extremity of every spray. You recollect with what amorous curiosity your thoughts and your looks were fixed upon that little whirl of whiz and hum, of wings of purple and azure, in the midst of which floated a form which your eye could not seize, veiled as it was by the very rapidity of its motion. The aërial being confusedly perceptible through all that fluttering of wings, appeared chimerical, imaginary, impossible to touch, impossible to see. But when, at last, the demoiselle settled on the point of a reed, and you could examine, holding in your breath all the while, the long gauze pinions, the long enamel robe, the two globes of crystal, what astonishment did you not experience, and what fear lest you should again see the form go off in shadow, and the being in chimera! Recall to your mind these impressions, and then you will easily understand what were the feelings of Gringoire in contemplating, under her visible and palpable form, that Esmeralda of whom, until then, he had only caught a glimpse amid a whirl of dance, song, and flutter."

Sinking deeper and deeper into his revery—

"So, then," said he to himself, as his eyes wandered over her, "I now see what this Esmeralda really is—a heavenly creature!—a dancer in the streets—so much, and yet so little! She it was who gave the finishing blow to my mystery this morning—she it is who saves my life to-night. My evil genius!—my good angel! A pretty woman, upon my word!—and who must love me to distraction, to have taken me as she has done. By-the-by," said he, suddenly rising up from his seat, with that feeling of the real which formed the substance of his character and of his philosophy, "I don't very well know how it happens—but I'm her husband!"

With this idea in his head, and in his eyes, he approached the young girl in so military and gallant a manner that she drew back. "What do you want with me?" said she.

"Can you ask me such a question, adorable Esmeralda?" returned Gringoire, in so impassioned a tone that he himself was astonished to hear himself utter it.

The gypsy opened her large eyes. "I don't know what you mean."

"What!" rejoined Gringoire, growing warmer and warmer, and reflecting that, after all, he had only to do with a virtue of the Court of Miracles, "am I not thine, my sweet friend?—art not thou mine?" And without more ado, he threw his arms around her waist.

The gypsy's corset slipped through his hands like the skin of an eel. She sprang from one end of the cell to the other, stooped down, and rose again with a small poniard in her hand, and all before Gringoire had even time to observe whence the poniard came—looking irritated and indignant, her lips puffed out, her nostrils distended, her cheeks all scarlet, and her eyeballs flashing. At the same time the little white goat placed itself before her, and presented a hostile front to Gringoire, lowering its two pretty gilt and very sharp horns. All this was done in the twinkling of an eye. The demoiselle turned wasp, and had every disposition to sting.

Our philosopher stood quite confused, looking sheepishly, first at the goat and then at its mistress. "Holy Virgin!" he exclaimed at last, as soon as his surprise permitted him to speak, "here are a pair of originals!"

The gypsy now broke silence. "You must be a very bold fellow!" she said.

"I ask your pardon, mademoiselle," said Gringoire, with a smile; "but why, then, did you take me for your husband?"

"Was I to let you be hanged?"

"So, then," rejoined the poet, a little disappointed in his amorous expectations, "you had no other intention in marrying me but to save me from the gallows?"

"Why, what other intention should I have had?"

Gringoire bit his lip. "Humph!" said he, "I'm not yet quite so triumphant in Cupido as I thought. But then what was the use of breaking that poor pitcher?"

Meanwhile the poniard of La Esmeralda and the horns of the goat were still in a posture of defense.

"Mademoiselle Esmeralda," said the poet, "let us

make a capitulation. As I am not registering clerk at the Châtelet, I shall not quibble with you about your thus carrying a dagger in Paris in the teeth of monsieur the provost's ordinances and prohibitions. You are aware, however, that Noël Lescrivain was condemned, only a week ago, to pay a fine of ten sous parisis for carrying a braquemard.* But that's no business of mine—and so, to the point. I swear to you, by my chance of salvation, that I will not approach you without your leave and permission. But pray, give me my supper."

The truth is, that Gringoire, like Despréaux, was "very little voluptuous." He was not of that cavalier and mousquetaire species who carry girls by assault. In a love affair, as in every other affair, he willingly resigned himself to temporizing and to middle terms; and a good supper, in comfortable tête-à-tête, appeared to him, especially when he was hungry, to be a very good interlude between the opening and the catastrophe of an amatory adventure.

The gypsy gave him no answer. She made her little disdainful mow; drew up her head like a bird; then burst into a laugh; and the little dagger disappeared, as it had come forth, without Gringoire's being able to discover whereabouts the wasp concealed its sting.

In a minute, there were upon the table a loaf of rye bread, a slice of bacon, some withered apples, and a jug of beer. Gringoire set to with perfect violence. To hear the furious clatter of his iron fork upon his earthenware plate, it seemed as if all his love had turned to hunger.

The girl, seated before him, witnessed his operations in silence, being evidently preoccupied by some other reflection, at which she smiled from time to time, while her delicate hand caressed the intelligent head of the goat, pressed softly between her knees.

---

* A sort of short cutlass which was worn hanging down by the thigh.

A candle of yellow wax lighted this scene of voracity and of musing.

And now, the first cravings of his stomach being appeased, Gringoire felt a twinge of false shame at seeing that there was only an apple left.

" Mademoiselle Esmeralda," said he, " you don't eat."

She answered by a negative motion of the head ; and then her pensive look seemed to fix itself upon the vault of the chamber.

" What the devil is she attending to ? " thought Gringoire ; " it can't be that grinning dwarf's face carved upon that keystone, that attracts her so mightily. The devil's in it if I can't bear that comparison at any rate."

He spoke louder—" Mademoiselle."

She seemed not to hear him.

He repeated, louder still, " Mademoiselle Esmeralda ! " It was all in vain. The girl's mind was wandering elsewhere, and Gringoire's voice was unable to bring it back. Luckily, the goat interfered. It began to pull its mistress gently by the sleeve. " What do you want, Djali ? " said the gypsy, sharply, as if starting out of her sleep.

" It's hungry," said Gringoire, delighted at an opportunity of entering into conversation.

La Esmeralda began to crumble some bread, which Djali gracefully ate out of the hollow of her hand.

Gringoire, however, allowed her no time to resume her revery. He ventured upon a delicate question : " You won't have me for your husband, then ? "

The girl looked steadily at him, and answered, " No."

" For your lover ? " proceeded Gringoire.

She thrust out her lip, and again answered, " No."

" For your friend ? " then demanded the poet.

Again she looked at him steadily ; and, after a moment's reflection, she said, " Perhaps."

This perhaps, so dear to philosophers, encouraged Gringoire. " Do you know what friendship is ? " he asked.

8

"Yes," answered the gypsy, "it is to be like brother and sister—two souls meeting without mingling—two fingers on the same hand."

"And love?" proceeded Gringoire.

"Oh! love!" said she—and her voice trembled, and her eye beamed—"that is, to be two and yet but one —a man and woman mingled into an angel—it is heaven!"

The street dancing-girl, while saying this, had a character of beauty which singularly struck Gringoire, and seemed to him to be in perfect harmony with the almost Oriental exaltation of her words. Her pure and roseate lips were half smiling. Her clear, calm forehead was momentarily ruffled by her thoughts, like the mirror dimmed by a passing breath. And from her long, dark, drooping lashes there emanated a kind of ineffable light, giving her profile that ideal suavity which Raphael afterward found at the mystic point of intersection of virginity, maternity, and divinity.

Gringoire, nevertheless, continued, "What must a man be, then, to please you?"

"He must be a man."

"And what am I, then?"

"A man has a helmet on his head, a sword in his hand, and gilt spurs at his heels."

"Good!" said Gringoire; "the horse makes the man. Do you love anybody?"

"As a lover?"

"Yes—as a lover."

She remained thoughtful for a moment. Then she said, with a peculiar expression, "I shall know that soon."

"Why not to-night?" rejoined the poet, in a tender tone. "Why not me?"

She gave him a grave look, and said: "I can never love a man who can not protect me."

Gringoire colored and took the reflection to himself. The girl evidently alluded to the feeble assistance he had lent her in the critical situation in which she had found herself two hours before. This recollection, effaced by his other adventures of the evening, now returned to him. He struck his forehead. "Apropos, mademoiselle," said he, "I ought to have begun with that—pardon my foolish distractions—how did you contrive to escape from the clutches of Quasimodo?"

At this question the gypsy started. "Oh! the horrid hunchback!" said she, hiding her face with her hands, and shivering violently.

"Horrid indeed!" said Gringoire, still pursuing his ideas. "But how did you manage to get away from him?"

La Esmeralda smiled, sighed, and was silent.

"Do you know why he had followed you?" asked Gringoire, striving to come round again to the object of his inquiry.

"I don't know," said the girl. Then she added sharply, "But you were following me too. Why did you follow me?"

"To speak honestly," replied Gringoire, "I don't know that either."

There was a pause. Gringoire was marking the table with his knife. The girl smiled, and seemed as if she had been looking at something through the wall. All at once she began to sing in a voice scarcely audible:

> Quando las pintadas aves
> Mudas estan, y la tierra . . . . .

She suddenly stopped short, and fell to caressing Djali.

"You've got a pretty animal there," said Gringoire.

"It's my sister," answered she.

"Why do they call you La Esmeralda?" asked the poet.

"I don't know at all."

"But why do they, though?"

She drew from her bosom a sort of small oblong bag, suspended from her neck by a chain of grains of adrez arach. A strong smell of camphor exhaled from the bag; it was covered with green silk, and had in the cen-

ter a large boss of green glass, in imitation of an emerald.
"Perhaps it's on account of that," said she.

Gringoire offered to take the bag, but she drew back
"Touch it not," she said, "it's an amulet. You would
do mischief to the charm, or the charm to you."

The poet's curiosity was more and more awakened.
"Who gave it you?" said he.

She placed her finger on her lip, and hid the amulet
again in her bosom. He tried a few more questions
but could hardly obtain any answer.

"What's the meaning of that word, La Esmeralda?"

"I don't know," she replied.

"What language does it belong to?"

"I think it's Egyptian."

"I suspected so," said Gringoire; "you're not a native of France?"

"I don't know."

"Are your parents living?"

She began to sing, to an old tune:

> "A bird was my mother;
> My father, another;
> Over the water I pass without ferry,
> Over the water I pass without wherry
> A bird was my mother;
> My father, another."

"Very good," said Gringoire. "At what age did you
come to France?"

"A very little girl."

"And when to Paris?"

"Last year. At the moment we were coming in by
the Porte Papale, I saw the reed linnet scud through
the air—it was at the end of August—I said, it'll be a
hard winter."

"It has been so," said Gringoire, delighted at this
commencement of conversation—"I've done nothing
but blow my fingers. So you've the gift of prophecy."

She fell into her laconics again. "No," she answered
dryly.

"That man whom you call the duke of Egypt is the chief of your tribe?"

"Yes."

"It was he, however, that married us," observed the poet, timidly.

She made that pretty little habitual grimace of hers —"I don't know so much as your name."

"My name?—If you wish to know it, it is this— Pierre Gringoire."

"I know a finer one," said she.

"Naughty girl!" rejoined the poet. "No matter— you shall not provoke me. Nay, you will perhaps love me when you know me better—and then, you have told me your history with such unreserved confidence that I am bound to give you some account of myself. You must know, then, that my name is Pierre Gringoire, and that I am the son of a farmer of the tabellionage of Gonesse, that is to say, of the office of notary in that seigneurial jurisdiction. My father was hanged by the Burgundians, and my mother ripped open by the Picards, at the time of the siege of Paris twenty years ago. At six years of age, then, I was an orphan, without any other sole to my foot than the pavement of Paris. How I got over the time from six years old to sixteen, I hardly know. Here a fruit woman used to give me a plum, and there a baker used to throw me a crust. At night I used to get myself picked up by the Onze-vingts, who put me in prison, and there I found a bundle of straw. All this did not prevent my growing tall and thin, as you see. In winter I warmed myself in the sun, under the porch of the Hôtel de Sens; and I thought it very ridiculous that the great fire on the feast of St. John should be reserved for the dog-days. At sixteen, I wished to choose a calling. I tried everything in succession. I turned soldier, but was not brave enough. I then turned monk, but was not devout enough—and besides, I'm a poor drinker. In despair, I apprenticed myself among the carpenters of the grande coignée, but I was not strong enough. I had more inclination to be a schoolmaster; to be sure, I couldn't read; but that needn't have hindered me. I perceived, at the end of a certain time, that I was in want of some requisite for everything—and so, finding that I was good for nothing, I, of my own free will and pleasure, turned poet and rhymester. 'Tis a calling that a man can always embrace when he's a vagabond; and it's better than robbing, as I was advised to do by some young plunderers of my acquaintance. Fortunately, I met, one fine day, with Don Claude Frollo, the reverend archdeacon of Notre-Dame. He took an interest in me; and to him I owe it that I am now a true man of letters, acquainted with Latin, from Cicero's Offices to the Mortuology of the Celestine fathers, and not absolutely barbarous either in scholastics, in poetics, or in rhythmics, nor yet in hermetics, that science of sciences. I am the author of the mystery that was performed to-day, with great triumph and concourse of people, all in the Grande Salle of the Palais. I've also written a book that will make six hundred pages, upon the prodigious comet of 1465, about which one man went mad. These are not the only successes I have had; being something of an artillery carver, I worked upon that great bombard of Jean Maugue, which you know burst at the bridge of Charenton the first time it was tried, and killed four-and-twenty of the spectators. You see that I'm not so indifferent a match. I know many sorts of very clever tricks, which I will teach your goat—for instance, to mimic the bishop of Paris, that cursed pharisee whose mill-wheels splash the passengers the whole length of the Pont-aux-Meuniers. And then, my mystery will bring me a good lump of hard cash, if I get paid. In short, I'm at your service— I, and my wit, and my science, and my letters—ready to live with you, damsel, as it shall please you—chastely or otherwise—as man and wife, if you think good—as brother and sister, if you like it better."

Here Gringoire was silent, awaiting the effect of his harangue upon the gypsy girl. Her eyes were fixed upon the ground.

"Phœbus," said she, with an emphasis upon the word, though in a half-whisper; then, turning to the poet, "Phœbus," said she "What does that mean?"

Gringoire, though not at all understanding what relation there could be between his address and this question, was not sorry to show off his erudition. He answered, bridling with dignity, "'Tis a Latin word, that signifies the sun."

"The sun!" repeated she.

"'Tis the name of a certain handsome archer, who was a god," added Gringoire.

"A god!" ejaculated his companion; and there was something pensive and impassioned in her tone.

At that moment, one of the bracelets came unfastened and dropped on the floor. Gringoire eagerly stooped to pick it up; and when he rose again, the girl and the goat had both disappeared. He heard the shoot of a bolt. It was a small door, communicating no doubt with an adjoining chamber, which some one was fastening outside.

"Has she, at any rate, left me a bed?" said our philosopher.

He made the tour of the chamber. There was no piece of furniture at all adapted to repose, except a very long wooden chest; and the lid of that was carved; so that it gave Gringoire, when he stretched himself upon it, a sensation much like that which the Micromegas of Voltaire's tale would experience, lying all his length upon the Alps.

"Come!" said he, making the best he could of it, "there's nothing for it but resignation. And yet this is a strange wedding night. 'Tis pity, too. That broken-pitcher marriage had something sweetly simple and antediluvian about it that quite pleased me."

BOOK III.

CHAPTER I.

THE CATHEDRAL OF NOTRE-DAME.

ASSUREDLY, the church of Our Lady at Paris is still, at this day, a majestic and sublime edifice. Yet, noble an aspect as it has preserved in growing old, it is difficult to suppress feelings of sorrow and indignation at the numberless degradations and mutilations which the hand of Time and that of man have inflicted upon the venerable monument, regardless alike of Charlemagne, who laid the first stone of it, and of Philip-Augustus, who laid the last.

Upon the face of this old queen of the French cathedrals, beside each wrinkle we constantly find a scar. *Tempus edax, homo edacior*—which we would willingly render thus—Time is blind, but man is stupid.

If we had leisure to examine one by one, with the reader, the traces of destruction imprinted on this ancient church, the work of Time would be found to form the lesser portion—the worst destruction has been perpetrated by men—especially by men of art. We are under the necessity of using the expression, men of art, seeing that there have been individuals who have assumed the character of architects in the two last centuries.

And first of all—to cite only a few leading examples— there are, assuredly, few finer architectural pages than that front of that cathedral, in which, successively and at once, the three receding pointed gateways; the decorated and indented band of the twenty-eight royal niches; the vast central circular window, flanked by the two lateral ones, like the priest by the deacon and sub-deacon; the lofty and slender gallery of trifoliated arcades, supporting a heavy platform upon its light and delicate columns; and the two dark and massive towers, with their eaves of slate—harmonious parts of one magnificent whole—rising one above another in five gigantic stories—unfold themselves to the eye, in combination unconfused—with their innumerable details of statuary, sculpture, and carving, in powerful alliance with the grandeur of the whole—a vast symphony in stone, if we may so express it—the colossal work of a man and of a nation—combining unity with complexity, like the Iliads and the Romanceros to which it is a sister production—the prodigious result of a draught upon the whole resources of an era—in which, upon every stone, is seen displayed, in a hundred varieties, the fancy of the workman disciplined by the genius of the artist—a sort of human Creation, in short, mighty and prolific as the Divine Creation, of which it seems to have caught the double character—variety and eternity.

And what is here said of the front must be said of the whole church—and what we say of the cathedral church of Paris must be said of all the churches of Christendom in the Middle Ages. Everything is in its place in that art, self-created, logical, and well-proportioned. By measuring the toe we estimate the giant.

But to return to the front of Notre-Dame, as it still appears to us when we go to gaze in pious admiration upon the solemn and mighty cathedral, looking terrible, as its chroniclers express it—*quæ mole suâ terrorem incutit spectantibus.*

Three things of importance are now wanting to this front: first, the flight of eleven steps by which it formerly rose above the level of the ground; then, the lower range of statues, which occupied the niches of the three portals; and lastly, the upper series, of the twenty-eight more ancient kings of France, which filled the gallery on the first story, beginning with Childebert

and ending with Philip-Augustus, each holding in his
hand the imperial ball.

As for the flight of steps, it is Time that has made it
disappear, by raising, with slow but resistless progress,
the level of the ground in the City. But while thus
swallowing up, one after another, in this mounting tide
of the pavement of Paris, the eleven steps which added
to the majestic elevation of the structure, Time has
given to the church, perhaps, yet more than he has
taken from it; for it is he who has spread over its face
that dark gray tint of centuries which makes of the old
age of architectural monuments their season of beauty.

But who has thrown down the two ranges of statues?
who has left the niches empty? who has cut, in the
middle of the central portal, that new and bastard
pointed arch? who has dared to hang in it that heavy,
unmeaning wooden gate, carved *à la* Louis XV., beside
the arabesques of Biscornette? The men, the architects,
the artists of our times.

And—if we enter the interior of the edifice—who has
overturned the colossal St. Christopher, proverbial for
his magnitude among statues as the Grande Salle of
the Palais was among halls—as the spire of Strasburg
among steeples? And those myriads of statues which
thronged all the inter-columniations of the nave and
the choir—kneeling—standing—equestrian—men, women, children—kings, bishops, warriors—in stone, in
marble, in gold, in silver, in brass, and even in wax—
who has brutally swept them out? It is not Time that
has done it.

And who has substituted for the old Gothic altar,
splendidly loaded with shrines and reliquaries, that
heavy sarcophagus of marble, with angels' heads and
clouds, which looks like an unmatched specimen from
the Val-de-Grâce or the Invalides? Who has stupidly
fixed that heavy anachronism of stone into the Carlovingian pavement of Hercandus? Was it not Louis
XIV. fulfilling the vow of Louis XIII.?

And who has put cold white glass in place of those
deep-tinctured panes which made the wandering eyes

of our forefathers hesitate between the round window over the grand doorway and the pointed ones of the chancel? And what would a subchanter of the six-teenth century say could he see that fine yellow-wash-ing with which the Vandal Archbishops have besmeared their cathedral? He would remember that it was the color with which the hangman brushed over such build-ings as were adjudged to be infamous—he would recol-lect the hôtel of the Petit-Bourbon, which had thus been washed all over yellow for the treason of the con-stable—"yellow, after all, so well mixed," says Sauval, "and so well applied, that the lapse of a century and more has not yet taken its color." He would believe that the holy place had become infamous, and would flee away from it.

And, then, if we ascend the cathedral—not to men-tion a thousand other barbarisms of every kind—what have they done with that charming small steeple which rose from the intersection of the cross, and which, no less bold and light than its neighbor, the spire (de-stroyed also) of the Sainte Chapelle, pierced into the sky yet further than the towers—perforated, sharp, so-norous, airy? An architect *de bon goût* amputated it in 1787, and thought it was sufficient to hide the wound with that great plaster of lead which resembles the lid of a porridge-pot.

Thus it is that the wondrous art of the Middle Ages has been treated in almost every country, and especially in France. In its ruin three sorts of inroads are distin-guishable, and have made breaches of different depths; first, Time, which has gradually made deficiencies here and there, and has gnawed over its whole surface; then, religious and political revolutions, which, blind and angry in their nature, have tumultuously wreaked their fury upon it, torn its rich garment of sculpture and carving, burst its rose-shaped windows, broken its bands of arabesques and miniature figures, torn down its statues, here for their mitre, there for their crown; and lastly, changes of fashion, growing more and more gro-tesque and stupid, which, commencing with the anarchical yet splendid deviations of the revival, have succeeded one another in the necessary decline of architecture. Fashion has done more mischief than revolutions. It has cut to the quick—it has attacked the very bone and framework of the art. It has mangled, dislocated, killed the edifice—in its form as well as in its meaning—in its consistency as well as in its beauty. And then, it has remade—which at least neither Time nor revolutions have pretended to do. It has audaciously fitted into the wounds of Gothic architecture its wretched gew-gaws of a day—its marble ribands—its metal pompoons —a very leprosy of ovolos, volutes, and entournements —of draperies, garlands, and fringes—of stone flames, brazen clouds, fleshy Cupids, and chubby cherubim— which we find beginning to devour the face of art in the oratory of Catherine de Médicis, and making it expire two centuries after, tortured and convulsed, in the boudoir of Madame Dubarry.

Thus, to sum up the points which we have here laid down, three kinds of ravages now disfigure Gothic architecture : wrinkles and knobs on the surface—these are the work of Time : violences, brutalities, contusions, fractures—these are the work of revolutions, from Luther down to Mirabeau : mutilations, amputations, dislocation of members, restorations—these are the labors, Grecian, Roman, and barbaric, of the professors according to Vitruvius and Vignola. That magnificent art which the Vandals had produced, the academies have murdered. To the operations of ages and of revolutions, which, at all events, devastate with impartiality and grandeur, have been added those of the cloud of school-trained architects, licensed, privileged, and patented, degrading with all the discernment and selection of bad taste—substituting, for instance, the *chichorées* of Louis XV. for the Gothic lacework, to the greater glory of the Parthenon. This is the kick of the ass at the expiring lion. 'Tis the old oak which, in the last stage of decay, is stung and gnawed by the caterpillars.

How remote is all this from the time when Robert Cenalis, comparing Notre-Dame at Paris to the famous temple of Diana at Ephesus, " so much vaunted by the ancient pagans," which immortalized Erostratus, thought the Gaulish cathedral " more excellent in length, breadth, height, and structure."

Notre-Dame, however, as an architectural monument, is not one of those which can be called complete, definite, belonging to a class. It is not a Roman church, nor is it a Gothic church. It is not a model of any individual order. It has not, like the abbey of Tournus, the solemn and massive squareness, the round broad vault, the icy bareness, the majestic simplicity, of the edifices which have the circular arch for their basis. Nor is it, like the cathedral of Bourges, the magnificent, airy, multiform, tufted, pinnacled, florid production of the pointed arch. It can not be ranked among that antique family of churches, gloomy, mysterious, lowering, crushed, as it were, by the weight of the circular arch—almost Egyptian, even to their ceilings—all hieroglyphical, all sacerdotal, all symbolical—more abounding, in their ornaments, with lozenges and zigzags than with flowers—with flowers than with animals—with animals than with human figures—the work not so much of the architect as of the bishop—the first transformation of the art—all stamped with theocratical and military discipline—having its root in the Lower Empire, and stopping at the time of William the Conqueror. Nor can this cathedral be ranked in that other family of lofty, airy churches, rich in sculpture and painted windows, of pointed forms and bold disposition—as political symbols, communal and citizen—as works of art, free, capricious, licentious—the second transformation of ecclesiastical architecture—no longer hieroglyphical, immutable, and sacerdotal, but artistical, progressive, and popular—beginning at the return from the crusades, and ending with Louis XI. Notre-Dame, then, is not of purely Roman race like the former, nor of purely Arabic race like the latter.

It is an edifice of the transition period. The Saxon architect was just finishing off the first pillars of the nave, when the pointed arch, arriving from the crusade,

came and seated itself as a conqueror upon the broad
Roman capitals which had been designed to support
only circular arches. The pointed arch, thenceforward
master of the field, constructed the remainder of the
building. However, inexperienced and timid at its
commencement, we find it widening its compass, and,
as it were, restraining itself, as not yet daring to spring
up into arrows and lancets, as it afterward did in so
many wonderful cathedrals. It might be said to have
been sensible of the neighborhood of the heavy Roman
pillars.

However, these edifices of the transition from the
Roman to the Gothic are not less valuable studies
than the pure models are. They express a gradation
of the art which would be lost without them. It is the
pointed species engrafted upon the circular.

Notre-Dame, in particular, is a curious specimen of
this variety. Each face, each stone, of this venerable
monument, is a page of the history, not only of the
country, but of the science and the art. Thus, to point
out here only some of the principal details; while the
small Porte-Rouge attains almost to the limits of the
Gothic delicacy of the fifteenth century, the pillars of
the nave, in their amplitude and solemnity, go back
almost as far as the Carlovingian abbey of St. Germain-
des-Près. One would think there were six centuries
between that door and those pillars. Not even the
hermetics fail to find, in the emblematical devices of
the great portal, a satisfactory compendium of their
science, of which the church of St. Jacques-de-la-
Boucherie was so complete a hieroglyphic. Thus the
Roman abbey—the hermetical church—Gothic art—
Saxon art—the heavy round pillar, which carries us
back to Gregory VII.—the hermetical symbolism by
which Nicholas Flamel anticipated Luther — papal
unity, and schism—St. Germain-des-Près, and St. Jacques-de-la-Boucherie—all are mingled, combined, and
amalgamated in Notre-Dame. This central and maternal church is, among the other old churches of Paris,
a sort of chimera; she has the head of one, the limbs

of another, the back of a third—something of every one.

We repeat it, these compound fabrics are not the least interesting to the artist, the antiquary, and the historian. They make us feel in how great a degree architecture is a primitive matter—demonstrating (as the Cyclopean vestiges, the Egyptian pyramids, and the gigantic Hindoo pagods likewise demonstrate) that the greatest productions of architecture are not so much the work of individuals as of society—the offspring rather of national efforts than of the conceptions of particular minds—a deposit left by a whole people—the accumulation of ages—the residue of the successive evaporations of human society—in short, a sort of formations. Each wave of time leaves its alluvion—each race deposits its strata upon the monument—each individual contributes his stone. So do the beavers—so do the bees—so does man. The great symbol of architecture, Babel, is a hive.

Great edifices, like great mountains, are the work of ages. Often the art undergoes a transformation while they are yet pending—*pendent opera interrupta*—they go on again quietly, in accordance with the change in the art. The altered art takes up the fabric, incrusts itself upon it, assimilates it to itself, develops it after its own fashion, and finishes it if it can. The thing is accomplished without disturbance, without effort, without reaction, according to a law natural and tranquil. It is a graft that shoots out—a sap that circulates—a vegetation that goes forward. Certainly there is matter for very large volumes, and often for the universal history of human nature, in those successive engraftings of several species of art at different elevations upon the same fabric. The man, the artist, the individual, are lost and disappear upon those great masses, leaving no name of an author behind. Human intelligence is there to be traced only in its aggregate. Time is the architect—the nation is the builder.

To consider in this place only the architecture of Christian Europe, the younger sister of the great ma-

sonries of the East; it presents to us an immense formation, divided into three superincumbent zones,
clearly defined; the Roman* zone; the Gothic zone;
and the zone of the Revival, which we would willingly
entitle the Greco-Roman. The Roman stratum, the
most ancient and the deepest, is occupied by the circular arch; which reappears rising from the Grecian column, in the modern and upper stratum of the Revival.
The pointed arch is found between the two. The edifices which belong to one or other of these three strata
exclusively, are perfectly distinct, uniform, and complete. Such is the abbey of Jumièges; such is the
cathedral of Rheims; such is the church of Sainte-
Croix at Orleans. But the three zones mingle and combine at their borders, like the colors of the prism. And
hence the complex fabrics—the edifices of gradation
and transition. One is Roman in its feet, Gothic in the
middle, and Greco-Roman in the head. This is when
it has taken six hundred years to build it. This variety
is rare: the donjon tower of Etampes is a specimen of
it. But the fabrics of two formations are more frequent. Such is the Notre-Dame of Paris, an edifice of
the pointed arch, which, in its earliest pillars, dips into
that Roman zone in which the portal of Saint-Denis
and the nave of St. Germain-des-Près are entirely immersed. Such is the charming semi-Gothic chapter
house of Bocherville, which the Roman layer mounts
half-way up. Such is the cathedral of Rouen, which
would have been entirely Gothic, had not the extremity
of its central spire pierced into the zone of the Revival.†

---

* The same which is also called, according to place, climate,
and species, Lombard, Saxon, or Byzantine. These are four
sister architectures, parallel to one another, having each its
particular character, but all deriving from the same principle,
the circular arch.

Facies non omnibus una,
Non diversa tamen, qualem, etc.

† This part of the spire, which was of timber, is precisely that
which was consumed by lightning in 1823.

However, all these gradations, all these differences, affect only the surface of the structures. It is only the art that has changed its coat—the conformation of the Christian temple itself has remained untouched. It is ever the same internal framework, the same logical disposition of parts. Whatever be the sculptured and decorated envelope of a cathedral, we constantly find underneath it at least the germ and rudiment of the Roman basilic. It eternally develops itself upon the ground according to the same law. There are invariably two naves crossing each other at right angles, the upper extremity of which cross is rounded into a chancel; there are constantly two low sides for the internal processions and for the chapels—a sort of lateral ambulatories communicating with the principal nave by the intercolumniations. This being once laid down, the number of the chapels, of the doorways, of the steeples, of the spires, is variable to infinity, according to the fancy of the age, of the nation, of the art. The performance of the worship being once provided for and ensured, architecture is at liberty to do what she pleases. Statues, painted glass, rose-shaped windows, arabesques, indentations, capitals, and bas-reliefs—all these objects of imagination she combines in such arrangement as best suits her. Hence the prodigious external variety of these edifices, in the main structure of which dwells so much order and uniformity. The trunk of the tree is unchanging—the vegetation is capricious.

CHAPTER II.

A BIRD'S—EYE VIEW OF PARIS.

WE have endeavored to repair for the reader the admirable church of Our Lady at Paris. We have briefly pointed out the greater part of the beauties which it

9

possessed in the fifteenth century, and which are want
ing to it now ; but we have omitted the principal—the
view of Paris as it then appeared from the summit of
the towers.

Indeed, when, after feeling your way up the long
spiral staircase that perpendicularly perforates the thick
walls of the steeples, you at last emerged all at once
upon one of the two elevated platforms inundated with
light and air, it was a fine picture that opened upon you
on every side, a spectacle *sui generis*, some idea of
which may easily be formed by such of our readers as
have had the good fortune to see a Gothic town, entire,
complete, homogeneous—of which description there are
still a few remaining, as Nuremberg in Bavaria, and
Vittoria in Spain—or even any smaller specimens, provided they be in good preservation, as Vitré in Brit-
tany, and Nordhausen in Prussia.

The Paris of three hundred and fifty years ago, the
Paris of the fifteenth century, was already a giant city.
The Parisians in general are mistaken as to the ground
which they think they have gained. Since the time of
Louis XI., Paris has not increased much more than a
third, and certainly it has lost much more in beauty
than it has gained in size.

Paris took its birth in that anciently-inhabited island
of the Cité, or City, which has indeed the form of a
cradle, lying about the center of the present town, and
embraced between the two channels of the Seine,
which, dividing at its eastern, meet again at its western
extremity. The strand of this island was its first enclosure ; the Seine its first trench. And for several
centuries Paris remained in its island state ; with two
bridges, one on the north, the other on the south ; and
two *têtes-de-ponts*, which were at once its gates and its
fortresses—the Grand Châtelet on the right bank of the
northern channel of the river, and the Petit Châtelet on
the left bank of the southern channel.

In the next place, under the first line of French
kings, being too much confined within the limits of its
island, behind which it could never return, Paris crossed

the water. Then on each side, beyond either Châtelet, a first line of walls and towers began to cut into the country on both sides of the Seine. Of this ancient enclosure some vestiges were still remaining as late as the last century; but now there is nothing left but the memory of it, with here and there a local tradition, as the Baudets or Baudoyer gate—*porta Bagauda*.

By degrees, the flood of houses, constantly impelled from the heart of the town toward the exterior, overflowed and wore away this enclosure. Philip-Augustus drew a fresh line of circumvallation. He imprisoned Paris within a circular chain of great towers, lofty and massive. For upwards of a century the houses pressed upon one another, accumulated, and rose higher in this basin, like water in a reservoir. They began to deepen —to pile story on story—to climb, as it were, one upon another. They shot out in height, like every growth that is compressed laterally; and strove each to lift its head above its neighbors, in order to get a breath of air. The streets became deeper and narrower, and every open space was overrun by buildings and disappeared. At last, we find the houses overstepping the wall of Philip-Augustus, and spreading themselves merrily over the plain in all manner of positions, without plan or arrangement, taking their unrestricted ease, and slicing themselves gardens out of the surrounding fields.

In 1367, the suburbs were already so extensive that another enclosure became necessary, and one was built by Charles V. But a town like Paris is perpetually on the increase—and it is only such towns that become capitals. They are a sort of funnels, which receive all the drains, geographical, political, moral, and intellectual, of a country—all the natural tendencies of a people—wells of civilization, as it were—and also sinks— where commerce, manufactures, intelligence, population —all the vital juices of a state—filter and collect incessantly, drop by drop, and century after century.

The circumvallation of Charles V., then, had the same fate as that of Philip-Augustus. At the end of the fifteenth century, a new suburb had collected beyond it, and in the sixteenth we find it rapidly receding, and becoming buried deeper and deeper in the old town, so dense was the new town becoming outside it. Thus, in the fifteenth century—to stop there—Paris had already worn away the three concentric circles of walls which, in the time of Julian, falsely called the Apostate, may be said to have been in embryo in the two castella, since called the Grand Châtelet, and the Petit Châtelet. The growing city had successively burst its four girdles of walls, like a child grown too large for its last year's clothes. In the reign of Louis XI., were to be seen rising here and there amid that sea of houses, some groups of ruinous towers belonging to the ancient bulwarks, like archipelagoes of the old Paris submerged under the inundation of the new.

Since then, Paris has undergone another transformation, unhappily for the eye of Taste ; but it has overleaped only one boundary more—that of Louis XV.—the wretched mud-wall, worthy of the king who built it, and of the poet who sang it in this magnificent line, too ingenious to be translatable—

"Le mur murant Paris rend Paris murmurant."

In the fifteenth century, Paris was still divided into three towns quite distinct and separate, having each its peculiar features, manners, customs, privileges, and history—the City, the University, and the Ville or Town properly so called. The City, which occupied the island, was the most ancient, the smallest, and the mother of the other two—looking squeezed (if we may be allowed such a comparison) like a little old woman between two fine flourishing daughters. The University covered the left bank of the Seine, from the Tournelle to the Tour de Nesle, the points answering to which, in modern Paris, are, to the former the Halle-aux-Vins or Wine Mart, and to the latter, the Monnaie or Mint. Its circuit included an ample slice of that tract in which Julian had constructed his baths, and comprised the hill of Ste. Geneviève. The apex of this curve of walls was the Porte Papale or Papal Gate,

that is to say, very nearly, the site of the present Pantheon. The Town, which was the largest of the three
portions of Paris, occupied the right bank. Its quay,
in which there were several breaks and interruptions,
ran along the Seine from the Tour de Billy to the Tour
du Bois, that is, from the spot where the Grenier
d'Abondance now stands, to that occupied by the Tuileries. These four points at which the Seine cut the
circumference of the capital; on the left, the Tournelle
and the Tour de Nesle; and on the right, the Tour de
Billy and the Tour du Bois; were called, by distinction,
the four towers of Paris. The Town projected yet
more deeply into the territory bordering on the Seine
than the University. The most salient points of its enclosure (the one constructed by Charles V.) were at the
Portes St. Denis and St. Martin, the sites of which were
precisely the same as those of the gates now so called.

As we have just before said, each one of these three
great divisions of Paris was a town—but it was a town
too peculiar to be complete in itself—a town which
could not dispense with the vicinity of the other two.
So, also, each had its characteristic aspect. In the City,
the churches abounded; in the Town, the palaces; in
the University, the colleges. Leaving apart the secondary original features of old Paris, and the capricious
dispositions attaching to the *droit de voirie*, or right of
road—and noting only the great masses in the chaos of
the communal jurisdictions—we may say in general,
that the island belonged to the bishop; the right bank,
to the *prévôt des marchands* or provost of the traders;
and the left bank to the rector of the University. The
provost of Paris, a royal and not a municipal officer,
had authority over all. Among the conspicuous edifices, the City had Notre-Dame; the Town, the Louvre
and the Hôtel-de-Ville; and the University, the Sorbonne. Again, the Town had the Halles; the City, the
Hôtel-Dieu; and the University, the Pré-aux-Clercs.
Offenses committed by the scholars on the left bank, in
their Pré-aux-Clercs, they were tried for in the island at
the Palais de Justice, and punished for on the right

bank at Montfaucon ; unless, indeed, the rector, feeling
the University to be strong at that particular time, and
the king weak, thought proper to interfere—for it was
a privilege of the scholars to be hanged at home, that
is to say, within the University precincts.

Most of these privileges (we may observe in passing),
and there were some of greater value than this, had
been extorted from the kings by revolts and disturbances.   Such has been the course of things time out of
mind.   As the French proverb saith, *Le roi ne lache que
quand le peuple arrache*—in plain English, the king
never leaves hold until the people pull too hard for him.
In one of the old French charters we find this popular
fidelity defined with great simplicity : *Civibus fidelitas
in reges, quæ tamen aliquoties seditionibus interrupta,
multa peperit privilegia.*

In the fifteenth century, the Seine embraced five
islands within the circuit of Paris ; the Ile Louviers, on
which there were then living trees, though there are
now only piles of wood ; the Ile aux Vaches and the
Ile Notre-Dame, both uninhabited, excepting only one
sorry tenement, both fiefs of the bishop's, which two
islands, in the seventeenth century, were made into
one, since built upon, and now called the Ile St. Louis ;
and the City, having, at its western extremity, the islet
of the Passeur-aux-Vaches, since lost under the esplanade of the Pont-Neuf.   The City had, at that time, five
bridges : three on the right, the Pont Notre-Dame, and
the Pont-au-Change, of stone, and the Pont-aux-Meuniers, of wood ; and two on the left, the Petit-Pont, of
stone, and the Pont St. Michel, of wood ; all of them
laden with houses.   The University had six gates, built
by Philip-Augustus ; which, to set out from the Tournelle, occurred in the following order : the Porte St.
Victor, the Porte Bordelle, the Porte Papale, the Porte
St. Jacques, the Porte St. Michel, and the Porte St
Germain.   The Town had also six gates, built by
Charles V., viz., setting out from the Tour de Billy, the
Porte St. Antoine, the Porte du Temple, the Porte St.
Martin, the Porte St. Denis, the Porte Montmartre, and

the Porte St. Honoré. All these gates were strong, and handsome withal—which latter attribute is by no means incompatible with strength. A wide and deep trench, having a running stream during the winter floods, washed the foot of the walls all round Paris; the Seine furnishing the water. At night the gates were shut, the river was barred at the two extremities of the town with massive iron chains, and Paris slept in tranquillity.

Seen in a bird's-eye view, these three great pieces of town, the City, the University, and the Ville, presented each an inextricable web of streets fantastically raveled. Yet a glance was sufficient to show the spectator that those three portions of a city formed but one complete whole. You at once distinguished two long parallel streets, without interruption or deviation, running almost in a straight line, and intersecting all the three towns, from one extremity to the other, from the south to the north, at right angles with the Seine, connecting and mingling them, and incessantly pouring the people of each into the precincts of the other, making the three but one. One of these two lines of street ran from the Porte St. Jacques to the Porte St. Martin ; and was called in the University, Rue St. Jacques ; in the City, Rue de la Juiverie (anglicè, Jewery or Jewry); and in the Town, Rue St. Martin. It crossed the water twice, under the names of Petit-Pont and Pont Notre-Dame. The other line, called, on the left bank, Rue de la Harpe ; in the island, the Rue de la Barillerie ; on the right bank, Rue St. Denis ; over one arm of the Seine, Pont St. Michel, and over the other Pont-au-Change ; ran from the Porte St. Michel in the University, to the Porte St. Denis in the Town. However, though under so many different names, they were still, in fact, only two streets ; but they were the two normal, the two mother streets—the two arteries of Paris, by which all the other veins of the triple city were fed, or into which they emptied themselves.

Independently of these two principal, diametrical streets, running quite across Paris, common to the entire capital, the Town and the University had each its own great street, running in the direction of their length, parallel to the Seine, and intersecting the two arterial streets at right angles. Thus, in the Town, you descended in a straight line from the Porte St. Antoine to the Porte St. Honoré; in the University, from the Porte St. Victor to the Porte St. Germain. These two great ways, crossing the two first-mentioned, formed with them the frame or skeleton upon which was laid, knotted, and drawn in every direction, the tangled network of the streets of Paris. In the unintelligible figure of this network, you might, however, also discover, upon attentive observation, two bunches, as it were, of large streets, the one in the University, the other in the Town, which ran diverging from the bridges to the gates. Somewhat of the same geometrical disposition still exists.

Now, what aspect did all this present when viewed from the top of the towers of Notre-Dame in 1482? We will endeavor to describe it.

The spectator, on arriving, out of breath, upon this summit, was first of all struck by a dazzling confusion of roofs, chimneys, streets, bridges, squares, spires, steeples. All burst upon the eye at once—the formally-cut gable, the acute-angled roofing, the hanging turret at the angles of the walls, the stone pyramid of the eleventh century, the slate obelisk of the fifteenth; the donjon tower, round and bare; the church tower, square and decorated; the large and the small, the massive and the airy. The gaze was for some time utterly bewildered by this labyrinth; in which there was nothing but proceeded from art—from the most inconsiderable carved and painted house-front, with external timbers, low doorway, and stories projecting each upon each, up to the royal Louvre itself, which, at that time, had a colonnade of towers. But the following were the principal masses that were distinguishable when the eye became steady enough to examine this tumultuous assemblage of objects in detail.

First of all, the City. The island of the City, as is

observed by Sauval, the most laborious of the old explorers of Parisian antiquity, who, amidst all his trashiness, has these occasional happinesses of expression—" The isle of the City is shaped like a great ship, sunk in the mud, and run aground lengthwise in the stream, about the middle of the Seine." We have already shown that, in the fifteenth century, this ship was moored to the two banks of the river by five bridges. This form of the hull of a vessel had also struck the heraldic scribes; for, from this circumstance, according to Favyn and Pasquier, and not from the siege by the Normans, came the ship emblazoned upon the old escutcheon of Paris. To him who can decipher it, heraldry is an emblematic language. The whole history of the latter half of the middle ages is written in heraldry, as that of the former half is in the symbolism of the churches of Roman architecture. 'Tis the hieroglyphics of feudality succeeding those of theocracy.

The City, then, first presented itself to the view, with its stern to the east and its prow to the west. Looking toward the prow, you had before you an innumerable congregation of old roofs, with the lead-covered bolster of Sainte-Chapelle rising above them broad and round, like an elephant's back with the tower upon it. Only that here the place of the elephant's tower was occupied by the boldest, openest, airiest, most notched and ornamented spire that ever showed the sky through its lacework cone. Close before Notre-Dame, three streets terminated in the parvis, or part of the churchyard contiguous to the grand entrance—a fine square of old houses. The southern side of this Place was overhung by the furrowed and rugged front of the Hôtel-Dieu, and its roof, which looks as if covered with pimples and warts. And then, right and left, east and west, within that narrow circuit of the City, were ranged the steeples of its twenty-one churches, of all dates, forms, and sizes; from the low and decayed Roman campanile of St. Denis-du-Pas (*carcer Glaucini*) to the slender spires of St. Pierre-aux-Bœufs and St. Laundry. Behind Notre-Dame extended northward, the cloister, with its Gothic galleries ; southward, the demi-Roman palace of the bishop ; and eastward, the uninhabited point of the island, called the terrain, or ground, by distinction. Amid that accumulation of houses the eye could also distinguish, by the high perforated mitres of stone, which at that period, placed aloft upon the roof itself, surmounted the highest range of palace windows, the mansion presented by the Parisians, in the reign of Charles VI., to Juvénal des Ursins ; a little farther on, the black, pitch-covered market-sheds of the Marché Palus ; and in another direction, the new chancel of St. Germain-le-Vieux, lengthened, in 1458, by an encroachment upon one end of the Rue-aux-Febves ; and then, here and there, were to be seen some cross-way crowded with people—some pillory erected at the corner of a street—some fine piece of the pavement of Philip-Augustus—a magnificent flagging, furrowed in the middle to prevent the horses from slipping, and so ill-replaced in the sixteenth century by the wretched pebbling called *pavé de la Ligue*—some solitary backyard, with one of those transparent staircase-turrets which they used to build in the fifteenth century, one of which is still to be seen in the Rue des Bourdonnais. And on the right of the Sainte-Chapelle, to the westward, the Palais de Justice rested its group of towers upon the water's brink. The groves of the royal gardens which occupied the western point of the island, hid from view the islet of the Passeur. As for the water itself, it was hardly visible from the towers of Notre-Dame, on either side of the City ; the Seine disappearing under the bridges, and the bridges under the houses.

And when you looked beyond those bridges, the roofs upon which were tinged with green, having contracted untimely mouldiness from the vapors of the water ; if you cast your eye on the left hand, toward the University, the first edifice that struck it was a large low cluster of towers, the Petit Châtelet, the gaping porch of which seemed to devour the extremity of the Petit-Pont. Then, if your view ranged along the shore from east to west, from the Tournelle to the Tour de Nesle, you beheld a long line of houses exhibiting sculptured beams, colored window-glass, each story overhanging that beneath it—an interminable zigzag of ordinary gables, cut at frequent intervals by the end of some street, and now and then also by the front or the corner of some great stone-built mansion, which seemed to stand at its ease, with its courtyards and gardens, its wings and its compartments, amid that rabble of houses crowding and pinching one another, like a grand seigneur amidst a mob of rustics. There were five or six of these mansions upon the quay, from the Logis de Lorraine, which shared with the house of the Bernardines the great neighboring enclosure of the Tournelle, to the Hôtel de Nesle, the principal tower of which formed the limit of Paris on that side, and the pointed roofs of which were so situated as to cut with their dark triangles, during three months of the year, the scarlet disc of the setting sun.

That side of the Seine, however, was the least mercantile of the two; there was more noise and crowd of scholars than of artisans; and there was not, properly speaking, any quay, except from the Pont-Saint-Michel to the Tour de Nesle. The rest of the margin of the river was either a bare strand, as was the case beyond the Bernardines, or a close range of houses with the water at their foot, as between the two bridges. There was a great clamor of washerwomen along the waterside, talking, shouting, singing, from morning till night, and beating away at their linen—as they do at this day, contributing their full share to the gayety of Paris.

The University, from one end to the other, presented to the eye one dense mass forming a compact and homogeneous whole. Those thousand thick-set angular roofs, nearly all composed of the same geometrical element, when seen from above, looked almost like one crystalization of the same substance. The capricious fissures formed by the streets did not cut this conglomeration of houses into slices too disproportionate. The forty-two colleges were distributed among them very equally, and were to be seen in every quarter. The amusingly varied summits of those fine buildings were a product of the same description of art as the ordinary roofs which they overtopped; being nothing more than a multiplication, into the square or cube, of the same geometrical figure. Thus they complicated the whole, without confusing it; completed without overloading it. Geometry itself is one kind of harmony. Several fine mansions, too, lifted their heads magnificently here and there above the picturesque attic stories of the left bank; as the Logis de Nevers, the Logis de Rome, the Logis de Reims, which have disappeared; and the Hôtel de Cluny, which still exists for the artist's consolation, but the tower of which was so stupidly shortened a few years ago. Near the Hôtel de Cluny, that Roman palace, with fine semicircular arches, were once the Baths of Julian. There were also a number of abbeys, of a beauty more religious, of a grandeur more solemn, than the secular mansions, but not less beautiful nor less grand. Those which first caught the attention were that of the Bernardines, with its three steeples; that of Sainte-Geneviève, the square tower of which, still existing, makes us so much regret the disappearance of the remainder; the Sorbonne, half-college, half-monastery, so admirable a nave of which yet survives; the fine quadrilateral cloister of the Mathurins, and, adjacent to it, the cloister of St. Benedict's; the house of the Cordeliers, with its three enormous and contiguous gables; that of the Augustines, the graceful spire of which formed, after the Tour de Nesle, the next lofty projection on that side of Paris, commencing from the westward. The colleges—which are in fact the intermediate link between the cloister and the world—held the medium in the architectural series between the great mansions and the abbeys, exhibiting a severe elegance, a sculpture less airy than that of the palaces, an architecture less stern than that of the convents. Unfortunately, scarcely anything remains of these structures, in which Gothic art held so just a balance between richness and economy. The churches (and they were numerous and splendid in the University, and of every architectural era, from the round arches of Saint-Julian to the Gothic ones of Saint-Severin)—the churches, we say, rose above the whole; and, as one harmony more in that harmonious mass, they pierced in close succession the multifarious indented outline of the roofs, with boldly-cut spires, with perforated steeples, and slender aiguilles, or needle spires, the lines of which were themselves but a magnificent exaggeration of the acute angle of the roofs.

The ground of the University was hilly. The Montagne Ste. Geneviève, on the southeast, made one grand swell; and it was curious to see, from the top of Notre-Dame, that crowd of narrow, winding streets (now the *pays Latin*), those clusters of houses which, scattered in every direction from the summit of that eminence, spread themselves in disorder, and almost precipitously down its sides, to the water's edge; looking, some as if they were falling, others as if they were climbing up, and all as if hanging to one another; while the continual motion of a thousand dark points crossing one another upon the pavement, gave the whole an appearance of life. These were the people in the streets, beheld thus from on high and at a distance.

And in the intervals between those roofs, those spires, those innumerable projections of buildings, which so fantastically bent, twisted, and indented the extreme line of the University, you distinguished here and there some great patch of moss-covered wall, some thick round tower, or some embattled, fortress-looking town gate— this was the enclosure of Philip-Augustus. Beyond extended the green meadows, across which the roads were seen diverging, having along their sides, at quitting the body of the town, a number of maisons de faubourg, or houses without the walls, which were seen more thinly scattered the greater their distances from the barriers. Some of these faubourgs were considerable. First of all (to go round from the Tournelle), there was the bourg St. Victor, with its bridge of one arch over the Bievre; its abbey, in which was to be read the epitaph of King Louis the Fat—*epitaphium Ludovici Grossi;* and its church with an octagonal spire flanked by four steeple turrets, of the eleventh century (such a one is still to be seen at Etampes). Then there was the bourg St. Marceau, which had already three churches and a convent. Then, leaving on the left the mill of the Gobelins and its four white walls, came the faubourg St. Jacques, with the fine sculptured cross in the middle of it ; the church of St. Jacques du Haut-Pas, then a charming Gothic structure ; that of St. Magloire, with its fine nave of the fourteenth century, which Napoleon turned into a hay-barn ; and that of Notre-Dame des Champs, or Notre-Dame-in-the-Fields, in which were to be seen some by-zantins. And after leaving in the open country the monastery of the Chartreux or Carthusians, a rich structure of the same period as the Palais de Justice, with its little compartmented gardens, and the haunted ruins of Vauvert, the eye fell toward the West, upon the three Roman-built spires of St. Germain-des-Près, St. Germain or Germanus-in-the-Meadows. The bourg St. Germain, already a large commune, formed fifteen or twenty streets in the rear, the sharp steeple of St. Sulpice indicating one of its corners. Close by it was to be distinguished the quadrilateral enclosure of the Foire St. Germain, where is now the market ; then the abbot's pillory, a pretty little round tower, well capped with a cone of lead ; farther on was the tuilerie or tile-kiln ; and the Rue du Four, which led to the four banal or manorial bakehouse, with the manorial mill perched upon its mound—a specimen of one of the most vexatiously tyrannical characteristics of " the good old times;" and the lazaretto, a small, detached, and half-seen building. But that which especially attracted the eye, and kept it long fixed upon this point, was the abbey itself. It is certain that this monastery, which had an aspect of grandeur both as a church and as a seigniory or temporal lordship—that abbatial palace, in which the bishops of Paris deemed themselves happy to sleep a single night—that refectory, to which the architect had given the air, the beauty, and the splendid rose-shaped window of a cathedral—that elegant chapel of the Vir gin—that monumental dormitory—those spacious gardens—that frowning portcullis and jealous drawbridge—that circuit of battlements which marked its indented outline upon the verdure of the meadows around—those courts in which the mail of men-at-arms shone mingled with golden copes—the whole grouped and rallied, as it were, about the three round-arched spires, solidly based upon a Gothic chancel—made a magnificent figure in the horizon.

When at length, after long contemplating the University, you turned toward the right bank to the Town, properly so called, the character of the scene was suddenly changed. The Town was not only much larger than the University, but also less uniform. At first sight it appeared to be divided into several masses, singularly distinct from each other. First of all, on the East, in that part of the Town which still takes its name from the marais or marsh in which Camulogenes entangled Cæsar, there was a collection of palaces, the mass of which extended to the waterside. Four great mansions almost contiguous—the Hôtels de Jouy, de Sens, and de Barbeau, and the Logis de la Reine—cast upon the Seine the reflection of their slated tops intersected by slender turrets. These four edifices occupied the space from the Rue des Nonaindières to the abbey of the Celestines, the small spire of which formed a graceful relief to their line of gables and battlements. Some sorry, greenish-looking houses overhanging the water did not conceal from view the fine angles of their fronts, their great square stone-framed windows, their Gothic porches loaded with statues, the boldly-cut borderings about their walls, and all those charming accidents of architecture which make Gothic art seem as if it recommended its combinations at every fresh structure. Behind those palaces ran in every direction, in some places cloven, palisaded, and embattled, like a citadel, in others veiled by large trees like a Carthusian monastery, the vast and multiform circuit of that wonderful Hôtel de St. Pol, in which the French king had room to lodge superbly twenty-two princes of the rank of the dauphin and the Duke of Burgundy, with their trains and their domestics, besides the grands seigneurs or superior nobles, and the emperor when he came to visit Paris, and the lions, who had a mansion to themselves within the royal mansion. And we must here observe, that a prince's lodgings then consisted of not less than eleven principal apartments, from the audience-room to the chamber appropriated to prayer; besides all the galleries, baths, stove-rooms, and other "superfluous places," with which each suite of apartments was provided; besides the private gardens of each one of the king's guests; besides the kitchens, cellars, pantries, and general refectories of the household; the basses-cours or backyards, in which there were two-and-twenty general offices, from the fourille or bakehouse to the échansonnerie or butlery; places for games of fifty different kinds, as mall, tennis, riding at the ring, etc.; aviaries, fish-ponds, menageries, stables, cattle-stalls, libraries, armories, and foundries. Such was, at that day, a palais de roy—a Louvre—a Hôtel St. Pol; it was a city within a city.

From the tower upon which we have placed ourselves, the Hôtel St. Pol, though almost half hidden from view by the four great mansions of which we have just spoken, was, nevertheless, very considerable and very wonderful to behold. You could clearly distinguish in it, although they had been skillfully joined to the main building by means of long windowed and pillared galleries, the three several mansions which Charles V. had thrown into one together with his former palace; the Hôtel du Petit-Muce, with the airy balustrade which gracefully bordered its roof; the hôtel of the abbot of St. Maur, presenting the variety of an entrance regularly fortified, with a massive tower, machicolations, shot-holes, moineaux de fer, and over the wide Saxony gateway, the abbot's escutcheon placed between the two notches for the drawbridge; the hôtel of the Count d'Etampes, the keep of which, being ruinous at the top, looked rounded and indented, like the crest of a cock; here and there three or four

old oaks, making together one great swelling tuft;
haunts of swans amid the clear waters the fish pre-
serves, all wavering in light and shade; the picturesque
corner of many a court; the Hôtel des Lions or mansions of the lions, with its low-pointed arches upon
short Saxon pillars, its iron portcullises and its perpetual roaring; then, shooting up above this group of objects, the scaly spire of the Ave-Maria; on the left, the
mansion of the provost of Paris, flanked by four turrets
delicately moulded and perforated; and, in the center
and heart of the whole, the Hôtel St. Pol itself,
properly so called, with its multiplied fronts, its successive enrichments since the time of Charles V., the
heterogeneous excrescences with which the fancy of
the artists had loaded it in the course of two centuries;
with all the chancels of its chapels, all the gables of its
galleries, its thousand weathercocks, and its two contiguous towers, the conical roof of which, surrounded
by battlements at its base, looked like a pointed hat
with the brim turned up.

In continuing to ascend the steps of that amphi-
theatre of palaces which thus displayed itself at a distance, after crossing a deep fissure in the roofs of the
Town, which marked the course of the Rue St.
Antoine, the eye traveled on to the Logis d'Angoulême,
a vast structure of several different periods, in which
there were some parts quite new and almost white,
scarcely better harmonizing with the rest than a red
waistcoat might with a blue doublet. However, the
singularly sharp and elevated roof of the modern
palace, bristling with carved sprout-ends, and covered
with sheets of lead, over which ran sparkling incrusta-
tions of gilt copper in a thousand fantastic arabesques
—that roof so curiously demaskened, sprang gracefully
up from amid the brown ruins of the ancient edifice,
the old massive towers of which were bellying with age
into the shape of casks, their height shrunk with decrepitude, and breaking asunder from top to bottom.
Behind rose the forest of spires of the Palais des
Tournelles. Nor was any assemblage of objects in the

world—not even at Chambord nor at the Alhambra—
more magical, more aërial, more captivating, than that
grove of spires, turrets, chimneys, weathercocks, spiral
staircases, airy lanterns, pavilions, spindle-shaped turrets, or tournelles, as they were then called—all differing in form, height, and position.

To the right of the Tournelles, that bundle of enormous towers perfectly black, growing, as it were, one
into another, and looking as if bound together by their
circular fosse; that donjon tower, looped much more
with shot-holes than with windows; that drawbridge
always lifted; that portcullis always down;—those are
the Bastille. Those objects like black beaks, projecting
between the battlements, and which, at this distance,
you would take for the mouth of spouts, are cannon.
Under their fire, at the foot of the formidable structure,
you may perceive the Porte St. Antoine, almost buried
between its two towers.

Beyond the Tournelles, as far as the wall of Charles
V., extended, in rich compartments of verdure and of
flowers, a tufted carpet of garden-grounds and royal
parks, in the midst of which was distinguishable, by its
labyrinth of groves and walks, the famous Dædalus
garden which Louis XI. had given to Coictier. The
doctor's observatory rose above the labyrinth, like a
great isolated column with a small house for its capital;
and in that study had been practiced astrologies of
terrible effect. That spot is now occupied by the
Palace Royale.

As we have already observed, the Palace and its
precincts, of which we have endeavored to give the
reader some idea, though by specifying only its most
prominent features, filled up the angle which Charles
V.'s enclosure made with the Seine on the east. The
center of the town was occupied by a heap of ordinary
houses. Indeed, it was there that the three bridges of
the City on the right bank discharged their stream of
passengers; and bridges led to the building of houses
before that of palaces. This accumulation of common
dwelling-houses, pressed against one another like the

cells in a hive, was not without its beauty. In the roofs of a capital, as in the waves of a sea, there is, at least, grandeur of outline. In the first place, then, the streets, crossed and intertwined, diversified the mass with a hundred amusing figures; around the Halles, it was like a star with a thousand rays. The Rues St. Denis and St. Martin, with their innumerable ramifications, ascended one after the other, like two great trees mingling their branches; and then there were tortuous lines, the Rue de la Plâtrerie, etc., winding about over the whole. There were also some fine edifices lifting their heads above the petrified undulation of this sea of gables. First, at the entrance of the Pont-aux-Changeurs, behind which the Seine was seen foaming under the mill-wheels at the Pont-aux-Meuniers, there was the Châtelet; no longer a Roman tower as under the Emperor Julian, but a feudal tower of the thirteenth century, and of a stone so hard, that in three hours the pick did not remove it to the depth of a man's fist. Then there was the rich square steeple of St. Jacques-de-la-Boucherie, its angles all rounded with sculptures, and already worthy of admiration, although it was not finished in the fifteenth century. (It wanted in particular those four monsters which, still perched at the four corners of its roof, look like so many sphinxes giving to the modern Paris the enigma of the ancient to unriddle. Rault, the sculptor, placed them there, not until the year 1526; and had twenty francs for his trouble.) Then, again, there was the Maison-aux-Piliers, overlooking that Place de Grève of which we have already given some description. There was the church of St. Gervais, which a doorway in good taste has since spoiled; that of St. Méry, the old pointed arches of which were almost approaching to the semicircular; and that of St. Jean, the magnificent spire of which was proverbial; besides twenty other structures which disdained not to bury their attractions in that chaos of deep, dark, and narrow streets. And to these the carved stone crosses, more abounding in the crossways even than the gibbets themselves; the

cemetery of the Innocents, of which you discovered at
a distance the architectural enclosure; the pillory of
the Halles, the top of which was visible between the
chimneys of the Rue de la Cossonnerie; the échelle of
the Croix-du-Trahoir, in its carrefour or opening, which
was constantly darkened with people; the circular
hovels of the Halle-au-Blé or Corn-market; the broken
fragments of the old wall of Philip-Augustus, distinguishable here and there, buried among the houses—
ivy-mantled towers, ruinous gateways—crumbling and
shapeless pieces of wall; the quay with its thousand
shops, and its bloody-looking écorcheries or skinning-
yards; the Seine covered with boats, from the Port-au-
Foin to the For-l'Evéque; and you will have some
general idea of the appearance presented, in 1482, by
the central trapezium or irregular quadrangle of the
Town.

Together with these two quarters, the one of palaces,
the other of houses, the third great feature then ob-
servable in the Ville, was a long zone or belt of abbeys
which bordered it almost in its whole compass on the
land side, from east to west, and, behind the line of
fortification by which Paris was shut in, formed a
second internal enclosure, consisting of convents and
chapels. Thus, close to the park of the Tournelles,
between the Rue St. Antoine and the old Rue du
Temple, there was St. Catherine's, with its immense
grounds, bounded only by the wall of Paris. Between
the old and the new Rue du Temple, there was the
Temple itself, a frowning bundle of towers, lofty, erect,
and isolated in the midst of an extensive embattled enclosure. Between the Rue Neuve du Temple and the
Rue St. Martin, in the midst of its gardens, stood St.
Martin's, a superb fortified church, whose girdle of
towers, whose tiara of steeples, were second in strength
and splendor only to St. Germain-des-Près. Between
the two Rues, St. Martin and St. Denis, was displayed
the circuit of the Trinité, or convent of the Trinity.
And between the Rue St. Denis and the Rue Montor-
gueil, was that of the Filles-Dieu. Close by the latter

were to be distinguished the decayed roofs and un-paved enclosures of the Cour des Miracles, the only profane link that obtruded itself into that chain of re-ligious houses.

Lastly, the fourth compartment which presented itself distinctly in the conglomeration of roofs upon the right bank, occupying the western angle of the great enclosure, and the water-side downward, was a fresh knot of palaces and great mansions crowding at the foot of the Louvre. The old Louvre of Philip-Augustus, that immense structure—the great tower of which mustered around it twenty-three principal towers, besides all the smaller ones—seemed, at a dis-tance, to be enchased, as it were, within the Gothic summits of the Hôtel d'Alençon and the Petit-Bour-bon. This hydra of towers, the giant keeper of Paris, with its four-and-twenty heads ever erect—with the monstrous ridges of its back sheathed in lead or scaled with slates, and all variegated with glittering metallic streaks—surprisingly terminated the configuration of the Town on the west.

This, an immense *pâté*—what the Romans called an insula or island—of ordinary dwelling-houses, flanked on either side by two great clusters of palaces, crowned, the one by the Louvre, the other by the Tournelles, and bordered on the north by a long belt of abbeys and cultivated enclosures—the whole mingled and amalga-mated in one view—and over those thousands of build-ings, whose tiled and slated roofs ran in so many fan-tastic chains, the steeples, engraved, embroidered, and inlaid, of the forty-four churches on the right bank—myriads of cross streets—the boundary, on one side, a line of lofty walls with square towers (those of the University wall being round), and on the other, the Seine, intersected by bridges and crowded with num-berless boats—such was the Town of Paris in the fif-teenth century.

Beyond the walls there were some faubourgs adjacent to the gates, but less numerous and more scattered than those on the University side. Thus, behind the

Bastille, there were a score of mean houses clustered around the curious carvings of the cross called the Croix-Faubin, and the buttresses of the abbey of St. Antoine-des-Champs, or St. Anthony's-in-the-Fields; then there was Popincourt, lost amid the corn fields; then, La Courtille, a merry village of cabarets or public houses; the bourg St. Laurent, with its church, the steeple of which, at a distance, seemed in contact with the pointed towers of the Porte St. Martin; the Faubourg St. Denis, with the extensive enclosure of St. Ladre; then, out at the Porte Montmartre, the Grange-Batelière, encircled with white walls; and behind it Montmartre itself, with its chalky declivities—Montmartre, which had then almost as many churches as windmills, but which has retained only the windmills, "for," observes our author, "society now seeks only bread for the body"—an observation which the reader may interpret in his own way. And then, beyond the Louvre, you saw, stretching into the meadows, the Fauborg St. Honoré, even then of considerable extent; and, looking green, La Petite-Bretagne or Little Britain; and, spreading itself out, the Marché-aux-Porceaux, or Hog-market, in the center of which heaved the horrible boiler used for executing those convicted of coining. Between La Courtille and St. Laurent your eye had already remarked, on the summit of a rising ground that swelled amidst a solitary plain, a sort of structure, which looked at a distance like a ruinous colonnade standing upon a basement with its foundation laid bare. This, however, was neither a Parthenon, nor a temple of the Olympian Jupiter; it was the dismal Montfaucon, already alluded to, and hereafter to be described.

Now, if the enumeration of so many edifices, brief as we have sought to make it, has not shattered, in the reader's mind, the general image of old Paris as fast as we have endeavored to construct it, we will recapitulate it in a few words. In the center was the island of the City, resembling in its form an enormous tortoise, extending on either side its bridges all scaly with tiles,

like so many feet, from under its gray shell of roofs.
On the left, the close, dense, bristling, and homogeneous
quadrangle of the University; and on the right, the
vast semicircle of the Town, much more interspersed
with gardens and great edifices. The three masses,
City, University, and Town, are veined with innumerable streets. Across the whole runs the Seine, "the
nursing Seine," as Father du Breul calls it, obstructed
with islands, bridges, and boats. All around is an immense plain, checkered with a thousand different sorts
of cultivation, and strewed with beautiful villages; on
the left, Issy, Vanvres, Vaugirard, Montrouge, Gentilly,
with its round tower and its square tower, etc.; and on
the right, twenty others, from Conflans to Ville-l'Evêque.
In the horizon a circle of hills formed, as it were, the
rim of the vast basin. And in the distance, on the east,
was Vincennes, with its seven quadrangular towers; on
the south, the Bicêtre, with its pointed turrets; on the
north, St. Denis and its spire; and on the west, St.
Cloud and its donjon. Such was the Paris beheld from
the summit of the towers of Notre-Dame by the crows
who lived in 1482.

And yet it is of this city that Voltaire has said, that
"before the time of Louis XIV. it possessed only four
fine pieces of architecture," that is to say, the dome of
the Sorbonne, the Val-de-Grâce, the modern Louvre,
and—we have forgotten which was the fourth—perhaps
it was the Luxembourg. Voltaire, however, was not the
less the author of "Candide" for having made this observation; nor is he the less, among all the men who
have succeeded one another in the long series of human
characters, the one who has possessed in the greatest
perfection the *rire diabolique*, the sardonic smile. This
opinion of his only affords one evidence, among so
many others, that a man may be a fine genius, and yet
understand nothing of an art which he has not studied.
Did not Molière think he was doing great honor to
Raphael and Michael Angelo when he called them
"those Mingards of their age"?

But to return to Paris and to the fifteenth century

It was not then a fine town only—but it was a homogeneous town—an architectural and historical production of the Middle Ages—a chronicle in stone. It was a city composed of two architectural strata only, the Romanish and the Gothic layer—for the true Roman layer had long disappeared, except in the Baths of Julian, where it still pierced through the thick incrustation of the Middle Ages—and as for the Celtic stratum, no specimen of that was now to be found, even in sinking a well.

Half a century later, when the Revival came and broke into that consistency so severe and yet so varied, with the dazzling profuseness of its systems and its fancies, rioting among Roman arches, Grecian columns, and Gothic depressions—its carving so delicate and so imaginative—its peculiar taste for arabesques and foliage—its architectural paganism contemporary with Luther—Paris was perhaps more beautiful still, though less harmonious to the eye and to the mind. But that splendid period was of short duration. The Revival was not impartial. Not content with erecting, it thought proper to pull down—it must be acknowledged, too, that it wanted room. So the Gothic Paris was complete but for a moment. Scarcely was the tower of St. Jacques-de-la-Boucherie finished, before the demolition of the old Louvre was begun.

Since then this great city has been daily sinking into deformity. The Gothic Paris, under which the Romanish Paris was disappearing, has disappeared in its turn ; but what name shall we give to the Paris that has taken its place?

There is the Paris of Catherine de Medicis at the Tuileries, the Paris of Henry II. at the Hôtel-de-Ville —two edifices which are still in fine taste ;—the Paris of Henry IV. at the Place Royale—a brick front, faced with stone, and roofed with slate—real tri-colored houses ;—the Paris of Louis XIII. at the Val-de-Grâce —of architecture crushed and squat—with basket-handle vaults, big-bellied columns, and a hump-backed dome ;— the Paris of Louis XIV. at the Invalides—great, rich,

gilded, and cold ;—the Paris of Louis XV. at St. Sulpice—with volutes, knots of ribbons, clouds, vermicelli,
and succory, all in stone ;—the Paris of Louis XVI. at
the Pantheon—St. Peter's at Rome ill-copied—and the
building has been awkwardly heightened, which has by
no means rectified its lines ;—the Paris of the Republic
at the School of Medicine—a poor Greek and Roman
style, just as much to be compared to the Coliseum or
the Parthenon, as the constitution of the year III. is to
the laws of Minos ; the French denomination for which
style in architecture is, *le goût messidor ;*—the Paris of
Napoleon, at the Place Vendôme—something sublime—
a brazen column composed of melted cannon ;—the
Paris of the Restoration, at the Bourse or Exchange—
a colonnade very white, supporting a frieze very smooth ;
the whole square, and costing twenty millions of francs.

To each of these characteristic structures is allied, by
similarity of style, manner, and disposition of parts, a
certain number of houses scattered over the different
quarters of the town, which the eye of the connoisseur
easily distinguishes and assigns to their respective dates.
When a man understands the art of seeing, he can trace
the spirit of an age and the features of a king even in
the knocker on a door.

The present Paris has therefore no general physiognomy. It is a collection of specimens of several different ages, and the finest of all have disappeared. This
capital is increasing in dwelling-houses only—and in
what dwelling-houses! If it goes on as it is now doing,
Paris will be renewed every fifty years. So, also, the
historical meaning of its architecture is daily wearing
away. Its great structures are becoming fewer and
fewer, seeming to be swallowed up one after another
by the flood of houses. "Our fathers," a Parisian of
the present day might exclaim, "had a Paris of stone—
our sons will have one of plaster."

As for the modern structures of the new Paris, we
shall gladly decline enlarging upon them. Not, indeed,
that we do not pay them all proper admiration. The
Ste. Geneviève of M. Soufflot is certainly the finest

Savoy cake that was ever made of stone. The Palace of the Legion of Honor is also a very distinguished piece of pastry. The Halle-au-Blé or Corn-market, is an English jockey-cap on a magnificent scale. The towers of Saint-Sulpice are two great clarinets; now, nobody can deny that a clarinet shape is a shape; and then, the telegraph, crooked and grinning, makes an admirable diversity upon the roof. The church of Saint-Rock has a doorway, with whose magnificence only that of St. Thomas d'Aquin can compare; it has also a plum-pudding Mount Calvary down in a cellar, and a sun of gilt wood; these, it must be owned, are things positively marvelous. The lantern of the labyrinth at the Jardin des Plantes, too, is vastly ingenious. As for the Palais de la Bourse or Exchange, which is Grecian in its colonnade, Roman by the circular arches of its doors and windows, and of the Revival by its great depressed ceiling, it is doubtless a structure in great correctness and purity of taste; one proof of which is, that it is crowned by an attic story such as was never seen at Athens, a fine straight line, gracefully intersected here and there by stovepipes. We must add, that if it be a rule that the architecture of a building should be so adapted to the purpose of the building itself, as that the aspect of the edifice should at once declare that purpose, we can not too much admire a structure which, from its appearance, might be either a royal palace, a chamber of deputies, a town-hall, a college, a riding-house, an academy, a repository, a court of justice, a museum, a barrack, a mausoleum, a temple, or a theatre —and which, all the while, is an Exchange. It has been thought, too, that an edifice should be made appropriate to the climate—and so this one has evidently been built on purpose for a cold and rainy sky.

It has a roof almost flat, as they are in the East; and, consequently, in winter, when it snows, the roof has to be swept—and does any one doubt that roofs are intended to be swept? As for the purpose of which we have just now been speaking, the building fulfills it admirably. It is an Exchange in France, as it would have been a temple in Greece. True it is that the architect has had much ado to conceal the clock-face, which would have destroyed the purity of the noble lines of the façade; but to make amends, we have that colonnade running round the whole structure, under which, on the grand days of religious solemnity, may be magnificently developed the schemes of money-brokers and stock-jobbers.

These, doubtless, are very superb structures. Add to these many a pretty street, amusing and diversified, like the Rue de Rivoli; and we need not despair that Paris shall one day present, as seen in a balloon flight, that richness of outline and opulence of detail—that peculiar diversity of aspect—that something surpassingly grand in the simple and striking in the beautiful—which distinguishes a draught-board.

However, admirable as you may think the present Paris, reconstruct in your imagination the Paris of the fifteenth century—look at the sky through that surprising forest of spires, towers, and steeples—spread out amidst the vast city, tear asunder at the points of the islands, and fold round the piers of the bridges, the Seine, with its broad green and yellow flakes, more variegated than the skin of a serpent—project distinctly upon a horizon of azure the Gothic profile of that old Paris—make its outline float in a wintry mist clinging to its innumerable chimneys—plunge it in deep night, and observe the fantastic play of the darkness and the lights in that gloomy labyrinth of buildings—cast upon it a ray of moonlight, showing it in glimmering vagueness, with its towers lifting their great heads from that foggy sea—or draw that dark veil aside, cast into shade the thousand sharp angles of its spires and its gables, and exhibit it all fantastically indented upon the glowing western sky at sunset—and then compare.

And if you would receive from the old city an impression which the modern one is quite incapable of giving you, ascend, on the morning of some great holiday, at sunrise, on Easter, or Whit-Sunday, to some elevated point from which your eye can command the whole capital—and attend the awakening of the chimes. Behold, at a signal from heaven—for it is the sun that gives it—those thousand churches starting from their sleep. At first you hear only scattered tinklings, going from church to church, as when musicians are giving one another notice to begin. Then, all on a sudden, behold—for there are moments when the ear itself seems to see—behold, ascending at the same moment, from every steeple, a column of sound, as it were, a cloud of harmony. At first the vibration of each bell mounts up direct, clear, and, as it were, isolated from the rest, into the splendid morning sky; then, by degrees, as they expand, they mingle, unite, are lost in each other, and confounded in one magnificent concert. Then it is all one mass of sonorous vibrations, incessantly sent forth from the innumerable steeples—floating, undulating, bounding, and eddying, over the town, and extending far beyond the horizon the deafening circle of its oscillations. Yet that sea of harmony is not a chaos. Wide and deep as it is, it has not lost its transparency; you perceive the windings of each group of notes that escapes from the several rings; you can follow the dialogue, by turns grave and clamorous, of the crecelle and the bourdon; you perceive the octaves leaping from one steeple to another; you observe them springing aloft, winged, light, and whistling, from the bell of silver; falling broken and limping from the bell of wood. You admire among them the rich gamut incessantly descending and reascending the seven bells of Saint-Eustache; and you see clear and rapid notes, running across, as it were, in three or four luminous zigzags, and vanishing like flashes of lightning. Down there you see Saint-Martin's Abbey, a shrill and broken-voiced songstress; here is the sinister and sullen voice of the Bastille; and at the other end is the great tower of the Louvre, with its counter-tenor. The royal chime of the Palais unceasingly casts on every side resplendent trillings, upon which fall, at regular intervals, the heavy strokes from the great bell of Notre-Dame, which strike sparkles from them like the hammer upon the anvil. At intervals, you perceive sounds pass by, of every form, from the triple peal of Saint-Germain-des-Près. Then, again, from time to time, that mass of sublime sounds half opens, and gives passage to the stretto of the Ave-Maria, which glitters like an aigrette of stars. Below, in the deepest of the concert, you distinguish confusedly the internal music of the churches, exhaled through the vibrating pores of their vaulted roofs. Here, certainly, is an opera worth hearing. Ordinarily, the murmur that escapes from Paris in the day-time, is the city talking; in the night, it is the city breathing; but here, it is the city singing. Listen, then, to this tutti of the steeples—diffuse over the whole the murmur of half a million of people—the everlasting plaint of the river—the boundless breathings of the wind—the grave and far quartet of the four forests placed upon the hills, in the distance, like so many vast organs—immersing in them, as in a demi-tint, all in the central concert that would otherwise be too rugged or too sharp; and then say whether you know of anything in the world more rich, more joyous, more golden, more dazzling, than this tumult of bells and chimes—this furnace of music—these thousand voices of brass, all singing together in flutes of stone three hundred feet high —this city which is all one orchestra—this symphony as loud as a tempest.

BOOK IV.

CHAPTER I.

A FOUNDLING.

IT was sixteen years before the period of our story that, on a fine morning of the first Sunday after Easter—called in England Low Sunday, and in France, *le dimanche de la Quasimodo*, or Quasimodo Sunday, from the word Quasimodo, which commences the Latin offertory appropriated to the mass of that day—that a young child had been deposited, after mass, in the cathedral church of Notre-Dame, upon the bedstead fixed in the pavement on the left hand of the entrance, opposite to that great image of St. Christopher which the stone figure of Messire Antoine des Essarts, knight, had been contemplating on his knees since the year 1413, at the time that it was thought proper to throw down both the saint and his faithful adorer. Upon this bedstead it was customary to expose foundlings to the charity of the public; any one took them that chose; and in the front of the bedstead was placed a copper basin for the reception of alms.

The sort of living creature that was found lying upon these planks on Low Sunday morning, in the year of our Lord 1467, appeared to excite, in a high degree, the curiosity of a very considerable group of persons which had collected round the bedstead, and which consisted, in great measure, of individuals of the fair sex. Indeed, they were nearly all old women.

In the front line of the spectators, and stooping the

most intently over the bedstead, were to be seen four
of them, who by their gray cagoule (a sort of cassock),
appeared to be attached to some devout sisterhood.
We know not why history should not hand down to
posterity the names of these discreet and venerable
demoiselles.   They were Agnès la Herme, Jehanne de
la Tarme, Henriette la Gaultièrre, and Gauchère la
Violette—all four widows, all four bonnes-femmes of
the Chapelle Etienne Haudry, who had come thus far
from their house, with their mistress's leave, and con-
formably to the statutes of Pierre d'Ailly, to hear the
sermon.

However, if these good Haudriettes were observing
for the moment the statutes of Pierre d'Ailly, assuredly
they were violating, to their heart's content, those of
Michel de Brache and the Cardinal of Pisa, which so
inhumanly prescribed silence to them.

"What ever can that be, sister?" said Agnès to
Gauchère, as she looked at the little exposed creature,
which lay screaming and twisting itself about upon the
bedstead, frightened at being looked at by so many
people.

"Bless you!" said Jehanne, "what's to become of us
all, if that's the way they make children now?"

"I'm no great judge of children," resumed Agnès,
"but it must surely be a sin to look at such a one as
this!"

"It's no child at all, Agnès—"

"It's a misshapen baboon," observed Gauchère.

"It's a miracle," said Henriette la Gaultière.

"Then," remarked Agnès, "this is the third since
Lætare Sunday; for it's not a week since we had the
miracle of the mocker of pilgrims divinely punished by
Our Lady of Aubervilliers; and that was the second
miracle of the month."

"This pretended foundling's a very monster of abomi-
nation," resumed Jehanne.

"He brawls loud enough to deafen a chanter," added
Gauchère; "hold your tongue, you little bellower."

"To say that it's monsieur of Reims that sends this

monstrosity to monsieur of Paris!" exclaimed La Gaultière, clasping her hands.

"I imagine," said Agnès la Herme, "that it's some strange animal—the offspring of some beastly Jew or other—something, at all events, that's not Christian, and so must be thrown into the water or into the fire."

"Surely," resumed La Gaultière, "nobody'll ask to have it!"

"Ah, my God!" exclaimed Agnès, "those poor nurses that live down there in the foundling-house at the bottom of the alley, going down to the river, close by the lord bishop's; suppose they were to go and take them this little monster to suckle! I'd rather give suck to a vampire."

"Is she a simpleton, that poor La Herme?" rejoined Jehanne. "Don't you see, my dear sister, that this little monster is at least four years old, and wouldn't have half so much appetite for your breast as for a piece of roast meat."

In fact, the "little monster" (for we ourselves should be much puzzled to give it any other denomination) was not a new-born infant. It was a little, angular, restless mass, imprisoned in a canvas bag marked with the cipher of Messire Guillaume Chartier, then bishop of Paris—with a head peeping out at one end of it. This head was very deformed, exhibiting only a forest of red hair, one eye, a mouth, and some teeth. The eye was weeping; the mouth was crying; and the teeth seemed to desire, above all things, to bite. The whole lump was struggling violently in the bag, to the great wonderment of the increasing and incessantly renewing crowd around it.

Dame Aloise de Gondelaurier, a wealthy and noble lady, holding by the hand a pretty little girl about six years of age, and drawing after her a long veil attached to the golden horn of her coif, stopped as she was passing before the bedstead, and looked for a moment at the unfortunate creature; while her charming little daughter, Fleur-de-Lys de Gondelaurier, all clad in silk and velvet, was spelling with her pretty finger, upon the

permanent label attached to the bedstead, the words
ENFANS TROUVES.

"Really," said the lady, turning away with disgust,
"I thought they exposed here nothing but children."

She turned her back; at the same time throwing into
the basin a silver florin, which rang among the liards,
and opened wide the eyes of the poor bonnes-femmes
of the Chapelle Etienne Haudry.

A moment afterward the grave and learned Robert
Mistricolle, king's prothonotary, passed by, with an
enormous missal under one arm, and his wife under the
other (Damoiselle Guillemette-la-Mairesse), having thus
at his side his two regulators, the spiritual and the temporal.

"Foundling, indeed!" said he, after examining the
living lump; "yes—found, apparently, upon the parapet of the river Phlegethon!"

"It has but one eye visible," observed Damoiselle
Guillemette; "it has a great wart upon the other."

"It's no wart," exclaimed Maître Robert Mistricolle;
"it's an egg, that contains just such another demon,
which has upon its eye another little egg enclosing another devil—and so on."

"How do you know that?" asked Guillemette-la-
Mairesse.

"I know it for very sufficient reasons," answered the
prothonotary.

"Monsieur the prothonotary," asked Gauchère, "what
do you prognosticate from this pretended foundling?"

"The greatest calamities," answered Mistricolle.

"Ah, my God!" said an old woman among the bystanders, "withal that there was a considerable pestilence last year, and that they say the English are going
to land in great company at Harfleur!"

"Perhaps that'll prevent the queen from coming to
Paris in September," observed another; "and trade's
so bad already!"

"I'm of opinion," cried Jehanne de la Tarme, "that
it would be better for the inhabitants of Paris, for that

11

little conjuror there to be lying upon a fagot than upon a board."

"A fine flaming fagot!" added the old woman.

"It would be more prudent," said Mistricolle.

For some minutes a young priest had been listening
to the argument of the Haudriettes and the oracular
sentences of the prothonotary.

He had a severe countenance, with a broad forehead
and a penetrating eye. He made way silently through
the crowd, examined the little conjuror with his eyes,
and stretched out his hand over him. It was time; for
all the devout old ladies were already regaling themselves with the anticipation of a fine flaming fagot.

"I adopt that child," said the priest. He wrapped
it in his cassock, and carried it away with him; the bystanders gazing after him with looks of affright. In a
minute he had disappeared through the Porte Rouge,
or red door, which at that time led from the church
into the cloisters.

When the first surprise was over, Jehanne de la Tarme
whispered in the ear of La Gaultière, "Did I not tell
you, sister, that that young clerk, Monsieur Claude
Frollo, is a sorcerer?"

CHAPTER II.

CLAUDE FROLLO.

CLAUDE FROLLO was in fact no vulgar person. He
belonged to one of those families of middle rank which
were called indifferently, in the impertinent language of
the last century, haute bourgeoisie or petite noblesse—
that is, high commoners or petty nobility. This family
had inherited from the brothers Paclet the fief of Tirechappe, which was held of the Bishop of Paris, and the
twenty-one houses of which had been, in the thirteenth

CLAUDE FROLLO.

century, the object of so many pleadings before the official. As possessor of this fief, Claude Frollo was one of the septvingt-un, or hundred and forty-one seigneurs, claiming censive, or manorial dues, in Paris and its faubourgs; and in that capacity his name was long to be seen inscribed between that of the Hôtel de Tancarville, belonging to Maître François Le Rez, and that of the college of Tours, in the chartulary deposited at Saint Martin-des-Champs.

The parents of Claude Frollo had destined him, from his infancy, for the ecclesiastical state. He had been taught to read in Latin; and had been bred to cast down his eyes, and to speak low. While yet a child, his father had cloistered him in the college of Torchi, in the University; and there it was that he had grown up, over the missal and the lexicon.

He was, moreover, a melancholy, grave, and serious boy, who studied ardently and learned with rapidity; he never shouted loud when at play; he mixed little in the bacchanalia of the Rue du Fouarre; knew not what it was to *dare alapas et capillos laniare;* nor had figured in that mutiny of 1463, which the annalists gravely record under the title of "Sixième Trouble de l'Université." It did not often happen to him to rally the poor scholars of Montaign upon their cappettes, from which they derived their University nickname; nor the fellows of the college of Dormans, upon their smooth tonsure and their tripartite frock, made of cloth, blue gray, blue, and violet—*azurini coloris et bruni*, as the charter of Cardinal des Quatre-Couronnes expresses it.

But, on the other hand, he was assiduous at the great and the little schools of the Rue Saint-Jean-de-Beauvais. The first scholar whom the abbot of Saint-Pierre-de-Val, at the moment of commencing his reading in canon law, always observed intently fixed, opposite to his chair, against a pillar of the école Saint-Vendregesile, was Claude Frollo, armed with his inkhorn, chewing his pen, scrawling upon his much-worn knee, and, in winter, blowing his fingers. The first auditor that Messire Miles d'Isliers, docteur en décret, saw arrive every Mon-

day morning, quite out of breath, at the opening of the
doors of the schools Du Chef Saint-Denis, was Claude
Frollo. Thus, at the age of sixteen, the young clerk
was a match, in mystical theology, for a father of the
Church; in canonical theology, for a father of the
Council; and in scholastic theology, for a doctor of the
Sorbonne.

Theology being passed through, he had then rushed
into the decrét, or study of the decretals. After the
Master of the Sentences, he had fallen upon the Capitularies of Charlemagne; and had successively devoured, in his appetite for knowledge, decretals upon decretals; those of Theodore, Bishop of Hispalis; those of
Bouchard, Bishop of Worms; those of Yves, Bishop of
Chartres; then the decrét of Gratian, which succeeded
the capitularies of Charlemagne; then the collection by
Gregory IX.; then the epistle Super specula of Hono-
rius III. He made himself clearly familiar with that
vast and tumultuous period of the civil and the canon
law, in collision and at strife with each other in the
chaos of the Middle Ages—a period which opens with
Bishop Theodore, in 618, and closes, in 1227, with Pope
Gregory.

Having digested the decretals, he plunged into medicine and the liberal arts. He studied the science of
herbs, the science of unguents. He became expert in
the treatment of fevers and of contusions, of wounds and
of imposthumes. Jacques d'Espars would have admitted him as a physician; Richard Hellain, as a surgeon.
In like manner he ran through every degree in the faculty of arts. He studied the languages Latin, Greek,
Hebrew; a triple sanctuary, then but very little frequented. He was possessed by an absolute fever of ac-
quiring and storing up science. At eighteen, he had
made his way through the four faculties; it seemed to
the young man that life had but one sole object, and
that was, to know.

It was just about this period that the excessive heat
of the summer of 1466 gave birth to the great plague
which carried off more than forty thousand souls within

the viscounty of Paris, and amongst others, says John of Troyes, "Maître Arnoul, the king's astrologer, a man full honest, wise, and pleasant." It was rumored in the University, that the Rue Tirechappe was one of those especially devastated by the pestilence. It was there, in the midst of their fief, that the parents of Claude resided. The young scholar hastened in great alarm to his paternal roof. On entering, he found that his father and his mother had both died the day before. A little brother, quite an infant, still in its swaddling clothes, was yet living, and crying abandoned in its cradle. It was all that remained to Claude of his family. The young man took the child under his arm, and went away pensive. Hitherto, he had lived only in science; he was now beginning to live in the world.

This catastrophe was a crisis in Claude's existence. An older brother, an orphan, and the head of a family at nineteen, he felt himself rudely aroused from the reveries of the school to the realities of this life. Then, moved with pity, he was seized with passion and devotion for this infant brother; and strange at once and sweet was this human affection to him who had never yet loved anything but books.

This affection developed itself to a singular degree; in a soul so new to passion it was like a first love. Separated since his childhood from his parents, whom he had scarcely known—cloistered and walled up, as it were, in his books—eager above all things to study and to learn—exclusively attentive, until then, to his understanding, which dilated in science—to his imagination, which expanded in literature—the poor scholar had not yet had time to feel that he had a heart. This little brother, without father or mother—this infant which suddenly dropped, as it were, from heaven into his charge—made a new man of him; he discovered that there was something else in the world besides the speculations of the Sorbonne and the verses of Homerus—that man has need of affections—that life without tenderness and without love, is but a piece of dry machinery, noisy and wearisome. Only he fancied—for he was still at that age when illusions are as yet replaced only by illusions—that the affections of blood and kindred were the only ones necessary; and that a little brother to love, was sufficient to fill up his whole existence.

He threw himself, then, into the love of his little Jehan, with all the warmth of a character which was already deep, ardent, concentrated. This poor, helpless creature, pretty, fair-haired, rosy, and curly—this orphan with another orphan for its only support—moved him to the inmost soul; and, like a grave thinker as he was, he began to reflect upon Jehan with a feeling of the tenderest pity. He bestowed all his solicitude upon him, as upon something extremely fragile, especially commended to his care: he was more than a brother to the infant—he became a mother to it.

Now, little Jehan having lost his mother before he was weaned, Claude put him out to nurse. Besides the fief of Tirechappe, he inherited from his father that of Moulin, which was held of the square tower of Gentilly; it was a mill standing upon a hill, near the Château de Winchestre, since corrupted into Bicêtre. The miller's wife was suckling a fine boy, it was not far from the University, and Claude carried his little Jehan to her in his own arms.

Thenceforward, feeling that he had a burden to bear, he began to look on life as a serious matter. The thought of his little brother became not only his recreation from study, but the object of his studies themselves. He resolved to devote himself entirely to the future life of the being for whom he thought himself answerable before God, and never to have any other spouse, any other offspring, than the happiness and the fortune of his brother. He attached himself, therefore, more devotedly than ever to his clerical vocation. His merit, his learning, his quality as an immediate vassal of the Bishop of Paris, opened wide to him the gates of the Church. At twenty years of age, by special dispensation from the Holy See, he was ordained priest; and performed the service, as the youngest of the chap-

lains of Notre-Dame, at the altar called, on account of
the late mass that was said at it, altare pigrorum, the
altar of the lazy.

There, more than ever immersed in his dear books,
which he quitted only to hasten for an hour to the fief
Du Moulin, this mixture of learning and austerity, so
rare at his age, had speedily gained him the admiration
and reverence of the cloister. From the cloister his
reputation for learning had been communicated to the
people, amongst whom it had been in some degree converted, as not unfrequently happened in that day, into
renown for sorcery.

It was at the moment of returning, on the Quasimodo
Sunday, from saying his mass of the slothful at their
altar, which was at the side of that gate of the choir
which opened into the nave, on the right hand, near the
image of the Virgin, that his attention had been awakened by the group of old women screaming around the
bed of the foundlings.

Then it was that he had approached the unfortunate
little creature, the object of so much hatred and menace.
That distress, that deformity, that abandonment, the
thought of his little brother—the idea which suddenly
crossed his mind that, were he himself to die, his dear
little Jehan, too, might chance to be miserably cast
upon those boards—all that had rushed upon his heart
at once—a deep feeling of pity had taken possession
of him, and he had borne off the child.

When he drew the infant out of the bag, he found it
to be very deformed indeed. The poor little imp had
a great lump covering its left eye—the head compressed between the shoulders—the spine crooked—the
breastbone prominent—and the legs bowed. Yet it
seemed to be full of life ; and although it was impossible to discover what language it spluttered, yet its cry
indicated a certain degree of health and strength.
Claude's compassion was increased by this ugliness ; and
he vowed in his heart to bring up this child for the love
of his brother ; in order that, whatever might in future
time be the faults of little Jehan, there might be placed

to his credit this piece of charity performed on his ac
count. It was a sort of putting out of good works a
interest, which he transacted in his brother's name—at
investment of good actions which he wished to make
for him beforehand—to provide against the chance o
the little fellow's one day finding himself short of that
sort of specie, the only kind taken at the gate of heaven

He baptized his adopted child by the name of Quasi
modo ; whether it was that he chose thereby to com
memorate the day which he had found him ; or that he
meant to mark by that name how incomplete and im-
perfectly moulded the poor little creature was. Indeed,
Quasimodo, one-eyed, hump-backed, and bow-legged,
could hardly be considered as anything more than an
almost.

CHAPTER III.

IMMANIS PECORIS CUSTOS, IMMANIOR IPSE.

Now, in 1482, Quasimodo had grown up, and had
been for several years ringer of the bells of Notre-
Dame, by the grace of his adoptive father, Claude
Frollo ; who was become Archdeacon of Joas, by the
grace of his suzerain, Messire Louis de Beaumont ; who
had become Bishop of Paris in 1472, on the death of
Guillaume Chartier, by the grace of his patron, Olivier
le Daim, barber to Louis XI., king by the grace of
God.

Quasimodo, then, was ringer general at Notre-Dame.

With time, a certain peculiar bond of intimacy had
been contracted between the ringer and the church.
Separated forever from the world by the double fatality of his unknown birth and his natural deformity—
imprisoned from his infancy within that double and im-
passable circle—the poor unfortunate had been accustomed to see nothing on this earth beyond the religious

walls which had received him into their shade. Notre-
Dame had been to him successively, as he grew up, the
egg—the nest—his house—his country—the world.

And certain it is, there was a sort of mysterious and
pre-existing harmony between this creature and this
edifice. When, while yet quite little, he used to drag
himself along, tortuously and tumblingly, under the
gloom of its arches, he seemed, with his human face
and his bestial members, the native reptile of that damp
dark floor, upon which the shadows of the Saxon capitals projected so many fantastic forms.

And, afterwards, the first time that he clung mechanically to the bell-rope in the towers, hung himself upon
it, and set the bell in motion, the effect upon Claude,
his adoptive father, was that of a child finding its tongue
and beginning to talk.

Thus it was that, gradually unfolding his being, which
constantly took its mould from the cathedral—living in
it—sleeping in it—scarcely ever going out of it—receiving every hour its mysterious impress—he came at
length to resemble it, to be fashioned to it as it were,
to make an integral part of it. His salient angles fitted
themselves (if we may be allowed the expression) into
the re-entering angles of the structure, and he seemed
to be not only its inhabitant, but even the natural tenant of it. He might almost be said to have taken its
form, as the snail takes that of its shell. It was his
dwelling place—his hole—his envelope. Between the
old church and himself, there was an instinctive sympathy so profound—so many affinities, magnetic as well
as material—that he in some sort adhered to it, like the
tortoise to its shell. The cathedral, with its time-
roughened surface, was his carapace.

It is needless to hint to the reader, that he is not to
accept literally the figures that we are here obliged to
employ in order to express that singular assimilation,
symmetrical—immediate—consubstantial, almost—of a
man to a building. Nor is it less evident to what a degree he must have familiarized himself with the whole
cathedral during so long and so intimate a cohabitation.

This was his own peculiar dwelling-place; it had no depth which Quasimodo had not penetrated, no height which he had not scaled. Many a time had he clambered up its front to one story after another, with no other help than the projections of its architecture and sculpture; the towers, over the external surface of which he was sometimes seen creeping, like a lizard gliding upon a perpendicular wall—those two giant cheeks of the building—so lofty, so threatening, so formidable—had for him neither giddiness, nor dizziness, nor terror. To see them so gentle under his hand, so easy to scale, one would have said that he had tamed them. By dint of leaping, climbing, sporting amid the abysses of the gigantic cathedral, he was become in some sort both monkey and chamois—like the Calabrian child, which swims before it can run, and plays in its infancy with the sea.

Moreover, not only did his body seem to have fashioned itself according to the cathedral, but his mind also. In what state was that soul of his? what bend had it contracted, what form had it taken, under that close-drawn envelope, in that savage mode of life? This it would be difficult to determine. Quasimodo was born one-eyed, hump-backed, limping. It was with great difficulty and great patience that Claude Frollo had succeeded in teaching him to speak. But a fatality pursued the poor foundling. Made ringer of Notre-Dame at fourteen years of age, a fresh infirmity had come to complete his desolation—the bells had broken his tympanum, and he had become deaf. The only door that nature had left him open to the external world, had been suddenly closed forever.

And in closing, it intercepted the sole ray of joy and light that still penetrated to the soul of Quasimodo. That moonlight was veiled in deep night. The poor creature's melancholy became incurable and complete as his deformity; add to which, his deafness rendered him in some sort dumb. For, that he might not make himself laughed at by others, from the moment that he found himself deaf, he resolutely determined to observe a silence which he scarcely ever broke, except when he was alone. He tied up voluntarily that tongue which Claude Frollo had had so much trouble to untie. And hence it was that, when necessity compelled him to speak, his tongue moved stiffly and awkwardly, like a door of which the hinges have grown rusty.

We are now to endeavor to penetrate to Quasimodo's soul through that thick, hard rind—could we sound the depths of that ill-formed organization—were it possible for us to look, as it were, with a torch in our hands, behind the non-transparency of those organs—to explore the darksome interior of that opaque being—to elucidate its obscure corners and absurd no-thoroughfares, and throw all at once a strong light upon the Psyche chained down in that drear cavern—doubtless we should find the poor creature in some posture of decrepitude, stunted and rickety—like those prisoners that used to grow old in the low dungeons of Venice, bent double in a stone chest too low and too short for them either to stand or to lie at full length.

It is certain that the spirit pines in a misshapen body. Quasimodo scarcely felt, stirring blindly within him, a soul made after his own image. The impressions of external objects underwent a considerable refraction before they reached his apprehension. His brain was a peculiar medium; the ideas which passed through it issued forth completely distorted. The reflection which proceeded from that refraction was necessarily divergent and astray.

Hence, he was subject to a thousand optical illusions, a thousand aberrations of judgment, a thousand wanderings of idea, sometimes foolish, sometimes idiotic.

The first effect of this fatal organization was to disturb the look which he cast upon external objects. He received from them scarcely any immediate perception. The external world seemed to him much farther off than it does to us.

The second effect of his misfortune was to render him mischievous. He was mischievous, indeed, because he was savage; and he was savage because he was ugly. There was a consequentiality in his nature as well as in ours. His strength, too, developed in so extraordinary a degree, was another cause of mischievousness *malus puer robustus,* says Hobbes.

Besides, we must do him the justice to observe that mischievousness, perhaps, was not inherent in him. At his very first steps among mankind, he had felt himself —and then he had seen himself—repulsed, branded, spit upon. Human speech had ever been to him a scoff or a malediction. As he grew up, he had found naught around him but hatred. What wonder that he should have caught it! He had but contracted his share of malice—he had but picked up the weapon that had wounded him.

And, after all, he turned but reluctantly toward mankind—his cathedral was sufficient for him. It was peopled with figures in marble—with kings, saints, bishops—who, at all events, did not burst out laughing in his face, but looked upon him with uniform tranquillity and benevolence. The other figures, those of the monsters and demons, had no hatred for him, Quasimodo. He was too much like them for that. They seemed much rather to be scoffing at the rest of mankind. The saints were his friends, and blessed him ; the monsters were his friends, and protected him. And, accordingly, he used to have long communings with them; he would sometimes pass whole hours squatted down before one of those statues, holding a solitary conversation with it; on which occasions, if any one happened to approach, he would fly like a lover surprised in his serenade.

And the cathedral was not only society to him—it was the world—it was all nature. He dreamt of no hedgerows but the stained windows ever in flower—no shades but the stone foliage which unfolds itself loaded with birds in the tufted Saxon capitals—no mountains but the colossal towers of the church—no ocean but Paris, murmuring at their feet.

That which he loved above all in his maternal edifice

·—that which awakened his soul, and made it stretch
forth its poor pinions, which it kept so miserably
folded up within its cavern—that which sometimes
made him happy—was, the bells. He loved them,
caressed them, talked to them, understood them. From
the carillon in the central steeple, to the great bell over
the doorway, they all shared his affections. The central
steeple and the two towers were to him three great
cages, the birds in which, taught by himself, sang for
him alone. It was, however, those same bells that had
made him deaf. But a mother is often the fondest of
that child which has cost her the most suffering.

It is true that their voices were the only ones that
he was still capable of hearing. On this account, the
great bell of all was his best beloved. She it was
whom he preferred among this family of noisy sisters
that fluttered about him on festival days. This
great bell was named Marie. She was placed in the
southern tower, where she had no companion but her
sister Jacqueline, a bell of smaller dimensions, shut up
in a smaller cage by the side of her own. This Jacqueline was so named after the wife of Jean Montagu,
which Jean had given her to the church—a donation,
however, which had not prevented him from going and
figuring without his head at Montfaucon. In the
northern tower were six other bells; while the six
smallest inhabited the central steeple, over the choir,
together with the wooden bell, which was rung only
from the afternoon of Maunday-Thursday until the
morning of Holy Saturday, or Easter-eve. Thus Quasimodo had fifteen bells in his seraglio; but the big
Marie was his favorite.

It is not easy to give an idea of his delight on those
days on which they rang in full peal. The moment
the archdeacon had set him off with the word "Go,"
he ascended the spiral staircase of the steeple quicker
than any other person would have descended it. He
rushed, all breathless, into the aërial chamber of the
large Marie; he gazed upon her for a moment intently
and fondly; then he addressed her softly; patted her

with his hand, like a good horse setting out on a long
journey; expressing sorrow for the trouble he was
going to give her. After these first caresses, he called out
to his assistants, placed in the lower story of the tower,
to begin. The latter then hung their weight at the ropes
the capstan creaked, and the enormous round of metal
swung slowly. Quasimodo, panting, followed it with
his eye. The first stroke of the clapper against the
brazen wall that encircled it shook the woodwork upon
which he stood. Quasimodo vibrated with the bell.
"Vah!" he would cry, with a burst of insensate laughter.
Meanwhile, the motion of the bell became quicker; and
as it went on, taking a wider and wider sweep, Quasimodo's eye, in like manner, opened wider and wider,
and became more and more phosphoric and flaming. At
length the great peal commenced—the whole tower
trembled—wood, lead, stone—all shook together—from
the piles of the foundation to the trifoliations at the
summit. Quasimodo was now in a violent perspiration,
running to and fro, and shaking, with the tower, from head
to foot. The bell, now in full and furious swing, presented alternately to each wall of the tower its brazen
throat, from whence escaped that tempest breath which
was audible at four leagues' distance. Quasimodo
placed himself before this gaping throat—squatted
down and rose up again at each turn of the bell—in-
haled that furious breath—looked by turns down upon
the Place which was swarming with people two hundred feet below him, and upon the enormous brazen
tongue which came, second after second, and bellowed
in his ear. It was the only speech that he understood—
the only sound that broke to him the universal silence.
His soul dilated in it, like a bird in the sunshine. All
at once he would catch the frenzy of the bell; and
then his look became extraordinary—he would wait the
next coming of the vast mass of metal, as the spider
waits for the fly, and then throw himself headlong
upon it. Now, suspended over the abyss, borne to
and fro by the formidable swinging of the bell, he
seized the brazen monster by the ears—griped it be-

tween his knees—spurred it with both his heels—and
redoubled, with the whole shock and weight of his
body, the fury of the peal. Meanwhile, the tower
trembled—while he shouted and ground his teeth—his
red hair bristling up—his breath heaving like the blast
of a forge—and his eye flaming—while his monstrous
steed was neighing and palpitating under him. Then
it was no longer either the great bell of Notre-Dame,
or Quasimodo the ringer—it was a dream—a whirl—a
tempest — dizziness astride upon clamor — a strange
centaur, half man, half bell—a sort of horrible Astolpho,
carried along upon a prodigious hippograff of living
bronze.

The presence of this extraordinary being breathed,
as it were, a breath of life through the whole cathedral.
There seemed to escape from him—so at least said the
exaggerating superstitions of the multitude—a mysterious emanation, which animated all the stones of Notre-
Dame, and heaved the deep bosom of the ancient
church. To know that he was there, was enough to
make you think you saw life and motion in the thousand statues of the galleries and doorways. The old
cathedral did indeed seem a creature docile and obedi-
ent to his hand; she waited his will, to lift up her loud
voice; she was filled and possessed with Quasimodo as
with a familiar spirit. One would have said that he
made the immense building breathe. He was to be
seen all over it; he multiplied himself upon every
point of the structure. Sometimes you beheld with
dread, at the very top of one of the towers, a fantastic
dwarfish-looking figure—climbing—twisting—crawling
about—descending outside over the abyss—leaping
from projection to projection—and then thrusting his
arm into the throat of some sculptured gorgon; it was
Quasimodo pulling the crows from their nests. Sometimes, in a dark corner of the church, you would stumble against a sort of living chimera, squatting and
dogged-looking—it was Quasimodo musing. Sometimes you espied, upon one of the steeples, an enormous head and a parcel of deranged limbs, swinging

furiously at the end of a rope—it was Quasimodo ringing the vesper-bell, or the Angelus. Often, at night, a hideous form was seen wandering upon the light delicate balustrade which crowns the towers and borders the top of the chancel—it was still the hunchback of Notre-Dame. Then, the good women of the neighborhood would say, something fantastic, supernatural, horrible, was to be seen in the whole church—eyes and mouths opened in it here and there—the stone dogs, griffons, and the rest, that watch day and night, with outstretched necks and open jaws, around the monstrous cathedral, were heard to bark. And if it was a Christmas night—while the great bell, that seemed to rattle in its throat, was calling the faithful to the blazing midnight mass, there was such an air spread over the gloomy front, that the great doorway seemed to be devouring the multitude, while the round window above it was looking down upon them—and all this came from Quasimodo. Egypt would have taken him for the god of this temple—the Middle Ages believed him to be its demon—he was in fact its soul.

So much was this the case that, to those who know that Quasimodo has existed, Notre-Dame is now solitary, inanimate, dead. They feel that something has disappeared. That vast body is empty—it is a skeleton—the spirit has quitted it—they see the place of its habitation, but that is all. It is like a skull, which still has holes for the eyes, but no look shining through them.

CHAPTER IV.

THE DOG AND HIS MASTER.

THERE was, however, one human creature whom Quasimodo excepted from the malice and hatred for the rest, and whom he loved as much, perhaps more, than his cathedral; this was Claude Frollo.

The case was simple enough. Claude Frollo had re-ceived him, adopted him, nursed him, brought him up. While yet quite little, it was between Claude Frollo's knees that he had been accustomed to take refuge when the dogs and the children ran yelping after him. Claude Frollo had taught him to speak, to read, to write. Claude Frollo, in fine, had made him ringer of the bells—and to give the great bell in marriage to Quasimodo, was giving Juliet to Romeo.

Accordingly, Quasimodo's gratitude was deep, ardent, boundless; and although the countenance of his adopt-ive father was often clouded and severe—although his mode of speaking was habitually brief, harsh, imperious —never had that feeling of gratitude wavered for a single instant. The archdeacon had in Quasimodo the most submissive of slaves, the most tractable of ser-vants, the most vigilant of watch-dogs. When the poor ringer had become deaf, there was established be-tween him and Claude Frollo a language of signs, mys-terious, and intelligible only to themselves. So that the archdeacon was the only human being with whom Quasimodo had preserved a communication. There were only two existences in this world with which he had any intercourse—Notre-Dame and Claude Frollo.

Unexampled were the sway of the archdeacon over the ringer, and the ringer's attachment to the archdea-con. One sign from Claude, and the idea of pleasing him would have sufficed to make Quasimodo throw himself from the top of the towers of Notre-Dame. There was something remarkable in all that physical strength, so extraordinarily developed in Quasimodo, and blindly placed by him at the disposal of another. In this there was undoubtedly filial devotion and do-mestic attachment; but there was also fascination of one mind by another mind. There was a poor, weak, awkward organization, hanging its head and casting down its eyes in the presence of a lofty and penetrating intellect, powerful and commanding. In fine, and above all the rest, there was gratitude — gratitude pushed to that extreme limit, that we know not to what

12

to compare it. This virtue not being one of those of which the finest examples are found amongst mankind, we must therefore say that Quasimodo loved the archdeacon as no dog, no horse, no elephant ever loved his master.

CHAPTER V.

FURTHER PARTICULARS OF CLAUDE FROLLO.

IN 1482, Quasimodo was about twenty years old, and Claude Frollo about thirty-six. The one had grown up; the other had grown old.

Claude Frollo was no longer the simple scholar of the Torchi college—the tender protector of a little boy—the young dreaming philosopher, who knew many things and was ignorant of many. He was a priest, austere, grave, morose—having cure of souls—Monsieur the Archdeacon of Joas—the second acolyte of the bishop—having charge of the two deaneries of Montlhéry and Châteaufort and of a hundred and seventy-four curés ruraux or country parochial clergy. He was an imposing and sombre personage, before whom trembled the chorister boys in aube and jaquette, the machicos, the brethren of St. Augustine, and the cercles matutinels of Notre-Dame, when he passed slowly under the lofty pointed arches of the choir, majestic, pensive, with his arms crossed, and his head so much inclined upon his breast that nothing could be seen of his face but his large bald forehead.

Dom Claude Frollo, however, had abandoned neither science nor the education of his brother, the two occupations of his life. But in the course of time, some bitterness had been mingled with these things which he had found so sweet. Little Jehan Frollo, surnamed Du Moulin from the place where he had been nursed, had not grown up in the direction which Claude had been desirous of giving him. The elder brother had reckoned upon a pupil pious, docile, learned, creditable. But the younger brother like those young plants which baffle the endeavors of the gardener, and turn obstinately toward that side alone from which they receive air and sunshine—the younger brother grew up, and shot forth full and luxuriant branches, only on the side of idleness, ignorance, and debauchery. He was a very devil—extremely disorderly—which made Dom Claude knit his brows—but very droll and very cunning—which made the elder smile. Claude had consigned him to that same college de Torchi in which he himself had passed his earlier years in study and modest seclusion ; and it grieved him that this sanctuary, once edificd by the name of Frollo, should be scandalized by it now. He sometimes read Jehan very long and very severe lectures upon the subject, which the latter intrepidly sustained. After all the young rake had a good heart —as all our comedies take care to assure us on a like occasion. But when the lecture was over, he did not the less quietly resume the course of his seditions and enormities. Sometimes it was a béjaune or yellow-beak, as a new-comer at the University was called, whom he had plucked for his entrance-money—a precious tradition, which has been carefully handed down to the present day. Sometimes he had set in motion a band of scholars, who had classically fallen upon a cabaret— *quasi classico excitati* — then had beaten the tavern-keeper *avec bâtons offensifs*, and merrily pillaged the tavern, even to the staving in of the hogsheads of wine in the cellar. And then there was a fine report, drawn up in Latin, which the sub-monitor of the Torchi college brought piteously to Dom Claude, with this dolorous heading—*Rixa* ; *prima causa vinum optimum potatum*. And, in fine, it was said—a thing quite horrible in a boy of sixteen—that his raking oftentimes led him as far as the Rue de Glatigny.

Owing to all this, Claude, saddened and discouraged in his human affections, had thrown himself the more ardently into the arms of science — that sister who, at all events, does not laugh in your face, but ever repays you (albeit in coin sometimes rather light) for the attention you have bestowed upon her. He became, then, more and more learned—and, at the same time, by a natural consequence, more and more rigid as a priest, more and more melancholy as a man. There are in each individual of us, certain parallelisms between our understanding, our manners, and our character, which develop themselves continuously, and are interrupted only by the greater disturbances of life.

As Claude Frollo had, in his youth, gone through nearly the whole circle of positive human knowledge, external and lawful, he was under the absolute necessity, unless he was to stop *ubi defuit orbis*, of going further, and seeking other food for the insatiable activity of his intellect. The ancient symbol of the serpent biting his tail is especially appropriate to science ; and it seems that Claude Frollo had experienced this. Many grave persons affirmed, that after exhausting the *fas* of human knowledge, he had ventured to penetrate into the *nefas*. He had, they said, successively tasted all the apples of the tree of knowledge; and, whether from hunger or disgust, he had ended with tasting of the forbidden fruit. He had taken his place by turns, as our readers have seen, at the conferences of the theologians at the Sorbonne ; at the meetings of the faculty of arts at the image of St. Hilary ; at the disputations of the decretists at the image of St. Martin ; at the congregations of the physicians at bénitier of Notre-Dame, *ad cupam nostræ dominæ*. All the viands, permitted and approved, which those four great cuisines called the four faculties could prepare and serve up to the understanding, he had devoured ; and he had been satiated with them before his hunger was appeased. Then he had penetrated further—lower—underneath all that finite, material, limited science ; he had perhaps risked his soul, and seated himself in the cavern, at that mysterious table of the alchemists, the astrologers, the hermetics, of which Averroës, Guillaume de Paris, and Nicolas Flamel occupy the lower extremity in the Middle Ages, and which extends in the East, under the light of the seven-branched candlestick, up to Solomon, Pythagoras, and Zoroaster. So, at least, it was supposed, whether rightly or not.

It is certain that the archdeacon often visited the cemetery of the Holy Innocents; in which, it is true, his father and mother had been buried, with the other victims of the plague of 1466; but that he testified much less devotion to the cross at the head of their grave, than to the strange figures upon the tomb of Nicolas Flamel and his wife Claude Pernelle, which stood close by it.

It is certain that he had often been seen to pass along the Rue des Lombards, and enter stealthily into a small house at the corner of the two streets, the Rue des Ecrivains and the Rue Marivaux. It was the house which Nicolas Flamel had built, in which he had died about the year 1417, and which, uninhabited ever since, was beginning to fall into ruins, so much had the hermetics and alchemists of all countries worn away its walls by simply engraving their names upon them. Some of the neighbors even affirmed, that they had once seen, through an air-hole, the archdeacon Claude digging and turning over the earth at the bottom of those two cellars, the buttresses in which had been scrawled over with innumerable verses and hieroglyphics by Nicolas Flamel himself. It was supposed that Flamel had buried the philosopher's stone in these cellars; and the alchemists for two centuries, from Magistri down to Father Pacifique, never ceased to turn about the ground, until the house itself, so mercilessly ransacked and turned inside out, had at last crumbled into dust under their feet.

It is certain, too, that the archdeacon had been seized with a singular passion for the symbolical doorway of Notre-Dame, that page of conjuration written in stone by Bishop William of Paris, who has undoubtedly been damned for attaching so infernal a frontispiece to the sacred poem eternally chanted by the rest of the structure. Archdeacon Claude had also the credit of having sounded the mysteries of the colossal St. Christopher, and of that long enigmatical statue which then stood at the entrance of the Parvis, and which the people had nicknamed Monsieur Legris. But what everybody might have remarked, was, the interminable hours which he would often spend, seated upon the parapet of the Parvis, in contemplating the sculptured figures of the portal—now examining the light maidens with their lamps turned upside down, and the prudent ones with their lamps the right end up—at other times calculating the angle of vision of that crow which clings to the left side of the doorway, casting its eye upon a mysterious point within the church—where the philosopher's stone is certainly hidden, if it be not in Nicolas Flamel's cellar.

It was a singular destiny (we may remark in passing) for the church of Notre-Dame, at that period, to be thus beloved in two different ways, and with so much devotion, by two beings so unlike as Claude and Quasimodo—loved by the one, a sort of half-human creature, instinctive and savage, for its beauty, for its stature, for the harmonies dwelling in the magnificent whole — loved by the other, a being of cultivated and ardent imagination, for its signification, its mystic meaning, the symbolic language lurking under the sculpture on its front, like the first text under the second in a palimpsest — in short, for the enigma which it eternally proposes to the understanding.

And, futhermore, it is certain that the archdeacon had fitted himself up, in that one of the two towers which looks upon the Grève, close by the cage of the bells, a little cell of great secrecy, into which no one entered—not even the bishop, it was said—without his leave. This cell had been constructed of old, almost at the top of the tower, among the crows' nests, by Bishop Hugo de Besançon,* who had played the necromancer there in his time. What this cell contained, no one knew. But from the strand of the Terrain, at night,

---

* "Hugo de Bisuncio," 1326-1332.

there was often seen to appear, disappear, and reappear, at short and regular intervals, at a small round window or luthern that admitted light into it from the back of the tower, a certain red, intermittent, singular glow, seeming as if it followed the successive puffings of a pair of bellows, and as if it proceeded from a flame rather than from a light. In the dark, at that elevation, it had a very odd appearance; and the good women of the neighborhood used to say: "There's the archdeacon blowing? Hell-fire's casting sparks up there!"

Not that here were, after all, any great proofs of sorcery; but still there was quite as much smoke as was necessary to make the good people suppose a flame; and the archdeacon had a reputation not a little formidable. We are bound to declare, however, that the sciences of Egypt—that necromancy—that magic—even the fairest and most innocent—had no more violent enemy, no more merciless denouncer before messieurs of the officiality of Notre-Dame, than himself. Whether it was sincere abhorrence, or merely the trick of the robber who cries Stop thief! this did not prevent the archdeacon from being considered by the learned heads of the chapter as one who had risked his soul upon the threshold of hell—as one lost in the caverns of the Cabala—feeling his way in the darkness of the occult sciences. Neither were the people blinded to the real state of the case; to the mind of every one possessed of the smallest sagacity, Quasimodo was the demon, and Claude Frollo the sorcerer; it was evident that the ringer was to serve the archdeacon for a given time, at the expiration of which he was to carry off his soul by way of payment. So that the archdeacon, despite the excessive austerity of his life, was in bad odor with all pious souls; and there was never a nose of a devotee, however inexperienced, but could smell him for a magician.

And if, as he grew older, he had formed to himself abysses in science, others had opened themselves in his heart. So at least they had reason to believe who narrowly observed that face of his, in which his soul shone forth only through a murky cloud. Whence that large bald forehead—that head constantly bent forward—that breast constantly heaved with sighs? What secret thought wreathed that bitter smile about his lips, at the same moment that his lowering brows approached each other fierce as two encountering bulls? Why were his remaining hairs already gray? What internal fire was that which occasionally shone in his glance, to such a degree as to make his eye look like a hole pierced through the wall of a furnace?

These symptoms of a violent moral preoccupation had acquired an especially high degree of intensity at the period to which our narrative refers. More than once had a chorister-boy fled affrighted at finding him alone in the church, so strange and fiery was his look. More than once, in the choir, at service-time, the occupant of the stall next his own had heard him mingle, in the plain-chant *ad omnem tonum*, unintelligible parentheses. More than once had the laundress of the Terrain, whose business it was " to wash the chapter," observed, not without dread, marks of finger-nails and clenched fingers in the surplice of Monsieur the Archdeacon of Joas.

However, he became doubly rigid, and had never been more exemplary. By character, as well as by calling, he had always kept at a distance from women ; and now he seemed to hate them more than ever. The mere rustling of a silken cotte-hardie brought his hood down over his eyes. On this point so jealous were his austerity and reserve, that when the king's daughter, the Lady of Beaujeu, came in December, 1481, to visit the cloister of Notre-Dame, he gravely opposed her entrance, reminding the bishop of the statute in the Livre Noir or Black Book of the chapter, dated St. Bartholomew's Eve, 1344, forbidding access to the cloister to every woman " whatsoever, old or young, mistress or maid." Whereupon the bishop having been constrained to cite to him the ordinance of the legate, Odo, which makes an exception in favor of certain ladies of high rank—*aliquæ magnates mulieres, quæ sine scandalo evitari non possunt*—the archdeacon still protested; objecting that the legate's ordinance being dated as far back as the year 1207, was a hundred and twenty-seven years anterior to the Livre Noir, and was consequently, to all intents and purposes, abrogated by it. And accordingly he had refused to make his appearance before the princess.

It was moreover remarked that, for some time past, his abhorrence of gypsy-women and zingari had been redoubled. He had solicited from the bishop an edict expressly forbidding the gypsies from coming to dance and play the tambourine in the Place du Parvis; and for the same length of time he had been rummaging among the mouldy archives of the official, in order to collect together all the cases of wizards and witches condemned to the flames or the halter for having been accomplices in sorcery with he-goats, she-goats, or sows.

CHAPTER VI.

UNPOPULARITY.

THE archdeacon and the bell-ringer, as we have already said, were but little esteemed among the little and great folks of the environs of the cathedral. When Claude and Quasimodo walked abroad on divers occasions, and they were observed in company traversing the clean, but narrow and dusky, streets of the neighborhood of Notre-Dame, the servant following his master, more than one malicious word, or ironical smile, or insulting jest, greeted them on their way; unless Claude Frollo—though this happened rarely—walked with head erect, exhibiting his stern and almost noble brow to the gaze of the astonished gossips.

The pair were in that neighborhood almost like the "poets," of whom Regnier speaks :

Toutes sortes de gens vont après les poètes,
Comme après les hiboux vont criant les fauvettes.

Sometimes an ill-natured body would risk his head and bones for the ineffable pleasure of running a pin into Quasimodo's hump. Sometimes a pretty girl, more full of frolic and boldness than became her, would rustle the priest's black gown, singing to his face the sarcastic song beginning: " Nestle, nestle, the Devil is caught." Sometimes a squalid group of old women, crouching down in the dusk along the steps of a porch, grumbled aloud as the archdeacon and the bell-ringer passed, or called after them with curses—this encouraging greeting: " Ho! here comes one with a soul as crooked as the other's body." Sometimes a band of scholars playing at hopscotch would jump up together and salute them classically with some cry in Latin, as *"Eia! eia! Claudius cum claudo!"*

BOOK V.

CHAPTER I.

A GLANCE AT THE ANCIENT MAGISTRACY.

RIGHT enviable personage, in the year of grace 1482, was noble homme Robert d'Estouteville, knight, Sieur of Beyne, Baron of Ivry and Saint Andry in Marche, councilor and chamberlain to the king, and keeper of the provostry of Paris. Already it was nearly seventeen years since he had received from King Louis, on the 7th of November, 1465, the year of the comet, that fine place of Provost of Paris, which was regarded rather as a seigneurie than as an office—*Dignitas*, says Joanes Lœmnœus, *quæ cum non exiguâ potestate politiam concernente, atque prærogativis multis et juribus conjuncta est.* It was a thing quite marvelous, that, in the year '82, there should be a gentleman holding the king's commission, whose letters of institution were dated as far back as the time of the marriage of Louis XI.'s natural daughter with monsieur the bastard of Bourbon. On the same day that Robert d'Estouteville had taken the place of Jacques de Villiers in the provostry of Paris, Maître Jean Dauvet succeeded Messire Hélye de Thorrettes in the first presidency of the court of parliament, Jean Jouvénel des Ursins supplanted Pierre de Morvilliers in the office of Chancellor of France, and Regnault des Dormans relieved Pierre Puy of the post of master of requests in ordinary to the king's household. Now, over how many heads had the presidency, the chancellorship, and the mastership traveled since Robert d'Estouteville had held the provostry of Paris? It had been "granted into his keeping," said the letters patent; and certainly he kept it well. He had clung to it, incorporated himself, identified himself with it, so thoroughly that he had escaped that rage for changes which possessed Louis XI., a distrustful, parsimonious, and laborious king, bent upon maintaining, by frequent appointments and dismissals, the elasticity of his power. Nay, more —the worthy chevalier had procured the reversion of his office for his son; and already, for two years, had the name of noble homme Jacques d'Estouteville, Esquire, figured at full length behind his own at the head of the register of the ordinary of the provostry of Paris—a rare, assuredly, and signal favor! True it is that Robert d'Estouteville was a good soldier; that he had loyally lifted his pennon against "the league of the public weal;" and that he had made a present to the queen, on the day of her entry into Paris in the year 14—, of a very wonderful stag, all made of confectionery. And, moreover, he had a good friend in Messire Tristan l'Hermite, provost-marshal of the king's household. So that Messire Robert enjoyed a very comfortable and agreeable existence. First of all, he had a very good salary; to which were attached, depending like so many additional bunches from his vine, the revenues of the registries, civil and criminal, of the provostry; then, the revenues of the Auditoires d'Embas, or inferior courts, of the Châtelet; besides some little toll from the bridges of Mante and Corbeil, and the profits of the tru on the esgrin of Paris, and on the measures of firewood and the meters of salt. Add to all this the pleasure of displaying, in his official rides through the town, in contrast with the gowns, half red and half tawny, of the échevins and the quarteniers, his fine military dress, which you may still admire sculptured upon his tomb at the abbey of Valmont in Normandy, as you may his richly embossed morion at Montlhéry. And then, was it nothing to have all supremacy over the sergeants of the douzaine, the keeper and the

watcher of the Châtelet (*auditores Castelleti*), the sixteen commissioners of the sixteen quarters of the city,
the jailor of the Châtelet, the four enfeoffed sergeants,
the hundred and twenty mounted sergeants, the hundred and twenty sergeants of the wand, and the knight
of the watch, with his men of the watch, the under-
watch, the counter-watch, and the rear-watch? Was it
nothing to exercise high and low justice, the right of
turning, hanging, and drawing, besides the jurisdiction
over minor offenses in the first resort (*in prima instantia,*
as the charters have it), over that viscounty of Paris, to
which were so gloriously appended seven noble bailiwicks? Can anything be imagined more gratifying
than to pass judgment and sentence, as Messire Robert
d'Estouteville daily did in the Grand Châtelet, under
the wide, depressed, Gothic arches of Philip-Augustus;
and to go, as was his wont, every evening to that
charming house situated in the Rue Galilee, within the
precints of the Palais-Royal, which he held in right of
his wife, Madame Ambroise de Loré, to repose from
the fatigue of having sent some poor devil to pass his
night in "that small cage in the Rue de l'Escorcherie,
which the provosts and échevins of Paris were wont to
make their prison; the dimensions of the same being
eleven feet in length, seven feet four inches in width,
and eleven feet in height?"

And not only had Messire Robert d'Estouteville his
particular justice as provost and viscount of Paris; but
also he had his share, both by presence and action, in
the grand justice of the king. There was no head of
any elevated rank but had passed through his hands before it came into those of the executioner. It was he
who had gone to the Bastille St. Antoine, to fetch Monsieur de Nemours from thence to the Halles; and to the
same place, to carry from thence to the Grève Monsieur
de St. Pol, who grumbled and complained, to the great
joy of monsieur the provost, who was no friend to monsieur the constable.

Here, assuredly, was more than enough to make a
man's life illustrious and happy, and to earn some day

a notable page in that interesting history of the prov-
osts of Paris, from which we learn that Oudard de
Villeneuve had a house in the Rue des Boucheries, that
Guillaume de Hangest bought the great and the little
Savoie; that Guillaume Thiboust gave his houses in the
Rue Clopin to the nuns of Ste. Geneviève; that Hugues
Aubriot lived in the Hôtel du Porc-Epic; with other
facts of the like importance.

And yet, with all these reasons for taking life patiently and cheerfully, Messire Robert d'Estouteville
had waked on the morning of the 7th of January, 1482,
very sulky—quite, indeed, in a massacring humor—
though for what cause he himself could not well have
told. Was it because the sky was dingy? or because
the buckle of his old Montlhéry sword-belt was ill fastened, and girded too militarily his provost-beseeming
portliness? or because he had seen the army of ribalds
marching through the street, four by four, under his
window, jeering at him as they passed by, in doublets
without shirts, under hats with their crowns out, and
scrip and bottle at their sides? Was it a vague presentiment of the three hundred and seventy livres sixteen sols eight deniers, which the future king, Charles
VIII., was to deduct the following year from the revenues of the provostry? Among these reasons, the reader
is at liberty to choose; for our own parts, we are much
inclined to believe that he was in an ill-humor simply
because he was in an ill-humor.

Besides, it was the day after a holiday—a day of disgust for everybody, and especially for the magistrate
whose business it was to sweep away all the filth, whether
in the literal or the figurative sense of the word, that a
holiday accumulated in Paris. And then he was to hold
a sitting in the Grand Châtelet; and the reader will
probably have remarked, that judges in general contrive
matters so, that their day of sitting shall also be their
day of ill-humor, in order that they may always have
some one upon whom to vent it conveniently, in the
name of the king and the law.

The magisterial operations, however, had commenced

without him. His deputies *au civil, au criminel,* and *au particulier,* were acting for him, according to custom; and as early as eight o'clock in the morning, some scores of townspeople, men and women, crowded together in a dark corner of the Auditoire d'Embas of the Châtelet, between the wall and a strong barrier of oak, were blissfully attending at the varied and exhilarating spectacle of the administration of civil and criminal justice by Maître Florian Barbedienne, auditor at the Châtelet, deputy of monsieur the provost—a little pell-mell, to be sure, and altogether at random.

The room was small, low, and vaulted. At the farther end was a table, figured over with fleur-de-lis, with a great arm-chair of carved oak for the provost, which was empty, and, on the left hand of it, a stool for the auditor, Maître Florian. Below sat the registrar, scribbling away. In front were the people; and before the door, and before the table, were a number of sergeants of the provostry in their violet hacquetons with white crosses upon them. Two sergeants of the Parloir-aux-Bourgeois, or Common-hall, in jackets half red and half blue, stood sentry before a low closed door, which was visible at the other end, behind the table. One solitary pointed window, straightly encased in the massive wall, threw a few pale January rays upon two grotesque countenances; that of the fantastic demon carved upon the key-stone of the vaulted ceiling, and that of the judge, seated at the extremity of the chamber, upon the fleurs-de-lis.

Indeed, figure to yourself, at the prevotal table, between two bundles of cases—leaning upon his elbows, with his foot upon the tail of his gown of plain brown cloth, and his face in its lining of white lamb-skin, with which his brows seemed to be of a piece—red-faced— harsh-looking—winking, carrying majestically the load of flesh upon his cheeks, which met from either side under his chin—Maître Florian Barbedienne, auditor at the Châtelet.

Now, the auditor was deaf—a slight defect for an auditor, and Maître Florian did not the less decide without appeal and quite competently. It is certainly quite sufficient that a judge should appear to listen ; and the venerable auditor the better fulfilled this condition, the only one essential to the good administration of justice, as his attention could not possibly be distracted by any noise.

However, there was among the audience a merciless censor of his deeds and gestures, in the person of our friend Jehan Frollo du Moulin, the little scholar of the day before—that stroller who was sure to be met with everywhere in Paris, except before the professor's chair.

"Look," said he to his companion Robert Poussepain, who was tittering beside him while he commented on the scenes that were passing before them ; there's Jehanneton du Buisson, the pretty girl at the Cagnard-au-Marché-Neuf ! On my soul, he's condemning her, the old fellow ! Then he's no more eyes than ears ! Fifteen sous four deniers parisis for wearing two strings of beads —that's rather dear. *Lex duri carminis*—Who's that ? —Robin Chief-de-Ville, hauberk-maker, for being passed and admitted a master in the said art and mystery. It's his entrance-money. Ah ! what ! two gentlemen among these rascals—Aiglet de Soins, Hutin de Mailly, two esquires !—*Corpus Christi !*—Oh ! they've been playing at dice. When shall we see our rector here, I wonder ? Fined a hundred livres parisis to the king ! Barbedienne hits like a deaf man as he is ! May I be my brother the archdeacon, if that shall hinder me from playing by day, playing by night, living at play, dying at play, and staking my soul when I've lost my shirt ! Holy Virgin ! what lots of girls !—one after another, my lambs. Ambrose Lécuyère ! Isabeau-la-Paynette ! Berarde Gironin ! I know them all, *par Dieu !* Fine them ! fine them ! We'll teach you to wear gilt belts ! Ten sols parisis a-piece, you coquettes !—Oh, the old muzzle of a judge, deaf and doting ! Oh, Florian the lubber ! Oh, Barbedienne the dolt ! There you see him at table —he dines off the pleader—he dines off the case—he eats—he chews—he swallows—he fills himself ! Fines —estrays—dues—expenses—costs—wages—damages—

torture—jail and stocks—are to him Christmas cami-
chons and midsummer marchpanes. Look at him,
the pig! Go on. Good again!—another amorous lady!
Thibaude-la-Thibaude, I declare, for going out of the
Rue Glatigny. What's this youth? Gieffroy Mabonne,
gendarme bearing the cross-bow—he's been profaning
the name of the Father. A fine for La Thibaude! a
fine for Gieffroy! a fine for them both! The old deaf
boy! he must have jumbled the two things together!
Ten to one but he makes the girl pay for the oath, and
the gendarme for the amour! Attention, Robin Poussepain! What are they bringing in now? Here are plenty
of sergeants, by Jupiter! all the hounds of the pack.
This must be the grand piece of game of all—a wild
boar, at least! It is one, Robin—it is one! and a fine
one, too!—Hercle! it's our prince of yesterday—our
fool's pope—our ringer—our one-eye—our hunchback
—our grin of grins! It's Quasimodo!"

It was he indeed. It was Quasimodo, bound, girded,
hooped, pinioned, and well guarded. The detachment
of sergeants that surrounded him were accompanied by
the chevalier du guet or knight of the watch, in person,
bearing the arms of France embroidered on his breast,
and those of the Town of Paris on his back. However,
there was nothing in Quasimodo, his deformity excepted, to justify all this display of halberts and arquebusses. He was gloomy, silent, and tranquil; his one
eye only just throwing, from time to time, a sullen and
resentful glance upon the bonds that covered him. He
cast the same look around him; but it seemed so dull
and sleepy, that the women pointed him out to each
other with their fingers in derision only.

Meanwhile, Maître Florian, the auditor, turned over
attentively the leaves of the written charge drawn up
against Quasimodo, and presented to him by the registrar; and, after taking that glance, appeared to be
meditating for a minute or two. Owing to this precau-
tion, which he was always careful to take at the moment of proceeding to an interrogatory, he knew before
hand the name, quality, and offense of the accused

13

made premeditated replies to answers foreseen; and so contrived to find his way through all the sinuosities of the interrogatory without too much betraying his deafness. The written charge was to him as the dog to the blind man. If it so happened that his infirmity discovered itself here and there, by some incoherent apostrophe or unintelligible question, it passed with some for profundity, with others for imbecility. In either case the honor of the magistracy did not suffer; for a judge had better be considered either imbecile or profound than deaf. So he took great care to disguise his deafness from the observation of all; and he commonly succeeded so well that he had come at last even to deceive himself about the matter—a species of deception, indeed, which is not so difficult as it may be thought; all hunchbacks walk with head erect; all stammerers are given to speechifying; and the deaf always talk in a whisper. For his part, the utmost admission that he made to himself on this point was, that his hearing was not quite so quick as some people's—it was the only concession in this respect that he could bring himself to make to public opinion, in his moments of candor and examination of conscience.

Having, then, well ruminated on the affair of Quasimodo, he threw back his head and half closed his eyes, by way of greater majesty and impartiality; so that, at that moment, he was blind as well as deaf—a double condition, without which no judge is perfect. It was in this magisterial attitude that he commenced the interrogatory:

"Your name?"

Now here was a case which had not been "foreseen by the law," that of one deaf man interrogated by another.

Quasimodo, receiving no intimation of the question thus addressed to him, continued to look fixedly at the judge, without making any answer. The deaf judge, on the other hand, receiving no intimation of the deafness of the accused, thought that he had answered, as the prisoners generally did; and continued, with his mechanical and stupid right-forwardness.

" Well—your age?"

Quasimodo made no more answer to this question than to the preceding one; but the judge, thinking it replied to, went on:

" Now—your calling?"

The culprit was still silent. The by-standers, however, were beginning to whisper and to look at each other.

" Enough!" added the imperturbable auditor, when he supposed that the accused had consummated his third answer. "You stand charged before us—*primo,* with nocturnal disturbance; *secundo,* with dishonest violence upon the person of a light woman—*in prejudicium meretricis; tertio,* of rebellion and disloyalty toward our lord the king's archers. Explain yourself on all these points. Registrar, have you taken down what the prisoner has said so far?"

At this unlucky question a burst of laughter was heard, caught by the audience from the registrar—so violent, so uncontrollable, so contagious, so universal, that neither of the deaf men could help perceiving it. Quasimodo turned round, shrugging up his hump in disdain; while Maître Florian, astonished like himself, and supposing that the laughter of the spectators had been excited by some irreverent reply from the accused, rendered visible to him by that shrug, apostrophised him indignantly.

" Fellow," said he, " you gave me an answer then that deserves the halter. Know you to whom you are speaking?"

This sally was not at all calculated to extinguish the explosion of the general merriment. It seemed to all present so incongruous and left-handed, that the wild laugh caught even the sergeants of the Parloir-aux-Bourgeois, a sort of serving-men carrying pikes, with whom stupidity was part of their uniform. Quasimodo alone preserved his gravity; for the very good reason, that he understood nothing at all of what was passing around him. The judge, growing more and more angry, thought himself bound to go on in the same tone, hoping thereby to strike a terror into the accused, which would react upon the bystanders, and bring them back to a proper sense of respect:

"So it seems, then, master, perverse and riotous that you are, that you presume to be impertinent to the auditor of the Châtelet; to the magistrate entrusted with the popular police of Paris; charged to make search into all crimes, offenses, and bad courses; to control all trades, and interdict monopolies; to repair the pavements; to prevent forestalling and regrating of poultry and wild-fowl; to superintend the measuring of firewood and other sorts of wood; to cleanse the town of mud, and the air of contagious distempers; in a word, to be doing continually the work of the public, without fee or reward, or expectation of any. Know you that my name is Florian Barbedienne, monsieur the provost's own proper deputy, and, moreover, commissioner, inquisitor, controller, and examiner, with equal power in provostry, bailiwick, conservatorship, and presidial court?"

There is no reason why a deaf man talking to a deaf man should ever stop. God only knows where and when Maître Florian would have come to anchor, launched thus in full career upon the main ocean of eloquence, had not the low door behind him opened all at once for the entrance of monsieur the provost in person.

At his entrance Maître Florian did not stop short; but, turning half round upon his heel, and suddenly aiming at the provost the harangue with which, the moment before, he had been battering Quasimodo, "Monsieur," said he, "I have to request such penalty as it shall please you, upon the accused here present, for flagrant and aggravated contempt of court."

Then he sat down again, quite out of breath, wiping away the big drops that fell from his forehead and moistened, like tears, the parchments spread out before him. Messire Robert d'Estouteville knitted his brow, and made a motion to Quasimodo to attend, in a manner so imperious and significant, that the deaf prisoner in some degree understood it.

The provost addressed him with severity. 'Rascal what hast thou done to be brought hither?"

The poor devil, supposing that the provost was asking him his name, now broke the silence which he habitually kept, and answered in a hoarse and guttural voice, " Quasimodo."

The answer so little corresponded to the question, that the loud laugh again began to go round ; and Messire Robert exclaimed, all reddening with anger: " What, you arrant rogue, you jest at me, too, do you ? "

" Ringer at Notre-Dame," answered Quasimodo, thinking that this time he was commanded to state to the judge who he was.

" Ringer ! " returned the provost, who, as we have already said, had got up that morning in so bad a humor that his fury needed not to be kindled by such unaccountable answers—" Ringer, indeed ! I'll make them ring a peal of rods on thy back through every street in Paris—dost thou hear, rascal ? "

" If it's my age you want to know," said Quasimodo, " I believe I shall be twenty next Martinmas."

This was rather too strong. The provost could endure it no longer.

" Ha ! so you jeer at the provostry, you wretch ! Messieurs the sergeants of the wand, you'll take this fellow to the pillory in the Grève, and there flog him and turn him for an hour. He shall pay for his impudence, *tête-Dieu !* And I order that this present sentence be proclaimed by four sworn trumpeters, in the seven castellanies of the viscounty of Paris."

The registrar set about drawing up the sentence forthwith.

" *Ventre Dieu !* but that's a good sentence," cried the little scholar, Jehan Frollo du Moulin, from his corner.

The provost turned round, and again fixed his eyes, all flashing, upon Quasimodo. " I believe the fellow said, *Ventre Dieu !* Registrar, add a fine of twelve deniers parisis for swearing; and let one-half of it go toward the repairs of St. Eustache's church—I've a particular devotion for St. Eustache."

In a few minutes the judgment was drawn out. The tenor of it was simple and brief. The custumel of the provostry and viscounty of Paris had not yet been elaborated by the president, Thibaut Baillet, and Roger Barmue, king's advocate; it was not yet obscured by that deep forest of chicanery and circumlocution which the two jurisconsults planted in it at the commencement of the sixteenth century. All was clear, expeditive, explicit, going direct to the point—and straight you saw before you, at the end of every path, without any thicket about it, or bend in the way to it, the wheel, the gibbet, or the pillory. You at least knew whither you were going.

The registrar presented the sentence to the provost, who affixed his seal to it, and then went away, to continue his round at the several auditories, in a temper of mind which seemed destined that day to fill every jail in Paris. Jehan Frollo and Robin Poussepain were laughing in their sleeves; while Quasimodo looked upon the whole with an air of indifference and astonishment.

However, the registrar, at the moment that Maître Florian Barbedienne was in his turn reading over the judgment previous to signing it, felt himself moved with pity for the poor devil under condemnation; and, in the hope of obtaining some mitigation of the penalty, he approached the auditor's ear as close as he could, and said to him, pointing to Quasimodo, "That man is deaf."

He hoped that a sense of their common infirmity would awaken some interest for the condemned in the breast of Maître Florian. But, in the first place, as we have already observed, Maître Florian did not care to have his deafness remarked; and, in the next place, his ear was so obtuse that he did not distinguish a single word of what the registrar said to him; nevertheless, choosing to seem as if he heard, he replied, "Ha, ha! that makes a difference—I didn't know that—in that case, let him have an hour more on the pillory." And he signed the sentence with this modification.

"Well done!" said Robin Poussepain, who still had a grudge against Quasimodo, "that'll teach him to handle folks so roughly."

CHAPTER II.

THE RAT-HOLE.

THE reader will now accompany us back to the Place de Grève, which we quitted yesterday with Gringoire, to follow La Esmeralda.

It is ten in the morning. We find everything denoting the day after a holiday. The ground is covered with shreds, ribbons, trimmings, feathers dropped from the plumes, drops of wax from the torch-lights, and fragments from the public banquet. A good many of the townspeople are sauntering about—turning over with their feet the extinguished brands of the bonfire—bursting into rapture before the Maison-aux-Piliers, at the recollection of the fine hangings exhibited there the day before, and now contemplating the nails that fastened them, the only remnant of the ravishing spectacle. The venders of beer and cider are rolling about their barrels among the several groups. On the other hand, some individuals are going this way and some that, evidently on business. The tradespeople are talking and calling to one another from their shop-doors. The holiday, the ambassadors, Coppenole, the Fools' Pope, are in every one's mouth; they seem to be striving who shall make the smartest comments and laugh the most. Meanwhile, however, four sergeants on horseback, who have just now posted themselves at the four sides of the pillory, have already concentrated around them a good part of the *populaire* that had been scattered over the Place, which crowd are condemning themselves to stand wearisomely waiting, in expectation of witnessing the punishment of some criminal.

If the reader will now, after contemplating this stirring and clamorous scene which is enacting upon every point of the square, turn his eyes toward that ancient house of demi-Romanish architecture, of the Tour-Roland, which stands at the western corner next the quay, he may remark, at the angle of its front, a large public breviary richly illuminated, protected from the rain by a small penthouse, and from thieves by a grating, which, however, allows the passenger to turn over its leaves. Close by this breviary is a narrow, pointed window-hole, guarded by two iron bars placed crosswise, and looking toward the square—the only aperture by which a little air and light are admitted into a small cell without a door, constructed on the level of the ground, in the thickness of the wall of the old mansion—and filled with a stillness the more profound, a silence the more dead, inasmuch as a public square, the most populous and the noisiest in Paris, is swarming and clamoring around.

This cell had been famous in Paris for three centuries, since Madame Rolande, of Roland's Tower, in mourning for her father who died in the crusades, had caused it to be hollowed out of the wall of her own house, to shut herself up in it forever, keeping of all her palace only this wretched nook, the door of which was walled up, and the window open to the elements, in winter as in summer—giving all the rest to God and to the poor. The desolate lady had, in fact, awaited death for twenty years in that anticipated tomb, praying day and night for the soul of her father, sleeping in ashes, without even a stone for her pillow, clad in black sackcloth, and living only upon such bread and water as the pity of the passers-by deposited upon the edge of her window-place—thus receiving charity after she had given it. At her death—at the moment of her passing into the other sepulchre—she had bequeathed this one in perpetuity to women in affliction, mothers, widows, or maidens, who should have many prayers to offer up for others or for themselves, and should choose to bury themselves alive in the greatness of their grief or their penitence. The poor of her time had honored her funeral with tears and benedictions; but to their great regret, the poor maiden had been unable, for want of patronage, to obtain the honors of canonization. Such of them as were a little given to impiety, had hoped that the thing would be done more easily in heaven than at Rome, and had actually presumed to offer up their prayers for the deceased to God Himself, in default of the Pope. Most of them, however, had contented themselves with holding Rolande's memory sacred, and converting the rags she left behind her into relics. The Town of Paris, too, had founded, in pursuance of the lady's intention, a public breviary, which had been permanently fixed near to the window of the cell, in order that the passengers might stop at it now and then, if only to pray; that prayer might make them think of almsgiving; and that the poor female recluses, inheriting the stony cave of Madame Rolande, might not absolutely die of famine and neglect.

Nor was it very rarely that these sort of tombs were to be found in the towns of the middle ages. There was not unfrequently to be met with, in the most frequented street, in the most crowded and noisy market-place—in the very midst—under the horses' feet and the wagon wheels, as it were—a cave—a well—a walled and grated cabin—at the bottom of which was praying, day and night, a human being, voluntarily devoted to some everlasting lamentation or some great expiation. And all the reflections that this strange spectacle would awaken in us of the present day—that horrid cell, a sort of intermediate link between the dwelling-house and the tomb, between the city and the cemetery—that living being cut off from the communion of mankind, and thenceforth numbered with the dead—that lamp consuming its last drop of oil in the darkness—that remnant of life already wavering in the grave—that breath, that voice, that everlasting prayer, encased in stone—that face forever turned toward the other world—that eye already illumined by another sun—that ear inclined intently to the walls of the sepulchre—that soul a prisoner in that body—that body a prisoner in that dungeon and under that double envelope of flesh and granite, the murmuring of that soul in pain—nothing of all that struck upon the apprehension of the multitude. The piety of that age, little reasoning and little refined, did not find in an act of religion so many different points of view. It took things in the gross; honoring, venerating, and, upon occasion, making the sacrifice; but not analyzing the sufferings attending it, nor feeling any depth of pity for them. It brought some pittance, from time to time, to the wretched penitent; looked through the hole, to see if he were yet living; knew not his name; scacely knew how many years it was since he had begun to die; and to the stranger, who questioned them respecting the living skeleton rotting in that cave, the neighbors would simply answer, " It's the recluse."

Thus it was that everything was then seen—unmetaphysically — without exaggeration — through no magnifying glass, but with the naked eye. The microscope was not yet invented for objects of mind any more that for those of matter.

However, little wonder or speculation as they excited, the instances of this sort of seclusion in the heart of towns, were, as we have already observed, in reality frequent. In Paris itself there were a considerable number of those cells of penitence and prayer; and nearly all of them were occupied. It is true that the clergy were rather solicitous that they should not be left empty, as that implied lukewarmness in the faithful; and that lepers were put into them when penitents were not to be had. Besides the logette or cell already described at the Grève, there were, one at Montfaucon, one at the charnel-house of the Holy Innocents, another we hardly recollect where—at the logis Clichon, we believe—and others at many different spots, where, in default of monuments, their memory is perpetuated by tradition. The University, too, had its share of them. On the Montagne Ste. Geneviève, a sort of Job of the middle ages sang for thirty years the seven penitential psalms, upon a dung-heap at the bottom of a cistern, beginning again immediately each time that he came to the end—singing louder in the night time, *magna voce per umbras ;* and the antiquary still fancies that he hears his voice, as he enters the Rue du Puits-qui-parle, or street of the talking well.

To confine ourselves here to the den in Roland's Tower—we are bound to declare that it had scarcely ever lain idle for want of a tenant. Since Madame Rolande's death, it had rarely been vacant even for a year or two. Many a woman had come and wept there until death over the memory of her parent, her lover, or her failings. The mischievousness of the Parisians, which meddles with everything, even with those things which concern them least, used to pretend that among the number there had been very few widows.

After the manner of the period, a Latin legend, inscribed upon the wall, indicated to the lettered passenger the pious purpose of the cell. This usage continued until the middle of the sixteenth century, of placing a brief explanatory motto above the entrance of a building. Thus in France we still read, over the wicket of the prison belonging to the seigniorial mansion of Tourville, *Sileto et spera ;* in Ireland, under the escutcheon placed above the great gateway of Fortescue Castle, *Forte scutum, salus ducum ;* and in England, over the principal entrance of the hospitable mansion of the Earls Cowper, *Tuum est.* Every edifice was then, as it were, a thought.

As there was no door to the walled-up cell of the Tour-Roland, there had been engraved, in great Roman capitals, over the window, these two words of invitation to prayer.

TU, ORA.

Whence it was that the people, whose straightforward good sense sees not so many subtleties in things, but readily translates Ludovico Magno into Porte-Saint-Denis, had given to this dark, damp, dismal cavity the name of Trou-aux-Rats*—an explanation less sublime, perhaps, than the other, but on the other hand, more picturesque.

---

* Signifying rat-hole, a possible vulgarization of the French mode of pronouncing the Latin, " Tu, ora."

CHAPTER III.

SISTER GUDULE.

At the period at which the principal events of this history occurred, the cell of the Tour-Roland was occupied. If the reader desires to know by whom, he has only to listen to the conversation of three fair gossips, who, at the moment that we have called his attention to the Trou-aux-Rats were directing their steps precisely to the same spot, going up the river side from the Châtelet toward the Grève.

Two of these women were attired after the manner of the good bourgeoises of Paris. The fine white gorget; the petticoat of tiretaine, with red and blue stripes; the white knitted stockings, worked in colors at the ankles, and drawn tight upon the leg; the square-toed shoes, of brown leather with black soles; and especially their head-dress, that sort of tinsel-covered horn, loaded with ribbons and lace, which is still worn by the Champenoises, or women of Champagne, in common with the grenadiers of the Russian imperial guard; announced that they belonged to that class of rich tradeswomen who hold the medium between what Parisian lackeys call a woman and what they call a lady. They wore neither rings nor golden crosses; but it was easy to perceive that this was owing, not to their poverty, but simply to their apprehension of the fine incurred by so doing. Their companion was decked out nearly in the same manner; but there were, in her mise and her tournure, that is to say in the arrangement of her dress, and in her carriage, that certain something which indicates the wife of a notaire de province, or country attorney. It was evident, from the shortness of her waist, that she had not been long in Paris; to which were to be added a gorgerette pellissée—knots of ribbon upon her shoes— her skirt striped across instead of downward—and fifty other enormities revolting to *le bon goût*.

The two first walked with the step peculiar to
Parisian women showing Paris to ladies from the country; and the provincial one held by the hand a big
chubby boy, who carried in his hand a large, thin cake
—and we are sorry to be obliged to add that, owing to
the severity of the season, his tongue was performing
the office of his pocket-handkerchief. This boy made
his mother drag him along, *haud passibus æquis*, as
Virgil says, and stumbling every moment, to her great
outcrying. It is true that he looked more at the cake
than upon the ground. Some grave reason, no doubt,
prevented him from setting his teeth in it (in the cake),
for he contented himself with looking at it affectionately. But the mother ought surely to have taken
charge of the cake herself; it was cruel thus to make a
Tantalus of the child.

Meanwhile the three damoiselles (for the epithet of
dame or lady was then reserved for women of the
noblesse) were all talking at once.

"Let us make haste, Damoiselle Mahiette," said the
youngest of the three, who was also the fattest, to the
provincial. "I'm very much afraid we shall get there
too late; they told us at the Châtelet that they were
going to carry him to the pillory directly."

"Ah, bah! what are you talking about, Damoiselle
Oudarde Musnier?" interrupted the other Parisian
lady. "He'll be two hours on the pillory. We've time
enough. My dear Mahiette, did you ever see anybody
pilloried?"

"Yes," said the provincial; "I have at Reims."

"Ah, bah! what's that? What's your pillory at
Reims? A paltry cage, where they turn nothing but
clowns. That's a great thing, to be sure!"

"What clowns?" said Mahiette. "Clowns in the
cloth-market at Reims! We've had very fine criminals
there, I can tell you—that had killed both father and
mother. Clowns indeed! What do you take us for,
Gervaise?"

It is certain that the country dame was on the point
of being in a passion for the honor of her pillory. For

tunately, the discreet Damoiselle Oudarde Musnier gave a timely turn to the conversation.

"By-the-by, Damoiselle Mahiette, what say you to our Flemish ambassadors? Have you any so fine at Reims?"

"I must acknowledge," answered Mahiette, "that it's only at Paris one can see such Flemings as those."

"Did you see, among the embassy, that great ambassador that's a hosier?" asked Oudarde.

"Yes," said Mahiette, "he looks like a very Saturn!'

"And that fat one, with a face looking like a naked paunch? And that little one with little eyes, and red eyelids all jagged and bearded like the head of a thistle?"

"It's their horses that are fine to see," said Oudarde, "all dressed as they are, after their country fashion."

"Ah! my dear," interrupted the provincial Mahiette, assuming in her turn an air of superiority, "what would you say, then, if you'd seen, in '61, at the coronation at Reims, one-and-twenty years ago, the horses of the princess and all the king's company! There were housings and caparisons of all sorts—some of Damascus cloth, fine cloth of gold, trimmed with sables—some of velvet, trimmed with ermine—some all loaded with gold-work and great gold and silver fringe. And then, the money that it all cost—and the beautiful boys, the pages, that were upon them!"

"But, for all that," replied Damoiselle Oudarde dryly, "the Flemings have very fine horses—and yesterday they'd a splendid supper given them by monsieur the provost-merchant, at the Hôtel-de-Ville; where they served up sweetmeats, hippocrass, spices, and such like singularities."

"What are you talking of, my dear neighbor?" said Gervaise—"it was at the lord cardinal's, at the Petit-Bourbon, that the Flemings supped."

"No, no—it was at the Hôtel-de-Ville."

"Yes, yes, I tell you—it was at the Petit-Bourbon."

"So surely was it at the Hôtel-de-Ville," returned Oudarde sharply, "that Doctor Scourable made them a Latin speech, and they were very well pleased with it. It was my husband that told me so—and he's one of the sworn booksellers."

"So surely was it at the Petit-Bourbon," returned Gervaise no less warmly, "that I'll just tell you what my lord cardinal's attorney made them a present of—twelve double quarts of hippocrass, white claret, and vermilion; four-and-twenty cases of gilt double Lyons marchpane; four-and-twenty wax-torches of two pounds a piece; and six demi-queues of Baune wine, white and claret, the best that could be found. I hope that's proof enough. I had it from my husband, whose cinquantenier at the Parloir-aux-Bourgeois, and who was making a comparison this morning between the Flemish ambassadors and those of Prester John and the Emperor of Trebizond, that came to Paris from Mesopotamia, in the last king's time, and that had rings in their ears."

"So true is it that they supped at the Hôtel-de-Ville," replied Oudarde, not a whit moved by all this display, "that never was there seen so fine a show of meat and sugar-plums."

"I tell you that they were waited on by Le Sec, town-sergeant, at the Hôtel du Petit-Bourbon—and that's what has deceived you."

"At the Hôtel-de-Ville, I tell you."

"At the Petit-Bourbon, my dear!—for they'd illuminated the word *Espérance* that's written over the great doorway, with magical glasses."

"At the Hôtel-de-Ville! at the Hôtel-de-Ville!—for Hussen-le-Voir was playing the flute to them."

"I tell you, no."

"I tell you, yes."

"I tell you, no."

The good plump Oudarde was preparing to reply; and the quarrel would perhaps have gone on to the pulling of caps, if Mahiette had not all at once exclaimed, "Look at those people there, gathered together at the end of the bridge. There's something among them that they're all looking at."

" I do indeed hear a tambourining," said Gervaise
" I think it's little Smeralda, doing her mummeries with
her goat. Make haste, Mahiette—double your pace,
and pull your boy along. You're come here to see all
the curiosities of Paris. Yesterday, you saw the Flemings
—to-day you must see the little gypsy."

" The gypsy ? " said Mahiette, turning sharply round,
and forcibly grasping her son's arms. " God preserve
me from her! She'd steal my child—Come along,
Eustache ! "

And she set off running along the quay toward the
Grève, until she had left the bridge far enough behind
her. The boy, too, whom she was dragging along,
stumbled and fell upon his knees ; and she herself was
out of breath. Oudarde and Gervaise now came up
with her.

" That gypsy steal your child ! " said Gervaise ;
" that's an odd fancy of yours ! "

Mahiette shook her head thoughtfully.

" It's curious enough," observed Oudarde, "that the
Sachette has the same notion about the Egyptian
women."

" What's the Sachette ? " inquired Mahiette.

" Why," said Oudarde, " It's Sister Gudule."

"And who's Sister Gudule ? " returned Mahiette.

" You must be very knowing—with your Reims—not
to know that ! " answered Oudarde, looking wise. " It's
the recluse of the Trou-aux-Rats."

" What ! " exclaimed Mahiette ; " that poor woman
that we're carrying this cake to ? "

Oudarde nodded affirmatively. " Precisely," said she,
" You'll see her directly, at her window-place on the
Grève. She looks as you do upon those vagabonds of
Egypt that go about tambourining and fortune-telling.
Nobody knows what has given her this horror of zin-
gari and Egyptians. But what makes you run away so,
Mahiette, at the very sight of them ? "

" Oh ! " said Mahiette, taking in both hands the
chubby head of her boy ; " I wouldn't have that hap
pen to me which happened to Pâquette-la-Chantefleurie ! "

"Ha, now you're going to tell us a story, my good Mahiette," said Gervaise, taking her arm.

"I'm quite willing," answered Mahiette; "but you must be very knowing—with your Paris—not to know that. I must tell you, then—but we needn't stand still to go through our story—that Pâquette-la-Chantefleurie was a pretty girl of eighteen when I was one too, that is to say eighteen years ago; and that it's her own fault if she's not now, as I am, a good fat fresh-looking mother of six-and-thirty, with a husband and a boy—but alack! from the time that she was fourteen years old, it was too late. I must tell you, then, that she was the daughter of Guybertaut, a boat-minstrel at Reims—the same who had played before King Charles VII. at his coronation; when he went down our river Vesle from Sillery to Muison, and Madame la Pucelle was in the boat. The old father died while Pâquette was quite a child, so that she had only her mother left, who was sister to Monsieur Matthieu Pradon, a master-brazier and tinman at Paris, Rue Parin-Garlin, who died last year. You see that she was of some family. The mother was a good simple woman unfortunately, and taught Pâquette nothing but a little needle-work and toy-making, which did not hinder the little girl from growing very tall and remaining very poor. They lived both of them at Reims, by the river side, Rue de Folle-Peine — mark that! for, I believe that's what brought misfortune to Pâquette. In '61, the year of the coronation of our King Louis XI., whom God preserve! Pâquette was so gay and so pretty, that everywhere they called her nothing but La Chantefleurie. Poor girl! she'd pretty teeth, and she was fond of laughing to show them. Now a girl that's fond of laughing is on the way to cry—fine teeth are the ruin of fine eyes; so she was La Chantefleurie. She and her mother got their bread hardly—they were fallen very low since the death of the musician — their needle-work brought them hardly above six deniers a week, which is not quite two liards à l'aigle. Where was the time when the father Guybertaut used to get twelve sols parisis, at a single coronation, for a song! One winter—it was in that same year '61—when the two women had neither logs nor fagots, and it was very cold — that gave such beautiful colors to La Chantefleurie, that the men would call after her 'Pâquette'—that some of them called her a 'Pâquerette'—and that she was ruined——Eustache, let me see you bite the cake, if you dare——We saw directly that she was ruined, one Sunday when she came to church with a gold cross on her neck. At fifteen!—only think of that! At first it was the young Viscount de Cormontreuil, who has his bell-tower three-quarters of a league from Reims; then, Messire Henri de Traincourt, the king's master of the horse; then, going down lower, Chiart de Beaulion, sergeant-at-arms; then lower still, Guery Aubergeon, king's carver; then Macé de Frépus, monsieur the dauphin's barber; then Thévenin le Moine, the king's first cook; then, still going on, from one to another, from the younger to the older, and from more noble to less noble, she came to Guillaume Racine, viol-player—and to Thierry-de-Mer, lamp-maker. Then, poor Chantefleurie, she was all things to all men—she was come to the last sou of her piece of gold. What think you, mesdamoiselles? At the coronation, in the same year '61, it was she that made the bed for the king of the ribalds! In the same year!—"

Mahiette sighed, and wiped away a tear that had started to her eyes.

"Here's a story," said Gervaise, "that's not very uncommon; and I find nothing in all that neither about gypsies nor children."

"Patience!" resumed Mahiette—"As for a child, there's one coming for you. In '66, it'll be sixteen years ago this month, on St. Paul's day, Pâquette was brought to bed of a little girl, unfortunate creature; she was in great joy at it—she'd long been wishing to have a child. Her mother, poor simple woman, who'd never known how to do anything but shut her eyes; her mother was dead. Pâquette had nothing in the world left to love or anything that loved her. For five

years past, since she had gone astray, poor Chantefleurie
had been a wretched creature. She was lone, lone in
this world; pointed at, shouted after, through the
streets; beaten by the sergeants; laughed at by the
little ragged boys. And then she had seen her twen-
tieth year—and twenty is old age for your amorous
women. Her way of life was beginning to bring her
no more than her needle-work had brought formerly.
For every wrinkle that came, a crown less found its
way into her pocket; she was beginning again to find
the winter severe; again was wood growing scarce in
her fire-place, and bread in her cupboard. She couldn't
work now; for in giving way to pleasure she'd given
way to idleness, and she suffered much more than formerly, because while giving way to idleness she'd given
way to pleasure. At least, that's the way that monsieur
the curé of St. Remy explains how it is that those sort
of women feel more cold and hunger than other poor
females do, as they get old—"

"Yes," interrupted Gervaise; but the gypsies?"

"Do wait a moment, Gervaise!" said Oudarde,
whose attention was less impatient; "what should we
have at the end, if everything was at the beginning?
Pray, Mahiette, go on. That poor Chantefleurie!—"

Mahiette continued:

"Well, then—she was very sorrowful, very wretched,
and furrowed her cheeks with her tears. But in her
shame, her infamy, and her abandonment, she thought
she would be less ashamed, less infamous, and less
abandoned, if there were something in the world, or
somebody, that she could love, and that could love her.
She knew it must be a child, because only a child could
be innocent enough for that. She was aware of this
after trying to love a thief, the only sort of man that
could have anything to say to her—but in a little time
she had found out that the thief despised her. Those
women of love must have a lover or a child to fill up
their hearts, else they are very unhappy. As she could
not have a lover, all her wishes turned toward having a
child; and, as she had all along been pious, she prayed

to God everlastingly to send her one. So God took
pity on her and gave her a little girl. I can not tell
you what was her joy—it was a fury of tears, kisses and
caresses. She suckled the child herself; she made it
swaddling-clothes out of her coverlet, the only one she
had upon her bed; and now she felt neither cold nor
hunger. Her beauty came again—an old maid makes
a young mother—so poor Chantefleurie came into fashion again, and once more had visitors. And out of all
those horrors she made baby-clothes—lace robes and
little satin caps—without so much as thinking of buy-
ing herself another coverlet——Master Eustache, I've
told you once not to bite of that cake——Sure enough
it is, that little Agnès—that was the child's name—its
christian name—for, as for a surname, it was long since
La Chantefleurie had lost hers!—certain it is that the
little thing was more wrapped about with ribbons and
embroidery than a dauphiness of Dauphiny. Among
other things, she'd a pair of little shoes, that it's certain
King Louis himself never had the like. Her mother
had stitched them and embroidered them herself; she'd
spent upon them all the art of a seamstress and all the
passequilles of a Holy Virgin's gown. Indeed, they
were the two prettiest little rose-colored shoes that ever
were seen. They were not longer than my thumb at
the most; and unless you saw the infant's little feet
come out of them, you could hardly have believed that
they had ever gone in. To be sure, the little feet were
so little, so pretty, so rosy—rosier than the satin of the
shoes! When you have children, Oudarde, you'll know
that nothing's so pretty as those little feet and those
little hands."

"I wish for nothing better," said Oudarde, sighing;
"but I must wait the good pleasure of Monsieur Andry
Musnier."

"And then," resumed Mahiette, "Pâquette's infant
had not pretty feet only. I saw her when she was only
four months old—she was a perfect little love. She
had eyes larger than her mouth, and such charming fine
black hair, that was curling already. She'd have made

a brave brunette at sixteen! Her mother grew fonder and fonder of her every day. She hugged her—kissed her—tickled her—washed her—dressed her out—devoured her. She thanked God for giving her this baby. In fact, it quite turned her head. Its pretty rosy feet especially—there was wondering without end—a very intoxication of joy. She was always pressing her lips to them—always admiring their littleness. She would put them into the little shoes—take them out again—admire them —wonder at them—hold them up to the light—pity them while she was teaching them to step one before the other upon her bed—and would gladly have passed her life upon her knees, covering and uncovering those little feet, as if they'd been the feet of an infant Jesus."

"The tale's all very fine and very good," said Gervaise, in a half whisper, "but what is there about gypsies in all that?"

"You shall hear," replied Mahiette. "One day there came to Reims a very odd sort of gentry. They were beggars and truands, strolling about the country, led by their duke and their counts. Their faces were tawny, their hair all curly, and they'd rings of silver in their ears. The women were still uglier than the men. Their faces were darker, and always uncovered; they wore a sorry roquet about their body; an old piece of linen cloth interwoven with cords, bound upon their shoulder; and their hair hanging like a horse's tail. The children that scrambled about their legs would have frightened as many monkeys. An excommunicated gang! They were all come in a straight line from lower Egypt to Reims, through Poland. The Pope had confessed them, it was said, and had set them for a penance to go through the world for seven years together without sleeping in a bed; and so they called themselves penitents, and smelt horribly. It seems they'd formerly been Saracens; and that's why they believed in Jupiter, and demanded ten livres tournois from all archbishops, bishops, and abbots that carried crosier and miter. It was a bull of the Pope that gave them that. They came to Reims to tell fortunes in the name of the King of Algiers and the Emperor of Germany. You may suppose that was quite enough for them to be forbidden to enter the town. Then the whole gang encamped of their own accord near the Braine gate, upon that mound where there's a windmill, close by the old chalk-pits. Then none of the folks in Reims could rest till they'd been to see them. They looked into your hand, and told you wonderful prophecies—they were bold enough to have foretold to Judas himself that he should be pope. At the same time there were shocking stories told about them—of child-stealing, purse-cutting, and eating of human flesh. The wise folks said to the foolish ones, 'Don't go!' and then went themselves by stealth. It was quite a rage. The fact is, that they said things enough to astonish a cardinal. Mothers made a great fuss with their children after the gypsy-women had read in their hands all sorts of miracles, written in Turkish and Pagan. One of them had got an emperor—another a pope—another a captain. Poor Chantefleurie was taken with curiosity—she'd a mind to know what she had got, and whether her pretty little Agnès wasn't some day to be Empress of Armenia, or something. So she carried her to the gypsies; and the gypsy-women admired the child, fondled it, kissed it with their black mouths, and wondered over its little hand—alas! to the great joy of its mother. Above all things they were delighted with the pretty feet and the pretty shoes. The child was not yet a year old. She was already beginning to splutter—laughed at her mother like a little mad thing—was so fat and plump—and had a thousand little gestures of the angels in paradise. She was very much frightened at the gypsy-women, and cried. But her mother kissed her the harder, and went away delighted at the good fortune which the conjuring women had told her Agnès. She was to be a beauty—a virtue—a queen. So the mother went back to her garret in the Rue Folle Peine, quite proud to carry with her a queen. The next day, she seized a moment when the child was sleeping upon

her bed (for she always had it to sleep with herself),
pulled the door to softly, and left it ajar, for fear of
disturbing the infant; and ran to relate to one of her
neighbors, in the Rue de la Séchesserie, that the day
was to come when her daughter Agnès was to be waited
on at table by the King of England and the Archduke
of Ethiopia—and a hundred other marvels. When she
came back, hearing no cry as she went up the staircase,
she said to herself, 'Good—the child's asleep still.'
She found her door more open than she had left it—
the poor mother, however, went in and ran to the bed.
The child was not there—the place was empty. Nothing was left of the baby but one of its pretty shoes.
She rushed out of the room, flew down-stairs, and
began to beat the walls with her head, crying out ' My
child ! my child ! who has taken my child ? ' The street
was solitary—the house stood alone—nobody could tell
her anything about it ; she went through the town—
she sought through every street—ran up and down the
whole day, wild, mad, terrible, peeping at the doors and
windows like a wild beast that has lost its little ones.
She was panting, disheveled, frightful to look upon—
and in her eyes there was a fire that dried her tears.
She stopped the people that she met, and cried, ' My
girl ! my girl ! my pretty little girl !—he that will restore
me my girl, I will be his servant—the servant of his
dog, and he shall eat my heart if he likes.' She met
monsieur the curé of St. Remy, and said to him,
' Monsieur le curé, I'll dig the ground with my nails—
but do give me back my child ! ' It was heart-rending,
Oudarde—and I saw a very hard-hearted man, Maître
Ponce Lacabre, the attorney, that shed tears. Ah ! the
poor mother ! At night she went back to her garret.
While she was away, one of her neighbors had seen two
gypsy-women steal up to it with a bundle in their arms ;
then go down again, after shutting the door, and make
haste away. After they were gone, a sort of crying of
a child was heard in Pâquette's room—the mother
laughed aloud—flew up the staircase as if she'd had
wings—burst in her door as if it was a cannon going

off, and entered the room. A frightful thing to tell
Oudarde!—instead of her sweet little Agnès, so fresh
and rosy, who was a gift from God, there was a sort of
little monster, hideous, shapeless, one-eyed, with its
limbs all awry, crawling and squalling upon the floor.
She turned her eyes away with horror. 'Oh!' said
she, 'can the witches have changed my girl into that
frightful animal!' They carried the little clump foot,
as quick as possible, out of her sight. He'd have driven
her mad. It was a monstrous child of some gypsy
woman given to the Devil. It was a boy, that seemed
to be about four years old, and spoke a language which
was not a human tongue—they were words that are
quite impossible. La Chantefleurie had thrown herself
upon the little shoe, all that was left her of all she had
loved. There she remained so long motionless, speechless, breathless, that they thought she was dead. All
at once her whole body trembled—she covered her relic
with frantic kisses, and sobbed violently, as if her heart
had burst. I assure you we all wept with her. She
said, 'Oh, my little girl! my pretty little girl! where
art thou?' and she said it in a tone that went to the
bottom of your heart. I weep yet when I think of it.
Our children, you see, are the very marrow of our
bones. My poor Eustache! thou art so handsome!
If you did but know how clever he is! Yesterday he
said to me, 'I'll be a gendarme.' Oh, my Eustache, if
I were to lose thee! La Chantefleurie got up all on a
sudden, and went running through Reims, crying out,
'To the gypsies' camp! to the gypsies' camp! Sergeants,
to burn the witches!' The gypsies were gone—it was
a dark night, so that they couldn't pursue them. The
next day, two leagues from Reims, on a heath between
Gueux and Tilloy, they found the remains of a great
fire, some ribbons that had belonged to Pâquette's
child, some drops of blood, and some goat's dung. The
night that was just gone over was a Saturday night.
Nobody doubted but the gypsies had kept their sabbath
upon that heath, and had devoured the baby in company with Beelzebub, as is done among the Mahomet

ans. When La Chantefleurie heard of these horrible things she shed no tears—she moved her lips as if to speak, but could not. The next day her hair was gray ; and the next but one, she had disappeared."

"A dreadful story, indeed !" said Oudarde, "enough to draw tears from a Burgundian ! "

"I don't wonder now," added Gervaise, "that the fear of the gypsies should haunt you so."

"And you have done the better," resumed Oudarde, "in running away just now with your Eustache; seeing that these, too, are gypsies from Poland."

"No," said Gervaise, "it's said they're come from Spain and Catalonia."

"Catalonia !—well, that may be," answered Oudarde ; " Polonia, Catalonia, Valonia—I always confound those three provinces. The sure thing is they are gypsies."

"And it's certain," added Gervaise, "that they've teeth long enough to eat little children. And I shouldn't be surprised if La Smeralda herself eats a little in that way, too, for all that she screws up her mouth so. That white goat of hers has got too many mischievous tricks for there not to be some wickedness behind."

Mahiette was walking on in silence. She was absorbed in that species of musing which is, as it were, a prolongation of a mournful story, and which does not stop until it has communicated the thrilling, from vibration to vibration, to the last fiber of the heart. Gervaise, however, addressed her : "And so it was never known what became of La Chantefleurie?" Mahiette made no answer—Gervaise repeated her question, at the same time shaking her by the arm and calling her by her name. Mahiette seemed to awake from her revery :

"What became of La Chantefleurie?" said she, mechanically repeating the words whose impression was yet fresh in her ear. Then, making an effort to bring her attention to the sense of those words—"Ah," said she, emphatically, " it was never known." And after a pause she added : " Some said they had seen her go out of Reims, in the dusk of the evening, at the Port

Fléchembault; others, at daybreak, by the old Port
Basée. A poor man found her gold cross hung upon
the stone cross in the close where the fair is held. It
was that trinket that had ruined her in '61. It was a
gift from the handsome Viscount de Cormontreuil, her
first lover. Pâquette would never part with it, even in
her greatest wretchedness—she clung to it as if it had
been her life. So that when we saw this cross abandoned, we all thought she was dead. However, there
were some people, at the Cabaret-les-Vautes, who said
they'd seen her go by on the Paris road, walking barefoot over the stones. But then she must have gone
out at the Porte de Vesle, and all those things don't
agree. Or rather I'm inclined to think that she did
indeed go out by the gate of the Vesle, but that she
went out of this world."

"I don't understand you," said Gervaise.

"The Vesle," answered Mahiette, with a melancholy
smile, "is the river."

"Poor Chantefleurie!" said Oudarde, shuddering;
"what, drowned?"

"Drowned," replied Mahiette. "And who would
have foretold to the good father Guybertaut, when he
was passing down the stream under the Tinqueux
bridge, singing in his boat, that his dear little Pâquette
should one day pass under that same bridge, but with
neither song nor boat!"

"And the little shoe?" inquired Gervaise.

"Disappeared with the mother," answered Mahiette.

"Poor little shoe!" said Oudarde.

Oudarde, a woman of full habit and tender fiber,
would have been quite content to sigh along with
Mahiette. But Gervaise, more curious, had not yet got
to the end of her questions.

"And the monster?" said she all at once to Mahiette.

"What monster?" asked the other.

"Why, the little gypsy monster that the witches left
at La Chantefleurie's in exchange for her daughter.
What did you do with it? I hope you drowned it
too."

"No," answered Mahiette, "we did not."

"What? burned it then? I'faith, that was a better way of disposing of a witch's child."

"We did neither the one nor the other, Gervaise. Monsieur the archbishop took an interest in the child of Egypt; he exorcised it, blessed it, carefully took the devil out of its body, and sent it to Paris to be exposed upon the wooden bed at Notre-Dame as a foundling."

"Those bishops!" muttered Gervaise; "because they're learned, forsooth, they can never do anything like other folks. Only consider, Oudarde—to think of putting the devil among the foundlings—for it's quite certain that little monster was the devil. Well, Mahiette, and what did they do with it at Paris? I'll answer for it that not one charitable person would take it."

"I don't know, indeed," answered the good lady of Reims. "It was just at that time that my husband bought the tabellionage of Beru, two leagues from the town; and we thought no more of all that story—for you must know, that just in front of Beru there are two mounds of Cernay, that take the towers of Reims cathedral out of your sight."

While talking thus, the three worthy bourgeoises had arrived at the Place de Grève. In the pre-occupation of their minds, they had passed by the public breviary of the Tour-Roland without observing it, and were proceeding mechanically toward the pillory, around which the crowd was every moment increasing. It is probable that the sight, which at that moment drew every eye toward it, would have made them completely forget the Trou-aux-Rats and the station they had intended to perform there, had not the big Eustache of six years old, whom Mahiette held by the hand, suddenly reminded them of it. "Mother," said he, as if some instinct apprised him that they had left the Trou-aux-Rats behind them, "now may I eat the cake?"

Had Eustache been more adroit, that is to say, less greedy, he would have waited a little longer; and not until they had reached home, in the University, at Maître Andry Musnier's, in the Rue Madame-la-Valence, when the two channels of the Seine and the five bridges of the city would have been between the cake and the Trou-aux-Rats, would he have hazarded that timid question—"Mother, now may I eat the cake?"

This same question, imprudent at the moment at which Eustache made it, aroused Mahiette's attention.

"By-the-by," exclaimed she, "we were forgetting the recluse! Show me this Trou-aux-Rats of yours, that I may carry her her cake."

"To be sure," said Oudarde, "it'll be a charity."

This was not the thing for Eustache. "Let me have my cake!" said he, rubbing first one of his ears upon his shoulder, and then the other—the sign in such cases, of supreme dissatisfaction.

The three women retraced their steps; and when they had nearly reached the house of the Tour-Roland, Oudarde said to the other two: "We must not all three look into the hole at once, lest we should frighten the Sachette. Do you two make as if you were reading Dominus in the breviary, while I peep in at the window hole. The Sachette knows me a little. I'll let you know when you may come."

She went by herself to the window-place. The moment that she looked in, profound pity depicted itself in all her features; her cheerful, open countenance changing its expression and its hue as suddenly as if it had passed out of a gleam of sunshine into one of moonlight; her eye moistened, and her mouth took that contraction which is the forerunner of weeping. A moment after, she laid her finger on her lip, and beckoned to Mahiette to come and look.

Mahiette came, tremulous, silent, and stepping on the points of her toes, like one approaching a death-bed.

It was in truth a sorrowful sight that presented itself to the eyes of the two women, while they looked, without stirring or drawing their breath, through the grated window of the Trou-aux-Rats.

The cell was of small dimensions, wider than it was

deep, with a gothic-vaulted ceiling, and looking, internally, much in the shape of the inner part of a bishop's mitre. Upon the bare flag-stones that formed its floor, in one corner, a woman was seated, or rather squatted down. Her chin was resting on her knees, with her arms, crossed before her, pressed close against her chest. Thus—gathered up, as it were, into a heap —clad in a brown sackcloth which wrapped her all round in large folds—with her long gray hair turned upon her forehead and hanging over her face, and down by her legs to her feet—she presented, at first sight, only a strange form, projected on the dark background of the cell—a sort of dusky triangle, which the daylight from the window-place crudely distinguished into two tints, the one light, the other dark. It was one of those spectres, half light, half shade, such as are seen in dreams, and in the extraordinary work of Goya—pale —motionless—dismal—squatting on a tomb, or reared against the grating of a dungeon. It was neither woman nor man, nor living being, nor definite form; it was a figure, a sort of vision, in which the real and the fanciful were intermingled like light and shadow. Beneath her hair, that fell all about it to the ground, scarcely could you distinguish a severe and attenuated profile, scarcely did there peep from under the hem of her flowing gown, the extremity of a naked foot, contracted upon the rigid and frozen pavement. The little of human form that was discernible under that mourning envelope made you shudder.

This figure, which looked as if it had been fixed in the floor, seemed to have neither motion, thought, nor breath. In that covering of thin, brown linen, in January, lying upon a pavement of granite, without fire, in the darkness of a dungeon, the oblique loophole of which admitted only the north-east wind, and never the sun—she seemed not to suffer, not even to feel. You would have thought that she had turned to stone with the dungeon, to ice with the season. Her hands were clasped, her eyes were fixed. At the first glance you took her for a specter; at the second, for a statue.

However, at intervals, her blue lips half opened with a breath, and trembled, but as deadly and mechanically as leaves parted by the wind. And from those dull, stony eyes, there proceeded a look, ineffable, profound, lugubrious, imperturbable, constantly fixed upon one angle of the cell, which could not be seen from the outside; a look which seemed to concentrate all the gloomy thoughts of that suffering spirit upon some mysterious object.

Such was the creature who from her tenement was called the recluse, and from her coarse linen or sacking garment, the Sachette.

The three women (for Gervaise had come up to Mahiette and Oudarde) were looking through the window-place. Their heads intercepted the feeble light of the dungeon, apparently without at all calling the wretched creature's attention in that direction. "Let us not disturb her," whispered Oudarde; "she's in her ecstasy, she's praying."

Meanwhile, Mahiette was gazing with a constantly increasing anxiety upon that wan, withered, disheveled head, and her eyes filled with tears. "That would be very singular!" muttered she.

She passed her head through the bars of the window, and succeeded in obtaining a glance into that angle of the cell upon which the unfortunate woman's look was immovably fixed. When she drew her head out again, her face was covered with tears.

"What is that woman's name?" said she to Oudarde.

Oudarde answered, "We call her Sister Gudule."

"And I," returned Mahiette, "call her Pâquette-la-Chantefleurie."

Then, laying her finger upon her lip, she made a sign to the amazed Oudarde, to put her head through the bars as she had done, and to look.

Oudarde looked and saw, in that corner upon which the eye of the recluse was fixed in that gloomy absorption, a little shoe of rose-colored satin, decorated all over with gold and silver spangles.

Gervaise looked after Oudarde; and then the three

women, gazing upon the unhappy mother, began to weep.

However, neither their looks nor their weeping had disturbed the recluse. Her hands remained clasped; her lips mute; her eyes fixed; and to any one who knew her story, that gaze of hers upon that little shoe was heart-rending.

The three women had not uttered a word; they dared not speak, even in a whisper. That deep silence, that deep forgetfulness, in which every object had disappeared, save one, had upon them the effect of a high altar at Easter or Christmas. They kept silence; they collected themselves; they were ready to kneel. They felt as if they had just entered a church on the Saturday in Passion-week.

At length Gervaise, the most curious of the three, and therefore the least sensitive, tried to make the recluse speak, by calling to her, "Sister! Sister Gudule!"

She repeated this call, to the third time, raising her voice higher every time. The recluse did not stir— there was not a word, not a look, not a sigh, not a sign of life.

Now, Oudarde herself, in a softer and kinder tone, said to her, "Sister—holy Sister Gudule!" There was the same silence, the same immobility.

"An odd woman!" exclaimed Gervaise, "that would not start at a bombard."

"Perhaps she's deaf," said Oudarde, with a sigh.

"Perhaps blind," added Gervaise.

"Perhaps dead," observed Mahiette.

It is certain that if the soul had not yet quitted that inert, torpid, lethargic body, it had at least retired within it, and hidden itself in depths to which the perceptions of the external organs did not penetrate.

"We shall be obliged, then," said Oudarde, "to leave the cake lying upon the window-case; and some lad or other will take it. What can we do to rouse her?"

Eustache, whose attention had until that moment been diverted by a little carriage drawn by a great dog, which had just passed them, all at once observed, that his three conductresses were looking at something through the hole in the wall; and his own curiosity being thus excited, he mounted upon a curb-stone, sprang up on his toes, and put his great rosy face to the opening, crying out, "Mother, let me see, too."

At the sound of this voice of a child, clear, fresh, and sonorous, the recluse started. She turned her head with the dry and sudden motion of a steel spring; her two long, fleshless hands threw aside her hair upon her forehead; and she fixed upon the child a look of astonishment, bitterness, and despair. That look was but a flash. "Oh, my God!" exclaimed she, all at once, hiding her head between her knees—and it seemed as if her hoarse voice tore her breast in passing—"at least don't show me those of others!"

"Good-day, madame," said the boy, gravely.

This shock, however, had, as it were, awakened the recluse. A long shiver ran over her whole body, from head to foot; her teeth chattered; she half raised her head, and said, pressing her elbows against her hips, and taking her feet in her hands, as if to restore their warmth, "Oh, the severe cold."

"Poor woman," said Oudarde, with deep pity, "will you have a little fire?"

She shook her head in token of refusal.

"Well," resumed Oudarde, offering her a flask, "here is some hippocrass, that will warm you. Drink."

She shook her head again, looked steadfastly at Oudarde, and answered, "some water!"

Oudarde insisted: "No, sister; that's not a January beverage. You must drink a little hippocrass, and eat this cake leavened with maize, that we've baked for you."

She rejected the cake, which Mahiette offered her, and said, "some black bread!"

"Here," said Gervaise, seized with charity in her turn, and taking off her woolen roquet—"here's a cloak rather warmer than yours—put this over your shoulders."

She refused the cloak as she had done the liquor and the cake at the same time answering "A sack!"

"But at all events," resumed the kind Oudarde, "you must be aware, I should think, that yesterday was a holiday."

"I am aware of it," said the recluse. "For two days past I have had no water in my pitcher."

She added, after a pause, "It's a holiday, and they forget me—they do well. Why should the world think of me, who think not of it? Cold ashes are fitting to a dead coal."

And then, as if fatigued with having said so much, she let her head drop upon her knees again. The simple and charitable Oudarde, thinking that she was to understand, from these last words, that the poor woman was still complaining of the cold, answered her with simplicity, "Then will you have a little fire?"

"Fire?" said the Sachette in a strange tone—"and will you make a little, too, for the poor little one that has been under ground these fifteen years?"

All her limbs trembled, her speech vibrated, her eye shone. She had risen up on her knees, she suddenly stretched out her white hands toward the child, which was gazing at her with an astonished look. "Take away that child!" she cried, "the gypsy woman's coming by."

Then she fell with her face to the ground, and her forehead striking the floor with the noise of a stone upon a stone. The three women thought she was dead. A minute afterwards she stirred, and they saw her crawl upon her hands and knees into the corner that contained the little shoe. Then they did not venture to look; they saw her no longer, but they heard a thousand kisses and sighs, intermingled with afflicting exclamations, and with dull strokes, like those of a head knocking against a wall; then, after one of these strokes, so violent that it startled them all three, all was silent.

"Has she killed herself, I wonder?" said Gervaise, venturing to put her head between the bars. "Sister! Sister Gudule!"

"Sister Gudule!" repeated Oudarde.

15

" Ah, my God, she doesn't stir ! " resumed Gervais. " Is she dead, think you ?—Gudule ! Gudule ! "

Mahiette, whose utterance had been choked until then, now made an effort. " Wait a moment," said she; and then, putting her head to the window, " Pâquette ! " she cried, " Pâquette-la-Chantefleurie ! "

A child that should blow unsuspectingly upon the ill-lighted match of a petard, and make it explode in his face, would not be more frightened than Mahiette was at the effect of this name thus suddenly breathed into the cell of Sister Gudule.

The recluse was agitated in every limb ; she rose erect upon her naked feet, and flew to the loop-hole with eyes so flaming that Mahiette and Oudarde, their companion and the child, all retreated as far as the parapet of the quay.

Meanwhile, the sinister visage of the recluse appeared close to the window-grate. " Oh, oh," she cried, with a frightful laugh, " it's the gypsy woman that calls me."

At that moment, a scene which was passing at the pillory arrested her haggard eye. Her forehead wrinkled with horror—she stretched out of her den her two skeleton arms, and cried out, with a voice that rattled in her throat :—" So, it's thou again, daughter of Egypt—it's thou that call'st me, thou child-stealer ! Well, cursed be thou ! cursed ! cursed ! cursed !——"

CHAPTER IV.

A TEAR FOR A DROP OF WATER.

THE concluding words of the foregoing chapter may be described as the point of junction of two scenes which, until that moment, had been simultaneously developing themselves, each upon its particular stage

the one, that which has just been related, at the Trou-
aux-Rats; the other, now to be described, at the
pillory. The former had been witnessed only by the
three women with whom the reader had just now been
made acquainted; the latter had had for spectators the
whole crowd which we have seen collect a little while
before upon the Place de Grève, around the pillory and
the gibbet.

This crowd, whom the sight of the four sergeants
posted from nine o'clock in the morning at the four
corners of the pillory, led to expect a penal exhibition
of some kind—not, certainly, a hanging—but a flogging,
a cutting off of ears, or something in that way—this
crowd, we say, had so rapidly increased, that the four
sergeants, finding themselves too closely invested, had
more than once been under the necessity of forcing it
back by the application of their whit-leather whips and
their horses' cruppers.

The populace, however, well drilled to the waiting
for this sort of spectacle, showed themselves tolerably
patient. They amused themselves with looking at the
pillory—a very simple sort of structure, in truth, consisting of a cubical mass of stone-work, some ten feet
high, and hollowed internally. A very steep flight of
steps, of unhewn stone, called by distinction the échelle
gave access to the upper platform, upon which was to
be seen a plain horizontal wheel made of oak wood.
The custom was to bind the sufferer upon this wheel,
on his knees, and his arms pinioned. An upright shaft
of timber, set in motion by a capstan concealed within
the interior of the small edifice, made the wheel re-
volve horizontally and uniformly, thus presenting the
face of the culprit successively to every point of the
Place. This was called "turning" the criminal.

It is clear that the pillory of the Grève was far from
possessing all the attractions of the pillory of the
Halles. There was nothing architectural, nothing monumental. There was no iron-cross roof—no octagonal
lantern—there were no slender colonnettes, opening
out against the border of the roof into capitals of

foliage and flowers—no monster-headed gutters—no carved woodwork—no bold and delicate sculpture. The spectator was obliged to content himself with those four faces of rough stone, surmounted by two side walls or parapets of stone still rougher, with a sorry stone gibbet, meagre and bare, standing beside them. The entertainment would have been pitiful enough for amateurs of Gothic architecture. But it is certain that none could be less curious in this way than the good cockneys of the middle ages, and that they took but little interest in the beauty of a pillory.

At last the culprit arrived, fastened at the tail of a cart, and as soon as he was hoisted upon the platform, so that he could be seen from every point of the Place, bound with cords and straps, upon the wheel of the pillory, a prodigious hooting, mingled with laughter and acclamations, burst from the assemblage in the square. They had recognized Quasimodo.

As regarded himself, the turn of affairs was somewhat striking—to be pilloried in that same square in which, the day before, he had been saluted and proclaimed pope and prince of the fools, in the train of the Duke of Egypt, the King of Tunis, and the Emperor of Galilee. Certain it is, however, that there was not one mind among the crowd—not even his own, though himself in turn the triumphant and the sufferer —that clearly drew this parallel. Gringoire and his philosophy were absent from this spectacle.

Anon, Michel Noiret, one of their lord the king's sworn trumpeters, after having silence cried to the manans, made proclamation of the sentence, pursuant to the ordinance and command of monsieur the provost. He then fell back behind the cart, with his men in their hacqueton uniform.

Quasimodo, quite passive, did not so much as knit his brow. All resistance was impossible to him by what was then called, in the style of the chancellerie criminelle, "the vehemence and firmness of the bonds" —that is to say, that the small straps and chains probably entered his flesh. "This, by-the-by," observes our author, "is a tradition which is not yet lost; the menottes or manacles still happily preserving it among ourselves, a people civilized, mild, and humane (the bagnio and the guillotine between parentheses)."

Quasimodo had let them lead him, thrust him, carry him along, hoist him up, bind and rebind him. Nothing was distinguishable in his countenance but the aston-ishment of a savage or an idiot. He was known to be deaf—he might have been taken to be blind.

They set him upon his knees on the circular plank, and stripped him to the waist—he made not the least resistance. They bound him down under a fresh sys-tem of straps and buckles—he let them buckle and strap him. Only from time to time he breathed heavily, like a calf, when its head hangs tossing about over the side of the butcher's cart.

"The dolt!" said Jehan Frollo du Moulin to his friend Robin Poussepain (for the two scholars had fol-lowed the sufferer, as in duty bound), "he understands no more about it than a cockchafer shut up in a box."

There was a wild laugh among the crowd when they saw, stripped naked to their view, Quasimodo's hump, his camel breast, his brawny and hairy shoulders. Dur-ing all this merriment, a man in the Town livery, short and thick-set, ascended the platform, and placed him-self by the culprit. His name was quickly circulated among the spectators—it was Maître Pierrat Torterue, sworn torturer at the Châtelet.

He commenced his operations by depositing on one corner of the pillory a black hour-glass, the upper cup of which was filled with red sand, which was filtering through into the lower recipient. Then he took off his parti-colored doublet; and there was seen dangling from his right hand a whip with long slender white lashes, shining, knotted, and armed with points of metal. With his left hand he carelessly turned up his shirt-sleeve, about his right arm, as high as the arm-pit.

Meanwhile Jehan Frollo cried out, lifting his light-haired, curly head above the crowd (for he had mounted

for that purpose on the shoulders of Robin Poussepain).
" Come and see—messieurs! mesdames!—they're going
peremptorily to flog Maître Quasimodo, ringer to my
brother monsieur the Archdeacon of Joas—a fellow of
oriental architecture, with his back like a dome, and
his legs like twisted columns!"

And the people laughed, especially the boys and
girls.

At last the torturer stamped with his foot. The
wheel began to turn; Quasimodo staggered under his
bonds. And the amazement that was suddenly depicted upon his deformed visage redoubled the bursts of
laughter all around.

All at once, at the moment when the wheel in its
rotation presented to Maître Pierrat Quasimodo's
mountainous back, Maître Pierrat lifted his arm, the
small lashes whistled sharply in the air like a handful
of vipers, and fell with fury upon the poor wretch's
shoulders.

Quasimodo made a spring as if starting from his
sleep. He now began to understand. He twisted
himself about in his toils. A violent contraction, expressive of surprise and pain, discomposed the muscles
of his face; but he breathed not a sigh. Only he
turned back his head first on the right side, then on
the left, balancing it backwards and forwards like a bull
stung in the flank by a gad-fly.

A second stroke followed the first—then a third—
then another—and another—and so on, without ceas-
ing; the wheel continuing to turn, and the lashes to
descend upon the sufferer. Soon the blood began to
flow; it was seen trickling in a thousand streaks over
the dark shoulders of the hunchback; and the keen
lashes, as they whistled through the air, scattered it in
drops among the multitude.

Quasimodo had resumed, in appearance at least, his
former passiveness. At first he had striven, silently
and without any great external shock, to burst his
bonds. His eye had been seen to kindle, his muscles
to contract, his limbs to gather themselves up, and the

straps and chains to be strained to their utmost tension. The effort was powerful, prodigious, desperate—but the old binders of the provostry resisted. They cracked; but that was all. Quasimodo sank exhausted; and, on his countenance, stupefaction was succeeded by an expression of bitter and deep discouragement. He closed his only eye, dropped his head upon his breast, and seemed as if he was dead.

Thenceforward he stirred not at all. Nothing could wring any motion from him—neither his blood, which continued to flow; nor the strokes of the whip, which fell with redoubled fury; nor the violence of the torturer, who worked himself up into a sort of intoxication; nor the keen whistling of the horrid lashes.

At length an usher of the Châtelet, clothed in black, mounted on a black horse, and stationed at the side of the échelle from the commencement of the punishment, pointed, with his ebony wand, to the hour-glass. The torturer held his hand, the wheel stopped, and Quasimodo's eye slowly reopened.

The flagellation was finished. Two assistants of the sworn torturer washed the bleeding shoulders of the sufferer, rubbed them with some kind of unguent, which immediately closed the wounds, and threw over his back a sort of yellow cloth cut in the form of a chasuble. Meanwhile Pierrat Torterue was letting the blood that soaked the lashes of his scourge drain from them in drops upon the ground.

However, all was not yet over for poor Quasimodo. He had still to undergo that hour on the pillory which Maître Florian Barbedienne had so judiciously added to the sentence of Messire Robert d'Estouteville—all to the greater glory of the old jeu de mots, physiological and psychological, of Jean de Cumène—*Surdus absurdus.*

So they turned the hour-glass, and left the hunchback bound down upon the wheel, that justice might be perpetrated to the end.

The people, in the inferior sense of the word, have hitherto been, in society, especially in the middle ages, what the child is in a family. So long as they remain in that state of primitive ignorance, of moral and intellectual nonage, it may be said of them as has been said of childhood—"that age is a stranger to pity." We have already shown that Quasimodo was generally hated—for more than one good reason, it is true. There was hardly a spectator among that crowd but either had or thought he had some cause of complaint against the mischievous hunchback of Notre-Dame. All had rejoiced to see him make his appearance on the pillory; and the severe punishment he had just undergone, and the piteous plight in which it had left him, so far from softening the hearts of the populace, had but rendered their hatred the more malicious by furnishing it with matter for merriment.

And accordingly the "public vengeance" being satisfied—the "vindicte publique," as it is called in the legal jargon of our neighbors—a thousand private revenges had now their turn. Here, as in the Grand Salle, it was the women that broke forth with the greatest violence. They all bore malice against him—some for his mischievousness, others for his ugliness. The latter were the most furious of the two.

"Oh! thou phiz of Antichrist!" exclaimed one.

"Thou broomstick-rider!" cried another.

"What a fine tragical grin!" bawled a third, "and one that would have made him Fools' Pope if to-day had been yesterday."

"Good!" chimed in an old woman. "This is the pillory grin; when is he to give us the gallows grin?"

"When art thou to have thy big bell clapped upon thy head a hundred feet under ground, thou cursed ringer?" shouted one.

"And yet it's this devil that rings the Angelus!"

"Oh! the deaf as a post! the one-eye! the hunchback! the monster!"

"He's a face to make a woman miscarry, better than any medicines or pharmacies."

And the two scholars, Jehan du Moulin and Robin Poussepain, sang out, as loud as they could bawl, the burden of an old popular song—

> A halter for the gallows rogue !
> A fagot for the witch !

A thousand other pieces of abuse were showered
upon him, and hootings, and imprecations, and bursts
of laughter, and here and there a stone.

Quasimodo was deaf, but he saw clearly; and the
public fury was not less forcibly expressed in the countenances of the people than by their words. Besides,
the stones that struck him explained the bursts of laughter.

At the first he bore it all very well. But, by degrees,
the patience which had braced up its fibres under the
lash of the torturer, relaxed and gave way under these
insect stings. The Asturian bull that has borne unmoved the attacks of the picador, is irritated by the
dogs and the banderillas.

First, he cast slowly around a look of menace upon
the crowd. But, bound hand and foot as he was, his
look had no power to chase away the flies that gnawed
his wound. Then he shook himself in his toils; and
his furious efforts made the old wheel of the pillory
creak upon its timbers, all which but increased the derision and the hooting.

Then the poor wretch, finding himself unable to
burst his wild beast's chain, once more became quiet;
only, at intervals, a sigh of rage heaved all the cavities
of his breast. In his face there was neither shame nor
blush. He was too far from the state of society, and
too near the state of nature, to know what shame was.
Besides, at that pitch of deformity, is infamy a thing
that can be felt? But resentment, hatred, and despair
were slowly spreading over that hideous visage a cloud
that grew more and more gloomy, more and more
charged with an electricity which shone in a thousand
flashes from the eye of the cyclop.

However, that cloud was dissipated for a moment at
the appearance of a mule which passed through the
crowd, carrying a priest upon its back. From the first
moment that he perceived that priest and that mule ap-

proaching, the poor sufferer's countenance became milder. The fury which had contracted it was succeeded by a strange smile, full of a softness, a gentleness, a tenderness inexpressible. As the priest came nearer, this smile became plainer, more distinct, more radiant. It was as if the unfortunate creature was hailing the coming of a Saviour. However, the moment that the mule had come near enough to the pillory for its rider to recognize the sufferer, the priest cast down his eyes, turned round abruptly, and spurred away his steed, as if in haste to escape humiliating appeals, and not at all anxious to be saluted and recognized by a poor devil in such a situation.

This priest was the Archdeacon Dom Claude Frollo; who, albeit he stood in much the same relation to Quasimodo as the knight of La Mancha did to his squire, was, in some respects, no more a Don Quixote than, in some others, Quasimodo was a Sancho Panza. And yet Sancho's blanket-tossing, from which the knight would have encountered any disgrace to have delivered him, was a mere trifle compared to this infliction undergone by the archdeacon's devoted servant.

And now the cloud fell darker than ever upon the face of Quasimodo. The smile was still mingled with it for a time; but it was bitter, disheartened, and profoundly sad.

The time was going on. He had been there for at least an hour and a half; lacerated, abused, mocked, and almost stoned to death. All at once he made another struggle in his chains, with redoubled desperation, that shook the whole woodwork upon which he was fixed; and, breaking the silence which until then he had obstinately kept, he cried out in a hoarse and furious voice, which was more like a dog's howl than a human shout, and which drowned the noise of the hooting, "Some drink!"

This exclamation of distress, far from exciting compassion, was an additional amusement to the good Parisian populace that surrounded the pillory, and who, it must be admitted, taken on the whole and as a multiude, were scarcely less cruel and brutal than that horrible tribe of the Truands, to which we have already introduced the reader, and which, indeed, was itself neither more nor less than the lowest stratum of the people. Not a voice was raised around the unhappy sufferer, except in mockery of his thirst. It is certain that at that moment his appearance was yet more grotesque and repulsive than it was pitiable—with his reddened and trickling face, his bewildered eye, his mouth foaming with rage and suffering, and his tongue half hanging out. We must observe, too, that had there even been among the multitude any good, charitable soul of a townsman or townswoman, who should have been tempted to carry a glass of water to that miserable creature in pain, there reigned around the ignominious steps of the pillory so strong an air of infamy in the prejudices of the time, as would have sufficed to repel the good Samaritan.

At the end of a few minutes more, Quasimodo cast around him a look of despair upon the crowd, and repeated in a voice yet more heart-rending, "Some drink!" And again they all laughed.

"Drink this!" cried Robin Poussepain, throwing in his face a sponge soaked in the kennel. "Here, you deaf scoundrel; I'm your debtor!"

A woman threw a stone at his head, saying: "That'll teach thee to wake us in the night with thy cursed ringing!"

"Well, my lad!" bawled a cripple, trying at the same time to reach him with his crutch, "wilt thou cast spells at us again from the top of the towers of Notre-Dame?"

"Here's a porringer to drink out of," said one man, hurling a broken pitcher at his breast. "It's thou that, with only passing before her, made my wife be brought to bed of a child with two heads!"

"And my cat of a kitten with six legs!" screamed an old woman as she flung a tile at him.

"Some drink!" repeated Quasimodo for the third time, panting. At that moment, he saw the populace making way for some one, and a young girl fantastically dressed, issued from the crowd. She was accompanied by a little she-goat with gilt horns, and carried a small tambourine in her hand.

Quasimodo's eyes sparkled. It was the gypsy girl whom he had attempted to carry off the night before, for which piece of presumption he had some confused notion that they were chastising him at that very moment—which, however, was by no means the case, seeing that he was punished only for the misfortune of being deaf and having had a deaf judge. He doubted not that she, too, was come to take her revenge, and to aim her blow at him like all the rest of them.

In fact, he beheld her rapidly ascend the steps. He was choking with rage and vexation. He wished that he could have crumbled the pillory to atoms; and if the flash of his eye could have destroyed, the gypsy would have been reduced to ashes before she could have reached the platform. Without uttering a word, she approached the sufferer, who was vainly writhing about to escape her; and then, unfastening a gourd-bottle from her belt, she held it out to the poor wretch's parched lips.

Then from that eye, hitherto so dry and burning, was seen to roll a big tear, which fell slowly down that deformed visage so long contracted by despair. Perhaps it was the first that the unfortunate creature had ever shed.

Meanwhile, he forgot to drink. The gypsy made her little accustomed grimace with impatience; and held up, smiling, the neck of the gourd to the jagged mouth of Quasimodo. He drank long draughts, for his thirst was burning.

When he had done, the poor wretch put out his black lips, undoubtedly to kiss the fair hand which had just relieved him; but the girl, who, remembering the violent attempt of the preceding night, was perhaps not without some mistrust, drew back her hand with the frightened look of a child afraid of being bitten by some animal.

Then the poor deaf creature fixed upon her a look reproachful and inexpressibly sad.

"HE DRANK LONG DRAUGHTS."

It would anywhere have been a touching spectacle, to see that beautiful girl, so fresh, so pure, so charming, and at the same time so weak, thus piously hastening to the relief of so much wretchedness, deformity, and malice; but on a pillory the spectacle was sublime. The people themselves were struck by it, and clapped their hands, shouting, "Noël, Noël!"

It was at that moment that the recluse, through the loophole of her cell, observed the gypsy girl upon the steps of the pillory, and cast at her the dismal imprecation, "Cursed be thou, daughter of Egypt! cursed! cursed!"

CHAPTER V.

THE CATASTROPHE OF THE CAKE.

ESMERALDA turned pale, and descended from the pillory, tottering; the voice of the recluse pursued her still. "Come down, come down, Egyptian thief! thou shalt go up there again!"

"The Sachette's in her crotchets," said the people, muttering—but that was all they did; for this sort of women were feared, and that made them sacred. Nobody in those days was willing to attack any one that prayed day and night.

The hour had now arrived for carrying back Quasimodo; they unfastened him from the pillory, and the crowd dispersed.

Near the Grand Pont, Mahiette, who was going away with her two companions, suddenly stopped short. "By-the-by, Eustache," said she, "what have you done with the cake?"

"Mother," said the boy, "while you were talking to that lady in the hole, there was a great dog came and bit of my cake—and then I bit of it too."

" What, sir ! " cried she ; " have you eaten it all ? "

" Mother, it was the dog. I told him so but he wouldn't listen to me. Then I bit a piece too—that's all."

" It's a shocking boy," said the mother, smiling and chiding at the same time. " What do you think, Oudarde—already he eats by himself all the cherries that grow upon the tree in our croft at Charlerange. So his grandfather says he'll be a captain. Let me catch you at it again, Master Eustache. Get along, you greedy fellow ! "

BOOK VI.

CHAPTER I.

SHOWING THE DANGER OF CONFIDING ONE'S SECRET
TO A GOAT.

SEVERAL weeks had elapsed. It was now the early part of the month of March. The sun, which Dubartas, that classic ancestor of periphrasis, had not yet named "the grand duke of the candles," was not, therefore, the less cheerful and radiant. It was one of those days of the early spring which are so mild and beautiful that all Paris turns out into the squares and promenades, to enjoy them as if they were holidays. On those days of clearness, warmth, and serenity, there is one hour in particular, at which you should go and admire the portal of Notre-Dame. It is that moment when the sun, already declining toward his setting, darts his rays almost directly upon the front of the cathedral. Becoming more and more horizontal, they gradually retire from the pavement of the Place, and mount up the perpendicular face of the structure, streaming full upon the thousand rotundities of its sculpture, while the great round central window flames like a cyclop's eye lit up by the reverberations of the forge.

At this hour it was that, opposite to the front of the lofty cathedral, reddened by the setting sun, upon the stone balcony constructed over the porch of a rich-looking Gothic house, at the angle formed by the Place with the Rue du Parvis, some handsome girls were laughing and talking together with all manner of grace and sportiveness. By the length of the veil which fell from the top of their pointed coif, all scrolled with pearls, down to their heels—by the fineness of the worked chemisette which covered their shoulders, revealing, according to the engaging fashion of that time, the swell of their fair virgin bosoms—by the richness of their under petticoats, yet more costly than the upper skirt (admirable refinement)! —by the gauze, the silk, and the velvet, with which the whole was loaded—and above all, by the whiteness of their hands—it was easy to divine that they were noble and wealthy heiresses. They were, in fact, Damoiselle Fleur-de-Lys de Gondelaurier, and her companions, Diane de Christeuil, Amelotte de Montmichel, Colombe de Gaillefontaine, and the little De Champchevrier, all girls of family, assembled at that moment at the mansion of the lady widow De Gondelaurier, on account of Monseigneur de Beaujeu and madame his wife, who were to come to Paris in April, to choose *accompagneresses d'honneur*, or maids of honor, to accompany the Dauphiness Marguerite, on the occasion of her reception in Picardy, at the hands of the Flemings, on her way to the court of France. Now, all the hobereaux or gentry for thirty leagues round, were seeking this honor for their daughters, and a good many of them had already brought or sent them to Paris. The young ladies in question had been entrusted by their parents to the discreet and reverend keeping of Madame Aloïse de Gondelaurier, widow of a ci-devant master of the king's cross-bowmen, now living in retirement with her only daughter, at her house in the Place du Parvis-Notre-Dame, at Paris.

The balcony at which these young ladies were amusing themselves, opened into an apartment richly hung with fawn-colored Flanders leather printed with golden foliage. The beams that ran across the ceiling, diverting the eye with a thousand fantastic carvings, painted and gilt. Splendid enamels were glittering here and there upon the lids of cabinets curiously carved; and a boar's head in china crowned a magnificent side-board, the two steps of which announced that the mistress of the house was the wife or widow of a knight banneret. At the upper end of the room, beside a lofty chimney-piece, covered with emblazonry from top to bottom, was seated, in a rich fauteuil of red velvet, the lady of Gondelaurier, whose fifty-five years of age were no less distinctly written on her dress than on her face. Beside her a young man was standing, of very imposing mien, though partaking somewhat of vanity and bravado—one of those fine fellows whom all women agree to admire, although their physiognomy is precisely that which makes grave and discerning men shake their heads. This young cavalier wore the brilliant uniform of a captain of archers of the ordonnance du roi or household troops—which uniform too closely resembled the costume of Jupiter, which the reader has already had an opportunity of admiring in the first chapter of this history, for us to weary him with a second description of it.

The young ladies were seated, part in the room, part in the balcony; the former on cushions of Utrecht velvet with gold corner-plates; the latter on oak stools carved in flowers and figures. Each of them held in her lap part of a large piece of tapestry, on which they were all at work, while one long end of it lay on the matting which covered the floor.

They were talking among themselves, in that whispering voice, and with those half-stifled laughs, so common in an assembly of young girls where there is a young man among them. The young man himself, whose presence had the effect of bringing into play all this feminine vanity, appeared, on his part, to care very little about it; and, while the lovely girls were vying with each other in endeavoring to attract his attention, he was specially occupied in polishing, with his doeskin glove, the buckle of his sword-belt.

From time to time, the old lady addressed him in a low voice, and he answered as well as he was able, with a sort of awkward and constrained politeness. From the smiles and significant gestures of Madame Aloïse as well as the glances which she threw toward her daughter Fleur-de-Lys as she spoke low to the captain, it was evident that the subject of their conversation was some previous betrothing, some marriage doubtless about to take place between the young man and Fleur-de-Lys. And from the cold embarrassed air of the officer, it was easy to see that so far at least as he was concerned, love had no longer any part in the matter. His whole demeanor conveyed an idea of constraint and ennui, which a modern French subaltern on garrison duty would admirably render by the exclamation, Quelle chienne de corvée!

The good lady, infatuated, like any other silly mother, with her daughter's charms, did not perceive the officer's want of enthusiasm, but exerted herself strenuously to point out in a whisper the infinite grace with which Fleur-de-Lys used her needle or wound her silk.

"Do look now, petit cousin," said she, pulling him by the sleeve toward her, and speaking in his ear. "Look at her! see, now she stoops."

"Yes, indeed," answered the young man, and fell back into his cold abstracted silence.

Shortly after, he had to lean again, on Dame Aloïse saying to him: "Did you ever see a more charming lightsome face than that of your betrothed? Can anything be more fair or more lovely? Are not those hands perfect? and that neck, does it not assume every graceful curve of the swan's?—How I envy you at times! and how happy you are, in being a man, wicked rogue that you are! Is not my Fleur-de-Lys adorably beautiful? and are you not passionately in love with her?"

"Assuredly," answered he, thinking all the time of something else.

"Speak to her, then," said Madame Aloïse, abruptly pushing him by the shoulder; "say something to her you're grown quite timid."

We can assure our readers that timidity was neither a virtue nor a defect of the captain's. He endeavored, however, to do as was bid.

"Belle cousine," said he, approaching Fleur-de-Lys, "what is the subject of this tapestry you are so busy with?"

"Beau cousin," answered Fleur-de-Lys, in a pettish tone, "I have already told you three times; it is grotto of Neptunus."

It was evident that Fleur-de-Lys saw more clearly than her mother through the cold, absent manner of the captain. He felt the necessity of entering into conversation.

"And for what is all this fine Neptune-work intended?" asked he.

"For the abbey of Saint-Antoine des Champs," said Fleur-de-Lys, without raising her eyes.

The captain took up a corner of the tapestry: "And pray, ma belle cousine, who is that big gendarme fellow there disguised as a fish, and blowing his trumpet till his cheeks are bursting?"

"This is Trito," answered she.

There was still a degree of pettishness in the tone of the few words uttered by Fleur-de-Lys. The young man understood that it was indispensable he should whisper in her ear some pretty nothing, some gallant compliment or other—no matter what. He accordingly leaned over, but his imagination could furnish nothing more tender or familiar than this: "Why does your mother always wear that petticoat with her arms worked upon it, like our great-grandmothers of Charles the VII.'s time? Pray tell her, belle cousine, that it's not the fashion of the present day, and that, all emblazoned in that way, her dress makes her look like a walking mantelpiece. 'Pon honor, no one sits under their banner in that way now, I assure you."

"Fleur-de-Lys raised her fine eyes toward his reproachfully: "Is that all you have to assure me of?" said she in a low tone.

Meanwhile the good Dame Aloïse, delighted to see them thus leaning over and whispering with each other, exclaimed, playing all the while with the clasps of her prayer-book: "Touching picture of love!"

The captain, more and more at a loss, passed to the subject of the tapestry again. "It is really a beautiful piece of work!" he cried.

At this juncture, Colombe de Gaillefontaine, another beautiful white-skinned blonde, dressed up to the neck in blue damask, ventured to put in a word, addressed to Fleur-de-Lys, but in the hope that the handsome captain would answer her: "My dear Gondelaurier, did you ever see the tapestry at the Hôtel de la Roche-Guyon?"

"Is that the hôtel where the garden is belonging to the Lingère of the Louvre?" asked Diane de Christeuil, laughing; for, having fine teeth, she laughed on all occasions.

"And where that big old tower is, part of the ancient wall of Paris?" added Amelotte de Montmichel, a pretty curly-headed fresh-looking brunette, who had a habit of sighing, just as the other laughed, without knowing why.

"My dear Colombe," said Dame Aloïse, "are you speaking of the hôtel which belonged to Monsieur de Bacqueville in the reign of Charles the VIth? There is indeed magnificent tapestry there, of the high warp."

"Charles the VIth! King Charles the VIth!" muttered the young captain, curling his moustaches. "Mon Dieu! what a memory the good lady has for everything old!"

Madame de Gondelaurier continued: "Superb tapestry indeed! So superior that it is considered unrivalled!"

At that moment, Bérangère de Champ-chevrier, an airy little creature of seven years of age, who was looking into the square through the tri-foliated ornaments of the balcony, cried out, "Oh! do look, dear god-mamma Fleur-de-Lys, at that pretty dancing-girl who is dancing in the street, and playing the tambourine in the midst of those common people!"

The sonorous vibration of a tambourine was, in fact, heard by the party. "Some gypsy girl from Bohemia," said Fleur-de-Lys, turning her head carelessly toward the square.

"Let us see! let us see!" cried her lively companions; and they all ran to the front of the balcony, while Fleur-de-Lys, musing over the coldness of her affianced

lover, followed them slowly; and the latter, relieved by
this incident, which cut short an embarrassed conversation, returned to the farther end of the room with the
satisfied air of a soldier relieved from duty. And yet no
unpleasing service was that of the lovely Fleur-de-Lys;
and such it had appeared to him formerly; but the captain had by degrees become dissipated, and the prospect
of an approaching marriage grew more and more repulsive to him every day. Besides, he was of a fickle disposition; and, if one may say so, of rather vulgar tastes.
Although of very noble birth, he had contracted, under
his officer's accoutrements, more than one habit of the
common soldier. He delighted in the tavern and its
accompaniments, and was never at his ease but amidst
gross language, military gallantries, easy beauties, and
as easy successes. He had notwithstanding received
from his family some education and some politeness of
manner; but he had too early been a rover, had too
early kept garrison, and each day the polish of the
gentleman became more and more worn away under the
friction of the gendarme's baldric. Though still continuing to visit her occasionally, through some small
remnant of common respect, he felt doubly constrained
with Fleur-de-Lys; first, because by dint of dividing his
love among so many different objects he had very little
left for her; and next, because, surrounded by a number of fine women of stiff, decorous, and formal manners,
he was constantly in fear lest his lips, accustomed to the
language of oaths, should inadvertently break through
their bounds and let slip some unfortunate tavern-slang
or other. The effect may be imagined!

And yet, with all this were mingled great pretensions
to elegance, taste in dress, and noble bearing. Let
these things be reconciled as they may—our office is
simply that of the historian.

He had been for some minutes thinking of something
or of nothing, leaning in silence against the carved mantelpiece, when Fleur-de-Lys turning suddenly round,
addressed him—for after all, the poor girl only pouted
in self-defense:

" Beau cousin, did you not tell us of a little gypsy girl you saved from a parcel of thieves about a month ago, as you were going the counter-watch at night?"

" I believe I did, belle cousine," said the captain.

" Well," rejoined she, " perhaps it is that very gypsy girl who is now dancing in the Parvis. Come and see if you recognize her, beau cousin Phœbus."

A secret desire of reconciliation was perceptible in the gentle invitation she gave him to draw near her, and in the care she took to call him by his name. Captain Phœbus de Chateupers (for it is he whom the reader has had before him from the beginning of this chapter) with tardy steps approached the balcony.

" Look," said Fleur-de-Lys tenderly, placing her hand on his arm, " look at that little girl, dancing there in the ring !—Is that your gypsy girl ? "

Phœbus looked, and said: " Yes—I know her by her goat."

"Ah !—so there is !—a pretty little goat!" said Amelotte, clasping her hands with delight.

"Are its horns really gold?" asked little Bérangère.

Without moving from her fauteuil, Dame Aloïse inquired : " Is it one of those gypsy girls that arrived last year by the Porte Gibard?"

" My dear mother," said Fleur-de-Lys gently, " that gate is now called Porte d'Enfer."

Mademoiselle de Gaundelaurier knew how much the captain's notions were shocked by her mother's antiquated modes of speech. Indeed he was already on the titter, and began to mutter between his teeth : " Porte Gibard! Porte Gibard! That's to make way for King Charles VI."

" Godmamma," exclaimed Bérangère, whose eyes, incessantly in motion, were suddenly raised toward the top of the towers of Notre-Dame, " who is that black man up there ? "

All the girls raised their eyes. A man in fact was leaning with his elbows upon the topmost balustrade of the northern tower, which looked toward the Grève. It was the figure of a priest ; and they could clearly dis-

ern both his costume and his face, which was resting
on his two hands. Otherwise he was as motionless as
a statue; his steady gaze seemed riveted to the Place.
There was in it something of the immobility of the kite
when it has just discovered a nest of sparrows and is
looking down upon it.

"It is monsieur the archdeacon of Joas," said Fleur-
de-Lys.

"You've good eyes if you know him at this distance,"
observed La Gaillefontaine.

"How he looks at the little dancing-girl," remarked
Diane de Christeuil.

"Let the gypsy girl beware," said Fleur-de-Lys; "for
he loves not Egypt."

"It's a great pity that man looks at her so," added
Amelotte de Montmichel; "for she dances delight-
fully."

"Beau cousin Phœbus," said Fleur-de-Lys, suddenly, "since you know this little gypsy girl, beckon
to her to come up. It will be an amusement for us."

"Oh, yes!" cried all her companions, clapping their
hands.

"It's really not worth while," answered Phœbus,
"she has forgotten me, I dare say; and I don't so
much as know her name. However, since you wish it,
ladies, I will see." And leaning over the balustrade of
the balcony, he began to call out—"Little girl!"

The dancing-girl was not at that moment playing her
tambourine; and, turning her head toward the point
from whence she heard herself called, her brilliant eyes
rested on Phœbus, and she stopped short suddenly.

"Little girl," repeated the captain, and he beckoned
to her to come in.

The young girl looked at him again; then blushed as
if a flame had risen to her cheeks; and, taking her tambourine under her arm, she made her way through the
midst of the gaping spectators, toward the door of the
house where Phœbus was, with slow and tottering steps,
and with the troubled air of a bird yielding to the fasci
nation of a serpent.

A moment or two after, the tapestry hanging at th
entrance was raised, and the gypsy girl made her ap
pearance on the threshold of the room, blushing, con
fused, and out of breath, her large eyes cast down, and
not daring to advance a step further.

Bérangère clapped her hands.

Meanwhile, the dancing-girl remained motionless a
the entrance of the apartment. Her appearance ha
produced on this group of young women a singula
effect. It is certain that a vague and undefined desir
of pleasing the handsome officer at once animated th
whole party; that the splendid uniform was the objec
at which all their coquetry was aimed; and that, fron
the time of his being present, there had arisen among
them a certain tacit, covert rivalry, scarcely acknowl
edged to themselves, but which did not the less constantly display itself in all their gestures and remarks.
Nevertheless, as they all possessed nearly the same degree of beauty, they contended with equal arms, and
each might reasonably hope for victory. The arrival of
the gypsy girl suddenly destroyed this equilibrium.
Her beauty was of so rare a cast that, the moment she
entered the apartment, she seemed to shed around it
a sort of light peculiar to herself. Within this enclosed
chamber, surrounded by its dusky hangings and wains-
cotings, she was incomparably more beautiful and
radiant than in the public square. She was as the
torch suddenly brought from the mid-day light into the
shade. The noble damsels were dazzled by it in spite
of themselves. Each felt that her beauty had in some
degree suffered; and, in consequence, their line of battle (if we may be allowed the expression) was changed
immediately, without a single word being uttered by
any of them. But they understood each other perfectly. The instincts of women comprehend and correspond with each other more quickly than the understandings of men. An enemy had arrived in the midst
of them; all felt it—all rallied. One drop of wine is
sufficient to tinge a whole glass of water; and to diffuse a certain degree of ill-temper throughout a com-

any of pretty women, it is only necessary for one still prettier to make her appearance—especially when there is but one man in the way. Thus the gypsy girl's reception proved mightily freezing. They eyed her from head to foot; then looked at each other; and that was enough—all was understood. Meanwhile the young girl, waiting for them to speak to her, was so much affected that she dared not raise her eyelids.

The captain was the first to break silence.

" 'Pon honor," said he, with his tone of brainless assurance, " here's a charming creature! What do you think of her, belle cousine?"

This observation, which a more delicate admirer would at least have made in an undertone, did not tend to dissipate the feminine jealousies which were on the alert in the presence of the gypsy girl.

Fleur-de-Lys answered the captain with a simpering affectation of contempt— "Ah, not amiss."

The others whispered together.

At length, Madame Aloïse, who was not the less jealous for being so on her daughter's account, addressed the dancing-girl:

" Come hither, little girl," said she.

" Come hither, little girl!" repeated, with comic dignity, little Bérangère, who would have stood about as high as her hip.

The gypsy girl advanced toward the noble lady.

" My pretty girl," said Phœbus, significantly, likewise advancing a few paces toward her, " I don't know whether I have the supreme felicity of being remembered by you."

She interrupted him by saying, with a look and smile of infinite sweetness, " Oh! yes."

" She has a good memory," observed Fleur-de-Lys.

" So," resumed Phœbus, " you contrived to make your escape in a hurry the other evening. Did I frighten you?"

" Oh! no," said the gypsy girl. There was, in the accent with which this " Oh! no," following immediately the " Oh! yes," was pronounced, an indescribable something which stung poor Fleur-de-Lys.

"You left me in your stead, my fair one," continued the captain, whose tongue became unloosed while speaking to the girl out of the street, "a rare grim-faced fellow, hump-backed and one-eyed, the ringer of the bishop's bells, I believe. They tell me he's an archdeacon's bastard and a devil by birth. He has a pretty name too; they call him Quatre-Temps,* Pâques-Fleuries,† Mardi-Gras,‡ I don't know what!—a bell-ringing, holiday name, in short. And so he thought fit to carry you off, as if you were made for such fellows as beadles! That is going a little too far. What the deuce could that screech-owl want with you? eh!"

"I don't know," answered she.

"Only imagine his insolence! a bell-ringer to carry off a girl like a viscount! a clown poaching the game of gentlemen! a rare piece of assurance, truly! But he paid pretty dear for it. Maître Pierrat Torterue is as rough a groom as ever curried a rascal; and your ringer's hide—if that will please you—got a thorough dressing at his hands, I warrant you."

"Poor man!" said the gypsy girl, the scene of the pillory brought back to her remembrance by these words.

The captain burst out laughing. "*Corne-de-bœuf!* your pity's about as well placed as a feather in a pig's tail. May I have a belly like a pope, if . . . . ." He stopped suddenly short. "Pardon me, ladies—I fear I was about to let slip some nonsense or other."

"Fie, monsieur!" said La Gaillefontaine.

"He speaks to this creature in her own language," added Fleur-de-Lys in an undertone, her vexation increasing every moment. This vexation was not diminished by seeing the captain, delighted with the gypsy girl, and above all with himself, turn round on his heel and repeat with naïve and soldier-like gallantry: "A lovely girl, upon my soul!"

"Very barbarously dressed!" said Diane de Christeuil, laughing to show her fine teeth.

---

* Quatre-Temps—Ember-week.
† Pâques Fleuries—Palm-Sunday.
‡ Mardi-gras—Shrove-Tuesday.

This remark was like a flash of light for the others It gave to view the gypsy's assailable point ; having noth ing to find fault with in her person, they all fell upon her dress.

"It's very true," said La Montmichel. "Pray, little girl, where did you learn to run about the streets in that way, without either neckerchief or tucker?"

"What a dreadful short petticoat!" added La Gaille-fontaine.

"You'll get yourself taken up, child, by the sergeants of the douzaine, for your gilt belt," continued Fleur-de-Lys harshly.

"Little girl, little girl," resumed Christeuil with an unmerciful smile, "if you had the decency to wear sleeves on your arms, they would not get so sun-burn-ed."

It was a sight worthy a more intelligent spectator than Phœbus, to watch how those fine girls, with their envenomed and angry tongues, turned, glided, and wound, as it were, around the street dancer ; they were at once cruel and courteous ; they searched and pried maliciously into every part of her poor wild dress of spangles and tinsel. Then followed the laugh, the iron-ical jest, humiliations without end. Sarcasms, haughty condescensions, and evil looks were poured upon the gypsy girl. One might have fancied them some of those young Roman ladies that used to amuse them-selves with thrusting golden pins into the bosom of some beautiful slave ; or have likened them to elegant greyhounds, turning, wheeling, with distended nostrils and eager eyes, around some poor hind of the forest whom nothing but their master's eye prevents them from devouring.

And what, in fact, was a poor dancing-girl of the pub-lic square to those high-born maidens? They did not seem so much as to recognize her presence ; but spoke of her, before her, and to herself, aloud, as of some-thing, pretty enough perhaps, but at the same time loathsome and abject.

The gypsy girl was insensible to these petty stings,

From time to time, a glow of shame or a flash of anger inflamed her eyes and cheeks—a disdainful exclamation seemed to hover on her lips—she made contemptuously the little grimace with which the reader is already familiar—but remained motionless, her eyes fixed, with a sweet, resigned, and melancholy expression upon Phœbus. In this look, too, were mingled delight and tenderness. It seemed as if she restrained herself for fear of being driven away.

As for Phœbus himself, he laughed, and took the gypsy girl's part, with a mixture of pity and impertinence. "Let them talk, little one," repeated he, jingling his gold spurs; "doubtless, your dress is a little wild and extravagant; but in a charming girl like you, what does that signify?"

"Mon Dieu!" exclaimed the blonde Gaillefontaine, drawing up her swan-like neck with a bitter smile, "I see that messieurs the king's archers take fire easily at bright gypsy eyes."

"And why not?" said Phœbus.

At this rejoinder, uttered carelessly by the captain, like a stone thrown at random, the fall of which one does not so much as turn to watch, Colombe began to laugh, as did Amelotte, Diane, and Fleur-de-Lys; while a tear rose at the same time to the eyes of the latter.

The gypsy girl, who had cast her eyes on the ground as Colombe and Gaillefontaine spoke, raised them all beaming with joy and pride, and fixed them again on Phœbus. She looked angelic at that moment.

The old lady, who observed this scene, felt herself piqued without well understanding why.

"Holy Virgin!" cried she suddenly, "what's that about my legs? Ah! the nasty animal!"

It was the goat, which had just arrived in search of its mistress, and which, in hurrying toward her, had got itself entangled by the horns in the pile of stuff which the noble lady's ample habiliments heaped around her whenever she was seated.

This made a diversion. The gypsy girl, without saying a word, disentangled the little creature's horns.

"Oh! here's the pretty little goat with the golden feet," cried Bérangère, jumping with joy.

The gypsy girl squatted on her knees, and pressed her cheek against the fondling head of the goat, as if to beg its pardon for having left it behind.

Meanwhile, Diane bent over and whispered in Colombe's ear: "Ah! mon Dieu! how is it I did not think of it before? It's the gypsy girl with the goat. They say she's a sorceress, and that her goat performs very miraculous tricks."

"Well," said Colombe, "let the goat amuse us now in its turn, and perform us a miracle."

Diane and Colombe eagerly addressed the gypsy girl. "Little girl, do let your goat perform a miracle."

"I don't know what you mean," said the dancing-girl.

"Why, a miracle—a conjuring trick—a feat of witch-craft."

"I do not understand," she replied. And she turned to caressing the pretty animal again, repeating, "Djali! Djali!"

At that moment Fleur-de-Lys remarked a little embroidered leathern bag hanging about the goat's neck. "What's that?" asked she of the gypsy girl.

The girl raised her large eyes toward her, and answered gravely, "That's my secret."

"I should like to know your secret," thought Fleur-de-Lys.

Meanwhile, the noble dame had risen angrily. "Come, come, gypsy girl; if neither you nor your goat have anything to dance to us, what do you do here?"

The gypsy girl, without answering, directed her steps slowly toward the door. But the nearer she approached it, the slower was her pace. An irresistible magnet seemed to arrest her steps. Suddenly, she turned her eyes moistened with tears toward Phœbus, and stood still.

"Vrai Dieu!" cried the captain, "you shall not go away thus. Come back and dance us something or other. By-the-by, sweet love, what's your name?"

" La Esmeralda," said the dancing-girl, without taking her eyes off him.

At this strange name the girls burst forth into an extravagant laugh.

" A formidable name indeed, for a young lady," said Diane.

" You see, plain enough," remarked Amelotte, " that she's an enchantress."

" My dear," cried dame Aloïse, seriously, "your parents never found that name for you in the baptismal font."

Meanwhile Bérangère, without any one's observing it, had, a few minutes before, enticed the goat into a corner of the room with a piece of sweet cake. In an instant they had become good friends; and the curious child had untied the little bag which hung at the goat's neck, had opened it, and spread its contents on the matting; it was an alphabet, each letter of which was inscribed separately on a small tablet of wood. No sooner were these toys displayed on the matting, than the child saw, with surprise, the goat (one of whose miracles, doubtless, it was) draw toward her, with her golden paw, certain letters, and arrange them, by pushing them about gently, in a particular order. In a minute, they formed a word which the goat seemed practiced in composing, so little was she at a loss in forming it; and Bérangère suddenly cried out, clasping her hands with admiration :

" Godmamma, Fleur-de-Lys—do see what the goat has been doing!"

Fleur-de-Lys ran to look, and started at the sight. The letters arranged on the floor formed, in the Gothic characters of the time, the word

$$\mathfrak{Phoebus}.$$

" Did the goat write that ?" asked she, with a faltering voice.

" Yes, godmamma," answered Bérangère. It was impossible to doubt it, for the child could not spell.

"Here's the secret!" thought Fleur-de-Lys. Meanwhile, at the child's exclamation they had all hurried forward to look; the lady mother, the young ladies, the gypsy, and the officer.

The gypsy girl saw the blunder the goat had committed. She turned red—then pale—and began to tremble like a guilty thing before the captain, who looked at her with a smile of satisfaction and astonishment.

"Phœbus!" whispered the girls, in amazement, "that's the captain's name!"

"You have a wonderful memory!" said Fleur-de-Lys to the petrified gypsy girl. Then bursting into sobs: "Oh!" stammered she sorrowfully, hiding her face between her two fair hands, "she is a sorceress!" while she heard a voice yet more bitter whisper from her inmost heart, "she is a rival!" And therewith she fainted away.

"My child! my child!" cried the terrified mother, "Begone, you diabolical gypsy."

La Esmeralda gathered together in a trice the unlucky letters, made a sign to Djali, and quitted the room at one door as Fleur-de-Lys was being carried out at the other.

Captain Phœbus, left alone, hesitated a moment between the two doors; then followed the gypsy girl.

CHAPTER II.

SHOWING THAT A PRIEST AND A PHILOSOPHER ARE DIFFERENT THINGS.

THE priest whom the young ladies had observed on the top of the northern tower, leaning over toward the square, and so attentive to the gypsy girl's dancing, was, in fact, the Archdeacon Claude Frollo.

Our readers have not forgotten the mysterious cell

which the archdeacon had appropriated to himself in this tower. By-the-way, we do not know whether it is not the same, the interior of which may be seen to this day through a small square window, opening toward the east, at about the height of a man from the floor, upon the platform from which the towers spring; a mere dog-hole now, naked, empty, and falling to decay; the ill-plastered walls of which are even at this time decorated here and there with a parcel of sorry yellow engravings representing cathedral fronts. We presume that this hole is jointly inhabited by bats and spiders, and that, consequently, a double war of extermination is carried on there against the flies.

Every day, an hour before sunset, the archdeacon ascended the staircase of the tower and shut himself up in this cell, where he sometimes passed whole nights. On this day, just as he had reached the low door of his little nook, and was putting into the lock the small key, with its intricate wards, which he always carried about him, in the escarcelle or large purse suspended at his side, the sound of a tambourine and castanets reached his ears. This sound proceeded from the Place du Parvis. The cell, as we have already said, had but one window, looking upon the back of the church. Claude Frollo had hastily withdrawn the key, and in an instant was on the summit of the tower, in that gloomy, thoughtful attitude in which the young ladies had first seen him.

There he was, grave, motionless, absorbed in one look, one thought. All Paris lay at his feet; with her thousand spires and her circular horizon of softly-swelling hills; with her river winding under her bridges, and her people flowing to and fro through her streets; with the cloud of her smoke; with her hilly chain of roofs pressing round Notre-Dame with redoubled folds; yet in all that city the archdeacon saw but one spot on its pavement, the Place du Parvis; in all that crowd, but one figure, that of the gypsy girl.

It would have been difficult to say what was the nature of that look, or whence arose the flame that issued from it. It was a fixed gaze, and yet full of trouble and tumult. And, from the profound stillness of his whole body, only just agitated at intervals by an involuntary shiver, like a tree shaken by the wind, his stiffened elbows more marble than the balustrade on which they leaned, and the petrified smile which contracted his countenance, one might have said that no part of Claude Frollo was alive but his eyes.

The gypsy girl was dancing, twirling her tambourine on the point of her finger, and throwing it aloft in the air as she danced the Provençal sarabands; agile, light, joyous, and unconscious of the formidable gaze which lighted directly on her head.

The crowd swarmed around her; occasionally, a man, tricked out in a red and yellow casaque or long loose coat, went round to make the people keep the ring; then returned to seat himself in a chair, a few steps off the dancer, and took the head of the goat upon his knees. This man appeared to be the companion of the gypsy girl. Claude Frollo, from the elevated spot on which he stood, could not distinguish his features.

No sooner had the archdeacon perceived this unknown, than his attention seemed to be divided between him and the dancer, and his countenance became more and more sombre. Suddenly he drew himself up, and a trembling ran through his whole frame. "Who's that man?" muttered he to himself; "I've always seen her alone before."

He then disappeared under the winding vault of the spiral staircase, and once more descended. Passing before the door of the bell-room, which was partly open, he saw something which struck him; it was Quasimodo, who, leaning toward an opening in those great slate eaves which resemble enormous projecting blinds, was likewise looking earnestly into the square. He was engaged in such profound contemplation that he did not observe his adoptive father passing by. His wild eye had in it a singular expression; it was a look at once tender and fascinated. "That's strange!"

17

murmured Claude; "is it at the gypsy girl that he is looking so?" He proceeded to descend. In a few minutes the moody archdeacon entered the square by the door at the bottom of the tower.

"What's become of the gypsy girl," said he, mingling with the group of spectators which the sound of the tambourine had collected together.

"I don't know," answered one of those nearest him; "she's just disappeared. I think she's gone to dance some fandango or other in the house opposite, whither they called her."

In the place of the gypsy girl, on that same carpet, the arabesques of which, but the moment before, seemed to vanish beneath the no less fantastic figures of her dance, the archdeacon saw no one but the red and yellow man, who, in order to gain a few testons in his turn, was parading around the circle, his elbows on his hips, his head thrown back, his face all red, his neck stretched out, with a chair between his teeth. On this chair he had fastened a cat, which a woman of the neighborhood had lent him, and which was swearing with terror.

"Notre Dame!" cried the archdeacon, just as the mountebank, the perspiration rolling off his face, was passing before him with his pyramid of chair and cat: "what does Maître Pierre Gringoire do there?"

The harsh voice of the archdeacon struck the poor devil with such commotion that he lost his equilibrium; and down fell the whole edifice, chair and cat and all, pell-mell upon the heads of the bystanders in the midst of inextinguishable hootings.

It is probable that Maître Pierre Gringoire (for he indeed it was) would have had a fine account to settle with the cat's proprietor, and all the bruised and scratched faces around him, if he had not hastily availed himself of the tumult to take refuge in the church, whither Claude Frollo beckoned him to follow.

The cathedral was already dark and solitary; the transepts were in thick darkness; and the lamps of the chapels were beginning to twinkle, so black had the

vaulted roofs become. The great central window of
the front alone, whose thousand tints were steeped in
one horizontal stream of the sun's declining rays, glis-
tened in the shade like a mass of diamonds, and cast
against the other extremity of the nave its dazzling
many-colored image.

When they had proceeded a few steps, Dom Claude,
leaning his back against a pillar, looked steadfastly at
Gringoire. This look was not the one which Gringoire
had apprehended, in his shame at being surprised by so
grave and learned a personage in his merry-andrew costume. There was in the priest's glance neither scoff
nor irony; it was serious, calm, and searching. The
archdeacon was the first to break silence.

" Come, Maître Pierre," said he, " you have many
things to explain to me. And first, how is it that I
have not seen you for the last two months, and that I
meet with you again in the public street, in rare guise,
i'faith, half red, half yellow, like a Caudebec apple!"

" Messire, a most marvellous gear is it indeed," said
Gringoire, piteously, " and behold me about as comfortable in it as a cat with a calabash clapped on her
head. Most hard is it, too, I acknowledge, that I
should subject those gentlemen, the sergeants of the
watch, to the risk of beating, under this casaque,
the humerus of Pythagorean philosopher. But what
would you, my reverend master? The fault is all in my
old coat, which basely forsook me in the depth of winter, under pretense that it was falling in tatters, and
that it was under the necessity of reposing itself in the
ragman's pack. What was to be done? Civilization has
not yet arrived at such a pitch that one may go quite
naked, as old Diogenes could have wished. Add to
this, that the wind blew very cold, and the month of
January is not the time to attempt successfully that
new step in refinement. This casaque offered itself—I
took it, and left off my old black souquenille, which,
for an hermetic philosopher like myself, was far from
being hermetically closed. Behold me, then, in my
buffoon's habit, like St. Genest. What would you

have? It's an eclipse. Apollo, you know, tended the flocks of Admetus."

"It's a fine trade you've taken up," replied the priest.

"I confess, my master, that it's better to philosophize than to poetize—to blow a flame in the furnace, or receive one from heaven—than to be carrying cats in triumph. And that's why, when you addressed me, I felt as silly as an ass before a roasting-jack. But what was to be done, messire!—one must eat every day; and the finest Alexandrine verses, to an empty stomach, are not to be compared to a piece of Brie cheese. Now, I composed for the Lady Margaret of Flanders, that famous epithalamium, you know; and the town has not paid me for it, pretending that it was not excellent —as if, for four écus, one could write a tragedy of Sophocles. Well, you see I was near dying of hunger. Fortunately for me, I am rather strong in the jaw; so I said to my jaw: 'Perform some feats of strength and equilibrium—find food for thyself—*Ale te ipsam.*' A parcel of vagabonds, who are become my good friends, taught me twenty different kinds of Herculean tricks; and now I feed my teeth every night with the bread they have earned in the day in the sweat of my brow. After all, *concedo*, I concede that it is but a sorry employ of my intellectual faculties, and that man is not formed to pass his life in tambourining and biting chairs. But, reverend master, it is not enough to pass one's life—one must do something to keep one's self alive."

Dom Claude listened in silence. All at once his sunken eyes assumed an expression so sagacious and penetrating, that Gringoire felt as if searched to his inmost soul by that look.

"Very well, Maître Pierre; but how is it that you are now in company with that dancing-girl of Egypt?"

"Why, just," said Gringoire, "because she is my wife and I am her husband."

The priest's dark eye took fire. "And hast thou done that, miserable man?" he cried, furiously grasping Gringoire's arm, "and hast thou been so abandoned of God as to lay thy hand upon that girl?"

"By my chance of paradise, monseigneur," answered Gringoire, trembling in every limb, "I swear to you that I have never touched her—if that be what disturbs you so."

"But what speak you, then, of husband and wife?" said the priest.

Gringoire eagerly related to him, as succinctly as possible, what the reader is already acquainted with—his adventure of the Cour des Miracles, and his broken-pitcher marriage—which marriage appeared, as yet, to have had no result whatever, the gypsy girl contriving to leave him every night, as she had done on the first, in single blessedness. "It's a bore," said he, "but that comes of my having had the misfortune to marry a maid."

"What do you mean?" inquired the archdeacon, whom this account had gradually appeased.

"It's very difficult to explain," answered the poet. "It's a superstition. My wife, as an old thief that's called among us the Duke of Egypt, has told me, is a foundling—or a lostling—which is the same thing. She wears about her neck an amulet, which they declare will some day make her find her parents again, but would lose its virtue if the girl lost hers. Whence it follows that we both of us remain quite virtuous."

"So," resumed Claude, whose brow was now clearing apace, "you believe, Maître Pierre, that this creature has not been approached by any man."

"Why, Dom Claude, what would you have a man do with a superstition? She has got that in her head. I do, indeed, believe it to be rarity enough, to find such a nunnish prudery keeping its wildness amidst all those gypsy girls so easily tamed; but she has three things to protect her: the Duke of Egypt, who has taken her under his safeguard, reckoning, perhaps, that he shall sell her to some jolly abbot or other; her whole tribe, who hold her in singular veneration, like an Our Lady; and a certain pretty little poniard, which the jade always carries about her in spite of the provost's ordinances, and which darts forth in her hand when you press her waist. It's a fierce wasp, I can tell you."

The archdeacon pressed Gringoire with questions.

La Esmeralda was, in Gringoire's opinion, a creature inoffensive, charming and pretty—allowance being made for a certain little grimace which was peculiar to herself—a girl artless and impassioned, ignorant of everything, and enthusiastic about everything, fond, above all things, of dancing, of bustle, of the open air—a sort of a bee of a woman, with invisible wings to her feet, and living in a continued whirl. She owed this nature to the wandering life she had always led. Gringoire had contrived to ascertain, that while quite a child, she had gone all through Spain and Catalonia, to Sicily, he thought, too, that the caravan of zingari to which she belonged, had carried her into the kingdom of Algiers—a country situated in Achaia —which Achaia was adjoining, on one side to Lesser Albania and Greece, on the other to the sea of the Sicilies, which was the way to Constantinople. The Bohemians, said Gringoire, were vassals to the King of Algiers, in his capacity of chief of the nation of the white Moors. Certain it was, that La Esmeralda had come into France while yet very young, by way of Hungary. From all those countries the girl had brought with her fragments of fantastic jargons, foreign songs and ideas, which made her almost as motley as her half Parisian, half African costume. However, the people of the quarters which she frequented loved her for her gayety, her gracefulness, her lively step, her dances, and her songs. In all the town, she believed herself to be hated by two persons only, of whom she often speaks with dread ; the Sachette of the Tour-Roland, a miserable recluse, that bore a strange malice against gypsy women, and was in the habit of heaping curses upon the poor dancing-girl every time she passed before her loop-hole ; and a priest who never met her without casting upon her looks and words that affrighted her. The mention of this latter circumstance visibly disturbed the archdeacon, but without Gringoire's much attending to his perturbation ; the two months that had elapsed having been quite sufficient

to make the poet forget the singular particulars of that
evening when he had first met with the gypsy girl, and
the apparent presence of the archdeacon on that occasion. For the rest, the little dancer, he said, feared
nothing. She did not tell fortunes, and so was secure
from those prosecutions for magic that were so frequently instituted against the gypsy women. And
then, Gringoire was as a brother to her, if not as a husband. After all, the philosopher very patiently endured
this kind of Platonic marriage. At all events there
were food and lodging for him; each morning he set
out from the truandry, most frequently in company
with the gypsy girl; he helped her to make in the
crossways her gathering of targes and petits-blancs;
each evening he returned with her under the same roof,
let her bolt herself in her own little chamber, and slept
the sleep of the just—a very agreeable existence on the
whole, said he, and very favorable to revery. And then,
in his heart and conscience, the philosopher was not
quite sure that he was desperately in love with the
gypsy. He loved her goat almost as much. It was a
charming animal, gentle, intelligent, clever, and knowing. Nothing was more common in the middle ages
than these knowing animals; at which the people
mightily wondered, and which frequently brought their
instructors to the stake. However, the sorceries of the
goat with the gilded feet were very harmless tricks
indeed. Gringoire explained them to the archdeacon,
whom these particulars seemed strongly to interest. In
most cases it was sufficient to present the tambourine
to the animal in such or such a manner, to obtain from
it the action desired. It had been trained to that by
its mistress, who had so singular a talent for that
species of tuition, that two months had been sufficient
for her to teach the goat to compose, with movable
letters, the word Phœbus.

"Phœbus!" said the priest. "Why Phœbus?"

"I don't know," replied Gringoire; "perhaps it's a
word that she thinks endowed with some magical and
secret virtue. She often repeats it in an undertone
when she thinks she's by herself."

"Are you sure?" rejoined Claude, with his penetrat ing look, "that it's only a word, and that it's not a name?"

"Name of whom?" said the poet.

"How should I know?" said the priest.

"This is what I imagine, messire; these gypsies are something of Guebres, and worship the sun—whence this Phœbus."

"That does not seem so clear to me as it does to you, Maître Pierre."

"Well, it's no matter to me. Let her mutter her Phœbus to her heart's content. It's a sure thing that Djali loves me already almost as much as she does."

"Who's Djali?"

"It's the goat."

The archdeacon placed his hand under his chin, and seemed ruminating for a moment. All at once he turned round abruptly to Gringoire:

"And you swear to me that you have not touched her?"

"Touched what?" said Gringoire. "The goat?"

"No—that woman."

"My wife? I swear to you I have not."

"And yet you are often alone with her."

"Every night for a full hour."

Dom Claude knit his brows. "Oh, oh," said he, "*Solus cum solâ non cogitabuntur orare Pater Noster.*"

"Upon my soul, I might say the *Pater*, and the *Ave Maria*, and the *Credo in Deum patrem omnipotentum*, without her taking any more notice of me than a hen does of a church."

"Swear to me by thy mother's womb," repeated the archdeacon with vehemence, "that thou hast not so much as touched that creature with thy finger's end."

"I could swear it, too, by my father's head," answered the poet. "But, my reverend master, just permit me to ask you a single question."

"Speak, sir."

"What does that signify to you?"

The pale countenance of the archdeacon reddened

like the cheek of a girl. He kept silence for a moment,
then answered with visible embarrassment : " Hearken,
Maître Pierre Gringoire. You are not yet damned,
that I know of. I feel interested for you, and wish
you well. Now, the slightest contact with that gypsy
girl of the demon would make you a vassal of Satan.
You know it's always the body that ruins the soul.
Woe to you if you approach that woman ! That's all
I have to say."

" I tried once," said Gringoire, scratching his ear ;
" it was the first day, but I only got myself stung."

"And had you that audacity, Maître Pierre ? " and
the priest's brow darkened again.

"Another time," continued the poet, smiling, " before
I went to bed, I looked through her keyhole, and indeed
I saw the most delicious damsel in her shift that ever
stepped upon a bedside with her naked foot."

" Go to the devil with you ! " cried the priest, with a
terrible look ; and pushing the amazed Gringoire by the
shoulders, he plunged his hasty strides under the darkest arches of the cathedral.

CHAPTER III.

THE BELLS.

SINCE the morning of his being pilloried, the inhabitants in the neighborhood of Notre-Dame thought
they perceived that Quasimodo's bell-ringing ardor had
remarkably abated. Before that time the bells were
going on all occasions ; long matin chimes which lasted
from Primes to Complins ; peals of the great bell for
high mass ; rich gamuts running up and down the small
bells for a wedding or a christening, and mingling in
the air like a rich embroidery of all sorts of delightful
sounds. The old church, all vibrating and sonorous,

was in a perpetual joyous whirl of bells. Some spirit of noise and whim appeared to be sending forth a never-ending carol through those brazen lips. Now that spirit seemed to have departed. The cathedral seemed to have grown wilfully sullen and silent. The holidays and interments had their simple accompaniment, bare and unadorned—just what the ritual demanded, and nothing more; of the double sound proceeding from a church, that of the organ within, and the bells without, the organ only was heard. It seemed as if there was no longer any musician in the steeples. Nevertheless, Quasimodo was still there; what had come to him, then? was it that the shame and desperation of the pillory scene still lingered about his heart, that the lashes of the torturer were ever present to his mind, and that his grief at such treatment had extinguished all feeling in him, even to his passion for the bells? Or was it rather that Marie had a rival in the heart of the ringer of Notre-Dame, and that the great bell and her fourteen sisters were neglected for something more beautiful and pleasing?

It happened that in the year of Our Lord 1482, the Annunciation fell on Tuesday, the 25th of March. On that day the air was so pure and light, that Quasimodo felt a little returning affection for his bells. He accordingly ascended the northern tower, while the beadle below threw wide the large doors of the church, which were formed, at that time, of enormous panels of strong wood, covered with leather, bordered with iron nails gilt, and encased with sculpture "very skillfully wrought."

Arrived in the high cage of the bells, Quasimodo fixed his eye for some time, with a sorrowful shake of the head, on his six songstresses, as if he sighed to think that something strange had intruded into his heart between himself and them. But when he had set them going—when he felt the whole cluster of bells moving under his hand—when he saw, for he did not hear it, the palpitating octave ascending and descending in the sonorous diapason like a bird hopping from branch to branch—when the demon of music, that demon who shakes a sparkling bundle of stretti, trills, and arpeggios, had taken possession of the poor deaf creature, then he became happy again ; he forgot everything, and the dilation of his heart expanded on his countenance.

He went to and fro, clapping his hands; he ran from one rope to another, animating the six songsters by his voice and gestures, like a leader of the band spurring on scientific musicians.

"Come, come, Gabrielle," said he, "pour forth all your sound into the square ; it's a holiday. Thibauld, none of your idleness. What ! you are lagging ! Get on with you. Are you grown rusty, lazybones ? That's it !—quick ! quick !—don't let the clapper be seen. Make them all as deaf as I am. Bravo ! Thibauld. Go it, Guillaume ! Guillaume, you are the biggest, and Pasquier's the least, and Pasquier goes best. I'll lay anything that those that can hear, hear him better than you. Well done, Gabrielle—harder ! harder ! Hey ! you there, The Sparrows, what are you both about ? I don't see you make the least noise. What's the meaning of those brazen beaks of yours, that seem to be gaping when they ought to be singing ? Come— work away ! it's the Annunciation. There's a fine sunshine, and we'll have a merry peal. Poor Guillaume— what ! are you out of breath, my old fellow ? "

He was fully occupied in goading on his bells, which were all six leaping one against another as in rivalry, and shaking their shining backs, like a noisy team of Spanish mules urged forward by the apostrophizings of the driver.

All at once, happening to cast his eye between the large slate scales which cover, at a certain height, the perpendicular wall of the steeple, he saw in the square a young girl fantastically dressed, who had stopped, and was laying down a carpet on which a little goat came and placed itself, and around whom a group of spectators was gathering. This view suddenly changed the course of his ideas, and cooled his musical enthusiasm. He stopped, turned his back to the bells, and squatted behind the slate eaves, fixing on the dancer that thoughtful, tender, and softened look which had already once astonished the archdeacon. Meanwhile, the forgotten bells all at once became utterly silent, to the great disappointment of the amateurs of ringing, who were listening to the peal in good earnest from off the Pont-au-Change, and who went away as confounded as a dog that has a bone offered him and a stone given him instead.

CHAPTER IV.

FATALITY.

IT happened, one fine morning in this same month of March—we believe it was on Saturday, the 29th, St. Eustache's day—that our young college friend, Jehan Frollo du Moulin, perceived, as he was dressing himself, that his breeches, containing his purse, emitted no metallic sound. "Poor purse!" said he, drawing it out of his fob. "What! not the smallest parisis! How cruelly have dice, Venus, and pots of beer disemboweled thee! Behold thee empty, wrinkled, and flabby! Thou art like the neck of a fury! I would ask you now, Messer Cicero and Messer Seneca, whose dog's-eared tomes I see there scattered upon the floor, of what use it is for me to know better than a governor of the mint, or a Jew of the Pont-aux-Changeurs, that a gold écu à la couronne is worth thirty-five unzains at twenty-five sous eight deniers parisis each; and that an écu au croissant is worth thirty-six unzains at twenty-six sous six deniers tournois apiece; if I've not one miserable black liard to risk upon the double-six? Oh! Consul Cicero! this is not a calamity from which one can extricate one's self by a periphrasis—by quemad-modums, and verumenimveros!"

He dressed himself with a sad heart. A thought came into his head as he was lacing his boots, which he at first repelled; it returned, however, and he put on his waistcoat wrong side outwards, an evident sign of a violent internal struggle. At length he threw his cap vehemently on the ground, and exclaimed: "Be it so! come what may, I'll go to my brother. I shall get a sermon, I know, but I shall get an écu as well."

He then put on hastily his fur-trimmed casaque, picked up his cap, and rushed out like a madman.

He turned down the Rue de la Harpe, toward the City. Passing the Rue de la Huchette, the odor from those admirable spits, which were then incessantly going, saluted his olfactory organs, and he cast an amorous look toward that cyclopean cookery which one day extorted from the cordelier Calatagirone the pathetic exclamation: *Veramente, queste rotisserie sono cosa stupenda?* But Jehan had not wherewithal to buy a breakfast; and he passed, with a profound sigh, through the gate of the Petit-Châtelet, that enormous double trefoil of massive towers which guarded the entrance to the City.

He did not so much as give himself time to throw, as was usual, a stone in passing at the miserable statue of that Perinet Leclerc, who had given up the Paris of Charles the Sixth to the English, a crime which his effigy, the face all battered with stones and soiled with mud, expiated during three centuries, as in an everlasting pillory, at the corner of the streets de la Harpe and de Bussy.

Having crossed the Petit-Pont, and strid down the Rue Neuve-Sainte-Geneviève, Jehan de Molendino found himself in front of Notre-Dame. Then all his indecision returned, and he walked about for some moments around the statue of M. Le Gris, repeating to himself with anguish, "The sermon is certain enough, the écru is doubtful."

He stopped a beadle who was coming out from the cloisters — "Where's Monsieur the Archdeacon of Joas?"

"I believe he's in his hiding-place in the tower," said the beadle; "and I advise you not to disturb him unless you come from some one like the Pope or the king himself."

Jehan clapped his hands. Bé diable! this is a prime opportunity for seeing the famous sorcery-box!"

Decided by this reflection, he advanced resolutely through the little dark doorway, and began to ascend the winding staircase of St. Gilles, which leads to the upper stories of the tower.

"I shall see!" he said, as he proceeded. "By the corbignolles of the Holy Virgin! it must be a curious concern, that cell which my reverend brother keeps so snugly to himself! They say he lights up hell's own fires there, and cooks at them the philosopher's stone. Egad! I care as little for the philosopher's stone as for a pebble; and I'd rather find over his furnace an omelet of Easter eggs fried in lard, than the biggest philosopher's stone in the world!"

Arrived at the gallery of the colonnettes, he took breath a moment, swearing against the interminable staircase by we know not how many million cart-loads of devils; he then continued his ascent by the narrow door of the northern tower, now closed to the public. In a few moments after, having passed by the cage of the bells, he came to a small landing contrived in a recess on one side, and, under the arched roof, a low pointed door; while a loophole opposite, in the circular wall of the staircase, enabled him to discern its enormous lock and strong iron bars. Persons in our day, desirous of visiting this door, might recently know it by this inscription, in white letters, on the black wall: J'ADORE CORALIE. 1823. *Signé, Ugène.* This diplomatic *Signé* is in the original.

"Whew!" said the scholar, "here it is, doubtless." The key was in the lock. The door was close by him; he pushed it gently, and put his head in at the opening.

The reader must have seen some of those admirable sketches by Rembrandt—who, in some respects, may be truly styled the Shakespeare of painting. Among so many wonderful engravings there is one in particular, an etching, representing, as is supposed, Doctor Faustus, which it is impossible to look at without astonishment. It represents a gloomy cell; in the middle is a table, loaded with hideous objects—death's heads, spheres, alembics, compasses, hieroglyphic parchments. The doctor is before this table, dressed in his wide great-coat, his head covered with a fur cap which reaches to his eye-brows. Only half of his body is seen. He has partly risen from his immense fauteuil, his bent knuckles are resting on the table, and he is gazing with curiosity and terror at a luminous circle, formed of magic letters, which are shining on the wall in the background like the solar spectrum in the camera obscura. This cabalistic sun seems to tremble before the eye, and fills the dim cell with its mysterious radiance. It is at once horrible and beautiful.

Something very similar to Faust's cell presented itself to the view of Jehan, when he ventured his head within the half-open door. It was a similar gloomy dim-lighted nook. There was also a large fauteuil and a large table; compasses; alembics; skeletons of animals suspended from the ceiling; a sphere rolling on the floor; hippocephales promiscuously with boccals in which were quivering leaves of gold; death's heads lying on sheets of vellum streaked all over with figures and characters; thick manuscripts piled up, all open, without any pity for the cracking corners of the parchment; in short, all the rubbish of science; dust and cobwebs covering the whole heap; but there was no circle of luminous letters, no doctor in ecstasy, contemplating the flaming vision as the eagle gazes at the sun.

Nevertheless the cell was not solitary. A man was seated in the fauteuil, and leaning over the table. Jehan, to whom his back was turned, could only see his shoulders and the back of his head; but he had no difficulty in recognizing that bald head, on which nature had bestowed an everlasting tonsure, as if to mark, by this external sign, the irresistible clerical vocation of the archdeacon

Jehan accordingly recognized his brother; but the door had been opened so gently that Dom Claude was not aware of his presence. The curious scholar availed himself of the opportunity to examine the cell for a few moments at his leisure. A large furnace, which he had not remarked at his first glance, was to the left of the fauteuil, under the small window. The ray of light which penetrated through this opening made its way through the circular web of a spider, who had tastefully traced her delicate rosace in the point of the window, and in the center of it the insect architect remained motionless, like the nave of this lace wheel. On the furnace were heaped in disorder all sorts of vessels—stone bottles, glass retorts, coal mattresses. Jehan observed with a sigh that there was neither frying-pan nor saucepan. "The kitchen apparatus is all cold!" thought he.

In fact, there was no fire in the furnace, and it seemed as if none had been lighted there for a long time. A glass mask, which Jehan remarked among the utensils of the alchemist, and which doubtless was used to protect the archdeacon's face when he was elaborating any formidable substance, lay in a corner, covered with dust, as if quite forgotten. By its side lay a pair of bellows, equally dusty, the upper side of which bore this motto encrusted in letters of copper—*Spira, spera !*

A great number of other mottoes were, according to the fashion of the hermetic philosophers, written upon the walls; some traced in ink, others engraved with a metallic point. Moreover, there were Gothic characters, Hebrew characters, Greek and Roman characters, pell-mell together; inscriptions overflowing at random, one upon the other, the more recent effacing the more ancient, and all entangled with each other, like the branches of a thicket, or pikes in a mêlée. It was, in fact, a strangely-confused mingling of all human reveries, all human science. Here and there one shone out above the rest like a banner amid the lances' heads, but for the most part they consisted of some brief Latin or Greek motto, after the ingenious fashion of the Middle

Ages; as thus: *Undè? indè?—Homo homini monstrum!
Astra, castra, nemen, numen.* Μέγα βιβλίον, μέλα
κακόν. *Sapere aude. Fiat ubi vult, etc.* Sometimes a
word apparently devoid of all meaning, as Ἀναγκοφαγία
—which perhaps concealed some bitter allusion to the
régime of the cloister; and sometimes it was a simple
maxim of clerical discipline, set forth in a regular hexameter:

"Cælestem dominum, terrestrem dicito domnum."

There were also scattered throughout pieces of Hebrew conjuration, about which Jehan, who was nothing
of a conjuror, and not even much of a Grecian, understood nothing; and the whole was crossed about in all
directions with stars, figures of men or animals, and triangles intersecting each other; which contributed in no
small degree to liken the daubed wall of the cell to a
sheet of paper over which a monkey has been dragging
about a pen full of ink.

The tout-ensemble of the retreat, in short, presented
a general aspect of neglect and ruin; and the sorry condition of the utensils led to the supposition that their
master had long been diverted from his labors by pur-
suits of some other kind.

This master, however, leaning over a vast manuscript,
adorned with singular paintings, appeared to be tormented by some idea which constantly mingled itself
with his meditations; so, at least, Jehan thought, as he
heard him exclaim, with the musing intermissions of a
waking dreamer, who thinks aloud:

"Yes; so Manou said and Zoroaster taught! the sun
is born of fire, the moon of the sun; fire is the soul of
the universe; its elementary atoms are diffused and in
constant flow throughout the world, by an infinite number of channels. At the points where these currents
cross each other in the heavens they produce light; at
their points of intersection in the earth they produce
gold. Light—gold; the same thing; fire in its con-
crete state; the difference between the visible and the

18

palpable, the fluid and the solid, in the same substance
—between vapor and ice—nothing more. These are
not chimeras—it is the general law of nature. But how
to extract from science the secret of this general law?
What! this light which bathes my hand is gold! these
same atoms dilated according to a certain law, it is only
necessary to condense them according to a certain other
law! How is it to be done? Some have thought of
burying a ray of the sun. Averroës, yes, it is Averroës
—Averroës buried one under the first pillar to the left
of the sanctuary of the Koran, in the grand mosque of
Cordova; but the vault was not to be opened, to see
whether the operation had suceeeded, under eight thousand years."

"The devil!" said Jehan to himself, "that's a long
time to wait for an écu."

"Others have thought," continued the archdeacon,
musing, "that it would be better to operate upon a ray
of Sirius. But it is difficult to get this ray pure, on account of the simultaneous presence of other stars,
whose rays mingle with it. Flamel considers that it is
more simple to operate on terrestrial fire. Flamel!
there's predestination in the name! Flamma! Yes,
fire. That is all. The diamond is in charcoal, gold in
fire. But how to extract it? Magistri affirms that
there are certain names of women which possess so
sweet and mysterious a charm that it is sufficient to
pronounce them during the operation. Let us hear
what Manou says about it : 'Where women are honored
the divinities are complacent; where they are despised,
it is useless to pray to God. The lips of a woman are
constantly pure ; they are as running waters, as rays of
the sun. A woman's name should be pleasing, soft, and
fanciful, should end with a long vowel, and resemble
words of benediction.' Yes, indeed, the sage is right;
Maria — Sophia — Esmeral . . . . Damnation! Ever
that thought."

And he closed the book with violence.

He passed his hand across his forehead, as if to chase
some idea which haunted him; then he took from off

the table a nail and a small hammer, the handle of which was ingeniously painted in cabalistic characters.

"For some time," said he, with a bitter smile, "I have failed in all my experiments ; one idea possesses me, and scorches my brain like a seal of fire. I have not so much as been able to discover the secret of Cassiodoros, whose lamp burned without wick or oil—a thing simple enough nevertheless."

"A plague upon it!" said Jehan through his teeth.

"One single miserable thought, then," continued the priest, "suffices to render a man weak and beside himself! Oh! how Claude Pernelle would laugh at me— she who could not for a moment turn aside Nicolas Flamel from his pursuit of the great work! What! I hold in my hand the magic hammer of Ezekiel! At each blow which, from the depth of his cell, the formidable rabbi struck upon this nail with this hammer, that one amongst his enemies whom he had condemned, even were he two thousand leagues off, sank a cubit's depth into the earth, which swallowed him up. The king of France himself, for having one evening inadvertently struck against the door of the thaumaturgus, sank up to the knees in his pavement of Paris. This happened three centuries ago. Well! I have the hammer and the nail, and yet these implements are no more formidable in my hands than a punching-tool in the hands of a smith. And yet it is only necessary to discover the magic word which Ezekiel pronounced as he struck upon the nail."

"What nonsense!" thought Jehan.

"Come, let us try," resumed the archdeacon, eagerly. "If I succeed, I shall see the blue spark fly out of the head of the nail. Emen-Hetan! Emen-Hetan! That's not it. Sigeani! Sigeani! May this nail open the grave for whosoever bears the name of Phœbus! . . . . . A curse upon it! still, again, eternally the same idea!"

And he threw aside the hammer angrily. He then sank so low into his fauteuil and upon the table, that Jehan lost sight of him behind the high back of his chair. For some minutes he could see nothing but his convulsed hand clenched over a book. All at once, Dom

Claude arose, took a pair of compasses, and engraved in silence on the wall, in capital letters this Greek word:

$$A'NA'\Gamma KH.$$

"My brother's a fool," said Jehan to himself; "it would have been much more simple to have written fatum—everybody's not obliged to know Greek."

The archdeacon reseated himself in his fauteuil, and leaned his head on his two hands, like a sick person whose temples are heavy and burning.

The scholar viewed his brother with surprise. He, for his part, knew not; he whose heart was as light as air—he, who observed no law in the world but the good old law of nature—he, who allowed his passions to flow according to their natural tendency, and in whom the lake of strong emotions was always dry, by so many fresh drains did he let it off daily, he knew not with what fury that sea of the human passions ferments and boils when it is refused all egress—how it gathers strength, swells, and overflows—how it wears away the heart—how it breaks forth in inward sobs and stifled convulsions, until it has rent away its dikes and even burst its bed. The austere and icy exterior of Claude Frollo, that cold surface of rugged and inaccessible virtue, had always deceived Jehan. The merry scholar never dreamed of the boiling, furious, and deep lava beneath the snowy brow of Etna.

We do not know whether any sudden perception of this kind crossed the mind of Jehan; but, giddy-brained as he was, he understood that he had seen what he should not have seen, that he had surprised the soul of his elder brother in one of its most secret frames—and that he must not let Claude discover it. Perceiving that the archdeacon had fallen again into his previous immobility, he withdrew his head very softly, and made a slight noise of steps behind the door, as of some one arriving and giving notice of their approach.

"Come in," cried the archdeacon from the interior of his cell "I was expecting you; I left the key in the door purposely; come in, Maître Jacques."

"TOOK A PAIR OF COMPASSES AND ENGRAVED IN SILENCE ON THE WALL."

The scholar entered boldly. The archdeacon, whom such a visit embarrassed extremely in such a place, shook in his fauteuil. "What! is it you, Jehan?"

"Still a J," said the scholar, with his ruddy, saucy, and joyous face.

The countenance of Dom Claude had recovered its severe expression. "What are you doing here?"

"Brother," answered the scholar, endeavoring to attain a decent, serious, and modest demeanor, twirling his cap in his hands with an air of innocence, "I came to ask—"

"What?"

"A moral lesson, of which I have great need." Jehan dared not add aloud, "And a little money, of which I have still greater need." This last member of the sentence remained unuttered.

"Sir," said the archdeacon coldly, "I am very much displeased with you."

"Alas!" sighed the scholar.

Dom Claude described a quarter of a circle with his fauteuil, and looked at Jehan earnestly: "I am very glad to see you."

This was a formidable exordium. Jehan prepared for a rough encounter.

"Jehan, I hear every day sad complaints of you. What was that scuffle about, in which you beat and bruised with a stick a certain little viscount, Albert de Ramonchamp?"

"Oh!" said Jehan; "a grand affair that! all about a good-for-nothing page that amused himself with splashing the scholars by galloping his horse through the mud."

"And what's this affair of Mahiet Fargel's, whose gown you have torn? *Tunicam dechiraverunt,* says the charge."

"Pshaw! a sorry Montaigu cappette! Isn't that it?"

"The accusation says tunicam—not cappettam. Do you understand Latin?"

Jehan made no answer.

"Yes, continued the priest, shaking his head; "see what study and letters are come to now! The Latin tongue is scarcely understood; the Syriac unknown; the Greek so odious, that it is not considered ignorance in the most learned to skip a Greek word without reading it, and to say: *Græcum est, non legitur.*"

The scholar raised his eyes boldly. " Brother, shall I tell you in good French the meaning of that Greek word on the wall?"

" What word?"

" *A'NA'ΓKH.*"

A slight blush spread itself over the mottled cheeks of the archdeacon, like a puff of smoke announcing externally the secret commotions of a volcano. The scholar scarcely remarked it.

" Well, Jehan," stammered out the elder brother, with difficulty, " what does the word mean?"

" Fate."

Dom Claude turned pale again, and the scholar continued carelessly: "And that word underneath, engraved by the same hand, *Aναγνεία,* signifies impurity. You see I know my Greek."

The archdeacon remained silent. This Greek lesson had set him musing. Master Jehan, who had all the finesse of a spoiled child, judged the moment favorable for venturing his request. So, assuming a particularly soft accent, he began:

" My dear brother, do you hate me so, then, as to look grim at me on account of a few poor scuffles and fisticuffs, dealt, all in fair play, amongst a pack of boys and marmosets, *quibusdam marmosetis ?* You see I know my Latin, brother Claude."

But all this fawning hypocrisy had not its accustomed effect on the severe elder brother. Cerebus did not snap at the honey-cake. The archdeacon's brow unfolded not a single wrinkle. " What is it you're aiming at?" said he.

" Well, then, the case is this," answered Jehan, bravely; " I want money."

At this audacious declaration the archdeacon's physiognomy completely assumed the pedagogic and paternal expression:

"You know, Mr. Jehan, that our fief of Tirechappe only brings in, including both the quit-rents and the rents of the twenty-one houses, thirty-nine livres eleven sous six deniers parisis. It's half as much again as in the time of the brothers Paclet; but it is not much."

"I want money," said Jehan, stoically.

"You know that the official decided that our twenty-one houses were held in full fee of the bishopric, and that we could only redeem this homage by paying to his reverence the bishop two marks of silver gilt, at six livres parisis each. Now I have not yet been able to get together these two marks; you know it well."

"I know that I want money," repeated Jehan, for the third time.

"And what do you want it for?" At this question a ray of hope shone in the eyes of Jehan. He put on his demure modest look.

"Hark you, my dear brother Claude—I do not come to you with any bad intention. I am not going to show off at taverns with your unzains, or to parade the streets of Paris in gold brocade trappings, with my lackey— *cum meo laquasio.* No, brother; it's for a good work."

"What good work?" asked Claude, a little surprised.

"Two of my friends wish to purchase some child bed-linen for a poor Haudriette widow—it's a charity—it will cost three florins, and I wish to subscribe to it."

"What are the names of your two friends?"

"Pierre l'Assommeur and Baptiste Croque-Oison."

"Humph!" said the archdeacon; "they are names that go about as fitly to a good work as a bombard would upon a high altar."*

It is certain that Jehan had very ill chosen the names of his two friends. He felt it when too late.

"And then," continued the shrewd Claude, "what sort of child bed-linen is it, to cost three florins, and that for the child of a Haudriette widow? And how long is it since Haudriette widows have begun to have brats in swaddling-clothes?"

---

* These two names are equivalent, in English, to Peter the Knocker-Down and Baptist, Filch-Gosling.

Jehan broke the ice once more.

"Well, then, I want some money, to go and see Isabeau-la-Thierrye, this evening, at the Val-d'Amour."

"Vile libertine!" exclaimed the priest."

"Ἀναγνεία!" said Jehan.

This quotation, which the scholar borrowed, perhaps mischievously, from the wall of the cell, had a singular effect upon the priest. He bit his lip, and his anger was lost in his confusion.

"Away with you," said he to Jehan, "I am expecting some one."

The scholar tried one more effort. "Brother Claude, give me, at least, one little parisis, to buy food."

"How far have you got with the decretals of Gratian?" asked Dom Claude.

"I've lost my copy-books."

"Where are you with the Latin classics?"

"Somebody has stolen my copy of Horatius."

"And whereabouts with Aristoteles?"

"'Faith, brother, what is the name of that father of the church who says, the errors of heretics have ever found shelter amid the thickets of Aristotle's metaphysics? A fig for Aristotle! I'll never mangle my religion with his metaphysics."

"Young man," continued the archdeacon, "at the last entry of the king, there was a gentleman named Philippe de Comines, who had embroidered on his horse's housings this motto of his, which I advise you to ponder over—*Qui non laborat non manducet.*"

The scholar remained a moment silent, his finger in his ear, his eyes bent on the ground, and his countenance chagrined. Suddenly he turned toward Claude with the lively quickness of a wagtail.

"So, my good brother, you refuse me a sou parisis, to buy me a crust at a tamellier's?"

"*Qui non laborat non manducet.*"

At this answer of the inflexible archdeacon, Jehan hid his head between his hands, like a woman sobbing, and exclaimed, with an expression of despair, "*O* τοτοτοτοτοι."

"What does all this mean, sir?" asked Claude, surprised at this freak.

"Well, what?" said the scholar? and he raised toward Claude his saucy eyes, into which he had been thrusting his fists, to make them look as if they were red with tears: "it's Greek—it is an anapæst of Æschylus which is admirably expressive of grief."

And here he burst into a fit of laughter so ludicrous and so violent that the archdeacon could not help smiling. It was in fact Claude's fault: why had he spoiled this boy?

"Oh, dear brother Claude," continued Jehan, emboldened by this smile, "look at my worn-out boots. Can any buskin in the world be more tragic than a boot with its poor sole hanging out its tongue so?"

The archdeacon had quickly recovered his former severity. "I will send you some new boots, but no money."

"Only one poor little parisis, brother," persisted the suppliant Jehan. "I'll learn Gratian by heart—I'll believe well in God—I'll be a perfect Pythagoras of science and virtue!—Only one little parisis, for pity's sake! Would you have me devoured by famine, which stands staring me in the face more with its gaping jaws, blacker, deeper, and noisome than Tartarus or a monk's nose?"

Dom Claude shook his wrinkled head—"*Qui non laborat . . .*"

Jehan did not let him finish.

"Well," cried he, "to the devil, then! huzza! I'll go to the tavern—I'll fight—I'll go and see the girls, and there shall be the devil to pay."

So saying, he threw his cap against the wall, and snapped his fingers like castanets.

The archdeacon looked at him seriously. "Jehan," said he, "you have no soul."

"In that case, according to Epicurus, I want a something, made of another something, which is without a name."

"Jehan, you must think seriously of amending your life."

"Oh, yes," cried the scholar, looking alternately at his brother and at the alembics on the furnace, " every thing's a-twist here, I see—ideas as well as bottles."

"Jehan, you are on the downward road; do you know whither you are going!"

"To the public-house," said Jehan.

"The public-house leads to the pillory."

"It's only another sort of lantern; and with that, perhaps, Diogenes would have found his man."

"The pillory leads to the gibbet."

"The gibbet is a balance, with a man at one end and the whole world at the other. It's fine to be the man."

"The gibbet leads to hell."

"That's a rousing fire."

"Jehan, Jehan! all this will have a bad end."

"It'll have had a good beginning."

At this moment the noise of steps was heard on the staircase.

"Silence!" said the archdeacon, putting his finger on his lips; "here's Maître Jacques. Hark you, Jehan," added he in a low voice, " beware of ever speaking of what you have seen and heard here. Hide yourself quickly under this furnace, and do not breathe."

The scholar skulked under the furnace, and just then a happy thought struck him.

"Apropos, brother Claude—a florin for not breath-ing!"

"Silence! I promise it to you."

"You must give it to me."

"Take it, then!" said the archdeacon, throwing him his purse angrily. Jehan crept under the furnace, and the door opened.

CHAPTER V.

THE TWO MEN IN BLACK.

THE person who now entered wore a black gown and a doleful mien. What, at the first glance, struck our friend Jehan (who, as may well be supposed, so placed himself in his corner as to be able to see and hear all at his good pleasure) was the perfect sadness both of the garment and the visage of this new-comer. There was, nevertheless, a certain meekness diffused over that countenance ; but it was the meekness of a cat, or of a judge—a sort of affected gentleness. He was very gray and wrinkled, was approaching his sixtieth year, had twinkling eyes, white eyebrows, a hanging lip and large hands. When Jehan saw that it was nothing more— that is to say, to all appearance, only a physician or a magistrate—and that this man's nose was very far from his mouth, a sign of stupidity, he ensconced himself in his hole, desperate at having to remain, he knew not how long, in such an uneasy posture, and in such bad company.

The archdeacon, in the meanwhile, had not so much as risen to receive this person. He motioned to him to be seated on a stool near the door ; and after a few moments' silence, during which he seemed to be carrying on some previous meditation, he said to him with a patronizing air, " Good-day to you, Maître Jacques."

" Your servant, maître," answered the man in black.

There was, in the two ways of pronouncing, on the one side, this Maître Jacques, and, on the other, this maître by distinction, the difference being monseigneur and monsieur, between domine and domne. It was evidently the meeting of the doctor and the disciple.

" Well," resumed the archdeacon, after another silence, which Maître Jacques did not care to disturb, " how do you succeed ?"

" Alas ! maître," said the other with a sorrowful smile, " I keep on blowing. As many cinders as I like, but not a spark of gold."

Dom Claude betrayed signs of impatience.

" I am not speaking to you of that, Maître Jacques Charmolue, but of the suit against your magician—Marc Cenaine, I think you call him—the butler of the Court of Accompts. Does he confess his sorcery ? Has the torture succeeded ?"

"Alas, no!" answered Maître Jacques, still with his sad smile, "we have not that consolation. That man's a perfect stone; we might boil him in the Marchéaux-Pourceaux, before he would say anything. However, we spare no pains to get at the truth. He has already every joint dislocated; we put all our irons on the fire, as says the old comic writer Plautus:

> Advorsum stimulos, laminas, crucesque, compedesque,
> Nervos, catenas, carceres, numellas, pedicas, boias.

But all to no purpose—that man's terrible—I quite lose my labor with him."

"You have found nothing fresh in his house?"

"Yes, yes," said Maître Jacques, feeling in his pouch, "this parchment. There are words in it which we do not understand. And yet, monsieur, the criminal advocate, Philippe Lheuiler, knows a little Hebrew, which he learned in that affair of the Jews of the Rue Kantersten at Brussels."

So saying, Maître Jacques unrolled a parchment. "Give it me," said the archdeacon. And casting his eyes over the scroll, "Pure magic, Maître Jacques!" cried he, "*Emen Hetan!* that's the cry of the witches when they arrive at their Sabbath. *Per ipsum, et cum ipso, et in ipso!* that's the command which chains the devil down in hell again. *Hax, pax, max!* that has to do with medicine; a spell against the bite of a mad dog. Maître Jacques, you are king's attorney in the ecclesiastical court—this parchment is abominable."

"We'll put the man to the torture again. Here's something else," added Maître Jacques, rummaging again in his bag, "which we found at Marc Cenaine's."

It was a vessel of the same family as those which covered the furnace of Dom Claude. "Ah!" said the archdeacon, "an alchemist's crucible!"

"I confess to you," replied Maître Jacques, with his timid and constrained smile, "that I have tried it over the furnace, but I have succeeded no better with it than with my own."

The archdeacon set about examining the vessel. "What has he engraved on his crucible?—*Och! och!*—a word to drive away fleas! This Marc Cenaine's an ignoramus. I can easily believe you'll not make gold with this! it will do to put in your alcove in the summer, and that's all."

"Since we are on the subject of errors," said the king's attorney, "I have just been studying, before I came up, the figures on the portal below; is your reverence quite sure that it's the opening of the book of natural philosophy that's represented there, on the side toward the Hôtel-Dieu, and that, among the seven naked figures at the feet of Our Lady, that which has wings at his heels is Mercurius?"

"Yes," answered the priest; "so Augustin Nypho writes, that Italian doctor who had a bearded demon which taught him everything. But we will go down, and I will explain to you from the text."

"Thank you, maître," said Charmolue, bending to the ground. "By-the-by, I had forgotten! When do you wish me to apprehend the little sorceress?"

"What sorceress?"

"That gypsy girl, you know, that comes and dances every day on the Parvis, in spite of the official's prohibition. She has a goat with devil's horns, which is possessed; it reads and writes, understands mathematics like Picatrix, and would be enough to hang all Bohemia. The prosecution is quite ready; and will soon be got through, take my word for it. She's a pretty creature, upon my soul, that dancing girl—the finest black eyes! —two Egyptian carbuncles! When shall we begin?"

The archdeacon was excessively pale.

"I will let you know," stammered he, in a voice scarcely articulate; he added with an effort, "Look you to Marc Cenaine."

"Never fear," said Charmolue, smiling; "when I get back I'll have him buckled on the bed of leather again. But he's a devil of a man—he tires out Pierrat Torterue himself, who has larger hands than I have. As says the excellent Plautus—

Nudus vinctus, centum pondo, es quando pendes perpedes.

"The torture with the roller is the most effectual—
we shall try it."

Dom Claude seemed sunk in gloomy abstraction.
He turned toward Charmolue. Maître Pierrat . . . .
Maître Jacques, I mean—look to Marc Cenaine."

"Yes, yes, Dom Claude. Poor man! he'll have suffered like Mummol. But what an idea! for a butler of
the Court of Accompts, who must know the text of
Charlemagne, *Stryga vel masca*, to attend the witches'
sabbath. As to the little one—Smelarda, as they call
her—I'll wait your orders. Ah! as we pass under the
portal, you'll explain to me that gardener painted in relief, that you see on entering the church—the Sower,
is it not? Eh, maître, what are you thinking about?"

Dom Claude, lost in his own thoughts, heard him
not. Charmolue, following the direction of his eyes,
saw that they had fixed themselves mechanically on the
large spider's web which hung like a drapery over the
small window. At that moment, a giddy fly, courting
the March sun, threw itself across the net, and got entangled in it. At the shaking of the web, the enormous
spider made a sudden movement from out his central
cell; then at one bound, rushed upon the fly, which he
bent double with his four feelers, while with his hideous
trunk he scooped out its head. "Poor fly!" said the
king's attorney in the ecclesiastical court; and he raised
his hand to save it. The archdeacon, as if starting out
of his sleep, held back his arm with convulsive violence.

"Maître Jacques," cried he, "let fate do its work!"

The king's attorney turned round quite scared. He
felt as if his arm was grasped with iron pincers. The
eye of the priest was motionless, haggard, glaring, and
remained fixed on the little horrible group of the spider
and the fly.

"Ah! yes," continued the priest, in a voice which
seemed to issue from the bottom of his heart; there is
a symbol of the whole!—She flies—she is joyous—she
emerges into life—she courts the spring, the open air,

liberty!—oh! yes, but she strikes against the fatal network—the spider issues from it, the hideous spider! Poor dancer! poor predestined fly! Maître Jacques leave it alone!—'tis fate! Alas! Claude, thou art the spider! Claude thou art the fly too! Thou didst hasten forward in search of knowledge, of the light, the sun—thy only care was to reach the pure air, the broad day-beams of eternal truth; but, rushing toward the dazzling loophole which opens on another world—a world of brightness, of intellect, of science—infatuated fly! insensate sage! thou didst not see the subtle spider's web, by destiny suspended between the light and thee—thou didst madly dash thyself against it, wretched maniac—and now thou dost struggle, with crushed head and mangled wings, between the iron antennæ of Fate! Maître Jacques, Maître Jacques, let the spider work on!"

"I assure you," said Charmolue, who looked at him without understanding him, "that I will not touch it. But let go my arm, maître, for pity's sake! you have a hand of iron."

The archdeacon heard him not. "Oh! madman!" continued he, without taking his eyes off the window. "And even couldst thou have broken through that formidable web, with thy gnat-like wings, thoughtst thou to have attained the light! Alas! that glass beyond—that transparent obstacle—that wall of crystal harder than brass, which separates all philosophy from the truth—how couldst thou have passed beyond it? Oh! vanity of science! how many sages have come fluttering from afar, to dash their heads against thee! —How many clashing systems buzz vainly about that everlasting barrier!"

He was silent. These last ideas, which had insensibly called off his thoughts from himself to science, appeared to have calmed him, and Jacques Charmolue completely brought him back to a sense of reality by addressing to him this question:—"Come, come, maître, when will you help me to make gold?—I long to succeed."

The archdeacon shook his head with a bitter smile. " Maître Jacques, read Michael Psellus, *Dialogus de energiâ et operatione dæmonum.* What we are doing is not quite innocent."

" Speak lower, maître! I have my doubts," said Charmolue. " But one may surely practice a little hermetic philosophy when one's only a poor king's attorney in the ecclesiastical court, at thirty crowns tournois a year. Only, let us speak low."

At that moment the noise of jaws in the act of mastication, issuing from under the furnace, struck the anxious ear of Charmolue.

" What's that ? " asked he.

It was the scholar, who, very tired and uneasy in his hiding-place, had just discovered a stale crust and a corner of mouldy cheese, and had begun to eat both, without any ceremony, by way of consolation and breakfast. As he was very hungry, he made a great noise, laying strong emphasis on each mouthful, and this it was that had roused and alarmed the king's attorney.

" It's a cat of mine," said the archdeacon, quickly, " feasting herself below, there upon some mouse or other."

This explanation satisfied Charmolue. " Why, indeed, maître," answered he, with a respectful smile, " all great philosophers have had some familiar animal. You know what Servius says—*Nullis enim locus sine genio est.*"

Meanwhile Dom Claude, fearing some new freak of Jehan's, reminded his worthy disciple that they had some figures on the portal to study together ; and they both quitted the cell, to the great relief of the scholar, who began seriously to fear that his knees would take the impression of his chin.

CHAPTER VI.

CAPTAIN PHŒBUS.

"TE DEUM LAUDAMUS!" exclaimed Maître Jehan issuing from his hole, " the two screech-owls are gone at last. *Och! och!— Hax! pax! max !*—fleas!—mad dogs!—the devil! I've had enough of their conversation! My head hums like a bell. Mouldy cheese into the bargain! Whew! let me get down and take the purse of my high and mighty brother, and convert all these coins into bottles."

He cast a look of tenderness and admiration into the interior of the precious escarcelle; adjusted his dress; rubbed his boots; dusted his poor furred sleeves, all white with ashes; whistled an air; pirouetted a movement; looked about the cell to see if there was anything else he could take; scraped up here and there from off the furnace some amulet in glassware by way of trinket to give to Isabeau-la-Thierrye; and finally, opened the door which his brother had left unfastened as a last indulgence, and which he in turn left open as a last piece of mischief; and descended the circular staircase skipping like a bird.

In the midst of the darkness of the spiral stairs he elbowed something, which moved out of the way with a growl; he presumed that it was Quasimodo; and his fancy was so tickled with the circumstance that he descended the rest of the stairs holding his sides with laughter, and was still laughing when he got out into the square.

He stamped his foot when he found himself on terra firma. "Oh!" said he, "most excellent and honorable pavement of Paris! Oh, cursed staircase, enough to wind the angels of Jacob's ladder! What was I thinking of to go and thrust myself into that stone gimlet which bores the sky, and all to eat bearded cheese and to see the steeples of Paris through a hole in the wall!"

He advanced a few steps, and perceived the two

19

screech-owls, that is to say, Dom Claude and Maître Jacques Charmolue, busy contemplating some sculpture on the portal. He approached them on tiptoe, and heard the archdeacon say in a whisper to Charmolue: "It was Guillaume de Paris that had a Job engraven on that stone of lapis-lazuli, gilt at the edges. By Job is meant the philosopher's stone, which must be tried and tortured to become perfect, as Raymond Lully says —*Sub conservatione formæ specificæ salva anima.*

"It's all one to me," said Jehan; "I've got the purse."

At that moment he heard a powerful and sonorous voice behind him uttering a series of formidable oaths: —"Sang-Dieu! Ventre-Dieu! Bé-Dieu! Corps de Dieu! Nombril de Belzébuth! Nom d'un pape! Corne et tonnerre!"

"My life for it," exclaimed Jehan; "that can be no other than my friend Captain Phœbus!"

This name of Phœbus reached the ears of the archdeacon just as he was explaining to the king's attorney the dragon concealing its tail in a bath from whence issue smoke and a king's head. Dom Claude started and stopped short, to the great astonishment of Charmolue, turned round, and saw his brother Jehan accosting a tall officer at the door of the Logis Gondelaurier.

It was, in fact, Captain Phœbus de Chateaupers. He was standing with his back against the corner of the house of his betrothed, and swearing like a Turk.

"I'faith, Captain Phœbus," said Jehan, taking him by the hand, "you swear with admirable unction."

"*Corne et tonnerre!*" answered the captain.

"*Corne et tonnerre* yourself," replied the scholar. "How now, my brave fellow? What's the meaning of this overflow of fine language?"

"Your pardon, friend Jehan," cried Phœbus, shaking him by the hand; "a spurred horse can't stop on a sudden. Now, I was swearing at full gallop. I've just left those silly women, and when I come away I've always my throat full of oaths, and if I didn't spit them out I should choke, *corne et tonnerre!*'

"Will you come and have something to drink?' asked the scholar.

This proposal tranquilized the captain.

"I would with all my heart, but I've no money."

"I have, though."

"Nonsense! let's see."

Jehan displayed the purse before the captain's eyes with dignity and simplicity. Meanwhile the archdeacon, having left Charmolue all aghast, had approached them, and stopped a few steps off, observing them both without their noticing him, so absorbed were they in the contemplation of the purse.

Phœbus exclaimed: "A purse in your pocket, Jehan! why it's the moon in a pail of water; one sees it but it's not there; there's nothing but the reflection. Egad! I'll lay anything they're pebble stones."

Jehan answered coolly, "These are the pebbles with which I pave my fob."

And without adding another word he emptied the purse upon a borne, or high curb-stone that was near, with the air of a Roman saving his country.

"Vrai Dieu!" growled out Phœbus—"Targes! grands blancs! petits blancs! mailles at two to a tournois! deniers parisis! and real eagle liards! It's enough to stagger one!"

Jehan remained dignified and immovable. A few liards rolled into the dirt; the captain, in his enthusiasm, stooped to pick them up. Jehan withheld him—"Fie, Captain Phœbus de Chateaupers!"

Phœbus counted the money; and, turning with solemnity toward Jehan, "Do you know, Jehan, said he, "that there are twenty-three sous parisis here? Whom have you been clearing out last night in Rue Coupe-Gueule?"

Jehan threw back his fair and curly head, and said, half closing his eyes as if in scorn, "What if one has a brother an archdeacon and a simpleton?"

"*Corne de Dieu!*" cried Phœbus, "the worthy man!"

"Let's go and drink," said Jehan.

"Where shall we go?" said Phœbus; "to the Pomme d'Eve?"

"No, captain, let's go to the Vieille *Science*—Une *vieille* qui *scie* une *anse*. That's a rebus, and I like a rebus."

"Deuce take the rebuses, Jehan; the wine's better at the Pomme d'Eve; and then, by the side of the door, there's a vine in the sun that cheers me when I'm drinking."

"Very well, then; here goes for Eve and her apple," said the scholar, taking Phœbus by the arm. "By-the-by, my dear captain, you said just now, Rue Coupe-Gueule. That's speaking very incorrectly; we are no longer so barbarous; we say Rue Coupe Gorge."

The two friends directed their steps toward the Pomme d'Eve. It is hardly necessary to say that they first gathered up the money, and that the archdeacon followed them.

The archdeacon followed them with a haggard and gloomy countenance. Was that the Phœbus whose accursed name, since his interview with Gringoire, had mingled with all his thoughts? He did not know; but, at any rate, it was a Phœbus; and that magic name was sufficient inducement for the archdeacon to follow the two thoughtless companions with a stealthy pace, listening to their words and observing their slightest gestures with anxious attention. However, nothing was easier than to hear all they said, so loud they talked, and so little did they care for the passers-by knowing their secrets. They talked of duels, girls, and pranks of all sorts.

At the turn of a street, the sound of a tambourine struck upon their ears from a neighboring crossway. Dom Claude heard the officer say to the scholar: "Tonnerre! let's quicken our steps."

"Why, Phœbus?"

"I'm afraid the gypsy will see me."

"What gypsy?"

"The little one with her goat."

"La Esmeralda?"

"That's it, Jehan. I always forget her devil of a name. Let's make haste; she'd recognize me, and I wouldn't have her accost me in the streets."

"Do you know her then, Phœbus?"

Here the archdeacon observed Phœbus chuckle, lean aside, and whisper something in Jehan's ear; Phœbus then burst out laughing, and tossed his head with a triumphant air.

"In very deed?" said Jehan.

"Upon my soul!" said Phœbus.

"This evening?"

"This evening!"

"Are you sure she'll come?"

"Are you a fool, Jehan? Does one ever doubt those sort of things?"

"Captain Phœbus, you are a happy gendarme."

The archdeacon overheard all this conversation. His teeth chattered; a visible shudder ran through his whole frame. He stopped a moment, leaned against a post like a drunken man, then followed the track of the two joyous boon companions.

Just as he came up to them again they had changed their conversation; and he heard them singing, at the full stretch of their lungs, the burden of an old song:

> "The lads the dice who merrily throw,
>   Merrily to the gallows go."

CHAPTER VII.

THE SPECTER MONK.

THE illustrious cabaret of the Pomme d'Eve was situated in the University, at the corner of the Rue de la Rondelle and the Rue du Bâtonnier. The principal room was on the ground floor, very large and very low, supported in the center by a heavy wooden pillar, painted yellow. There were tables all round; shining pewter pots hung up against the wall; a constant abundance of drinkers, and girls in plenty; a large casement looking to the street; a vine at the door, and over the door a creaking iron plate, with an apple and a woman painted upon it, rusted by the rain, and turning with the wind upon an iron pin. This sort of weather-cock looking toward the highway, was the sign of the house.

Night was falling; the street was dark; the cabaret, full of lighted candles, flamed afar like a forge in the darkness, and emitted the noise of glasses, of feasting, of oaths, of quarrels, all escaping through the broken panes. Through the mist which the heat of the room diffused over the long casement in front, were seen a multitude of figures confusedly swarming; and now and then there burst forth a loud peal of laughter. The people going along the street upon their business, passed by this tumultuous casement without casting their eyes that way. Only now and then some little tattered boy would spring up on his toes until he could just see in at the window, and shout into the cabaret the old bantering cry with which it was then the custom to follow drunkards: *Aux Houls, saouls, saouls, saouls !*

One man, however, was walking backward and forward imperturbably before the noisy tavern, looking toward it incessantly, and stepping no farther away from it than a pikeman from his sentry-box. He was cloaked up to the nose. He had just bought the cloak at a ready-made clothes shop near to the Pomme d'Eve, doubtless to secure himself from the cold of a March night—perhaps also to conceal his costume. From time to time he stopped before the dim lattice-leaded casement, listening, looking, and beating with his foot.

At length the door of the cabaret opened, and for that he seemed to have been waiting. A pair of boon companions came out. The gleam of light that now issued through the doorway cast a glow for a moment on their jovial faces. The man in the cloak went and placed himself on the watch under a porch on the other side of the street.

"*Corne et tonnerre !*" said one of the two companions, " it's on the stroke of seven. It's the hour of my assignation."

" I tell you," said the other, speaking thick, " that I don't live in the Rue des Mauvaises Paroles—*Indignus qui inter mala verba habitat*. I lodge in the Rue Jean-Pain-Mollet—*in vico Joannis-Pain-Mollet*—and you're a wry-brained fellow if you say the contrary. Everybody knows that he that gets once upon a bear's back is never afraid—but you've a nose for smelling out a dainty bit, like St. Jacques-de-l'Hôpital."

" Jehan, my friend, you're drunk," said his companion.

The other answered, staggering all the while : " It pleases you to say so, Phœbus, but it's proved that Plâto had the profile of a hound."

Doubtless the reader has already recognized our two worthy friends, the captain and the scholar. It seems that the man who was watching them in the dark had recognized them too ; for he followed with slow steps all the zigzags which the reeling scholar forced the captain to make, who, being a more seasoned drinker, had retained all his self-possession. By listening attentively, the man in the cloak overheard the whole of the interesting conversation which follows :

" *Corbacque !* try to walk straight, monsieur the bachelor ; you know that I must leave you. It's seven o'clock, and I have to meet a woman."

" Leave me, then. I can see stars and squibs. You're like Dampmartin Castle, that's bursting with laughter."

" By my grandmother's warts, Jehan, but this is talking nonsense a little too hard. By-the-by, Jehan, have you no money left ? "

" Monsieur the rector, it's no fault of mine. The *petit boucherie—parva boucheria—*"

" Jehan—friend Jehan—you know I've promised to meet that little girl at the end of the Pont St. Michel ; that I can take her nowhere but to La Falourdel's, the old woman's on the bridge, and that I must pay for the room. The old white-whiskered jade won't give me credit. Jehan, I pray you, have we drunk all the contents of the curé's pouch? Haven't you a single parisis left?"

"The consciousness of having spent our other hours well is a just and savory sauce to our table."

"*Ventre et boyaux!* a truce with your gibberish. Tell me—the devil's own Jehan—have you any coin left? Give it me, Bé-Dieu! or I'll search you all over, though I should find you as lousy as Job, and as scabby as Cæsar."

"Monsieur, the Rue Galiache is a street with the Rue de la Verrerie at one end of it, and the Rue de la Tixeranderie at the other."

"Well—yes—my good friend Jehan—my poor comrade—the Rue Galiache—good—very good. But, in heaven's name, come to your senses. I want but one sou parisis, and seven o'clock's the time."

"Silence around and attention to the song:

> "'When mice have every case devour'd,
> The King of Arras shall be lord;
> When the sea, so deep and wide,
> Is frozen over at Midsummer tide,
> Then all upon the ice you'll see,
> The Arras men their town shall flee.'"

"Well, scholar of Antichrist, the devil strangle thee!' exclaimed Phœbus; and he roughly pushed the intoxicated scholar, who reeled against the wall, and fell down gently upon the pavement of Philip-Augustus. Through a remnant of that fraternal pity which never absolutely deserts the heart of a bottle companion, Phœbus rolled Jehan with his foot upon one of those pillows of the poor man which Providence keeps ready against every curbstone and post in Paris, and which the rich scornfully stigmatize with the name of dungheaps. The captain reared up Jehan's head on an inclined plane of cabbage-stalks, and forthwith the scholar began to snore a most magnificent bass. However, all malice had not entirely left the heart of the captain. "So much the worse for thee, if the devil's cart picks

tnee up as it goes by," said he to the poor sleeping
clerk; and he went on his way.

The man in the cloak, who had kept following him,
stopped for a moment before the recumbent scholar, as
if agitated by some feeling of indecision; then heaving
a deep sigh, he went on also after the captain.

Like them, we will now leave Jehan sleeping under
the benevolent eye of the fair starlight; and, with the
reader's permission, we will track their steps.

On turning into the Rue St. André-des-Arcs, Captain
Phœbus perceived that some one was following him.
He saw, while accidentally casting round his eyes, a
sort of shadè creeping behind him along the walls. He
stopped—it stopped; he went on—then the shade went
on again also. This, however, gave him very little concern. "Ah! bah!" said he to himself, "it matters little—I've not a sou about me."

In front of the Collège d'Autun he made a halt. It
was at that college that he had shuffled through what
he was pleased to call his studies; and through a certain habit of a refractory schoolboy which still clung to
him, he never passed before the front of that college
without stopping to pay his compliments to the statue
of Cardinal Pierre Bertrand, which stood on the right
hand of the gateway. While pausing, as usual, before
the effigy of the cardinal, and snuffing the wind, the
street being there quite solitary, he saw the shadow approaching him slowly—so slowly that he had full time
to observe that this same shade had a cloak and a hat.
When it had nearly come up to him, it stopped, and remained almost as motionless as the statue of Cardinal
Bertrand itself. But it fixed upon Phœbus two steadfast
eyes, full of that vague sort of light which issues in the
night-time from the pupils of a cat.

The captain was brave, and would have cared very
little for a robber with a rapier in his hand. But this
walking statue, this petrified man, made his blood run
cold. At that time there were certain strange rumors
afloat about a specter monk that ranged the streets of
Paris in the night-time, and they recurred confusedly to

his recollection. He stood confounded for a few minutes, then broke silence, at the same time endeavoring to laugh. "Sir," said he, "if you be a thief, as I hope is the case, you're just now for all the world like a heron attacking a walnut-shell. My dear fellow, I'm a ruined youth of family. Try your hand hard by here. In the chapel of this college there's some wood of the true cross, set in silver."

The hand of the shade came forth from under its cloak, and fell upon Phœbus' arms with the force of an eagle's gripe, the shade at the same time opening its lips, and saying with emphasis, "Captain Phœbus de Chateaupers!"

"What the devil!" said Phœbus; "do you know my name?"

"I not only know your name," returned the man in the cloak, with his sepulchral voice; "but I also know that you have an appointment to-night."

"Yes," answered Phœbus, in amazement.

"At seven o'clock."

"In a quarter of an hour."

"At La Falourdel's."

"Exactly so."

"The old woman's on the Pont St. Michel."

"Yes—St. Michel-Archange, as the Paternoster says."

"Impious man!" muttered the specter. "With a woman?"

"*Confiteor.*"

"Whose name is——"

"La Smeralda," said Phœbus with alacrity, all his carelessness having gradually returned to him.

At that time, the gripe of the specter shook Phœbus' arm furiously. "Captain Phœbus de Chateaupers, you lie!"

Any one who could have seen, at that moment, the fiery countenance of the captain—the spring which he made backward, so violent that it disengaged him from the clutch which had seized him—the haughty mien with which he laid his hand upon the hilt of his sword —and, in the presence of all that passionate anger, the sullen stillness of the man in the cloak; any one who could have seen all that would have been affrighted There was somewhat of the combat of Don Juan and the statue.

"Christ and Satan!" cried the captain; "that's a word that seldom assails the ear of a Chateaupers! Thou durst not repeat it."

"You lie!" said the specter, coolly.

The captain ground his teeth. Specter monk—phantom—superstitions—all were forgotten at that moment. He now saw nothing but a man and insult. "Ha, ha! this goes well!" spluttered he in a voice choking with rage. He drew his sword; then, still stammering, for anger as well as fear makes a man tremble—"Hither!" said he, "directly! Come on! Swords! swords! Blood upon these stones!"

Meanwhile, the other did not stir. When he saw his adversary on his guard, and prepared to defend himself; "Captain Phœbus," said he, and his accent vibrated with bitterness, "you forget your assignation."

The angry fits of such men as Phœbus are like boiling milk, of which a drop of cold water allays the ebullition. These few words brought down the point of the sword which glittered in the captain's hand.

"Captain," continued the man, "to-morrow—the next day—a month hence—ten years hence—you'll find me quite ready to cut your throat. But first go to your assignation."

"Why, in truth," said Phœbus, as if seeking to capitulate with himself, "a sword and a girl are two charming things to meet in a rendezvous—but I don't see why I should miss one of them for the sake of the other, when I can have them both." And so saying, he put up his sword.

"Go to your assignation," resumed the unknown.

"Monsieur," answered Phœbus, with some embarrassment, "many thanks for your courtesy. It will, in fact, be time enough to-morrow, to make slashes and buttonholes upon each other in father Adam's doublet. I'm much obliged to you for giving me leave to pass one pleasant quarter of an hour more. I was indeed in hopes to have laid you quietly in the gutter, and still have arrived in time for the lady—the more so as it is debonnaire to make a woman wait for you a little on such an occasion. But you seem to me to be a fellow of mettle—so that the safest way is, to put off our game till to-morrow. So now I go to my rendezvous. Seven o'clock's the time, as you know." Here Phœbus scratched his ear. "Ah! Corne Dieu! I'd forgotten! I've not a sou to pay the hire of the garret—and the old hag will want to be paid beforehand—she won't trust me."

"Here is wherewith to pay."

Phœbus felt the cold hand of the unknown slip into his a large piece of money. He could not help taking the money, and grasping the hand. "Vrai Dieu!" he exclaimed, "but you're a good fellow!"

"One condition," said the stranger. "Prove to me that I've been wrong, and that you spoke truth. Hide me in some corner whence I may see whether this woman be really she whose name you have uttered."

"Oh," answered Phœbus, "it's just the same to me. We shall take the St. Martha room. You can see to your heart's content from the kennel that's on one side of it."

"Come, then," rejoined the shade.

"At your service," said the captain—"I know not indeed whether you be not Messer Diabolus *in propriâ personâ*. But let us be good friends to-night; and to-morrow I'll pay you all my debts, of the purse and of the sword."

They went forward at a rapid pace, and in a few minutes the noise of the river below announced to them that they were upon the Pont St. Michel, then loaded with houses. "I'll first introduce you," said Phœbus; "then I'll go and fetch the lady, who was to wait for me near the Petit-Châtelet." His companion made no answer; since they had been walking side by side, he had not uttered a word. Phœbus stopped against a low door, and gave it a rough jolt. A light

made its appearance through the crevices of the door
" Who's there?" cried a toothless voice. " *Corps-Dieu !
tête-Dieu ! ventre Dieu !* " answered the captain. The
door opened immediately, and exhibited to the new-
comers an old woman and an old lamp, both of them
trembling. The old woman was bent double—clothed
in tatters—her head shaking, wrapped in a duster by
way of coiffure, and perforated by two small eyes—
wrinkled all over, her hands, her face, her neck—her
lips turning inward, underneath her gums—and all
round her mouth she had tufts of white hair, giving her
the whiskered and demure look of a cat. The interior
of this dog-hole was in no less decay than herself;
there were walls of chalk; black beams in the ceiling;
a dismantled fire-place; cobwebs in every corner; in
the middle a tottering company of maimed stools and
tables; a dirty child in the ash-heap; and at the back,
a staircase, or rather a wooden ladder, ascending to a
trap-door in the ceiling. As he entered this den, Phœbus' mysterious companion pulled his cloak up to his
eyes. Meanwhile the captain, swearing all the while
like a Saracen, lost no time in producing his écu, saying,
as he presented it, " The St. Martha room."

The old woman received him like a grandee, and
shut up the écu in a drawer. It was the piece which
Phœbus had received from the man in the black coat.
While her back was turned, the little long-haired tattered boy that was playing among the ashes, went slyly to
the drawer, took out the écu, and put there instead of
it a dry leaf which he had plucked from a fagot.

The old woman beckoned to the two gentlemen, as
she called them, to follow her, and ascended the ladder
before them. On reaching the upper story, she set
down her lamp upon a chest; and Phœbus, as one accustomed to the house, opened a side door which was
the entrance to a dark and out-of-the-way nook. " Go
in there, my dear fellow," said he to his companion.
The man in the cloak obeyed without answering a word;
the door closed upon him; he heard Phœbus bolt it
outside, and, a moment afterward, go down-stairs again
with the old woman. The light had disappeared.

CHAPTER VIII.

CONVENIENCE OF THE WINDOWS LOOKING UPON THE RIVER.

CLAUDE FROLLO (for we presume that the reader, better informed than Phœbus, has seen in all this ad-venture no other specter monk than the archdeacon himself) groped about him for some moments in the dark corner in which the captain had bolted him up. It was one of those which builders sometimes reserve in the angle formed by the roof with the wall that sup-ports it. The vertical section of this kennel, as Phœ-bus had so aptly termed it, would have been a triangle. It had neither window nor skylight, and the incline plane of the roof prevented a man's standing up in it. Claude was therefore under the necessity of squatting down in the dust and the plaster that cracked under-neath him ; and at the same time his head was burning. In ferreting about him with his hands, he found upon the floor a piece of broken glass, which he applied to his forehead, and the coolness of which gave him some little relief.

What was passing at that moment in the dark soul of the archdeacon ? He and God alone could tell.

According to what fatal order was he disposing in his thoughts La Esmeralda, Phœbus, Jacques Charmolue, his young brother, of whom he was so fond, abandoned by him in the mud, his archdeacon's cassock, his repu-tation perhaps, thus dragged to La Falourdel's—all those images—all those adventurers? We know not, but it is certain that these ideas formed a horrible group in his mind.

He had been waiting for a quarter of an hour, and he felt as if he had grown older by fifty years. All at once he heard the wooden staircase creak, as some one ascended. The trap-door opened again, and again a light made its appearance. In the worm-eaten door of his nook there was a slit of considerable width, to which

he put his face, so that he could see all that passed in
the adjoining chamber. First of all, the old woman
with the cat's face issued through the trap-door with
her lamp in her hand; then Phœbus, curling his moustaches; then a third person, that beautiful and graceful figure, La Esmeralda. The priest saw her issue from
below like a dazzling apparition. Claude trembled; a
cloud spread itself over his eyes; his pulses beat violently; his brain was in a whirl; he no longer saw or
heard anything.

When he came to himself again, Phœbus and La
Esmeralda were alone, seated upon the wooden chest,
beside the lamp, the light of which exhibited to the
archdeacon those two youthful figures, and a wretched-
looking couch at the farther end of the room.

Close to the couch there was a window, the casement
of which, burst like a spider's web upon which the rain
has beaten, showed through its broken meshes a small
patch of sky, with the moon reposing upon a pillow of
soft clouds.

The young girl was blushing, confused, palpitating.
Her long drooping lashes shaded her glowing cheeks.
The officer, to whom she dared not lift her eyes, was
quite radiant. Mechanically, and with a charming air
of unconsciousness, she was tracing incoherent lines
with the end of her finger upon the wooden seat, and
looking at the finger. Her foot was not visible, for the
little goat was lying upon it.

The captain was very gallantly arrayed. Upon his
neck and his wrists he had tufts of fancy trimming, a
great elegancy of that day.

It was not without difficulty that Dom Claude could
overhear their conversation, through the humming of
the blood that was boiling in his temples.

A dull affair enough, the talk of a pair of lovers—a
perpetual "I love you"—a musical strain the reception
of which is very monotonous and very insipid to all indifferent hearers when it is not set off with a few fiori-
ture. But Claude was no indifferent hearer.

"Oh!" said the young girl, without lifting her eyes,

" do not despise me, Monseigneur Phœbus—I feel that
I am doing what is wrong."

"Despise you, my pretty girl," returned the officer
with an air of gallantry *supérieure et distinguée*—" despise
you, *tête-Dieu!* and why should I?"

"For having followed you."

"On that score, my charmer, we don't at all agree. I
ought not only to despise you, but to hate you."

The young girl looked at him in affright. "Hate
me!" exclaimed she. "Why, what have I done?"

"For having taken so much soliciting."

"Alas!" said she, "it is that I'm breaking a vow—I
shall never find my parents—the amulet will lose its
virtue—but what then? What occasion have I for father
and mother now?"

So saying, she fixed upon the captain her large black
eyes moist with joy and tenderness.

" Deuce take me, if I understand you," cried Phœbus.

La Esmeralda remained silent for a moment; then a
tear issued from her eyes, a sigh from her lips, and she
said, "Oh, monseigneur, I love you."

There was around the young girl such a perfume of
chastity, such a charm of virtue, that Phœbus did not
feel quite at his ease with her. These words, however,
emboldened him. "You love me!" said he with trans-
port, and he threw his arm round the gypsy girl's waist;
he had only been waiting for that opportunity.

The priest beheld it; and thereupon he felt with his
finger's end the point of a dagger which he bore concealed in his breast.

"Phœbus," continued the gypsy girl, gently disen-
gaging her waist from the tenacious hands of the captain, "you are good—you are generous—you are handsome—you have saved me—me, who am but a poor girl
lost in Bohemia. I had long dreamt of an officer that
was to save my life. It was of you that I dreamt, before I knew you, my Phœbus. The officer in my dream
had a fine uniform like you—a grand look—a sword;
your name is Phœbus—it's a fine name—I love your
sword. Do draw your sword, Phœbus, that I may see it.'

"Child!" said the captain, and he unsheathed his rapier, smiling. The gypsy girl looked first at the hilt, then at the blade; examined with wonderful curiosity the cypher upon the guard; and kissed the sword, saying, "You are the sword of a brave man—I love my captain."

Again, Phœbus availed himself of the opportunity to impress upon her beautiful neck, bent aside in the act of looking, a kiss which made the young girl draw herself up again all crimson, and made the priest grind his teeth in the dark.

"Phœbus," resumed the gypsy girl, "let me speak to you. Do just walk a little, that I may see you at your full height, and hear the sound of your spurs. How handsome you are!"

The captain rose to comply, chiding her at the same time with a smile of satisfaction. "Really, now, you are such a child! By-the-by, my dear, have you seen me in my state hacqueton?"

"Alas, no!" answered she.

"Ha, that's the finest thing of all!"

Phœbus came and seated himself beside her again, but much nearer than before. He began, "Just listen, my dear—"

The gypsy girl gave him several little taps of her pretty hand upon the lips, with childish and graceful sportiveness. "No, no," said she, "I will not listen to you. Do you love me? I want you to tell me whether you love me."

"Whether I love you, sweet angel?" cried the captain, bending one knee to the floor. "My blood, my soul, my property—all are thine—all at thy disposal. I love thee, and have never loved any but thee."

The captain had so many times repeated this sentence, on many a like occasion, that he delivered it all in a breath, and without a single blunder. At this impassioned declaration, the gypsy girl raised to the dingy ceiling which here held the place of heaven, a look full of angelic happiness. "Oh!" murmured she, "such is the moment at which one ought to die!" Phœbus

20

found "the moment" convenient for snatching from her another kiss, which went to torture the wretched archdeacon in his corner.

"To die!" cried the amorous captain; "what are you talking about, my angel? It's the time to live—or Jupiter is but a blackguard. Die at the beginning of such a pleasant thing! *Corne-de-bœuf!* what a joke! Not so, indeed. Just listen, my dear Similar—Esmeralda—Pardon me, but you've got a name so prodigiously Saracen that I can't run it off my tongue—I get entangled in it like a brier."

"Mon Dieu!" said the poor girl, "and I, now, used to think that name pretty for its singularity. But since it displeases you, I'm quite willing to call myself Goton."

"Ha! no crying about such a little matter, my charmer! It's a name that one must get used to, that's all. When once I know it by heart, it'll come ready enough. So hark ye, my dear Similar. I adore you to a very passion—I love you, so that really it's quite miraculous—I know a little girl that's dying with rage about it."

The jealous girl interrupted him. "Who's that?" said she.

"Oh, what does that signify to us?" said Phœbus; "do you love me?"

"Oh!" said she.

"Well, then, that's enough. We shall see how I love you, too. May the great devil Neptunus stick his pitch-fork into me, if I don't make you the happiest creature alive. We'll have a pretty little lodging somewhere or other. I'll make my archers parade under your windows—they're all on horseback, and cut out Captain Mignon's. There are bill-men, cross-bow-men, and culverin-men. I'll take you to the great musters of the Parisians at the Grange de Rully. It's very magnificent. Eighty thousand men under arms—thirty thousand white harnesses, jaques or brigandines—the sixty-seven banners of the trades—the standards of the parliament, of the Chamber of Accompts, of the trésor des généraux, of the aides des monnaies—the devil's own turn-out, in short. And then, I'll take you to see the lions of the Hôtel du Roi—that are wild beasts, you know. All the women are fond of that."

For some moments the young girl, absorbed in her pleasing reflections, had been musing to the sound of his voice, without attending to the meaning of his words.

"Oh, you'll be so happy!" continued the captain, at the same time gently unbuckling the gypsy's belt. "What are you doing?" said she sharply. This movement had aroused her from her revery.

"Nothing at all," answered Phœbus. "I was only saying that you must put off all that wild street-running dress when you're with me."

"When I'm with you, my Phœbus!" said the young girl, tenderly. And again she became pensive and silent.

The captain, emboldened by her gentleness, threw his arm round her waist without her making any resistance; then began softly to unlace the poor girl's corsage, and so violently displaced her gorgerette, that the priest, all panting, saw issue from underneath the lawn the charming bare shoulder of the gypsy girl, round and dusky like the moon rising through a misty horizon.

The young girl let Phœbus have his way. She seemed unconscious of what he was doing. The captain's eyes sparkled. All at once she turned round to him. "Phœbus," said she, with an expression of boundless love, "instruct me in your religion."

"My religion!" cried the captain, bursting into a laugh. "Instruct you in my religion! *Corne et tonnerre!* what do you want with my religion?"

"That we may be married," answered she. The captain's face took a mingled expression of surprise, disdain, unconcern, and libidinous passion. "Ah, bah," said he, "is there any marrying in the case?"

The gypsy turned pale, and her head dropped mournfully upon her breast. "My sweet love," said Phœbus, tenderly, "what signifies all that nonsense? Marriage is a grand affair, to be sure! Shall we love one another any the worse for not having Latin gabbled to us in a priest's shop?" And while saying this in his softest tone, he approached extremely near the gypsy girl; his fondling hands had resumed their position about that waist so slender and so pliant, and his eye kindled more and more.

Meanwhile, Dom Claude observed everything from his hiding-place. Its door was made of puncheon ribs, quite decayed, leaving between them ample passage for his look of a bird of prey. It was, it must be owned, a trying spectacle for a brown-skinned, broad-shouldered priest, condemned until that moment to the austere virginity of the cloister. He felt extraordinary movements within him; and any one who could then have seen the wretched man's countenance close against the worm-eaten bars, might have thought they saw a tiger's face looking out from his cage upon some jackal devouring a gazelle.

All at once, by a sudden movement, Phœbus snatched the gypsy's gorgerette completely off. The poor girl, who had remained pale and thoughtful, started up as if out of her sleep; she hastily drew back from the enterprising officer; and casting a look over her bare neck and shoulder, blushing, confused, and mute with shame, she crossed her two lovely arms upon her bosom to hide it. But for the flame that was glowing in her cheeks, to see her standing thus silent and motionless, one might have taken her for a statue of Modesty. Her eyes were bent upon the ground.

This action of the captain's had laid bare the mysterious amulet which she wore about her neck. "What's that?" said he, laying hold of this pretext for going up to the beautiful creature that he had just scared away from him.

"Touch it not," answered she warmly; "it's my guardian. It's that by which I shall find my family again, if I keep worthy. Oh, leave me, monsieur le capitaine! My mother! my poor mother! where are you? Come to my help! Do, Monsieur Phœbus, give me back my gorgerette."

Phœbus drew back, and said coldly, "Oh, mademoiselle, how plainly do I see that you don't love me."

"Not love him!" exclaimed the poor unfortunate girl ; and at the same time she clung with an air of fondness to the captain, whom she made sit down beside her. "Not love you, my Phœbus! What is it you are saying, wicked man, to rend my heart? Oh, come—take me—take me—do what you will with me —I am yours. What is the amulet to me now? What is my mother to me now? You are my mother, since I love you. Phœbus, my beloved Phœbus, dost thou see me? 'Tis I. Look at me. 'Tis that little girl whom thou wilt not spurn from thee—who comes, who comes herself to seek thee. My soul, my life, my person—all are yours, my captain. Well, then, let it be so—let us not marry—it is not thy wish—and besides, what am I but a wretched girl of the common way—while you, Phœbus, are a gentleman. A fine thing it would be, truly, for a dancing-girl to marry an officer! I was mad to think of it. No, Phœbus, no—I will be your mistress—your amusement—your pleasure—when you will—a girl that will be yours, and yours only. For that alone was I made—to be stained, despised, dishonored—but what then?—loved! I shall be the proudest and the happiest of women. And when I shall grow old and ugly, Phœbus—when I shall no longer be fit to love you, monseigneur, you will still suffer me to serve you. Others will embroider scarfs for you—I, your servant, will take care of them. You will let me polish your spurs, brush your hacqueton, and dust your riding-boots. Will you not, my Phœbus, have that pity? And in the meanwhile take me to yourself. Here, Phœbus, all belongs to you. Only love me. That is all we gypsy girls have occasion for —air and love."

So saying, she threw her arms around the officer's neck, raising her eyes to him supplicantly and smiling through her tears. Her delicate neck was chafed by the woolen-cloth doublet and its rough embroidery. The captain, quite intoxicated, pressed his glowing lips to those lovely African shoulders, and the young girl, her eyes cast upward to the ceiling, was all trembling and palpitating under his kisses.

All at once, above the head of Phœbus, she beheld another head—a strange, livid, convulsive countenance with the look of a demoniac; and close by that face, there was a hand holding a poniard. They were the face and hand of the priest; he had contrived to make his way through the crazy door of his hiding-place, and there he was. Phœbus could not see him. The young girl remained motionless, frozen, dumb under the influence of the frightful apparition—like a dove that should raise her head at the moment that the osprey is looking into her nest with his round fearful eyes.

She was unable even to utter a cry. She saw the poniard descend upon Phœbus, and rise again all reeking. "Malédiction!" exclaimed the captain, and he fell upon the floor.

She fainted. At the moment that her eyes closed and all sense was forsaking her, she thought she felt a touch of fire impressed upon her lips, a kiss more burning than the executioner's branding iron.

When she recovered her senses, she found herself, surrounded by soldiers of the watch; they were carrying off the captain weltering in his blood; the priest had disappeared; the window at the back of the chamber, looking upon the river, was wide open; they were picking up from the floor a cloak which they supposed to belong to the officer, and she heard them saying around her, "It's a witch has been poniarding a captain."

BOOK VII.

CHAPTER I.

THE CROWN TRANSFORMED INTO A WITHERED LEAF.

RINGOIRE and the whole Court of Miracles were in a state of mortal anxiety. For a whole month it was not known what had become of La Esmeralda, which sadly grieved the Duke of Egypt and his friends the Truands; nor what had become of her goat, which redoubled the grief of Gringoire. One evening the gypsy girl had disappeared; since which time she had held no communication with them. All search had been fruitless. Some teasing sabouleux told Gringoire they had met her that same evening in the neighborhood of the Pont Saint-Michel, walking off with an officer; but this husband *à la mode de Bohème* was an incredulous philosopher; and besides, he knew better than any one his wife's extreme purity; he had been enabled to judge how impregnable was the chastity resulting from the two combined virtues of the amulet and the gypsy herself, and he had mathematically calculated the resistance of this chastity multiplied into itself. On that score, at least, his mind was at ease.

Still he could not account for her sudden disappearance, which was a source of deep mortification to him. He would have grown thinner upon it, if the thing had been possible. He had, in consequence, neglected everything, even to his literary tastes, even to his great work, *De figuris regularibus et irregularibus*, which he

intended printing with the first money he should get.
For he raved upon printing ever since he had seen the
Didascolon of Hugues de Saint-Victor printed with the
celebrated types of Vindelin of Spires.

One day, as he was passing sorrowfully before the
Tournelle Criminelle, he observed a crowd at one of
the doors of the Palais de Justice. "What's all that
about?" asked he of a young man who was coming
out.

"I don't know, monsieur," answered the young man.
"They say there's a woman being tried for the murder of
a gendarme. As there seems to be some witchcraft in
the business, the bishop and the official have interposed
in the cause; and my brother, who's archdeacon of
Josas, can think of nothing else. Now I wished to
speak to him; but I have not been able to get near
him for the crowd—which annoys me sadly, for I want
money."

"Alas! monsieur," said Gringoire, "I would I could
lend you some; but though my breeches are in holes,
it's not from the weight of crown-pieces."

He dared not tell the young man that he knew his
brother, the archdeacon, toward whom he had not ventured to return since the scene of the church—a neglect
which embarrassed him much.

The scholar passed on, and Gringoire proceeded to follow the crowd which was ascending the staircase of the
Grande Chambre. To his mind there was nothing
equal to the spectacle of a trial in a criminal court for
dissipating melancholy, the judges are generally so de-
lightfully stupid. The people with whom he had mingled were moving on and elbowing each other in
silence. After a slow and tiresome pattering through
a long gloomy passage, which wound through the
Palais like the intestinal canal of the old edifice, he arrived at a low door opening into a salle or great public
room, which his tall figure permitted him to explore
with his eyes, over the waving heads of the multitude.

The hall was spacious and gloomy, which latter circumstance made it appear still more spacious. The

day was declining; the long pointed windows admitted only a few pale rays of light, which were extinguished before they reached the vaulted ceiling, an enormous trellis-work of carved wood, the thousand figures of which seemed to be moving about confusedly in the shade. There were already several candles lighted here and there upon tables, and glimmering over the heads of the greffiers or registrars, buried amidst the bundles of papers. The lower end of the room was occupied by the crowd; on the right and left were gentlemen of the gown at tables; at the extremity, upon an estrade or raised platform, were a number of judges, the farther rows just vanishing in the distance—motionless and sinister visages. The walls were strewed with numberless fleurs-de-lis. Over the judges might be vaguely distinguished a large figure of Christ; and in all directions pikes and halberds, the points of which were tipped with fire by the reflection of the candles.

"Monsieur," asked Gringoire of one of those next him, "who are all those persons yonder, ranged like prelates in council?"

"Monsieur," said his neighbor, "they are the Councilors of the Grande Chambre on the right; and those on the left are the councilors of the inquests, the maîtres in black gowns, and the messires in red ones."

"And there, above them," continued Gringoire, "who's that great red-faced fellow all in a perspiration?"

"That's monsieur the president."

"And those sheep behind him?" proceeded Gringoire, who, as we have already said, loved not the magistracy; which was owing, perhaps, to the ill-will he bore the Palais de Justice ever since his dramatic misadventure.

"They are messieurs, the masters of requests of the king's household."

"And before him, that wild boar?"

"That's the registrar of the court of parliament."

"And to the right, that crocodile?"

"Maître Philippe Lheulier, king's advocate extraordinary."

" And to the left, that great black cat?"

" Maître Jacques Charmolue, king's attorney in the ecclesiastical court, with the gentlemen of the officiality."

" Ah, well, monsieur," said Gringoire, " and what, pray, are all those good folks about?"

" They're trying some one."

" Trying whom? I see no prisoner."

" It's a woman, monsieur. You can not see her. Her back is toward us, and she is concealed by the crowd. Look, there she is, amidst that group of partisans."

" Who is the woman?" asked Gringoire. " Do you know her name?"

" No, monsieur; I am only just arrived. I suppose, however, that there's some sorcery in the matter, since the official's engaged on the trial."

" Now then," said our philosopher, " we are going to see all these men of the gown play the part of cannibals. Well, one sight's as good as another."

" Do you not think, monsieur," observed his neighbor, " that Maître Jacques Charmolue looks very mild?"

" Humph!" answered Gringoire, " I'm rather distrustful of mildness with a pinched-up nose and thin lips."

Here the bystanders imposed silence on the two talkers. An important deposition was being heard.

" Messeigneurs," said, from the middle of the room, an old woman whose face was so buried under her clothes that she might have been taken for a walking bundle of rags—" messeigneurs, the thing is as true as that I am La Falourdel, for forty years a housekeeper on the Pont St. Michel, and paying regularly my rent, dues, and quit-rent; my door opposite the house of Tassin Caillart the dyer, who lives on the side looking up the river. An old woman now! a pretty girl once, messeigneurs! A few days ago, some one said to me, ' Don't spin too much of an evening, La Falourdel—the devil's fond of combing old women's distaffs with his horns. It's certain that the specter monk that was last

year about the Temple, is now wandering about the
City. Take care, La Falourdel, that he doesn't knock
at your door.' One evening I was turning my wheel;
some one knocks at my door. 'Who is it?' says I.
Some one swears. I open the door. Two men come
in; a man in black, with a handsome officer. One
could see nothing of the black man but his eyes—two
live coals. All the rest was cloak and hat. And so
they say to me—'The Saint Martha room.' That's my
upper room, messeigneurs—my best. They give me an
écu. I lock the écu in my drawer, and I says, 'That
will buy some tripe to-morrow at the slaughter-house
De la Gloriette.' We go upstairs. When we'd got up,
while I turned my back, the black man disappears.
This astounds me a little. The officer, who was as handsome as a great lord, goes down with me. He leaves
the house. In about time enough to spin a quarter of
a skein, he comes in again with a pretty young girl—
quite a paragon, messeigneurs—that would have shone
like a sun, if she'd had her hair dressed. She had with
her a goat, a great he-goat, black or white, I don't remember which. This sets me thinking. The girl—
that doesn't concern me;—but the goat! I don't like
those animals, with their beards and their horns—it's
so like a man. Besides, it has a touch of the sabbath.
However, I said nothing. I had the écu. That's only
fair, you know, my lord judge. I show the captain and
the girl into the upstairs room, and leave them alone—
that's to say with the goat. I go down, and get to my
spinning again. I must tell you that my house has a
ground-floor and a story above; it looks out at the back
upon the river, like the other houses on the bridge, and
the ground-floor window and the first-floor window open
upon the water. Well, as I was saying, I had got to
my spinning. I don't know why, but I was thinking
about the specter monk which the goat had put into
my head—and then the pretty girl was rather queerly
tricked out. All at once I hear a cry overhead, and
something fall on the floor, and the window open. I
run to mine which is underneath, and I see pass before

my eyes a black heap, and it falls into the water. It was a phantom dressed like a priest. It was moonlight, I saw it quite plain. It was swimming toward the City. All in a tremble, I call the watch. The gentlemen of the douzaine come in; and, at first, not knowing what was the matter, as they were merry, they began to beat me. I explained to them. We go upstairs, and what do we find? My poor room swimming in blood—the captain stretched at his length with a dagger in his neck—the girl pretending to be dead—and the goat all in a fright. 'Pretty work!' says I—'I shall have to wash the floor for a fortnight and more. It must be scraped. It'll be a terrible job.' They carry off the officer, poor young man, and the girl, all in disorder. But stop. The worst of all is, that the next day, when I was going to take the écu to buy my tripe, I found a withered leaf in its place."

The old woman ceased. A murmur of horror ran through the audience. "That phantom, that goat, all that savors of magic," said one of Gringoire's neighbors. "And that withered leaf!" added another. "No doubt," continued a third, "that it's some witch that's connected with the specter monk to plunder officers." Gringoire himself was not far from considering this ensemble at once probable and terrific.

"Woman Falourdel," said monsieur the president with majesty, "have you nothing further to say to the court?"

"No, monseigneur," answered the old woman, "unless it is, that in the report my house has been called an old tumble-down offensive hovel—which is most insulting language. The houses on the bridge are not very good-looking, because there are such numbers of people; but the butchers live there for all that, and they are rich men, married to pretty proper sort of women."

The magistrate, who had reminded Gringoire of a crocodile, rose. "Silence," said he; "I beg you, gentlemen, to bear in mind that a poniard was found on the accused. Woman Falourdel, have you brought the leaf into which the écu was changed that the demon gave you?"

"Yes, monseigneur," answered she, "I've found it. Here it is."

An usher of the court passed the withered leaf to the crocodile, who, with a doleful shake of the head, passed it to the president; who sent it on to the king's attorney in the ecclesiastical court; so that it made the round of the room. "It's a beech leaf," said Maître Jacques Charmolue, "an additional proof of magic."

A councilor then began: "Witness, two men went up-stairs in your house at the same time; the black man, whom you at first saw disappear, then swim across the Seine in priest's clothes; and the officer. Which of them gave you the crown?"

The old woman reflected a moment, and then said, "It was the officer."

A murmur ran through the crowd.

"Ha," thought Gringoire, "that creates some doubt in my mind."

Meanwhile, Maître Philippe Lheulier, king's advocate extraordinary, again interposed. "I would remind you, gentlemen, that the murdered officer, in the deposition written at his bedside, while stating that a vague notion had crossed his mind, at the instant when the black man accosted him, that it might be the specter monk, added that the phantom had eagerly pressed him to go and meet the prisoner, and, on his (the captain's) observing that he was without money, he had given him the écu which the said officer had paid La Falourdel. Thus the écu is a coin from hell."

This concluding observation appeared to dissipate all the doubts, both of Gringoire and the other skeptics among the auditory.

"Gentlemen, you have the bundle of documents," added the king's advocate, seating himself; "you can consult the deposition of Phœbus de Chateaupers."

At that name the prisoner rose; her head was now above the crowd; and Gringoire, aghast, recognized La Esmeralda.

She was pale; her hair, formerly so gracefully braided and spangled with sequins, fell in disorder; her lips were blue; her hollow eyes were terrific. Alas!

"Phœbus!" said she, wildly; "where is he? Oh, messeigneurs! before you kill me, for mercy's sake, tell me if he yet lives!"

"Hold your tongue, woman," answered the president, "that's not our business."

"Oh, for pity's sake, tell me if he is living," continued she, clasping her beautiful wasted hands; and her chains were heard as they brushed along her dress.

"Well," said the king's advocate roughly, "he is dying. Does that content you?"

The wretched girl fell back on her seat, speechless, tearless, white as a form of wax.

The president leaned over to a man at his feet, who was dressed in a gilt cap and black gown; and had a chain round his neck and a wand in his hand. "Usher, bring in the second prisoner."

All eyes were now turned toward a small door, which opened, and, to the great trepidation of Gringoire, made way for a pretty she-goat with gilt feet and horns. The elegant animal stopped a moment on the threshold, stretching out her neck, as if, perched on the point of a rock, she had before her eyes a vast horizon. All at once she caught sight of the gypsy girl; and leaping over the table and a registrar's head, in two bounds she was at her knees; she then rolled herself gracefully over her mistress's feet, begging for a word or a caress; but the prisoner remained motionless, and even poor Djali herself obtained not a look.

"Ay, ay; that's the horrid beast," said the old Falourdel, "and well I know them both again."

Jacques Charmolue interposed; "If you please, gentlemen, we will proceed to the examination of the goat."

The goat was, in fact, the second prisoner. Nothing was more common in those times than a charge of sorcery brought against an animal. Among others, in the Provostry Accompts for 1466, may be seen a curious detail of the expenses of the proceeding against Gillet

Soulart and his sow, executed "for their demerits" at Corbeil. Everything is there; the cost of the pit to put the sow in; the five hundred bundles of wood from the wharf of Morsant; the three pints of wine and the bread, the sufferer's last repast, shared in a brotherly manner by the executioner; and even the eleven days' custody and feed of the sow, at eight deniers parisis per day. Sometimes they went further even than animals. The capitularies of Charlemagne and Louis le Débonnaire impose severe penalties on the fiery phantoms which might think fit to appear in the air.

Meanwhile the king's attorney in the ecclesiastical court had exclaimed: "If the demon which possesses this goat, and which has resisted all exorcisms, persist in his sorceries—if he astound the court with them—we forewarn him, that we shall be obliged to have recourse against him to the gibbet or the stake."

Gringoire was all in a cold perspiration. Charmolue took up from a table the gypsy girl's tambourine, and, presenting it in a certain manner to the goat, he asked her, " What's o'clock?"

The goat looked at him with a sagacious eye, raised her gilt foot, and struck it seven times. It was indeed seven o'clock. A movement of terror ran through the crowd. Gringoire could bear it no longer.

" She'll be her own ruin," cried he aloud, " you see she does not know what she's about!"

" Silence! you people at the end of the room!" said the usher, sharply.

Jacques Charmolue, by means of the same manœuvres with the tambourine, made the goat perform several other tricks, about the day of the month, the month of the year, etc., which the reader has already witnessed. And, by an optical illusion peculiar to judicial proceedings, those same spectators who, perhaps, had more than once applauded in the public streets the innocent performances of Djali, were terrified at them under the roof of the Palais de Justice. The goat was indisputably the devil.

It was still worse when, the king's attorney having

emptied on the floor a certain leathern bag full of movable letters, which Djali had about her neck, they saw
the goat kick out with her foot from among the scattered alphabet the fatal name Phœbus. The sorcery of
which the captain had been the victim seemed unan-
swerably proved ; and, in the eyes of all, the gypsy girl,
that charming dancer, who had so often dazzled the
passers-by with her airy grace, was neither more nor less
than a frightful witch.

She, on her part, gave no signs of life ; neither the
graceful evolutions of Djali, nor the threatenings of the
men of law, nor the stifled imprecations of the auditory
—nothing now reached her apprehension.

She could only be roused by a sergeant shaking her
pitilessly, and the president raising his voice with solemnity :—" Girl, you are of Bohemian race, given to
sorcery. You, with your accomplice, the enchanted
goat, implicated in the charge, did, on the night of the
29th of March last, wound and poniard, in concert with
the powers of darkness, by the aid of charms and spells,
a captain of the king's archers, Phœbus de Chateaupers
by name. Do you persist in denying it ? "

" Horrible ! " cried the young girl, hiding her face
with her hands. " My Phœbus ! Oh, it's hellish ! "

" Do you persist in denying it ? " asked the president,
coolly.

" Do I deny it ! " said she, in a terrible accent ; and
she rose, and her eyes flashed.

The president continued straightforwardly, " Then
how do you explain the facts laid to your charge ? "

She answered in a broken voice, " I've already said
I don't know. It's a priest—a priest that I do not
know—an infernal priest, that pursues me ! "

" Just so," replied the judge ; " the specter monk ! "

" Oh, gentlemen, have pity upon me ! I'm only a
poor girl—"

" Of Egypt," said the judge.

Maître Jacques Charmolue commenced with mildness
—" Seeing the painful obstinacy of the accused, I de-
mand the application of the torture."

"Granted," said the president.

A shudder ran through the whole frame of the unhappy girl. She rose, however, at the order of the partisan-men, and walked with a tolerably firm step, preceded by Charmolue and the priests of the officiality, between two rows of halberds, toward a false door, which suddenly opened and shut again upon her, having the effect upon Gringoire of a mouth gaping to devour her.

When she disappeared, a plaintive bleating was heard. It was the little goat crying.

The sitting of the court was suspended. A councilor having observed that the gentlemen were fatigued, and that it would be long to wait for the conclusion of the torture, the president answered that a magistrate must sacrifice himself to his duty.

"What a troublesome, vexatious jade!" said an old judge, "to make one give her the torture when one has not supped!"

CHAPTER II.

THE QUESTION CHAMBER.

AFTER ascending and descending several flights of steps as they proceeded through passages so gloomy that they were lighted with lamps at midday, La Esmeralda, still surrounded by her lugubrious attendants, was pushed forward by the sergeants of the Palais into a dismal chamber. This chamber, of a circular form, occupied the ground floor of one of those large towers which still in our day appear through the layer of recent edifices with which modern Paris has covered the ancient one. There were no windows to this vault; no other opening than the low overhanging entrance of an enormous iron door. Still it did not want for light a furnace was contrived in the thickness of the wall; a large fire was lighted in it, which filled the vault with its crimson reflection, and stripped of every ray a miserable candle placed in a corner. The sort of portcullis which was used to inclose the furnace, being raised at the moment, only gave to view at the mouth of the flaming edifice, which glared upon the dark wall, the lower extremity of its bars, like a row of black sharp teeth set at regular distances, which gave the furnace the appearance of one of those dragon's mouths which vomit forth flames in ancient legends. By the light which issued from it, the prisoner saw all around the chamber frightful instruments of which she did not understand the use. In the middle lay a mattress of leather almost touching the ground, over which hung a leathern strap with a buckle, attached to a copper ring held in the teeth of a flat-nosed monster carved in the keystone of the vault. Pincers, nippers, large plowshares, were heaped inside the furnace, and were heating red-hot, promisucously upon the burning coals. The sanguine glow of the furnace only served to light up throughout the chamber an assemblage of horrible things.

This Tartarus was called simply la chambre de la question.

Upon the bed was seated unconcernedly, Pierrat Torterue, the sworn torturer. His assistants, two square-faced gnomes, with leathern aprons and tarpaulin coats, were turning about the irons on the coals.

In vain had the poor girl called up all her courage; on entering this room she was seized with horror.

The sergeants of the bailiff of the Palais were ranged on one side; the priests of the officiality on the other. A registrar, a table, and writing materials were in one corner. Maître Jacques Charmolue approached the gypsy girl with a very soft smile. " My dear child," said he, "you persist, then, in denying everything ? "

" Yes," answered she, in a dying voice.

" In that case," resumed Charmolue, " It will be our painful duty to question you more urgently than we should otherwise wish. Have the goodness to sit down on that bed. Maître Pierrat, make room for mademoiselle, and shut the door.

Pierrat rose with a growl. "If I shut the door," muttered he, "my fire will go out."

"Well, then, my good fellow," replied Charmolue, "leave it open."

Meanwhile La Esmeralda remained standing. The bed of leather, upon which so many poor wretches had writhed, scared her. Terror froze her very marrow; there she stood bewildered and stupefied. At a sign from Charmolue, the two assistants took her and seated her on the bed. They did not hurt her; but when those men touched her—when that leather touched her —she felt all her blood flow back to her heart. She cast a wandering look around the room. She fancied she saw moving and walking from all sides toward her, to crawl upon her body and pinch and bite her, all those monstrous instruments of torture, which were, to the instruments of all kinds that she had hitherto seen, what bats, centipedes and spiders are to birds and insects.

"Where is the physician?" asked Charmolue.

"Here," answered a black gown that she had not observed before.

She shuddered.

"Mademoiselle," resumed the fawning voice of the attorney of the ecclesiastical court, "for the third time, do you persist in denying the facts of which you are accused?"

This time she could only bend her head in token of assent—her voice failed her.

"You persist, then?" said Jacques Charmolue. "Then I'm extremely sorry, but I must fulfill the duty of my office."

"Monsieur, the king's attorney," said Pierrat gruffly, "what shall we begin with?"

Charmolue hesitated a moment, with the ambiguous grimace of a poet seeking rhyme. "With the brodequin," said he at last.

The unhappy creature felt herself so completely

abandoned of God and man, that her head fell on her chest like a thing inert, which has no power within itself.

The torturer and the physician approached her both at once. The two assistants began rummaging in their hideous armory. At the sound of those frightful irons the unfortunate girl started convulsively. "Oh," murmured she, so low that no one heard her, "Oh, my Phœbus!" She then sank again into her previous insensibility and petrified silence. This spectacle would have torn any heart but the hearts of judges. She resembled a poor sinful soul interrogated by Satan at the crimson wicket of hell. The miserable body about which was to cling that frightful swarm of saws, wheels and chevalets—the being about to be handled so roughly by those grim executioners and torturing pincers—was, then, that soft, fair, and fragile creature; a poor grain of millet, which human justice was sending to be ground by the horrid millstones of torture.

Meanwhile the callous hands of Pierrat Torterue's assistants had brutally stripped that charming leg, that little foot, which had so often astonished the passers-by with their grace and beauty, in the streets of Paris. "It's a pity," growled out the torturer as he remarked the grace and delicacy of their form. If the archdeacon had been present, he certainly would have remembered at that moment his symbol of the spider and the fly. Soon the unhappy girl saw approaching through the mist which was spreading over her eyes, the brodequin or wooden boot; soon she saw her foot, encased between the iron-bound boards, disappear under the terrific apparatus. Then terror restored her strength. "Take that off," cried she, angrily, starting up all disheveled; "mercy!"

She sprang from the bed to throw herself at the feet of the king's attorney; but her leg was caught in the heavy block of oak and iron-work, and she sank upon the brodequin more shattered than a bee with a heavy weight upon its wing.

At a sign from Charmolue they replaced her on the

bed, and two coarse hands fastened round her small waist the leathern strap which hung from the ceiling.

"For the last time, do you confess the facts of the charge?" asked Charmolue, with his imperturbable benignity.

"I am innocent," was the answer.

"Then, mademoiselle, how do you explain the circumstances brought against you?"

"Alas, monseigneur, I don't know."

"You deny, then?"

"All!"

"Proceed," said Charmolue to Pierrat.

Pierrat turned the screw; the brodequin tightened; and the wretched girl uttered one of those terrible cries which are without orthography in any human tongue.

"Stop," said Charmolue to Pierrat.

"Do you confess?" said he to the gypsy girl.

"Ah!" cried the wretched girl. "I confess! I confess! Mercy!"

She had not calculated her strength in braving the torture. Poor child! whose life hitherto had been so joyous, so pleasant, so sweet—the first pang of acute pain had overcome her.

"Humanity obliges me to tell you," observed the king's attorney, "that, in confessing, you have only to look for death."

"I hope so," said she. And she fell back on the bed of leather, dying, bent double, letting herself hang by the strap buckled round her waist.

"Come, come, my darling, hold up a bit," said Maître Pierrat, raising her. "You look like the gold sheep that hangs about Monsieur of Burgundy's neck."

Jacques Charmolue raised his voice:

"Registrar, write down. Young Bohemian girl, you confess your participation in the love-feasts, sabbaths, and sorceries of hell, with wicked spirits, witches, and hobgoblins?—Answer."

"Yes," said she, so low that the word was lost in a whisper.

"You confess having seen the ram which Beelzebub

causes to appear in the clouds to assemble the sabbath and which is only seen by sorcerers?"

"Yes."

"You confess having adored the heads of Bohomet, those abominable idols of the Templars?"

"Yes."

"Having held habitual intercourse with the devil, under the form of a familiar she-goat, included in the prosecution?"

"Yes."

Lastly, you avow and confess having, with the assistance of the demon, and the phantom commonly called the specter monk, on the night of the twenty-ninth of March last, murdered and assassinated a captain named Phœbus Chateaupers?"

She raised her large fixed eyes toward the magistrate; and answered, as if mechanically, without effort or emotion, "Yes!" It was evident her whole being was shaken.

"Write down, registrar," said Charmolue. And addressing himself to the torturers: "Let the prisoner be unbound and taken back into court."

When the brodequin was removed, the attorney of the ecclesiastical court examined her foot, still paralyzed with pain. "Come," said he, "there's not much harm done. You cried out in time. You could dance yet, my beauty!" He then turned toward his acolytes of the officiality: "At length justice is enlightened! that's a relief, gentlemen! Mademoiselle will at least bear this testimony, that we have acted with all possible gentleness."

CHAPTER III.

THE SENTENCE.

WHEN, pale and limping, she re-entered the court, a general hum of pleasure greeted her. On the part of the auditory, it was that feeling of satisfied impatience which is experienced at the theatre, at the expiration of the interval between the last two acts of a play, when the curtain is raised, and "the end," according to the French expression, "is about to begin." On the part of the judges, it was the hope of soon getting their supper. The little goat, too, bleated with joy. She would have run to her mistress, but they had tied her to the bench.

Night had quite set in. The candles, whose number had not been increased, gave so little light, that the walls of the spacious room could not be seen. Darkness enveloped every object in a sort of mist. A few apathetic judges' faces were just visible. Opposite to them, at the extremity of the long apartment, they could distinguish an ill-defined white point standing out amid the gloomy background. It was the prisoner.

She had crawled to her place. When Charmolue had magisterially installed himself in his, he sat down; then rose and said, without exhibiting too much of the self-complacency of success, "The accused has confessed all."

"Bohemian girl," continued the president, "you have confessed all your acts of sorcery, prostitution, and assassination upon Phœbus de Chateaupers?"

Her heart was full. She was heard sobbing amid the gloom. "Whatever you will," answered she feebly; "but make an end of me quickly."

"Monsieur, the king's attorney in the ecclesiastical court," said the president, "the chamber is ready to hear your requisitions."

Maître Charmolue exhibited a frightful scroll; and began to read over, with much gesticulation and the exaggerated emphasis of the bar, a Latin oration, in which all the evidence of the trial was drawn out in Ciceronian periphrases, flanked by quotations from Plautus, his favorite comic author. We regret that it is not in our power to present our readers with this extraordinary piece of eloquence. The orator delivered it with marvelous action. He had not concluded the

exordium before the perspiration began to start from
his forehead, and his eyes from his head. All at once,
in the middle of a finely turned period, he broke off,
and his countenance, which was generally mild enough,
and, indeed, stupid enough, became terrible. "Gentlemen," cried he (this time in French, for it was in the
scroll), "Satan is so mixed up in this affair that, behold!
he is present at our councils, and makes a mock of their
majesty. Behold him!" So saying, he pointed to the
little goat, which, seeing Charmolue gesticulating,
thought it quite proper she should do the same, and
had seated herself on her haunches, mimicking as well
as she could, with her fore feet and shaggy head, the
pathetic action of the king's attorney in the ecclesiastical court. It was, if we remember right, one of her prettiest talents. This incident, this last proof, produced a
great effect. They tied the goat's feet; and the king's
attorney resumed the thread of his eloquence. It was
a long thread, indeed; but the peroration was admirable. The last sentence ran thus—we leave the reader's
imagination to combine with it the hoarse voice and
broken-winded gestures of Maître Charmolue: "*Ideò,
domni, coram stryga demonstrata, crimine patente, inten-
tione criminis existente, in nomine sanctæ ecclesiæ Nostræ-
Dominæ Parisiensis quæ est in saisina habendi omnimodam
altam et bassam justitiam in illa hac intemerata Civi-
tatis insula, tenore præsentium declaramus nos requirere,
primo, aliquamdam pecuniariam indemnitatem; secundo,
amendationem honorabilem ante portalium maximum
Nostræ-Dominæ, ecclesiæ cathedralis; tertio, sententiam
in virtute cujus ista stryga cum sua capella, seu in trivio
vulgariter dicto* la Grève, *seu in insula exeunte in fluvio
Secanæ, juxta pointam jardini regalis, executatæ sint!*"*

---

* It may be as well to attempt a translation for the reader, of
this delicate specimen of the barbarous Latin and the legal jargon of the Middle Ages:

"Therefore, gentlemen, the witchcraft being proved, and the
crime made manifest, as likewise the criminal intention—in the
name of the holy church of Our Lady of Paris, which is seised
of the right of all manner of justice, high and low, within this

He put on his cap again, and re-seated himself.

"*Eheu!*" muttered Gringoire, quite overwhelmed; "*bassa latinitas!*"

Another man in a black gown then rose near the prisoner; it was her advocate or counsel. The fasting judges began to murmur.

"Mr. Advocate, be brief," said the president.

"Monsieur the president," answered the advocate, "since the defendant has confessed the crime, I have only one word to say to these gentlemen. I hold in my hand a passage of the Salic law: 'If a witch has eaten a man, and is convicted of it, she shall pay a fine of eight thousand deniers, which make two hundred sous of gold.' Let the chamber condemn my client to the fine."

"An abrogated clause," said the king's advocate extraordinary.

"*Nego,*" replied the prisoner's advocate.

"Take the votes," said a councilor; "the crime is manifest; and it is late."

The votes were taken without going out of court. The judges voted by the lifting of their caps—they were in haste. Their hooded heads were seen uncovering one after another in the shade, at the lugubrious question addressed to them in a low voice by the president. The poor prisoner seemed to be looking at them, but her bewildered eye no longer saw anything.

Then the registrar began to write; then he handed to the president a long scroll of parchment. Then the unhappy girl heard the people stirring, the pikes clashing, and a freezing voice saying:

"Bohemian girl, on such day as it shall please our

inviolate island of the City—we declare, by the tenor of these presents, that we require, firstly, some pecuniary compensation; secondly, penance before the great portal of the cathedral church of Our Lady; thirdly, a sentence, by virtue of which this witch, together with her she-goat, shall, either in the public square, commonly called La Grève, or in the island standing forth in the river Seine, adjacent to the point of the royal gardens, be executed."

lord the king, at the hour of noon, you shall be taken in a tumbrel, in your shift, barefooted, with a rope round your neck, before the great portal of Notre-Dame ; and there you shall do penance wlth a wax torch of two pounds weight in your hand ; and from thence you shall be taken to the Place de Grève, where you shall be hanged and strangled on the Town gibbet, and your goat likewise ; and shall pay to the official three lions of gold, in reparation of the crimes by you committed and confessed, of sorcery, magic, prostitution and murder, upon the person of the sieur Phœbus de Chateaupers. So God have mercy on your soul ! "

"Oh ! it's a dream ! " murmured she ; and she felt rude hands bearing her away.

CHAPTER IV.

LASCIATE OGNI SPERANZA.

IN the Middle Ages, when an edifice was complete, there was almost as much of it within the ground as above it. Except, indeed, it was built upon piles, like Notre-Dame, a palace, a fortress, or a church had always a double bottom. In the cathedrals it was, as it were, another cathedral, subterraneous, low, dark, mysterious, blind, and dumb, under the aisles of the building above, all flooded with light and resounding night and day with the music of bells and organs. Sometimes it was a sepulchre. In the palaces and the bastiles it was a prison—sometimes a sepulchre too—and sometimes it was both together. Those mighty masses of masonry of which we have explained elsewhere the mode of formation and vegetation, had not foundations merely ; they might be said to have roots, branching out under ground in chambers, galleries, and staircases, like the structure above. Thus all of them, churches, palaces,

and bastiles stood half within the earth. The subterraneous vaults of an edifice formed another edifice, in
which you descended instead of ascending, and the
underground stories of which extended downward beneath the pile of external stories of the structure, like
those inverted forests and mountains which are seen in
the liquid mirror of a lake, underneath the forests and
mountains on its borders.

At the Bastile St. Antoine, at the Palais de Justice
of Paris, and at the Louvre, these subterraneous edifices
were prisons. The stories of these prisons, as they went
deeper into the ground, grew narrower and darker.
They formed so many zones, presenting, as by a gradu-
ated scale, deeper and deeper shades of horror. Dante
could find nothing better for the construction of his
hell. These dungeon funnels usually terminated in a
low hollow, shaped like the bottom of a tub, in which
Dante has placed his Satan, and in which society placed
the criminal condemned to death. When once a miserable human existence was there interred—then farewell
light, air, life, ogni speranza; it never went out again
but to the gibbet or the stake. Sometimes it rotted
there, and human justice called that forgetting. Between mankind and himself the condemned felt weighing upon his head an accumulation of stones and jail-
ers; and the whole prison together, the massive bastile,
was now but one enormous complicated lock that barred
him out of the living world.

It was in one of these low damp holes, in the oubli-
ettes excavated by St. Louis in the *in pace* of the Tournelle, that—for fear of her escaping, no doubt—they
had deposited La Esmeralda condemned to the gibbet,
with the colossal Palais de Justice over her head—a
poor fly that could not have stirred the smallest of its
stones.

Assuredly, Providence and society had been alike un-
just; such a profusion of misfortune and of torture was
not necessary to shatter so fragile a creature.

She was there, lost in darkness, buried, walled up.
Any one that could have seen her in that state, after

having seen her laughing and dancing in the sunshine, would have shuddered. Chill as night, chill as death, no longer a breath of air in her locks, no longer a human voice in her ear, no longer a glimpse of daylight in her eyes, broken in two, as it were, crushed with chains, bent double beside a pitcher and a loaf of bread upon a little straw in the pool of water that formed itself under her from the oozings of the dungeon, without motion, almost without breath, she was now scarcely sensible even to suffering. Phœbus, the sunshine, noonday, the open air, the streets of Paris, her dancing amid the applauses of the spectators, her soft prattlings of love with the officer, and then the priest, the old woman, the poniard, blood, the torture, the gibbet—all that was indeed still floating in her mind, now as a harmonious and golden vision, then as a frightful nightmare; but her apprehension of it all was now but that of a vaguely horrible struggle involved in darkness, or of a distant music that was still playing above ground, but was no longer audible at the depth to which the unfortunate girl had fallen. Since she had been there she neither waked nor slept; in that misery, in that dungeon, she could no more distinguish waking from sleeping, dreams from reality, than she could the day from the night. All was mingled, broken, floating, confusedly scattered in her thoughts. She no longer felt, no longer knew, no longer thought—at most she only dreamed. Never had living creature been plunged more deeply into annihilation.

Thus benumbed, frozen, petrified, scarcely had she remarked, at two or three different times, the noise of a trap-door which had opened somewhere above her, without even admitting a ray of light, and through which the hand of some one had thrown her a crust of black bread. Yet this was her only remaining communication with mankind—the periodical visit of the jailer. One thing alone still mechanically occupied her ear; over her head the damp filtered through the mouldy stones of the vault, and at regular intervals, drop after drop, thus collected, fell into the pool of water beside her, with a plashing to which in her stupor she involuntarily listened.

The drop of water falling into that pool was the only movement still perceptible about her, her only clock to mark the time, the only noise that reached her of all the noise that is made upon the earth, except, indeed, that she also felt, from time to time, in that sink of mire and darkness, something cold passing here and there over her foot or her arm, and making her shiver.

How long had she been there? She knew not. She had some recollection of a sentence of death pronounced somewhere upon some one, that then they had carried herself away, and that she had awoke in darkness and silence, freezing. She had crawled along upon her hands, then she had felt iron rings cutting her ankles, and chains had clanked. She had discovered that all around her was wall, that underneath her were flagstones covered with wet, and a bundle of straw, but there was neither lamp nor ventilator. Then she had seated herself upon that straw, and sometimes, for a change of posture, upon the lowest step of a stone flight which there was in her dungeon. At one moment she had endeavored to count the dark minutes which the drops of water measured to her ear, but soon that mournful employment of her sick brain had broken itself off, and left her in stupor again.

At length, one day, or one night (for midnight and noon had the same hue in this sepulchre), she heard above her a louder noise than that which the turnkey generally made when he brought her her loaf of bread and pitcher of water. She raised her head, and saw a reddish light through the crevices of the sort of trap-door made in the vault of the *in pace*. At the same time the heavy iron creaked, the trap-door grated on its rusty hinges, turned back, and she saw a lantern, a hand, and the lower part of the bodies of two men, the door being too low for her to see the upper. The light affected her eyes so sensibly that she closed them.

When she reopened them the door was closed, the lantern was placed on a step of the staircase; a man alone was standing before her. A cagoule fell to his feet, a caffardum of the same color concealed his face. Nothing was seen of his person, neither his face nor his hands. It was a long black winding-sheet standing on end, and under which something was perceived to move. She looked steadily for some minutes at this sort of specter. Meanwhile neither of them spoke. They were like two statues confronting each other. Two things alone seemed to have life in the vault: the wick of the lantern, which crackled owing to the humidity of the atmosphere, and the drop of water from the roof, which broke this irregular crepitation by its monotonous plash, and made the reflection of the lantern tremble in concentric circles upon the oily water of the pool.

At length the prisoner broke silence. "Who are you?"

"A priest."

The word, the accent, the sound of the voice made her start.

The priest continued in a hollow tone: "Are you prepared?"

"For what?"

"For death."

"Oh!" said she; "will it be soon?"

"To-morrow."

Her head, which she had raised joyfully, fell back again upon her bosom. "That's very long!" murmured she; "what could it signify to them if it had been to-day?"

"You are very wretched, then?" asked the priest after a short silence.

"I'm very cold," answered she.

She took her feet between her hands, an habitual gesture with poor creatures extremely cold, and which we have already remarked in the recluse of the Tour-Roland, and her teeth chattered.

The priest's eyes appeared to be wandering from under his hood around the dungeon. "Without light! without fire! in the water! 'Tis horrible!"

"Yes," answered she with the bewildered air which misery had given her. "The day is for every one—why do they give me nothing but night?"

"Do you know," resumed the priest, after another silence, "why you are here?"

"I think I knew it once," said she, passing her thin fingers across her brow, as if to assist her memory, "but I don't know now."

All at once she began to weep like a child. "I want to go away from here, monsieur. I'm cold—I'm afraid—and there are creatures crawling over me."

"Well, then, follow me."

So saying, the priest took her arm. The poor girl was frozen to her very vitals, and yet that hand felt cold to her.

"Oh!" murmured she, "it's the icy hand of death. Who are you?"

The priest raised his hood—she looked—it was that ominous visage which had so long pursued her—that demon's head which had appeared to her at La Falourdel's over the adored head of her Phœbus—that eye which she had the last time seen glaring by the side of a poniard.

This apparition, ever so fatal to her, and which had thus pushed her on from misfortune to misfortune, even to an ignominious death, roused her from her stupor. It seemed to her as if the sort of veil which had woven itself upon her memory, was rent away. All the details of her dismal adventure, from the nocturnal scene at La Falourdel's to her condemnation at the Tournelle, were at once brought back to her mind, not vague and confused as hitherto, but distinct, decided, breathing, terrible. These recollections, almost obliterated by excess of suffering, were revived at the sight of the gloomy figure before her, as the approach of fire brings out afresh upon the white paper the invisible letters traced on it with sympathetic ink. It seemed as if all the wounds of her heart were at once reopened and bleeding.

"Ha!" cried she, her hands before her eyes, and with a convulsive shiver "it's the priest!"

She then let fall her unnerved arms, and remained sitting, her head cast down, her eyes fixed on the ground, speechless, and continuing to tremble.

The priest looked at her with the eye of a kite which has been long hovering from the upmost heaven around a poor lark cowering in the corn, and has been gradually and silently contracting the formidable circles of its flight, until it suddenly darts down like lightning upon its prey, and holds it panting between its talons.

She began to murmur in a low tone, " Finish! finish! the last blow!" And her head sank between her shoulders, like a sheep awaiting the stroke of the butcher.

" You have a horror of me, then," said he at length. She did not answer.

" Have you a horror of me?" repeated he.

Her lips contracted as if she was smiling. "Yes," said she; "the executioner taunts the condemned! For months he pursues me—threatens me—terrifies me. But for him, my God, how happy I was! It is he that has cast me into this abyss! Oh, heavens! it is he that killed—it is he that killed him—my Phœbus!" Here, bursting into sobs, and raising her eyes toward the priest: "Oh! wretch! who are you? what have I done to you? do you hate me so, then? Alas! what have you against me?"

" I love thee!" cried the priest.

Her tears suddenly ceased; she looked at him with an idiotic air. He had fallen on his knees, and was looking her through with eyes of fire.

" Dost thou hear? I love thee!" cried he again.

" What love?" said the wretched girl, shuddering.

He continued—" The love of the damned!"

Both remained for some minutes silent, crushed under the weight of their emotions—he maddened—she stupefied.

" Listen," said the priest at length; and a strange calm came over him: "thou shalt know all. I am about to tell thee what hitherto I have scarcely dared tell myself, when secretly I have interrogated my conscience, in those deep hours of the night when it has been so dark that it seemed as if God could no longer see me. Listen—before I met thee, young girl, I was happy—"

"And I too!" sighed she feebly.

"Interrupt me not! Yes—I was happy; at least I thought myself so. I was pure—my soul was filled with limpid light. No head ever rose more lofty or more radiant than mine. Priests consulted me upon chastity, doctors upon doctrine. Yes, science was everything to me; it was a sister—and a sister sufficed me. Not but that, with age, other ideas came across my mind. More than once my blood was roused by the passing of a female form. That force of sex and blood which, foolish youth, I had thought stifled forever, had more than once shaken convulsively the chain of the iron vows which bind me, miserable wretch, to the cold stones of the altar. But fasting, prayer, study, the macerations of the cloister had again restored the soul's empire over the body. And then I avoided women. Besides, I had only to open a book, for all the impure vapors of the brain to evaporate before the splendor of science. In a few minutes, I saw flee before me the gross things of earth; and again I became tranquil, beguiled, and serene before the calm radiance of eternal truth. So long as the Demon only sent to encounter me vague shadows of women, passing here and there before my eyes, in the church, in the streets, in the fields, and which were scarcely retraced in my dreams, I vanquished him easily. Alas! if victory stayed not with me, the fault is in God, who made not man and the Demon of equal strength. Listen—one day—"

Here the priest stopped; and the prisoner heard issuing from his bosom sighs which seemed to rend him. He resumed:

"One day, I was leaning against the window of my cell. What book was I reading then? Oh! all that's confusion in my head. I was reading. The window overlooked a square. I heard the sound of a tambourine and music. Angry at being thus disturbed in my revery, I look into the square. What I saw, there were others that saw it too—and yet it was not a spectacle

for human eyes. There, in the middle of the pavement
—it was noon—a burning sun—a creature was dancing
—a creature so beautiful, that God would have preferred her to the Virgin—would have chosen her for
His mother—would have been born of her, if she had
existed when He became man. Her eyes were black
and splendid; amidst her raven locks, a few single hairs,
through which the sunbeams shone, were glistening like
threads of gold. Her feet were lost in the rapidity of
their movement. Around her head, amongst her ebon
tresses, were plates of metal, which sparkled in the sun,
and formed about her temples a diadem of stars. Her
dress, thick-set with spangles, twinkled, all blue and
studded with sparkles, like a summer's night. Her
brown and pliant arms twined and untwined themselves
about her waist like two silken scarfs. Her form was
effulgent with beauty. Oh! the resplendent figure,
which stood out like something luminous even in the
sunlight itself! Alas! young girl, it was thou! Surprised, intoxicated, enchanted, I suffered myself to look.
I looked at thee so long, that all at once I shuddered
with affright. I felt that fate was laying hold on me."

The priest, overcome, again ceased a moment; then
commenced:

"Already half fascinated, I strove to cling to something that might break my fall. I recalled to mind the
snares which Satan had already laid before me. The
creature before me was of that preternatural beauty
which can only be of heaven or hell. That was no
mere girl made of a little of our clay, and feebly lighted within by the vacillating ray of a woman's soul. It
was an angel, but of darkness—of flame, not of light.
At the moment when thinking thus, I saw near thee a
goat, a beast of the sabbath, which looked at me laugh-
ingly. The mid-day sun gilded its horns with fire.
Then I caught a glimpse of the Demon's snare, and I
no longer doubted that thou camest from hell, and that
thou camest for my perdition. I believed so."

Here the priest looked in the face of the prisoner, and
added coolly:

"I believe so still. Meanwhile, the charm operated by degrees; thy dancing whirled in my brain; I felt the mysterious spell at work within me. All that should have kept awake fell asleep in my soul; and, like those who die in the snow, I found pleasure in yielding to that slumber. All at once thou didst begin to sing. What could I do, wretch that I was? Thy song was still more bewitching than thy dance. I would have fled—I felt it impossible. I was nailed, rooted to the ground. It seemed as if the marble flags had risen to my knees. I was obliged to stay to the end. My feet were ice—my brain was boiling. At length thou didst, perhaps, take pity on me; thou didst cease to sing; thou didst disappear. The reflection of the dazzling vision, the reverberation of the enchanting music vanished by degrees from my eyes and ears. Then I fell into the corner of the window, more stiff and helpless than a loosened statue. The vesper bell awoke me. I rose—I fled; but, alas! there was something within me fallen to rise no more—something come upon me from which I could not flee!"

He made another pause, and resumed:

"Yes; from that day forward, there was within me a man I knew not. I had recourse to all my remedies—the cloister—the altar—labor—books. Folly! Oh! how hollow does science sound when a head full of passions in despair strikes against it! Knowest thou, young girl, what I ever after saw between the book and me? It was thyself, thy shade, the image of the luminous apparition which had one day crossed the space before me. But that image no longer wore the same hue—it was gloomy, funereal, darksome—like the black circle that long hangs about the vision of the imprudent one who has been gazing steadfastly at the sun.

"Unable to get rid of it—constantly hearing thy voice warbling in my ears—constantly seeing thy feet dancing on my breviary—constantly feeling at night, in my dreams, thy form in contact with my own—I wished to see thee again—to touch thee—to know who thou wert —to see whether I should find thee indeed equal to the idea. image that had remained of thee—to dispel, perhaps, my dream with the reality. At all events I hoped a fresh impression would efface the former one, and the former was become insupportable. I sought thee. I saw thee again. Misery! When I had seen thee twice, I wished to see thee a thousand times—I wished to see thee always! Then, how to stop short on that hellish declivity? Then I was no longer my own. The other end of the thread which the Demon had tied about my pinions was fastened to his foot. I became vagrant and wandering like thyself—I waited for thee under porches —I spied thee out at the corners of streets—I watched thee from the top of my tower. Each evening, I re-entered within myself more charmed, more desperate, more fascinated, more undone!

"I had learned who thou wast—a gypsy—a Bohemian—a gitana—a zingara. How could I doubt of the magic? Listen. I hoped that a prosecution would rid me of the charm. A sorceress had bewitched Bruno of Asti; he had her burned, and was cured. I knew it. I wished to try the remedy. I first endeavored to get thee prohibited the Parvis Notre-Dame, hoping to forget thee if thou camest no more. Thou heededst it not. Thou camest again. Then arose the idea of carrying thee off. One night I attempted it. There were two of us. Already we had laid hold on thee, when that wretched officer came upon us. He delivered thee. Thus was he the beginning of thy misfortunes, of mine, and of his own. At length, not knowing what to do or what to become of me, I denounced thee to the official. I thought I should be cured like Bruno of Asti. I thought, also, confusedly, that a prosecution would place thee at my disposal—that in a prison I should hold thee, I should have thee—that there thou couldst not escape me—that thou hadst possessed me long enough for me to possess thee in my turn. When one does evil, one should do it thoroughly. 'Tis madness to stop midway in the monstrous! The extremity of crime has its delirium of joy. A priest and a witch may mingle in its ecstasies upon the straw of a dungeor. floor!

"So I denounced thee. 'Twas then that I used to terrify thee whenever I met thee. The plot which I was weaving against thee, the storm which I was brewing over thy head, burst from me in muttered threats and lightning glances. Still, however, I hesitated. My project had its appalling points of view, which made me shrink back.

"Perhaps might I have renounced it—perhaps might my hideous thought have withered in my brain without bearing any fruit. I thought it would always depend upon myself either to follow up or set aside this prosecution. But every evil thought is inexorable, and will become an act; and there, where I thought myself all-powerful, fate was more powerful than I. Alas! alas! 'tis fate has laid hold on thee, and cast thee amid the terrible machinery of the engine I had darkly constructed! Listen—I have almost done.

"One day—it was another day of sunshine—I see pass before me a man who pronounces thy name and laughs; he carries profligacy in his eyes. Damnation! I followed. Thou knowest the rest."

He was silent. The young girl could only find one word to utter—"Oh, my Phœbus!"

"No more of that name!" said the priest, seizing her arm with violence. "Pronounce not that name! Oh! wretched that we are, 'tis that name that has undone us! or rather we have undone one another, all through the inexplicable play of fate! Thou art suffering, art thou not? thou art cold; darkness blinds thee; the dungeon wraps thee round; but perhaps hast thou still some light yet shining within thee — were it only thy childish love for that empty being that was trifling with thy heart? while I—I bear the dungeon within me; within me is the winter, the ice, the despair; I have the darkness in my soul. Knowest thou all that I have suffered? I was present at thy trial. I was seated on the bench of the official. Yes—under one of those priestly hoods were the contortions of a damned spirit. When thou wast brought in, I was there; when thou wast interrogated, I was there. The den of wolves! 'Twas my own crime, 'twas my own gibbet they were slowly constructing over thy head! At each deposition, at each proof, at each pleading, I was there; I could count each one of thy steps in the way of sorrow; I was there, too, when that wild beast . . . . . Oh! I had not foreseen the torture! Listen. I followed thee into the chamber of anguish. I saw thee undressed and half naked under the vile hands of the torturer. I saw thy foot—that foot, to have imprinted a kiss on which and to have died, I would have given an empire—that foot, to have had my head crushed under which I should have felt so much ecstasy—that foot I saw put into the horrible brodequin—that brodequin which makes the limb of a living being all one bloody clod! Oh! miserable wretch! while I was looking on, with a poniard I had under my gown I was lacerating my breast. At the cry thou utteredst, I plunged it in my flesh; at a second cry, it would have entered my heart. Look—I think the wound is bleeding still."

He opened his cassock. His chest was indeed torn as if by a tiger's claws; and in his side was a large ill-closed wound.

The prisoner shrank back with horror.

"Oh!" said the priest, "young girl, take pity on me! Thou thinkest thyself miserable. Alas! alas! thou knowest not what misery is. Oh! to love a woman— to be a priest—to be hated—to love with all the powers of one's soul—to feel that one would give for the least of her smiles one's blood, one's vitals, one's fame, one's salvation, immortality and eternity, this life and that which is to come—to regret one is not a king, a genius, an emperor, an archangel, God, that one might place a greater slave under her feet—to clasp her day and night in one's dreams, in one's thoughts; and to see her in love with the trappings of a soldier, and have nothing to offer her but a priest's poor cassock, at which she will feel fear and disgust! To be present with one's jealousy and one's rage, while she lavishes on a wretched imbecile fanfaron those treasures of love and beauty! To behold that form which maddens you, that voluptuous bosom, that flesh panting and blushing under the kisses of another! Oh heavens! to love her foot, her arm, her shoulder—to think of her blue veins, of her brown skin, till one writhes for nights together on the pavement of one's cell; and to see all those caresses one has dreamed of end in her torture! to have succeeded only in laying her on the bed of leather! Oh, these are the true pincers heated at the fires of hell! Oh! blessed is he that is sawn asunder between two boards, or torn to pieces by four horses! Knowest thou what that torture is, endured through long nights, from boiling arteries, a breaking heart, a bursting head, and teeth-gnawed hands—fell tormentors which are unceasingly turning you, as on a burning gridiron, over a thought of love, jealousy, and despair! Young girl, mercy! A truce for a moment! A few ashes on this living coal! Wipe away, I conjure thee, the perspiration that streams in large drops from my brow! Child! torture me with one hand—but caress me with the other! Have pity, young girl! have pity on me."

The priest rolled himself on the wet floor and beat his head against the angles of the stone steps. The young girl listened to him, looked at him. When he ceased, exhausted and panting, she repeated in an undertone, "Oh, my Phœbus!"

The priest crept toward her on his knees.

"I implore thee," cried he, "if thou hast any bowels of compassion, repulse me not! Oh! I love thee! I am a wretch! When thou utterest that name, unhappy girl, it is as if thou wert grinding between thy teeth every fibre of my heart! Mercy! If thou comest from hell, I go thither with thee. I have done enough for that. The hell where thou art, shall be my paradise—the sight of thee is more to be desired than that of God. Oh! say! wilt thou none of me, then? I should have thought the very mountains would have been removed before a woman would have repulsed such a love. Oh! if thou wouldst! . . . . Oh! how happy could we be! We would fly—I would contrive thy escape—we would go somewhere—we would seek that spot on the earth where the sun is the brightest, the trees most luxuriant, the sky the bluest. We would love each other—our two souls should be poured out into each other—and each of us should have an inextinguishable thirst for the other which we would quench incessantly and in common at that inexhaustible fountain of love!"

She interrupted him with a horrible and thrilling laugh. "Look, father! you have blood upon your fingers!"

The priest remained for some moments as if petrified, his eyes fixed on his hand.

"Yes—'tis well," continued he at length with singular calmness; "insult me—taunt me—overwhelm me with scorn! but come, come away. Let us hasten. 'Tis to be to-morrow, I tell thee. The gibbet of the Grève, thou knowest? It still awaits thee. 'Tis horrible—to see thee carried in that cart! Oh! mercy! Never did I feel as now I do how much I love thee. Oh! follow me. Thou shalt take time to love me after I have saved thee. Thou shalt hate me as long as thou wilt. But come. To-morrow! to-morrow! the gibbet! thy execution! Oh! save thyself! spare me!"

He took her arm—he was wild—he offered to drag her away.

She fixed on him a steady gaze. "What's become of Phœbus?"

"Ah!" said the priest, letting go her arm, "you have no pity!"

"What's become of Phœbus!" repeated she coldly.

"He's dead!" cried the priest.

"Dead!" said she, still frozen and motionless; "then why do you talk to me of living?"

He was not listening to her. "Oh, yes!" said he, as if speaking to himself, "he must be dead enough. The blade entered deep. I think I reached his heart with the point. Oh! my very soul was in that dagger's point!"

The young girl rushed upon him like a furious tigress, and pushed him against the flight of steps with supernatural strength. "Begone, monster! begone, murderer! leave me to die! May the blood of both of us be an everlasting stain upon thy forehead! Be thine! priest! Never! never! nothing shall unite us! not hell itself! Begone, accursed! Never!"

The priest had stumbled against the stairs. He silently disengaged his feet from the folds of his gown, took up his lantern, and began slowly to ascend the steps leading to the door; he reopened the door, and went out. All at once the young girl saw his head reappear; its expression was terrible; and he cried out, hoarse with rage and despair, "I tell thee, he's dead!"

She fell with her face to the floor; and no other sound was now to be heard in the dungeon, save the trickling of the drop of water which ruffled the surface of the pool in the darkness.

CHAPTER V.

THE MOTHER.

WE doubt whether there be anything in the world more gladdening to the heart of a mother than the ideas awakened by the sight of her infant's little shoe; above all, when it is the holiday, the Sunday, the christening shoe—the shoe embroidered to the very sole—a shoe in which the child has not yet taken one step. The shoe so tiny, has such a charm in it—'tis so impossible for it to walk—that it is to the mother as if she saw her child. She smiles at it, she kisses it, she talks to it, she asks herself, can it really be that there's a foot so small? and, should the child be absent, the little shoe suffices to bring back to her view the soft and fragile creature. She thinks she sees it—sees it all—living, joyous, with its delicate hands, its round head, its pure lips, its clear eyes, with their whites so blue. If it be winter, there it is crawling on the carpet, climbing laboriously up a stool; and the mother trembles lest it should go near the fire. If it be summer, it creeps about the yard, the garden—plucks up the grass from between the stones—gazes with artless wonder, and without fear, at the great dogs, the great horses—plays with the shell-work, the flowers, and makes the gardener scold when he finds the gravel on the beds and the mould in the walks. Everything smiles, everything is bright, everything plays around it, like itself—even to the zephyr and the sunbeam, which sport in rivalry amidst its wanton curls. The shoe brings all this home to the mother; and her heart melts before it as wax before the fire.

But when the child is lost, those thousand images of joy, of delight, of tenderness which swarmed around the little shoe, become so many sources of horror. The pretty little embroidered shoe is now only an instrument of torture, wearing away incessantly the heart of the mother. It is still the same chord which vibrates, the fibre the most sensitive, the most profound—but instead of its being touched by an angel, it is now wrenched by a demon.

One morning, as the May sun was rising on one of those dark-blue skies in which Garofolo loves to place his descents from the cross, the recluse of the Tour-Roland heard a noise of wheels, of horses, and the clanking of irons, in the Place de Grève. She was but little roused by it; fastened her hair over her ears to deaden the sound; and on her knees resumed her contemplation of the inanimate object which she had been thus adoring for fifteen years. That little shoe, we have already said, was to her the universe. Her thoughts were locked up in it, and were never to quit it until death. What bitter imprecations she had breathed to heaven, what heart-rending complaints, what prayers and sobs about this charming, rosy, satin toy, the gloomy cave of the Tour-Roland only knew. Never was more despair lavished upon a thing more charming or more graceful. That morning, it seemed as if her grief was venting itself still more violently than usual; and she was heard from without, lamenting in a loud and monotonous voice that went to the heart.

"Oh! my child," said she, "my chi.d! my poor dear
little babe, I shall see thee then no more!—all's over
then! It seems to me always as if it was done but yesterday! My God! my God! to take her from me so
soon—it would have been better not to have given her
to me! You do not know, then, that our children are
of our own bowels, and that a mother that has lost her
child believes no longer in God? Ah! wretched that
I am—to have gone out that day!—Lord! Lord! to
take her from me so! You never saw me with her,
then—when I warmed her all joyous at my fire—when
she laughed at me as I gave her suck—when I made
her little feet creep up my bosom to my lips? Oh! if
you had but seen that, my God! you would have had
pity on my joy—you would not have taken from me
the only thing I had left to love! Was I such a
wretched creature, then, Lord, that you could not look
at me before you condemned me?—Alas! alas! there's
the shoe—but the foot, where is it?—where is the rest!
—where is the child? My babe! my babe! what have
they done with thee? Lord, give her back to me!
For fifteen years have I worn my knees in praying to
thee, my God!—is that not enough? Give her back to
me for one day, one hour, one minute—but one minute,
Lord! and then cast me to the evil one forever! Oh!
if I knew where lay but the hem of your garment, I
would cling to it with both hands, and you would be
obliged to give me back my child! Her pretty little
shoe, have you no pity on it, Lord? Can you condemn a poor mother to this fifteen years' torture?
Good Virgin! good Virgin of heaven! my own infant
Jesus, they have taken it from me—they have stolen it
—they have eaten it on the wild heath—they have
drunk its blood—they have gnawed its bones? Good
Virgin! have pity on me? My girl! I must have my
girl! What care I that she's in heaven? I'll none of
your angel, I want my child! I am the lioness, I want
my whelp! Oh, I'll writhe upon the ground—I'll dash
my forehead against the stones—I'll damn myself, and
curse you, Lord, if you keep from me my child! You

see how my arms are gnawed all over, Lord! Has the
good God no pity! Oh, give me only black bread and
salt, only let me have my child to warm me like a sun!
Alas! Lord God, I am only a vile sinner, but my
child made me pious. I was full of religion for her
sake, and I saw you through her smile as through an
opening of heaven. Oh, let me only once, once again,
one little once, put this shoe on her pretty little rosy
feet—and I will die, good Virgin, blessing you! Ah!
fifteen years! she would be grown up now! Unhappy
child!—What! is it true, then, I shall never see her
more, not even in heaven? for I shall never go there.
Oh, what misery! to have to say, 'There is her shoe,
and that is all!'"

The wretched woman had thrown herself on this
shoe, for so many years her consolation and despair;
and her heart was rent with sobs as at the first day—
for to a mother that has lost her child, it is always the
first day—that grief never grows old. In vain may the
mourning garments wear out and lose their dye—the
heart remains dark as at first!

At that moment some fresh and joyous children's
voices passed before the cell. Whenever any children
met her eye or ear, the poor mother used to rush in the
darkest corner of her sepulchre, and seemed as if she
would plunge her head into the stone that she might
not hear them. This time, on the contrary, she started
up, and listened eagerly. One of the little boys had
just said, "They're going to hang a gypsy woman to-
day."

With a sudden bound, like that of the spider which
we have seen rush upon a fly at the shaking of her web,
she ran to her loophole, which looked out, as the reader
is aware, upon the Place de Grève. There, indeed, was
a ladder reared up against the permanent gibbet; and
the hangman's assistant was busy adjusting the chains
rusted by the rain. Some people were standing around.

The smiling group of children was already far off.
The Sachette sought with her eyes some passer-by
whom she might interrogate. Close to her cell she

caught sight of a priest, who seemed to be reading in the public breviary, but whose mind was much less occupied with the lattice-guarded volume than with the gibbet, toward which he cast from time to time a stern and gloomy look. She recognized Monsieur the Archdeacon of Josas, a holy man.

"Father," asked she, "Who's going to be hanged there?"

The priest looked at her without answering; she repeated the question, and then he said, "I don't know."

"There were some children here just now, that said it was a gypsy woman," continued the recluse.

"I believe it is," said the priest.

Then Paquette la Chantefleurie burst into a hyena laugh.

"Sister," said the archdeacon, "you hate the gypsy woman heartily then?"

"Hate them!" cried the recluse; "they are witches —child-stealers! They devoured my little girl—my child—my only child! I have no heart left—they have devoured it!"

She was frightful. The priest looked at her coldly.

"There's one of them that I hate above all, and that I've cursed," resumed she; "a young one, who's the age my girl would be if her mother had not eaten my girl. Every time that young viper passes before my cell, she makes my blood boil."

"Well, sister, be joyful now," said the priest, as icy cold as a sepulchral statue; "that's the one you are going to see die."

His head fell upon his breast, and he withdrew slowly. The recluse writhed her arms with joy.

"I had foretold it to her that she would go up there again. Thank you, priest," cried she; and then she began to pace with rapid steps before the bars of her window-place, her hair disheveled, her eyes glaring, striking her shoulder against the wall, with the wild air of a caged she-wolf that has long been hungry and feels that the hour of her repast is approaching.

CHAPTER VI.

THREE HEARTS OF DIFFERENT KINDS.

PHŒBUS, however, was not dead. Men of his description are not easily killed. When Maître Philippe
Lheulier, the king's advocate extraordinary, had said to
the poor Esmeralda, "he's dying," it was by mistake
or in jest. When the archdeacon had repeated to the
condemned, "he is dead," the fact was that he knew
nothing about the matter, but that he believed so, that
he calculated it must be so, and fully hoped it was so.
He could ill have brooked the giving to the woman he
was in love with, any good news of his rival. "Any
man in his place," our author ingenuously remarks,
"would have done likewise."

Not, indeed, that Phœbus's wound had not been serious ; but it had been less so than the archdeacon flattered himself. The surgeon—the maître-myrrhe, as he
was then called—to whose residence the soldiers of the
watch had conveyed him in the first instance, had, for
a week, been in fear for his life, and had even told him
so in Latin. However, the vigor of a youthful constitution had triumphed ; and as often happens, notwithstanding prognostics and diagnostics, Nature amused
herself with saving the patient, in spite of the physician.
It was while he was yet lying upon the sick-bed of the
son of Esculapius, that he underwent the first inter-
rogatories of Philippe Lheulier and the official's enquê-
teurs or inquest men, which he had found especially
wearisome. And so, one fine morning, feeling himself beaten, he had left his gold spurs in payment
to the man of medicine and taken himself off. This,
however, had by no means impeded the framing
of the indictment and preparation of the evidence.
The justice of that day was very little anxious
about clearness and precision in the proceedings
against a criminal. Provided only that the accused got
hanged, that was sufficient. And then, the judges had

quite proof enough against La Esmeralda—they had believed Phœbus to be dead—and that was decisive.

Phœbus himself had fled to no great distance. He had merely, and very naturally, gone to join his company, then on garrison duty at Queue-en-Brie, in the Isle of France, a few stages from Paris.

After all, he felt that it would be by no means agreeable for him to appear personally in that trial. He had a vague impression that he would look rather ridiculous in it. In fact, he did not very well know what to think of the whole affair. Superstitious without devotion, like every soldier who is nothing more than a soldier, when he questioned himself upon the particulars of that adventure, he was not altogether without his suspicions respecting the little goat—the odd circumstances under which he had first met with La Esmeralda—the manner no less strange in which she had seemed to betray to him the secret of her passion—her being a gypsy—and last, but not least, the specter monk. In all those incidents he thought he could discern much more magic than love—probably a sorceress—perhaps the devil—a sort of drama, in short—or, to speak the language of that day, a mystery — very disagreeable indeed — in which he played a very awkward part, that of the personage beaten and laughed at. The captain felt abashed at this; he experienced that species of shame which Lafontaine has so admirably defined :

As ashamed as a fox would be, caught by a hen.

Besides, he hoped that the affair would not be rumored about—that, himself being absent, his name would hardly be pronounced in connection with it, or, at any rate would not be heard beyond the court-room of the Tournelle. Nor was he mistaken in that respect; there was not then any *Gazette des Tribunaux ;* and as hardly a week passed in which there was not some coiner boiled to death, some witch hanged, or some heretic burned, at some one of the innumerable justices of Paris, people were so much accustomed to see, at every crossway, the old feudal Themis, with her arms bare and her sleeves turned up, at work at her gibbets, her échelles, and her pillories, that scarcely any notice was taken of the matter. The *beau monde* of that age hardly knew the name of the sufferer that passed by at the corner of the street ; and, at most, it was only the populace that regaled themselves with that unsavory viand. An execution was one of the incidents habitually met with in the public way, like the braisière of the talmellier, or the slaughter-house of the écorcheur. The executioner was but a sort of butcher rather more versed in his trade than ordinary.

Phœbus, therefore, very soon set his mind to rest with respect to the enchantress Esmeralda, or Similar, as he called her, the stab which he had received from the gypsy girl, or from the specter monk (it mattered little to him which), and the issue of the trial. But no sooner was his heart vacant on that side, than the image of Fleur-de-Lys returned to it—for the heart of Captain Phœbus, like the natural philosophy of the day, abhorred a vacuum.

Moreover, he found it very dull staying at Queue-en-Brie, a village of farriers and milk-women with chapped hands ; a long string of mean houses and hovels, bordering the highway on both sides for half a league ; a tail, in short, as its name imports.

Fleur-de-Lys was his last flame but one—a pretty girl—a charming portion ; and so, one fine morning, being quite cured of his wound, and fairly presuming that after two months had elapsed, the affair of the gypsy girl must be over and forgotten, the amorous cavalier arrived, prancing in full feather, at the door of the Logis Gondelaurier.

He paid no attention to a very numerous crowd that was collecting in the Place du Parvis, before the entrance of Notre-Dame. He recollected that it was the month of May—he supposed that there was some procession, some Whitsuntide or other holiday exhibition—fastened his horse's bridle to the ring at the porch, and gayly ascended the staircase in search of his fair betrothed. He found her and her mother alone.

Fleur-de-Lys had still weighing upon her heart the scene of the sorceress with her goat and its accursed alphabet, and the lengthened absence of Phœbus. Nevertheless, when she saw her captain enter, she thought he looked so well, and wore so fresh a hacqueton, so shining a baldrick, and so impassioned an air, that she blushed with pleasure. The noble damoiselle herself was more charming than ever. Her magnificent fair locks were braided to perfection; she was clad in all that heavenly blue which so well becomes a fair complexion (a piece of coquetry which she had learned from her acquaintance, Colombe), and her eyes were steeped in that amorous languor which becomes it better still.

Phœbus, who had seen no description of beauty since he quitted the country wenches of Queue-en-Brie, was absolutely intoxicated with the sight of Fleur-de-Lys— which rendered our officer's manner so gallant and assiduous, that his peace was made immediately. Madame de Gondelaurier herself, still maternally seated in her great fauteuil, had not resolution to scold him. As for Fleur-de-Lys's reproaches, they died away in tender cooings.

The young lady was seated near the window, still embroidering her grotto of Neptunus. The captain stood leaning over the back of her chair, while she murmured to him her gentle upbraidings.

" Wherever have you been for full two months past, you wicked man ?"

" I swear," answered Phœbus, a little embarrassed by the question, " that you are beautiful enough to make an archbishop dream."

She could not help smiling. Very good, very good, monsieur. But leave my beauty alone, and answer me. Fine beauty, to be sure !"

" Well, my dear cousin—I was recalled to keep garrison."

" And where was that, if you please ? and why did you not come and bid me adieu ?"

" It was Queue-en-Brie."

2 3

Phœbus was delighted that the first question had helped him to elude the second.

"But that's quite near, monsieur. How happened it that you did not come once to see me?"

Here Phœbus was very seriously perplexed. "Because—the service—and besides, my charming cousin, I've been unwell."

"Unwell!" exclaimed she in alarm.

"Yes—wounded."

"Wounded!"

The poor girl was quite overcome.

"Oh, don't be frightened about that," said Phœbus, carelessly; "it's nothing at all. A quarrel—a crossing of swords—what does that signify to you, my dear?"

"What does it signify to me!" exclaimed Fleur-de-Lys, lifting her beautiful eyes filled with tears. "Oh! you don't think what you say. What was that crossing of swords? I want to know all about it."

"Well, my fair one, I've had a quarrel with Mahé Fédy, you know, the lieutenant of St. Germain-en-Laye; and each of us have ripped open a few inches of the other's skin—that's all."

The lying captain was well aware that an affair of honor always set a man off to advantage in the eyes of a woman. And, in fact, Fleur-de-Lys looked him in the face with mingled sensations of fear, pleasure, and admiration. However, she did not yet feel completely reassured.

"So that you are but perfectly cured, my Phœbus!" said she. "I don't know your Mahé Fédy—but he must be a vile fellow. And what was this quarrel about?"

Here Phœbus, whose imagination was not over creative, began to be rather at a loss how to dispose conveniently of his prowess.

"Oh, I don't know—a mere nothing at all—a horse—a word dropped. *Belle cousine*," said he, by way of turning the conversation, "what's that noise about in the Parvis?" He went to the window—"Oh, *mon Dieu! belle cousine*, there's a great crowd in the Place."

"I don't know," said Fleur-de-Lys ; "it seems there's a witch going to do penance this morning before the church, on her way to be hanged."

So absolutely did the captain believe the affair of La Esmeralda to be terminated, that he was little affected by these words of Fleur-de-Lys. Nevertheless, he asked her one or two questions.

"What's the witch's name?"

"I don't know," she answered.

"And what do they say she's done?"

Again she shrugged her white shoulders, and replied, "I don't know."

"Oh, *mon Dieu Jésus!*" exclaimed her mother, "there are so many sorcerers nowadays that I dare say they burn them without knowing their names. It would be of no more use than to try to know the name of every cloud in the sky. But, after all, we may make ourselves easy—God above keeps his register." Here the venerable dame rose and went to the window. "Signeur!" she cried, "you're right, Phœbus—there is indeed a great crowd of the populaire. There they are, blessed be God! even up to the house-tops! Do you know, Phœbus, that reminds me of my young days— the entry of King Charles VII.—when there was such a concourse too—I don't recollect what year it was. When I talk to you about that now, it sounds to you (doesn't it?) like something old, and to me like something young. Oh! there was a far finer crowd of people than there is now. There were some even upon the machicolations of the Porte St. Antoine. The king had the queen on a pillion behind him ; and after their highnesses came all the ladies mounted behind the sig- neurs. I remember there was much laughing ; for by the side of Amanyon de Garlande, who was very short, there was the Sire Matefelon, a knight of giant stature, who had killed heaps of English. It was very fine in- deed. A procession of all the gentlemen of France, with their oriflammes waving red before you. There were those of the pennon, and those of the banner. Let me see—there was the Sire de Calan, with his pennon; Jean de Chateaumorant, with his banner; the Sire de Coucy, with his banner—and a richer one, too, than any of the others, except the Duke of Bourbon's. Alas! how melancholy to think that all that has existed, and that all has passed away!"

The two lovers were inattentive to the reminiscences of the venerable dowager. Phœbus had returned to lean over the back of the chair of his betrothed—a charming situation, from which his libertine glance could invade all the openings of Fleur-de-Lys's collarette, which yawned so conveniently, revealed to him so many exquisite things, and led him to divine so many others, that Phœbus, quite ravished with that satiny-glowing skin, said to himself, "How can a man love any but a fair beauty?" They both remained silent. The young lady lifted up to him, from time to time, her eyes full of gentleness and delight; and their hair mingled in the beams of the vernal sun.

"Phœbus," said Fleur-de-Lys all at once, in a whisper, "we are to be married in three months—swear to me that you have never loved any woman but myself."

"I swear it, fair angel!" answered he; and, to convince Fleur-de-Lys, an impassioned look was added to the sincere tone of his voice. Perhaps, indeed, at that moment, he himself believed what he was saying.

Meanwhile, the good mother, delighted to see the two fiancés on such excellent terms with each other, had quitted the apartment to attend to some household matter. Phœbus remarked it; and they being left thus alone so much emboldened the adventurous captain, that some very strange ideas entered his brain. Fleur-de-Lys loved him—he was engaged to her—they were alone—his old inclination for her had revived, not in all its freshness indeed, but in all its ardor — after all, there could be no great crime. We know not exactly whether all these thoughts actually crossed his mind, but this is certain—that Fleur-de-Lys was all at once alarmed at the expression of his countenance. She looked around her, and saw that her mother was gone.

"*Mon Dieu!*" said she, blushing and uneasy, "I'm very hot!"

"I think, indeed," returned Phœbus, "it must be almost noon. The sun becomes annoying—there's no remedy but to draw the curtains."

"No, no!" cried the poor girl, "on the contrary, I've occasion for air."

And, like a hind that scents the breath of the approaching pack, she rose, hurried to the window, opened it, and rushed upon the balcony. Phœbus, little gratified at this movement, followed her thither.

The Place du Parvis Notre-Dame, upon which, as the reader is aware, the balcony looked, presented, at that moment, an odd and dismal spectacle, which suddenly altered the nature of the timid Fleur-de-Lys's alarm.

An immense crowd of people, extending into all the adjacent streets, covered the Place properly so called. The low wall inclosing the Parvis itself, would not have sufficed to keep that interior space clear, but that it was lined by dense ranks of the sergeants of the Onze-vingts, and of hack-buteers, culverin in hand. Owing, however, to this grove of pikes and arquebusses, the Parvis was empty. Its entrance was guarded by a body of the bishop's own halberdiers. The great doors of the church were shut, thus contrasting with the numberless windows round the Place, which, being all open up to the very gables, exhibited thousands of heads piled in heaps, something like the balls in a park of artillery.

The surface of the multitude was dingy and dirty-looking. The sight which they were waiting to see was evidently one of those whose privilege it is to bring out and call together all that is most unclean in the population of a city. Nothing could be more hideous than the murmur that rose from that swarm of yellow caps and dirty heads. In this crowd there were fewer shouts than peals of laughter, fewer men than women.

From time to time some shrill voice pierced through the general hum.

"I say—Mahiet Baliffre—are they going to hang her there?"

"You simpleton! this is to be the penance in her

shift. God Almighty's going to cough Latin in her face. That's always done here at noon. If it's the gallows you want, you must go to the Grève."

" I'll go there after."

* * * * *

" Do just tell me, La Boucanbry, is it true that she's refused to have a confessor?"

" It seems it is, La Bechaigne."

"Oh! the pagan!"

* * * * *

" Sir, it's the custom. The bailiff of the Palais is bound to deliver the malefactor, ready sentenced, for execution—if it's a layman, to the provost of Paris—if it's a clerk, to the official of the bishopric."

" Thank you, sir."

* * * * * * *

" Oh, my God!" said Fleur-de-Lys—" the poor creature!"

This thought filled with sadness the look which she cast over the populace. The captain, whose attention was much more occupied by herself than by that congregation of the rabble, was amorously fingering her waist behind. She turned around with a look half smiling and half entreating. " Now, do leave me alone, Phœbus!—if my mother were to come in she would see your hand."

At that moment, the clock of Notre-Dame slowly struck twelve. A murmur of satisfaction burst from the crowd. The last vibration of the twelfth stroke had hardly expired on the air, when the heads of the multitude were all set in motion like the waves before a sudden gale, and an immense shout arose at once, from the ground, from the windows, and from the roofs, of " Here she comes!"

Fleur-de-Lys put her hands before her eyes, that she might not see.

" My charmer," said Phœbus, " will you go in?"

" No," answered she ; and those eyes which she had just closed through fear, she opened again through curiosity.

A tumbrel drawn by a strong Norman dray-horse, and quite surrounded by horsemen in the violet uniform with the white crosses, had just entered the Place from the Rue Saint-Pierre-aux-Bœufs. The sergeants of the watch made way for it through the multitude by a vigorous use of their whit-leather boullayes. By the side of the tumbrel rode some officers of justice and of police, distinguishable by their black costume and their awkwardness on horseback. Maître Jacques Charmolue paraded at their head. In the fatal cart a young girl was seated, with her hands tied behind her, and without any priest at her side. She was in her shift ; her long black hair (for it was then the custom not to cut it until reaching the foot of the gibbet) fell unbound upon her neck and over her half-uncovered shoulders.

Across those disheveled and undulating locks, more shining than a raven's plumage, was seen, twisted and knotted, a thick brown cord, which roughly chafed the poor girl's pretty fragile neck, encircling it like an earthworm twined about a flower. Beneath that rope glittered a small amulet, ornamented with green glass, which, no doubt, she had been allowed to keep merely because it was thought not worth while to refuse it to one just going to die. The spectators up at the windows could discern at the bottom of the tumbrel her naked legs, which she strove to conceal under her as if through a last remaining instinct of her sex. At her feet was a little she-goat, with its limbs also bound. The condemned was holding together with her teeth her ill-tied chemise. It seemed as if she still suffered in her misery from being thus exposed almost naked before all eyes. Alas ! it was not for shudderings like this that feminine modesty was designed.

" Jesus ! " said Fleur-de-Lys sharply to the captain, " look there, beau cousin—it's that vile gypsy girl with the goat."

So saying, she turned around to Phœbus. His eyes were fixed upon the tumbrel, and he looked very pale.

"What gypsy girl with the goat?" said he, stammering.

"Why," rejoined Fleur-de-Lys, "don't you remember?"

Phœbus interrupted her—"I don't know what you mean."

He made one step to go in; but Fleur-de-Lys, whose jealousy, but lately so vehement, so strongly excited by that same gypsy girl, was now re-awakened, cast at him a glance full of penetration and mistrust. At that moment, she vaguely recollected having heard speak of a captain whose name had been mixed up in the trial of that sorceress.

"What's the matter with you?" said she to Phœbus; "one would think that woman had discomposed you."

Phœbus strove to force a titter. "Me!" said he—"not the least in the world. Me, indeed!"

"Stay, then," said she in a commanding tone, "and let us see it out."

The unlucky captain had no chance but to remain. However, it encouraged him a little, to see that the condemned kept her eyes fixed upon the bottom of the tumbrel. It was but too truly La Esmeralda. In this last stage of ignominy and misfortune, she was still beautiful—her large black eyes looked larger for the sinking of her cheeks, and her livid profile was pure and sublime. She resembled what she had been, just in the degree that one of Masaccio's Virgins resembles one of Raphael's—looking weaker, slenderer, thinner.

As for her mien—she seemed to be all tossing about, as it were—everything, except as far as modesty dictated, being left to chance—so thoroughly had her spirit been broken by stupor and despair. Her form rebounded at every jolt of the tumbrel, like something dead or dislocated—her look was fixed and unconscious—a tear was still to be seen in her eye, but motionless, as if it had been frozen there.

Meanwhile, the dismal cavalcade had traversed the crowd, amid shouts of rejoicing and attitudes of curiosity. Nevertheless, historical fidelity calls upon us to testify that on seeing her so beautiful and so over-whelmed with affliction, many were moved to pity, even among the most hard-hearted. The tumbrel had entered the Parvis, and had stopped before the central doorway of the church.

The escort drew up in a line on either side. The crowd were now silent; and amid that silence so solemn and anxious, each half of the great door turned, as if of itself, upon its hinges, which creaked like the sound of a fife. Then the deep interior of the church was seen in its whole extent, gloomy, hung with mourning, faintly lighted by a few wax tapers twinkling afar off upon the high altar, yawning like a cavern amidst the Place inundated with light. Quite at the farther end, in the shade of the chancel, was dimly distinguished a gigantic silver cross, gleaming against a piece of black drapery, which hung from the vaulted ceiling down to the floor. The nave was quite solitary; but the heads of some priests were seen confusedly stirring in the distant stalls of the choir; and at the moment that the great door opened, there burst from the interior of the church a solemn and monotonous chant, which cast, as in successive puffs, upon the head of the condemned, fragments of dismal psalms:—

" . . . . *Non timebo millia populi circumdantis me; exsurge, Domine : salvum me fac, Deus !* " *

" . . . . *Salvum me fac, Deus, quoniam intraverunt aquæ usque ad animam meam.*" †

" . . . . *Infixus sum in limo profundi; et non est substantia.*" ‡

At the same time another voice, isolated from the choir, gave out from the steps of the high altar, this melancholy offertory:

" . . . . *Qui verbum meum audit, et credit ei qui*

---

* . . . . I will not fear the thousands of the people gathered about me; arise, O Lord! save me, O my God.

† . . . . Save me, O God; albeit the waters have entered in even unto my soul.

‡ . . . . Behold, I am set fast in the slime of the great deep and there is no ground under my feet.

misit me, habet vitam æternam, et in judicium non venit ;
sed transit a morte in vitam." *

This chant, which some old men, lost to view in the
darkness of the church, were thus pouring forth over
that beautiful creature full of youth and life, wooed by
the tepid airs of spring, and wrapped in sunshine, was
the mass for the dead.

The multitude listened in mute attention.

The unfortunate girl, quite bewildered, seemed to
lose her view and her consciousness in the dark interior
of the cathedral. Her pale lips moved as if uttering a
prayer ; and when the executioner's assistant approached to help her down from the tumbrel, he heard her
repeat, in a whisper, the word "Phœbus."

They untied her hands, and made her descend from
the vehicle, accompanied by her goat, which they
also unbound, and which bleated with joy to feel itself
at liberty. They then made her walk barefoot over
the pavement, to the bottom of the great steps of entrance ; the rope that was passed round her neck trail-
ing behind her, and looking like a serpent closely pursuing her.

Then there was a pause in the chant within the
church. A great cross of gold and a file of wax-tapers
were seen beginning to move in the dark distance. The
halberds of the motley-dressed yeomen of the bishop
were heard to clang upon the floor ; and in a few minutes a long procession, of priests in their chasubles and
deacons in their dalmatics, coming, psalm-singing,
slowly along, developed itself to the view of the condemned and to that of the multitude. But her eye
fixed itself upon the one who walked at their head, immediately after the cross-bearer. "Oh !" said she to
herself in a low whisper, shuddering as she spoke, "'tis
he again ! the priest !"

It was in fact the archdeacon. On his left walked

---

* . . . . Whoso heareth my word, and believeth in him that
sent me, hath life everlasting ; he cometh not into judgment, but
from death he passeth unto life.

the sub-chanter; and on his right, the precentor, carrying
his staff of office. He advanced with his head thrown
back, his eyes wide open and fixed, singing in a strong
voice:

"*De ventre inferi clamavi, et exaudisti vocem meam.*[*]
"*Et projecisti me in profundum in corde maris, et
flumen circumdedit me.*"[†]

At the moment that he appeared in the broad daylight, under the high pointed doorway, wrapped in an
ample silver cope, marked with a black cross, he was so
pale, that some among the crowd actually thought that
one of the marble bishops kneeling on the tombstones
in the choir had risen upon his feet, and was come to
receive on the threshold of the grave her who was going
to die.

She herself, no less pale and statue-like, had scarcely
perceived that they had put into her hand a heavy
lighted taper of yellow wax. She had not hearkened
to the clamorous voice of the registrar, reading over the
fatal tenor of the amende honorable; only, when they
had told her to answer amen, she had answered,
"Amen!"

She was not brought back to some slight consciousness of life and strength, until she saw the priest make
a sign to her guards to retire, and himself advanced
toward her. But now she felt her blood boiling in her
head, and a remaining spark of indignation was kindled
in that spirit already benumbed and cold.

The archdeacon approached her slowly. Even in
that her dire extremity, she perceived him cast over her
exposed form an eye sparkling with jealousy and lascivious desire. Then he said to her in a loud voice,
"Young woman, have you asked pardon of God for
your sins and your offenses?" He leaned to her ear,
and added (while the spectators supposed he was re-

---

[*] Out of the bowels of the earth I have called unto thee, and
thou hast heard my voice.

[†] And thou hast cast me into the depths of the sea, and the
waters have gone about me.

ceiving her last confession), "Will you have anything to say to me? I can save you yet!"

She looked him steadfastly in the face and said, "Begone, you demon, or I denounce you!"

He smiled—a horrid smile—"They'll not believe you—you will be but adding a scandal to a crime—answer me quickly—will you have anything to say to me?"

"What have you done with my Phœbus," she returned.

"He's dead," said the priest.

At that moment, the wretched archdeacon raised his head mechanically, and saw, at the opposite side of the Place, on the balcony of the Logis Gondelaurier, the captain himself, standing close by Fleur-de-Lys. He staggered, passed his hands over his eyes, looked again, muttered a malediction, and every line of his face was violently contracted.

"Well, then, die thou!" said he, between his teeth; "no one shall have thee!" Then lifting his hand over the gypsy girl, he exclaimed, in a sepulchral voice, "*I nunc anima anceps, et sit tibi Deus misericors.*" *

This was the awful formula with which it was the custom to close that gloomy ceremonial. It was the preconcerted signal given by the priest to the executioner.

Hereupon the people knelt down.

"*Kyrie Eleison!*" † said the priests, remaining under the great arched doorway.

"*Kyrie Eleison!*" repeated the multitude, with that murmuring noise which runs over a sea of heads, like the plashing of the waves of the sea itself when in agitation.

"Amen!" said the archdeacon.

He turned his back upon the condemned; his head fell upon his breast; his hands crossed themselves; he returned to his train of priests, and in a minute he was

---

* Go thy way now, lingering soul, and may God have mercy upon thee!

† Lord, have mercy upon us!

seen to disappear with the cross; the tapers and the copes, under the dim arches of the cathedral, and his sonorous voice gradually died away in the choir while chanting this verse of despair:

"*Omnes gurgites tui et fluctus tui super me trans-ierunt!*" ‡

At the same time, the intermitted clang of the iron-covered butt-ends of the yeomen's pikes, dying away successively under the several intercolumniations of the nave, sounded like the hammer of a clock striking the last hour of the condemned.

Meanwhile the doors of Notre-Dame remained open, showing the interior of the church, empty, desolate, in mourning, torchless, and voiceless.

The condemned remained motionless on the spot where they had placed her, waiting to be disposed of. It was necessary for one of the sergeants of the wand to give information of the circumstance to Maître Charmolue, who, during all this scene, had set himself to study that bas-relief of the grand portal which represents, according to some, Abraham's sacrifice, according to others the magnum opus, the grand alchemical operation, the sun being figured by the angel, the fire by the fagot, and the operator by Abraham.

They had much ado to draw him away from this contemplation; but at last he turned round, and at the sign which he made them, two men dressed in yellow, the executioner's assistants, approached the gypsy girl to tie her hands again.

The unfortunate girl at the moment of re-ascending the fatal cart, and moving on toward her final scene, was seized, perhaps, by some last overwhelming clinging to life. She lifted her dry reddened eyes to heaven, to the sky, to the sun, to the silvery clouds, intermingled with patches of brilliant blue; then she cast them around her upon the ground, the people, the houses. All at once, while the man in yellow was pinioning her,

---

‡ All thy whirlpools, O Lord, and all thy waves, have gone over me!

she uttered a terrible cry, a cry of joy. At that balcony over there, at the angle of the Place, she had distinguished his form, the form of him, her friend, her lord, Phœbus, that other apparition of her life! The judge had lied! the priest had lied! it was he indeed, she could not doubt it. He was there, living, beautiful, clad in his brilliant uniform, with the plume on his head and the sword by his side.

"Phœbus!" she cried, "my Phœbus!" and she would have stretched out to him her arms all trembling with love and delight, but they were bound.

Then she saw the captain knit his brows; a fine young woman, leaning upon his arm, looked at him with scornful lip and angry eye; then Phœbus uttered some words which did not reach her ear, and then he and the lady both hastily disappeared behind the casement of the balcony, which immediately closed.

"Phœbus!" cried the unfortunate, "can it be that thou believest it?"

A monstrous idea had just suggested itself to her. She recollected that she had been condemned for murder committed on the person of Phœbus de Chateaupers.

She had supported everything until now, but this last blow was too severe. She fell senseless upon the ground.

"Come," said Charmolue, "carry her into the cart, and let us finish."

No one had yet remarked, in the gallery of royal statues carved immediately above the arches of the portal, a strange-looking spectator, who, until then, had been observing all that passed with such absolute passiveness, a neck so intently stretched, a visage so deformed, that, but for his habiliments, half red and half violet, he might have been taken for one of the stone monsters through whose mouths the long gutters of the cathedral have disgorged themselves for six hundred years. No visible circumstance of all that had been transacted before the entrance of Notre-Dame since the hour of twelve had escaped this spectator. And at the very commencement, without any one's noticing the action, he had fastened firmly to one of the small columns of the gallery a strong knotted rope, the other end of which fell down below upon the top of the steps of entrance. This being done, he had set himself to look quietly on, only whistling from time to time when some blackbird flew by him. All at once, at the moment that the chief executioner's two assistants were preparing to execute Charmolue's phlegmatic order, he strided over the balustrade of the gallery, gripped the cord with his feet, his knees, and his hands; then he was seen to slide down over that part of the façade, like a drop of rain gliding down a pane of glass, run up to the two sub-executioners with the speed of a cat just dropped from a housetop, knock them both down with a pair of enormous fists, carry off the gypsy girl with one hand, as a child does a doll, and leap, at one bound, into the church, lifting the girl above his head, and crying out with a formidable voice, " Sanctuary!"

This was done with such rapidity that, had it been night, the whole might have been seen by the glare of a single flash of lightning.

" Sanctuary! sanctuary!" repeated the crowd; and the clapping of ten thousand hands made Quasimodo's only eye sparkle with joy and pride.

This shock brought the condemned to her senses. She lifted her eyelids, looked at Quasimodo, then suddenly dropped them again, as if terrified at her deliverer.

Charmolue, the executioners, and the whole escort were confounded. The fact was that within the walls of Notre-Dame the condemned was inviolable. The cathedral was a recognized place of refuge; all temporal jurisdiction expired upon its threshold.

Quasimodo had stopped under the grand doorway. His broad feet seemed to rest as solidly upon the floor of the church as the heavy Roman pillars themselves. His great disheveled head looked compressed between his shoulders, like that of a lion, which animal, in like manner, has a mane but no neck. He held the young girl, all palpitating, suspended in his horny hands, like a piece of white drapery, but he bore her so cautiously that he seemed to be afraid of breaking or withering her. It was as if he felt that she was something delicate, exquisite, precious, made for other hands than his. At some moments he looked as if not daring to touch her, even with his breath. Then, all at once, he would strain her closely in his arms to his angular breast, as if she were his only good, his treasure, as the mother of that child would have done. His gnome's eye, bent down upon her, poured over her a flood of tenderness, grief, and pity, and then again it was lifted up all flashing. Then the women laughed and wept, the crowd stamped their feet with enthusiasm, for at that moment Quasimodo had really a beauty of his own. Yes, that orphan, that foundling, that outcast was fair to look upon. He felt himself august in his strength. He stood erect, looking full in the face that society from which he was banished, yet in which he was displaying so powerful an intervention; that human justice from which he had snatched its prey; all those tigers whose longing jaws he forced to remain empty; all those police-agents, those judges, those executioners; all that force of the king which he, poor and helpless as he was, had broken with the force of God.

And then, there was something affecting in that protection falling from a being so deformed upon one so unfortunate; in the circumstance of a poor girl condemned to death being saved by Quasimodo. It was the extremity of natural and that of social wretchedness, meeting and assisting each other.

Meanwhile, after a few minutes' triumph, Quasimodo had suddenly plunged, with his burden, into the darksome interior of the church. The people, fond of any display of prowess, sought him with their eyes under the gloomy nave, regretting that he had so quickly withdrawn himself from their acclamations. All at once he was seen to reappear at one extremity of the gallery of the royal statues. He passed along it, running like a madman, lifting up his conquest in his arms,

ind shouting "Sanctuary!" Fresh plaudits burst from
the multitude. Having traversed the gallery, he plunged
again into the interior of the church. A minute afterward he appeared upon the upper platform, still bearing the gypsy in his arms, still running wildly along,
still shouting "Sanctuary!" and the crowd still ap-
plauding. At last he made a third appearance on the
summit of the tower of the great bell : from thence he
seemed to show exultingly to the whole city the fair
creature he had saved ; and his thundering voice, that
voice which was heard so seldom, and which he never
heard at all, thrice repeated with frantic vehemence,
even in the very clouds, "Sanctuary! Sanctuary! Sanctuary!"

"Noël! Noël! cried the people in their turn ; and
that multitudinous acclamation resounded upon the
opposite shore of the Seine, to the astonishment of the
crowd assembled in the Place de Grève, and of the recluse herself, who was still waiting with her eyes fixed
upon the gibbet.

24

BOOK VIII.

CHAPTER I.

DELIRIUM.

CLAUDE FROLLO was no longer in Notre-Dame when his adopted son thus abruptly cut the fatal knot in which the unhappy archdeacon had bound the gypsy girl and caught himself. On returning into the sacristy, he had torn from his shoulders the albe, the cope, and the stole; thrown them all into the hands of the amazed verger; made his escape through the private door of the cloister; had ordered a wherryman of the Terrain to convey him to the left bank of the Seine, and plunged into the hilly streets of the University, going he knew not whither; meeting, at every step, parties of men and of women pressing joyously toward the Pont St. Michel, in the hope that they should still " get there in time " to see the witch hanged—looking pale and wild, more troubled, more blinded, and more scared than some bird of night let fly and pursued by a troop of children in broad daylight. He knew not where he was, what he thought, what he dreamed. He went forward, walking, running, taking each street at random, making no selection of his route, only still urged on by that Grève, that horrible Grève, which he confusedly felt to be behind him.

In this manner he proceeded the whole length of the Montagne Ste. Geneviève, and at last issued out of the town by the Porte St. Victor. He continued his flight so long as, turning round, he could see the towered enclosure of the University, and the scattered houses of the faubourg; but when at last a ridge of ground had taken completely out of his view that hateful Paris—when he could imagine himself a hundred leagues from it—in the country—in a desert—he stopped, and felt as if he breathed more freely.

Then frightful ideas rushed upon his mind. He saw down clear into his soul, and shuddered. He thought of that unfortunate girl who had destroyed him, and whom he had destroyed. He cast a haggard eye over the two winding paths, along which fate had driven their separate destinies, to that point of intersection at which she had pitilessly shattered them against each other. He thought of the folly of everlasting vows—the emptiness of chastity, science, religion, virtue—the inutility of God. He took his fill of these bad thoughts; and, while plunging deeper into them, he felt as if the fiend were laughing within him.

And, while thus diving into his soul, when he saw how large a space nature had assigned in it to the passions, he smiled more bitterly still. He stirred up from the bottom of his heart all his hatred, all his wickedness; and he discovered, with the cool eye of a physician examining a patient, that this hatred, this wickedness, were but vitiated love—that love, the source of every virtue in man, turned to things horrible in the heart of a priest—and that a man constituted as he was, by making himself a priest, made himself a demon. Then he laughed frightfully, and all at once he grew pale again, in contemplating the worst side of his fatal passion—of that love, corroding, venomous, malignant, implacable—which had driven one of them to the gibbet, the other to hell-fire; her to condemnation, him to damnation.

And then his laugh came again, when he reflected that Phœbus was living—that the captain was alive, gay, and happy, had finer hacquetons than ever, and a new mistress, whom he brought to see the old one hanged. And he sneered at himself with redoubled bitterness, when he reflected that, of the living beings whose death he had desired, the only one whom he did not really hate, was the only one he had not failed to kill.

Then his thoughts wandered from the captain to the assembled multitude, and he was seized with a jealousy of a novel kind. He reflected that the people, too, the whole people, had had before their eyes the woman whom he loved, exposed almost in a state of nudity. He writhed his arms with agony at the idea that that woman, but a glimpse of whose form caught by himself alone in the darkness, would have been to him the very height of happiness, had been given thus, in broad daylight, at the very noontide, to the gaze of a whole multitude, clad as for a bridal night. He wept with rage over the thought that all those mysteries of love should be thus profaned, sullied, stripped, withered forever. He wept with rage as he figured to himself how many impure looks that ill-attached vesture had gratified—that this lovely girl, this virgin lily, this cup of purity and delight, which he could not have approached with his lips but in trembling, had been converted, as it were, into a public trough, at which the vilest of the Parisian populace, the thieves, the beggars, the lackeys, had come to drink in common of a pleasure shameless, impure, and depraved.

And then, when he thought to picture to his imagination the happiness which he might have found upon earth, had not she been a gypsy and he a priest, had Phœbus not existed, and had she but loved him—when he figured to himself that a life of serenity and love would have been possible for him too—that at that very moment there were happy couples to be found here and there upon the earth, whiling away the hours in sweet and devious converse, in orange groves—on the side of rivulets—by the setting sun, or under a starry sky—and that, had it been God's will, he might have formed with her one of those blissful couples—his heart melted in tenderness and despair.

Oh, she—still she! It was that fixed idea that haunted him incessantly—that tortured him—that gnawed his brain and corroded his heart. He did not regret,

he did not repent; all that he had done, he was ready
to do again; he liked better to see her in the hands of
the executioner than in the arms of the captain. But
he was suffering, suffering so violently, that at some
moments he tore handfuls of hair from his head, to see
if it were not whitening.

There was one moment, among the rest, at which it
entered his mind that, perhaps at that very minute, the
hideous chain which he had seen in the morning, was
drawing its noose of iron about that neck so slender
and so graceful; this thought brought the perspiration
boiling through his pores.

There was another moment at which, in the midst of
a diabolical laugh at himself, he pictured to his imagination, at one and the same time, La Esmeralda as he
had seen her for the first time—lively, careless, joyous,
gayly attired, dancing, winged, harmonious—and La
Esmeralda at her last hour, in her scanty shift, with the
rope about her neck, ascending slowly with her naked
feet the sharp-cornered steps of the gibbet. He drew
this picture to himself so vividly that he uttered a terrific cry.

While this hurricane of despair was overturning,
breaking, tearing up, bending to the earth, uprooting
all within him, he looked upon the face of nature
around him. At his feet some fowls were stirring
about among the bushes, pecking the scaly insects that
were running in the sunshine. Over his head were
some groups of dappled clouds, gliding over a deep
blue sky. In the horizon, the spire of St. Victor's abbey shot up its obelisk of slate above the intervening
ridge of ground. And the miller of the Butte Copeaux
was whistling light-heartedly while he looked at the
steady-turning sails of his mill. All those objects, instinct with a life active, organized, and tranquil, recur-
ring around him in a thousand forms, were painful to
him; and again he began to fly.

Thus he hurried on through the country until the
evening. This flight of his, from nature, from life,
from himself, from man, from God, from everything,

lasted the whole day. Sometimes he threw himself with his face to the ground, and tore up with his nails the young blades of corn. Sometimes he stopped in the solitary street of a village, and his thoughts were so insupportable, that he would take his head between both his hands, as if to tear it from his shoulders and dash it on the stones.

Toward the hour of sunset, he examined himself again, and found himself almost mad. The storm that had been raging within him ever since the moment that he had lost all hope and wish to save the gypsy girl, had left him unconscious of a single sound idea, a single rational thought. His reason lay prostrate, almost utterly destroyed. Only two distinct images remained in his mind, La Esmeralda and the gallows—all beside was utter darkness. Those two images, appearing together, presented to him a frightful group ; and the more he fixed upon them such power of attention and contemplation as remained to him, the more he saw them increase according to a fancied progression— the one in grace, in charm, in beauty, in light—the other in deformity and horror—until, at last, La Esmeralda appeared to him as a star, the gibbet as an enormous fleshless arm.

It is remarkable that, during all this torture, he was visited by no serious thought of dying. So the wretched man was constituted—he clung to life—perhaps, indeed, he really saw hell in prospect.

Meanwhile, the daylight was declining. The living spirit still existing within him began confusedly to think of return. He thought himself far from Paris ; but, on striving to ascertain its bearing, he discovered that he had only been traveling round the circuit of the University. The spire at St. Sulpice and the three lofty needles of St. Germain-des-Près, shot up above the horizon on his right. He bent his steps in that direction. When he heard the "*Qui-vive !*" of the abbot's men-at-arms around the embattled circumvallation of St. Germain's, he turned aside, took a path that lay before him, between the abbey mill and the Maladerie or lazaretto of the bourg, and in a few minutes found himself upon the border of the Pré-aux-Clercs. This Pré was celebrated for the tumults that arose in it night and day; it was a hydra to the poor monks of St. Germain's —*Quod monachis Sancti Germani Pratensis hydra fuit, clericis nova semper dissidiorum capita suscitantibus.* The archdeacon was afraid of meeting some one there; he dreaded to encounter any human face; he had avoided the University, and the Bourg St. Germain, and he wished to enter the streets again at the latest hour possible. He passed along the side of the Pré-aux-Clercs, took the solitary path which lay between it and the Dieu-Neuf, and at length reached the water-side. There Dom Claude found a boatman, who, for a few deniers parisis, conveyed him up the Seine to the extremity of the island of the City, and landed him upon that uninhabited tongue of land on which the reader has already seen poor Gringoire musing, and which extended beyond the king's gardens, parallel to the islet of the Passeur-aux-Vaches.

The monotonous rocking of the boat, and the dashing of the water, had in some degree lulled the unhappy Claude. When the wherryman had taken his departure, he remained standing in stupor upon the bank, looking straight before him, but perceiving objects only through such magnifying objects as made all a sort of phantasmagoria to him. The exhaustion of a violent grief will often produce this effect upon the mind.

The sun had set behind the lofty Tour de Nesle, and it was now the twilight hour. The sky was white, and so was the surface of the river. Between these two sheets of white, the left bank of the Seine, upon which his eyes were fixed, projected its dark mass, which, gradually tapering away in the perspective, shot out into the gray horizon like a huge black spire. It was loaded with houses, of which nothing was distinguishable but the dark outline of the whole, boldly marked upon the clear light tint of the sky and the water. Here and there the windows were beginning to twinkle from the lights within. That immense black obelisk, thus isolated between the two white expanses of the sky and the river (at that place very broad), had a singular appearance to Dom Claude, similar to that which would be experienced by a man lying with his back to the ground at the foot of the steeple of Strasburg, and looking up at the enormous spire piercing into the sky above him in the dim twilight. Only there was this difference—that here Claude was erect, and the obelisk was horizontal; but as the river, by reflecting the sky, deepened indefinitely the abyss beneath him, the vast promontory seemed springing as boldly into the void as any cathedral spire, and the impression was the same. Here, indeed, the impression was in this respect stronger and more profound—that, although it was indeed the steeple of Strasburg, it was the steeple of Strasburg two leagues high—something unexampled, gigantic, immeasurable—a structure such as no human eye had seen, except it were the Tower of Babel. The chimneys of the houses, the battlements of the walls, the fantastically-cut gables of the roofs, the spire of the Augustines, the Tour de Nesle—all those projections which indented the profile of the colossal obelisk—added to the illusion by their odd resemblance to the outline of a florid and fanciful sculpture. Claude, in the state of hallucination in which he then was, thought he saw with his living eyes the very steeple of hell. The thousand lights scattered over the whole height of the fearful tower, seemed to him to be so many openings of the vast internal furnace; while the voices and the noises that escaped from it were so many shrieks and groanings of the damned. Then he was terror-struck; he put his hands to his ears that he might hear no longer, turned his back that he might no longer see, and strode hastily away from the frightful vision. But the vision was in himself.

When he came into the streets again, the people passing to and fro in the light of the shop-fronts appeared to him like an everlasting movement of specters about him. He had strange noises in his ears, and extraordinary fancies disturbed his brain. He saw neither the houses, nor the pavement, nor the vehicles, nor the men and women—but a chaos of undefined objects merging one into another. At the corner of the Rue de la Barillerie, there was a chandler's shop, which had the penthouse above its window, according to immemorial custom, garnished all round with tin hoops, from each of which was suspended a circle of wooden candles, clattering against each other in the wind with a noise like that of castanets. He thought he heard, rattling one against another in the dark, the bundles of skeletons at Montfaucon.

"Oh!" muttered he, "the night wind drives them one against another, and mixes the rattle of their chains with the rattle of their bones. Perhaps she is there in the midst of them!"

Quite bewildered, he knew not whither he was going. After advancing a few steps farther, he found himself upon the Pont St. Michel. There was a light at a ground-floor window—he went up to it. Through the cracked panes he saw a dirty room, which awakened in his mind a confused recollection. In that room, ill-lighted by a meager lamp, there was a young man, fair and fresh-looking, with a joyous face, throwing his arms, with boisterous laughter, about a girl very immodestly attired; and near the lamp there was an old woman spinning and singing with a tremulous voice. As the young man's laughter was not heard at every moment, the old woman's song made its way in fragments to the ear of the priest; it was something unintelligible yet frightful:

> "Growl, Grève! bark Grève!
> Spin away, my distaff brave!
> Let the hangman have his cord,
> That whistles in the prison-yard.
> Growl, Grève! bark, Grève!

> "Hemp, that makes the pretty rope—
> Sow it widely, give it scope—
> Better hemp than wheaten sheaves;
> Thief there's none that ever thieves
> The pretty rope, the hempen rope.

"Bark, Grève! growl Grève!
 To see the girl of pleasure brave
  Dangling on the gibbet high,
  Every window is an eye—
 Bark, Grève! growl, Grève!"

Hereupon the young man was laughing and caressing the girl. The old woman was La Falourdel; the girl was a girl of the town; and the young man was his brother Jehan.

He continued looking; this sight pleased him then as well as any other.

He saw Jehan go to a window at the farther end of the room, open it, look out upon the quay, where a thousand lighted windows were shining in the distance; and then he heard him say, as he shut the window again:

"Upon my soul, but it's night already! The towns-folk are lighting their candles, and God Almighty his stars."

Then Jehan returned to the wench, and broke a bottle that stood by them on a table, exclaiming: "Empty already, cor-bœuf! and I've no more money. Isabeau, my darling, I shall not be satisfied with Jupiter till he's changed your two white nipples into two black bottles, that I may suck Beaune wine from them day and night."

This fine piece of wit made the courtezan laugh; and Jehan took his departure.

Dom Claude had only just time to throw himself on the ground, in order to escape being met, looked in the face, and recognized by his brother. Fortunately the street was dark, and the scholar was drunk. Nevertheless, he espied the archdeacon lying upon the pavement in the mud. "Oh! oh!" said he, "here's one that's had a merry time of it to-day."

He pushed Dom Claude with his foot, the archdeacon holding his breath the while.

"Dead drunk!" resumed Jehan. "Bravo! he's full! a very leech dropped off a wine-cask. He's bald," added he, stooping over him; "it's an old man—*Fortunate senex!*"

Then Dom Claude heard him go away, saying: "It's

all one—reason's a fine thing—and my brother the arch-deacon's a lucky fellow to be wise and have money!"

The archdeacon then got up again, and hurried straight to Notre-Dame, the big towers of which he could see rising in the dark over the houses.

At the moment that he arrived, all panting, at the Place du Parvis, he shrunk back, and dared not lift his eyes toward the fatal edifice. "Oh," whispered he to himself, "and can it really be, that such a thing took place here to-day—this very morning!"

And now he ventured a glance at the church. Its front was dark—the sky behind was glittering with stars —the crescent moon, in her flight upward from the horizon, at that moment reached the summit of the right-hand tower, and seemed to have perched upon it, like a luminous bird, on the edge of the dark trifoliated balustrade.

The gate of the cloister was shut; but the archdeacon always had with him the key of the tower containing his laboratory, and he now made use of it to enter the church.

He found within it the darkness and the silence of a cavern. By the great shadows that fell from all sides in broad masses, he perceived that the hangings of the morning ceremony were not yet taken away. The great silver cross was glittering amid the darkness, sprinkled over with a number of glittering points, like the milky-way of that sepulchral night. The long windows of the choir showed, above the black drapery, the upper ex-tremities of their pointed arches, the stained glass of which, as shown by the moonlight, had only the doubt-ful colors of the night, a sort of violet, white, and blue, of a tint to be found nowhere else but on the faces of the dead. The archdeacon, on observing all round the choir those pale pointed window tops, thought he saw so many mitres of bishops gone to perdition. He closed his eyes; and when he opened them again, he thought they were a circle of pale visages looking down upon him.

He began to flee away through the church. Then it

seemed to him as if the church itself took life and motion—that each massive column became an enormous leg that beat the ground with its broad foot of stone, and that the gigantic cathedral had become a sort of prodigious elephant, breathing and walking along, with its pillars for legs, its two towers for tusks, and the immense black drapery for its caparison.

Thus his fever, or his madness, had arrived at such a pitch of intensity, that the whole external world was become to the unhappy man a sort of apocalypse, visible, palpable, frightful.

For one moment he felt some relief; on plunging into the side aisles, he perceived issuing from behind a group of pillars, a reddish light; he rushed toward it as toward a star of salvation. It was the feeble lamp that lighted day and night the public breviary of Notre-Dame under its iron trellis-work. He cast his eye eagerly upon the sacred book, in the hope of finding there some sentence of consolation or encouragement. The volume was open at this passage of Job, over which he ran his burning eye: "And a spirit passed before my face; and I heard a little breath; and the hair of my flesh stood up."

On reading this dismal sentence, his sensations were those of a blind man when he feels himself pricked by the staff he has picked up. His knees dropped under him, and he sank upon the pavement, thinking of her who had died that day. He felt so many monstrous fumes inundating his brain, that it seemed to him as if his head was become one of the chimneys of hell.

It appears that he remained long in this posture—thinking no more, but overwhelmed and passive under the power of the demon. At last some strength returned to him; he thought of going and taking refuge in the tower, near to his faithful Quasimodo. He rose; and, as fear was upon him, he took the lamp of the breviary to light him. This was a sacrilege—but he was now beyond regarding so slight a consideration.

He climbed slowly up the staircase of the towers, filled with a secret dread, which was likely to be communicated even to the few passengers at that hour through the Place du Parvis, by the mysterious light of his lamp ascending so late at night from loophole to loophole, to the top of the steeple.

All at once he felt some coolness upon his face, and found himself under the doorway of the upper gallery. The air was cold; the sky was streaked with clouds, the broad white flakes of which drifted one upon another like river ice breaking up after a frost. The crescent moon gleaming amid them, looked now like some celestial vessel set fast among those icebergs of the air.

He cast his eyes downward, and gazed for a moment through the curtain of slender columns that connects the towers, afar off, through a light veil of mist and smoke—upon the silent multitude of the roofs of Paris —pointed, innumerable, crowded, and small, like the waves of a tranquil sea in a summer's night. The moon cast a feeble light, which gave to earth and sky an ashy hue.

At that moment the cathedral clock lifted its harsh, broken voice. It struck twelve. The priest thought of noon—it was twelve o'clock come again. "Oh," he whispered to himself, "she must be cold now."

Suddenly a puff of wind extinguished his lamp, and almost at the same time there appeared to him, at the opposite angle of the tower, a shade, a something white, a shape, a female form. He started. By the side of that female form was that of a little goat, that mingled its bleating with the last sounds of the clock.

He had resolution enough to look—it was she!

She was pale—she was sad. Her hair fell upon her shoulders as in the morning, but no rope was round her neck, no cord upon her hands—she was free—she was clad in white, and over her head was thrown a white veil.

She came toward him slowly, looking up to heaven, the unearthly goat following her. He felt himself of stone—too stiff to fly. At each step that she came forward, he made one backward, and that was all. In this manner he re-entered under the dark vault of the staircase. He froze at the idea that she perhaps was going to enter there too; had she done so, he would have died of terror.

She arrived indeed before the staircase door, stopped there for some moments, looked steadfastly into the dark cavity; then, without appearing to perceive the priest there, she passed on. He thought she looked taller than when she was alive—he saw the moon through her white robe—and was near enough to hear her breathing.

When she had passed by, he began to redescend the staircase with the same slowness which he had observed in the specter, thinking himself a specter too—all haggard, his hair erect, the lamp still extinguished in his hand; and, as he descended the spiral stairs, he distinctly heard a voice laughing and repeating in his ear: "And a spirit passed before my face; and I heard a little breath; and the hair of my flesh stood up."

CHAPTER II.

HUMP-BACKED, BLEAR-EYED, AND LAME.

EVERY town in the Middle Ages, and down to the time of Louis XII., every town in France had its places of sanctuary. These sanctuaries, amid the deluge of penal laws and barbarous jurisdictions that inundated the state, were a sort of islands rising above the level of human justice. Every criminal that landed upon any one of them was saved. In each banlieue there were almost as many of these places of refuge as there were of execution. It was the abuse of impunity beside the abuse of capital punishments—two bad things endeavoring to correct each other. The royal palaces, the mansions of the princes, and especially the churches, had right of sanctuary. Sometimes a whole town that happened to want repeopling, was converted for the time into a place of refuge for criminals; thus Louis XI. made all Paris a sanctuary in 1467.

When once he had set foot within the asylum, the criminal's person was sacred; but it behooved him to beware how he quitted it again; but one step out of the sanctuary—and he fell back into the flood. The wheel, the gibbet, and the strappado kept close guard around the place of refuge, watching incessantly for their prey, like sharks about a ship. Thus individuals under condemnation have been known to grow gray, confined to a cloister, to the staircase of a palace, the grounds of an abbey, or the porch of a church; so far, the sanctuary itself was but a prison under another name. It now and then happened that a solemn decree of the parliament violated the asylum, and reconsigned the condemned to the hands of the executioner—but this was a rare occurrence. The parliaments stood in fear of the bishops; for when the two gowns, the spiritual and the secular, happened to chafe each other, the simar had the worst of it in its collision with the cassock. Occasionally, however, as in the case of the assassins of Petit-Jean, the Paris executioner, and in that of Emery Rousseau, who had murdered Jean Valleret, temporal justice overleaped the pretensions of the Church, and went on to the execution of its sentences. But except by virtue of a decree of the parliament, woe to him that forcibly violated a place of sanctuary! It is well known what was the end of Robert de Clermont, marshal of France, and Jean de Châlons, marshal of Champagne; and yet it was all about one Perrin Marc, a money-changer's man and a wretched assassin; but the two marshals had forced the doors of St. Mary's church—there was the enormity.

Around the places of sanctuary there floated such an atmosphere of reverence that, according to tradition, it sometimes affected even animals. Aymoin relates that a stag, hunted by King Dagobert, having taken refuge at the tomb of St. Denis, the hounds stopped short, barking.

The churches had usually a cell prepared for the re

ception of the suppliants. In 1407, Nicolas Flamel caused to be built for them over the vaulted roof of the church of St. Jacques-de-la-Boucherie, a chamber which cost him four livres six sols sixteen deniers parisis.

At Notre-Dame it was a cell constructed over one of the side aisles, under the buttresses, and looking toward the cloister, precisely at the spot where the wife of the concierge or keeper of the towers, in 1831, had made herself a garden—which was, to the hanging gardens of Babylon, as a lettuce to a palm tree, or as a porter's wife is to a Semiramis.

There it was that, after his frantic and triumphal course along the towers and galleries, Quasimodo had deposited La Esmeralda. So long as that course lasted, the girl had remained almost without consciousness, having only a vague perception that she was ascending in the air, that she was floating, flying there, that something was carrying her upward from the earth. From time to time she heard the bursting laugh, the loud voice of Quasimodo, at her ear; she half opened her eyes; and then she saw, confusedly, beneath her, Paris, all checkered over with its thousand roofs of tile and slate, like a red and blue mosaic-work; and just above her head, Quasimodo's frightful and joy-illumined face. Then her eyelids dropped again; she believed that all was over—that she had been executed while in her fainting-fit; and that the deformed genius that had ruled her destiny had now laid hold of her spirit and was bearing it away. She dared not look at him, but resigned herself to this power.

But when the poor ringer, all disheveled and panting, had deposited her in the cell of refuge—when she felt his clumsy hands gently untying the cord that had cut into her arms—she felt that sort of shock which startles out of their sleep the passengers in a vessel that strikes the bottom in the middle of a dark night. So were her ideas awakened, and they returned to her one after another. She saw that she was in Notre-Dame; she remembered having been snatched from the hands of the executioner; that Phœbus was living, that

Phœbus loved her no longer; and these two ideas, of which the latter shed so much bitterness over the former, presenting themselves jointly to the poor sufferer, she turned to Quasimodo, who kept standing before her, and whose countenance affrighted her, and said to him, " Why have you saved me?"

He looked at her anxiously, as if striving to divine what she was saying to him. She repeated her question. He then gave her another look of profound sadness, and hastened away, leaving her in astonishment.

In a few minutes he returned, carrying a bundle, which he threw down at her feet. It was some wearing apparel which certain charitable women had deposited at the threshold of the church. Then she cast down her eyes over her own person, found herself almost naked, and blushed. Life was now returning to her.

Somewhat of this feeling of modest shame seemed to communicate itself to Quasimodo. He veiled his eye with his broad hand, and once more went away, but with tardy steps.

She dressed herself in haste. There were a white gown and a white veil; it was the habit of a novice of the Hôtel-Dieu.

She had scarcely finished her toilet before she saw Qausimodo return, carrying a basket under one arm, and a mattress under the other. This basket contained a bottle, with some bread and other provisions. He set the basket on the ground, and said to her, " eat." He spread out the mattress upon the flag-stones, and said, "sleep." It was his own meal, his own bed, that the poor ringer had been to fetch.

The gypsy girl raised her eyes to thank him, but could not articulate a word. The poor devil was in truth horrible to look upon. She cast down her eyes again, shuddering.

Then he said to her: " I frighten you—I'm very ugly —am not I? Don't look at me—only listen to me. In the daytime, you'll stay here—at night, you can walk

25

about the whole church. But don't go out of the church either by day or night. You'd be ruined. They'd kill you—and I should die."

Affected at his words, she raised her head to answer him, but he had disappeared. She found herself alone, musing upon the singular sentences of this almost monstrous being, and struck by the tone of his voice, so hoarse and yet so gentle.

Then she examined her cell. It was a little room, some six feet square, with a small window and a door upon the gently inclined plane of the roofing of flat stones. A number of spout-ends in the figure of animals seemed bending around her, outside, and stretching out their necks to look at her through the little window. Over the verge of the roof, she discerned a thousand chimney-tops casting up before her the smoke from the multitudinous fires of Paris—a melancholy sight to the poor gypsy girl—a foundling—a convict capitally condemned—an unfortunate creature, with no country, no family, no home.

At the moment that the thought of her loneliness in the world was oppressing her more poignantly than ever, she felt a hairy, shaggy head gliding between her hands, upon her lap. She startled (for everything frightened her now), and looked down. It was the poor little goat, the nimble Djali, which had escaped after her at the moment that Quasimodo had scattered Charmolue's brigade, and had been lavishing its caresses at her feet for nearly an hour without obtaining so much as a single look. Its mistress inundated it with kisses. "Oh, Djali," said she, "how I had forgotten thee! So thou still think'st of me. Oh, thou art not ungrateful!" At the same time, as if some invisible hand had lifted the weight that had so long repressed her tears within her heart, she began to weep; and as the tears flowed, she felt as if what was sharpest and bitterest in her grief was departing with them.

When evening came, she thought the night so fine, the moonlight so soft, that she went quite round the high gallery that encircles the cathedral; and this little promenade gave her some relief, so calm did the earth seem to her, viewed from that elevation.

CHAPTER III.

THE SYLPH AND THE GNOME.

THE next morning the poor gypsy girl perceived, on waking, that she had slept—a thing which astonished her—she had been so long unaccustomed to sleep! Some cheerful rays of the rising sun streamed through her window, and fell upon her face. At the same time with the sun, she saw at the window the unfortunate face of Quasimodo. Involuntarily her eyes closed again, but in vain—she still thought she saw, through her roseate eyelids, that gnome's visage, one-eyed and gap-toothed. Then, still keeping her eyes shut, she heard a rough voice saying, very gently, "Don't be afraid. I'm your friend. I was come to look at you sleeping. That doesn't hurt you, does it—that I should come and see you asleep? What does it signify to you my being here when you have your eyes shut? Now I'm going away. There. I've put myself behind the wall—now you may open your eyes again."

There was something yet more plaintive than these words; it was the tone in which they were uttered. The gypsy girl, affected at them, opened her eyes. He had, in fact, gone away from the window. She went up to it, and saw the poor hunchback crouching in an angle of the wall, in a posture of sorrow and resignation. She made an effort to overcome the repugnance which she felt at the sight of him. "Come hither," said she, softly. From the movement of her lips Quasimodo thought that she was bidding him go away; then he rose up and retreated, limping, slow, hanging his head, not venturing to lift up to the young girl his despairing countenance. "Come hither, I say," cried she; but he continued to move away. Then she hurried out of the cell, ran after him, and laid hold of his arm. On feeling the pressure, Quasimodo trembled in every limb. He lifted a suppliant eye; and finding that she was trying to draw him toward her, his whole face beamed with joy and tenderness. She tried to make him enter her cell; but he persisted in remaining on the threshold. "No, no," said he, "the owl goes not into the nest of the lark."

Then she gracefully squatted down upon her couch, with her goat asleep at her feet. Both parties remained motionless for a few minutes, absorbed in the contemplation—he, of so much grace—she, of so much ugliness. Every moment she discovered in Quasimodo some additional deformity. Her eye wandered over him, from his bow legs to his hump back, from his hump back to his one eye. She could not understand how a being so awkwardly fashioned could be in existence. Yet, over the whole there was diffused an air of so much sadness and gentleness, that she was beginning to be reconciled to it.

He was the first to break silence. "So you were telling me to come back."

She nodded affirmatively, and said, "Yes."

He understood the motion of her head. "Alas!" said he, as if hesitating to finish the sentence, "you see, I'm deaf."

"Poor man!" exclaimed the gypsy girl, with an expression of benevolent pity.

He smiled sorrowfully. "You thought that was all I wanted—didn't you? Yes, I'm deaf. That's the way I'm made. It's horrible, isn't it? You now, you're so beautiful."

In the poor creature's tone there was so deep a feeling of his wretchedness, that she had not resolution to say a word. Besides, he would not have heard it. He continued:

"Never did I see my ugliness as I do now. When I compare myself to you, I do indeed pity myself, poor

"THEN SHE GRACEFULLY SQUATTED DOWN UPON HER COUCH."

unhappy monster that I am. You must think I look like a beast. Tell me, now. You, now, are a sunbeam —a dewdrop—a bird's song. But me—I'm something frightful—neither man nor brute—a sort of a thing that's harder, and more trod upon, and more unshapely than a flint-stone."

Then he laughed—a heart-rending laugh. He went on:

"Yes, I'm deaf—but you'll speak to me by gestures and signs. I've a master that talks to me that way. And then, I shall know your will very quickly, by seeing how your lips move, and how you look."

"Well then," said she, smiling, "tell me why you saved me."

He looked at her intently while she was speaking.

"Oh, I understand," he replied, "you ask me why it was I saved you. You've forgotten a poor wretch that tried to carry you off one night—a poor wretch that you brought relief to, the very next day, on their shameful pillory—a drop of water and a little pity. There was more than I can pay you back with all my life. You've forgotten that poor wretch—but he remembers."

She listened to him with deep emotion. A tear stood in the poor ringer's eye—but it did not fall—he seemed to make it, as it were, a point of honor to retain it. "Just hear me," said he, when he was no longer afraid that this tear would escape him—"We've very high towers here—if a man was to fall from one, he'd be dead before he got to the ground; when you like me to fall in that way, you'll not so much as have to say a word—a glance of your eye will be enough."

Then he rose up from his leaning posture. This odd being, unhappy as the gypsy girl herself was, yet awakened some compassion in her breast. She motioned to him to remain.

"No, no," said he, "I mustn't stay too long—I'm not at my ease. It's all for pity that you don't turn away your eyes. I'm going somewhere, from whence I shall see you and you won't see me—that will be better."

He drew from his pocket a small metal whistle. "There," said he; "when you want me—when you wish me to come—when you'll not be too much horrified at the sight of me—you'll whistle with that. I can hear that noise."

He laid the whistle on the ground and went his way.

CHAPTER IV.

EARTHENWARE AND CRYSTAL.

DAY after day passed over, and tranquillity returned, by degrees, to the spirit of La Esmeralda. Excessive grief, like excessive joy, being violent in its nature, is of short duration. The human heart is incapable of remaining long in an extreme. The gypsy girl had suffered so much, that astonishment at it was all that she now felt.

With the feeling of security, hope had returned to her. She was out of society, out of life; but she had a vague sense that it was not quite impossible for her to return to them. It was as if one of the dead should have in reserve a key to open the tomb.

She felt gradually departing from her mind the terrible images which had so long beset her. All the hideous phantoms, Pierrat Torterue, Jacques Charmolue, were vanishing from her—not excepting the priest himself.

And then, Phœbus was living—she was sure of it—she had seen him. To her the fact of his being alive was everything. After the series of fatal shocks which had overturned everything in her soul, she had found nothing still keeping its place there but one feeling, her love for the captain. For love is like a tree—vegetating of itself—striking deep roots through all our being —and often continuing to grow greenly over a heart in ruins.

And, inexplicable as it is, the blinder is this passion the more it is tenacious. It is never more firmly seated than when it is without a shadow of reason. Assuredly La Esmeralda could not think of the captain without feelings of bitterness. Assuredly it was dreadful that he too should have been deceived—that he should have believed such a thing possible—that he should have conceived of a stab with a poniard coming from her who would have given a thousand lives to save him. And yet, he was not so excessively to blame; for had she not acknowledged the crime? had she not yielded, weak woman as she was, to the torture? All the fault was her own—she ought rather to have let them tear the nails from her feet than such an avowal from her lips. But then, could she but see Phœbus once more, for a single minute—a word, a look, would suffice to unde-ceive him, to bring him back. She doubted it not. She also strove to account to herself for many singular things—for Phœbus's happening to be present on the day of the penance at the church door, and for his being with that young lady. It was his sister, no doubt—an explanation by no means plausible, but with which she contented herself, because she needed to believe that Phœbus still loved her, and her alone. Had he not sworn it to her? And what stronger assurance did she need, all simple and credulous as she was? And be-sides in the sequel of the affair, were not appearances much more strongly against herself than against him? So she waited and hoped.

We may add that the church itself—that vast edifice —wrapping her, as it were, on all sides—protecting her —saving her—was a sovereign tranquilizer. The sol-emn lines of its architecture; the religious attitude of all the objects by which the girl was surrounded; the pious and serene thoughts escaping, as it were, from every pore of those venerable stones—acted upon her unconsciously to herself. The structure had sounds too, of such blessedness and such majesty, that they soothed that suffering spirit. The monotonous chant of the performers of the service; the responses of the people to the priests, now inarticulate, now of thundering loudness; the harmonious trembling of the casements; the organs bursting forth like the voice of a hundred trumpets; the three steeples humming like hives of enormous bees—all that orchestra, over which bounded a gigantic gamut, ascending and descending incessantly, from the voice of a multitude to that of a bell—lulled her memory, her imagination, and her sorrow. The bells especially had this effect. It was as a powerful magnetism which those vast machines poured in large waves over her. Thus each successive sunrise found her less pale, more tranquilized, and breathing more freely. In proportion as her internal wounds healed, her grace and her beauty bloomed again on her countenance, but more collected and composed. Her former character also returned—something even of her gayety, her pretty grimace, her fondness for her goat, her love of singing, her feminine bashfulness. She was careful to dress herself in the morning, in the corner of her little chamber, lest some inhabitant of the neighboring garrets should see her through the little window.

When her thinking of Phœbus allowed her leisure, the gypsy girl sometimes thought of Quasimodo. He was the only link, the only means of communication with mankind, with the living, that remained to her. Unfortunate creature! she was more out of the world than Quasimodo himself. She knew not what to make of the strange friend whom chance had given her. Often she reproached herself for not having a gratitude which could shut its eyes—but, positively, she could not reconcile herself to the sight of the poor ringer—he was too ugly.

She had left the whistle he had given her lying on the ground. This, however, did not prevent Quasimodo from reappearing, from time to time, during the first days. She strove hard to restrain herself from turning away with too strong an appearance of disgust when he came and brought her the basket of provisions or the pitcher of water; but he always perceived the smallest motion of that kind, and then he went away sorrowful.

Once he happened to come at the moment she was caressing Djali. He stood for a few minutes pensively contemplating that graceful group of the goat and the gypsy, and then he said, shaking his heavy and ill-formed head : " My misfortune is, that I'm still too much like a man—I wish I were a beast outright, like that goat."

She raised her eyes toward him with a look of astonishment. To this look he answered, " Oh, I well know why ! " and went his way.

Another time he presented himself at the door of the cell (into which he never entered) at the moment when La Esmeralda was singing an old Spanish ballad, the words of which she did not understand, but which had dwelt in her ear because the gypsy woman had lulled her to sleep with it when a child. At the sight of that shocking countenance appearing suddenly in the middle of her song, the girl broke it off with an involuntary gesture of affright. The unfortunate ringer fell upon his knees on the threshold, and clasped with a suppliant look his great shapeless hands. " Oh ! " said he, with a sorrowful accent, " go on, I entreat you, and don't send me away." She was unwilling to pain him ; and so, all trembling, she resumed her romance. Her fright, however, dissipated by degrees, and she abandoned herself wholly to the expression of the plaintive air she was singing. He, the while, had remained upon his knees, with his hands clasped as in prayer—attentive—hardly drawing his breath—his look fixed upon the beaming eyes of the gypsy. It seemed as if he was reading her song in those eyes.

At another time, again, he came to her with a look of awkwardness and timidity. " Listen," said he, with an effort ; " I have something to say to you." She made him a sign that she was listening. Then he began to sigh, half opened his lips, seemed for a moment to be on the point of speaking, then looked her in the face, made a negative motion with his head, and slowly withdrew, with his hand pressed to his forehead, leaving the gypsy girl in amazement.

Among the grotesque figures carved upon the wall, there was one for which he had a particular affection, and with which he often seemed to be exchanging fraternal looks. On one occasion, the gypsy heard him saying to it, "Oh! why am I not made of stone like thee!"

At length, one morning, La Esmeralda, having advanced to the verge of the roof, was looking into the Place, over the sharp ridge of the church of Saint-Jean-le-Rond. Quasimodo was present, behind her. He used so to place himself of his own accord, in order to spare the young girl as much as possible the disagreeableness of seeing him. Suddenly the gypsy started—a tear and a flash of joy shone at once in her eyes—she knelt down on the edge of the roof, and stretched out her arms in anguish toward the Place, crying out, "Phœbus! oh come! come hither! one word! but one word, in heaven's name!—Phœbus! Phœbus!" Her voice, her face, her gesture, her whole figure had the heart-rending aspect of a shipwrecked mariner making the signal of distress to some gay vessel passing in the distant horizon in a gleam of sunshine. Quasimodo leaned over toward the Place, and saw that the object of this tender and agonizing prayer was a young man, a captain, a handsome cavalier, all glittering in arms and gay attire, who was passing by caracoling in the square beneath, and saluting with his plume a fine young lady smiling at her balcony. The officer, however, did not hear the call of the unfortunate girl, for he was too far off.

But the poor deaf ringer heard it. A deep sigh heaved his breast; he turned round; his heart was swelled with all the tears which he restrained from flowing; his hands, clenched convulsively, struck against his head, and when he drew them away there came with each of them a handful of his rough red hair.

The gypsy girl was paying no attention to him. He said, in an undertone, grinding his teeth: "Damnation! So that's how a man should be; he need only be handsome outside!"

Meanwhile, she had remained upon her knees, crying out with extraordinary agitation: " Oh, there! he's getting off his horse. He's going into that house. Phœbus! He does not hear me. Phœbus! What a wicked woman that is to talk to him at the same time that I do. Phœbus! Phœbus!"

The deaf man had his eye upon her all the while. He understood this (to him) dumb show. The poor ringer's eyes filled with tears, but he let not one of them fall. All at once he pulled her gently by the extremity of the sleeve. She turned round. He had assumed a tranquil air, and said to her, " Should you like me to go and fetch him?"

She uttered an exclamation of joy. " Oh, yes, go! go! run! quick!—that captain—that captain—bring him to me and I'll love you!" She clasped his knees. He could not help shaking his head sorrowfully. " I'll bring him to you," said he, in a faint voice. Then he turned his head, and strode hastily to the staircase, his heart bursting with sobs.

When he reached the Place, he found only the fine horse fastened at the door of the Logis Gondelaurier; the captain had just entered. He looked up to the roof of the church; La Esmeralda was still there, at the same spot, in the same posture. He made her a melancholy sign of the head; then set his back against one of the posts of the porch of the mansion, determined to wait until the captain came out.

It was, at the Logis Gondelaurier, one of those gala days that precede a marriage; Quasimodo saw many people enter, and nobody come away. Now and then he looked up to the roof of the church, and he saw that the gypsy girl did not stir from her place any more than himself. There came a groom, who untied the horse, and led him to the stable of the mansion.

The whole day was passed in this manner, Quasimodo against the post, La Esmeralda upon the roof, and Phœbus, no doubt, at the feet of Fleur-de-Lys.

At length night came, a dark, moonless night. In vain did Quasimodo fix his eye upon La Esmeralda;

she soon faded into something white glimmering in the twilight, then quite disappeared from his view. All had vanished, all was black. Quasimodo now saw the light shining through the windows from top to bottom of the front of the Logis Gondelaurier; he saw the other windows of the Place lit up one after another; one after another, too, he saw the light disappear from them till every one was dark, for he remained the whole evening at his post. The officer did not come away. When the latest passengers had returned home, when all the windows of the other houses were darkened, Quasimodo remained entirely alone, entirely in the dark. There was not then any luminaire in the Parvis of Notre-Dame.

However, the windows of the Logis Gondelaurier remained lighted, even after midnight. Quasimodo, motionless and attentive, saw passing to and fro behind the many-colored panes a multitude of lively dancing shadows. Had he not been deaf, in proportion as the murmur of slumbering Paris died away, he would have heard more and more distinctly, from within the Logis Gondelaurier, the sounds of an evening entertainment, of laughter, and of music.

About one in the morning the company began to depart. Quasimodo, wrapped in darkness, looked at them all as they passed under the flambeau-lighted porch, but none of them was the captain.

He was full of melancholy thoughts; now and then he looked up into the air, like one weary of waiting. Great black clouds, heavy, torn, riven, were hanging like ragged festoons of crape under the starry arch of night.

At one of those moments he suddenly saw the long folding window that opened upon the balcony, whose stone balustrade projected above him, mysteriously open. The light glazed door admitted two persons through it upon the balcony, then softly closed behind them. They were a male and a female figure. It was not without difficulty that Quasimodo, in the dark, could recognize in the man the handsome captain, in

the woman the young lady whom he had seen in the
morning bidding the officer welcome from the same
balcony. The Place was perfectly dark, and a double
crimson curtain, which had fallen behind the glass door
at the moment it had closed, intercepted almost every
ray of light from the apartment within.

The young man and woman, as far as our deaf spectator could judge without hearing a word of what they
said, appeared to abandon themselves to a very tender
tête-à-tête. The young lady seemed to have permitted
the officer to encircle her waist with his arm, and was
gently resisting a kiss.

Quasimodo witnessed from below this scene, the
more attractive as it was not intended to be witnessed.
He contemplated that happiness, that beauty with feelings of bitterness. After all, nature was not altogether
silent in the poor devil, and his nervous system, strangely
distorted as it was, was yet susceptible of excitement
like another man's. He thought of the wretched share
which Providence had dealt him; that woman, that the
pleasures of love, were destined everlastingly to pass
under his eyes without his ever doing more than witness the felicity of others. But that which pained him
most of all in this spectacle—that which mingled indignation with his chagrin—was to think what the gypsy
girl would suffer were she to behold it. True it was
that the night was very dark, that La Esmeralda, if she
had remained at the same place, as he doubted not she
had, was very far off, and that it was all that he himself
could do to distinguish the lovers on the balcony—this
consoled him.

Meanwhile the conversation above became more and
more animated. The young lady seemed to be entreating the officer to solicit nothing more from her. All
that Quasimodo could distinguish was the fair clasped
hands, the mingled smiles and tears, and the uplifted
eyes of the young woman, and the eyes of the captain
fixed ardently upon her.

Fortunately for the young lady, whose resistance was
growing weaker, the door of the balcony suddenly re-

opened, and an old lady made her appearance, where upon the young one looked confused, the officer cha-grined, and they all three went in again.

A minute afterward a horse came prancing under the porch, and the brilliant officer, wrapped in his night cloak, passed rapidly before Quasimodo.

The ringer let him turn the corner of the street, and then ran after him, with his monkey nimbleness, shout-ing, " Ho ! there ! captain ! "

The captain stopped his horse. " What does the rascal want with me ? " said he, espying in the dark that sort of out-of-the-way figure running hobblingly toward him.

Meanwhile Quasimodo had come up to him, and boldly taken his horse by the bridle, saying, " Follow me, captain ; there's somebody here that wants to speak to you."

" Corne-Mahom ! " grumbled Phœbus, " here's a vil-lainous ragged bird that I think I've seen somewhere before. Hollo ! master ! won't you leave hold of my bridle ? "

" Captain," answered the deaf man, " aren't you ask-ing me who it is ? "

" I tell thee to let go my horse," returned Phœbus, impatiently. " What does the fellow want, hanging at my charger's rein ? Dost thou take my horse for a gallows ? "

Quasimodo, so far from leaving hold of the horse's bridle, was preparing to make him turn round. Unable to explain to himself the captain's resistance, he hastily said to him : " Come along, captain ; it's a woman that's waiting for you ; " then, with an effort, he added, " a woman that loves you."

" A rare scoundrel ! " said the captain, " that thinks me obliged to go after every woman that loves me, or says she does. And then, if she is but like thee, thou owl-faced villain ! Tell her that sent thee that I'm going to be married, and that she may go to the devil."

" Hark ye ! " cried Quasimodo, thinking to overcome his hesitation with a single word ; " come along, mon-seigneur ; it's the gypsy girl that you know of."

This word did in fact make a great impression upon Phœbus, but it was not that which the deaf man expected from it. It will be remembered that our gallant officer had retired from the balcony with Fleur-de-Lys a few minutes before Quasimodo delivered the penitent out of the hands of Charmolue. Since then, in all his visits at the Logis Gondelaurier, he had been very careful to avoid mentioning that young woman, the recollection of whom, after all, was painful to him, and Fleur-de-Lys, on her part, had not deemed it politic to tell him that the gypsy girl was living. So Phœbus believed poor Similar, as he called her, to have been dead for a month or two. To which we must add that the captain had been thinking for a few moments of the profound darkness of the night, the supernatural ugliness and sepulchral voice of the messenger, that it was past midnight, that the street was as solitary as it had been the evening that the specter monk had accosted him, and that his horse snorted at the sight of Quasimodo.

"The gypsy girl!" cried he, almost in a fright. "How now! Art thou come from the other world?" and so saying he laid his hand upon his dagger-hilt.

"Quick! quick!" said the deaf man striving to turn the horse round; "this way!"

Phœbus struck him a violent blow in the chest with the point of his boot.

Quasimodo's eyes sparkled. He made a movement to throw himself upon the captain. But checking himself, he said: "Ah! how happy you are to have some one that loves you!"

He laid strong emphasis upon the words some one, and leaving hold of the horse's bridle, he said, "Go your way."

Phœbus spurred off swearing. Quasimodo watched him plunge into the dark shades of the street. "Oh!" whispered the poor deaf creature to himself, "to refuse that!"

He returned into Notre-Dame, lighted his lamp, and went up the tower again. As he had supposed, the gypsy girl was still at the same spot. The moment she perceived him coming she ran to meet him.

"Alone!" cried she, clasping her beautiful hands in agony.

"I could not find him again," said Quasimodo coolly.

"You should have waited for him all night," returned she passionately.

He observed her angry gesture, and understood the reproof. "I'll watch him better another time," said he, hanging down his head.

"Get you gone," said she.

He left her. She was dissatisfied with him. He had preferred being chided by her, to giving her greater affliction. He had kept all the grief to himself.

From that day forward, the gypsy saw no more of him —he came no longer to her cell. Now and then, indeed, she caught a distant glimpse of the ringer's countenance looking mournfully upon her from the top of one of the towers; but as soon as she perceived him, he constantly disappeared.

We must admit that she was little afflicted by the voluntary absence of the poor hunchback. At the bottom of her heart, she felt obliged to him for it. Nor was Quasimodo himself under any delusion about the matter.

She saw him no more, but she felt the presence of a good genius about her. Her provisions were renewed by an invisible hand during her sleep. One morning, she found against her window a cage of birds. Over her cell there was a piece of sculpture that frightened her. She had repeatedly testified this in Quasimodo's presence. One morning (for all these things were done in the night-time) she saw it no longer—it had been broken off. He who had climbed up to that piece of carving, must have risked his life.

Sometimes, in the evening, she heard the voice of one concealed under the penthouse of the steeple, singing, as if to lull her to sleep, a melancholy and fantastic song, without rhyme or rhythm, such as a deaf man might make:

Oh, look not at the face,
    Young maid look at the heart:
The heart of a fine young man is often deformed;
There are some hearts will hold no love a long while.

Young maid, the pine's not fair to see,
    Not fair to see as the poplar is,
    But it keeps its leaves in winter-time.
Alas! it's vain to talk of that—
    What is not fair ought not to be—
    Beauty will only beauty love—
    April looks not on January.

Beauty is perfection,
    Beauty can do all,
Beauty is the only thing that does not shine by halves.

The crow flies but by day;
    The owl flies but by night;
    The swan flies night and day.

On waking one morning, she saw in her window two
bunches of flowers; one of them in a glass vessel, very
beautiful and brilliant, but cracked; it had let all the
water escape, and the flowers it contained were faded.
The other vessel was of earthenware, rude and common,
but had kept all the water, so that its flowers remained
fresh and blooming.

We know not whether she did it intentionally, but
La Esmeralda took the faded nosegay and wore it all
day in her bosom.

That day she did not hear the voice from the tower
sing.

She felt little concern about it. She passed her days
in caressing Djali, watching the door of the Logis Gondelaurier, talking low to herself about Phœbus, and
crumbling her bread to the swallows.

And then she had altogether ceased to see or to hear
Quasimodo. The poor ringer seemed to have departed
from the church. One night, however, as she lay awake,
thinking of her handsome captain, she heard a strong
breathing near her cell. She rose up affrighted, and
saw, by the moonlight, a shapeless mass lying across the
front of her door. It was Quasimodo sleeping there
upon the stones.

26

CHAPTER V.

THE KEY OF THE PORTE-ROUGE.

MEANWHILE public rumor had acquainted the arch-deacon with the miraculous manner in which the gypsy girl had been saved. When he learned this, he felt he knew not what. He had reconciled his mind to the thought of La Esmeralda's death, and so he had become calm; he had gone to the bottom of the greatest grief possible. The human heart (and Dom Claude had meditated upon these matters) can not contain more than a certain quantity of despair. When the sponge is thoroughly soaked, the sea may pass over it without its imbibing one tear more.

Now, La Esmeralda being dead, the sponge was thoroughly soaked; all was over for Dom Claude upon this earth. But to feel that she was alive, and Phœbus too —that was the recommencement of torture, of pangs, of alternations, of life—and Dom Claude was weary of all that.

When this piece of intelligence reached him, he shut himself up in his cloister cell. He appeared neither at the conferences of the chapter, nor at the services in the church. He shut his door against every one, even against the bishop. He kept himself thus immured for several weeks. He was thought to be ill, and so indeed he was.

What was he doing, shut up thus? With what thoughts was the unfortunate man contending? Was he making a final struggle against his formidable passion? Was he combining some final plan of death for her and perdition for himself?

His Jehan, his cherished brother, his spoiled child, came once to his door, knocked, swore, entreated, announced himself ten times over—but Claude kept the door shut.

He passed whole days with his face close against the casement of his window. From that window, situated in the cloister, he could see the cell of La Esmeralda; he often saw herself, with her goat—sometimes with Quasimodo. He remarked the deaf wretch's assiduities, his obedience, his delicate and submissive behavior to the gypsy girl. He recollected—for he had a good memory, and memory is the tormentor of the jealous—he recollected the singular look which the ringer had cast upon the dancing-girl on a certain evening. He asked himself what motive could have urged Quasimodo to save her. He was an eye-witness to a thousand little scenes that passed between the gypsy and the ringer; the action of which, as seen at that distance and commented on by his passion, he thought very tender. He had his misgivings with respect to feminine capriciousness. Then he felt confusedly arising within him a jealousy such as he had never anticipated—a jealousy that made him redden with shame and indignation. "As for the captain," thought he, "that might pass—but this one!" And the idea quite overpowered him.

His nights were dreadful. Since he had learned that the gypsy girl was alive, all those cold images of specters and the grave, which had beset him for a whole day, had vanished from his spirit, and the flesh began again to torment him.

Each night his delirious imagination represented to him La Esmeralda in all the attitudes that had most strongly excited his passion. He beheld her leaning faint upon the poniarded captain—her eyes closed—her fair naked neck crimsoned with the blood of Phœbus—at that moment of wild delight at which the archdeacon had imprinted on her pale lips that kiss of which the unfortunate girl, half dying as she was, had felt the burning pressure. Again, he beheld her undressed by the savage hands of the torturers, letting them thrust all naked into the horrid iron-screwed boot her little foot, her round and delicate leg, her white and supple knee; and then he saw that ivory knee alone appearing, all below it being enveloped in Torterue's horrible apparatus. And again, he figured to himself the young girl, in her slight chemise, with the rope about her neck, with bare feet and uncovered shoulders, as he had seen her on the day of penance. These voluptuous images made him clench his hands, and sent a shiver through his nerves.

One night in particular, they so cruelly inflamed his priestly virgin blood, that he tore his pillow with his teeth, leaped out of bed, threw a surplice over his night-gown, and went out of his cell with his lamp in his hand, half naked, wild, with fire in his eyes.

He knew where to find the key of the Porte-Rouge, or Red Door, opening from the cloister into the church; and, as the reader is aware, he always carried about him a key of the tower staircase.

CHAPTER VI.

SEQUEL TO THE KEY OF THE PORTE-ROUGE.

That night La Esmeralda had fallen asleep in her little chamber, full of forgetfulness, of hope, and of flattering thoughts. She had been sleeping for some time, dreaming, as usual, of Phœbus; when she thought she heard some noise about her. Her sleep was light and airy—the sleep of a bird; the slightest thing awakened her. She opened her eyes. The night was very dark. Yet she discerned at the little window a face looking in upon her—there was a lamp which cast its light upon this apparition. The moment that it perceived itself to be observed by La Esmeralda, that face blew out the lamp. Nevertheless, the young girl had caught a glimpse of its features; her eyelids dropped with terror. "Oh!" said she in a faint voice, "the priest!"

All her past misfortune flashed upon her mind, and she fell back frozen with horror upon her bed.

A moment after, she felt a contact the whole length

of her body, which made her shudder so violently that she started and sat up in bed wide awake and furious. The priest had glided up to her, and threw both his arms around her. She strove to cry out, but could not.

"Begone, monster! begone, murderer!" said she, in a voice low and faltering with anger and dread.

"Mercy! mercy!" murmured the priest, pressing his burning lips to her shoulders.

She seized his bald head between her hands by its remaining hairs, and strove to repel his kisses as if he had been biting her.

"Mercy!" repeated the wretched man. "Didst thou but know what is my love for thee! 'tis fire! 'tis molten lead! 'tis a thousand daggers in my heart!"

And he held back both her arms with superhuman strength.

Quite desperate, "Let me go," she cried, "or I spit in your face!"

He left hold. "Vilify me—strike me—be wicked—do what thou wilt!" said he, "but, oh, have mercy, and love me!"

Then she struck him with the fury of a child. She drew up her pretty hands to tear his face. "Begone, demon!"

"Love me! love me! love me! for pity's sake!" cried the poor priest, answering her blows with his unwelcome caresses.

All at once she felt that he was overpowering her. "There must be an end of this," said he, grinding his teeth. She felt a lascivious hand wandering over her. "Help me! help me! a vampire! a vampire!"

But nothing came. Only Djali was awake and bleated with anguish.

"Silence!" said the panting priest.

Suddenly, in the midst of her struggling, the gypsy's hand came in contact with something cold and metallic —it was Quasimodo's whistle. She seized it with a convulsion of hope, put it to her lips, and blew with all her remaining strength. The whistle sounded clear, shrill, and piercing.

" What's that ?" said the priest.

Almost at the same instant he felt himself dragged away by a vigorous arm. The cell was dark; he could not clearly distinguish who it was that held him thus; but he heard some one's teeth clattering with rage, and there was just light enough scattered in the darkness for him to see shining over his head a large cutlass blade.

The priest thought he could discern the form of Quasimodo. He supposed it could be no one else. He recollected having stumbled, in entering, against a bundle of something that was lying across the doorway outside. Yet, as the new-comer uttered not a word, he knew not what to think. He threw himself upon the arm that held the cutlass, crying out, " Quasimodo !" forgetting, at that moment of distress, that Quasimodo was deaf.

In a trice the priest was thrown upon the floor, and felt a knee of lead weighing upon his breast. By the angular impression of that knee he recognized Quasimodo. But what was he to do ? how was he to make himself known to the other? Night made the deaf man blind.

He was lost. The young girl, pitiless as an enraged tigress, interfered not to save him. The cutlass was approaching his head—the moment was critical. Suddenly his adversary appeared seized with hesitation. " No blood upon her !" said he, in an under voice. It was, in fact, the voice of Quasimodo.

Then the priest felt the great hand dragging him by the foot out of the cell—outside he was to die. Luckily for him, the moon had been risen for a few moments.

When they had crossed the threshold of the chamber, its pale rays fell upon the features of the priest. Quasimodo looked in his face ; a tremor came over him ; he quitted his hold of the priest and shrank back.

The gypsy girl, having come forward to the door of her cell, was surprised to see them suddenly change parts ; for now it was the priest that threatened, and Quasimodo was the suppliant.

The priest, heaping gestures of anger and reproof upon the deaf man, motioned to him passionately to withdraw.

The deaf man cast down his eyes; then came and knelt before the gypsy girl's door. " Monseigneur," said he, in a tone of gravity and resignation, " afterwards you will do what you please—but kill me first."

So saying, he presented his cutlass to the priest; and the priest, who had lost all command of himself, was going to seize it. But the girl was quicker than he; she snatched the cutlass out of Quasimodo's hands, and burst into a frantic laugh. "Approach!" said she to the priest.

She held the blade aloft. The priest hesitated. She would certainly have struck. "You dare not approach now, you coward," she resumed. Then she added, in a pitiless accent, and well knowing that it would be plunging a red-hot iron into the heart of the priest, "Ha! I know that Phœbus is not dead."

The priest gave Quasimodo a kick, which threw him down upon the stones; and then plunged back, all trembling with rage, under the vault of the staircase.

When he was gone, Quasimodo picked up the whistle that had just saved the gypsy girl. "It was growing rusty," said he, as he gave it to her, and then he left her to herself.

The young girl, quite overpowered by this violent scene, fell exhausted upon her couch, and began to sob and weep bitterly; again her horizon was growing dismal.

As for the priest, he had groped his way back into his cell.

'Twas done—Dom Claude was jealous of Quasimodo. He repeated pensively to himself his fatal sentence: " No one shall have her."

BOOK IX.

CHAPTER I.

GRINGOIRE HAS SEVERAL BRIGHT IDEAS ONE AFTER THE OTHER IN THE RUE DES BERNARDINS.

FROM the time that Pierre Gringoire had seen the turn that all this affair was taking, and that hanging by the neck, and other disagreeables, were decidedly in store for the principal characters of this drama, he had felt no anxiety to take part in it. The Truands, amongst whom he had remained, considering as he did that, after all, they were the best company in Paris—the Truands had continued to feel interested for the gypsy girl. He thought that very natural in people who, like herself, had nothing but Charmolue and Torterue in prospect, and did not, like him, Gringoire, mount aloft in the regions of imagination between the wings of Pegasus. He had learned from their discourse that his bride of the broken pitcher had found refuge in Notre-Dame, and he was very glad of it. But he did not even feel tempted to go and see her there. He sometimes thought of the little goat, and that was all. In the day-time, he performed feats of strength to get his bread; and, at night, he was elaborating a paper against the Bishop of Paris, for he remembered being drenched by his mill-wheels, and bore malice against him for it. He was also engaged in writing a commentary upon the fine work of Baudry-le-Rouge, Bishop of Noyon and Tournay, De cupâ petrarum, which had given him a violent inclination for architecture, a propensity which had supplanted in his breast his passion for hermetics, of which, too, it was but a natural consequence, seeing that there is an intimate connection between the hermetical philosophy and stone-work. Gringoire had passed from the love of an idea to the love of the substance.

One day he had stopped near the church of Saint-Germain-l'Auxerrois, at the corner of a building called le For-l'Evêque, which was opposite another called le For-le-Roi. There was at this For-l'Evêque a beautiful chapel of the fourteenth century, the chancel of which was toward the street; Gringoire was examining devoutly its external sculpture. It was one of those moments of selfish, exclusive, and supreme enjoyment, in which the artist sees nothing in the world but his art, and the world itself in that art. All at once, he felt a hand placed heavily on his shoulder; he turned round —it was his old friend, his old master, the archdeacon. He was quite confounded. It was long since he had seen the archdeacon; and Dom Claude was one of those grave and ardent beings a meeting with whom always disturbs the equilibrium of a skeptical philosopher.

The archdeacon, for some moments, kept silence, during which Gringoire had leisure to observe him. He found Dom Claude much altered—pale as a winter morning; his eyes hollow, his hair almost white. The priest was the first to break this silence, by saying, in a calm but freezing tone, "How are you, Maître Pierre?"

"As to my health," answered Gringoire, "why, it's so so, I believe, on the whole, pretty good. I do not take too much of anything. You know, master, the secret of being well, according to Hippocrates—*id est : cibi, potus, somni, venus, omnia moderata sint.*"

"You have no care, then, Maître Pierre?" resumed the archdeacon, looking steadfastly at Gringoire.

"'Faith, not I!"

"And what are you doing now?"

"You see, master, I am examining the cutting of these stones, and the style in which this bas-relief is thrown out."

The priest began to smile, but with that bitter smile

which raises only one of the extremities of the mouth. "And that amuses you?"

"It's paradise!" exclaimed Gringoire. And, leaning over the sculpture with the fascinated air of a demonstrator of living phenomena—"Now, for example, do you not think that that metamorphosis, in baissetaille, is executed with a great deal of skill, delicacy, and patience? Look at that small column—was ever capital entwined with leaves more graceful or more exquisitely touched by the chisel? Here are three alto-relievos by Jean Maillevin. They are not the finest specimens of that great genius. Nevertheless, the simplicity, the sweetness of those faces, the sportiveness of the attitudes and the draperies, and that undefinable charm which is mingled with all the imperfections, make the miniature figures so very light and delicate—perhaps even too much so. You do not find it interesting?"

"Oh, yes!" said the priest.

"And if you were to see the interior of the chapel!" continued the poet, with his loquacious enthusiasm. "Sculpture in all directions! It's as full as the heart of a cabbage! The style of the chancel is most heavenly; and so peculiar that I have never seen anything like it anywhere else!"

Dom Claude interrupted him: "You are happy, then?"

"Upon my honor, yes! At one time I loved women, then animals; now I love stones. They are quite as amusing as animals or women, and not so false."

The priest passed his hand across his forehead. It was a gesture habitual with him. "Indeed!"

"Hark you," said Gringoire; "one has one's enjoyments." He took the arm of the priest, who yielded to his guidance, and led him under the staircase turret of the For-l'Evêque. "There's a staircase!" he exclaimed. "Whenever I see it I am happy. That flight of steps is the most simple and the most uncommon in Paris— every step is hollowed underneath. Its beauty and simplicity consist in the circumstance of the steps, which are a foot broad or thereabouts, being interlaced, morticed, jointed, enchained, enchased, set one in the other, and biting into each other, in a way that's truly both substantial and pretty."

"And you desire nothing?" said the priest.

"No!"

"And you regret nothing?"

"Neither regret nor desire. I have arranged my mode of life."

"What man arranges," said Claude, "circumstances disarrange."

"I am a Pyrrhonian philosopher," answered Gringoire, "and I hold everything in equilibrium."

"And how do you earn your living?"

"I still write epopees and tragedies now and then; but what brings me in the most is that industrious talent of mine which you are aware of, master—carrying pyramids of chairs on my teeth."

"A low occupation for a philosopher!"

"It's equilibrium, though," said Gringoire. "When one gets an idea in one's head, one finds it in everything."

"I know it," answered the archdeacon.

After a short silence, the priest continued: "And yet you are poor enough?"

"Poor—yes—but not unhappy."

At that moment the sound of horses was heard; and our two interlocutors saw filing off at the end of the street a company of the king's archers, with their lances raised, and an officer at their head. The cavalcade was brilliant, and its march resounded on the pavement.

"How you look at that officer!" said Gringoire to the archdeacon.

"I think I know him!" was the reply.

"How do you call him?"

"I believe," said Claude, "his name is Phœbus de Chateaupers."

"Phœbus! a curious sort of a name! There's Phœbus, too, Count of Foix. I recollect I knew a girl once who never swore by any other name."

"Come hither," said the priest, "I have something to say to you."

Since the passing of that troop, a degree of agitation was perceptible through the frozen exterior of the archdeacon. He walked on. Gringoire followed him, accustomed to obey him, like all who had once approached that being so commanding. They reached in silence the Rue des Bernardins, which was pretty clear of people. Dom Claude stopped.

"What have you to say to me, master?" asked Gringoire.

"Do you not think," answered the archdeacon, with an air of profound reflection, "that the dress of those cavaliers whom we have just seen, is handsomer than yours and mine?"

Gringoire shook his head. "No—'faith, I like my red and yellow gonelle better than those iron and steel scales. A pleasant sort of thing, to make a noise in going along like an iron-wharf in an earthquake?"

"Then, Gringoire, you have never envied those fine fellows in their warlike hacquetons?"

"Envied what, monsieur the archdeacon? their strength, their armor, their discipline? Give me rather philosophy and independence in rags. I would rather be the head of a fly than the tail of a lion."

"That's singular," said the musing priest. "A fine uniform is a fine thing nevertheless."

Gringoire, seeing him pensive, left him to go and admire the porch of a neighboring house. He returned, clapping his hands. "If you were less occupied with the fine clothes of the soldiers, monsieur the archdeacon, I would beg you to go and see that doorway. I have always said that the Sieur Aubry's house has the finest entrance that ever was seen."

"Pierre Gringoire," said the archdeacon, "what have you done with the little gypsy dancing-girl?"

"La Esmeralda? You change the conversation very abruptly."

"Was she not your wife?"

"Yes, by dint of a broken pitcher. We were in for it for four years. By-the-by," added Gringoire, looking at the archdeacon with a half-bantering air, "you think of her still, then?"

"And you—do you no longer think of her?"

"Not much. I have so many things!—My God, how pretty the little goat was!"

"Did not that Bohemian girl save your life?"

"Egad, that's true."

"Well—what became of her? what have you done with her?"

"I can't tell you. I believe they've hanged her."

"You believe?"

"I'm not sure. When I saw there was hanging in the case, I kept out of the business."

"And that's all you know about her?"

"Stay. I was told she had taken refuge in Notre-Dame, and that she was there in safety—and I am delighted at it—and I've not been able to find out whether the goat escaped with her—and that's all I know about the matter."

"I will tell you more about it," cried Dom Claude; and his voice, till then low, deliberate, and hollow, had become like thunder. "She has indeed taken refuge in Notre-Dame. But in three days justice will drag her again from thence, and she will be hanged at the Grève. There is a decree of the parliament for it!"

"That's a pity," said Gringoire.

The priest in a moment had become cool and calm again.

"And who the devil," continued the poet, "has taken the trouble to solicit a sentence of reintegration? Could they not leave the parliament alone? Of what consequence can it be that a poor girl takes shelter under the buttresses of Notre-Dame among the swallows' nests?"

"There are Satans in the world," answered the archdeacon.

"That's a devilish bad piece of work," observed Gringoire.

The archdeacon resumed, after a short silence: "She saved your life, then?"

"Among my good friends the Truands, I was within an inch of being hanged. They would have been sorry for it now."

" Will you then do nothing for her ? "

" I should rejoice to be of service, Dom Claude ; but if I were to bring a bad piece of business about my ears ! "

" What can it signify ? "

" The deuce ! what can it signify ! You are very kind, master ! I have two great works begun."

The priest struck his forehead. In spite of his affected calmness, from time to time a violent gesture revealed his inward struggles.

" How is she to be saved ? "

" Master," said Gringoire, " I will answer you—*Il padelt*—which means in the Turkish, ' God is our hope.' "

" How is she to be saved ? " repeated Claude, ruminating.

Gringoire, in his turn, struck his forehead.

" Hark you, master—I have some imagination—I will find expedients for you. What if we were to entreat the king's mercy ? "

" Mercy ! of Louis XI. ! "

" Why not ? "

" Go take from the tiger his bone ! "

Gringoire began to rummage for other expedients.

" Well—stay—shall I address a memorial to the midwives, declaring that the girl is pregnant ? "

" At this the priest's sunken eyeballs glared.

" Pregnant ! fellow ! do you know anything about it ? "

Gringoire was terrified at his manner. He hastened to say : " Oh, not I. Our marriage was a regular forismaritagium. I'm altogether out of it. But at any rate one should obtain a respite."

" Madness ! infamy ! hold thy peace ! "

" You are wrong to be angry," muttered Gringoire. " One gets a respite—that does no harm to anybody, and it puts forty deniers parisis into the pockets of the midwives, who are poor women."

The priest heard him not. " She must go from thence, nevertheless," murmured he. " The sentence is to be put in force within three days. Otherwise, it would not be va'id. That Quasimodo ! Women have very depraved tastes!" He raised his voice: "Maître Pierre, I have well considered the matter. There is but one means of saving her."

"And what is it? For my part, I see none."

"Hark ye, Maître Pierre; remember that you owe your life to her. I will tell you candidly my idea. The church is watched day and night; no one is allowed to come out but those who have been seen to go in. Thus you can go in. You shall come, and I will take you to her. You will change clothes with her. She will take your doublet, and you will take her petticoat."

"So far so good," observed the philosopher; "and what then?"

"What then? Why, she will go out in your clothes, and you will remain in hers. You may get hanged, perhaps—but she will be saved."

Gringoire scratched his ear with a very serious air.

"Well!" said he, "that's an idea would never have come into my head of itself."

At Dom Claude's unexpected proposal, the open and benignant countenance of the poet had become instantaneously overcast, like a smiling Italian landscape when an unlucky gust of wind suddenly dashes a cloud across the sun.

"Well, Gringoire—what say you to the plan?"

"I say, master, that I shall not be hanged perhaps, but that I shall be hanged indubitably."

"That does not concern us."

"The plague!" said Gringoire.

"She saved your life. It's a debt you have to pay."

"There are many others I don't pay."

"Maître Pierre, it must absolutely be so."

The archdeacon spoke imperiously.

"Hark you, Dom Claude," answered the poet in great consternation. "You cling to that idea, and you are wrong. I don't see why I should get myself hanged instead of another."

"What can you have to attach you so strongly to life?"

"Ah! a thousand reasons.'

" What are they, pray ? "

" What are they !   The air—the sky—the morning—
the evening—the moonlight—my good friends the Truands—our merry-making with the old women—the fine
architecture of Paris to study—three great books to
write, one of them against the bishop and his mills—
more than I can tell.   Anaxagoras used to say he had
come into the world to admire the sun.   And then, I
have the felicity of passing the whole of my days, from
morning till night, with a man of genius—no other than
I myself—and that's very agreeable."

" Oh, thou head, fit only to make a rattle of ! " muttered the archdeacon.   " Speak, then ; who preserved
that life thou makest out to be so charming ? To whom
art thou indebted for the privilege of breathing that air,
of seeing that sky, of being still able to amuse thy lark-
like spirit with trash and fooleries ?   Had it not been
for her, where wouldst thou be ?   Thou wilt have her
die then—she through whom thou livest ; thou wilt
have her die—that creature so lovely, so sweet,
so adorable—a creature necessary to the light of the
world—more divine than divinity itself ; while thou,
half sage, half fool, a mere sketch of something, a sort
of vegetable which fancies it walks and thinks, wouldst
continue to live with the life thou hast stolen from her,
as useless as a taper at noonday !   Come, Gringoire, a
little pity ! be generous in thy turn—she has set the example."

The priest was vehement.   Gringoire listened to him
at first with an air of indecision, then became moved,
and concluded with making a tragical grimace which
likened his wan countenance to that of a new-born child
in a fit of the colic.

" You are very pathetic ? " said he, wiping away a
tear.   " Well ! I'll think of it.   That's an odd idea of
yours.   After all," pursued he, after a moment's silence,
" who knows ? perhaps they'll not hang me—there's
many a slip between the cup and the lip.   When they
find me in that box, so grotesquely muffled, in cap and
petticoat, perhaps they'll burst out laughing.   And if

they do hang me, what then? The rope—that's a death like any other. Or rather, it is not a death like any other. It's a death worthy of the sage who has been wavering all his life—a death which is neither fish nor flesh, like the mind of the true skeptic—a death fully marked with Pyrrhonism and hesitation—which holds the medium between heaven and earth—which leaves you in suspense. It's the death of a philosopher, and I was predestined to it, perhaps. "'Tis fine to die as one has lived—"

The priest interrupted him: "Is it agreed?"

"What is death, after all?" continued Gringoire, heroically. "A disagreeable moment—a turnpike-gate —the passage from little to nothing. Some one having asked Cercidas of Megalopolis, whether he could die willingly: 'Why should I not?' answered he; 'for after my death, I shall see those great men, Pythagoras among the philosophers, Hecatæus among the historians, Homer among the poets, Olympus among the musicians!'"

The archdeacon held out his hand to him. "Then it's settled? you will come to-morrow?"

This gesture brought Gringoire back to reality.

"'Faith no!" said he, with the tone of a man just awaking. "Be hanged; it's too absurd! I will not."

"Fare you well, then;" and the archdeacon added between his teeth, "I shall find thee again."

"I don't wish that devil of a man to find me again so," thought Gringoire; and he ran after Dom Claude. "Stay, monsieur the archdeacon," said he; "old friends should not fall out. You take an interest in that girl— my wife, I mean. That's all right. You have thought of a stratagem for getting her safe out of Notre-Dame; but your plan is extremely unpleasant for me, Gringoire. Now, if I could suggest another, myself!—I beg to say, a most luminous inspiration has just come over me. If I had an expedient for extricating her from her sorry plight, without compromising my neck in the smallest degree with a slip knot, what would you say?

27

—would not that suffice you? Is it absolutely necessary that I should be hanged to satisfy you?"

The priest was tearing the buttons from his cassock
with impatience. "Thou everlasting stream of words!
what is your plan?"

"Yes," continued Gringoire, talking to himself, and
touching his nose with his forefinger in sign of deep
cogitation—"that's it! The Truands are fine fellows!
The tribe of Egypt love her! They will rise at the
first word! Nothing easier! A bold stroke. By means
of the disorder, they will easily carry her off! To-morrow evening. Nothing would please them better."

"The means!—speak!" said the priest, shaking him.

Gringoire turned majestically toward him: "Let me
alone!—you see I am composing!" He reflected again
for a few seconds; then began to clap his hands at his
thought, exclaiming, "Admirable!—certain success!"

"The means? repeated Claude, angrily. Gringoire
was radiant.

"Come hither," said he—"Let me tell you in a whisper. It's a counterplot that's really capital, and that
will get us all out of the scrape. Egad! you must
allow I'm no simpleton!"

He stopped short: "Ah! and the little goat—is she
with the girl?"

"Yes—the devil take thee!"

"Why, they would have hanged her too, wouldn't
they?"

"What's that to me?"

"Yes, they would have hanged her. They hanged a
sow last month, sure enough. The executioner likes
that—he eats the animal after. To think of hanging
my pretty Djali! poor little lamb!"

"A curse upon thee!" cried Dom Claude. "The
hangman is thyself. What means of safety hast thou
found, fellow! Wilt thou never be delivered of thy
scheme?"

"Softly, master! You shall hear."

Gringoire leaned aside and spoke very low in the
archdeacon's ear, casting an anxious look from one end

of the street to the other, where, however, no one was passing. When he had done, Dom Claude took his hand, and said, coolly, "'Tis well. Till to-morrow fare you well."

"Till to-morrow," repeated Gringoire; and while the archdeacon withdrew one way, he went off the other, saying low to himself: "This is a grand affair, Monsieur Pierre Gringoire. Never mind—it's not to be said that because one's of little account one's to be frightened at a great undertaking. Biton carried a great bull on his shoulders—wagtails, linnets and buntings, across the ocean."

CHAPTER II.

TURN VAGABOND!

ON re-entering the cloister, the archdeacon found at the door of his cell his brother, Jehan du Moulin, who was waiting for him, and who had whiled away the tediousness of expectation by drawing on the wall, with a piece of charcoal, a profile of his elder brother, embellished with a nose of immoderate dimensions.

Dom Claude scarcely looked at his brother; he was full of other ruminations. That joyous roguish countenance, the irradiation of which had so often cleared away the gloom from the physiognomy of the priest, had now no power to dissipate the mist which was each day gathering thicker and thicker over that corrupt, mephitic, and stagnant soul.

"Brother," said Jehan timidly, "I am come to see you."

The archdeacon did not so much as raise his eyes toward him. "Well?"

"Brother," continued the hypocrite, "you are so good to me, and give me such excellent advice, that I always come back to you."

"What next?"

"Alas! brother, you were very right when you used to say to me : ' Jehan! Jehan, *cessat doctorum doctrina, discipulorum disciplina.* Jehan, be prudent. Jehan, be studious. Jehan, do not go out of college at night without lawful occasion and leave of the master. Do not beat the Picards. *Noli, Joannes, verberrare Picardos.* Do not grow old like an unlettered ass, *quasi asinus illiteratus,* amidst the litter of the schools. Jehan, go every evening to chapel, and sing an anthem with a verse and prayer to our lady the glorious Virgin Mary.' Alas! how excellent was that advice!"

"And what then?"

"Brother, you see before you a guilty wretch, a criminal, a miscreant, a libertine, a monster! My dear brother, Jehan has treated your gracious counsels as grass and straw, fit only to be trampled under foot. Well am I chastised for it—and God Almighty is exceeding just. So long as I had money, I spent it in feasting, folly, and joviality. Oh! how grim-faced and vile to look back upon, is that debauchery which appears so charming in prospect! Now I have not a single blanc left ; I have sold my table-cloth, my shirt, and my towel. A merry life no longer!—the bright taper is extinguished, and nothing is left me but its noisome snuff, which stinks under my nostrils. The girls mock at me. I drink water. I am tormented with remorse and creditors."

"Go on," said the archdeacon.

"Alas! dearest brother, I would fain lead a better life. I come to you full of contrition. I am penitent. I confess my faults. I beat my breast with heavy blows. You are very right to wish I should one day become a licentiate and sub-monitor of the Torchi College. I now feel a remarkable vocation for that office. But I have no ink left—I must buy some ; I have no pens left —I must buy some ; I have no paper left, no books left —I must buy some. I have a great need of a little money for those purposes ; and I come to you, brother with my heart full of contrition."

"Is that all?"

"Yes," said the scholar. "A little money."

"I have none."

The scholar then said, with an air at once grave and decided: "Well, brother, I am sorry to inform you that I have received from other quarters very advantageous offers and proposals. You will not give me any money?—No?—In that case I will turn Truand."

On pronouncing this monstrous word, he assumed the port of an Ajax expecting to see the thunderbolt fall on his head.

The archdeacon said to him coolly, "Turn Truand then."

Jehan made him a low bow, and re-descended the cloister staircase whistling.

Just as he was passing through the court of the cloisters, under the window of his brother's cell, he heard that window open, raised his head, and saw the archdeacon's severe face looking through the opening. "Get thee to the devil!" said Dom Claude; "this is the last money thou shalt have of me."

So saying the priest threw out a purse to Jehan, which raised a large lump on his forehead, and with which he set off, at once angry and pleased, like a dog that has been pelted with marrow-bones.

CHAPTER III.

VIVE LA JOIE!

THE reader will not, perhaps, have forgotten that a part of the Court of Miracles was enclosed within the ancient walls of the Town, a great number of the towers of which were beginning, at that time, to fall into decay. One of these towers had been converted into a place of entertainment by the Truands. There was a

cabaret or public-house on the lowest floor, and the rest
was carried on in the upper stories. This tower was
the point the most alive, and consequently the most
hideous, of the Truandry. It was a sort of monstrous
hive, which was humming day and night. At night,
when all the remainder of the rabble were asleep—when
not a lighted window was to be seen in the dingy fronts
of the houses in the square—when not a sound was
heard to issue from its innumerable families, from those
swarms of thieves, loose women, and stolen or bastard
children — the joyous tower might always be distinguished by the noise which proceeded from it, by the
crimson light which, gleaming at once from the air-
holes, the windows, the crevices in the gaping walls, escaped, as it were, from every pore.

The cellar, then, formed the public-house. The descent to it was through a low door and down a steep
staircase. Over the door there was, by way of sign, a
marvelous daub representing new-coined sols and dead
chickens, with this punning inscription underneath :
Aux sonneurs pour les trépassés—that is, " The ringers
for the dead."

One evening, at the moment when the curfew bell
was ringing from all the steeples in Paris, the sergeants
of the watch, had they been permitted to enter the
formidable Court of Miracles, might have remarked that
still greater tumult than usual was going on in the tavern of the Truands, that they were drinking deeper and
swearing louder. Without, in the square, were a number of groups, conversing in low tones as if some great
plot was hatching ; and here and there a fellow, squatted down, was sharpening a sorry iron blade upon a
stone.

Meanwhile, in the tavern itself, wine and gaming diverted the minds of the Truandry so powerfully from
the ideas which had occupied them that evening, that
it would have been difficult to have divined from the
conversation of the drinkers what was the affair in agi
tation. Only they had a gayer appearance than usual,
and between the legs of each of them was seen glitter-

ing some weapon or other, a pruning-hook, an axe, a large backsword, or the crook of an old hackbut.

The apartment, of a circular form, was very spaçious; but the tables were so close together and the tipplers so numerous, that the whole contents of the tavern, men, women, benches, beer-jugs, the drinkers, the sleepers, the gamblers, the able-bodied, the crippled, seemed thrown pell-mell together with about as much order and arrangement as a heap of oyster shells. A few greasy candles were burning upon the tables; but the grand luminary of the tavern, that which sustained in the pot-house the character of the chandelier in an opera house, was the fire. That cellar was so damp that the fire was never allowed to go out in it even in the height of summer; an immense fire-place, with a carved mantelpiece, and thick-set with heavy iron dogs and kitchen utensils, had in it, then, one of those large fires composed of wood and turf, which, at night, in a village street on the Continent, cast so red a reflection through the windows of some forge upon the wall opposite. A large dog, gravely seated in the ashes, was turning before the glowing fuel a spit loaded with different sorts of meat.

In spite of the confusion, after the first glance, amid this multitude three principal groups might be distinguished, pressing around three several personages with whom the reader is already acquainted. One of these personages, fantastically bedizened with many an Oriental gaud, was Mathias Hungadi Spicali, Duke of Egypt and Bohemia. The old rogue was seated on the table, with his legs crossed and his finger in the air, exhibiting, in a loud voice, his skill in white and black magic, to many a gaping face which surrounded him. Another set were gathering thick around our old friend, the valiant King of Tunis, armed to the teeth; and Clopin Trouillefou, with a very serious air and in a low voice, was superintending the ransacking of an enormous cask full of arms, staved wide before him, from which were issuing in profusion axes, swords, fire-locks, coats of mail, lance and pike heads, cross-bow bolts and arrows, like apples and grapes out of a cornucopia. Each one was taking something from the heap; one a morion, another a long rapier, and a third, the cross-handled *misericorde* or small dagger. The children themselves were arming; and even the veriest cripples without either legs or thighs, all barbed and cuirassed, were moving about on their seats between the legs of the drinkers, like so many large beetles.

And lastly, a third audience, the most noisy, the most jovial, and the most numerous of all, were crowding the benches and tables from the midst of which a flute-like voice, haranguing and swearing, proceeded from under a heavy suit of armor all complete from the casque to the spurs. The individual who had thus screwed himself up in full panoply, was so lost under his warlike trappings that nothing was seen of his person but a red, impudent, turned-up nose, a lock of fair hair, red lips, and a pair of bold-looking eyes. His belt was full of daggers and poniards; a large sword hung by his side; a rusty cross-bow was on his left, and an immense wine-pot before him : besides a strapping wench with her breast all open, seated on his right. All the mouths around him were laughing, swearing, and drinking.

Add to these twenty secondary groups; the waiters, male and female, running backward and forward with pitchers on their heads; the gamesters stooping over the billes (a rude sort of billiards), the merèlles, the dice, the vachettes, the exciting game of the tringlett (a kind of backgammon); quarrels in one corner—kisses in another; and some idea may then be formed of the whole collective scene; over which wavered the light of a great flaming fire, making a thousand grotesque and enormous shadows dance upon the tavern walls.

With respect to noise, the place might be likened to the interior of a bell in full peal.

The great dripping-pan before the fire, in which a shower of grease was crackling from the spit, filled up, with its unintermitted yelping, the intervals of those thousand dialogues which crossed each other in all directions from one side to another of the great circular room.

Amidst all this uproar there was, quite at one side of the tavern, upon the bench within the great open fireplace, a philosopher meditating, with his feet in the ashes, and his eyes upon the burning brands. It was Pierre Gringoire.

"Come! quick! make haste! get under arms! we must march in an hour," said Clopin Trouillefou to his Argotiers.

A girl was humming an air:

> "Father and mother, good-night;
> The latest up rake the fire."

Two card players were disputing—"Knave," cried the reddest-faced of the two, shaking his fist at the other "I'll mark thee. Thou might go and take Mistigri's place in messeigneur the king's own card party."

"O Lord!" bawled one whom his nasal pronunciation showed to be a Norman, "we're all heaped together here like the saints at Caillouville!"

"My lads," said the Duke of Egypt to his auditory, speaking in an affected canting tone, "the witches of France go to the sabbath without ointment, broomstick, or anything to ride on, with a few magical words only. The witches of Italy have always a he-goat that waits for them at their door. All of them are bound to go out up the chimney."

The voice of the young fellow armed cap-à-pie was heard above the general hum. "Noël! Noël!" cried he, "so this is my first day in armor! A Truand! I'm a Truand, ventre de Christ! Fill my glass. Friends, my name is Jehan Frollo du Moulin, and I'm a gentleman. It's my opinion that if God were a gendarme, he'd turn housebreaker. Brethren, we're going upon a noble expedition. We're of the valiant. Besiege the church—force the doors—bring away the pretty girl—save her from the judges—save her from the priests—dismantle the cloister—burn the bishop in his house—all that we shall do in less time than a burgomaster takes to eat a spoonful of soup. Our cause is just—we'll plunder Notre-Dame—and that's all about it. We'll hang up Quasimodo. Do you know Quasimodo, mesdemoiselles? Have you ever seen him work himself out of breath upon the big bell on a Whitsun holiday? Corne du Père! but it's very fine. You'd say it was a devil mounted upon a great gaping muzzle. Hark ye, my friends, I'm a Truand from the bottom of my heart—I'm an Argotier in my soul—I'm a Cagou born. I was very rich, and I've spent all I had. My mother wanted to make me an officer; my father, a sub-deacon; my aunt, a councilor of the inquests; my grandmother, king's prothonotary; my great aunt, treasurer of the short robe; but I would make myself a Truand. I told my father so, and he spit his male-diction in my face. I told my mother so, and she, poor old lady, began to cry and slobber like that log upon that iron dog there. Let's be merry! I'm a very Bicètre in myself. Landlady, my dear, some more wine! I've got some money left yet. But mind, I'll have no more of that Surène wine—it hurts my throat. I'd as lief gargle myself, cor-bœuf, with a basket!"

Meanwhile, the company around applauded with boisterous laughter; and, finding that the tumult was redoubling around him, the scholar exclaimed: "Oh, what a glorious noise! *Populi debacchantis populosa debacchatio!*" Then he began to sing out, with an eye as if swimming in ecstasy, and the tone of a canon leading the vesper chant: "*Quæ cantica! quæ organa! quæ cantilenæ! quæ melodiæ hic sine fine decantatur! Sonant melliflua hymnorum organa, suavissima angelorum melodia, cantica canticorum mira!*"—He stopped short. "Hey, you there, the devil's own barmaid; let me have some supper."

There was a moment of something approaching to silence, during which the shrill voice of the Duke of Egypt was heard in its turn, instructing his Bohemians in the mysteries of the black art. "The weazel," said he, "goes by the name of Aduine; a fox is called Blue-foot, or the Woodranger; a wolf, Gray-foot or Gilt-foot; a bear, the Old one, or the Grandfather. A gnome's cap makes one invisible, and makes one see in-

visible things. Whenever a toad is to be christened, it
ought to be dressed in velvet, red or black, with a little
bell at its neck and one at its feet. The godfather
holds it by the head, and the godmother by the hinder
parts. It's the demon Sidragasum that has the power
of making girls dance naked."

"By the mass," interrupted Jehan, "then I should
like to be the demon Sidragasum!"

Meanwhile, the Truands continued to arm, whispering to one another at the other side of the tavern.

"That poor Esmeralda!" exclaimed one of the gypsy
men; "she's our sister; we must get her out of that
place."

"So she's still at Notre-Dame, is she?" asked a Marcandier with a Jewish look.

"Yes, pardieu!" was the reply.

"Well, comrades," resumed the Marcandier; "to
Notre-Dame then! All the more, because there, in the
chapel of Saints Féréol and Ferrution, there are two
statues, the one of St. John the Baptist, the other of
St. Anthony, of solid gold, weighing together seventeen gold marks and fifteen esterlins; and the pedestals,
of silver gilt, weigh seventeen marks five ounces. I
know it, for I'm a goldsmith."

Here they served up Jehan his supper. He called
out, throwing himself back upon the bosom of the girl
that sat by him, "By Saint-Voult-de-Lucques, called by
the people Saint Goguelu, now I'm perfectly happy. I
see a blockhead there, straight before me, that's looking at me with a face as smooth as an archduke. Here's
another, at my left hand, with teeth so long that one
can't see his chin. And then, I'm like the Maréchal de
Gié at the siege of Pontoise; I've my right resting upon
a mamelon. Ventre-Mahom! comrade! you look like
a tennis-ball merchant—and you come and sit down by
me; I'm noble, my friend; and trade's incompatible
with nobility. Get thee away. Hollo! you, there!
don't fight! What! Baptiste Croque-Oison! with a
fine nose like thine; wilt thou go and risk it against
that blockhead's great fists? You simpleton! *Non*

cuiquam datum est habere nasum. Truly, thou'rt divine,
Jacqueline Rouge-Oreille! it's a pity thou hast no hair
on thy head! Hollah! do you hear? My name's Jehan Frollo, and my brother's an archdeacon—the devil
fly away with him! All that I tell you's the truth. By
turning Truand I've jocundly given up one half of a
house situate in Paradise, which my brother had promised me—*dimidam domum in paradiso*—those are the
very words. I've a fief in the Rue Tirechappe—and
all the women are in love with me—as true as it is that
St. Eloi was an excellent goldsmith, and that the five
trades of the good city of Paris are the tanners, the
leather-dressers, the baldric-makers, the purse-makers,
and the cordwainers; and that St. Laurence was broil-
ed over egg-shells. I swear to you, comrades,

> For full twelve months I'll taste no wine,
> If this be any lie of mine!

"My charmer, it's moonlight. Just look there,
through that air-hole, how the wind rumples those
clouds—just as I do thy gorgerette! Girls, snuff the
candles and the children. Christ et Mahom, what am
I eating now, in the name of Jupiter? Hey, there, old
jade! the hairs that are not to be found on thy wenches'
heads, we find in the omelets. Do you hear, old woman?
I like my omelets bald. The devil flatten thy nose! A
fine tavern of Beelzebub is this—where the wenches
comb themselves with the forks!"

And thereupon he broke his plate upon the floor,
and began to sing out with all his might,

> "Et je n'ai moi,
> Par la Sang-Dieu!
> Ni foi, ni loi,
> Ni feu, ni lieu,
> 　Ni roi,
> 　Ni Dieu!"

Meanwhile, Clopin Trouillefou had finished his dis-
tribution of weapons. He went up to Gringoire, who

seemed absorbed in profound revery, with his feet against one of the iron dogs in the fireplace. "Friend Pierre," said the King of Tunis, "what the devil art thou thinking about?"

Gringoire turned round to him with a melancholy smile; "I'm fond of the fire, my dear seigneur, not for any such trivial reason as that the fire warms our feet or boils our soup, but because it throws out sparks. Sometimes I pass whole hours in looking at the sparks. I discover a thousand things in those stars that sprinkle the dark back of the chimney-place. Those stars themselves are worlds."

"Tonnerre, if I understand thee," said the Truand. "Dost thou know what o'clock it is?"

"I don't know," answered Gringoire.

Clopin then went up to the Duke of Egypt. "Comrade Mathias," said he, "this is not a good time we've hit upon. They say King Louis the Eleventh's at Paris."

"The more need to get our sister out of his clutches," answered the old gypsy.

"You speak like a man, Mathias," said the King of Tunis. "Besides, we shall do the thing well enough. There's no resistance to fear in the church. The canons are like so many hares, and we're in force. The parliament's men will be finely balked when they come there for her to-morrow. *Boyaux du Pape!* I wouldn't have them hang the pretty girl!"

Clopin then went out of the cabaret.

Meantime, Jehan was crying out in a voice hoarse with bawling: "I drink—I eat—I'm drunk—I'm Jupiter! Hey! you there, Pierre l'Assommeur, if you look at me in that way again, I'll fillip the dust off your nose."

Gringoire, on the other hand, startled from his meditations, had set himself calmly to contemplate the passionate, clamorous scene around him, and muttered between his teeth: "*Luxuriosa res vinum et tumultuosa ebrietas.* Ah, what good reason have I to abstain from drinking! and how excellent is the saying of St. Bene dict: *Vinum apostatare facit etiam sapientes!*"

At that moment Clopin re-entered, and cried out in a voice of thunder, " Midnight ! "

At this word, which operated upon the Truands as the order to mount does upon a regiment halting, the whole of them—men, women, and children—rushed out of the tavern, with a great clatter of arms and iron implements.

The moon was now obscured by clouds, and the Court of Miracles was entirely dark. Not a single light was to be seen in it ; but it was far from being solitary. There was discernible in it a great crowd of men and women talking to one another in a low voice. The hum of this multitude was to be heard, and all sorts of weapons were to be seen glittering in the darkness. Clopin mounted upon a large stone. " To your ranks, Argot ! " cried he ; " to your ranks, Egypt ! to your ranks, Galilee ! " Then there was a movement in the darkness. The immense multitude seemed to be forming in column. In a few minutes the King of Tunis again raised his voice : " Now, silence ! to march through Paris. The password is, *Petite flambe en bagne-naud*. The torches must not be lighted till we get to Notre-Dame. March ! "

And in ten minutes after, the horsemen of the night-watch were flying terrified before a long procession of men descending in darkness and silence toward the Pont-au-Change, through the winding streets that intersect in every direction the close-built neighborhood of the Halles.

CHAPTER IV.

AN AWKWARD FRIEND.

THAT same night Quasimodo slept not. He had just gone his last round through the church. He had not remarked, at the moment when he was closing the doors, that the archdeacon had passed near him and had displayed a degree of ill-humor at seeing him bolt and padlock with care the enormous iron bars which gave to their large folds the solidity of a wall. Dom Claude appeared still more abstracted than usual. Moreover, since the nocturnal adventure of the cell, he was constantly ill-treating Quasimodo ; but in vain he used him harshly, even striking him sometimes ; nothing could shake the submission, the patience, the devoted resignation of the faithful ringer. From the archdeacon he could endure anything—ill-language, menaces, blows—without murmuring a reproach, without uttering a complaint. At most he would follow Dom Claude anxiously with his eye, as he ascended the staircase of the towers ; but the archdeacon had of himself abstained from again appearing before the gypsy girl.

That night, then, Quasimodo, after casting one look toward his poor forsaken bells, Jacqueline, Marie, and Thibauld, ascended to the top of the northern tower, and there, placing his well-closed dark lantern on the leads, set himself to contemplate Paris. The night, as we have already said, was very dark. Paris, which, comparatively speaking, was not lighted at that period, presented to the eye a confused heap of black masses, intersected here and there by the silvery windings of the Seine. Not a light could Quasimodo see except from the window of a distant edifice, the vague and gloomy profile of which was distinguishable, rising above the roofs in the direction of the Porte St. Antoine. There, too, was some one wakeful.

While his only eye was thus hovering over that horizon of mist and darkness, the ringer felt within himself an inexpressible anxiety. For several days he had been upon the watch. He had seen constantly wandering around the church, men of sinister aspect, who never took off their eyes from the young girl's asylum. He feared lest some plot should be hatching against the unfortunate refugee. He fancied that she was an object of popular hatred as well as himself, and that something might probably very shortly happen. Thus he remained on his tower, on the lookout *rêvant dans son rêvoir*, as Rabelais says, his eye by turns cast upon the cell and upon Paris, keeping safe watch like a trusty dog, with a thousand suspicions in his mind.

All at once, while he was reconnoitering the great city with that eye which nature, as if by way of compensation, had made so piercing that it almost supplied the deficiency of other organs in Quasimodo, it struck him that there was something unusual in the appearance of the outline of the quay of the Vielle Pelleterie, that there was some movement upon that point, that the line of the parapet which stood out black against the whiteness of the water was not so straight and still like that of the other quays, but that it undulated before the eye like the waves of a river, or the heads of a crowd in motion.

This appeared strange to him. He redoubled his attention. The movement seemed to be coming toward the city. No light was to be seen. It remained some time on the quay, then flowed off it by degrees, as if whatever was passing along was entering the interior of the island ; then it ceased entirely, and the line of the quay became straight and motionless again.

Just as Quasimodo was exhausting himself in conjectures, it seemed to him that the movement was reappearing in the Rue du Parvis, which runs into the City perpendicularly to the front of Notre-Dame. In fine, notwithstanding the great darkness, he could see the head of a column issuing from that street, and in an instant a crowd spreading over the square, of which he could distinguish nothing further than that it was a crowd.

This spectacle was one of terror to Quasimodo. It is probable that that singular procession which seemed so anxious to conceal itself in profound darkness, observed a silence no less profound. Still some sound must have escaped from it, were it only the pattering of feet. But even this noise did not reach our deaf hero ; and that great multitude of which he could scarcely see anything, from which he could hear nothing, and which, nevertheless, was walking and in agitation so near him, produced on him the effect of an assemblage of the dead, mute, impalpable, lost in vapor. He seemed to see advancing toward him a mist peopled with men, to see shades moving in the shade.

Then his fears returned; the idea of an attempt against the gypsy girl presented itself again to his mind. He had a vague feeling that he was about to find himself in a critical situation. In this crisis he held counsel with himself, and his reasoning was more just and prompt than might have been expected from a brain so ill-organized. Should he awaken the gypsy girl? assist her to escape? Which way? The streets were beset; behind the church was the river; there was no boat, no egress! There was but one measure to be taken: to meet death on the threshold of Notre-Dame; to resist at least until some assistance came, if any were to come, and not to disturb the sleep of La Esmeralda. The unhappy girl would be awake time enough to die. This resolution once taken, he proceeded to reconnoiter the enemy more calmly.

The crowd seemed to be increasing every moment in the Parvis. He concluded, however, that very little noise was made, since the windows of the streets and the square remained closed. All at once a light shone out, and in an instant seven or eight lighted torches were waved above the heads, shaking their tufts of flame in the deep shade. Quasimodo then saw distinctly in commotion, in the Parvis, a frightful troop of men and women in rags, armed with scythes, pikes, pruning-hooks, partisans, their thousand points all sparkling. Here and there black pitchforks formed horns to those hideous visages. He had a confused recollection of that populace, and thought he recognized all the heads which, a few months before, had saluted him Pope of the Fools. A man holding a torch in one hand and a boullaye in the other mounted a boundary-stone and appeared to be haranguing. At the same time the strange army performed some evolutions, as if taking post around the church. Quasimodo took up his lantern and descended to the platform between the towers, to observe more closely and to deliberate on the means of defense.

Clopin Trouillefou, having arrived before the principal door of Notre-Dame, had, in fact, placed his troops in battle array. Although he did not anticipate any resistance, yet, like a prudent general, he wished to preserve such a degree of order as would, in case of need, enable him to face a sudden attack of the watch or the onze-vingts. He had accordingly drawn out his brigade in such a manner that, seen from on high and at a distance, it might have been taken for the Roman triangle of the battle of Ecnoma, the pig's head of Alexander, or the famous wedge of Gustavus Adolphus. The base of this triangle was formed along the back of the square, so as to bar the entrance to the Rue du Parvis ; one of the sides looked toward the Hôtel-Dieu, the other toward the Rue Saint-Pierre-aux-Bœufs. Clopin Trouillefou had placed himself at the point, with the Duke of Egypt, our friend Jehan, and the boldest of the sabouleux.

An enterprise such as the Truands were now attempting against Notre-Dame was no uncommon occurrence in the cities of the Middle Ages. What we in our day call police, did not then exist. In populous towns, in capitals especially, there was no central power, sole and commanding all the rest. Feudality had constructed those great municipalities after a strange fashion. A city was an assemblage of innumerable seigneuries, which divided it into compartments of all forms and sizes. From thence arose a thousand contradictory establishments of police, or rather no police at all. In Paris, for example, independently of the hundred and forty-one lords claiming censive or manorial dues, there were twenty-five claiming justice and censive—from the Bishop of Paris, who had five hundred streets, to the Prior of Notre-Dame-des-Champs, who had only four. All these feudal justiciaries only recognized nominally the paramount authority of the king. All had right of highway-keeping. All were their own masters. Louis

XI., that indefatigable workman who commenced on so large a scale the demolition of the feudal edifice, carried on by Richelieu and Louis XIV. to the advantage of the royalty, and completed in 1789 to the advantage of the people—Louis XI. had indeed striven to burst this network of seigneuries which covered Paris, by throwing violently athwart it two or three ordinances of general police. Thus, in 1465, the inhabitants were ordered to light candles in their windows at nightfall, and to shut up their dogs, under pain of the halter. In the same year they were ordered to close the streets in an evening with iron chains, and forbidden to carry daggers or other offensive weapons in the streets at night. But in a short time all these attempts at municipal legislation fell into disuse. The townspeople allowed the candles at their windows to be extinguished by the wind, and their dogs to stray; the iron chains were only stretched across in case of siege; and the prohibition against carrying daggers brought about no other changes than that of the name of the Rue Coupe-gueule into Rue Coupe-gorge, which, to be sure, was a manifest improvement. The old framework of the feudal jurisdictions remained standing—an immense accumulation of bailiwicks and seigneuries, crossing one another in all directions throughout the city, straitening and entangling each other, interwoven with each other, and projecting one into another—a useless thicket of watches, under-watches, counter-watches, through the midst of which the armed hand of brigandage, rapine, and sedition was constantly passing. Thus it was no unheard-of event, in this state of disorder, for a part of the populace to lay violent hands on a palace, a hotel, or any ordinary mansion, in the quarters the most thickly inhabited. In most cases, the neighbors did not interfere in the affair unless the pillage reached themselves. They stopped their ears against the report of the musketry, closed their shutters, barricaded their doors, and let the struggle exhaust itself with or without the watch; and the next day it would be quietly said in Paris,

" Last night, Etienne Barbette had his house forced ; ' or, " The Maréchal de Clermont was laid hold of," etc. Hence, not only the royal residences—the Louvre, the Palais, the Bastile, the Tournelles—but such as were simply seigneurial, the Petit-Bourbon, the Hôtel-de-Sens, the Hôtel d'Angoulême, etc.—had their battle-mented walls and their machicolated gates. The churches were protected by their sanctity. Some of them, nevertheless, among which was Notre-Dame, were fortified. The Abbey of Saint-Germain-des-Près was castellated like a baronial mansion, and more weight of metal was to be found there in bombards than in bells. This fortress was still to be seen in 1630, but now barely the church remains.

To return to Notre-Dame.

When the first arrangements were completed—and we must say, to the honor of Truand discipline, that Clopin's orders were executed in silence and with ad-mirable precision—the worthy leader mounted the parapet of the Parvis, and raised his hoarse and sullen voice, his face turned toward Notre-Dame, and shak-ing his torch, the light of which, agitated by the wind and veiled at intervals by its own smoke, made the glowing front of the church by turns appear and disappear before the eye:

" Unto thee, Louis de Beaumont, Bishop of Paris, councilor in the court of parliament: thus say I, Clopin Trouillefou, King of Tunis, Grand-Coësre, Prince of Argot, Bishop of the Fools: Our sister, falsely condemned for magic, has taken refuge in thy church. Thou art bound to give her shelter and safeguard Now, the court of parliament wants to take her thence, and thou consentest to it ; so that she would be hanged to-morrow at the Grève, if God and the Truands were not at hand. We come to thee, then, bishop. If thy church is sacred, our sister is so, too ; if our sister is not sacred, neither is thy church. Wherefore we summon thee to give up the girl, if thou wilt save thy church ; or we will take the girl, and will plunder the church. Which will be well and good. In witness whereof, I here set up my standard. And so, God help thee, Bishop of Paris."

Quasimodo, unfortunately, could not hear these words, which were uttered with a sort of sullen savage majesty. A Truand presented the standard to Clopin, who gravely planted it between two of the paving-stones. It was a pitchfork, from the prongs of which hung, all bloody, a quarter of carrion meat.

This done, the King of Tunis turned about, and cast his eyes over his army, a ferocious multitude whose eyes glared almost as much as their pikes. After a moment's pause: "Forward, boys!" cried he. "To your work, Hutins."

Thirty stout men, square-limbed, and with pick-lock faces, stepped out from the ranks, with hammers, pincers, and iron crows on their shoulders. They advanced toward the principal door of the church; ascended the steps; and directly they were to be seen stooping down under the pointed arches of the portal, heaving at the door with pincers and levers. A crowd of Truands followed them, to assist or look on; so that the whole eleven steps were covered with them. The door, however, stood firm. "Diable! but she's hard and headstrong," said one. "She's old, and her gristles are tough," said another. "Courage, my friends!" cried Clopin. "I'll wager my head against a slipper that you'll have burst the door, brought away the girl, and undressed the great altar, before there's one beadle of 'em all awake. There—I think the lock's going."

Clopin was interrupted by a frightful noise which at that moment resounded behind him. He turned round; an enormous beam had just fallen from on high, crushing a dozen of the Truands upon the church steps, and rebounding upon the pavement with the sound of a piece of artillery; breaking here and there the legs of others among the vagabond crowd, which shrunk away from it with cries of terror. In a trice the confined inclosure of the Parvis was empty. The Hutins, though protected by the deep retiring arches of the doorway, abandoned the door, and Clopin himself fell back to a respectful distance from the church.

"Egad, I've had a narrow escape!" cried Jehan; "I felt the wind of it, tête-bœuf! but Pierre the Knocker down's knocked down at last."

The astonishment mingled with dread which fell upon the brigands with this unaccountable piece of timber is indescribable. They remained for some minutes gazing fixedly upward, in greater consternation at this piece of wood than they would have been at twenty thousand king's archers. "Satan!" growled the Duke of Egypt, "but this smells of magic!"

"It's the moon that's been throwing that log at us," said Andry-le-Rouge.

"Why," remarked François Chanteprune, "you know, they say the moon's a friend of the Virgin's."

"Mille-papes!" exclaimed Clopin, "you're all simpletons together." Yet he knew not how to account for the fall of the beam.

All this while nothing was distinguishable upon the grand front of the building, to the top of which the light from the torches did not reach. The ponderous beam lay in the middle of the Parvis; and groans were heard from the miserable wretches who had received its first shock, and been almost cut in two upon the angles of the stone steps.

At last the King of Tunis, his first astonishment being over, hit upon an explanation which his comrades thought plausible. "Gueule-Dieu!" said he, "are the canons making a defense? If that be it, then, A sac! à sac!"

"A sac!" repeated the mob with a furious hurrah; and they made a general discharge of cross-bows and hackbuts against the front of the church.

This report awoke the peaceable inhabitants of the neighboring houses; several window-shutters were seen to open; and nightcaps and hands holding candles appeared at the casements. "Fire at the windows!" cried Clopin. The windows were immediately shut again, and the poor citizens, who had scarcely had time to cast a bewildered look upon that scene of glare and tumult, went back trembling to their wives, asking themselves whether it was that the witches now held their sabbath in the Parvis Notre-Dame or that they were assaulted by the Burgundians as in the year sixty-four.

"A sac!" repeated the Argotiers; but they dared not approach. They looked first at the church and then at the marvelous beam. The beam lay perfectly still; the edifice kept its calm and solitary look; but something froze the courage of the Truands.

"To your work, Hutins!" cried Trouillefou. "Come —force the door."

Nobody advanced a step.

"Barbe et ventre!" said Clopin; "here are men afraid of a rafter!"

An old Hutin now addressed him. "Captain, it's not the rafter that we care about; it's the door, that's all overlaid with iron bars. The pincers can do nothing with it."

"What should you have, then, to burst it open with?" asked Clopin.

"Why, we should have a battering ram."

The king of Tunis ran bravely up to the formidable piece of timber, and set his foot upon it. "Here's one!" cried he; "the canons have sent it you;" and, making a mock reverence to the cathedral, "Thank you canons," he added.

This bravado had great effect—the spell of the wonderful beam was broken. The Truands recovered courage; and soon the heavy timber, picked up like a feather by two hundred vigorous arms, was driven with fury against the great door which it had already been attempted to shake. Seen thus, by the sort of half light which the few scattered torches of the Truands cast over the Place, the long beam, borne along by that multitude of men rushing on with its extremity pointed against the church, looked like some monstrous animal, with innumerable legs, running, head foremost, to attack the stone giantess.

At the shock given by the beam, the half metal door sounded like an immense drum. It was not burst in but the whole cathedral shook, and the deepest of its internal echoes were awakened. At the same moment, a shower of great stones began to fall from the upper part of the front upon the assailants. "Diable!" cried Jehan, "are the towers shaking down their balustrades upon our heads?" But the impulse was given. The King of Tunis stuck to his text. It was decidedly the bishop making a defense. And so they only battered the door the more furiously, in spite of the stones that were fracturing their skulls right and left.

It must be remarked that these stones all fell one by one; but they followed one another close. The Argotiers always felt two of them at one and the same time, one against their legs, the other upon their heads. Nearly all of them took effect; and already the dead and wounded were thickly strewn, bleeding and panting under the feet of the assailants, who, now grown furious, filled up instantly and without intermission the places of the disabled. The long beam continued battering the door with periodical strokes, the stones to shower down, the door to groan, and the interior of the cathedral to reverberate.

Undoubtedly, the reader has not yet to divine that this unexpected resistance which had exasperated the Truands proceeded from Quasimodo. Accident had unfortunately favored our deaf hero's exertions.

When he had descended upon the platform between the towers, his ideas were all in confusion. He ran to and fro along the gallery for some minutes, like one insane; beholding from on high the compact mass of the Truands ready to rush against the church; imploring the powers celestial or infernal to save the gypsy girl. He once thought of ascending the southern steeple, and sounding the tocsin; but then before the loud voice of Marie could have uttered a single sound, would there not be interval enough for the door of the church to be forced ten times over! It was just the moment at which the Hutins were advancing toward it with their burglarious instruments. What was to be done?

All at once he recollected that some masons had been

at work the whole day, repairing the wall, the wood-work, and the roofing of the southern tower. This was a beam of light to him. The wall was of stone; the roofing was of lead; and then there was the woodwork, so prodigious, and so thick-clustering, that it went by the name of the forest.

Quasimodo ran to this tower. The lower chambers of it were, in fact, full of materials. There were piles of building stone, sheets of lead rolled up, bundles of laths, strong beams already shaped by the saw, heaps of rub-bish—in short, an arsenal complete.

Time pressed. The levers and the hammers were at work below. With a strength multiplied tenfold by the feeling of imminent danger, he lifted an end of one of the beams, the heaviest and longest of all. He managed to push it through one of the loopholes; then, laying hold of it again outside the tower, he shoved it over the outer angle of the balustrade surrounding the platform, and let it fall into the abyss beneath.

The enormous beam, in this fall of a hundred and sixty feet, grazing the wall, breaking the sculptured fig-ures, turned several times upon its center, like one of the two cross arms of a windmill, going by itself. At length it reached the ground; a horrid cry arose; and the dark piece of timber rebounded upon the pavement, like a serpent rearing itself and darting.

Quasimodo saw the Truands scattered by the fall of the beam like ashes by the blowing of a child; and while they fixed their superstitious gaze upon the im-mense log fallen from the sky, and peppered the stone saints of the portal with a discharge of bolts and bullets, Quasimodo was silently piling up stones and rubbish, and even the masons' bags of tools, upon the verge of that balustrade from which he had already hurled the large timber.

And accordingly, as soon as they began to batter the great door, the shower of great stones began to fall, making them think that the church must be shaking it-self to pieces upon their heads.

Any one who could have seen Quasimodo at that mo

ment, would have been affrighted. Independently of the missiles which he had piled up on the balustrade, he had got together a heap of stones upon the platform itself. As soon as the great stones heaped upon the external border were spent, he had recourse to this latter heap. Then he stooped down, rose up, stooped, and rose again, with incredible agility. He thrust his great gnome's head over the balustrade; then there dropped an enormous stone—then another—then another. Now and then he followed some big stone with his eye; and when he saw that it did good execution, he ejaculated a "hum!" of satisfaction.

The beggars, meanwhile, did not lose courage. Already above twenty times had the massive door which they were so furiously assailing, shaken under the weight of their oaken battering-ram, multiplied by the strength of a hundred men. The panels cracked—the carvings flew in splinters—the hinges, at each shock, danced upon their hooks—the planks were forced out of their places—the wood was falling in dust, bruised between the sheathings of iron. Fortunately for Quasimodo's defense, there was more iron than wood.

Nevertheless he felt that an impression was being made upon the great door. Each stroke of the battering ram, notwithstanding that he did not hear it, awakened not only the echoes within the church, but a pang of apprehension in his heart. As he looked down upon the Truands, he beheld them full of exultation and of rage, shaking their fists at the dark front of the edifice; and he coveted, for the gypsy girl and himself, the wings of the owls that were flocking away affrighted over his head. His shower of stones did not suffice to repel the assailants.

It was in this moment of anguish that he fixed his eyes a little below the balustrade from which he had been crushing the Argotiers, upon two long stone gutters which discharged themselves immediately over the grand doorway. The internal orifice of these gutters was in the floor of the platform. An idea occurred to him. He ran and brought a fagot from the little lodge

which he occupied as ringer; laid over the fagot a
number of bundles of laths and rolls of lead—ammunition of which he had not yet made any use; and,
after placing this pile in the proper position as regarded
the orifice of the gutters, he set fire to it with his lantern.

While he was thus employed, as the stones no longer
fell, the Truands ceased looking up into the air. The
brigands, panting like a pack of hounds at baying the
wild boar in his lair, were pressing tumultuously round
the great door, all disfigured and shapeless from the
strokes of the ram, but still erect. They waited in a
sort of shuddering anxiety for the grand stroke of all,
the stroke which was to burst it in. They were all striving to get nearest, in order to be the first, when it should
open, to rush into that well-stored cathedral—a vast repository in which had been successively accumulating
the riches of three centuries. They reminded one another, with roars of exultation and greedy desire, of the
fine silver crosses, the fine brocade copes, the fine silver
gilt monuments, of all the magnificence of the choir, the
dazzling holiday displays, the Christmas illuminations
with torches, the Easter suns, all those splendid solemni-
ties, in which shrines, candlesticks, pixes, tabernacles,
and reliquaries, embossed the altars as it were with a
covering of gold and jewels. Certain it is that, at that
flattering moment, cagoux and malingreux, archisuppôts and rifodés, were all of them thinking much less
about delivering the gypsy girl than about plundering
Notre-Dame. Nay, we could even go so far as to believe that, with a good many of them, La Esmeralda
was merely a pretext—if, indeed, thieves could have
need of a pretext.

All at once, at the moment that they were crowding
about the battering-ram for a final effort, each one holding in his breath and gathering up his muscles, so as to
give full force to the decisive stroke, a howling more
terrific yet than that which had burst forth and expired
under the fall of the great beam, arose from the midst
of them. They who had not cried out, they who were

still alive, looked, and saw two jets of melted lead falling from the top of the edifice into the thickest of the
crowd. The waves of that human sea had shrunk under the boiling metal, which, at the two points where
it fell, had made two black and reeking hollows in the
crowd, like the effect of hot water thrown upon snow.
There were to be seen dying wretches burned half to a
cinder, and moaning with agony. Around the two
principal jets, there were drops of that horrible rain
falling scatteredly upon the assailants, and entering
their skulls like fiery gimlet points.

The outcry was heart-rending. They fled in disorder,
throwing down the beam upon the dead bodies—the
boldest of them as well as the most timid—and the
Parvis was left empty for the second time.

All eyes were now cast upward to the top of the
church, and they beheld an extraordinary sight. On
the topmost gallery, higher than the great central window, was a great flame ascending between the two
steeples, with clouds of sparks—a great flame, irregular
and furious, a portion of which, by the action of the
wind, was at intervals enveloped in the smoke. Underneath that flame, underneath the trifoliated balustrade showing darkly upon its glare, two monster-headed gutters were vomiting incessantly that burning
shower, the silver-trickling of which shone out upon
the darkness of the lower part of the grand front. As
they approached the ground, the two jets of liquid lead
spread out into myriads of drops like water sprinkled
from the small holes of a watering-pan. Above the
flame the huge towers, of each of which two faces were
to be seen in all their sharpness of outline, the one quite
black, the other quite red, seemed huger still by all the
immensity of shadow which they cast into the sky.
Their innumerable sculptured demons and dragons assumed a formidable aspect. The restless flickering
light from the unaccountable flame, made them seem as
if they were moving. Some of the guivres seemed to
be laughing—some of the gargouilles you might have
fancied you heard yelping; there were salamanders

puffing at the fire—tarasques sneezing in the smoke.
And among those monsters, thus awakened from their
stony slumber by that unearthly flame, by that unwont-
ed clamor, there was one walking about and seen from
time to time to pass before the blazing front of the pile
like a bat before a torch.

Assuredly, this strange beacon-light must have awak
ened the far woodcutter on the Bicêtre hills, startled to
see wavering upon his coppices the gigantic shadows of
the towers of Notre-Dame.

The silence of terror now took place among the Tru
ands; during which nothing was heard but the cries of
alarm from the canons, shut up in their cloisters and
more uneasy than the horses in a burning stable—the
stealthy sound of windows opened quick and shut yet
quicker—the stir in the interior of the houses and of
the Hôtel-Dieu—the wind agitating the flame—the last
groans of the dying—and the continued crackling of
the shower of boiling lead upon the pavement.

Meanwhile the principal Truands, having retreated
under the porch of the Logis Gondelaurier, were there
holding a council of war. The Duke of Egypt, seated
upon a boundary-stone, was contemplating with religious awe the phantasmagoric pile blazing two hundred
feet aloft in the air. Clopin Trouillefou was gnawing
his great fists with rage. "Not possible to get in!"
muttered he to himself.

"An old elf of a church!" growled the old Bohemian, Mathias Hungadi Spicali.

"By the Pope's whiskers!" added a gray-headed narquois who had once been in actual service, "but there
are two church gutters that spit molten lead at you
better than the machicolles at Lectoure!"

"Do you see that demon, going backward and forward before the fire?" cried the Duke of Egypt.

"Par-Dieu!" said Clopin, "it's the damned ringer—
it's Quasimodo."

The Bohemian shook his head. "I tell you, no,"
said he; "it's the spirit Sabnac, the great marquis, the
demon of fortifications. Out of an armed soldier he's

been making a lion's head. Sometimes he's mounted on a frightful horse. He turns men into stones, and builds towers of them. He commands fifty legions. It's he, sure enough. I know him again. Sometimes he has on a fine robe of gold, figured after the Turkish fashion."

" Where's Bellevigne-de-l'Etoile ? " asked Clopin.

" He's dead," answered a female Truand.

Here Andry-le-Rouge observed, laughing idiotically, " Notre-Dame's finding work for the Hôtel-Dieu."

" Is there no way to force that door, then ? " said the King of Tunis, stamping his foot.

Hereupon the Duke of Egypt pointed with a melancholy look to the two streams of boiling lead, which streaked the dark front of the building, looking like two long phosphoric distaffs. " There have been churches known to defend themselves so," observed he with a sigh. " St. Sophia's, at Constantinople—some forty years ago—threw down to the ground three times, one after another, the crescent of Mahound—just by shaking her domes, which are her heads. William of Paris, that built this here, was a magician."

" And are we to slink away pitifully, then, like so many running footmen ? " said Clopin. " What ! leave our sister there, for those ugly hooded fellows of canons to hang to-morrow ! "

" And the sacristy—where there are cartloads of gold ! " said a Truand, with whose name we are sorry to say that we are not acquainted.

" Barbe-Mahom ! " exclaimed Trouillefou.

" Let us try once more," rejoined the Truand.

Mathias Hungadi shook his head. " We shall not get in at the door," said he. " We must find out some seam in the old elf's armor—a hole—a false postern—a joint of some sort or other."

" Who's for it ? " said Clopin. " I'll go at it again. By-the-by, where's the little scholar, Jehan, that had cased himself up so ? "

" He's dead, no doubt," answered some one, " for nobody hears him laugh."

The King of Tunis knit his brows. "So much the worse!" said he. "There was a stout heart under that iron case. And Maître Pierre Gringoire?"

"Captain Clopin," said Andry-le-Rouge, "he stole away before we had got as far as the Pont-aux-Changeurs."

Clopin stamped with his foot. "Gueule-Dieu!" he cried, "that fellow pushed us into this business, and then leaves us here just in the thick of the job. A prating nightcap-helmeted coward!"

"Captain Clopin," cried Andry-le-Rouge, looking up the Rue de Parvis, "here comes the little scholar!"

"Blessed be Pluto!" said Clopin. "But what the devil is he pulling after him?"

It was in fact Jehan, coming up as quick as he found practicable under his ponderous knightly accoutrements, with a long ladder, which he was dragging stoutly over the pavement, more out of breath than an ant which has harnessed itself to a blade of grass twenty times its own length.

"Victory! Te Deum!" shouted the scholar. "Here's the ladder belonging to the unladers of St. Landry's wharf."

Clopin went up to him. "My lad," said he, "what are you going to do, corne-Dieu! with that ladder?"

"I have it," answered Jehan, panting. "I knew where it was. Under the shed of the lieutenant's house. There's a girl there, that I'm acquainted with, that thinks me quite a Cupido for beauty. It was through her I tried to get the ladder—and now I have the ladder, Pasque-Mahom! The poor girl came out in her shift to let me in."

"Yes, yes," said Clopin; "but what do you want to do with this ladder?"

Jehan gave him a roguish, knowing look, and snapped his fingers. At that moment he was quite sublime. He had upon his head one of those overloaded helmets of the fifteenth century which affrighted the enemy with their monstrous-looking peaks. The one which he wore was jagged with no less than ten beaks of steel so that Jehan might have contended for the formidable epithet of δεκεμβολ ᵒς with the Homeric ship of Nestor.

"What do I want to do with it, august King of Tunis?" said he. "Do you see that row of statues there, that look like blockheads, over the three doorways?"

"Yes. Well?"

"It's the gallery of the Kings of France."

"What's that to me?" said Clopin.

"Wait a bit. At the end of that gallery there's a door that's always on the latch. With this ladder I get up to it, and then I'm in the church."

"Let me get up first, lad," said the other.

"No, comrade; the ladder's mine. Come along—you shall be the second."

"Beelzebub strangle thee!" said Clopin, turning sulky. "I'll not go after anybody."

"Then, Clopin, go look for a ladder."

And therewith Jehan set off again across the Place, dragging along his ladder, and shouting, "Follow me, boys!"

In an instant the ladder was reared up, and the top of it placed against the balustrade of the lower gallery, over one of the side doorways. The crowd of the Truands, raising great acclamations, pressed to the foot of it for the purpose of ascending. But Jehan maintained his right, and was the first that set foot on the steps of the ladder. The passage to be made was a long one. The gallery of the French kings is, at this day, about sixty feet from the ground; to which elevation was, at that period, added the height of the eleven steps of entrance. Jehan ascended slowly, much encumbered with his heavy armor, with one hand upon the ladder and the other grasping his cross-bow. When he was half way up, he cast down a melancholy glance upon the poor dead Argotiers, strewed upon the steps of the grand portal. "Alas!" said he, "here's a heap of dead worthy the fifth book of the Iliad!" Then he continued his ascent. The Truands followed him. There was one upon each step of the ladder. To see that line of mailed backs thus rise undulating in the dark, one might

have imagined it a serpent with steely scales, rearing itself up to assail the church, but that the whistling of
Jehan, who formed its head, was not exactly the ser-
pent-like sound requisite to complete the illusion.

The scholar at length reached the parapet of the gallery, and strode lightly over it, amid the applauses of
the whole Truandry. Thus master of the citadel, he
uttered a joyful shout—but stopped short all at once,
confounded. He had just discovered, behind one of
the royal statues, Quasimodo in concealment, his eye
all flashing in the dark.

Before another of the besiegers had time to gain footing on the gallery, the formidable hunchback sprang to
the head of the ladder; took hold without saying a
word, of the ends of the two uprights with his two
powerful hands; heaved them away from the edge of
the balustrade; balanced for a moment, amid cries of
anguish, the long bending ladder, covered with Truands
from top to bottom; then suddenly, with superhuman
strength, he threw back that cluster of men into the
Place. For a moment or two the most resolute felt
their hearts palpitate. The ladder thus hurled backward with all that living weight upon it, remained perpendicular for an instant, and its inclination seemed
doubtful; then it wavered; then, suddenly describing
a frightful arc of eighty feet radius, it came down upon the pavement, with its load of brigands, more swift-
ly than a drawbridge when its chains give way. There
arose one vast imprecation—then all was still, and a few
mutilated wretches were seen crawling out from under
the heap of dead.

A mixed murmur of pain and resentment among the
besiegers succeeded their first shouts of triumph.
Quasimodo, unmoved, his elbows resting upon the balustrade, was quietly looking on, with the mien of some
old long-haired king looking out at his window.

Jehan Frollo, on the other hand, was in a critical situation. He found himself in the gallery with the redoubtable ringer—alone, separated from his companions
by eighty feet of perpendicular wall. While Quasi-

modo was dealing with the ladder, the scholar had run to the postern, which he expected to find on the latch. No such thing. The ringer, as he entered the gallery, had fastened it behind him. Jehan had then hidden himself behind one of the stone kings, not daring to draw breath, but fixing upon the monstrous hunchback a look of wild apprehension—like the man who, upon a time, making love to the wife of a menagerie-keeper, and going one evening to meet her in an assignation, scaled the wrong wall, and suddenly found himself tête-à-tête with a white bear.

For the first few moments the hunchback took no notice of him; but at length he turned his head and drew up his limbs, for the scholar had just caught his eye.

Jehan prepared for a rude encounter; but his deaf antagonist remained motionless; only his face was turned toward the scholar, at whom he continued looking.

" Ho, ho ! " said Jehan, " what dost thou look at me for with that one melancholy eye of thine ? " And so saying, the young rogue was stealthily making ready his cross-bow. " Quasimodo," he cried, " I'm going to change thy surname. They shall call thee the blind."

Jehan let fly the winged shaft, which whistled through the air, and struck its point into the left arm of the hunchback. This no more disturbed Quasimodo than a scratch would have done his stone neighbor, King Pharamond. He laid his hand upon the arrow, drew it out of his arm, and quietly broke it over his clumsy knee. Then he dropped, rather than threw, the two pieces on the ground. But he did not give Jehan time to discharge a second shaft. As soon as the arrow was broken, Quasimodo, breathing strongly through his nostrils, bounded like a grasshopper upon the scholar, whose armor this shock of his flattened against the wall.

Then, through that atmosphere in which wavered the light of the torches, was dimly seen a sight of terror.

Quasimodo had grasped in his left hand both the

arms of Jehan, who made no struggle, so utterly did he give himself up for lost. With his right hand the hunchback took off, one after another, with ominous deliberation, the several pieces of his armor, offensive and defensive—the sword, the daggers, the helmet, the breastplate, the armpieces—as if it had been a monkey peeling a walnut. Quasimodo dropped at his feet, piece after piece, the scholar's iron shell.

When the scholar had found himself disarmed and un-cased, feeble and naked, in those formidable hands, he did not offer to speak to his deaf enemy; but he fell to laughing audaciously in his face, and singing, with the careless assurance of a boy of sixteen, a popular air of the time:

> " Elle est bien babillée,
> La ville de Cambrai ;
> Marafin l'a pillée . . ."

He had not time to finish. Quasimodo was now seen standing upon the parapet of the gallery, holding the scholar by the feet with one hand only, and swing-ing him round like a sling over the external abyss. Then a noise was heard like some box made of bone dashing against a wall; and something was seen fall-ing, but it stopped a third part of the way down, being arrested in its descent by one of the architect-ural projections. It was a dead body which remained suspended there, bent double, the loins broken, and the skull empty.

A cry of horror arose from the Truands. "Re-venge!" cried Clopin. "*A sac !*" answered the mul-titude. "Assault! assault!" Then there was a pro-digious howling, mixed up of all languages, all dialects, and all tones of voice. The poor scholar's death inspired the crowd with a frantic ardor. They were seized with shame and resentment at having been so long kept in check, before a church, by a hunchback. Their rage found them ladders, multiplied their torches, and in a few minutes Quasimodo, in con-fusion and despair, saw a frightful swarm ascending from all sides, to the assault of Notre Dame. They who had not ladders had knotted ropes; and they who had not ropes climbed up by means of the projections of the sculpture. They hung at one another's tattered habiliments. There was no means of resisting this rising tide of frightful visages. Fury seemed to writhe in those ferocious countenances; their dirty foreheads were streaming with perspiration; their eyes flashed; and all those varieties of grimace and ugliness were besetting Quasimodo. It seemed as if some other church had sent her gorgons, her dogs, her drées, her demons, all her most fantastic sculptures, to assail Notre-Dame. It was a coat of living monsters covering the stone monsters of the façade.

Meanwhile a thousand torches had kindled in the Place. This disorderly scene, buried until then in thick obscurity, was wrapped in a sudden blaze of light. The Parvis was resplendent, and cast a radiance on the sky, while the pile that had been lighted on the high platform of the church still burned and illumined the city far around. The vast outline of the two towers, projected afar upon the roofs of Paris, threw amid that light a huge mass of shade. The whole town seemed now to be roused from its slumber. Distant tocsins were mournfully sounding; the Truands were howling, panting, swearing, climbing; and Quasimodo, powerless against so many enemies, trembling for the gypsy girl, seeing all those furious faces approaching nearer and nearer to his gallery, was imploring a miracle from heaven, and writhing his arms in despair.

CHAPTER V.

THE RETREAT IN WHICH MONSIEUR LOUIS OF FRANCE SAYS HIS PRAYERS.

THE reader has probably not forgotten that Quasimodo, a moment or two before he perceived the noc-

turnal band of the Truands in motion, while looking
over Paris from the top of his steeple, saw but one
single remaining light, twinkling at a window in the
topmost story of a lofty and gloomy building, close by
the Porte St. Antoine. That building was the Bastile:
and that twinkling light was Louis XI.'s candle.

Louis XI. had, in fact, been at Paris for the last two
days. He was to set out again the next day but one
for his citadel of Plessis, or Montilz-les-Tours. He
seldom made his appearance in this good city of Paris,
and when he did appear, it was during very short intervals, as he did not there feel himself surrounded by a
sufficient abundance of pitfalls, gibbets, and Scottish
archers.

He had come that day to sleep at the Bastile. His
grand chamber at the Louvre, five toises square, with
its grand chimney-piece loaded with twelve great beasts
and thirteen great prophets, and his great bed, eleven
feet by twelve, were little to his taste. He felt himself
lost amidst all those grandeurs. This good homely
king preferred the Bastile with a chamber and a bed of
humbler dimensions; and, besides, the Bastile was
stronger than the Louvre.

The chamber which Louis XI. reserved to himself in
the famous state prison, notwithstanding its comparative smallness, was positively spacious, occupying the
upper story of a secondary tower adhering to the donjon or great keep of the fortress. It was a circular
apartment, hung with matting of shining straw; ceiled
with wooden beams decorated with raised fleurs-de-lys
of gilt metal, with colored spaces between them, and
wainscoted with rich carvings interspersed with rosettes
of white metal, and painted of a fine light green made
of orpiment and fine indigo.

There was but one window, a long pointed one, latticed with iron bars and brass wire, and still further
darkened with fine glass painted with the arms of the
king and queen, each pane of which had cost two-and-
twenty sols.

There was but one entrance, a modern doorway under

an overhanging circular arch, furnished inside with a piece of tapestry, and outside with one of those porches of Irish wood (*bois d'Irelande*), as it was called—frail structures of curious cabinet-work, which were still to be seen abounding in old French mansions a hundred and fifty years ago. "Although they disfigure and encumber the places," says Sauval in despair, "yet our old gentlemen will not put them out of the way, but keep them in spite of everybody."

No description of ordinary furniture was to be seen in this chamber; neither benches, nor trestles, nor forms, nor common box stools, nor fine stools supported by pillars and counter pillars, at four sols a-piece; there was only one easy arm-chair, a very magnificent one; the wood of it was painted with roses upon a red ground, and its seat was of red morocco, decorated with long silken fringe and with abundance of gold-headed nails. The soleness of this chair testified that one person alone was entitled to be seated in the chamber. By the chair, and close to the window, there was a table, the cover of which was figured with birds. On the table were a gallemard or standish, spotted with ink, some scrolls of parchment, some pens, and a hanap or large cup of silver chased. A little further on were a chauffe-doux, and, for the purpose of prayer, a prie-Dieu or small pew of crimson velvet set off with golden bosses. And behind was a plain bed of yellow and pink damask, without any sort of tinsel decoration, having only an ordinary fringe. It was this same bed, famous for having borne the sleep or the sleeplessness of Louis XI., that was still to be beheld two hundred years back, at the house of a councilor of state, where it was seen by the aged Madame Pilou, celebrated in the great romance of "Cyrus" under the name of *Arricidie* and that of *La Morale Vivante*. Such was the chamber which was then popularly styled "the closet where Louis of France says his prayers."

At the moment at which we have introduced the reader into it, this closet was very dark. The curfew had rung an hour ago; it was dark night; and there

was but one wavering wax candle set upon the table to
light five different persons variously grouped in the
chamber.

The first upon whom the light fell was a seigneur
splendidly attired in a doublet and hose of scarlet
striped with silver, and a cloak with mahoîtres, or
shoulder pieces, of cloth of gold with black figures.
This splendid costume, as the light played upon it,
glittered flamingly at every fold. The man who wore
it had upon his breast his arms embroidered in brilliant
colors—*un chevron accompagné en pointe d'un daim
payssant.* The escutcheon was accosté on the right by
an olive branch, and on the left by a stag's horn.
This man wore in his girdle a rich dagger, the hilt
of which, of silver gilt, was chased in the form of a
helmet top, and surmounted by a count's coronet.
His air was unprepossessing, his look haughty and stiff.
At the first glance you saw arrogance in his face; at
the second, cunning.

He was standing bareheaded, with a long written
scroll in his hand, behind the easy-chair, upon which
was seated, with his body ungracefully bent double, his
knees thrown one across the other, and his elbow resting on the table, a person in very indifferent habiliments. Imagine, indeed, upon the rich morocco seat,
a pair of crooked joints, a pair of lean thighs poorly
wrapped in a web of black worsted, a trunk wrapped in
a loose coat of linsey-woolsey, the fur trimming of which
had much more leather left than hair, and, to crown the
whole, an old greasy hat of the meanest black cloth,
garnished all round with a band of small leaden figures.
Such, together with a dirty skull-cap beneath which
hardly a single hair was visible, was all that could be
distinguished of the sitting personage. He kept his
head so much bent down over his chest that nothing
was visible of his face thus thrown into shadow, except
only the extremity of his nose, upon which a ray of
light fell, and which, it was evident, must be a long
one. The thinness of his wrinkled hand showed it to
be an old man. It was Louis XI.

At some distance behind them there were talking in a low voice two men habited after the Flemish fashion, who were not so completely lost in the darkness but that any one who had attended the performance of Gringoire's mystery could recognize in them two of the principal Flemish envoys, Guillaume Rym, the sagacious pensionary of Ghent, and Jacques Coppenole, the popular hosier. It will be recollected that these two men were concerned in the secret politics of Louis XI.

And quite behind all the rest, near the door, there was standing in the dark, motionless as a statue, a stout, brawny, thick-set man, in military accoutrements, with an emblazoned casaque, whose square face, with its prominent eyes, its immense cleft of a mouth, its ears concealed each under a great mat of hair, and with scarcely any forehead, seemed a sort of compound of the dog and the tiger.

All were uncovered except the king.

The seigneur standing by him was reading over to him a sort of long official paper, to which his majesty seemed to be attentively listening, while the two Flemings were whispering to each other behind.

"Croix-Dieu!" muttered Coppenole, "I'm tired of standing. Is there never a chair here?"

Rym answered by a negative gesture, accompanied with a circumspect smile.

"Croix-Dieu!" resumed Coppenole, quite wretched at being obliged thus to lower his voice, "I feel a mighty itching to sit myself down on the floor, with my legs across, hosier-like, as I do in my own shop."

"You had better beware of doing so, Maître Jacques," was the reply.

"Hey-day! Maître Guillaume—so, then, here a man can be nohow but on his feet?"

"Or on his knees," said Rym.

At that moment the king raised his voice, and they ceased talking.

"Fifty sols for the gowns of our valets, and twelve livres for the mantles of the clerks of our crown! That's the way! Pour out gold by tons? Are you mad, Olivier?"

So saying the old man had raised his head. The golden shells of the collar of St. Michael were now seen to glitter about his neck. The candle shone full upon his meager and morose profile. He snatched the paper from the hands of the other.

"You're ruining us," cried he, casting his hollow eyes over the schedule. "What's all this? What need have we of so prodigious a household? Two chaplains at the rate of ten livres a month each, and a chapel clerk at a hundred sols! A valet-de-chambre at ninety livres a year! Four squires of the kitchen at a hundred and twenty livres a year each! A roaster, a potagier, a saucier, a chief cook, an armory-keeper, two sumpter-men, at the rate of ten livres a month each! Two turnspits at eight livres! A groom and his two helpers at four-and-twenty livres a month! A porter, a pastry-cook, a baker, two carters, each sixty livres a year! And the marshal of the forges a hundred and twenty livres! And the master of our exchequer chamber twelve hundred livres! And the comptroler five hundred! And God knows what besides! Why, it's absolutely monstrous! The wages of our domestics are laying France under pillage! All the treasure in the Louvre will melt away in such a blaze of expense! We shall have to sell our plate! And next year, if God and Our Lady" (here he raised his hat from his head) "grant us life, we shall drink our ptisans out of a pewter pot!"

So saying, he cast his eye upon the silver goblet that was glittering on the table. He coughed, and continued:

"Maître Olivier! princes who reign over great seigneuries, as kings and emperors, ought not to let sumptuousness be engendered in their households, for 'tis a fire that will spread from thence into their provinces. And so, Maître Olivier, set this down for certain—that the thing displeases us. What! Pasque-Dieu! until the year '79, it never exceeded thirty-six thousand livres; in '80, it rose to forty-three thousand six hundred and nineteen livres—I've the figures in my head; in '81, it came to sixty-six thousand six hundred and eighty; and this year, by the faith of my body, it will amount to eighty thousand livres! Doubled in four years! Monstrous!"

He stopped quite out of breath, then resumed with vehemence: "I see none about me but people fattening upon my leanness. You suck money from me at every pore!"

All kept silence. It was one of those fits of passion which must be allowed to run its course. He continued:

"It's just like that Latin memorial from the body of the French seigneurs, requesting us to re-establish what they call the great offices of the crown. Ha! messieurs, you tell us that we are no king to reign *dapifero nullo, buticulario nullo*. But we'll show you, Pasque-Dieu! whether we're a king or not."

Here he smiled in the consciousness of his power; his ill-humor was allayed by it, and he turned round to the Flemings:

"Look you, Compère Guillaume, the grand baker, the grand butler, the grand chamberlain, the grand seneschal, are not so useful as the meanest valet. Bear this in mind, Compère Coppenole—they're of no service whatever. Keeping themselves thus useless about the king, they put me in mind of the four evangelists that surround the face of the great clock of the Palais, and that Philippe Brille has just now been renovating. They're gilt indeed, but they don't mark the hour, and the hand of the clock can do very well without them."

He remained thoughtful for a moment, and then added, shaking his aged head, "Ho, ho! by Our Lady, but I'm not Philippe Brille, and I'm not going to re-gild the great vassals. Proceed, Olivier."

The person whom he designated by that name again took the sheet in his hands, and went on reading aloud:

"To Adam Tenon, keeper of the seals of the provostry of Paris, for the silver, workmanship, and engraving of the said seals, which have been made new, because the former ones, by reason of their being old and worn out, could no longer be used—twelve livres parisis.

"To Guillaume, his brother, the sum of four livres four sols parisis, for his trouble and cost in having fed and nourished the pigeons of the two pigeon-houses at the Hôtel des Tournelles, during the months of January, February, and March of this year, for the which he has furnished seven sextiers of barley.

"To a cordelier, for confessing a criminal, four sols parisis."

The king listened in silence. From time to time he coughed; then he lifted the goblet to his lips, and swallowed a draft of its contents, at which he made a wry face.

"In this year have been made," continued the reader, "by judicial order, by sound of trumpet, through the streets of Paris, fifty-six several cries. Account not made up.

"For search made in divers places, in Paris and elsewhere, after treasure said to have been concealed in the said places, but nothing has been found, forty-five livres parisis——"

"Burying an écu to dig up a sou!" said the king.

"For putting in, at the Hôtel des Tournelles, six panes of white glass, at the place where the iron cage is, thirteen sols. For making and delivering, by the king's command, on the day of the musters, four escutcheons, bearing the arms of our said lord, and wreathed all round with chaplets of roses, six livres. For two new sleeves to the king's old doublet, twenty sols. For a box of grease to grease the king's boots, fifteen deniers. A new sty for keeping the king's black swine, thirty livres parisis. Divers partitions, planks, and trap-doors, for the safe keeping of the lions at the Hôtel St. Pol, twenty-two livres."

"Dear beasts, those!" said Louis XI. "But no matter; it's a fair piece of royal magnificence. There's a great red lion that I love for his pretty behavior. Have you seen him, Maître Guillaume? Princes must have those wondrous animals. For dogs we kings should have lions, and for cats, tigers. The great befits a crown. In the time of the pagans of Jupiter, when

the people offered up at the churches a hundred oxen
and a hundred sheep, the emperors gave a hundred
lions and a hundred eagles. That was very fierce and
noble. The Kings of France have always those roar-
ings about their throne. Nevertheless, this justice will
be done me, to admit that I spend less money in that
way than my predecessors, and that I have a more
moderate stock of lions, bears, elephants, and leopards.
Go on, Maître Olivier—only we had a mind to say so
much to our Flemish friends."

Guillaume Rym made a low bow, while Coppenole,
with his gruff countenance, looked much like one of
the bears of whom his majesty spoke. The king did
not observe it; he had just then put the goblet to his
lips, and was spitting out what remained in his mouth
of the unsavory beverage, saying, " Foh ! the nauseous
ptisan !" His reader continued :

" For the food of a rogue and vagabond, kept for the
last six months in the lock-up house of the Ecorcherie,
until it should be known what was to be done with
him, six livres four sols."

" What's that ?" interrupted the king, sharply.
" Feeding what ought to be hanged ? Pasque-Dieu !
I'll not give a single sol toward such feeding. Olivier,
you'll arrange that matter with Monsieur d'Estouteville, and this very night you'll make preparations for
uniting this gentleman in holy matrimony to a gallows.
Now go on with your reading."

Olivier made a mark with his thumb-nail at the rogue
and vagabond article, and went on :

" To Henriet Cousin, executioner-in-chief at the justice of Paris, the sum of sixty sols parisis, to him adjudged by monseigneur the provost of Paris, for having
bought, by order of the said lord the provost, a large
broad-bladed sword, to be used in executing and be-
heading persons judicially condemned for their delin-
quencies, and had it furnished with a scabbard and all
other appurtenances, as also for repairing and putting
in order the old sword which had been splintered and
jagged by executing justice upon Messire Louis of
Luxemburg, as can be more fully made appear——"

Here the king interrupted him. "Enough," said he; "I shall give the order for that payment with all my heart. Those are expenses I make no account of. I have never grudged that money. Proceed."

"For making a great new cage—"

"Ha!" said the king, laying each hand upon an arm of his chair, "I knew I was come to this Bastile for something or other. Stop, Maître Olivier—I will see that cage myself. You shall read over to me the cost of it while I examine it. Messieurs the Flemings, you must come and see that—it's curious."

Then he rose, leaned upon the arm of his interlocutor, made a sign to the sort of mute who kept standing before the doorway to go before him, made another to the two Flemings to follow him, and went out of the chamber.

The royal train was recruited at the door by men-at-arms ponderous with steel, and slender pages carrying flambeaux. It proceeded for some time in the interior of the gloomy donjon, perforated by staircases and corridors even into the thickness of the walls. The captain of the Bastile walked at its head, and directed the opening of the successive narrow doors, before the old sickly and stooping king, who coughed as he walked along.

At each doorway, every one was obliged to stoop in order to pass, except only the old man bent with age. "Hum!" said he, between his gums, for he had no teeth left—"We're quite ready for the door of the sepulchre. A low door needs a stooping passenger."

At length, after making their way through the last door of all, so loaded with complicated locks that it took a quarter of an hour to open it, they entered a spacious and lofty chamber, of Gothic vaulting, in the center of which was discernible, by the light of the torches, a great cubical mass of masonry, iron, and wood-work. The interior was hollow. It was one of those famous cages for state prisoners which were called familiarly les fillettes du roi. In its walls there were two or three small windows, so thickly latticed with massive iron bars as to leave no glass visible. The door consisted of a single large flat stone, like that of a tomb—one of those doors that serve for entrance only. The difference was, that here the tenant was alive.

The king went and paced slowly round this small edifice examining it carefully, while Maître Olivier, following him, read out his paper of expenses aloud:

"For making a great wooden cage, of heavy beams, joists, and rafters, measuring inside nine feet long by eight broad, and seven feet high between the planks; morticed and bolted with great iron bolts; which has been fixed in a certain chamber of one of the towers of the Bastile St. Antoine; in which said cage is put and kept, by command of our lord the king, a prisoner, that before inhabited an old, decayed, and worn-out cage. Used, in making the said new cage, ninety-six horizontal beams and fifty-two perpendicular; ten joists, each three toises long. Employed, in squaring, planing and fitting all the said wood-work, in the yard of the Bastile—nineteen carpenters for twenty days—"

"Very fine heart of oak," said the king, rapping his knuckles against the timbers.

"Used in this cage," continued the other, "two hundred and twenty great iron bolts, nine feet and a half long—the rest of a medium length—together with the plates and nuts for fastening the said bolts—the said irons weighing altogether three thousand seven hundred and thirty-five pounds; besides eight heavy iron equières for fixing the said cage in its place; with the cramp-irons and nails; weighing altogether two hundred and eighteen pounds; without reckoning the iron for the trellis-work of the windows of the chamber in which the said cage has been placed, the iron bars of the door of the chamber, and other articles—"

"Here's a deal of iron," observed the king, "to restrain the levity of a spirit."

"The whole amounts to three hundred and seventeen livres, five sols, seven deniers."

"Pasque-Dieu!" cried the king.

At this oath, which was the favorite one of Louis

XI., some one seemed to be aroused in the interior of the cage. There was a noise of chains clanking on its floor; and a feeble voice was heard, which seemed to issue from the tomb, exclaiming—" Sire, sire! mercy, mercy!" It could not be seen who uttered this exclamation.

" Three hundred and seventeen livres, five sols, seven deniers!" repeated Louis XI.

The voice of lamentation which had issued from the cage chilled the blood of all present, even that of Maître Olivier. The king alone looked as if he had not heard it. At his command, Maître Olivier resumed his reading; and his majesty coolly continued his inspection of the cage.

" Besides the above, there has been paid to a mason for making the holes to fix the window-grates and the floor of the chamber containing the cage, because the other floor would not have been strong enough to support such cage, by reason of its weight—twenty-seven livres, fourteen sols parisis—"

Again the voice began to complain—" Mercy, sire! I assure you that it was Monsieur the Cardinal of Angers that committed the treason, and not I!"

" The mason is a rough hand," said the king. " Proceed, Olivier."

Olivier continued—" To a joiner for window-frames, bedstead, close-stool, and other matters, twenty livres two sols parisis—"

The voice still continued—" Alas, sire! will you not listen to me? I protest it was not I that wrote that matter to Monseigneur of Guyenne—it was monsieur the Cardinal Balue."

" The joiner charges high," observed the king. " Is that all?"

" No, sire—To a glazier for the window glass of the said chamber, forty-six sols eight deniers parisis."

" Have mercy, sire!" cried the voice again. " Is it not enough that all my property has been given to my judges—my plate to Monsieur de Torcy—my library to Maître Pierre Doriolle—and my tapestry to the governor of Roussillon? I am innocent. It is now fourteen years that I have been shivering in an iron cage! Have mercy, sire! and you will find it in heaven!"

"Maître Olivier," said the king, "what is the sum total?"

"Three hundred and sixty-seven livres eight sols three deniers parisis."

"Our Lady!" exclaimed the king. "Here's a cage out of all reason!"

He snatched the account from the hands of Maître Olivier, and began to reckon it up himself upon his fingers, examining, by turns, the paper and the cage. Meanwhile, the prisoner was heard sobbing within. The effect, in the darkness, was dismal in the extreme; and the faces of the bystanders turned pale and looked at one another.

"Fourteen years, sire! It is fourteen years since April, 1469. In the name of the holy mother of God, sire, hearken to me. All that time you have been enjoying the warmth of the sun—and shall I, wretched that I am! never again see the light? Mercy, sire!— be merciful! Clemency is a noble virtue in a king, that turns aside the stream of wrath. Does your majesty think that at the hour of death it is a great satisfaction for a king to have left no offense unpunished? Besides, sire, it was not I that betrayed your majesty—it was Monsieur of Angers. And I have a very heavy chain to my foot, with a huge ball of iron at the end of it, much heavier than is needful. Oh, sire, do have pity on me!"

"Olivier," said the king, shaking his head, "I observe that they put me down the bushel of plaster at twenty sols, though it's only worth twelve. You'll draw out this account afresh."

He turned his back on the cage, and began to move toward the door of the chamber. The wretched prisoner judged by the withdrawing of the torchlight and the noise, that the king was going away. "Sire! sire!" cried he in despair. The door closed again, and he no longer distinguished anything but the hoarse voice of

the turnkey, humming in his ears a popular song of the
day:

> Maître Jehan Balue
> Has lost out of view
> His good bishoprics all:
> Monsieur de Ferdum
> Can not now boast of one;
> They are gone, one and all.

The king reascended in silence to his closet, followed
by the persons of his train horror-struck at the last
groanings of the condemned. All at once his majesty
turned round to the Governor of the Bastile. "By-
the-by," said he, "was there not some one in that cage!"

"Par-Dieu, yes, sire!" answered the governor as-
tounded at the question.

"And who, pray?"

"Monsieur the Bishop of Verdun."

The king knew that better than any one else, but this
was a mania of his.

"Ha!" said he, with an air of simplicity, as if he was
thinking of it for the first time—"Guillaume de Haran-
court, the friend of Monsieur the Cardinal Balue. A
good fellow of a bishop."

A few moments after, the door of the closet had reopened and then closed again upon the five persons
whom the reader had found there at the beginning of
this chapter, and who had severally resumed their
places, their postures, and their whispering conversation.

During the king's absence, some dispatches had been
laid upon the table, of which he himself broke the seal.
Then he began to read them over diligently one after
another; motioned to Maître Olivier, who seemed to act
as his minister, to take up a pen; and, without communicating to him the contents of the dispatches, he began, in a low voice, to dictate to him the answers, which
the latter wrote, very uncomfortably to himself, on his
knees before the table.

Guillaume Rym was on the watch.

The king spoke so low that the Flemings could hear

3°

nothing at all of what he was dictating, except here and there a few isolated and scarcely intelligible fragments, as thus: "To maintain the fertile places by commerce, the sterile ones by manufactures—To show the English lords our four bombards, the Londres, the Brabant, the Bourg-en-Bresse, the St. Omer—It is owing to artillery that war is now more judiciously carried on—To our friend Monsieur de Bressuire—The armies can not be kept on foot without contributions—" etc.

Once he spoke aloud: "Pasque-Dieu! Monsieur the King of Sicily seals his letters with yellow wax like a King of France! Perhaps we do wrong to permit him. My fair cousin of Burgundy gave no arms on a field gule. The greatness of a house is secured by maintaining the integrity of its prerogatives. Note that down, Compère Olivier."

At another moment, "Oh, oh," said he, "the bold message! What is our friend the emperor demanding of us?" Then casting his eyes over the missive, interrupting his perusal here and there with brief interjections: "Certes, that Germany is so large and powerful that it's hardly credible! But we don't forget the old proverb. The finest country is Flanders; the finest duchy, Milan; the finest kingdom, France! Is it not so, messieurs the Flemings?"

This time, Coppenole bowed as well as Guillaume Rym. The hosier's patriotism was tickled.

The last dispatch of all made Louis XI. knit his brows. "What's that?" he exclaimed. "Complaints and petitions against our garrisons in Picardy! Olivier, write with all speed to Monsieur the Marshal de Rouault. That discipline is relaxed. That the gendarmes of the ordonnance, the nobles, the free archers, the Swiss, do infinite mischief to the inhabitants. That the military, not content with what they find in the houses of the husbandmen, compel them, with heavy blows of staves or bills, to go and fetch from the town, wine, fish, groceries, and other unreasonable articles. That the king knows all that. That we mean to protect our people from annoyance, theft and pillage. That such is our will, by Our Lady! That furthermore, it does not please us, that any musician, barber, or servant-at-arms should go clad like a prince, in velvet, silk, and gold rings. That such vanities are hateful to God! That we, who are a gentleman, content ourselves with a doublet made of cloth at sixteen sols the Paris ell. That messieurs the serving-men of the army may very well come down to that price likewise. Order and command. To our friend, Monsieur de Rouault. Good."

He dictated this letter aloud, in a firm tone, and in short abrupt sentences. At the moment of his finishing it, the door opened, and admitted a fresh person, who rushed all aghast into the chamber, crying: "Sire! sire! there's a sedition of the populace in Paris!"

The grave countenance of Louis XI. was contracted for a moment; but all that was visible in his emotion passed away like a flash. He contained himself, and said with a tone and look of quiet severity: "Compère Jacques, you enter very abruptly."

"Sire, sire, there's a revolt!" resumed Compère Jacques, quite out of breath.

The king, who had risen from his seat, seized him roughly by the arm, and said in his ear, so as to be heard by no one else, with an expression of internal anger, and an oblique glance at the Flemings, "Hold your tongue—or speak low!"

The new-comer understood, and set himself to make to the king a very terrified narration, to which the latter listened calmly, while Guillaume Rym was calling Coppenole's attention to the face and dress of the news-bearer—his furred capuce or hood (*caputia fourrata*)—his short épitoge (*epitogia curta*) and his black velvet gown, which bespoke a President of the Court of Accompts.

No sooner had this person given the king some explanations, than Louis XI. exclaimed with a burst of laughter: "Nay, in sooth, speak aloud, Compère Coictier. What occasion have you to whisper so? Our Lady knows we have no secrets with our good Flemish friends."

"But, sire—'

"Speak up!" said the king.

Compère Coictier remained mute with surprise.

"Come, come," resumed the king; "speak out, sir.
There's a commotion of the people in our good city of
Paris?"

"Yes, sire."

"And which is directed, you say, against Monsieur
the Bailiff of the Palais de Justice?"

"So it appears," said the compère, who still stammered out his words, quite confounded at the sudden
and inexplicable change which had taken place in the
mind of the king.

Louis IX. resumed: "Whereabouts did the watch
meet with the mob?"

"Coming along from the great Truandry toward the
Pont-aux-Changeurs, sire. I met it myself as I was coming hither in obedience to your majesty's orders. I
heard some of them crying, 'Down with the Bailiff of
the Palais!'"

"And what grievances have they against the bailiff?"

"Ah," said Compère Jacques, "that he is their seigneur."

"Is it really so?"

"Yes, sire. They are rascals from the Court of Miracles. They have long been complaining of the bailiff,
whose vassals they are. They will not acknowledge him
either as justiciary or as keeper of the highways."

"So, so," said the king, with a smile of satisfaction,
which he strove in vain to disguise.

"In all their petitions to the parliament," continued
Compère Jacques, "they pretend that they have only
two masters—your majesty, and their God, whom I believe to be the Devil."

"Oh, oh," said the king.

He rubbed his hands; laughed with that internal
laugh which irradiates the countenance; and was quite
unable to dissemble his joy, though he now and then
strove to compose himself. None of those present
could at all understand his hilarity—not even Maître

Olivier.   At length his majesty remained silent or a moment, with a thoughtful but satisfied air.

All at once he asked, " Are they in force ? "

" Yes, sire ; that they certainly are," answered Compère Jacques.

" How many ? "

" At least six thousand."

The king could not help saying, " Good ! "   He went on : " Are they armed ? "

" Yes, sire, with scythes, pikes, hackbuts, pickaxes, all sorts of most violent weapons."

The king seemed to be not at all disturbed by this awful detail.   Compère Jacques thought proper to add : " Unless your majesty sends speedy succor to the bailiff, he is lost ! "

" We will send," said the king, with affected seriousness.   " Good ! certainly we will send.   Monsieur the bailiff is our friend.   Six thousand ! They're determined rogues !   Their boldness is marvelous, and deeply are we wroth at it.   But we have few men about us to-night.   It will be time enough to-morrow morning."

Compère Jacques could not help exclaiming : " Directly, sire.   They'll have time to sack the bailiff's house twenty times over, violate the seigneury, and hang the bailiff himself.   For God's sake, sire, send before to-morrow morning."

The king looked him full in the face.   " I have told you to-morrow morning."   It was one of those looks to which there is no reply.

After a pause, Louis XI. again raised his voice.   " My Compère Jacques, you should know that.   What was . . . . ." (he corrected himself).   " What is the bailiff's feudal jurisdiction ? "

" Sire, the Bailiff of the Palais has the Rue de la Calandre, as far as the Rue de l'Herberie ; the Place St. Michel, and the places commonly called Les Mureaux, situated near the church of Notre-Dame-des-Champs " (here the king lifted the brim of his hat), " which mansions amount to thirteen ; besides the Court of Miracles, and the lazaretto called the Banlieue ; and all the highway beginning at the lazaretto and ending at the Porte St. Jacques. Of those several places he is keeper of the ways—chief, mean, and inferior justiciary—full and entire lord."

"So ho!" said the king, scratching his left ear with his right hand, "that makes a good slice of my town! So, monsieur the bailiff was king of all that, eh?"

This time he did not correct himself. He continued ruminating and as if talking to himself: "Softly, monsieur the bailiff, you had a very pretty slice of our Paris in your clutches, truly."

All at once he broke forth; "Pasque-Dieu! what are all these people that pretend to be highway-keepers, justiciaries, lords, and masters along with us, that have their toll-gate at the corner of every field, their justice and their bourreau at every cross-way among our people? so that, as the Greek thought he had as many gods as he had springs of water, and the Persian as many as he saw stars, so the Frenchman reckons up as many kings as he sees gibbets. Par-Dieu! this thing is evil, and the confusion of it displeases me. I should like to be told, now, if it be God's pleasure that there should be at Paris any highway-keepers but the king——any justiciary but our parliament—any emperor but ourself in this empire. By the faith of my soul, but the day must come when there shall be in France but one king, one lord, one judge, one headsman, as there is but one God in heaven."

Here he lifted his cap again, and continued, still ruminating, and with the look and accent of a huntsman cheering on his pack: "Good, my people! Well done! Shatter those false seigneurs! Do your work! On, on! Pillage—hang—sack them! So, you want to be kings, messeigneurs? On, my people, on!'

Here he suddenly stopped himself; bit his lip, as if to recall his half-wandering thoughts; fixed his piercing eye in turn upon each of the five persons around him; and then, all at once taking his hat between both hands, and looking steadfastly at it, he said, "Oh, I would burn thee, if thou couldst know what I have in my head!"

Then once more casting around him the cautious anxious look of a fox stealing back into his hole: "No matter," said he; "we will send succor to monsieur the bailiff. Unluckily, we have very few troops here at this moment, against such a number of the populace. We must wait till to-morrow. Order then shall be restored in the city; and all who are taken shall be hanged up forthwith."

"Apropos, sire," said Compère Coictier; "I had forgotten that in my first perturbation. The watch have seized two stragglers belonging to the gang. If it be your majesty's pleasure to see the men, they are here."

"If it be my pleasure!" exclaimed the king. "What, Pasque-Dieu! Canst thou forget such a thing as that? Run—quick! Olivier—go and fetch them in."

Maître Olivier went out, and returned in a minute with the two prisoners surrounded by archers of the ordonnance. The first of the two had a great idiotic, drunken, and wonder-struck visage. He was clothed in tatters, and walked with one knee bent and the foot dragging along; the other had a pale, half-smiling countenance, with which the reader is already acquainted.

The king scrutinized them a moment, without saying a word; then suddenly addressing the first of the two prisoners, "What is thy name?" he asked.

"Geoffroy Pincebourde."

"Thy trade?"

"A Truand."

"What wast thou going to do in that damnable sedition?"

The Truand looked at the king, swinging his arms the while with an air of sottish stupidity. His was one of those heads of awkward conformation, in which the intellect is about as much at its ease as a light under an extinguisher. "I don't know," said he. "They were going—and so I went."

"Were you not going outrageously to attack and plunder your lord the bailiff of the Palais?"

"I know they were going to take something at somebody's—and that's all."

Here a soldier showed the king a pruning-hook, which had been found upon the Truand.

"Dost thou know that weapon?" asked the king.

"Yes—it's my pruning-hook. I'm a vine-dresser."

"And dost thou know that man for thy comrade?" asked Louis XI., pointing to the other prisoner.

"No, I don't know him."

"Enough," said the king; and motioning with his finger to the silent person standing motionless by the door, whom we have already pointed out to the reader, "Compère Tristan," said he, "there's a man for you."

Tristan l'Hermite bowed to his majesty, and then whispered an order to a couple of archers, who thereupon carried away the poor Truand.

Meanwhile, the king had addressed the second prisoner, who was perspiring profusely, "Thy name?"

"Sire, it is Pierre Gringoire."

"Thy trade?"

"A philosopher, sire."

"How comes it, fellow, that thou hast the audacity to go and beset our friend Monsieur the bailiff of the Palais? and what hast thou to say about this popular commotion?"

"Sire, I was not in it."

"Come, come, paillard, wast thou not apprehended by the watch in that company?"

"No, sire—there's a mistake. It's a fatality. I write tragedies, sire. I implore your majesty to hear me. I am a poet. It's the hard lot of men of my profession to be going about the streets at night. By mere chance I happened to be going by there this evening. They took me up without reason. I am quite innocent of this civil storm. Your majesty saw that the Truand did not recognize me. I entreat your majesty—"

"Hold your tongue," said the king, between two draughts of his ptisan—"you split our head!"

Tristan l'Hermite stepped forward, and said, pointing to Gringoire: "Sire, may we hang that one too?" This was the first word he had uttered.

"Oh, why," answered the king, carelessly, "I don't see any objections."

"But I see many," said Gringoire.

At this moment, our philosopher's countenance was horribly livid. He saw, by the cool and indifferent manner of the king, that he had no resource but in something excessively pathetic; and he threw himself at the feet of Louis XI. with gestures of despair:

"Sire, your majesty will vouchsafe to hear me. Sire, burst not in thunder upon so poor a thing as I am. God's great thunderbolts strike not the lowly plant. Sire, you are an august and most puissant monarch— have pity on a poor honest man, as incapable of fanning the flame of revolt as an icicle of striking a spark. Most gracious sire, mildness is the virtue of a lion and of a king. Alas! severity does but exasperate; the fierce blasts of the north wind make not the traveler lay aside his cloak; but the sun darting his rays by little and little, warms him so that at length he will gladly strip himself. Sire, you are the sun. I protest to you, my sovereign lord and master, that I am not a companion of Truands, thievish and disorderly. Rebellion and pillage go not in the train of Apollo. I am no man to go and rush into those clouds which burst in seditious clamor. I am a faithful vassal of your majesty. The same jealousy which the husband has for the honor of his wife—the affection with which the son should requite his father's love—a good vassal should feel for the glory of his king. He should wear himself out for the upholding of his house and the promoting of his service. Any other passion that should possess him would be mere frenzy. Such, sire, are my maxims of state; do not, then, judge me to be seditious and plundering because my garment is out at the elbows. If you show me mercy, sire, I will wear it out at the knees in praying for you morning and night. Alas! I am not extremely rich, it is true—indeed I am rather poor; but I am not wicked for all that. It is no fault of mine. Everybody knows that great wealth is not to be acquired by the belles-lettres; and that the most accomplished writers have not always a great fire in winter time. The gentlemen of the law take all the wheat to themselves, and leave nothing but the chaff for the other learned professions. There are forty most excellent proverbs about the philosopher's threadbare cloak. Oh, sire, clemency is the only light that can enlighten the interior of a great soul. Clemency carries the torch before all the other virtues. Without her they are but blind, and seek God in the dark. Mercy, which is the same thing as clemency, produces loving subjects, who are the most powerful body-guard of the prince. What can it signify to your majesty, by whom all faces are dazzled, that there should be one poor man more upon the earth? a poor innocent philosopher, creeping about in the darkness of calamity, with his empty fob lying flat upon his empty stomach. Besides, sire, I am a man of letters. Great kings add a jewel to their crown by patronizing letters. Hercules did not disdain the title of Musagetes. Matthias Corvinus showed favor to Jean de Monroyal, the ornament of mathematics. Now, 'tis an ill way of patronizing letters, to hang up the lettered. What a stain to Alexander if he had had Aristoteles hanged! The act would not have been a small patch upon the face of his reputation to embellish it, but a virulent ulcer to disfigure it. Sire, I wrote a very appropriate epithalamium for Mademoiselle of Flanders and Monseigneur the most august Dauphin. That was not like a firebrand of rebellion. Your majesty sees that I am no dunce—that I have studied excellently—and that I have much natural eloquence. Grant me mercy, sire. So doing, you will do an act grateful to Our Lady; and I assure you, sire, that I am very much frightened at the idea of being hanged!"

So saying, the desolate Gringoire kissed the king's slippers; while Guillaume Rym whispered to Coppenole: "He does well to crawl upon the floor; kings are like the Jupiter of Crete—they hear only through their feet." And, quite inattentive to the Cretan Jupiter, the hosier answered, with a heavy smile, and his eyes fixed upon Gringoire, "Ah, that's good! I could fancy I heard the Chancellor Hugonet asking me for mercy."

When Gringoire stopped at length quite out of breath,

he raised his eyes, trembling, toward the king, who was scratching with his finger-nail a spot which he saw upon his breeches' knee, after which his majesty took another draught from the goblet. But he uttered not a syllable —and this silence kept Gringoire in torture. At last the king looked at him. "Here's a terrible prater," said he. Then, turning to Tristan l'Hermite : "Pshaw! let him go."

Gringoire fell backward upon his posteriors, quite thunderstruck with joy.

"Let him go!" grumbled Tristan. "Is it not your majesty's pleasure that he should be caged for a little while?"

"Compère," returned Louis XI., "dost thou think it is for birds like this that we have cages made at three hundred and sixty-seven livres eight sols three deniers apiece? Let him go directly, the paillard; and send him out with a drubbing."

"Oh," exclaimed Gringoire, in ecstasy, "this is indeed a great king."

Then, for fear of a countermand, he rushed toward the door, which Tristan opened for him with a very ill grace. The soldiers went out with him, driving him before them with hard blows of their fists, which Gringoire endured like a true stoic philosopher.

The good humor of the king, since the revolt against the bailiff had been announced to him, manifested itself in everything. This unusual clemency of his was no small sign of it. Tristan l'Hermite, in his corner, was looking as surly as a mastiff dog balked of his meal.

Meanwhile the king was gayly beating with his fingers upon his chair arm, the Pont-Audemer march. Though a dissembling prince, he was much better able to conceal his sorrow than his rejoicing. These his external manifestations of joy on the receipt of any good news, sometimes carried him great lengths; as, for instance, at the death of Charles the Rash of Burgundy, to that of vowing balustrades of silver to St. Martin of Tours; and, on his accession to the throne, to that of forgetting to give orders for his father's funeral.

"Ha, sire!" suddenly exclaimed Jacques Coictier "what is become of the sharp pains on account of which your majesty sent for me?"

"Oh!" said the king, "truly, my compère, I am suffering greatly. I've a singing in my ears, and teeth of fire raking my breast."

Coictier took the king's hand, and began to feel his pulse with a knowing look.

"Look there, Coppenole," whispered Rym. "There you see him between Coictier and Tristan. That's his whole court—a physician for himself, and a hangman for other people."

While feeling the king's pulse, Coictier was assuming a look of greater and greater alarm. Louis XI. looked at him with some anxiety; while the physician's countenance grew more and more dismal. The king's bad health was the only estate the good man had to cultivate, and accordingly he made the most of it.

"Oh! oh!" muttered he at last, "this is serious, indeed!"

"Is it not?" said the king, uneasy.

"*Pulsus creber, anhelans, crepitans, irregularis,*" continued the physician.

"Pasque-Dieu!" exclaimed his majesty.

"This might carry a man off in less than three days!"

"Our Lady!" cried the king. "And the remedy, compère?"

"I'm thinking of it, sire."

He made the king put out his tongue; shook his head; made a wry face; and in the midst of this grimacing, "Par-Dieu, sire," said he, all on a sudden, "I must inform you that there is a receivership of episcopal revenues vacant, and that I have a nephew."

"I give the receivership to thy nephew, Compère Jacques," answered the king; "but take this fire out of my breast!"

"Since your majesty is so gracious," resumed the physician, "I am sure you will not refuse to assist me a little in the building of my house in the Rue St. André-des-Arcs."

"Heu!" said the king.

"I'm at the end of my cash," said the doctor; "and it would really be a pity that the house should be left without a roof—not for the sake of the house itself, which is quite plain and homely; but for the sake of the paintings by Jehan Fourbault, that adorn its wainscoting. There's a Diana flying in the air—so excellently done—so tender—so delicate—of an action so artless—her head so well dressed, and crowned with a crescent—her flesh so white—that she leads into temptation those who examine her too curiously. Then, there's a Ceres—and she, too, is a very beautiful divinity. She's sitting upon corn sheaves, and crowned with a goodly wreath of ears of corn intertwined with purple goat's-beard and other flowers. Never were seen more amorous eyes, rounder legs, a nobler air, or a more gracefully flowing skirt. She's one of the most innocent and most perfect beauties ever produced by the pencil."

"Bourreau!" grumbled Louis XI., "what art thou driving at?"

"I want a roof over these paintings, sire; and, although it is but a trifle, I have no money left."

"What will thy roof cost?"

"Oh . . . . why . . . . a roof of copper, figured and gilt . . . . not above two thousand livres."

"Ha! the assassin!" cried the king. "He never draws me a tooth but he makes a diamond of it."

"Am I to have my roof?" said Coictier.

"Yes—the devil take you! but cure me."

Jacques Coictier made a low bow, and said: "Sire, it is a repellent that will save you. We shall apply to your loins the grand defensive, composed of cerate, bole armoniac, white of eggs, oil, and vinegar. You will continue your ptisan—and we will answer for your majesty's safety."

A lighted candle never attracts one gnat only. Maître Olivier, seeing the king in a liberal mood, and deeming the moment propitious, approached in his turn:—
"Sire!"

"What next?" said Louis XI.

"Sire, your majesty is aware that Maître Simon Radin is dead."

"Well?"

"He was king's councilor for the jurisdiction of the treasury."

"Well?"

"Sire, his place is vacant."

While thus speaking, Maître Olivier's haughty countenance had exchanged the arrogant for the fawning expression—the only alternation that ever takes place in the countenance of a courtier. The king looked him full in the face, and said, dryly, "I understand."

His majesty resumed: "Maître Olivier, Marshal de Boucicault used to say, 'There's no good gift but from a king; there's no good fishing but in the sea.' I see that you are of the marshal's opinion. Now, hear this. We have a good memory. In the year '68, we made you groom of our chamber; in '69 castellan of the bridge of St. Cloud, with a salary of a hundred livres tournois —you wanted them parisis. In November, '73, by letters given at Gergeaule, we appointed you keeper of the Bois de Vincennes, in lieu of Gilbert Acle, esquire; in '75, warden of the forest of Rouvray-les-Saint-Cloud, in the place of Jacques Le Maire; in '78, we graciously settled upon you, by letters-patent sealed on extra label with green wax, an annuity of ten livres parisis, to you and your wife, upon the Place-aux-Marchands, situated at the Ecole St. Germain. In '79, we made you warden of the forest of Senart, in room of that poor Jehan Daiz; then captain of the castle of Loches; then governor of St. Quentin; then captain of the bridge of Meulan, of which you call yourself count. Out of the fine of five sols paid by every barber that shaves on a holiday, you get three, and we get what you leave. We were pleased to change your name of Le Mauvais, which was too much like your countenance. In '74, we granted you, to the great displeasure of our nobility, armorial bearings of a thousand colors, that make you a breast like a peacock. Pasque-Dieu! have you not your fill? Is not the draught of fishes fine and miraculous enough? And are you not afraid lest a single salmon more should be enough to sink your boat? Pride will ruin you, my compère. Pride is ever followed close behind by ruin and shame. Think of that, and be silent."

These words, uttered in a low tone of severity, brought back the chagrined physiognomy of Maître Olivier to its former insolent expression. "Good!" muttered he, almost aloud. "It's plain enough that the king's ill to-day, for he gives all to the physician."

Louis XI., far from taking offense at this piece of presumption, resumed, with some mildness: "Stay—I forgot to add that I made you ambassador to Madame Marie at Ghent. Yes, gentlemen," added the king, turning to the Flemings; "this man has been an ambassador. There, my compère," continued he, again addressing Maître Olivier, "let us not fall out—we're old friends. It's getting very late. We've got through our work. Shave me."

Our readers have doubtless already recognized in Maître Olivier that terrible Figaro whom Providence, the great dramatist of all, so artfully mixed up in the long and sanguinary play of Louis XI.'s reign. We shall not here undertake to develop, at full length, that singular character. This barber to the king had three names. At court he was called politely Olivier-le-Daim, from the daim, or stag, upon his escutcheon; and among the people Olivier-le-Diable, or the Devil. But, by his right name, he was called Olivier-le-Mauvais, or the Bad.

Olivier-le-Mauvais then stood motionless, looking sulkily at the king, and enviously at Jacques Coictier. "Yes, yes—the physician!" muttered he.

"Well, yes—the physician!" resumed Louis XI. with singular good humor; "the physician has yet more influence than thyself. It's a matter of course. He has got our whole body in his hands; and thou dost but hold us by the chin. Come, come, my poor barber, there's nothing amiss. What wouldst thou say, and what would become of thy office, if I were a king like King Chilperic, whose way it was to hold his beard with one hand. Come, my compère, perform thy office, and shave me—go and fetch thy tools."

Olivier, seeing that the king had resolved to take the matter in jest, and that there was no means even of provoking him, went out, grumbling, to execute his commands. The king rose from his seat, went to the window, and suddenly opening it in extraordinary agitation—"Oh, yes!" exclaimed he, clapping his hands; "there's a glare in the sky over the city. It's the bailiff burning; it can not be anything else. Ha! my good people, so you help me, then, at last, to pull down the seigneuries!"

Then turning to the Flemings: "Gentlemen," said he, "come and see. Is not that a fire that glares so red?"

The two Gantois came forward to look.

"It's a great fire," said Guillaume Rym.

"Oh," added Coppenole, whose eyes all at once began to sparkle, "that reminds me of the burning of the house of the Seigneur d'Hymbercourt. There must be a stout revolt there."

"You think so, Maître Coppenole?" said the king; and he looked almost as much pleased as the hosier himself. "Don't you think it will be difficult to resist it?" he added.

"Croix-Dieu! sire, it may cost your majesty many a company of good soldiers."

"Ha! cost me! that's quite another thing," returned the king. "If I chose—"

The hosier rejoined boldly: "If that revolt be what I suppose, you would choose in vain, sire."

"Compère," said Louis XI., "two companies of my ordonnance, and the discharge of a serpentine, are quite sufficient to rout a mob of the common people."

The hosier, in spite of the signs that Guillaume Rym was making to him, seemed determined to contest the matter with the king. "Sire," said he, "the Swiss were common people, too. Monsieur the Duke of Burgundy was a great gentleman, and made no account of that canaille. At the battle of Grandson, sire, he called out, 'Cannoneers, fire upon those villains!' and he swore by St. George. But the avoyer, Scharnactal, rushed upon the fine duke with his club and his people; and at the shock of the peasants, with their bull-hides, the shining Burgundian army was shattered like a pane of glass by a flint-stone. Many a knight was killed there by those base churls; and Monsieur de Château-Guyon, the greatest lord in Burgundy, was found dead, with his great gray horse in a little boggy field!"

"Friend," returned the king, "you're talking of a battle; but here it's only a riot, and I can put an end to it with a single frown, when I please." The other replied, unconcernedly, "That may be, sire. In that case the people's hour is not yet come."

Guillaume Rym thought he must now interfere. "Maître Coppenole," said he, "you are talking to a mighty king."

"I know it," answered the hosier, gravely.

"Let him go on, Monsieur Rym, my friend," said the king; "I like this plain speaking. My father, Charles VII., used to say that truth was sick! for my part I thought she was dead, and had found no confessor; but Maître Coppenole shows me I was mistaken."

Then clapping his hand familiarly upon Coppenole's shoulder, "You were saying then, Maître Jacques—"

"I say, sire, that perhaps you are right—that the people's hour is not yet come with you."

Louis XI. looked at him with his penetrating eye: "And when will that hour come, maître?"

"You will hear it strike."

"By what clock, pray?"

Coppenole, with his quiet and homely self-possession, motioned to the king to approach the window. "Hark you, sire," said he; "here there are a donjon, an alarm-bell, cannon, townspeople, soldiers. When the alarm-bell shall sound—when the cannon shall roar—when, with great clamor the donjon walls shall be shattered —when townspeople and soldiers shall shout and kill each other—then the hour will strike."

The countenance of Louis XI. became gloomy and

thoughtful. He remained silent for a moment; then tapping gently with his hand against the massive wall of the donjon, as if patting the crupper of a war-horse, "Ah, no, no!" said he, "thou wilt not so easily be shattered, wilt thou, my good Bastile?"

Then, turning abruptly round to the bold Fleming, he said: "Have you ever seen a revolt, Maître Jacques?"

"I have made one," said the hosier.

"What do you do?" said the king, "to make a revolt?"

"Oh!" answered Coppenole, "it's not very hard to do. There are a hundred ways. First of all, there must be dissatisfaction in the town. That's nothing uncommon. And then, one must consider the character of the inhabitants. Those of Ghent are prone to revolt. They always like the son of the prince, but never the prince himself. Well, now, one morning, we'll suppose, somebody comes into my shop, and says, Father Coppenole, it's so and so—as that the Lady of Flanders wants to save her ministers—that the high bailiff is doubling the toll on vegetables—or what not—anything you like. Then I throw by my work, go out into the street, and cry—*A sac!* There's always some empty cask or other in the way. I get upon it, and say with a loud voice, the first words that come into my head—what's uppermost in my heart—and when one belongs to the people, sire, one has always something upon one's heart. Then a crowd gets together—they shout—they ring the tocsin—the people get arms by disarming the soldiers—the market people join the rest —and then they go to work; and it will always be so, so long as there are seigneurs in the seigneuries, towns-people in the towns, and country-people in the country."

"And against whom did you rebel thus?" asked the king. "Against your bailiffs—against your lords?"

"Sometimes. That's as it may happen. Against the duke, too, sometimes."

Louis XI. returned to his seat, and said, with a smile, "Ah! but here they have not yet got farther than the bailiffs."

At that moment Olivier-le-Daim re-entered, followed by two pages carrying the apparatus for dressing his majesty; but what struck Louis XI. was to see him also accompanied by the provost of Paris and the knight of the watch, who seemed both in consternation. There was consternation, too, in the look of the mortified barber; but there was satisfaction lurking under it. It was he that spoke first. " Sire, I beg pardon of your majesty for the calamitous news I bring you."

The king, turning sharply round, grazed the mat upon the floor with the feet of his chair. "What's it about?" said he.

"Sire," returned Olivier, with the malicious look of a man rejoicing that he has to deal a violent blow, "it is not against the bailiff of the Palais that this popular sedition is driving."

"Against whom, then?"

"Against you, sire."

The aged king rose upon his feet, and erect, like a young man. "Explain, Olivier, explain—and look well to thy head, my compère—for I swear to thee, by the cross of St. Lô, that if thou speakest false in this matter, the sword that cut Monsieur of Luxemburg's throat is not so dinted but it shall saw thine, too."

The oath was formidable. Louis XI. had never but twice in his life sworn by the cross of St. Lô. Olivier opened his lips to reply. " Sire—"

"Down on your knees!' interrupted the king, with violence. "Tristan, keep your eye upon this man."

Olivier fell upon his knees, and said composedly: "Sire, a witch has been condemned to death by your court of parliament. She has taken refuge in Notre-Dame. The people want to take her from thence by main force. Monsieur the provost and monsieur the knight of the watch who are come straight from the spot, are here to contradict me if I speak not the truth. It is Notre-Dame that the people are besieging."

"Ah, ah," said the king, in an undertone, all pale and trembling with passion; " Notre-Dame! They are besieging Our Lady, my good mistress, in her own cathedral! Rise, Olivier. Thou are right; I give thee Simon Radin's office. Thou art right; it is me they're attacking. The witch is under the safeguard of the church; the church is under my safeguard, and I, who thought all the while that it was only the bailiff, 'tis against myself!"

Then, invigorated by passion, he began to pace hurriedly to and fro. He laughed no longer; he was terrible. The fox was changed into a hyena. He seemed to be choking with rage; his lips moved without utterance, and his withered hands were clenched. All at once he raised his head; his hollow eye seemed full of light, and his voice burst forth like a clarion: "Upon them, Tristan! Fall upon the knaves! Go, Tristan, my friend! Kill! kill!"

When this paroxysm was over, he went once more to his seat, and said, with a cool and concentrated passion: "Here, Tristan! We have with us in this Bastile the fifty lances of the Viscount de Gif, making three hundred horse; you'll take them. There's also Monsieur de Chateaupers's company of the archers of our ordonnance; you'll take them. You are provost-marshal, and have the men of your provostry; you'll take them. At the Hôtel St. Pol, you'll find forty archers of Monsieur the Dauphin's new guard; you'll take them. And, with the whole, you'll make all speed to Notre-Dame. Ha! messieurs the commons of Paris— so you presume to fly in the face of the crown of France, the sanctity of Our Lady, and the peace of this commonwealth. Exterminate, Tristan! exterminate! and let not one escape except for Montfaucon!"

Tristan bowed. "'Tis well, sire."

He added after a pause: "And what shall I do with the witch?"

This question set the king ruminating. "Ha," said he, "the witch! Monsieur d'Estouteville, what did the people want to do with her?"

"Sire," answered the provost of Paris, "I imagine that, as the people are come to drag her away from her sanctuary of Notre-Dame, it is her impunity that offends them, and they want to hang her."

The king seemed to reflect deeply; then, addressing himself to Tristan l'Hermite, he said: "Well, my compère, exterminate the people and hang the witch."

"Just so," whispered Rym to Coppenole. "Punish the people for wishing, and do what they wish."

"Enough, sire," answered Tristan. "If the witch be still in Notre-Dame, must we take her away in spite of the sanctuary?"

"Pasque-Dieu! the sanctuary!" said the king, scratching his ear; "and yet that woman must be hanged."

Here, as if a thought had suddenly occurred to him, he knelt down before his chair, took off his hat, placed it upon the seat, and looking devoutly at one of the leaden figures with which it was loaded: "Oh," said he, clasping his hands, "Our Lady of Paris, my gracious patroness, pardon me. I will only do it this once. That criminal must be punished. I assure you, O Lady Virgin, my good mistress, that she is a witch, unworthy of your kind protection. You know, Lady, that many very pious princes have trespassed upon the privileges of churches, for the glory of God and the necessity of the state. Saint Hugh, an English bishop, permitted King Edward to seize a magician in his church. My master, Saint Louis of France, transgressed for the like purpose in the church of Monsieur St. Paul, as did also Monsieur Alphonse, King of Jerusalem, in the church of the Holy Sepulchre itself. Pardon me, then, for this once, Our Lady of Paris. I will never do so again; and I will give you a fine statue of silver like that which I gave last year to Our Lady of Ecouys. So be it."

He crossed himself, rose from his knees, put on his hat, and said to Tristan: "Make all speed, my compére. Take Monsieur de Chateaupers with you. You'll have the tocsin rung. You'll crush the populace. You'll hang the witch. That's settled. You yourself will defray all charges of the execution, and bring me in an account of them. Come, Olivier, I shall not lie down to-night. Shave me."

Tristan l'Hermite bowed and departed. Then the king, motioning to Rym and Coppenole to retire:

"God keep you, messieurs, my good Flemish friends!"
said he. "Go and take a little rest. The night is fast
wearing away; we are nearer the morning than the
evening."

They both withdrew, and on reaching their apartments, to which they were conducted by the captain
of the Bastile, Coppenole said to Guillaume Rym:
"Humph! I've had enough of this coughing king.
I've seen Charles of Burgundy drunk, but he was not
so mischievous as Louis XI. sick."

"Maître Jacques," answered Rym, with mock solemnity, "that is because a king finds less cruelty in his
wine than in his barley-water."

CHAPTER VI.

THE PASSWORD.

ON quitting the Bastile, Gringoire ran down the Rue
St. Antoine with the speed of a runaway horse. When
he had reached the Porte Baudoyer, he walked straight
up to the stone cross standing in the middle of the
open space there, as if he could have discerned in the
dark the figure of a man clothed and hooded in black,
sitting upon the steps of the cross. "Is it you, master?" said Gringoire.

The person in black rose. "Death and passion! you
drive me mad, Gringoire!" said he. "The man upon
St. Gervais's tower has just been calling half-past one
in the morning!"

"Oh," returned Gringoire, "it's no fault of mine, but
of the watch, and of the king. I've had a narrow escape. Yet I always just miss being hanged—it's my
predestination."

"You just miss everything," said the other. "But
come along quick Have you the password?"

" Only think, master. I've seen the king. I've just left him. He wears worsted breeches. It's an adventure, I can tell you."

" Oh, thou spinner of words! What's thy adventure to me? Hast thou got the password of the Truands?"

" I've got it. Make yourself easy. It's *Petite flambe en baguenaud.*"

" Very well. Otherwise we should not have been able to make our way to the church. The Truands block up the streets. Fortunately, it seems, they've met with resistance. Perhaps we shall still get there in time."

" Yes, master; but how shall we get into Notre-Dame?"

" I have the key of the towers."

"And how shall we get out again?"

" There's a small door, behind the cloister, which leads to the Terrain, and so to the water-side. I have taken possession of the key, and I moored a boat there this morning."

" I've had a nice miss of being hanged," repeated Gringoire.

" Ah—well—come along quick," said the other; and they both walked off at a great rate toward the City.

CHAPTER VII.

CHATEAUPERS TO THE RESCUE.

THE reader probably bears in his recollection the critical situation in which we left Quasimodo. The brave ringer, assailed on all sides, had lost, though not all courage, at least all hope of saving—not himself— he thought not of himself—but the gypsy girl. He ran wildly to and fro along the gallery. Notre-Dame was on the point of being carried by the Truands, when all at once a great galloping of horses filled the neighboring streets, and, with a long file of torches, and a dense column of horsemen, lances and bridles lowered these furious sounds came rushing into the Place like a hurricane: " France! France! Cut down the knaves! Chateaupers to the rescue! Provostry! provostry!"

The Truands in terror faced about.

Quasimodo, though he heard nothing, saw the drawn swords, the flambeaux, the spear-heads—all that cavalry, at the head of which he recognized Captain Phœbus; he saw the confusion of the Truands, the terror of some of them, the perturbation of the stoutest-hearted among them, and this unexpected succor so much revived his own energies, that he hurled back from the church the most forward of the assailants, who were already striding over into the gallery.

It was in fact the king's troops that had just arrived.

The Truands bore themselves bravely, and defended themselves desperately. Attacked in flank from the Rue Saint-Pierre-aux-Bœufs, and in rear from the Rue du Parvis—pressed against Notre-Dame, which they were still assailing, and which Quasimodo was defending—at once besieging and besieged—they were in the singular situation which, subsequently, at the famous siege of Turin, in 1640, was that of Count Henri d'Harcourt, between Prince Thomas of Savoy, whom he was besieging, and the Marquis of Leganez, who was blockading him— *Taurinum obsessor idem et obsessus*, as his epitaph expresses it.

The mêlée was frightful. Wolves' flesh calls for dog's teeth, as Father Matthieu phrases it. The king's horsemen, amid whom Phœbus de Chateaupers bore himself valiantly, gave no quarter, and they who escaped the thrust of the lance fell by the edge of the sword. The Truands, ill-armed, foamed and bit with rage and despair. Men, women, and children threw themselves upon the cruppers and chests of the horses, and clung to them like cats with their teeth and claws; others struck the archers in the face with their torches; and others, again, aimed their bill-hooks at the necks

of the horsemen, striving to pull them down, and mangled such as fell.   One of them was seen with a large
glittering scythe, with which, for a long time, he mowed
the legs of the horses.   He was terrific ; he went on,
singing a song with a nasal intonation, taking long and
sweeping strokes with his scythe.   At each stroke he
described around him a great circle of severed limbs.
He advanced in this manner into the thickest of the
cavalry, with the quiet slowness, the regular motion of
the head and drawing of the breath, of a harvest-man
putting the scythe into a field of corn.   This was Clopin
Trouillefou.   He fell by the shot of an arquebus.

Meantime, the windows had opened again.   The
neighbors, hearing the war-shouts of the king's men,
had taken part in the affair, and from every story bullets were showered upon the Truands.   The Parvis
was filled with a thick smoke, which the flashing of the
musketry streaked with fire.   Through it were confusedly discernible the front of Notre-Dame, and the de-
crepit Hôtel-Dieu, with a few pale-faced invalids looking from the top of its roof checkered with skylights.

At last the Truands gave way.   Exhaustion, want of
good weapons, the terror struck into them by this surprise, the discharges of musketry from the windows,
and the spirited charge of the king's troops, all combined to overpower them.   They broke through the
line of their assailants, and fled in all directions, leaving
the Parvis covered with their dead.

When Quasimodo, who had not for a moment ceased
fighting, beheld this rout, he fell upon his knees, and
lifted his hands to heaven.   Then, intoxicated with joy,
he mounted with the quickness of a bird up to that cell
the approaches of which he had so intrepidly defended.
He had now but one thought—it was, to go and fall
upon his knees before her whom he had saved for the
second time.

When he entered the cell, however, he found it
empty.

BOOK XI.

CHAPTER I.

THE LITTLE SHOE.

T the moment when the Truands had assailed the church, La Esmeralda was asleep. But soon, the constantly increasing clamor about the edifice, and the plaintive bleating of her goat, which was awakened before herself, had chased away her slumber. She had then sat up in bed, listened, and looked around her; and then, frightened at the light and the noise, she had hurried out of the cell and gone to see what was the matter. The aspect of the Place; the strange vision that was moving in it; the disorder of that nocturnal assault; that hideous crowd leaping about like a cloud of frogs, half distinguishable in the darkness; the croaking of that hoarse multitude; the few red torches running backward and forward, passing and re-passing one another in the dark, like those meteors of the night that play over the misty surface of a marsh; all together seemed to her like some mysterious battle commenced between the phantoms of a witches' sabbath and the stone monsters of the church. Imbued from her infancy with the superstitions which at that day possessed the minds of many of her tribe, the notion that first suggested itself to her was, that she had come unawares upon the magic revels of the beings proper to the night. Then she ran back in terror to cower in her cell, and ask of her humble couch some less horrible vision.

By degrees, however, the first fumes of her terror had dispersed from her brain; and by the constantly increasing noise, together with other signs of reality, she discovered that she was beset, not by specters, but by human beings. Then her fear, though it had not increased, had changed its nature. She had thought of the possibility of a popular rising to drag her from her asylum. The idea of once more losing life, hope, Phœbus, who still was ever present to her hopes; her extreme helplessness; all flight barred; her abandonment; her solitariness; these and a thousand other cruel thoughts had quite overwhelmed her. She had fallen upon her knees, with her head upon her couch, and her hands clasped upon her head, full of anxiety and trepidation; and gypsy, idolatress, and heathen as she was, she had begun, sobbing, to ask mercy of the God of the Christians, and to pray to Our Lady her hostess. "For," says our author, "whether one believes anything or nothing, there are moments in life when one is always of the religion of the temple nearest at hand."

She remained thus prostrate for a considerable time; trembling, indeed, yet more than she prayed; her blood running cold as the breath of that furious multitude approached nearer and nearer; ignorant of the nature of this popular storm—of what was in agitation—of what was doing—of what was intended; but feeling a presentiment of some dreadful result.

In the very midst of all this anguish, she heard footsteps approaching her. She turned her head. Two men, one of whom carried a lantern, had just entered her cell. She uttered a feeble cry.

" Don't be afraid," said a voice to which she was not a stranger. " 'Tis I."

" 'Tis who?" asked she.

" Pierre Gringoire."

This name encouraged her. She raised her eyes, and saw that it was indeed the poet. But close by him there was a dark figure, veiled from head to foot, the sight of which struck her dumb.

"Ah!" resumed Gringoire, in a reproachful tone, "Djali had recognized me before you did."

The little goat, in fact, had not waited for Gringoire to announce himself. No sooner had he entered than she had begun to rub herself affectionately against his knees, covering the poet with caresses and with white hairs, for she was changing her coat. Gringoire returned her caresses with the greatest cordiality.

"Who is that with you?" whispered the gypsy girl.

"Make yourself easy," answered Gringoire; "it's a friend of mine."

Then the philosopher, setting his lantern on the floor, squatted down upon the stones, and exclaimed with enthusiasm, clasping Djali in his arms: "Oh! it's a charming animal!—more remarkable, to be sure, for beauty and cleanliness than for size; but clever, cunning, and lettered as a grammarian! Let us see, now, my Djali, if thou rememberest all thy pretty tricks. How does Maître Jacques Charmolue go—"

The man in black did not let Gringoire finish. He came up to him, and pushed him forcibly by the shoulder. Gringoire got up again. "True," said he; "I'd forgotten that we're in haste. However, master, that's no reason for using folks so roughly. My pretty dear," said he, addressing the gypsy girl, "Your life's in danger, and Djali's too. They want to hang you again. We're your friends and have come to save you. Follow us."

"Is that true?" exclaimed she, quite overcome.

"Yes—quite true. Come, quick."

"I will," faltered she; "but why does not that friend of yours speak?"

"Ha!" said Gringoire; "that's because his father and mother were whimsical people, and made him of a silent disposition."

She was obliged to content herself with this explanation. Gringoire took her by the hand. His companion took up the lantern from the floor, and walked first.

Fear made the young girl quite passive; she let them lead her along. The goat skipped after them, so delighted to see Gringoire again that she made him stumble at almost every step, with thrusting her horns against his legs. "Such is life," said the philosopher, once that he was very near being laid prostrate; "it is often our best friends that occasion our fall."

They rapidly descended the staircase of the towers, crossed the interior of the church, which was all dark and solitary, but resounded from the uproar without, thus offering a frightful contrast; and went out by the Porte Rouge into the court of the cloisters. The cloisters themselves were deserted, the canons having taken refuge in the bishop's house, there to offer up their prayers in common; only some terrified serving-men were skulking in the darkest corners. They proceeded toward the small door leading from that court to the Terrain. The man in black opened it with a key which he had about him. Our readers are aware that the Terrain was a slip of ground enclosed with walls on the side next the City, and belonging to the chapter of Notre-Dame, which terminated the island eastward, behind the church. They found this enclosure perfectly solitary. Here, too, they found the tumult in the air sensibly diminished. The noise of the assault by the Truands reached their ears more confusedly and less clamorously. The cool breeze which follows the current of the river, stirred the leaves of the only tree planted at the point of the Terrain, with a noise which was now perceptible to them. Nevertheless, they were still very near the danger. The buildings nearest to them were the bishop's palace and the church. There was evidently great confusion within the residence of the bishop. Its dark mass was tracked in all directions by lights hurrying from one window to another; just as, after burning a piece of paper, there remains a dark structure of ashes, over which bright sparks are running in a thousand fantastic courses. And close by it, the huge towers of Notre-Dame, seen thus from behind, with the long nave over which they rear themselves, showing black upon the vast red light which glowed above the Parvis, looked like the gigantic uprights of some Cyclopean fire-grate.

What was visible of Paris seemed wavering on all sides in a sort of shadow mingled with light, resembling some of Rembrandt's backgrounds.

The man with the lantern walked straight to the projecting point of the Terrain; where, at the extreme verge of the water, were the decayed remains of a fence of stakes with laths nailed across, upon which a low vine spread out its few meagre branches like the fingers of an open hand. Behind this sort of lattice-work, in the shade which it cast, a small boat lay hidden. The man motioned to Gringoire and the young woman to enter it; and the goat jumped in after them. The man himself got in last of all. Then he cut the rope; pushed off from the shore with a long boat-hook; and laying hold of a pair of oars, he seated himself in front, and rowed with all his might across the stream. The Seine is very rapid at that place, and he found considerable difficulty in clearing the point of the island.

Gringoire's first care, on entering the boat, was to place the goat upon his lap. He placed himself in the hinder part of the boat; and the young girl, whom the sight of the stranger filled with indescribable uneasiness, went and seated herself as close as possible to the poet. When our philosopher felt the boat in motion, he clapped his hands, and kissed Djali upon the forehead.

"Oh!" cried he, "now we are all four saved!" He added, with the look of a profound thinker, "We are indebted sometimes to fortune, sometimes to contrivance, for the happy issue of a great undertaking."

The boat was making its way slowly toward the right bank. The young girl watched the movement of the unknown with a secret terror. He had carefully turned off again the light of his dark lantern; and he was now discernible, like a specter, at the head of the boat. His hood, which was constantly down, was a sort of mask over his face; and every time that, in rowing, he half opened his arms, upon which he had large black hanging sleeves, they looked like a pair of enormous bat's wings. But he had not yet breathed a single syllable. There was a perfect stillness in the boat, excepting only the periodical plash of the oars, and the rippling of the water against the side of the skiff.

"Upon my soul!" exclaimed Gringoire, all at once, "Here we go, as gay and as merry as owlets! We're as silent as so many Pythagoreans, or so many fish. Pasque-Dieu! my friends—I should like somebody to talk to me. The human voice is music to the human ear. That's not a saying of mine, but of Didymus of Alexandria—and a capital sentence it is. Certes, Didymus of Alexandria is no mean philosopher. One word, my pretty dear—do just say one word to me, I beg. By-the-by, you used to have a curious odd little mow of your own—do you make it still? You must know, my dear, that the parliament has full jurisdiction over all places of sanctuary, and that you were in great peril in that little box of yours at Notre-Dame. Alas! the little bird, the trochylus, maketh its nest in the crocodile's mouth. Master, here's the moon coming out again. So that they don't discover us! We're doing a laudable act in saving mademoiselle. And yet they'd hang us up in the king's name if they were to catch us. Alas! every human action has two handles. One man gets praised for what another gets blamed for. One man admires Cæsar, and reproaches Catiline. Is it not so, master? What say you to this philosophy? I possess the philosophy of instinct, of nature, *ut apes geometriam*, as the bees do geometry. So, nobody answers me. What a plaguey humor you're both in! I'm obliged to talk all by myself. That's what we call, in tragedy, a monologue. Pasque-Dieu! I'd have you to know that I've just now seen King Louis XI., and that it's from him I've caught that oath. Pasque-Dieu! then, they're still making a glorious howl in the City. He's a vile mischievous old king. He's all wrapped about with furs. He still owes me the money for my epithalamium; and he has all but hanged me to-night, which would have been very awkward for me indeed.

He's niggardly to men of merit. He should e'en read Salvian of Cologne's four books *adversus Avaritiam.* In sooth, he's a king very paltry in his dealings with men of letters—and that commits very barbarous cruelties. He's a sponge sucking up the money that's raised from the people. His savings are as the spleen, that grows big upon the pining of the other members. And so the complaints of the hardness of the times turn to murmurs against the prince. Under this mild and pious lord of ours the gibbets are overloaded with carcasses, the blocks stream with gore, the prisons are crammed to bursting. This king strips with one hand and hangs with the other. He's grand caterer to Dame Gabelle and Monseigneur Gibet. The high are stripped of their dignities, and the low are everlastingly loaded with fresh burdens. It's an exorbitant prince. I don't like this monarch. What say you, master?"

The man in black let the loquacious poet run on. He was still struggling against the strong compressed current which separates the prow of the City from the stern of the Ile Notre-Dame, now called, l'Ile Saint-Louis.

"By-the-by, master," resumed Gringoire suddenly, "just as we reached the Parvis through the enraged Truands, did your reverence observe that poor little devil, whose brains that deaf man of yours seemed in a fair way to knock out upon the balustrade of the gallery of the royal statues? I'm short-sighted, and could not distinguish his features. Who might it be, think you?"

The unknown answered not a word. But he suddenly left off rowing; his arms dropped as if they had been broken; his head fell upon his breast; and La Esmeralda could hear him sighing convulsively. She started —she had heard sounds like those before.

The boat, left to itself, followed for some moments the impulse of the stream. But at length the man in black recovered himself; seized the oars again, and again set himself to row against the current. He doubled the point of the Ile Notre-Dame, and made for the landing place at the Port-au-Foin or Hay-wharf

"Ha!" said Gringoire, "over there is the Logis Barbeau. There, master, look, that group of black roofs, that make such odd angles—there, just underneath that heap of low, dirty, ragged clouds, where the moon is all crushed and spread about like the yolk of an egg when the shell's broken. It's a fine mansion. There's a chapel with a little vaulted roof, lined with enrichments excellently cut. You may discern the bull-turret above it, very delicately perforated. There's also a pleasant garden, consisting of a pond, an aviary, an echo, a mall, a labyrinth, a wild-beast house, and plenty of thick-shaded walks very agreeable to Venus. And then there's a rogue of a tree which they call *le luxurieux*, because it once favored the pleasures of a famous princess and a certain constable of France, a man of wit and gallantry. Alas! we poor philosophers are to a constable of France, as a cabbage-plot or a radish bed is to a grove of laurels. After all, what does it signify? Human life is a mixture of good and evil for the great as well as for us. Sorrow ever attends upon joy—the spondee upon the dactyl. Master, I must tell you that story about the Logis Barbeau. It ends tragically. It was in 1319, in the reign of Philip the Fifth, the longest of all the French kings. The moral of the story is, that the temptations of the flesh are pernicious and malign. Let us not look too steadfastly upon our neighbor's wife, how much soever our senses may be taken with her beauty. Fornication is a very libertine thought. Adultery is a prying into another man's pleasure. Eh! what! the noise grows louder there!"

The tumult was in fact increasing around Notre-Dame. They listened, and could very distinctly hear shouts of victory. All at once, a hundred flambeaux, the light of which glittered upon the helmets of men-at-arms, spread themselves over the church at all elevations—on the towers—on the galleries—under the buttresses. Those torches seemed to be carried in search of something; and soon those distant clamors reached distinctly the ears of the fugitives: "The gypsy!" they cried: "the witch! death to the gypsy!"

The head of the unfortunate girl dropped upon her hands, and the unknown began to row with violence toward the bank. Meanwhile our philosopher was reflecting. He pressed the goat in his arms, and sidled away very gently from the gypsy girl, who kept pressing closer and closer to him, as to her only remaining protection.

It is certain that Gringoire was in a cruel perplexity. He reflected that the goat too, *d'après la législation existante*, would be hanged if she were retaken—that it would be a great pity, poor Djali! that two condemned females thus clinging to him would be too much for him, and that his companion would be most happy to take charge of the gypsy girl. Yet a violent struggle was taking place in his mind; wherein, like the Jupiter of the Iliad, he placed in the balance alternately the gypsy girl and the goat; and he looked first at one of them, then at the other, his eyes moist with tears, and muttering between his teeth, " And yet I can not save you both! "

The striking of the boat at length apprised them that they had reached the shore. The fearful acclamations were still resounding through the city. The unknown rose, came up to the gypsy girl, and offered to take her arm in order to help her out of the boat. She pushed him away from her, and laid hold of Gringoire's sleeve, when he, in turn, being fully occupied with the goat, almost repulsed her. Then she jumped ashore by herself. She was in such perturbation that she knew not what she was doing nor whither she was going. She remained thus for a few moments, quite stupefied, watching the water as it flowed. When she recovered a little, she found herself alone upon the landing-place with the unknown. It appears that Gringoire had availed himself of the moment of their going ashore, to make off with the goat into the mass of houses of the Rue Grenier-sur-l'Eau.

The poor gypsy girl shuddered to find herself alone with that man. She strove to speak, to cry out, to call Gringoire; but her tongue refused its office, and no

sound issued from her lips. All at once she felt the
hand of the stranger placed upon her own; the hand
was cold and strong. Her teeth chattered. She turned
paler than the moonbeams that were shining upon her.
The man said not a word. He began to walk up the
river side at a rapid pace, toward the Place de Grève,
holding her by the hand. At that moment she had a
vague feeling of the irresistibleness of destiny. No
muscular strength remained to her; she let him drag
her along, running while he walked. The quay, at that
place, was somewhat rising before them; and yet it
seemed to her as if she was going down a declivity.

She looked on all sides, but not a passenger was to be
seen; the quay was absolutely solitary. She heard no
sound, she perceived no one stirring, except in the glaring and tumultuous city, from which she was separated
only by an arm of the Seine, and from which her name
reached her ear mingled with shouts of " Death ! " The
rest of Paris lay spread around her in great masses of
shade.

Meanwhile the unknown was still dragging her on,
in the same silence and with the same rapidity. She
had no recollection of any of the places through which
she was passing. As they were going by a lighted window, she made one effort, suddenly drew up, and cried
out, " Help ! "

The master of the house opened the windows, showed
himself in his nightgown with his lamp in his hand,
looked out between sleeping and waking on the quay,
uttered some words which she did not hear, and closed
his shutter again. It was the extinction of her last ray
of hope.

The man in black uttered not a syllable. He held
her fast, and walked on yet quicker than before. She
made no more resistance, but followed him like a thing
utterly powerless.

Now and then, indeed, she gathered just strength
enough to say, with a voice interrupted by the uneven-
ness of the pavement and the rapidity of her motion,
which had almost taken her breath, " Who are you?
who are you?" But he made no answer.

In that manner, keeping constantly along the quay, they arrived at a square of considerable size. There was then a little moonlight. It was the Grève. A sort of black cross was discernible, standing in the middle of it; that was the gibbet. She observed all this, and then she knew where she was.

The man stopped, turned toward her, and lifted his hood. "Oh!" faltered she, almost petrified, "I knew it was he again!"

It was in fact the priest. He looked like the ghost of himself. It was an effect of the moonlight—a light by which one seems to see only the specters of objects.

"Listen," said he; and she shuddered at the sound of that ill-omened voice, which it was long since she had heard. He continued, speaking with that short and gasping utterance which bespeaks deep internal heavings, "listen. We are here. I have to talk to thee. This is the Grève. This is an extreme point. Fate gives up each of us to the other. I am going to dispose of thy life—thou, of my soul. Beyond this place and this night, nothing is to be seen. Listen to me, then. I'm going to tell thee. . . . . First of all, don't talk to me of thy Phœbus." So saying, he paced backward and forward, like a man incapable of standing still, dragging her after him. "Talk not of him. Mark me, if thou utter his name, I know not what I shall do, but it will be something terrible!"

Then, like a body finding its center of gravity again, he once more became motionless; but his words betrayed no less agitation. His voice grew lower and lower. "Don't turn thy head aside so. Hearken to me. 'Tis a serious matter. First of all, I'll tell thee what has happened. There will be no laughing about this, I assure thee. What was I saying? remind me—Ah! it is that there's a decree of the parliament, delivering thee over to execution again. I've just now taken thee out of their hands. But there they are pursuing thee. Look."

He stretched out his arm toward the City; where, indeed, the search seemed to be eagerly continued. The clamor came nearer. The tower of the lieutenant's house, situated opposite to the Grève, was full of noise and lights; and soldiers were running over the quay opposite with torches in their hands, shouting: "The gypsy woman! where is the gypsy woman? Death? Death!'

"Thou seest plainly enough," resumed the priest, "that they're pursuing thee, and that I tell no falsehood. I love thee. Open not thy lips. Rather, speak not a word, if it be to tell me that thou hatest me. I'm determined not to hear that again. I've just now saved thee. First, let me finish. I can save thee quite. I've made all things ready. Thou hast only to will it. As thou wilt, I can do."

Here he violently checked himself. "No, that is not what I had to say."

And with hurried step—making her hurry too, for he never let go her arm—he went straight up to the gibbet, and pointing to it: "Choose between us," said he, coolly.

She tore herself from his grasp, fell at the foot of the gibbet, and clasped that dismal supporter; then she half turned her beautiful head, and looked at the priest over her shoulder. She had the air of a Madonna at the foot of the cross. The priest had remained quite still, his finger raised toward the gibbet, and his gesture unchanged like a statue.

At length the gypsy girl said to him, "It is less horrible to me than you are."

Then he let his arm drop slowly, and cast his eyes upon the ground in deep dejection. "If these stones could speak," muttered he—"yes, they would say, Here is, indeed, an unhappy man!"

He resumed. The young girl, kneeling before the gibbet, enveloped in her long flowing hair, let him speak without interrupting him. His accent was now mild and plaintive, contrasting mournfully with the haughty harshness of his features:

"I love you! Oh, still, 'tis very true I do! And is nothing, then, perceivable without, of that fire which

consumes my heart? Alas! young girl—night and
day—yes, night and day! does that deserve no pity!
'Tis a love of the night and the day, I tell you—'tis a
torture! Oh, I suffer too much, my poor child—'tis a
thing worthy of compassion, I do assure you. You see
that I speak gently to you. I would fain have you
cease to abhor me. For, after all, when a man loves a
woman, 'tis not his fault. Oh, my God! What! will
you never forgive me, then? will you hate me always?
and is it all over? That is what makes me wicked, do
you see, and horrible to myself. You don't so much as
look at me. You are thinking of something else, perhaps, while I talk to you as I stand shuddering on the
brink of eternity to both of us! But, of all things,
don't talk to me of the officer! What! I might throw
myself at your feet! What! I might kiss—not your
feet—you would not permit it—but the ground under
your feet. What! I might sob like a child—I might
heave from my breast—not words—but my very heart
—to tell you that I love you! and yet all would be in
vain—all! And yet there is nothing in your soul but
what is kind and tender. You are all beaming with the
loveliest gentleness—all sweet, all merciful, all charming! Alas! you have no malevolence but for me alone.
Oh, what a fatality!"

He hid his face in his hands. The young girl heard
him weeping. It was the first time. Standing thus
erect, and convulsed by sobbing, he looked even more
wretched and suppliant than on his knees. For a while
he continued weeping.

"But come," he continued, as soon as these first tears
were over—"I find no words. And yet I had well
meditated what I had to say to you. Now I tremble
and shiver—I stagger at the decisive moment—I feel
that something transcendent wraps us round—and my
voice falters. Oh, I shall fall to the ground if you do
not take pity on me, pity on yourself. Do not condemn us both. If you did but know how much I love
you! What a heart is mine! Oh, what desertion of
all virtue! what desperate abandonment of myself! A

doctor, I mock at science—a gentleman, I tarnish my name—a priest, I make my missal a pillow of desire, I spit in the face of my God! All that for thee, enchantress! to be more worthy of thy hell! and yet thou rejectest the reprobate! Oh, let me tell thee all—more still—something more horrible—oh, yet more horrible!"

As he uttered these last words, his look became utterly bewildered. He was silent for a moment; then resumed, as if talking to himself, and in a strong voice, "Cain, what hast thou done with thy brother?"

He paused again; and then continued: "What have I done with him, Lord? I have taken him to myself—nourished him, brought him up, loved him, idolized him—and killed him! Yes, Lord, just now, before my eyes, have they dashed his head upon the stones of thine house—and it was because of me—because of this woman—because of her!"

His eye was haggard—his voice was sinking—he repeated several times over, mechanically, at considerable intervals, like the last stroke of a clock prolonging its vibration, "Because of her—because of her." Then his tongue articulated no perceptible sound, though his lips continued to move. All at once, he sank down, like something falling to pieces, and remained upon the ground with his head between his knees.

A slight movement of the young girl, drawing away her foot from under him, brought him to himself. He passed his hand slowly over his hollow cheeks, and looked for some moments, in stupor, at his fingers, which were wet. "What," murmured he, "have I been weeping!"

And turning suddenly to the gypsy girl, with inexpressible anguish: "Alas! you have beheld me weep, unmoved! Child, dost thou know that those tears are tears of fire? And is it, then, so true, that from the man we hate nothing can move us? Thou wouldst see me die, and thou wouldst laugh the while. Oh, I wish not to see thee die! One word—one single word of forgiveness! Tell me not that thou lovest me—tell me only that thou art willing—that will suffice, and I will save thee. If not—— Oh, the time flies! I entreat thee, by all that is sacred, wait not until I am become of stone again, like this gibbet which claims thee too! Think, that I hold both our destinies in my hand—that I am maddened—'tis terrible—that I may let all go— and that there is beneath us, unhappy girl, a bottom- less abyss, wherein my fall will pursue thine for all eter- nity! One word of kindness—say one word—but one word!"

She opened her lips to answer him. He threw him- self on his knees before her, to receive with adoration the word, perhaps of relenting, which was about to fall from those lips. She said to him, "You are an as- sassin!"

The priest took her in his arms with fury, and laugh- ed an abominable laugh. "Well—yes—an assassin," said he—"and I will have thee. Thou wilt not have me for thy slave—thou shalt have me for thy master. I will have thee! I have a den, whither I will drag thee. Thou shalt follow me—thou must follow me, or I deliver thee over! You must die, my fair one, or be mine—the priest's—the apostate's—the assassin's—this very night—dost thou hear? Come— joy! Come! kiss me, silly girl! The grave! or my couch!"

His eyes were sparkling with rage and licentiousness; and his lascivious lips were covering the young girl's neck with scarlet. She struggled in his arms, and he kept loading her with furious kisses.

"Don't bite me, monster!" she cried. "Oh, the hateful poisonous monk! Leave me! I'll pull off thy vile gray hair, and throw it by handfuls in thy face!"

He turned red—then pale—then left hold of her, and gazed upon her with a dismal look. She now thought herself victorious, and continued: "I tell thee, I be- long to my Phœbus—that it is Phœbus I love—that 'tis Phœbus who is handsome! Thou priest, art old! thou art ugly! Get thee gone!"

He uttered a violent cry, like some wretch under a branding-iron. "Die, then!" said he, grinding his teeth. She saw his frightful look, and offered to fly.

But he seized her again, shook her, threw her upon the ground, and walked rapidly toward the angle of the Tour-Roland, dragging her after him by her beautiful hands.

When he had reached that corner of the square, he turned round to her and said : " Once for all, wilt thou be mine?"

She answered him with emphasis, " No !"

Then he called out in a loud voice, "Gudule! Gudule! here's the gypsy woman! take thy revenge!"

The young girl felt herself seized suddenly by the arm. She looked; it was a fleshless arm extended through a window-place in the wall, and grasping her with a hand of iron.

" Hold fast !" said the priest; " it's the gypsy woman escaped. Don't let her go. I'm going to fetch the sergeants. Thou shalt see her hanged."

A guttural laugh from the interior of the wall, made answer to these deadly words—" Hah! hah! hah!" The gypsy girl saw the priest hurry away toward the Pont Notre-Dame, in which direction a trampling of horses was heard.

The young girl had recognized the malicious recluse. Panting with terror, she strove to disengage herself. She twisted herself about, made several bounds in agony and despair, but the other held her with incredible strength. The lean bony fingers that pinched her were clenched and met round her flesh; it seemed as if that hand was riveted to her arm. It was more than a chain—more than an iron ring; it was a pair of pincers, with life and understanding, issuing from a wall.

Quite exhausted, she fell back against the wall, and then the fear of death came over her. She thought of all the charms of life—of youth—of the sight of the heavens—of the aspect of nature—of love—of Phœbus —of all that was flying from her; and then, of all that was approaching—of the priest betraying her—of the executioner that was coming—of the gibbet that was there. Then she felt terror mounting even to the roots of her hair—and she heard the dismal laugh of the recluse, saying low to her: "Ha! ha! thou'rt going to be hanged!"

She turned with a dying look toward the window of her cell, and she saw the wild countenance of the Sachette through the bars. "What have I done to you?" said she, almost inarticulately.

The recluse made no answer, but began to mutter, in a singing, irritated, and mocking tone, "Daughter of Egypt! daughter of Egypt! daughter of Egypt!"

The unfortunate Esmeralda let her head drop under her long flowing hair, understanding that it was no human being she had here to deal with.

All at once the recluse exclaimed, as if the gypsy's question had taken all that time to reach her apprehension: "What hast thou done to me, dost thou say? Ha! what hast thou done to me, gypsy woman? Well, hark thee! I had a child—dost thou see—I had a child—a child, I tell thee—a pretty little girl—my Agnès!" she continued wildly, kissing something in the dark. "Well, dost thou see, daughter of Egypt, they took my child from me—they stole my child—they ate my child! That is what thou hast done to me!"

The young girl answered, like the lamb in the fable: "Alas! perhaps I was not then born!"

"Oh, yes," rejoined the recluse; "thou must have been born then. Thou wast one of them—she would have been of thy age. For fifteen years have I been here—fifteen years have I been suffering—fifteen years have I been knocking my head against these four walls. I tell thee, they were gypsy women that stole her from me—dost thou hear that? and that ate her with their teeth. Hast thou a heart? Only think what it is to see one's own child playing, sucking, sleeping; it's so innocent! Well, that's what they've taken from me—what they've killed. God Almighty knows it well. Now, it's my turn; I'm going to eat some gypsy woman's flesh. Oh, how I would bite thee, if the bars didn't hinder me—my head's too big. Poor little thing —while she was asleep! And if they woke her with taking her away, in vain might she cry—I was not there! Ha! you gypsy mothers—you ate my child—now come and look at yours!"

Then she laughed, or ground her teeth—for the two things were alike in that frantic countenance. The day was beginning to dawn, dimly spreading over this scene an ashy tint, and the gibbet was growing more and more distinctly visible in the centre of the Place. On the other side, toward the Pont Notre-Dame, the poor condemned girl thought she heard the noise of the horsemen approaching.

"Madame!" she cried, clasping her hands and falling upon her knees, disheveled, wild, distracted with extremity of dread, "madame, have pity! They're coming. I've done nothing to you. Can you wish me to die in that horrible manner before your eyes? You pity me, I am sure. 'Tis too dreadful! Let me fly for my life—let me go, for mercy's sake! I wish not to die so!"

"Give me back my child!" said the recluse.

"Mercy! mercy!"

"Give me back my child!"

"Let me go, in heaven's name!"

"Give me back my child!"

And now, again, the young girl sank exhausted, powerless, having already the glazy eye of one in the grave. "Alas!" faltered she, "you seek your child—I seek my parents!"

"Give me back my little Agnès!" continued Gudule. "Knowest thou not where she is? Then, die! I'll tell thee! I was once a girl of pleasure; I had a child; they took my child from me—it was the gypsy women. Thou seest plain enough that thou must die. When the gypsy mother comes to ask for thee, I shall say to her 'Mother, look at that gibbet.' Else, give me back my child! Dost thou know where she is, little girl? Here—let me show thee—here's her shoe, all that's left me of her. Dost thou know where the fellow to it is? If thou dost, tell me; and if it's only at the other end of the earth, I'll go thither on my knees to fetch it!"

So saying, with her other arm extended through the

window-place, she showed the gypsy girl the little embroidered shoe. There was already daylight enough to distinguish its shape and its colors.

The gypsy girl, starting, said, " Let me see that shoe. Oh, heavens ! " And at the same time, with the hand she had at liberty, she eagerly opened the little bag with green glass ornaments which she wore about her neck.

" Ha, there ! " muttered Gudule, " rummage thy amulet of the foul fiend—" She suddenly stopped short, her whole frame trembled, and she cried in a voice that came from her inmost heart, " My daughter ! "

The gypsy girl had just taken out of the bag a little shoe exactly matching the other. To the little shoe was attached a slip of parchment, upon which was written this rude couplet :

> " When thou the like to this shalt see,
>   Thy mother'll stretch her arms to thee."

With lightning quickness the recluse had compared the two shoes, read the inscription on the parchment, and then put close to the window bars her face all beaming with a celestial joy, exclaiming, " My daughter ! my daughter ! "

" My mother ! " answered the gypsy girl.

Here all description fails us.

The wall and the iron bars were between them. " Oh, the wall ! " cried the recluse. " To see her and not embrace her ! Thy hand ! thy hand ! "

The young girl passed her arm through one of the openings. The recluse threw herself upon that hand, pressed her lips to it, and there she remained, absorbed in that kiss, giving no sign of animation but a sob which heaved her sides from time to time. Meanwhile she was weeping in torrents, in the silence and the darkness, like rain falling in the night. The poor mother was pouring out in floods upon that adored hand that deep dark well of sorrow into which all her grief had filtered, drop by drop, for fifteen years.

All at once she rose up, threw her long gray hair from off her forehead, and without saying a word, strove with both hands, and with the fury of a lioness, to shake the bars of her window hole. But the bars were not so to be shaken. She then went and fetched from one corner of her cell a large paving-stone, which served her for a pillow, and hurled it against them with such violence that one of the bars broke, casting numberless sparks. A second stroke completed the bursting out of the old iron cross that barricaded the window-place. Then, exerting both hands, she managed to loosen and remove the rusty stumps of the bars. There are moments when the hands of a woman are possessed of superhuman strength.

The passage being thus cleared—and it was all done in less than a minute—she took her daughter by the middle, and drew her through into the cell. "Come," murmured she, "let me drag thee out of the abyss!"

As soon as she had her daughter within the cell, she set her gently on the ground, then took her up again, and, carrying her in her arms as if she were still only her little Agnès, she passed to and fro in her narrow lodge intoxicated, frantic with joy, shouting, singing, kissing her daughter, talking to her, laughing aloud, melting into tears—all at once and all vehemently.

"My daughter! my daughter!" said she, "I have my daughter! Here she is! God Almighty has given her back to me! Ha! you—come all of you—is there anybody there to see that I've got my daughter? Lord Jesus, how beautiful she is! You have made me wait fifteen years, O my God, but it was that you might give her back to me so beautiful. So the gypsy women had not eaten her! Who said that they had? My little girl! my little girl! kiss me! Those good gypsy women! I love the gypsy women! So, 'tis thou indeed. So it was that that made my heart leap every time thou didst go by. And I took that for hatred! Forgive me, my Agnès—forgive me! Thou thoughtest me very malicious, didst thou not? I love thee. Hast thou that little mark on thy neck yet? Let me see. She has it yet. Oh, thou art so handsome! It was I that gave you those large eyes, mademoiselle. Kiss me. I love thee. What matters it to me that other mothers have children? I can laugh at them now! They have only to come and look. Here is mine. Look at her neck, her eyes, her hair, her hand. Find me anything so handsome as that? Oh, I'll answer for it, she'll have plenty of lovers. I've wept for fifteen years. All my beauty has gone away, and is come again in her—Kiss me."

She said a thousand other extravagant things to her, of which the accent in which they were uttered made all the beauty; disordered the poor girl's apparel, even till she made her blush; smoothed out her silken tresses with her hand; kissed her foot, her knee, her forehead, her eyelids; was enraptured with everything. The young girl was quite passive the while, only repeating at intervals, very low and with infinite sweetness, " My mother!"

"Look you, my little girl," resumed the recluse, constantly interrupting her words with kisses, "look you— I shall love you so dearly. We will go away from here. We shall be so happy. I've inherited something at Reims, in our country. You know Reims. Oh, no, you don't know that—you were too little. If you did but know how pretty you were at four months old. Such little feet, that people came to see all the way from Epernay, which is five leagues off. We shall have a field and a house. Thou shalt sleep in my own bed. Oh, my God! who would believe it? I have my daughter again!"

"Oh, my mother!" said the young girl, gathering strength at last to speak in her emotion, "the gypsy woman had told me so. There was a good gypsy among our people that died last year, and that had always taken care of me like a foster-mother. It was she that had put this little bag on my neck. She used always to say to me: 'Little girl, take care of this trinket—it's a treasure—it will make thee find thy mother again. Thou wearest thy mother about thy neck.' She foretold it—the gypsy woman."

Again the Sachette clasped her daughter in her arms. "Come," said she, "let me kiss thee. Thou sayest that so prettily! When we get into the country, we'll put the little shoes on the feet of an infant Jesus in a church. We owe as much to the good Holy Virgin. Mon Dieu! what a pretty voice thou hast. When thou wast talking to me just now, it was like music. Ah, my Lord God! so I have found my child again! But is it to be believed now—all that story? Surely nothing will kill one—or I should have died of joy."

And then she clapped her hands again, laughing, and exclaiming, "We shall be so happy."

At that moment the cell resounded with a clattering of arms and galloping of horses, which seemed to be issuing from the Pont Notre-Dame, and approaching nearer and nearer along the quay. The gypsy girl threw herself in agony into the arms of the Sachette; "Save me! save me! my mother—they are coming!"

The recluse turned pale again. "Oh, Heaven! what dost thou say? I'd forgotten: They're pursuing thee. Why, what hast thou done?"

"I don't know," answered the unfortunate girl, "but I'm condemned to die."

"To die!" exclaimed Gudule, tottering as if struck by a thunderbolt. "To die!" she repeated slowly, looking upon her daughter with her fixed eye.

"Yes, my mother," repeated the young girl, with wild despair, "they want to kill me. They're coming to hang me. That gallows is for me. Save me, save me! They're here. Save me!"

The recluse remained for a few moments in petrified silence, then shook her head doubtingly, then, suddenly falling into a burst of laughter, but of that former frightful laughter which had now returned to her: "Oh, oh, no!" said she, "it's a dream thou art telling me of. Ah! what! that I should have lost her; that should have lasted fifteen years; and that then I should find her again, and that should last only a minute. That they should take her from me again, now that she's handsome—that she's grown up—that she talks to me

—that she loves me ; that now they should come and devour her before my own eyes, who am her mother. Oh, no ! such things can not be ; God Almighty permits nothing like that."

Now the cavalcade seemed to stop, and a voice at a distance was heard saying : " This way, Messire Tristan. The priest says we shall find her at the Trou-aux-Rats." The trampling of horses was then heard to re-commence.

The recluse started up with a cry of despair : " Fly, fly, my child. I remember it well. Thou art right. 'Tis thy death ! Oh, horror ! malediction ! fly ! "

She put her head to the loophole, and drew it back again hastily. " Stay," said she, in an accent low, brief, and dismal, pressing convulsively the hand of the gypsy girl, who was already more dead than alive. " Stay, don't breathe. There are soldiers all about. You can't go out. There's too much daylight."

Her eyes were dry and burning. For a few moments she said nothing, only pacing hurriedly to and fro in the cell, and stopping now and then plucking her gray hairs in frenzy from her head.

All at once she said : " They're coming near. I'll speak to them. Hide thee in that corner. They'll not see thee. I'll tell them that thou art run away—that I let thee go, i'faith."

She set down her daughter (for she had constantly been carrying her in her arms) in an angle of the cell which was not visible from without. She made her squat down ; arranged all carefully, so that neither foot nor hand should project from out the shade ; unbound her black hair, and spread it over her white gown, to mask it from view ; and set before her her pitcher and her paving-stone—the only articles of furniture she had —imagining that that pitcher and that stone would conceal her. And when all was finished, finding herself more calm, she knelt down and prayed. As the dawn was only just breaking, there was still great darkness in the Trou-aux-Rats.

At that instant, the voice of the priest—that infernal

voice—passed very near the cell, crying, " This way.
Captain Phœbus de Chateaupers."

At that name, from that voice, La Esmeralda, squatted in her corner, made a movement. " Don't stir," said
Gudule.

Scarcely had she said this, before a tumultuous crowd
of men, swords, and horses, stopped around the cell.
The mother, rising quick from her knees, went and
posted herself before her loophole, to cover the aperture. She beheld a strong body of armed men, horse
and foot, drawn up on the Grève. Their commander
dismounted and walked up to her. " Old woman," said
this man, whose features had an atrocious expression,
" we're seeking a witch, to hang her. We've been told
that you had got her."

The poor mother, assuming as indifferent an air as
she was able, replied, " I don't very well understand
what you mean."

The other resumed : " Tête-Dieu ! Then what sort
of a tale was that wild, staring archdeacon telling us?
Where is he ? "

" Monseigneur," said a soldier, " he's disappeared."

" Come, come, old mad woman," resumed the commander, " don't tell me any lies. There was a witch
given you to keep. What have you done with her ? "

The recluse would not give a flat denial, for fear of
awakening suspicion, but answered, in a downright and
surly tone, " If you're talking of a tall young girl that
was given to me to hold just now, I can tell you that
she bit me, and I let her go. That's all. Leave me at
rest."

The commander made a grimace of disappointment.
" Let me have no lying, old specter," he resumed once
more. " My name's Tristan l'Hermite, and I am the
king's compère. Tristan l'Hermite ! Dost thou hear ? "
he added, casting his eyes around the Place de Grève,
" It's a name that has echoes here."

" If you were Satan l'Hermite," rejoined Gudule,
gathering hope, " I should have nothing else to tell
you ; nor should I be afraid of you."

"Tête-Dieu," said Tristan, "here's a commère. Ha! so the witch-girl has got away. And which way is she gone?"

Gudule answered, in a tone of unconcern, "By the Rue du Mouton, I believe."

Tristan turned his head, and motioned to his men to make ready for resuming their march. The recluse took breath.

"Monseigneur," said an archer all at once, "just ask the old elf how it is that her window-bars are broken out so?"

This question plunged the heart of the wretched mother in anguish again. Still she did not lose all presence of mind. "They were always so," stammered she.

"Pshaw!" returned the archer; "no longer ago than yesterday they made a fine black cross that it made one devout to look at."

Tristan cast an oblique glance at the recluse. "I think the commère's perplexed," said he.

The unfortunate woman felt that all depended upon keeping her self-possession; and so, though death was in her soul, she began to jeer at them. Mothers are equal to efforts like this. "Bah!" said she, "that man's drunk. It's above a year since the back of a cart laden with stones ran against my window-place, and burst out the bars. I well remember how I scolded the driver."

"It's true," said another archer; "I was by when it happened."

There are always to be found, in all places, people who have seen everything. This unlooked-for testimony of the archer's revived the spirits of the recluse, who, in undergoing this interrogatory, was crossing an abyss upon the edge of a knife.

But she was doomed to a perpetual alternation of hope and alarm.

"If a cart had done that," resumed the first soldier "the stumps of the bars must have been driven inward but you see that they've been forced outward."

"Ha, ha!" said Tristan to the soldier, "thou hast the nose of an inquisitor at the Châtelet. Answer what he says, old woman."

"Mon Dieu!" exclaimed she, reduced to the last extremity, and bursting into tears in spite of herself, "I assure you, monseigneur, that it was a cart that broke those bars. You hear, that man saw it. And besides, what has that to do with the gypsy girl you talk of?"

"Hum!" growled Tristan.

"Diable!" continued the soldier, flattered by the provost's commendation, "the iron looks quite fresh broken!"

Tristan shook his head. She turned pale. "How long is it, do you say, since this cart affair?" he asked.

"A month—perhaps a fortnight, monseigneur. I don't recollect."

"At first she said above a year," observed the soldier.

"That looks queer!" said the provost.

"Monseigneur," cried she, still standing up close to the loophole, and trembling lest suspicion should prompt them to put their heads through and look round the cell—"monseigneur, I do assure you, it was a cart that broke this grating; I swear it to you by all the angels in paradise. If it was not done by a cart, I wish I may go to everlasting perdition, and I deny my God!"

"Thou art very hot in that oath of thine," said Tristan with his inquisitorial glance.

The poor woman felt her assurance deserting her more and more. She was already making blunders, and had a terrible consciousness that she was saying what she should not have said.

And now another soldier came up, crying: "Monseigneur, the old elf lies. The witch has not run away by the Rue du Mouton; the chain of that street has been stretched across all night, and the chain-keeper has seen nobody go by."

Tristan, the expression of whose countenance was every moment growing more sinister, again interrogated the recluse: "What hast thou to say to that?"

Still she strove to bear up against this fresh incident. 'That I don't know, monseigneur," she replied—"that I may have been mistaken. In fact, I think she went across the water."

"That's on the opposite side," said the provost. "And yet it's not very likely that she should have wanted to go into the City again, where they were making search for her. You lie, old woman."

"And besides," added the first soldier, "there's no boat, neither on this side the water nor on the other."

"She might swim across," replied the recluse, defending her ground inch by inch.

"Do women swim?" said the soldier.

"Tête-Dieu! old woman! you lie! you lie!" replied Tristan angrily; "I've a good mind to leave the witch and take thee. A quarter of an hour's questioning will perhaps get the truth out of thy throat. Come—thou shalt go along with us."

She caught eagerly at these words: "Just as you please, monseigneur. Do as you say. The question, the question. I'm quite willing. Carry me with you. Quick, quick!—let us go directly." In the meantime, thought she, my daughter will make her escape.

"Mort-Dieu!" said the provost, "what an appetite for the chevalet. This mad woman's quite past my comprehension."

An old gray-headed sergeant of the watch now stepped out of the ranks, and, addressing the provost, said: "Mad, in truth, monseigneur! If she let the gypsy go, it's not her fault, for she's no liking for gypsy women. For fifteen years have I been on this duty, and every night I hear her cursing against those Bohemian dames with execrations without end. If the one we are seeking be, as I believe she is, the little dancing-girl with the goat, she detests her above all the rest."

Gudule made an effort, and repeated, "Her above all the rest."

The unanimous testimony of the men of the watch confirmed to the provost what the old sergeant had said. Tristan l'Hermite, despairing of getting anything out of the recluse, turned his back upon her; and she, with inexpressible anxiety, watched him pace slowly back toward his horse. "Come," said he, grumblingly, "forward! we must continue the search. I will not sleep until the gypsy woman be hanged."

Still he hesitated for a while before mounting his horse. Gudule was palpitating between life and death while she beheld him throwing around the Place that restless look of a hound that feels himself to be near the lair of the game and is reluctant to go away. At last he shook his head, and sprang into his saddle.

Gudule's heart, which had been so horribly compressed, now dilated; and she said in a whisper, casting a glance upon her daughter, at whom she had not yet ventured to look since the arrival of her pursuers, "Saved!"

The poor girl had remained all this time in her corner, without breathing or stirring; with the image of death staring her in the face. No particular of the scene between Gudule and Tristan had escaped her, and each pang of her mother's had vibrated in her own heart. She had heard, as it were, each successive cracking of the thread which had held her suspended over the abyss; oftentimes had she thought she perceived it breaking asunder; and it was only now that she was beginning to take breath and to feel the ground steady under her feet. At that moment she heard a man saying to the provost—"Cor-bœuf! monsieur the provost, it's not my business, who am a man-at-arms, to hang witches. The rabble rout of the populace is put down. I leave you to do your own work by yourself. You'll allow me to go back to my company, who are waiting for their captain." The voice, as the reader will probably have divined, was that of Phœbus de Chateaupers. What passed in the breast of the gypsy girl, it is not easy to describe. So he was there—her friend—her protector—her support—her shelter—her Phœbus! She started up; and before her mother could prevent her, she had sprung to the loophole, crying out, "Phœbus! hither! my Phœbus!"

Phœbus was no longer there. He had just galloped round the corner of the Rue de la Coutellerie. But Tristan was not yet gone away.

The recluse rushed upon her daughter with a roar of agony, and drew her violently back, her nails entering the flesh of the poor girl's neck; but the grasp of a tigress mother can not be nicely cautious. It was too late, however—Tristan had observed.

"Ha, ha," he cried, with a laugh that showed all his teeth, and made his face resemble the muzzle of a wolf, "two mice in the trap."

"I suspected as much," said the soldier.

Tristan slapped him on the shoulder, saying, "Thou art a good cat! Come," he added, "where is Henriet Cousin?"

A man who had neither the dress nor the mien of a soldier, now stepped out of their ranks. He wore a suit half gray, half brown—his hair combed out flat—leathern sleeves—and carried a bundle of ropes in his large hand. This man constantly attended upon Tristan, who constantly attended upon Louis XI.

"Friend," said Tristan l'Hermite, "I presume that this is the witch we were seeking. Thou wilt hang me that one. Hast thou thy ladder with thee?"

"There's one under the shed of the Maison-aux-Piliers," answered the man. "Is it at that justice there that we're to do the job?" continued he, pointing to the stone gibbet.

"Yes."

"So ho!" said the man, with a loud laugh, more brutal still than that of the provost, "we shall not have far to go!"

"Make haste," said Tristan, "and do thy laughing after."

Meanwhile, since the time that Tristan had observed her daughter, and all hope was lost, the recluse had not yet uttered a word. She had thrown the poor gypsy girl, half dead, into the corner of the cell, and resumed her post at the loophole, her two hands resting upon the bottom of the stone window case, like the clutches of some animal. In that attitude she was seen throwing intrepidly over all those soldiers her look, which was become wild and frantic again. At the moment that Henriet Cousin approached the place, she looked at him so savagely that he shrank back.

"Monseigneur," said he, turning back to the provost, "which must I take?"

"The young one."

"So much the better, for the old one seems none so easy to take."

"Poor little dancing-girl with the goat!" said the old sergeant of the watch.

Henriet Cousin again approached the window-place. The mother's eye made his own droop. He said very timidly, "Madame—"

She interrupted him in a voice very low but furious: "What do you want?"

"Not you," said he, "but the other."

"What other?"

"The young one."

She began to shake her head, crying, "There's nobody! there's nobody! there's nobody!"

"Yes, there is somebody, you know it well enough," returned the hangman. "Let me take the young one; I don't want to do you any harm."

She answered, with a strange sneering expression, "Ha! you don't want to do me any harm!"

"Let me have the other, madame," said the man. "It's the will of monsieur the provost."

She replied, with a look of insanity, "There's nobody!"

"I tell you there is," rejoined the hangman. "We've all seen that there were two of you."

"You'd better look!" said the recluse, with her strange sneer. "Thrust your head through the window."

The man observed the threatening nails of the mother, and did not venture.

"Make haste!" cried Tristan, who had just drawn up his troops in a circle about the Trou-aux-Rats, and had stationed himself on horseback near the gibbet.

Henriet once more went back to the provost, quite perplexed. He had laid his ropes upon the ground, and, with a sheepish look, was turning about his hat in his hands. "Monseigneur," he asked, "how must I get in?"

"Through the door."

"There is none."

"Through the window, then."

"It's not wide enough."

"Widen it then," said Tristan, angrily. "Hast thou no picks with thee?"

The mother, from the interior of the cave, was still steadfastly watching them. She had ceased to hope— she no longer knew what she wanted—except that she wanted them not to take from her her daughter.

Henriet Cousin went and fetched the box of tools of the bass-œuvres (that is, the implements for the use of the sub-executioners) from under the hangar or long shed of the Maison-aux-Piliers. He also brought out from the same place the double ladder, which he immediately set up against the gibbet. Five or six of the provost's men provided themselves with pickaxes and crowbars, and Tristan went up with them to the window of the cell.

"Old woman," said the provost, in a tone of severity, "give us up the girl quietly."

She looked at him like one who does not understand.

"Tête-Dieu!" resumed Tristan; "what good can it do thee to hinder that witch from being hanged as it pleases the king?"

The wretched woman fell a-laughing with her wild laugh. "What good can it do me? She's my daughter!"

The tone in which this word was uttered produced a shudder in Henriet Cousin himself.

"I'm sorry for it," returned the provost; "but it's the king's pleasure."

She cried, laughing her terrific laugh with redoubled loudness, "What's thy king to me? I tell thee it's my daughter!"

" Make a way through the wall," said Tristan.

To make an opening sufficiently large, it was only necessary to loosen one course of stone underneath the window-place. When the mother heard the picks and the levers sapping her fortress, she uttered a dreadful cry. Then she began to go with frightful quickness round and round her cell—a habit of a wild beast, which her long residence in that cage had given her. She no longer said anything, her eyes were flaming. The soldiers felt their blood chilled to the very heart.

All at once she took up her paving-stone, laughed, and threw it with both hands at the workmen. The stone, ill-thrown (for her hands were trembling), touched no one, but fell quite harmless at the feet of Tristan's horse. She gnashed her teeth.

Meanwhile, although the sun was not yet risen, it was become broad daylight, and a fine roseate tint beautified the old decayed chimneys of the Maison-aux-Piliers. It was the hour when the windows of the earliest risers in the great city opened cheerfully upon the roofs. A few rustics, a few fruit-sellers, going to the Halles upon their asses, were beginning to cross the Grève, stopped for a moment before that group of soldiers gathered about the Trou-aux-Rats, gazed at it with looks of astonishment, and passed on.

The recluse had gone and seated herself close to her daughter, covering her with her own figure—her eyes fixed—listening to the poor girl, who stirred not, but was murmuring low her only word—" Phœbus ! Phœbus !" In proportion as the work of the demolishers seemed to be advancing, the mother mechanically shrunk away, pressing the young girl closer and closer against the wall. All at once, the recluse saw the course of stone (for she was on the watch, and had her eye constantly fixed upon it) beginning to give way, and she heard the voice of Tristan encouraging the workmen. Then starting out of the sort of prostration into which her spirit had sunk for some minutes, she cried out— and, as she spoke, her voice now tore the ear like a saw, now faltered as if every species of malediction had crowded to her lips to burst forth at one and the same time—"Ho, ho, ho! but it's horrible! You are robbers! Are you really going to take my daughter from me? I tell you she's my daughter! Oh, the cowards! oh, the hangman lackeys! the miserable murdering suttlers! Help! help! fire! And will they take my child from me so? Who is it, then, that they call the good God of heaven?"

Then, addressing herself to Tristan, with foaming mouth and haggard eyes, on all fours, and bristling like a panther—"You'd better come and take my daughter. Dost thou not understand that this woman tells thee it's her daughter? Dost thou know what it is to have a child, eh? thou he-wolf! Hast thou never laid with thy mate? Hast thou never had a cub by her? And if thou hast little ones, when they howl is there nothing stirs within thee?"

"Down with the stones!" said Tristan; "they're quite loose now."

The crowbars now heaved up the heavy course of stone. It was, as we have said, the mother's last bulwark. She threw herself upon it—she would fain have held it in its place—she scratched the stones with her nails; but the heavy mass, put in motion by half a dozen men, escaped her grasp, and fell gently down to the ground along the iron levers.

The mother, seeing the breach effected, threw herself on the floor across the opening, barricading it with her body, writhing her arms, beating her head against the flag-stones, and crying in a loud voice, hoarse and nearly inarticulate with exhaustion—"Help, help!—fire, fire!"

"Now, take the girl," said Tristan, still imperturbable.

The mother looked at the soldiers in so formidable a manner, that they had more disposition to retreat than to advance.

"Now for it!" resumed the provost. "You, Henriet Cousin."

Nobody advanced a step.

The provost swore. "Tête-Christ! my fighting men! Afraid of a woman!"

"Monseigneur," said Henriet, "do you call that a woman?"

"She has a lion's mane," said another.

"Come!" continued the provost; "the gap's large enough. Enter three abreast, as at the breach of Pontoise. Let's get done with it, mort-Mahom! The first man that gives back, I'll cleave him in two."

Placed thus between the provost and the mother, the soldiers hesitated a moment; then made up their minds, and went up to the Trou-aux-Rats.

When the recluse saw this, she suddenly reared herself upon her knees, threw aside her hair from her face, then dropped her lean, grazed hands upon her hips. Then big tears issued one by one from her eyes, coursing each other down her furrowed cheeks, like a stream down the bed that it has worn itself. At the same time she began to speak, but in a voice so suppliant, so gentle, so submissive, so heart-piercing, that more than one old hardened argousin among those who surrounded Tristan wiped his eyes.

"Messeigneurs," said she, "messieurs the sergeants! one word! There's a thing I must tell you. It's my daughter, do you see—my dear little daughter, that I had lost. Listen; it's quite a history. Consider that I'm very well acquainted with messieurs the sergeants. They were always good to me in those times when the little boys used to throw stones at me because I was a girl of pleasure. So you see—you'll leave me my child when you know all! I was a poor woman of the town. It was the gypsy women that stole her away from me —by the same token that I've kept her shoe these fifteen years. Look! here it is. She'd a foot like that. At Reims—La Chantefleurie—Rue Folle-Peine. Perhaps you know all that. It was I. In your youth—in those days—it was a merry time—and there were merry doings. You'll have pity on me, won't you, messeigneurs? The gypsy women stole her from me. They hid her from me for fifteen years. I thought she was dead! Only think, my good friends; I thought she was dead! I've passed fifteen years here—in this cave—without fire in the winter. It's hard, that! The poor dear little shoe! I cried so much that at last God Almighty heard me. This night he has given me back my daughter. It's a miracle of God Almighty's. She was not dead. You'll not take her from me—I'm sure you won't. If it were myself, now, I can't say—but to take her, a child of sixteen! Let her have time to see the sun. What has she done to you? Nothing at all. Nor I neither. If you did but know, now, that I have but her—that I am old—that it's a blessing the holy Virgin sends me! And then, you're all of you so good! You didn't know it was my daughter—but you know now. Oh, I love her so. Monsieur the grand-provost, I would rather have a stab in my side than a scratch upon her finger! It's you that look like a good seigneur! What I tell you now, explains the thing to you, doesn't it? Oh, if you have had a mother, monseigneur! You are the commander, leave me my child. Only consider that I am praying to you on my knees, as they pray to a Christ Jesus! I ask nothing of anybody. I am of Reims, messeigneurs—I've a little field there that was Mahiet Pradon's. I am not a beggar. I want nothing —but I want to keep my child. God Almighty, who is master of all, has not given her back to me for nothing. The king—you say, the king. It can't be any great pleasure to him that they should kill my little girl. Besides, it's my daughter—it's my daughter—mine—she's not the king's—she's not yours! I want to go away from here—we both want to go—and when two women are going along, mother and daughter, you let them go quietly. Let us go quietly. We belong to Reims. Oh, you're so good, messieurs the sergeants —I love you all. You'll not take my dear little one away from me—it's impossible? Is it not, now, quite impossible? My child! my child!"

We shall not attempt to give an idea of her gesture, her accent—the tears which she drank in while speaking —the clasping and the writhing of her hands, the agonizing smiles, the swimming looks, the sighs, the moans, the miserable and piercing cries which she mingled with these disordered, wild, and incoherent words. When she ceased, Tristan l'Hermite knit his brows, but it was to conceal a tear that was standing in his tiger's eye. However, he overcame this weakness, and said, with brief utterance, "the king wills it."

Then he whispered in the ear of Henriet Cousin, "Get done quickly." It might be that the redoubtable provost felt his own heart failing him—even his.

The executioner and the sergeants entered the cell. The mother made no resistance; she only crept up to her daughter, and threw herself madly upon her. When the gypsy girl saw the soldiers approaching, the horror of death gave her strength again. "My mother," cried she, in a tone of indescribable distress; "oh, my mother! they are coming; defend me!" "Yes, my love, I am defending you!" answered the mother, in a faint voice; and clasping her closely in her arms, she covered her with kisses. To see them both thus upon the ground the mother upon the daughter, was truly piteous.

Henriet Cousin took hold of the gypsy girl just below her beautiful shoulders. When she felt his hands touching her, she cried, "Heuh!" and fainted. The executioner, from whose eye big tears were falling upon her drop by drop, offered to carry her away in his arms. He strove to unclasp the embrace of the mother, who had, as it were, drawn her hands in a knot about her daughter's waist; but the grasp which thus bound her to the person of her child was so powerful that he found it impossible to unloose it. Henriet Cousin then dragged the young girl out of the cell, and her mother after her. The eyes of the mother were closed as well as those of the daughter.

The sun was rising at that moment; and already there was a considerable collection of people upon the Place, looking from a distance to see what they were thus dragging along the ground toward the gibbet. For

this was a way of the Provost Tristan's at executions—
he had a rage for preventing the curious from coming
near.

There was nobody at the windows. Only there were
to be seen at a distance, on the top of that one of the
towers of Notre-Dame which looks upon the Grève, two
men, whose figures stood darkly out against the clear
morning sky, and who seemed to be looking on.

Henriet Cousin stopped with what he was dragging
along, at the foot of the fatal ladder; and, with troubled
breath—such a pity did he think it—he passed the rope
round the young girl's lovely neck. The unfortunate
girl felt the horrible contact of the hempen cord. She
raised her eyelids, and beheld the skeleton arm of the
stone gibbet extended over her head. Then she shook
herself, and cried, in a loud and agonizing voice, "No!
no! I won't! I won't!" The mother, whose head was
quite buried under her daughter's attire, said not a word;
but a long shudder was seen to run through her whole
frame, and she was heard multiplying her kisses upon
the form of her child. The executioner seized that moment to unclasp, by a strong and sudden effort, the arms
with which she held fast the condemned; and, whether
from exhaustion or despair, they yielded. Then he
took the young girl upon his shoulder, from whence her
charming figure fell gracefully bending over his large
head. And then he set his foot upon the ladder in
order to ascend.

At that moment, the mother, who had sunk upon the
ground, quite opened her eyes. Without uttering any
cry, she started up with a terrific expression of countenance; then, like a beast rushing upon its prey, she threw
herself upon the executioner's hand, and set her teeth
in it. This was done with the quickness of lightning.
The executioner howled with pain. They came to his
relief, and with difficulty liberated his bleeding hand
from the bite of the mother. She kept a profound
silence. They pushed her away with brutal violence,
and it was remarked that her head fell back heavily up-

on the ground. They raised her up—she fell back again. The fact was, that she was dead.

The executioner, who had kept his hold of the young girl, began again to ascend the ladder.

CHAPTER II.

LA CREATURA BELLA, BIANCO VESTITA.

WHEN Quasimodo saw that the cell was empty—that the gypsy girl was gone—that she had been carried off while he had been defending her—he grasped his hair with both hands, and stamped with surprise and grief; then he went running over the whole church, seeking his young Bohemian—bawling strange cries at every corner—strewing his red hair upon the pavement. It was just the moment when the king's archers were entering victorious into Notre-Dame, likewise in search of the gypsy girl. The poor deaf ringer assisted their search without in the least suspecting their fatal intentions; he thought that the enemies of the gypsy girl were the Truands. He himself showed Tristan l'Hermite the way into every possible nook of concealment; opened him the secret doors, the false backs of the altars, the inner sacristies. Had the unfortunate girl been still there, it would have been he himself that would have put her in their hands. When the irksomeness of seeking in vain had tired out Tristan, who was not to be tired out easily, Quasimodo continued the search by himself. Twenty times, a hundred times over, did he make the circuit of the church, from one end to the other, and from top to bottom—ascending, descending, running, calling, shouting, peeping, rummaging, ferreting, putting his head into every hole, thrusting a torch under every vault, desperate, mad, haggard, and moaning as a beast that had lost his mate. At length, when he had made himself sure, quite sure, that she was gone—that all was over—that they had stolen her

from him—he slowly reascended the tower staircase—
that staircase which he had mounted so nimbly and
triumphantly on the day that he had saved her. He
now passed by the same spots, with drooping head,
voiceless, tearless, and hardly drawing breath. The
church had become solitary and silent again. The archers had quitted it to pursue the sorceress into the City.
Quasimodo, left alone in that vast Notre-Dame, the
moment before so besieged and so tumultuous, took his
way once more toward the cell in which the gypsy girl
had slept for so many weeks under his protection. As
he approached it, he could not help fancying to himself
that perhaps, on arriving, he should find her there again.
On reaching that bend of the gallery which looks upon
the roof of the side aisle, he could see the narrow re-
ceptacle, with its little window and its little door, lying
close under one of the great buttresses, like a bird's
nest under a bough. The poor fellow's heart failed him,
and he leaned against a pillar to keep himself from
falling. He figured to himself that perhaps she might
have come back thither—that some good genius had no
doubt brought her back—that that little nest was too
quiet, too safe, and too charming for her not to be there
—and he dared not advance a step farther, for fear of
dispelling the illusion. "Yes," said he to himself,
"she's sleeping, perhaps—or praying—I mustn't disturb her." At last he summoned up courage, approached on tip-toe, looked, entered. Empty! the cell was
still empty! The unhappy man moved slowly round it,
lifted up her couch, and looked underneath it, as if she
could have been hidden between the mattress and the
stones; then he shook his head, and stood stupefied.
All at once he furiously stamped out his torchlight,
and without uttering a word or breathing a sigh, he
rushed with all his force head-foremost against the wall,
and fell senseless upon the floor.

When his senses returned, he threw himself upon the
bed, rolling about, and frantically kissing the yet warm
place where the young girl had slept! then he remained
for some minutes motionless, as if he was expiring there

then he rose again, streaming with perspiration, panting, frenzied; and fell to beating the walls with his head,
with the frightful regularity of the stroke of a clock,
and the resolution of a man determined to fracture his
skull. At length he sank exhausted a second time.
Then he crawled to the outside of the cell, and remained
crouching in an attitude of astonishment in front of the
door, for a full hour, with his eye fixed upon the solitary dwelling-place—more gloomy and pensive than a
mother seated between the cradle and the coffin of her
departed child. He uttered not a word; only at intervals, a violent sob agitated his whole frame—but it was
a sobbing devoid of tears.

It seems to have been that, striving to divine, amidst
his desolate ruminations, who could have been the unexpected ravisher of the gypsy girl, he thought of the
archdeacon. He recollected that Dom Claude alone had
a key of the staircase leading to the cell. He remembered his nocturnal attempts upon La Esmeralda—the
first of which he, Quasimodo, had aided—the second of
which he had prevented. He called to mind a thousand various particulars; and soon he felt quite con-
vinced that it was the archdeacon that had taken the
gypsy girl from him. Yet such was his reverence for
the priest—his gratitude, his devotedness, his love for
that man were so deeply rooted in his heart—that they
resisted, even at this dire moment, the fangs of jealousy
and despair.

He reflected that the archdeacon had done it; and
that sanguinary, deadly resentment which he would
have felt for it against any other individual, was turned
in the poor ringer's breast, the moment that Claude
Frollo was concerned, simply into an increase of sorrow.

At the moment that his thoughts were thus fixing
themselves upon the priest, while the buttresses were
whitening in the daybreak, he beheld, on the upper
story of Notre-Dame, at the angle formed by the external balustrade which runs round the top of the chancel, a figure walking. The figure was coming toward
him. He recognized it, it was that of the archdeacon

Claude was pacing along gravely and slowly. He did not look before him as he advanced, directing his steps toward the northern tower; his face was turned aside toward the right bank of the Seine; and he carried his head erect, as if striving to obtain a view of something over the roofs. The owl has often that oblique attitude, flying in one direction and looking in another. In this manner the priest passed above Quasimodo without seeing him.

The deaf spectator, whom this sudden apparition had confounded, saw the figure disappear through the door of the staircase of the northern tower, which, as the reader is aware, is the one commanding a view of the Hôtel-de-Ville. Quasimodo rose up and followed the archdeacon.

Quasimodo ascended the tower staircase to learn why the priest was ascending it, but the poor ringer knew not what he himself was going to do, what he was going to say, what he wanted. He was full of rage and full of dread. The archdeacon and the gypsy girl clashed together in his heart.

When he had reached the top of the tower, before issuing from the shade of the staircase upon the open platform, he cautiously observed whereabouts the priest was. The priest had his back toward him. An open balustrade surrounds the platform of the steeple. The priest, whose eyes were bent upon the town, was leaning his breast upon that one of the four sides of the balustrade which looks upon the Pont Notre-Dame.

Quasimodo stole up behind him to see what he was looking at so, and the priest's attention was so completely absorbed elsewhere that he heard not the step of his deaf servant near him.

It is a magnificent and captivating spectacle, and at that day it was yet more so, to look down upon Paris from the summit of the towers of Notre-Dame, in the fresh light of a summer dawn. The day in question might be one of the early ones of July. The sky was perfectly serene. A few lingering stars were fading away in different directions, and eastward there was one very brilliant, in the lightest part of the heavens The sun was on the point of making his appearance. Paris was beginning to stir. A very white, pure light showed vividly to the eye the endless varieties of outline which its buildings presented on the east, while the giant shadows of the steeples traversed building after building from one end of the great city to the other. Already voices and noises were to be heard from several quarters of the town. Here was heard the stroke of a bell—there that of a hammer—and there again the complicated clatter of a dray in motion. Already the smoke from some of the chimneys was escaping scatteredly over all that surface of roofs, as if through the fissures of some vast sulphur-work. The river, whose waters are rippled by the piers of so many bridges and the points of so many islands, was wavering in folds of silver. Around the town, outside the ramparts, the view was lost in a great circle of fleecy vapors, through which were indistinctly discernible the dim line of the plains and the graceful swelling of the heights. All sorts of floating sounds were scattered over that halfawakened region. And eastward, the morning breeze was chasing across the sky a few light locks plucked from the fleecy mantle of the hills.

In the Parvis some good women, with their milk-pots in their hands, were pointing out to one another, in astonishment, the singularly shattered state of the great door of Notre-Dame, and the two congealed streams of lead all down the crevices of the front. It was all that remained of the tumult of the night before. The pile kindled by Quasimodo between the towers was extinct. Tristan had cleared the ground of the Place, and had the dead thrown into the Seine. Kings like Louis XI. take care to clean the pavements quick after a massacre.

Outside the balustrade of the tower, exactly underneath the point where the priest had stopped, was one of those fantastically carved stone gutters which diversify the exterior of Gothic buildings; and in a crevice of the gutter, two pretty wallflowers in full bloom, shaken and vivified as it were by the breath of the morning, made sportive salutation to each other, while over the towers, far above in the sky, were heard the cheerful voices of early birds.

But the priest neither saw nor heard anything of all that. He was one of those men to whom there are neither mornings, nor birds, nor flowers. In all that immense horizon, spread around him with such diversity of aspect, his contemplation was concentrated upon one single point.

Quasimodo burned to ask him what he had done with the gypsy girl, but the archdeacon seemed at that moment to be rapt out of the world. He was evidently in one of those violent passages of existence when the earth itself might fall to ruin without our perceiving it.

With his eyes invariably fixed upon a certain spot, he remained motionless and silent ; and in that silence and immobility there was something so formidable that the savage ringer shuddered at the contemplation, and dared not intrude upon them. All that he did—and it was one way of interrogating the archdeacon—was to follow the direction of his vision, which thus guided the view of the unfortunate hunchback to the Place de Grève.

In this manner he discovered what the priest was looking at. The ladder was erected against the permanent gibbet. There were some people in the Place, and a number of soldiers. A man was dragging along the ground something white, to which something black was clinging. This man stopped at the foot of the gibbet. Here something took place which Quasimodo could not very distinctly see—not that his only eye had not preserved its long reach—but there was a body of soldiers in the way, which prevented him from distinguishing all. Moreover, at that instant the sun appeared, and such a flood of light burst over the horizon, that it seemed as if every point of Paris—spires, chimneys, and gables—were taking fire at once.

Meantime, the man began to ascend the ladder. Then Quasimodo saw him distinctly again. He was carrying a female figure upon his shoulder—a young

"HE PUSHED DOM CLAUDE OVER INTO THE ABYSS."

girl clad in white. There was a noose round the young girl's neck. Quasimodo recognized her. It was she!

The man arrived with his burden at the top of the ladder. There he arranged the noose. And now the priest, to have a better view, set himself on his knees upon the balustrade.

All at once the man pushed away the ladder with his heel; and Quasimodo, who for some moments had not drawn his breath, saw wavering at the end of the cord, about two toises above the ground, the form of the unfortunate girl with that of the man squatted upon her shoulders. The cord made several turns upon itself, and Quasimodo beheld horrible convulsions agitating the frame of the gypsy girl. On the other hand, the priest, with outstretched neck and starting eyeballs, was contemplating that frightful group of the man and the girl—the spider and the fly!

At the moment when it looked the most horrible, a demoniacal laugh—a laugh such as can come only from one who is no longer human—burst from the livid visage of the priest. Quasimodo did not hear that laugh, but he saw it. The ringer made a few steps backward from behind the archdeacon, and then rushing furiously upon him, thrusting both his large hands against his back, he pushed Dom Claude over into the abyss toward which he had been leaning.

The priest cried out, " Damnation ! " and fell.

The gutter-head over which he had been leaning arrested his fall. He clung to it with desperate gripe; but, at the moment that he was opening his lips to cry out again, he saw passing along the verge of the balustrade above him the formidable and avenging countenance of Quasimodo, and was silent.

Beneath him was the abyss—a fall of full two hundred feet—and the pavement. In this dreadful situation the archdeacon said not a word, breathed not a groan. Only he writhed upon the gutter, making incredible efforts to re-ascend; but his hands had no hold of the granite, his feet constantly slid away upon the blackened wall. They who have ascended to the top of the towers of Notre-Dame know that the stone-work swells out immediately below the balustrade. It was on the re-entering angle of this ridge that the miserable archdeacon was exhausting his efforts. It was not with a wall merely perpendicular that he was striving, but with a wall that sloped away from under him.

Quasimodo would only have had to stretch out his hand to him to draw him from the gulf, but he did not so much as look at him. He was looking on the Grève —he was looking on the gibbet—he was looking on the gypsy girl. The poor deaf creature had leaned his elbows on the balustrade in the very place where the archdeacon had been the moment before, and there, keeping his eye fixed upon the only object of which at that moment he was conscious, he was mute and motionless as one struck by the thunderbolt—except that a long stream of tears was flowing from that eye which until then had never shed but one.

Meanwhile the archdeacon was panting; his bald forehead was streaming with perspiration; his nails were bleeding against the stones; he was grazing his knees against the wall. He could hear his cassock, which had caught hold of the gutter, tearing more and more at each jerk that he gave it; and to complete his misfortune, the gutter itself terminated in a leaden pipe, which he could feel slowly bending under the weight of his body. The wretched man was saying to himself, that when his hands should be worn out with fatigue—when his cassock should be rent asunder— when that lead should be completely bent—he must of necessity fall—and terror froze his vitals. Now and then he looked down bewilderedly upon a sort of small table formed some ten feet lower by projections of sculpture; and he implored heaven from the bottom of his agonizing soul, that he might be permitted to spend the remainder of his life upon that narrow space of two feet square, though it were to last a hundred years. Once he ventured to look down into the Place below him, but when he turned his head upward again, it was with closing eyes and hair erect.

There was something frightful in the silence of these two men. While the archdeacon was agonizing in that horrible manner but a few feet from him, Quasimode was weeping and looking upon the Grève.

The archdeacon, finding that all his efforts to raise himself served only to warp the one feeble point of support that remained to him, had at length resolved to remain quite still. There he was—clasping the gutter—scarce drawing his breath—stirring not at all—without any other motion than that mechanical convulsion of the viscera which is felt in a dream when we fancy we are falling. His fixed eyes were wide open with a stare of pain and astonishment. Meanwhile he felt himself going by degrees; his fingers slipped upon the gutter; he felt more and more the weakness of his arms and the weight of his body; the bending piece of lead that supported him inclined more and more downward. He saw beneath him, frightful to look upon, the sharp roof of the church of Saint-Jean-de-Rond, small as a card bent double. He looked, one after another, at the imperturbable sculptures of the tower—like him suspended over the precipice—but without terror for themselves or pity for him. All around him was of stone—before his eyes, the gaping monsters; in the Place below, the pavement; over his head, Quasimodo weeping.

Down in the Parvis there were some groups of worthy starers, quietly striving to guess what madman it could be that was amusing himself after so strange a fashion. The priest could hear them saying—for their voices mounted up to him clear and shrill—" Why, he'll surely break his neck."

Quasimodo was weeping.

At length the archdeacon, foaming with rage and dread, felt that all was unavailing. However, he gathered what strength he had remaining for one last effort. He drew himself up on the gutter, sprung from against the wall with both his keees, hung his hands in a cleft of the stonework, and succeeded, perhaps, in climbing up with one foot; but the force which he was obliged to use gave a sudden bend to the leaden beak that supported him ; and the same effort rent his cassock asunder. Then, finding everything under him give way—having only his benumbed and powerless hands by which to cling to anything—the unhappy man closed his eyes, left hold of the gutter, and fell.

Quasimodo looked at him falling.

A fall from such a height is seldom perpendicular. The archdeacon, launched through the void, fell at first with his head downward and his arms extended—then he turned round several times. The wind carried him against the top of one of the houses, upon which the miserable man was first dashed. However, he was not dead when he reached it. The ringer could perceive him still make an effort to cling to the gable with his hands, but the slope was too quick, and he had no strength left. He glided rapidly down the roof, like a loosened tile, then dashed upon the pavement, and there he lay quite still.

Quasimodo then lifted his eye to look upon the gypsy girl, whose body, suspended from the gibbet, he beheld quivering afar, under its white robe, in the last struggles of death ; then again he dropped it upon the archdeacon, stretched a shapeless mass at the foot of the tower, and he said, with a sob that heaved his deep breast to the bottom, " Oh !—all that I've ever loved ! "

CHAPTER III.

THE MARRIAGE OF CAPTAIN PHŒBUS.

WHEN, toward the evening of that day, the judicial officers of the bishop came to remove the shattered body of the archdeacon, Quasimodo had disappeared from Notre-Dame.

This circumstance gave rise to various rumors. It

was considered unquestionable that the day had at
length arrived when, according to compact, Quasimodo
—that is to say the Devil—was to carry off Claude
Frollo, that is to say the sorcerer. It was presumed
that he had broken up the body in taking the soul, as
a monkey cracks the shell to get at the nut.

It was for this reason that the archdeacon was not
interred in consecrated ground.

Louis XI. died the following year in August, 1483.

As for Pierre Gringoire, he not only succeeded in
saving the goat, but obtained considerable success as
a writer of tragedy. It appears that after dabbling in
astrology, philosophy, architecture, hermetics—in short
in every vanity, he came back to tragedy, which some
people think the vainest pursuit of all. This he called
coming to a tragical end. On the subject of his dramatic triumphs, we read in the " Ordinary's Accounts
for 1483," as follows :

" To Jehan Marchand and Pierre Gringoire, carpenter
and composer, for making and composing the mystery
performed at the Châtelet of Paris on the day of the
entry of Monsieur the Legate ; for duly ordering the
characters, with properties and habiliments proper for
the said mystery, and likewise for making the wooden
stages necessary for the same—one hundred livres."

Phœbus de Chateaupers also came to a tragical end ;
he married.

CHAPTER IV.

THE MARRIAGE OF QUASIMODO.

WE have already said that Quasimodo disappeared
from Notre-Dame on the day of the death of the gypsy
girl and the archdeacon. In fact he was never seen
again, nor was it known what had become of him.

In the night immediately following the execution of

Esmeralda, the executioner's men had taken down her body from the gibbet, and, according to custom, had carried it away and deposited it in the great charnel vault of Montfaucon.

Montfaucon, to use the words of the antiquary Sauval was the most ancient and the most superb gibbet in the kingdom. Between the faubourg of the Temple and St. Martin, at the distance of about one hundred and sixty toises from the walls of Paris, and a few bow-shots from the village of La Courtille, was to be seen on the summit of an almost imperceptibly rising ground, but on a spot sufficiently elevated to be visible for several leagues around, an edifice of a strange form, much resembling a Druidical cromlech, and having, like the cromlech, its human sacrifices.

Let the reader imagine a great oblong mass of stone-work, fifteen feet high, thirty feet wide, and forty long, based upon a pile of plaster, and having a door, an external railing, and an upper platform. Standing upon this platform are sixteen enormous pillars of unhewn stone, thirty feet high, ranged in a colonnade around three of the four sides of the huge block supporting them, and connected at the top by heavy beams, from which chains are hanging at short intervals. At each of those chains are a group of skeletons—not far off, in the plain, are a stone cross and two secondary gibbets, rising like shoots from the great central tree, and in the sky, hovering over the whole, a perpetual flock of carrion crows. Such was Montfaucon.

At the end of the fifteenth century this formidable gibbet, which had stood since 1328, was already much dilapidated; the beams were decayed, the chains were corroded with rust, the pillars green with mould, the courses of hewn stone were all gaping at their joints, and the grass was growing upon that platform to which no foot reached. The structure showed a horrible profile against the sky—especially at night time—when the moonlight gleaming upon those whitened skulls, or when the breeze of evening sweeping past the chains and skeletons, made them rattle in the darkness. The presence of this gibbet communicated a dismal character to the surrounding landscape.

The mass of stonework that formed the base of the repulsive edifice was hollow. An immense cavern had been constructed within it, the entrance of which was closed with an old battered iron grating, and into which were thrown not only the human relics taken down from the chains of Montfaucon, but also the carcasses of the sufferers at all the other permanent gibbets of Paris. To that deep charnel-house, wherein so many human remains, and the memories of so many crimes, have festered and been confounded together, many a great one of the earth, and many of the innocent, at one time or other, contributed their bones—from Enguerrand de Marigni, and who was one of the just, down to the Admiral De Coligni, who had the last, and was of the just also.

As for Quasimodo's mysterious disappearance, all that we have been able to ascertain respecting it is this :

About a year and a half or two years after the events that conclude this history, when search was made in the cave of Montfaucon for the body of Olivier le Daim, who had been hanged two days before, and to whom Charles VIII., son and successor of Olivier's kind master, granted the favor of being interred at the church of St. Laurent in better company, there were found among all those hideous carcasses, two skeletons, the arms of one of which were thrown round the other. One of the two, that of a woman, had still about it some tattered fragments of a garment, apparently of a stuff that had once been white ; and about its neck was a string of grains of adrezarach, together with a small silken bag, ornamented with green glass, which was open and empty. These articles had been of so little value, that the executioner, doubtless, had not cared to take them. The other skeleton, which held this one close in its arms, was that of a man. It was remarked in the latter, that the spine was crooked, the head compressed between the shoulder-blades, and that one leg was shorter than the other. It was also remarkable there was no rupture of the vertebræ at the nape of the neck, whence it was evident that he had not been hanged. Hence it was inferred that the man must have come hither of himself, and died there. When they strove to detach this skeleton from the one it was embracing, it fell into dust.

THE END.